Courageous Lady

Courageous Lady

A woman's Alaskan quest for Native
American spirituality

Mark Allen North

Fresh Ink Group
Roanoke

Courageous Lady
A woman's Alaskan quest for Native American spirituality

Fresh Ink Group
An Imprint of:
The Fresh Ink Group, LLC
PO Box 525
Roanoke, TX 76262
Email: info@FreshInkGroup.com
www.FreshInkGroup.com

Edition 1.0	2006
Edition 2.0	2012
Edition 3.0	2016

Book design by Ann E. Stewart

Cover design by Stephen Geez/Fresh Ink Group

Inspired by the artwork of Frank Minnick

Cataloging-in-Publication Recommendations: General Fiction; Multi-cultural (Fiction); Contemporary Women (Fiction); Cultural Heritage (Fiction); Action & Adventure (Fiction); Mythology (Fiction); Alaska; Alaskan Wilderness; Tlingit Culture; Native American; Wilderness Survival; Women's Fiction

Library of Congress Control Number: 2012938627

ISBN-13: 978-1-936442-12-6

For

Marjorie Broome-Redick
and
Frank Milton Redick

who taught me everything, by example

Acknowledgements

Writing *Courageous Lady*, *Intrepid Lady*, and the last installment, *Valiant Lady*, would not have been possible without a great deal of help. Leigh's experiences could not have reached this form without the contributions of many people. In many ways, both obvious and obscure, it is a collaborative work.

I want to express my gratitude to the people who helped develop the "Lady Series" along the way: Dave and Becky Halverstadt, Shirley Sampier, Gay Lynn Redick-Cookson, Tom Redick, Denium Roman, Anne Arnold, Betsy and Bill Ince, Carol and Chuck Jennings, Dave and Kay Wagner, Chuck and Non Rycenga, Pam and Bill Gnodtke, Glenn Bongard, Lyman Jones, Janet Curio, Ian Lamb, Robert Tiran, Scott Detloff, and Henry Phillips. Whether through financial or literary support, they all saved me from the more obvious forms of embarrassment when I used words to express my thoughts.

I am particularly thankful to Leonard Gasco (full-blooded Odawa Indian elder) for his counsel on Native American customs and traditions.

For her inspiration, I thank Madeline Kiser.

Thanks to George Parker for his faithful support.

Many thanks to Francis S. Minnick, whose artwork inspired the covers for all three books.

For his contribution of many storyline ideas, scientific insight, financial support, marketing ideas, and counsel, I thank Big Brother Milton Duane Redick. He's my best friend and supporter.

Heartfelt thanks go to Ann Stewart and Stephen Geez of Fresh Ink Group for the file creation, book design, and cover design.

Ultra-thanks go to my agent and ever-present advocate, LeAnne Redick-Wilson, who managed and coordinated publication with Fresh Ink Group—I couldn't do this without her help.

Of special note, I acknowledge my friend, David Duyst, Sr., whose constructive criticism was always welcome and whose creative ideas enhanced the story throughout.

Finally, thanks to my confidant and teacher, Stephen Geez, for his invaluable editorial opinions. He's a mentor, author, and patient artisan of words who contributed immeasurably to the book's readability.

I beg readers' forgiveness for any errors in the text, and for omitting any helpful people I have overlooked.

Author's Note

It has been an extremely rewarding endeavor writing *Courageous Lady*, a story of Leigh West's adventures in Alaska. Its penning served as a release, a purge, of the memory of a love lost and finding a new consciousness, a restored life. As a result of this cleansing there is a personal bias interwoven in the design of the story.

Native Americans tell many stories about the relationship between animals and human beings; these stories appear in various tribes and languages throughout the north. The versions that I expressed may differ from others collected by scholars and folklorists. The seed that became a secondary story of animals interacting with humans has been a combination of many traditional stories involving ravens, owls, wolves, and yes, even a mouse. Many are coastal stories from Southeastern Alaska and the others come from the northern interior. This novel is not meant to displace or contradict any of the scholarly work that has been done by authors preceding my efforts. However, rest assured, characters and events of the episodes are products of my imagination. Captivating Alaska, of course, remains very real.

The cities of Juneau, Skagway, Haines, the Leland Canal, and majestic Tongass National Forest are easily found on the map. The proud and distinguished Tlingit Tribe around which much of the story line revolves is present in Southeastern Alaska as are their neighbors, the Haida, and Tsimshian Tribes. Native American Beliefs in the Natural World and its Creator, their God, "the hero with a thousand faces," strengthens their commitment to preserve Mother Earth and Father Sky, as the backbone of tribal unions to hold off white man's intrusion to their land, and its "taking" policies. The landscape in and around Leigh's hut on the meadow and the Tlingit Settlements are fictional.

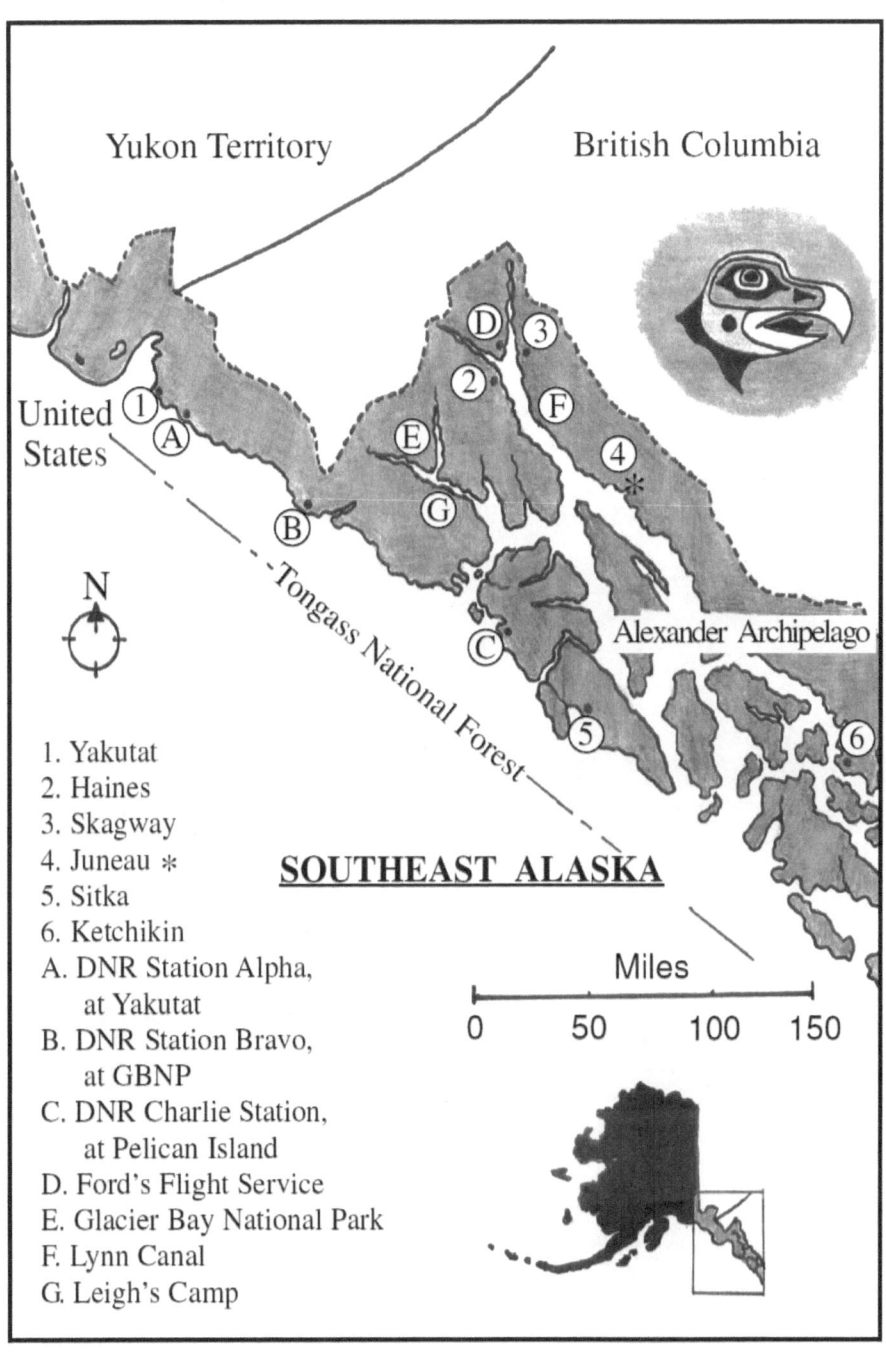

Yukon Territory

British Columbia

United States

Tongass National Forest

N

Alexander Archipelago

SOUTHEAST ALASKA

1. Yakutat
2. Haines
3. Skagway
4. Juneau *
5. Sitka
6. Ketchikin
A. DNR Station Alpha,
   at Yakutat
B. DNR Station Bravo,
   at GBNP
C. DNR Charlie Station,
   at Pelican Island
D. Ford's Flight Service
E. Glacier Bay National Park
F. Lynn Canal
G. Leigh's Camp

Miles

0   50   100   150

Chapter 1

A Journey To Discover

Never did she imagine that coming to the Alaskan wilderness to live amid nature and write a book would bring her to this: a long, desperate night protecting the mangled and bloody bodies of her friends from scavengers and grizzly bears.

*　　*　　*

The Northern Rockies provided a special kind of isolation. With its scarcity of conventional roadways and landing strips, the forest provided a perfect environment for those seeking seclusion—simple solitude, alone by choice. Leigh West would certainly need a little more time than Thoreau's twenty-six months at Walden Pond. She embraced his fundamental logic and would attempt to interweave his thoughts as she chose freely her estrangement from mankind. His opus, *On Solitary Retreat*, reflected her feelings:

"I went to the woods because I wished to live life deliberately."

It seemed ideal at first, building the shelter from components air-delivered by bush pilot Ford Harrison, learning native Indian beliefs from local Shaman Walkswithwater, appreciating the companionship of her faithful pointer, Boy, and testing herself to learn what truly matters here in the spectacular Tongass rainforest. The sun had risen much earlier, but the temporary campsite still lurked in the shadows of the Coastal Range's soaring peaks.

Although silent to others, dawn appeared as a loud crack, bursting like liquid sunshine, pouring onto the distant hillsides along the river. Startled, Leigh raised her head. As her auburn locks billowed to her shoulders, she scanned where the sun had fully enveloped the range to the west. She looked up to the water-soaked air above the river as it transformed to a captivating, mysterious mist. Eerie, concealing but natural, the mist would be short-lived as the sun continued to rise in the southeast. Brightness awakened Mother Earth.

Silence embraced the vigor of dawn—powerful but deafening. The muffled beauty of sunshine triggered memories of Leigh's past, and what would never be again . . . . The new day in a new life in a new locale had begun as she mumbled aloud, "Let's get moving."

She scanned the horizon, treetops, river, pathway, and finally the banks of the Bitterroot River. The shroud of evaporating mist revealed the landscape to the west. Strange how what is true at first light belies the scene of darkness as dawn reveals the magnitude of the forest.

Absent the mask of mist, the river unveiled several ducks quietly foraging, others running on water and flapping to escape an unseen adversary. Small shore birds also moved along the narrow sand bank like Sir Charlie Chaplin.

Step, step, step, tilt head—listen—peck.

Step, step, step, tilt head—listen—peck.

Then a *sound* would startle them, and they'd fly away, and repeat . . .

Step, step, step, tilt head—listen—peck . . .

The shadow of pine and fir provided a gossamer lace of beauty as the birds darted through the outline of the canopy near the sandy bank. The birds were also busy trying to survive as part of the food chain. They, too, were proving that only the fittest remain to subsist and breed. There is no free lunch in the wild. Likewise, Leigh belonged to the chain and had experienced the trauma of its cycle in the lower forty-eight. She had become displeased with the establishment—yes, mankind—after marital abuse and the resulting pain. She felt that the Tongass and writing would clear her mind and test her skills for the future. Upset with the norms that judged popular opinion, religious myths, and a full range of conservative to liberal beliefs, she, like e.e. cummings, had had enough of conformity:

> "To be yourself in a world that is trying
> night and day to make you just like everyone
> else is to fight the hardest battle anyone
> has ever fought, and keep on fighting."

She felt like a million bucks after a good night's sleep in the open, absorbing the intrinsic rewards, if not rapture, of the evening under the stars hopefully without any serious animal intrusion to the camp larder. She stretched and looked to the left to check the three-person pup tent. Then, while straining her sleepy body, she checked the elevated bear-proof food cache hanging in the tree. As planned, it hung in one of the "twin pines" that marked her spot on the river for Ford. Landmarks like these are a critical element for bush pilots since their location is the only way to ensure that campers can be found again for resupply or recovery. Nevertheless, she felt a little more secure with her satellite phone and other electronic aids, certainly more in touch with the world than Sacagawea with Lewis and Clark in 1804.

At some point in life, knowing very well there is a scoreboard and that you win some, lose some, every person should let safety take a second position to adventure by embracing the wonder of nature up close and personal. In Leigh's case, she felt that if laws of the food chain terminate an individual—so be it. Of course, she had no plans to toss caution to the wind, either. With luck, she would want to have at least twenty years left of good-time living.

It's early, she thought.

Should I get up?

The dew is still on the sleeping bag.

Maybe a few more minutes.

Yeah, that's what I'll do; maybe thirty minutes more . . .

Suddenly, she heard the telltale signs of enthusiastic Boy . . .

Huff-huff-huff! Lick-lick! Whine . . .

The decision had been made; there would be no more rest. She would have to get up because Boy now stood over her, soaking wet. Apparently he had been the adversary chasing ducks that she had seen earlier. Thankfully, Boy's presence gave Leigh the assurance that she'd never really be alone. Ford had insisted that Boy go with her into the forest for the extra eyes, ears, and nose in this hostile environment.

Boy's presence at dawn and again at sunset always gave her a secure feeling. Even in the tent, his fine-tuned whine indicated when she needed to respond. Friend or foe, he let her know. In daylight, she loved watching the movement of his ears, even with his head down resting between his paws. Observing him react to windward scents presented animation at its very best. If his head came out of his paws, she'd look; otherwise, she'd pass on any action or response. His eyes would also soften at her sight, but then quickly harden to brittle yellow jewels as he scanned the edge of the river or the shadows deep in the foreboding timber for potential danger.

Many mornings, Leigh would pull her aging body out of the poly-sack and stretch her uppers, lowers, and neck to pump life back into her well-tuned body. After watching, Boy would repeat every motion horizontally as if he had viewed his own TV doggie exercise show, too. With his ungainly four legs, toothy yawn, and bobbing tail, he would lie down and wait for her next move.

I've got to get going, she mused.

Boy, you've made the difficult decision for me.

I'm getting out and up, right now.

Come on, girl, drag your fanny out of the bag.

Getting ready for the hut-building project gave Leigh the mental goose she needed to get going. The building area was thirty feet up the sandbank, and the two of them had a lot of site preparation work ahead. She had planned for a schedule to complete the airdropped hut in ten days.

"Let's get going, Boy. Daylight's burning."

*   *   *

The hut would be phased, over three or four flights, in prefabricated sections. With good weather, good luck, and skillful assembly, it would provide comfort and security from Alaska's extreme climate and animals of the forest for three years. Boy would be her helper, fetching tools, getting parts, and just being there to provide security or to complain to about difficulties or to brag about successes. The designers in Skagway had said it would take about two weeks to assemble with her limited non-powered tools, simple erection tripods and ramps—plus a lot of good old common sense.

"Okay, Boy, you like to play hard; now we're going to work hard and start erecting this Jessie," said Leigh. Boy's ears perked up as he seemed to sense her change in mood. "Come on, Boy, let's roll."

Their temporary camp was on the flood-plain, so she started lugging the first pallet of four separate boxes, dropped earlier, up from the river's edge to higher ground.

"Christ!" Leigh exclaimed. "There goes one of the boxes downriver. It must have broken loose in the water during impact. Yikes! It's taking off as if in a horse race. Whoa! Damn it, box—hold on. Boy, what are we going to do?"

The box moved suddenly to the center of the river. She quickly secured the remaining boxes on the pallet, called Boy, and ran along the bank hoping for an intercept along the river's edge. Running, jumping, and leaping over roots and deadfalls, she charged downriver much faster than the current.

"Ha, I've got you now," she declared as the heavy half-exposed box jostled toward the slower eddy current at the bend. Boy thought it was a game of tag or hide-and-seek as he enjoyed the on-bank declarations of Leigh.

"You're mine now, baby, come on. Just a little more this way and I'll snatch you from Neptune's grasp," Leigh proclaimed. "Just a little more."

Then it happened.

Snap echoed along the river as the limb broke under her weight with gravity taking care of the rest.

Splash!

A water-laced "son-of-a-bitch" followed along the ridge as Leigh proclaimed her plight to all those in the Tongass with ears. Wallowing in the mud-bottomed, whirlpool-like eddy, she managed to keep her fingers around the twine-tied box. She struggled to stand up and regain her footing while still holding on to the box. It was a difficult task while spread-eagled, but on the fourth try she stood and cleared her eyes of the muddy silt-laden mask of the 'Root.

Then she heard it.

Splash!

Her eyes barely clear now, she mused, "*What the hell was that?*" Boy had jumped in and was paddling around as if they were playing tag again. As she continued clearing her eyes, she gave him a piece of her mind. "No, Boy, not now, I'm trying to get out of here." His frolicking stopped as he finally got the message.

"Get out, Boy, you're just stirring up the water . . . get out!" The splashing had stirred up some previously trapped flotsam now surrounding her and the entire surface of the oxbow. Boy struggled through the debris to the river's edge. As he leaped to shore, he accidentally released another trapped mass. She continued struggling in the flotsam while clearing her eyes and holding on to the box. She noticed a large clump of something floating straight at her; before she could react, a bloated, partially decomposed deer knocked her over, pushing her under the surface. On top of her submerged body, the deer hung up on Leigh and the box.

Panic shot through her as her attempt to surface was thwarted by the weight of the bloated deer.

She could not move.

She could not breathe.

The deer remained over her while she *still* held on to the box.

She had to make a decision quickly.

Then she heard the muffled sound of Boy's energized barking on the bank.

He must sense that I need help.

Boy jumped in the river and thrashed about, searching for Leigh's submerged torso. He pushed the deer carcass aside with a powerful thrust. Then submerging, he found Leigh and nudged her trembling body. She felt his presence, which triggered two quick actions to save her life—she released the box and pushed the carcass totally away with both hands, then darted to the surface and took a deep breath.

It worked.

She was free.

The box drifted downriver.

The putrid carcass tumbled into the current and moved serpentine fashion to the next snag in the river.

Boy exclaimed, "Woof!" with his welcome-back bark.

She rinsed her putrid-smelling hands, cleaned her face of muck and decomposed hide, and being totally exhausted, staggered to the bank to rest. "Come, Boy, *we made it.* That calls for a big kiss and hug. Thanks." After holding Boy's warm body and reassessing what had happened, she savored the moment in cheating death on her second day in camp.

"One thing is certain, Boy; I've got to get cleaned up. The center of the river by the shallows, up river, nearer camp, is next on my agenda. To hell with the box floating downriver; the S.O.B. almost cost me my life. Screw it! We'll get it later."

Carefully wading into the cool swift waters of the river, Leigh doffed all her muddy silt-stained clothes. She rinsed her mucked-up, bare-assed, goose-bumped body and clothes in a frisky, animated fashion. The water was cold. Boy joined in as if nothing had happened and it was a typical "playtime" with Leigh.

"Oops! There goes my brassiere downstream . . . Dang it. Oh well, I'll swing around and hang low a couple days. Who cares up here? Not I." Her wrists were sore and her shoulder was strained, but everything else seemed to be functioning.

"Thank goodness I'm still in one piece," she exclaimed to Boy, "and thank you again for helping out back there in the muck."

Suffering the dilemma of donning wet clothes in the middle of the river, she looked to see if the box had hung up on anything along the bank. Nothing in sight, she figured her next task was wading or walking the edge of the 'Root's downriver course.

"Dang, I must have a handful of sand in my pants. For Christ's sake, that's all I need. Okay, girl, assume the position." Her dad had told her many years ago how to purge the ocean's sand from the gates of hell . . . he was quite a character.

While facing the upriver current, Leigh dropped her Wranglers, knelt in the flow, shook her pants in the current, and stood up slowly while shaking out the sand traps.

How was the cold-water rinse? her father would have said, for he was always on the edge of being indecent. *Dad left no room for modesty; emotions were hung out on the clothesline of life experiences.*

Still soaking wet, she and Boy left the river and stumbled farther downstream to seek the errant box. Finally, after a hundred meters, they had some luck. Trapped in a root system on the edge of the rapids, the box was snagged right along the edge on their side of the river. The retrieval point was also shallow and clear so she simply rolled the box up the bank to the primitive game trail.

"What say you, Boy? How's that for a slick recovery? Let's drag it back to camp. Dang, this is hard work," she exclaimed as they reached the temporary camp and started moving the boxes to the permanent hut site. "Okay, Boy, one more time. Up, you mule, up, up, ha mule, up, up! Geez, I do sound like a mule skinner. Trouble is, I'm barking at myself."

Leigh had selected the east bank in the shadow of the tall timber at dawn for several reasons. She personally preferred sunsets to sunrises. This far north, she welcomed the late impingement of the setting sun on her camp.

At the best possible site now, she unpacked the tools and tripods for erecting the unit. With Boy's help she spent most of the afternoon leveling the site for proper drainage and placement of foundation supports. The black Mylar vapor barrier would be next, weighted down with rocks followed by large aluminum blocks placed in preassigned locations to support the octagon frames. They would be airdropped on the next flight.

"Voila! That didn't take long, Boy. I hope the rest of the project goes as well," Leigh proclaimed. Then she rested while bathing in the afternoon sun, drinking in its warmth while enjoying the lush aromas of summer.

"Can you picture us lounging in the hut in a couple months, or better yet, snuggled in our beds as a blanket of snow envelopes the Tongass? Guess what, we'll soon savor the scene from our secure abode."

While petting Boy, she looked up at the forest canopy. Late July had matured the leaves, and the crown metamorphosed into early changes of stunning yellow tints, soon to be followed by crimson reds and finally terminal brown. Visibility into the forest would improve and the animals, masked earlier by leaves, would appear for her enjoyment as they made their way around the hut in the meadow.

Man seems so insignificant, she thought, in the larger sense of the Earth's evolution. Would her token presence make any measurable contribution to life on this planet? Probably not. Would anyone even care? Most likely not.

"Come on, Boy, I'm tired, sore, and sleepy. Let's call it a day," Leigh said. She slipped into her sack as Boy snuggled to her side with his muzzle on her arm.

A pair of ravens appeared in the sky, circled camp, descended, and silently perched in one of the twin pines.

Leigh thought about her newfound love, Ford, the bush pilot who dropped her and Boy into the forest. He was her primary contact with civilization. She felt very dependent on him. He was her emotional base camp in her little corner of the world. The consequences of her choice, while separated from him in the wilds, became much easier in knowing he seemed to need her, too. She could count on him for anything—which is the basis for true love—giving of oneself for the pleasure of the other, without judgment, unconditionally.

Nevertheless, she had to get him out of her mind; she was getting just a little too romantic—or was it the adjustment of being alone? She must really be hooked on this warm but irascible old-time timber-duster pilot; just thinking about his cleverness made her feel more confident and comforted. It's strange how a few rolls in the hay with Ford made her tingle all over. She felt very wholesome about the guy. She knew, he knew, that they were stuck on each other.

Why Ford? Why live alone? Why Alaska?

*　　*　　*

Few knew Ford as a space program scientist—or anything about him. Likewise, he told very few of his experiences in Mexico and Spain while training to fight El Toro, the bull. It really didn't matter. His injuries did not affect his flying skills or judgment while ferrying personnel and equipment into the bush. And he knew very well to be careful, remembering, as the saying goes:

THERE ARE A LOT OF BOLD PILOTS
BUT THERE ARE NO OLD BOLD PILOTS.

Flying westward over the Tongass, Ford relished the challenges of piloting Big Red Bird, a powerful C-190 Cessna floatplane, in the Alaskan wilderness. While scanning the horizon, he thought of his most recent conversations with Leigh and his warm memories of how they had connected.

She was a welcome breath of fresh air from the first day she contacted Ford Flying Service (FFS) in Skagway. What a relief to talk to a confident, classy woman with a sound mind and hard body. She appeared a little brazen at first, but they quickly connected. He and his men tackled the hurry-up job to design, fabricate, and deliver the well-planned hut to her pastoral meadow along the Bitterroot River in the foothills of Mount Elias.

Ford needed a change. He just finished, thank God, a terrible two-year charter/supply contract with a Christian missionary group whose contract agreement turned sour and cost him a bundle. But a quote cannot be withdrawn and an oral contract is binding—even if it is a loser. The error was his. But for some strange reason the deacon in charge of the remote retreat felt that Ford should provide a lot of "gimmies" just because they were Christians. However, he had told them more than once, "Excuse me, I'm a businessman, an agnostic who believes the existence of any *ultimate reality*, of a creator, is unknown and probably unknowable; I'm uninterested in donating to your belief system. I've demonstrated time and time again over the years that I'm a loving and caring man to *everyone*, based on their actions, not their beliefs."

He felt he was living proof that life's goodness and appreciation could be embraced within elemental ethical logic, which certainly outweighed many corporate religions so prevalent in modern times. He could have shown his outrage to those who believe theirs is the only belief, but he didn't; Christians and Muslims in particular needed to learn to recognize that spirituality comes in many forms.

In a nutshell, he judged people on their actions when alone or how they behaved under stress—not their "institutional" belief system.

He, too, was about to experience aerial stress.

The collision occurred about ten miles west of Haines, at 2,600 feet mean sea level (MSL), about 2,000 feet above the ground in broken cumulus clouds. Ford had noticed a flock of geese in formation circling below, near the marsh area south of town. However, the C-190 being a high-wing type, he was unaware of the formation of a dozen or so stragglers descending from 3,000.

Two seconds after sighting the birds, Ford instinctively pushed the yoke forward and rotated it to the right to minimize the impact mass of the plane to the honking horde.

"What the . . . hell. Damn birds . . . Look out, you buggars! For Christ's sake . . . Oh no!" exclaimed Ford.

The plane rolled to starboard and descended . . . one bird never knew what was about to happen . . . and shredded through the propeller as blood and feathers. The bloody mass impacted the plane's cowling, windshield, and side windows . . .

One did not escape. Others, unseen, may have suffered the same fate. He also felt several birds impact the leading edge of the wing, pontoons, and undercarriage cargo-rack. Those who did were probably mortally wounded.

"Damn. What a sickening sight. That poor soul could have gone through the windshield and been sitting on my face." Visibility was restricted now, but the integrity of the windshield and fuselage appeared to be intact, albeit bloodied and feathered.

"You're a lucky camper, Ford. I hope the cargo-rack isn't full of dead birds. We'll soon find out when we land on the canal. Then I'll be able to check the vertical and horizontal stabilizer when I inspect this Jessie."

He returned to thoughts of the number one person in his life—Leigh. Her beliefs, in contrast, were in deism, believing in a supernatural creator, God, whose hands formed the universe, a belief based on human morality and reason rather than divine revelation, and that God had no part in man's daily activities. Pray to a deity, if you choose, was her view, remembering that it's only a "construct" of man.

Ford mused, *That's enough analysis of belief systems. I've never doubted an individual's need for a "construct" of God to help in time of personal crisis, nor that the prophet Jesus walked the Earth. It's trinitarianism that I could not embrace.*

He had read with keen interest the writings of the theological philosopher Joseph Campbell. He described how each civilization, separated over time, all developed deities to give thanks for their life on Earth. That sounded normal and expected if it helped the faithful develop positive character traits.

"I've sure been talking to the sky, the yoke, and empty co-pilot's seat for a while. I'd better see about landing this old bird," uttered Ford. The lights of Skagway appeared on the horizon straight ahead. Ford called Air Traffic Control (ATC) at the airport and asked for clearance to the landing area, local traffic conditions, and weather, then indicated he was descending from 2,000 feet for landing to the north on the waters of Lynn Canal in fifteen minutes.

"Roger, C-190. Winds easterly at five miles per hour, visibility twenty miles, temperature forty degrees Fahrenheit, minor chop on water of six inches. Clear to land. Flight Service Station, Skagway ATC on standby."

"Roger, ATC, this is ninety. Thanks for the good report; I'll let you know when the old bird is down, wet, and right side up. Ninety to standby."

ATC is generally all business, but Ford used humor as a distraction to imply everything on board was A-okay. If the truth were to be known—it wasn't A-okay. The multiple bird strikes may have damaged any number of items affecting the landing. However, experience with the FAA had given him a reason to be cautious about mentioning the bird strikes. He'd only report it as an incident if there were critical damage . . . since FAA's paperwork to Washington, D.C., would sink a battleship. Truly conservative, if anything was severely damaged he'd report it . . . but *only* if it impacted the flight-worthiness of Big Red. He hated that thought, hoping it was dark enough that the tower didn't notice part of Big Red's color was . . . blood red.

Ford gently coaxed the plane down, flaring precisely at water contact while pushing through the minor surface chop. The pontoon parted the water much like the burst of a breaching whale, then gradually separated the waters like a silent knife. A perfect water landing, like this one, is an awesome sight. The unauthorized hitchhikers—white, gray, and black goose feathers —were thankfully masked in the water spray. Easing into the frigid midnight-blue water, Big Bird coasted to the FFS docks.

"ATC, this is ninety, down, wet, and right side up. Thanks again. This is one-ninety, out."

He tied up the plane, inspected her for damage, hosed off the remaining hitchhiking avian anatomy, counted his blessings, and finally thanked her for another safe flight. His mistress of the sky had served him well—again.

"Damn, I sure miss Boy and Leigh. Well, it's off to Snug Harbor Saloon to wash down the day's in-flight trauma and loneliness of single life. Good night, old bird," Ford said, leaving the moonlight-basked docks.

*   *   *

After a good night's sleep under the stars, Leigh was lounging over an extended breakfast coffee in the clearing by the 'Root when she heard an airplane to the east. She hoped it was Ford circling the Cessna as he prepared for another drop at the river's broadest point. Then she heard what sounded like an explosion when suddenly the thunder of Big Bird's radial four-hundred burst over the treetops.

"There he is, Boy! Here we are, Ford! Hi, Babe!" she exclaimed. She splashed through the water, waving her hands as Ford tilted his wings slightly and roared by at 80 knots.

"Okay, girl, get organized. Get your hand-held radio so we can talk." Boy looked indifferent. He had not recovered from being pushed out of a perfectly good airplane at five hundred feet. He lay low in a water hole, his body and legs bruised and sore; wallowing in the water was just about all he could handle right now.

"DC 1, I have visual contact; let her rip any time now. Over," she called into her radio.

"DC 2, this is DC 1. Well, you made it. Congratulations! You're no longer a leg."

Woop! Snap! Flutter! The chute opened; the supplies were on the way. Leigh yelled at the top of her voice, "Yea! The package made it, Boy. We'll eat and sleep tonight in a little more comfort once I get the pallet out of the river."

"DC 2, this is DC 1. I'm headed back to the airport. I'll start bringing up the hut tomorrow. Over."

"Roger, Babe, thanks for the lift. Boy is still looking kind of beat and puzzled. He never knew quite what to expect with your dog harness-chute assembly. He still looks up when you pass, with an expression of disgust for you."

"He'll get over it," Ford related. "He's tough like me. Now remember, load your forty-four immediately, and get the supplies under cover, odors squelched, and generally buttoned up before dark sets in. Over."

"Okay, okay, we've been over this a hundred times. I'll behave, maybe. . . . Over."

"Well, don't be too good; I might lose interest," he joked. "Say, I'll be out of line-of-sight communications soon. I've got to head back anyway; remember our 'sked' to talk every third day at 0600 hours. Over."

"Roger all that, dear. Now don't worry if I miss one call. Love you, take care. This is DC 2. Out."

"This is DC 1. Roger wilco, out," said Ford in an anxious voice. He was very concerned about Leigh's remoteness and the dangers of the Tongass.

A raven appeared suddenly, gracefully circling the site and descending to perch quietly in one of the eloquent twin pines at the river's edge.

She now felt very alone after all the preflight preparation, the flight, landing by chute, and the successful airdrop of pallet number one of five. Not wanting to worry him, she had said nothing about the loose box and recovery trauma. She'd survived, learning how hazardous living on one's own could be. She had a little concern for her safety, too, but quickly shed the "Did I do the right thing?" analysis since that was not going to change. One thing certainly helped minimize her doubts—she looked around and savored the most magnificent spot possible in the mighty Tongass National Forest. Awestruck, she thought, *those trees are huge.*

"Boy, where are you?"

Woof, sounded from a distant stand of cattails.

"Come over here and help your mom! Sorry to bark at you, but if you're okay now, we've got to get these supplies secured, tent erected, food protected, and the permanent river camp established.

While walking back to the river's edge, she gasped. Another box had broken loose from the pallet.

"Oh no! No! Christ! Here we go again, Boy! Look! One of the boxes is floating away," Leigh exclaimed.

She ran toward the edge of the river and lunged into the water. Too late and too dangerous, she flailed her way back to the bank and Boy. She looked at him, then the box bobbing merrily away, and had an idea. She had to act quickly, and with haste she did. "Boy, you're going to get that box—fetch!"

Boy looked around, barked, and spun again in excitement looking for a "bird-like" retrieval opportunity. He jumped up and barked again. He saw no bird to retrieve. Puzzled, he looked at Leigh.

"Fetch that box . . . the box, Boy," as she now pointed to the eluding bobbing box. Boy now seemed to get the idea. He looked at the box, and back at Leigh for assurance, and again at the box.

"Fetch. That's right, Boy, fetch!"

Fetch he did. In an instant, he leaped into the water, bounded until unable to contact bottom, and finally dog-paddled to the box. Without additional instructions, he nipped at the loose twine several times until his teeth held fast, then started pulling to the river's edge.

By now he had drifted downriver several meters where Leigh met him with a robust, water-soaked hug. The box was retrieved in quick order, and she received a celebratory drenching as Boy shook off the river water.

"Thank you, my dear dog. What a wonderful friend to have in camp. I'm blessed. First you help me recover, and now you score as a first-rate retriever of the errant box. Come on, Boy, let's roll," she said as they returned to the clearing with the box in tow.

With a lot of tugging, lugging, and sweat, she started working on a more complete camp, and in less than an hour of sawing and nailing she built a rustic bench at the edge of the river.

"Well, if I don't say so myself, this is a beautiful provincial bench, Boy. Come, let's give it a sit-test; come on, big fella," she bragged to Boy.

The raven continued to watch like a stoic sentinel, never moving, as he witnessed their progress.

Sitting on the bench, she inhaled the beauty of the temporary camp. The peace it radiated soon embraced her heart and soul. She felt with her every move that her mission was now underway, and that it would purge the doubts of her past. Delusion would soon perish, and her body and soul slowly find Nirvana.

Peace of mind would soon be in her grasp.

She recalled one of her favorite 16th-century French authors, Montaigne, whose work had dramatically affected her life. He wrote so clearly in one fine passage that paralleled her beliefs and reflections on her life:

> "And if you have lived a day, you have seen
> everything. One day is equal to all days, there
> is no other light, no other night. This sun, this
> moon, these stars, the way they are arranged, all
> is the same your ancestors enjoyed, and that will
> entertain your grandchildren."

She surveyed the captivating camp in the clearing and gave it a wink and nod of approval as the sun cast early-afternoon shadows across the river.

"Slide over here, Boy; I need another nostalgic hug . . . thanks, I needed that," Leigh said as she bathed in the afternoon sun.

*   *   *

Jumping off the bench, Leigh exclaimed, "Oops, we must have nodded off to sleep, Boy. It's getting late, about three. Let's get some fresh air on one of those ridges." She looked around at the beautiful oaks and conifers jutting out of the ridgelines encircling the meadow, trying to decide which one to climb.

"Let's attack the ridgeline to the west."

They meandered up the steep slope around deadfalls, leaped over fallen giants, and inched their way up the ridge to an open meadow-like flat clearing on top. The climb was more like an obstacle course to reach the crest.

"This looks a little better. In fact, it's gorgeous up here. Come on, big guy; now I can race you to the other side of the clearing and see what's there. Slow down, Boy," Leigh hollered as she raced after him, never expecting him to obey; he always wanted to show off his speed. He loved to run, whether on land or in the water. Halfway across the clearing she paused to rest and scan the horizon with her binoculars. She was awestruck by the dancing clouds and sunlight glittering on the river. The western sawtooth range fulfilled her vision of the forest's true natural beauty, unspoiled and untouched by man. Blue-gray to azure shadows added depth to the endless undulating ridges of the distant sea. Her only worthy description for the area: "glorious."

"Oops," she exclaimed as Boy's nose nudged her crotch. "I give up on teaching you a more socially acceptable attention getter."

Her dad had said long ago, "It's no accident; they know what they're doing . . . and it gets your attention . . . doesn't it?" Boy was back and ready to race again.

"Okay, let's go." Off they went across the clearing, lickety-split. Looking around more than at where she was going, she tripped over a partially concealed rock. Her binoculars raced ahead without her, disappearing into tall, dense grass. Cautiously searching on her hands and knees for the Nikons, she moved through the grass like a cat seeking mice, one slow step at a time, with deliberate placement of one paw after another, her stealthy movements feline-like, looking forward, over her shoulder, and sideways until a rise in the earth stopped her for a moment.

She felt uneasy. The surroundings now seemed different. She knew not why. *A raven appeared on a branch at the edge of the meadow.*

Leigh's pounding heart seemed to be echoing across the clearing. Her mouth was dry and metallic as she swallowed again and again to moisten. She also sensed a change in the intensity and pitch of the wind in the stoic pines . . . as if a whispering voice were warning her of danger in what she was doing in the clearing.

Unsure how to explain it, she felt as though someone or something watched all her movements. Could it be her imagination? She experienced a strange, mystical-type feeling. An eerie spell seemed to envelop the clearing. She was uncertain as to just what was happening.

She shook, and then shivered.

The air in the meadow changed, a palpable heaviness pervading her senses. She felt afraid. Picking up the pace of her search, she quickly felt around the tall grass until she found a round, rough-surfaced object on the edge of a slight depression. Separating the tall grass for a better look, she gasped! She had discovered a half-buried, bleached and charred skull lying next to the Nikons.

She scrambled away, stood up, and caught her breath. Boy joined her quickly as if sensing her surprise. "No problem, Boy, just a skull," she said in an astonished voice. Shocked, they both froze in place, Leigh wondering what to do next. They looked around the clearing. . . .

"Did you hear that?"

He must have heard something, for he had suddenly stiffened to a point, his hackles raised, growling at a sound in the direction of the skull. He crept closer to investigate, but he backed away, too, whimpered, lowered his head in an unusually submissive fashion, looked at Leigh, and waited for her to say something. She wondered how the hell fate could deal her a situation like this on her first full day in camp. Coincidence? It seemed more than accidental that the binoculars came to rest next to a skull . . . what appeared to be a human skull.

Finding herself face-to-face with the vestiges of death, she retrieved the binoculars and bolted up and away again, then stopped. She wondered, could this have been a lost hunter? *The remains of an ancient one, abandoned by the tribe? The sacrifice to some mythical god?* She fretted. . . .

Several more ravens circled the clearing and descended to the trees on its perimeter.

Unsure of these possibilities, she returned to the site to investigate further. Poking around the bones might provide some clues. Why the charring? The rest of the skeleton appeared to be on the top of a large, partially buried stone slab. She found a large dead branch, broke it to fashion a crude digging stick, and moved the bones to the surface. Boy sniffed until he found a stray bone and tried to play with it, which upset Leigh.

"Boy, drop that!" Obedient, he gave the large femur-like bone back to her. She still felt strange disturbing the skeleton; it didn't seem right. And it did seem a little spurious in the openness of the clearing. Leigh continued digging to help clear the site around the granite-like slab. Boy joined in now as unearthing the slab progressed rapidly. They stopped periodically to examine their progress, and nervously searched the surrounding timber with their eyes. Still feeling queasy and nervous about what they were doing, she saw at least a hundred ravens congregating on the perimeter of the clearing.

She shivered again, as the birds called . . .

Caw—Caw—Caw.

Suddenly, she noticed a mass of ravens descending toward them from the trees, and before she could react, a dozen or so swooped down on both of them. Boy barked and she ducked as they came within inches of their heads. Rising again, the birds turned in flight and dove back again.

"Get down, Boy," she shouted as he jumped at them on the second pass. "What the hell is going on here? Would you believe it? It's as though we're in the Hitchcock thriller *The Birds*. Down, Boy, they may be coming back."

Then as abruptly as they attacked, the birds returned to their aerial perch. Arms akimbo, Leigh stared at the treetops in disbelief.

Without warning, something moved near the slab.

Nudging her aside, Boy moved aggressively toward the mound, stopped, and growled while on the rock-hard point.

The slab moved again. The movement allowed for the surface debris to completely cover the exposed skeleton.

"Okay, Boy, that's enough; it's getting too spooky around here. Let's finish up and get out of here. I think we must have unsettled the slab while digging. These things must have a logical explanation . . . don't you think? At least I hope that's the case."

On her knees, she mused. *It's got to have been our digging. I certainly hope it is not something else . . . a warning? Something isn't right here. We better take one more look and leave this menacing site.*

To her surprise, she found a secondary shelf on legs of four large boulders elevating the slab. *It was now evident that they had found an altar* of some sort; she felt more certain that, indeed, it could be a sacrificial worship site of the native Indians. Was it a place of honor or dishonor? Was the body a villain or an important member of a tribe? But so small a bone structure. . . .

Still on her knees, she looked around again. There were still several hundred ravens in the trees watching like silent sentinels.

"Okay, you ebony scoundrels, we'll soon be gone. Hold on a little longer."

She noticed the slightly higher elevation at the site, and the area appeared to be on the highest ridge along the valley. While standing parallel to the slab, she also observed how the spectacular view to the west revealed the Bitterroot River meandering its way through the sister peak's cleavage and out to the western plains on the horizon.

Another coincidence: she noted that allowing for the current month's sun angle, the summer solstice sun would align straight down the cleavage in the mountain in June, directly impacting the tilted slab. She had an idea. Then, as if commanded, she cleared the top surface of the block, being careful not to disturb the skeleton. Her bare fingers felt the chiseled grooves, and she cleared the etched path along the surface. She now felt a concave circular shape at the end of the groove. The circular shape had radiating patterns emanating from its center . . . like the rays of a sun.

"Bingo! That's it. The slab is an altar aligned to the sun's rays at solstice. I know it. It's right here. I'm right!"

Since recorded time, the solstice had been observed when the sun reaches the point farthest north of the equator, its angle predictable and repeatable. The tribal leaders and shamans must have observed and recorded . . . and placed the altar accordingly.

She felt just a bit irreverent, having clearly violated the ceremonial shrine-like alcove of an earlier tribal nation. It all fit together—precise solar alignment of the sun to the south, known presence of Tlingit tribes in the area, and a history of native sacrifices.

Was her imagination getting the best of her? She didn't think so. Nevertheless, the spot appeared to be so sacred and so peaceful that she felt as if she were a part of a truly unique experience. Death is celebrated in many special ways by various cultures, and she was in the center of this one. Looking around, she felt it now . . . she felt the presence of death, and the need to restore the site.

She replaced most of the disturbed soil and debris. Why she did it was unclear, but like Buddhist worshippers she slowly backed out and away from the alcove in respect of the tribes' beliefs. "What a relief," she whispered.

Looking for Boy somewhere in the clearing, she reflected on a contrasting view of death by Utah's Cactus Ed Abbey:

"Please leave me to my mistress, the southwest desert, and let the sun, buzzards, coyotes, and rodents scatter my bones across Mother Earth from whence I came. And please tell no one where I lay. Some things are private. I want no honors, only the glory of returning to a desert grave. . . ."

This situation was similar in conviction, but divergent in reverence. She hoped the intrusion would be forgiven.

"Come on, Boy, let's get going. We'll return at a later date with some background information about the local tribes. Come on, those mice you're digging at will wait. Plus, that flock of ravens could still cause us big trouble. They must have been guarding this site for years. And, yes, we're probably intruding. Let's go."

As Leigh walked down the ridge, the ravens rose from their perches and soared to the thermals without a sound.

She had a pretty good idea that she'd be returning to the site. Someone in Skagway's Native American population would know about this section of the Tongass. Wondering if she was over-reacting about the site's origin, she thought, *Maybe I'm reading too much Michener.* Time would tell; there would be another day.

Arriving at camp, she found herself still yelling at Boy to join her and leave the mice alone. It was getting dark. "Boy! Come on, let's grab a sandwich and get some sack time. Come on!"

She unzipped the tent, and in they went. Settling in, she heard the sounds of the night like a symphony of music, both melodic and soothing. She wondered, *Is that an owl? And isn't that a night hawk?* What's that? *Stop*, she said to herself. *You'll never figure out all these sounds. Get to sleep.*

Finally, "Good night, Boy."

Boy's muzzle sought Leigh's arm while he moaned in a throaty sound. His ears, once lifting to every sound outside, were now finally at rest. He laid his head beside his mistress and slept.

A raven landed silently in the tree above the tent.

Under the cool starlit night, the only sound heard on the edge of the meadow was the babbling bubbles of the Bitterroot. It had been a day to remember.

Nightly denizens of the meadow now appeared silently in the moon's eerie shadows. One, a large silver-tip bruin, emerged from the nearby swamp, scattering several smaller animals in the meadow, for they knew very well that he ruled the night. . . .

Chapter 2

Discovering

Outside the morning wind moaned and shrieked as if the Mountain Spirit resented this invasion of his ancient domain. The sounds nudged Leigh and Boy from their deep restful sleep. Leigh's presence in the forest was in fact the result of dramatically taking control of her life in its last quartile.

She asked, "What should we do with our lives as time occupies more space?" Thoreau, again, offers this advice:

> "Do what you love. Know your own bone; gnaw at it, bury it, and gnaw at it still . . .
> Be not simply good—be good for something.
> Live experiences and growth, not just doing something well."

Both Montaigne's and Thoreau's writings had encouraged uncompromising independence.

Thoreau wrote:

> ". . . yes, apply those thoughts found in school—but to live a life of simplicity—of independence—of magnanimity and trust—such as all should live." Furthermore, ". . . *do not adopt my mode* of living on any account, for beside that, before he has fairly learned it, I may have found out another for myself. Pursue your own way—many ways—and not your father's or mother's or neighbor's instead."

Leigh had always valued the advice of scholars. It was time for change in her character,

too; Thoreau was very convincing about living and writing in a remote locale. She decided to look at things in a new and different way, and the northern climes would serve that need. She would rediscover herself, one way or another.

A choice to be alone in the Northern Forest was just what Leigh needed to get away and "write the flames in her heart." The past twenty years had altered her opinion of certain institutions in society.

"Come on, Boy, it's time to get up and at it." She hollered, "If dogs could talk, I don't think the response would be very positive." He had, after all, explored the highlands above the river and dug until tuckered, or should she say was "dog tired." They repeated the morning stretching now, in unison. "Come on, Boy, Jane Fonda I'm not. Let's go, our hut work is awaitin'. Damn, I've got some digging and hiking pains, too, but the day's work will assuredly take the kinks out of this old bod. You know, Boy, I'm just not what I used to be . . . but is anybody?" She cried, "No!"

Camp was inspected by the nose of the best as Boy sniffed every nook and cranny in and around the site. Of course he had to leave his mark, again, as if to say, "Yep, that's me, I'm still here . . . beware."

"Please, Boy, not on the tent," she called. "Let's hit the water and clean up."

He aggressively walloped the water in the stream as she freshened up for the day's activities. She thought it would be nice to do that, but splashing naked did not seem to be on her list this morn, maybe this noon. The hell with it—why not right now—she didn't care if she was bare-assed at ten-hundred hours in the Bitterroot with the dog and 10,000 pines. No one was here to look, care, or even judge. She felt, screw 'em; she'd decide, not anyone else. *Remember, you're not beholden to some of the prudish ethics of the lower 48.*

Well, a "romp" in the nude is sensitive if done in the fountain in front of the League at U of M at midnight, which she did in the '60s as part of a not-so-sober challenge . . . but she did it!

"*But you're not there now,* she said to herself. *Stop it, Leigh; quit thinking about 'others' all the time, especially up here in the northern environs. Now is the time for change, and change was needed. Right? Right! Enough,* she thought, *get on with it.*

They had a lot of work remaining to finish erecting the hutch so they could vacate the tent and start writing and exploring. The aboriginal altar was still on her mind. If Tlingit, as they're known to be indigenous to the area, were there any settlements still around? She wondered. She also wondered if they knew of its location. They were certainly unaware of her discovery. She also wondered if she should share this unusual find, or keep its uniqueness to herself. She wondered. What's fair?

Pondering for many moments, Leigh came to a decision. *It will remain my discovery, my covert secret, unless conditions are present by a Tlingit that merits changing my mind.*

She strongly believed certain aspects of life and its unique experiences and discoveries should remain personal, even to death—unless, of course, sharing that information would save your fellow man, your family or those you love. She thought there were few secrets to protect that affect others. She was referring to personal experiences, personal exposure to one's soul, error in judgment, and personal relationships that provided an extreme exposure to life or death and love or loss of love.

As she undressed along the river's edge, the well-worn Levi denim and the *Michigan* sweatshirt dropped to the primitive log bench. Boy stopped, frozen in place. He knew something was amiss, different, and well, puzzling! The dog staring at her was hard to explain, except that he'd never seen her undress outside or away from the tent. Oh well, things change dramatically up here; there are few rules . . . *Go for it, girl . . . whatever you're up to*, he mused.

Dang, she's fully undressed now, what next?

SPLISH-SPLASH—CRASH ON YOUR ASS!

Leigh thought, *What the hell is the difference, even if a hunter, pilot or native saw me at a distance.* Boy gave her a big helping of confidence with his protective presence. She recalled an earlier accidental 12-second exposure at school when one of the "Fratters" told their buddies, "I saw Leigh's black patch and nips!"

Well, if that's what turns 'em on, so be it, at least this time she wasn't dashing from the shower in a coed dorm. Still cautious, more of bears and wolves, she enjoyed the "romp" with Boy, throwing sticks, retrieving and chasing irretrievable submerged stones. What a way to start the day! She sang, "Splish, splash, I'm gonna crash . . . come on, fall on your ass."

OOPS! What was that . . . She was standing on a crawfish. It dashed away, backwards, she hoped without injury. Suddenly, she laughed with the uncontrolled robust laughter as she thought of Michigan's Greek sororities' traditional Spring song:

THE FIRST OF MAY, THE FIRST OF MAY
OUTDOOR SCREWING STARTS TODAY
HOORAY—HOORAY! LET'S PLAY

In hindsight, she would not change many events in her life, be it friends and fun, as humorously referenced, involvement with family, men, or sex. Her dad had another oblique reference to being careful with boys as a teenager. It was actually from G.B. Shaw. An actress, in the 1800s related her (Shaw's) feelings about sex in one of his plays:

"It doesn't matter what you do in the bedroom as long as you
don't do it in the street and scare the horses."

While watching Boy and drying her svelte 120-pound, sixty-eight-inch body, she mused . . . *I have so much to be thankful for:* her family who stayed the course during one crisis, after unfathomable expense and separation, balanced by the loving support of friends who never faltered. And, of course, there was Ford. Everyone needs an anvil of emotional stability and unwavering love when thrust into a new and unknown environment, and that was Ford. Having said that, she still espoused the opportunity she chose to be alone while still cleaving to her man and rediscovering herself, her final goals, and writing.

The sun was at its zenith and, as her dad used to say, "Sunlight is awaiting, let's get going!"

"Come on, Boy," she said, "let's level and grade the site today, unroll the black poly sheeting, secure it with rocks, and drag the foundation rocks into place. Then we'll be ready for the hut sill beams. We'll be out of this tent soon." Boy looked, cocked his head, got that puzzled expression on his face, barked, and seemed to think, *Something good must be happening soon.* Jumping for joy for what, he probably didn't know, but both had an added skip in their step as they reached the building site. They both hustled and got the shovel, rake, and rope to move some real estate.

After leveling the site 20' x 20" (400 sq. ft.), she unrolled the plastic, weighted down with large rocks, and edges trimmed and buried; her eyes indicated this looked good, even if she said so herself.

The large rocks were heavy, and she needed a total of sixteen 18-inch-diameter boulders along the sill beam within plus/minus one inch of accuracy. Shims would ensure true leveling and tie downs would ensure the plate remained on the rock foundations—water acted as a compaction means prior to emplacement. She thought it would be nice to have surveyors' optics or a laser beam-leveling device. No sweat, she'd get it very close to level. She had fashioned a simple stone-boat with a rope tie down and harness (people type) for skidding the rocks to the site. It was slave labor reborn for four hours of Egyptian-style toil. But, it worked and all boulders were in place by 1800 hours. Boy seemed to sense that she was tired, so he snuggled her body with care, the exertion having sapped her strength. There was enough left to stroke his ears and neck. "Good boy. Your old mom will be up and at it again soon, but for now I'm just going to flop." She groaned. He, too, was accustomed to being on Leigh's side, his head on leg, or head on arm, or head on her lap, as a show of affection to her.

A soaring eagle banked, circled and glided by to inspect this intrusion into his terrain. After three passes his curiosity was satisfied; he screeched and headed west with the evening thermals. A squirrel, accustomed to an undisturbed lair, repeated his warning, chattering, "This is my meadow; this is my hideaway—scram" again and again, but it didn't work. The dog and lady were undaunted by the challenge. Frustrated, the squirrel was apparently not sure what he'd do about this; maybe nothing, since dogs don't climb trees. "I guess they can stay; I guess it's okay to have some visitors. Hope their stay is short-lived . . . Ooops, hide, here comes that grumpy old gray squirrel heading this way. Bully, he is, always strutting for the girls."

"Listen, Boy," said Leigh, holding him to her chest. "Listen to that sound upon the ridge." They would soon know, elk were getting ready for the fall "rut" as the forest rang out to the bone-on-bone sounds of bulls knocking their antlers against trees and each other.

"You know, Boy, let's take another swim in the river to cast off today's soil and freshen up this old tired bod. Remember, Ford is due to drop our second package tomorrow, so let's clean up and eat before sack time. It will be a real challenge for both the fly-boy above and the construction team below tomorrow as our 'Manor' starts to take shape.

"Last one in is a dirty rascal," she said, knowing very well that Boy would be soaking wet and chomping/drinking the water before she ever got her shoes off. Sure enough his eyes said, *What's the holdup, girl; I'm waiting to play*! Submerged, she wallowed like a walrus, sans tusks, as the afternoon sun sank to four fingers from the horizon. A beautiful yellowish-orange glow reflected on the Bitterroot pool. It was a glorious scene. Not a cloud appeared in the sky, not even a haze generally found at 50 degrees latitude; only cool breezes moved casually across the landscape. Alaska is like that, a masterpiece of nature, and an area to make the heart glad that man is an animal who can love the entire earth as a deer loves the cool highlands, or a bear as it scavenges for those beloved berries and honey. Yet in autumn, when the seasons are about to change, it has a special beauty, and if great thoughts have sometimes come from this small region, it is partly because of the magnificence of this land. The magnificence that lies in familiar earthly things, rather than in the similar beauty of great oceans, has always impressed itself upon the people who lived in the area.

A splendid silence of whispering pines, screeching eagles, and soft fluttering wings of their own little shore birds embraced life on the 'Root. Wasn't that a little presumptuous? She felt that they were her birds; well, they stayed with her after she and Boy intruded on their domain, so they must be hers. She sank below, away from the modulated din of the forest. It was heavenly silence below the calm waters. *Ooops, up you go, girl; you do not have gills. Heavenly, yep; that's what it is; wait a minute, what's that?* Something startled her. She threw back her auburn locks. "What's up, Boy? Boy, are you there?"

Woof, as if to say, "over here."

The sound was Boy's growl. He stood frozen in a four-legged muscular stance with neck and back hair erect, pointing at the opposite side of the 'Root. Leigh's eyes followed Boy's to a white wolf that was equally frozen in place at 200 feet. . . . Here she was, naked, a visiting wolf and her side arm twenty feet away.

Not good. Neither canine moved, nor did Leigh. All three just stared at each other. She slowly inched her way toward her clothes. Another sound roared into the scene.

It continued . . . Could there be a storm front plowing its way through the sky, or was it the wind in the pines? "No. It's a plane!"

The noise must have startled the white wolf. He bolted and ran into the trees. Luckily, Boy did not pursue. "Good boy. . . Come."

"It's Ford; what's he doing here? He's a day early! Not only a day early, but late in the afternoon of the same day!"

Buck naked, she stood up, hands on hips, arms akimbo, and stared upward at that unpredictable, unbridled hunk as he passed over on his downwind leg. She could just hear him saying:

"Damn, I think I'll land and roll around with that she-fish while she's already stripped to her scales." She knew him only too well.

"Damn you!" she said as he dipped his wing and glared at the naked lady below—she knew his thoughts. Don't most women? "Okay, so you saw the hips and tits in broad daylight by sneaking up on me . . . you big funk."

She ran, splashing toward her clothes on the bench to get to her transceiver.

"Stop, Boy, I'm not playing. It's Ford, I've got to get to the hand-held. Sorry, Boy, later.

I'm proud of you for standing down that white wolf and not chasing. "Good boy."

"DC2, this is DC 1, over," Ford radioed.

"DC1, I read you loud and clear, over," Leigh responded.

"You have made my day—the whole body parade with hips, nips, and tits; saluting me was great, not to mention the 'other.'"

She knew he'd say or think something like that. "Okay, this is my bathtub, you know; what are you doing here a day early? Over."

"A long story, weather problems tomorrow, so get dressed, or I'll land this bird and fly my bird to your nest."

"Some FAA official may be listening."

"Yeah, at this latitude, I doubt it. Seriously, I'll be dropping the first pallet in a moment; get dressed, I'm getting overly stressed sexually. Over."

"Okay, Babe, see you on the up-wind leg in a few minutes. Love you. Out."

*   *   *

He thought to himself, *I love you, too* . . . but back to work.

Ford banked and turned 180 degrees to align the plane with the river's E/W orientation. He went over his mental checklist: flaps at 20, throttle at 50% power, true air speed (TAS) about 100 knots (remember Kn x 1.15 = MPH); let's see, stall speed is about 60 Kn with this load; that should do it. He descended to the treetops at about 500 feet; the 190 with its underslung module floated on the treetops with minimal buffeting; there were few thermals in the evening to contend with.

"Remember, fella, you've got a damn ugly box, a 1,000-pound load to release, and you're going to 'leap' into the air, so be mindful of that."

He thought, there's the river. Steady as she goes. Just a little lower altitude. Better use flaps. Don't want to drop below 3,000 rpm; its risky when power is needed to pull out. Naval flyers on carriers have the same concerns for a "no-hook" contingency; as such they land at "full power." Why? If the plane's hook "missed" the fourth wire, knowing very well they were to grab the second wire, they had to be airborne in three seconds, for there is no more runway under the plane.

Steady as she goes, there's the drop zone, marked with a great dog and a greater broad. Okay, the "D" ring was in his lap, flaps to 10; back to full power, he grabbed the ring and pulled.

Load released, the plane leaped into the air and the chute bellowed out as the static line deployed the pilot chute and the main. At positive G's, gravity pull increased downward on buttocks, intestinal gas resulting in another rush of flatulent air. He gained altitude prior to banking and did a full 180 turn to check out his water drop zone.

He chuckled as he remembered the "gilded words" on the Ready-Room Doorway during flight training:

THE THREE MOST USELESS THINGS TO A PILOT:
1. Altitude, Above,
2. Gas at the Pump,
3. Runway Behind.

He had to maintain altitude, *below*.

Right now, he needed to watch his fuel and give attention to No. 2 fuel, so he finished his climb and banked to a position for his last pass at the site. He spotted Leigh and Boy at the edge of the river about two meters from the edge of the bank. It was a good drop, and the package appeared to be in one piece.

"DC 2, this is DC 1, over."

"DC 1, read you 5x5, and the pallet/hutch parts are fine, A-Okay, Babe!" Leigh said.

"Great, gotta go, daylight is burning and gas, too, so I'll be heading over the horizon on this, my last pass. I've got a night landing as it is and a front is coming through very soon."

"Wait, Babe, can't you talk?"

"Nope, but thanks for the 'treat' earlier. Love you; this is DC 1, out."

"Love you, too; see you in two days; this is DC2, out."

*   *   *

As the Cessna disappeared over the horizon and the radio broke contact, Leigh noticed the hut components were now aluminum versus plywood. A note from Ford and the fabricator indicated the change added expense but reduced weight for aircraft hauling and erection. Plus, the honeycomb (fiber) sandwich construction provided not only space-age strength but also insulation characteristics far beyond wood. Sounded good to her: lighter, thinner, stronger, and easier to assemble. Good going, boys. Of course, at mounting points, or strength locations, there was the typical 6061- T6 aluminum angle to secure the panels and add the requisite rigidity.

She removed the skid with its components from the impact pallet. *Good kindling wood*, she thought. The impact pallet had six eight-inch crush-blocks that did, in fact, stroke and crush to four inches upon impact. Who knows, the chute may also be usable but; if not, she was still instructed to clean, dry, fold and stow it, if possible. If torn, she would bury it.

Pulling the aluminum components was at her "threshold of strength," but away she went under harness like a Belgium. "Boy, get off that load! I can ill afford another eighty pounds. Get!"

She sensed a smile or smirk on his face . . . "Buggar, I don't need your playtime right now."

Hinged and pinned, the floor sections were integrated to the walls with temporary bracing to hold them in place until the companion units were received and erected with their sister units and finally tied-in as a complete floor. Marked by position on a clock, she placed the pallet at 12 o'clock and unlashed the three-legged tripod "A" frame hoist for lifting the units into place. Telescopic and lightweight, it was assembled and positioned without any problem. The winch and hook assembly mounted to its apex and was attached to the first panel while still on the pallet. Slowly the first unit rose from its resting place and swung up and over the foundation with determined cadence, up-1, over-2, open-3, lock-4, down-5. To her surprise, it worked as advertised, up twelve feet over as planned and onto the boulders . . . cool, man. Impressed, she hollered, "Hooray!"

She jockeyed the unit to its exact location and installed the locking-pins (ball detent type like on sailboat rigging), then ensured the floor configuration was secure; she then braced the outer wall with local aspen logs and weighted the floor with local boulders. Finally, one quarter of the octagon was in place! Satisfied with the stability of the quartile, she removed the "A" frame and moved it to the next section. The pallet was moved, winch attached, and the second floor/wall unit was erected in place. The same process was repeated and it, too, dropped in place, lock-pins installed, and half of the unit was up. After bracing and weights were secure, she checked the interlocks and, surprisingly, they were all okay. Her aegis hut was close to reality. What finesse. She expected to be hammering and twisting bent interfaces from the airdrop . . . into the night to straighten them out. With Boy at her heels, she braced the "baby" and wrapped it up for the night. She said, "Careful, don't go near the edges until fully assembled. Some of those exposed panels are sharp enough to tear you up."

Again, the subsurface appeared to be forgiving as she rotated or twisted the earthen tie-downs into the ground so the sill beams would be anchored. Upon completion, the SS cable was looped between the beam and the anchor, and the C-clamps were installed. Never saddle a loose horse, meaning saddle the long end, she thought. Construction guys would understand. A quick once-over and double checking for good bracing; then the "team" stepped back about 50 meters to view their handiwork. They sat. They relished the actions and success of a good day. The river looked inviting . . .

Splish-splash and who cares about a bare ass . . . it was their section of the river. It was a great way to end the day; refreshing, relaxing, and invigorating. Boy played fetch as he ran wild in and out of the water.

At least this time she knew Ford would *not* be buzzing her "pond" at 500 feet. It was twenty-hundred hours and well past his flight limits. Submerged, alone, and at peace, she reflected on the day's events. She knew Ford was doing likewise, she just knew. The encounter was unique, with her naked as a jaybird, and both enjoying the pleasure of the rapture of their mutual fantasia at 500-foot separation. She loved showing him her body, but middle-class mores taught her it was improper. Balderdash! It felt good to show her lover his "treats." Damn, she wanted him now. Not possible, she thought, submerging while thinking of him, the good day of construction, and the anxiousness of the pleasure expected in the coming days.

Tonight the tent was especially nice, and Boy made it even nicer by providing that little bit of companionship for a woman above 50 degrees latitude. Even solace that's chosen needs a little "bump" or "rub" by another . . . Boy provided that. Add her akimbo naked display to Ford, and her fantasies were on overdrive. Why not, it never hurt to imagine an encounter . . .

"Ha!" She laughed so loud that Boy looked startled. "It's okay, Boy, I'm just reliving the hilarious meeting with 'fly-boy' on the river while in my birthday suit earlier today. I'd sure like to wrap these legs around that hunk right now . . . but your attention will do for now." He'd always been that way, surprising her when she thought things would be typical. There was no "usual" for him. Maybe that's why she liked him so much. She never knew what would develop when they were together. And yes, they would be together again when the time was right. And yes, she would find the right time; it would come in the not-too-distant future. "Patience, Leigh, hang in there; you'll be together soon enough. Just as soon as you can handle a close relationship.

"Remember, you don't want to 'get burned' again. Amen."

Now restless, she glanced at her watch and decided a moonlight walk along the river and meadow was just what the doctor ordered. It was 2200 hours, but who cared; danger lurked many places in this changing world. She called, "Come on, Boy, let's take a little stroll along the river's edge." He was game, always would be when given a chance to stretch that fine-tuned body. She slipped on a tunic and grabbed her six-cell and meandered to the edge of the river. The rustling of tiny feet echoed from the cook-tent as curious rodents and whatever scattered to their safe havens with the night's sudden appearance of a dog and his mistress.

As a precaution, Leigh scanned the edge of the riverbank on either side and the perimeter of the tree line at the meadow. Two eyes reflected in the light . . . *Crash!*—a "mulie" and two fawns lurched from their late-night feeding; they bounded as if pogo sticks and abruptly stopped; frozen in place, they stared back at them as if to say, "What's up—what are you doing 'out' at our time of night?" Irritated, the doe stomped the ground, turned away, and bounded off.

The beam was now directed to the sleeping fish in the crystal-clear river. Wondering, she thought, Do fish sleep? Boy stared back with one of those looks—what are you doing? She'd soon ask some ichthyologist next time while "cocktailing." "No, you can't go in the water, Boy, if you want to sleep in the tent—do so and you're 'outside.' Come on, big fella, sit with me on the bench. Maybe this new moon will reveal some animal activity."

Think of this setting: a woman alone with a dog at 2330 hours, hundreds of miles from civilization, shear guts or courage to protect her from the local carnivores. Well, there was Boy, and the Colt .44 Magnum Special in her tunic, but in reality she was at risk, whether on the bench or in the tent (or anywhere on the building site) until the hut was built, and that was weeks away; she was living on the edge. Weather permitting, Ford would drop a pallet every other day for five days, so the hut might be two weeks from completion.

"Look, Boy, another family of deer, mulies again, across the river in those cedars and on the sandbar at the edge. Okay, Boy, they're okay right where they are; settle down, they've already heard your whine; steady, Boy, they're okay. Sit! Isn't the forest beautiful when bathed in the moonlight, stunning yet eerie since there's much more out there that we can't see? Maybe we can convince Ford to drop us his night-vision goggles. Well, we can ask anyway. I know what he'll say: *"What are you doing out at night; don't you know that's dangerous?"*

Always the father figure, looking out for me. He'll never change.

They wandered down to check the natural little log dam, and to see if it had affected the river depth by the bend. "Look out for those exposed tree roots; better walk farther away from the edge or they'd go ass over teakettle walking here." They noticed it had an effect on the height and depth. The birch roots were below water now, and the water was cascading over the logs. Maybe a beaver would see this and take over. They hoped so. In any event, they would watch the development of the pond and, if necessary, raise the height one more log, knowing very well the spring thaw with its ice and logs would blow it out. But they'd try raising the pond anyway. They wandered back to the bench to enjoy the night breezes.

Not only was the moon bright, but the pre-dawn Northern Lights, a.k.a. Aurora Borealis, also graced the sky with its wonder. A seldom-viewed phenomenon since people were usually asleep, the luminous streams of light "danced" in the upper atmosphere of the planets' magnetic polar regions. Caused by the emission of light from atoms, excited by electrons accelerated along the planet's magnetic field lines, it reflected on her dad's earlier explanation on an overnight scouting experience in '48. He said, "It's the wonder of the mythical Goddess Aurora, the Roman Deity of Dawn, who is energizing the electrical field (atoms) around the poles."

"Who?" she said.

"My child, for these things we cannot explain, man created deities, as we continue to now. The Bible, Koran, and many other beliefs and cultures create mythical gods to explain their individual and corporate worlds; the Romans on or about 1000 BCE (Before Common Era) explained the Northern Lights via Aurora. So, in the Northern Hemisphere we call them Aurora Borealis and in the Southern Hemisphere, Aurora Australis (southern dawn)." That was probably an adequate explanation. She remembered it well.

The impact of the moonlit night was dramatic on both Boy and Leigh. Eerie shadows stretched across the eddies of the gurgling river and climbed up the opposite banks along the cattails that scattered the silhouettes randomly on the forest floor.

Interestingly, even though the foreground had some muffled noise, the absence of background sound was deafening, nothing, yet periodically there would be a rustle of leaves, the chatter of gossiping grosbeaks and the whisper of stately pines at the apex of their growth. Almost like . . . Voices of the Wind.

Yes, much as if the spirit of the earlier aboriginal inhabitants still resided in the area, she felt their presence in the whispered silence of the pines and the babbling brook. In fact, E. E. Clark said it well in her writings about Indians in *Native American Legends*:

"North American Indians believed that spirit life dwelled in all of nature. So very much of the North American Indian's way of life was related to their spiritual beliefs and to the rituals of daily life for each tribe. They believed that everything in nature possessed a life or spirit (like the enormous Thunderbird who ruled over storms) within—even the sky, earth, mountains, trees, waters, animals, birds and man.

"The North American Indian believed all rain or hail from the sky contained its own special spirit song for his sensitive ear, a challenge to him for further endeavor or perhaps a warning of things to come. Indians believed every wind breathed forth the spirit of the one who made the wind blow, however far away, and they had their own special names for the many spirit 'Voices of the Wind.' Indians heard them in every sigh, whisper, bluster, roar, moan, or whistle of the wind, each filled with spirit life and power for the one who listened, as described by many Native Grandparents.

"The Indians believed the happenings in every river, waterfall, echo, thunder, and even the changing position of stars in the sky, resulted from actions by their indwelling spirits. They believed these spirits of nature controlled nature itself, the way good or bad spirits living in man seem to control much of his behavior.

"Did the North American Indians think certain spirits in nature seemed more powerful than others? Many legends tell about the Great Spirit, probably meaning their most awesome spirit. Other Indians also speak of the Chief of the Sky Spirits. Is it possible that both the Great Spirit and the Chief of the Sky Spirits were the Indians' interpretation of the white man's God or Supreme Being?"

"Boy, do you realize that we too, alone, at night, are witness to the same environment that our predecessors were exposed to two-hundred years ago? I wonder if in time we, too, here together, would be fortunate to hear an echo of the Voices of the Wind.

"Let's linger a little while longer . . . and listen."

Chapter 3

The Tongass

The beautiful experience of the previous moonlit night swirled through her mind. She felt closer to nature and the Voices of the Wind. Could there be native Tlingits in the area? Somehow she felt the presence of these mysterious yet cultured people.

The year to head north and find solace was not chosen by her; nevertheless, factors beyond her control had evolved and here she was in the year 1999. It was a few years later than "Erik the Red," Norwegian navigator and explorer, who sought the new world for similar goals in 1000 C.E.

Many ask about the new standard worldwide use of C.E. (Common Era) and B.C.E. (Before Common Era), versus the earlier use of B.C. (Before Christ), and A.D. (Anno Domini), medieval Latin meaning "In the year of the Lord." The reason stems from the *new* pluralistic society with many beliefs beyond the Christian myth whose Gergorian calendar all use. This allows all to be on the same page, even though the Christian group is much smaller now with the growth of Muslim, Hindu, Buddhist, Judaic, Unitarian, Deist, Agnostic, and other varied beliefs, which do not revolve around the Jesus myth. Just as all longitude was measured from an English observatory near London, whether Anglophobes liked it or not, B.C.E. and C.E. are also accepted by all political and religious beliefs.

Leigh had found her new place in life, knowing that suffering was inherent in life and one can be liberated from it by mental self-purification. She was hoping that this location, at the river by the meadow, and her writings would help her to achieve enlightenment, much like the Buddhist belief.

A daily time-line was not important up here, but the erection of the hut did have an exact relationship to air drops by Ford. As preplanned at the manufacturer, the assembly should take about ten days' total at the site, with the drops approximately every other day. Ford had given her this tentative schedule for the octagonal hut.

First Day	Three drops	Leigh, Boy, & tools
Third Day	One drop	Quadrants #1 & #2 & tripod
Fifth Day	One drop	Quadrants #3 & #4 w/hardware
Seventh Day	One drop	Eight roof sections w/pillars

Ninth Day   One drop   Internal components, food, etc.

Sure enough, there would be changes due to weather and plane problems, but this was the plan. The schedule was very aggressive, but not beyond "doable," as Ford would say. The last drop would have many key components, very small but very well designed and efficient to make the hut a home, such as:

- Combination gas stove and refrigerator
- Combination sink and metal cabinet w/pots & pans
- Gas furnace with vent pipes, w/SS chimney
- Collapsible bed, table, chairs, linens
- Recycling (self-contained) commode
- Canned food and gas cylinders
- Miscellaneous supplies

Later flyovers would provide food for a month, spare parts, and consumables such as batteries, cylinders, and the like.

Future flights would be on a two-week interval based on consumption factors preplanned for food, heating/cooling gas (many are not aware of the gas "fridge"), and unexpected needs of the "Hermitage." Yep, she had several names for her forest home.

It was day three, and things were under control so far. At least she thought so. Leigh wandered down to the river bench to read and relax with a little anxiousness over the next few days of closure with the hut airdrops, assembly and final erection. She returned to the site and double-checked the stability of the braces and the half-shell sturdiness. Yep, it would make it through the day, as long as there was no "square dancing." They had started the long weekend of July 4th, so if everything worked out i.e., flights, weather, and minimal drop damage—they should be closed-in by the 15th at the latest.

"Well, Boy, how does that sound?" she said. He cocked his head and, with a whine, she knew he had a little idea of her world; then again, maybe he hadn't a clue. . . .

*   *   *

Her location in Glacier Bay National Park, which was a part of the Tongass National Forest, provided an address of sorts, but certainly many miles from civilization: almost 200 km, NNW of the Capital, Juneau (population: 27,000); 150 km SW of Whitehorse, Canada (Yukon Territory); 100 km WSW of Skagway (population: 700); 90 km SW of Yakuatut (population: 100); and about 90 km +/-

20 km west (via the Bitterroot River) to the Gulf of Alaska in the Northern Pacific.

A splendid virgin forest, the Tongass provided a beautiful venue for rediscovery of herself, her future, and her writing. At 59 degrees latitude, temperatures ranged from 0 to -10 degrees Fahrenheit in January and 50 to 55 degrees Fahrenheit in July. The coastal warming effect provided this mild range of temperatures. Also, much like in a tropical rain forest, the coastal range forced all the moisture out of the clouds, causing the Tongass to have an annual rainfall of 140 (+/- 10) inches. Due to the frequent rainfall, most when working outdoors were accustomed to wearing "slickers" and rubber boots.

Outside the Park's boundaries, about 90 kilometers wide, local forest products, lumbering, iron ore mines, and fisheries operations were well established and active both by plane and ship along the coastal waters. There were no roads except for a "two track" here and there left over from lumbering interests that went nowhere and stopped everywhere. There were, of course, a very limited number of roads along the coastal area, but they did not traverse inland. The terrain prohibited it, and the population just was not of the density to warrant roadways, so most of the inland population *flew* into their lakeside home or cabin, or hut, like Ford to Leigh. Some never landed, either, like her. Because of this, there are more pilots and planes registered in Alaska than any other state in the USA.

She was aware that there might be contact with others working in the coastal region. The US Geological Survey was in the middle of a five-year study called The Greater Glacier Area Bear DNA Project. Ford had given her some background reading in case they happened upon her camp some day. Apparently they were developing the biggest revolution in wildlife management since radio telemetry (collars). DNA sampling was much more effective, especially for those secretive forest creatures that are difficult to catch and monitor. In short, the Project was trying to improve its database through DNA records rather than the dangerous tasks associated with catching, sedating, collaring, and tracking by air 300- to 800-pound grizzly bears. Even positioned cameras by bait piles with trip lines frequently failed. Many a bear tried to eat the "flashing" camera, and one actually did.

This new project systematically collected grizzly bear hair samples. These non-invasive genetic techniques were less stressful, less disruptive, and more efficient. Previous readings indicated live capture at only about 25 bears a year. But with DNA sampling over the same 12-week period in 1999, enough hair was obtained to identify 212 individual grizzly bears. Leigh noted that in the study area where she made camp about 350 bears ranged or traversed from the Yukon Territory to the coast and SE into British Columbia—food for thought.

Interestingly, DNA tests of hair revealed the bears' paternity, pedigree, and inter-population count. Neat stuff. She wanted to know how they got the hair samples. "I bet it takes some sort of 'baiting' with an adhesive strip on a bar, or something like that. Maybe we'll find out, sooner or later."

*   *   *

She heard a hum, a growl, then a roar . . . It's Ford. Here he comes again. Right on time.

Splashing to the center of the sandbar, the two scanned the sky—she, akimbo again, dressed this time, Boy wagging his tail.

"There he is," Leigh cried out as the 190 dipped its wing and slowly banked to the North with the 400 screaming at the wind as the engine strained while working at lower altitudes. Non-flyers should know that higher altitudes are an engine's friend where the air is thinner and drag reduced. A slower air speed is another unwelcome guest. The wings struggle and in fact buffet as stall speed thresholds creep up on the wing's lift. The 180-degree turn added complexity to the plane's task, since sideslipping is another unwelcome guest. Also consider the additional caution of inherent pontoon drag. Ford knew how to handle Bernoulli's principle, which explains why the upper portion of a wing is curved as opposed to the flat lower portion allowing the wing to "lift." The plane is allowed to be airborne with the thrust provided by the propeller, another airfoil. Of course the constant enemy, drag, prevents unlimited speed. Unfortunately, drag increases as the square of the speed. In fact, an "airfoil" is also the reason why a sail on a sailing ship can "tack," close-hauled, and sail into the wind. Aren't the laws of physics wonderful, yet immutable? Leigh thought. All this positioned the overloaded 190 for an upwind pass. But Ford was good at it.

Her heart pounded for his powerful hands, which had caressed her many times, and had left their fingerprints on her heart. The "old boy" was barreling down the river cut at over 150 as he spoke, "DC2, this is DC1, over."

"DC 1, this is DC2, read you loud and clear . . . Hi, Babe, how was the flight from Skagway? Over."

"Okay, Babe, how the hell are you? I had a dream about us last night, but better not talk about it on the air. It was nice. Anyway, how'd the first two units go up? Over."

"Good. Tell the fabricators the Aluminum honey-comb panels are stronger than hell, lightweight, and fit together like a glove. Over."

"Well, now, isn't that good news? Hope these two I'm dropping fit as well. You know, Babe, the fabricators are old-time Apollo sages from down-under. I'm about to turn; I'll be off the air while I get things ready . . . kinda busy up here during the release. I'll call after the release. Over."

"Roger, out."

She reflected on their good times together as he cleared the treetops and disappeared downwind. She looked once more to the fading sound of Ford's plane. Have a safe "drop," my friend.

Little did she know that Ford was also concerned about safety and was part of the Federal Aviation Administration's (FFA) new program with the Global Positioning System (GPS) navigation plan as the enabling technology. They installed an avionics suite being tested in Alaska that offers bush pilots many of the safety benefits that have long been standard in commercial jets. The FAA "Capstone" program provides an avionics suite that brings GPS satellite navigation, digital terrain database, and data link to selected general aviation-type aircraft. The program's goal is to improve flight safety by decreasing Controlled Flight Into Terrain (CFIT), pronounced "see fit"—also known as "wings and smoke in a hole." Ford was one of the 150 general aviation-type aircraft flown by small commercial operators in the rugged Yukon, British Columbia, and U.S. coastal areas of SW Alaska. The local FAA Director said CFIT and unpredictable, extreme weather were killers up there. There were a total of 1,665 aviation accidents in Alaska for the 10-year period of 1990-99, an average of an accident every other day, with a fatality every nine days, making aviation the most dangerous profession in Alaska; 11 % would die in accidents, compared with 2.5% average in the other 49 states combined.

At this lower altitude (500'), the turbocharger was "screaming" in its effort to "ram more air into the engine." The floatplane appeared as if an out-of-water leviathan, swooping over the treetops while straining against its constant companions, drag and gravity. The plane's plight of fighting gravity was not unlike older humans who fight this physical law of gravity "pulling-flesh" to the fullest after 60.

"DC2, this is DC1, over."

"DC1, we're waiting. Give her hell! Aim for me; I'll get out of the way. I'd be your bull's eye, any day, over."

"Enough suggestive talk. Here she comes." 'D' ring pulled, latch released, static line will deploy pilot chute, two seconds . . . 'POP' main opened, fluttered, swung and drifted with a bellow of beauty; beautiful!

Kerplop, the chute folded on itself, the risers flopped over the pallet, and a woman and dog dragged the sealed pallet to the bank. Two down, three to go.

"DC2, this is DC1, gotta go. How'd the drop go?"

"Great, have a safe flight, over."

"Roger, wilco out."

"Okay, Babe, C-you, love-you, miss-you, DC2, out."

"Come on, Boy, wanna watch yo mamma haul ass? We're gonna move that pallet with this little ass right now!"

"Up, girl, up-up-up! I think that's what Dad said to the horses under harness, so I can say that, too. Let's call it self-motivation; it worked on the horses, didn't it?" Leigh exclaimed!

Eighty meters and twenty-eight minutes later the pallet with quadrants three and four were positioned under the tripod for placement. While unlashing the tie-down straps she discovered a little "note" from the sages of Apollo. It was taped to a nice box of candy with a poem for her. She wondered if it was fit for a proper girl. It was a poem by Dion Cathrop, British artist and writer, from "The Charm of Gardens," (1910):

> "The art of leisure lies, to me, in the power of absorbing without effort the spirit of one's surroundings; to look, without speculation, at the sky and sea; to become part of a green plain; to rejoice with a tranquil mind, in the feast of color in a bed of flowers."

She thought, I think the boys must be reminding me that the work will end and leisure will be here soon.

Thinking to herself, she thanked the boys, knowing she could even afford the calories since this was a 5,000-calorie day anyway. She gave Boy a soft marshmallow candy; have two, they're small. With a chuckle, she knew dogs could not chew hard candies without looking like fools as the treat continued rolling around and around with his tongue, as it stuck to each tooth as an immovable object; enough, Boy. She removed it and gave him a soft cream, and it disappeared. Boy seemed to wonder, What was that all about? I think I was set up; I'll get you for that, girl!

Enough of this fooling around. She hooked up the tripod and got the units in place. Quadrant number three lifted and swung into place without any problem. Quad four, likewise, but in being the last part of the pie, engagement and locking were presenting a little problem of mass . . . her ass was smaller than the quad's mass. A weight problem. How could 120 pounds push 600 pounds into an engagement/lock position? Well, she found a way. Like trying to put a pie back together. She wished she weighed more, or that Ford's 220 was here. She had an idea; she'd get back 20 feet and run at the wall and use the good old $E=mc^2$ (energy = mass X speed of light squared) to move that quad into a locking position. "Look out! Here I come, Boy!" He looked at her in that weird way, like, What the heck is she up to? Still suspended on the tripod, the quad waited defiantly for her 120-pound assault.

BANG! CRASH! KERPLUNK! The quad did not move an inch. However,

Leigh's shoulder seemed to move an inch out of place—"#$%0&*#"—Dad said it was okay to swear when you did a dumb thing or were bit on the ass by an ill-mannered horse or sheep. Again, "?*&%$#, what do you think you're doing? Use your head, not your body. There isn't enough there; you do, however, have brains."

Boy couldn't figure what was going on; he'd heard swearing when she hit her finger with a hammer, but didn't she mean to "throw her body at the wall?" Women! I'll never figure them out. Ford asked me once if she loved him. Now there's a dumb question. What was I to do, bark "Yes," lick him and have him figure it out. He had already said no one could figure out females. I'm confused. Oh, well, "people." Boy lamented, My little dog back home knows what I need and when; she is a wonderful mate and friend.

Leigh had a great idea. Get a pry-bar, log, and push the unit into place. "Let's use these braces; we won't need them soon anyway. Get out of the way! Damn dog . . . okay, I'm sorry, but get!" There, this should do it; in the ground on the edge of the sill, and Push! Push! Hold it, Leigh; lower the quad a little—Push *Clunk*—it's locked! "Good show, girl, if I do say so myself."

The last section had the door and step module, so they were extended and locked into place. Now if this doesn't look cool, she thought as she walked up the steps. "Look, Boy, we've even got a key for the door, actually four on a ring; guess they think we'll lose a few. We'll hide one later. Step up my friend and enter our abode. Hold it; check your paws. Just kidding; thank God the rules are not as strict as with the tent." The outer octagon walls were still a little unstable without the integrated ridge beams, roof panels and pillars, but all in all the outer shell was very firm. Like him—a private joke between "him" and her.

She checked the integrated dual axis bubble levels and shimmed the sill plates at two locations to within one-half degree of true level. Boy was having a little difficulty keeping up with her and trying to figure out what she was up to. Looks goofy to him, he thought. Oh. Well, one thing did develop as he shadowed every move. The porch steps were unnecessary for him . . . one bound and he was up and in!

Leigh augured-in the tie-down anchors and attached the hold-down cables; "Never saddle a dead horse," as Dad had said many times.

She decided to camp and pitch the tent in the shell now for the night. Before she knew it, everything was in the unit, the tent erected, and the kitchen "fly" reassembled, too. Kinda cozy for both. "Just wait; we'll soon have a roof and all the (limited) comforts of home. We'll find a blanket bed for you, too. You're not sleeping with me anymore. Okay, maybe if there's lightning, but that's it!"

While sitting on the steps watching the sunset at two fingers, she noted, "What's that?" The woods exploded in the northern direction. "Hummm, an elk, mulie, or bear? By now, most of the critters probably know we're here, camping on the meadow's fringe; at least the mulies do. We see them every night as they graze in the eastern meadow. Elk are more arcane and avoid open country except when seeking a mate in the fall, and then anything goes, as *he* pursued *her*. Their actions are not unlike ours. I've done some pretty goofy things to get a man's attention, and likewise men to women. I wonder how the grizzly operates. One thing is certain; some traits you'll never know about."

Bear have their own realm, both mysterious and unpredictable, as stories abound about their prowess along the river-highways to the west. Most were embellished to gain attention to the hunter's skill, meaning to his ego and attention to his prowess. Certainly among the bear species, Black, Polar, and Grizzly, the "Grizz" would be her eminent neighbor for the next two years. Although they are solitary and skittish to humans, she hoped that encounters would be rare, infrequent, and at a distance. Nine times out of ten they will want no part of people or her camp, unless hungry, injured/sick, unable to forage, cornered, or overtly protecting cubs.

Her studies of the bear led to the reality of bruin life, that there is no bear family as depicted in stories for kids. The male is solitary and ranges with the female only when breeding every other year in June, and then only for a week of continuous copulation. Eat your heart out, boys . . . but remember, it's only every two years. They depart, or she may chase him away, and they both feed up to 18 hours a day to fatten up for the winter hibernation. She delivers up to three 12-ounce cubs seven and one-half months later in her den. They suckle their sleeping mom, unaided, and triple their weight every month for their "coming out" into the world in March at approximately ten pounds each. Snow is still on the ground then, so they enjoy sliding down to the river's edge with Mom.

Lewis and Clark recorded grizzly ferocity and frequent encounters on the westward trails. Most have surmised that their temper is defensive, not aggressive, unless they feel cornered or threatened. Even though the bears always flee man, experienced hikers and hunters prefer to avoid tall grass and closely knit tag-elders, or the like, in lowlands, favorite habitats of resting or sleeping bears. They don't go there unless they can see at least 50 meters ahead or to the side or, if they must, they go with a partner, a gun (30 caliber or greater) at the ready.

Leigh had recorded the factors to avoid encounters with or ward-off Grizz:

- Avoid lowlands and marshes around rivers.
- Avoid thickets which block vision up to 50 meters.
- Avoid salmon fishing spots in the fall.
- Avoid camping near a mud or snow slide by the river

or on their trails; scat and tracks tell.

- Keep food odors secured in metal cans and elevated at least 25 feet via a rope (a cache).

But many stories *are just not true*! An example is this "Rookie's" story of hunting the Grizz in the early 1900s in Montana, by William H. Wright, in *Grizzly*, 1910:

> "I was told to sit with my rifle and let my scent blow downwind into the hills, like 'chumming' for fish, and the ferocious Bear would work its way upwind with the intention of eating me . . . since I was in his or her terrain."

Leigh mused, "If we've got a grizzly in the area we'll soon find out. Let's look for tracks and scat in the morning. Hopefully the bear was just passing through . . . hopefully!"

Unfortunately there was a small wetland near the camp. Not big, but it was there; it was overlooked while surveying the area from the air. She looked at the positive aspects of the swamp and figured maybe it would draw deer and elk in the winter; it would be their feedlot and entertainment. They'd enjoy the company, and again nodded that, hopefully, if it was a bear, it was just passing through!

They had enjoyed a good day and were going to sleep in a little more secure place that night—by sleeping in the shell, with side wall protection and the ability to see the stars and moon without a roof. Before turning in, they went back and double-checked the old campsite. It had a better view to the river and melodic babble, but the new site had a better view to the meadow; it was a tossup of complimentary beauty.

They walked quietly back to the hut, *without* the beam of the flashlight for guidance so they could spot some game in the meadow. Stealthily and carefully they eased their way up the path through the shadow and over the numerous deadfalls of decay. The moon was waxing toward full at about 80% with cloud cover absent—all making for a clear, cold, and brightly lit evening. It was as like early evening nautical twilight, that period after the sun has set over the horizon but its brilliance still fills the sky with refracted light. One difference here, however: it was 0100 hours and Leigh could see up to 100 meters across the meadow. With his sensitive eyes, Boy could probably see 300.

It was like daylight here at fifty degrees latitude, with the clear beauty of this uncluttered sky. Not only was there less particulate in the air but also absolutely no scattered light from man-made sources. Part of the eerie and mystical aspects of the night were the added deception of the staggered silhouettes and moving shadows of the gentle side-to-side oscillation of aerial limbs, ebbing and flowing in a light wind. Their elevated exposure did not always reflect the nadir of the calmer existence below. Some of the monarchs taunted the lower stratus clouds as if to investigate or probe their lower limits to its upper reach to the sky. In awe, she lay on her back at the base of these imposing giants of the forest. Boy plunked down next to her and watched her moves, the leaves, and finally he too watched the trees' and limbs' gentle sway that seemed to be in excess of ten feet fore and aft in their dance on the stage of their own private canopy in the sky. Actually, Boy wondered what the heck Leigh was up to, by just looking "up" at nothing. How-ever, always vigilant, he was also scanning the forest's edge, too, as her aegis of the meadow.

"There's our good old friend, the moon, peeking over the horizon in its splendor as the second brightest object in the sky." Naturally inconstant by nature, many myths surrounded its travels over the sky. Leigh remembered her dad's lessons well.

Many early Native Americans would never understand that their location, latitude and longitude, plus seasonal variances (Earth axis) affected where the moon appeared in the sky and for how long. It was much later (1500) that sailors finally discovered the key to navigation using not only the moon but also our planets and stars both near and far.

The discovery of a circular Earth was certainly, in part, understood as most natives observed a canoe and its occupant disappear over the horizon at about six kilometers, 3-4 miles; there was always a "sharp" observer in camp no matter what period of history. They may not have documented those thoughts, but they were observed and noted orally in their unwritten stories imparted at the communal campfires.

The visible outer planets, Mars, Jupiter, and Saturn, appear everywhere near or along the ecliptic plane or orbit around the sun, and disappear in the sun's glare frequently. Of Mercury, Venus, Earth, Mars, Jupiter, Saturn, Uranus, Neptune, and Pluto, in that order, and with only the naked eye to observe, early natives only dealt with the first five—the others being so far away and infrequent to our observation, partially due to their heliacal risings as the sun and Earth traverse through the galaxy and the variable locations in the sky. Little was known of the planets, so many relied on the moon for their calendar. It was predictable.

In addition to observing and charting the motions and appearances of celestial objects, Leigh wondered how their leaders or shamans attempted to understand and explain the irregular occurrence of eclipses, meteors, and comets, as well as unusual atmospheric phenomena such as the "Northern Lights" (auroras). Her recollection was that most early civilizations took these appearances for portents, usually possessing negative connotations. Because of the dramatic effect to all living things, solar and lunar eclipses were especially impressive appearances to Leigh, who had witnessed both.

As she scanned the sky, she recalled her dad saying a lunar eclipse, which can occur only when the Earth comes between the sun and the moon, begins as a brightly curved shadow starts to work its way across the bright lunar surface. After one hour the moon appears to take on a disturbing, deep blood-red color, which darkens as the shadow deepens, then lightens again as the darkest part of the shadow moves in—only to have brightness reappear soon and lighten the sky again.

She remembered him saying a *total* solar eclipse in many respects is more impressive. During the progression of the solar eclipse, when the moon passes between the Earth and the sun, the moon takes a larger bite out of the sun. The sky darkens at the edge of the area of totality about 2,000 km in diameter, with the darker almost midnight-appearing center of totality being approximately 120 km in diameter, where "daylight" takes on an eerie quality. Finally, the sun turns totally dark and the stars become visible. She remembered the pinhole mask held over the white surface of the box her dad made for her as she observed the eclipse without looking at the sun's harmful rays. Amazingly, during the eight to ten minutes of totality, diurnal animals often act as if night has fallen. Birds are silent, and other animals prepare for sleep. Many are confused. She had only been on the outside path of totality, but daylight under even these conditions had taken the color from all living things. The earth turned black and gray, without any color.

The following moving historical description by British author *Virginia Woolf* (1953) captures the "feel" of a total solar eclipse on the Yorkshire moors in 1927:

> "Rapidly, very, very quickly, all the colors faded; it became darker and darker as at the beginning of a violent storm; the light sank and sank; we kept saying this is the shadow; and we thought now it is over—this is the shadow; when suddenly the light went out. We had fallen. It was extinct. There was no color. The earth was dead. That was an astonishing moment . . . then astonishingly the light rebounded, color returned; it had been much worse than we had expected; as though we were kneeling and got up to our ethereal tie to light; we had seen the world dead and suddenly it came back. This, we were reminded, was in the power of nature."

Thank goodness, on the average, there are only four eclipses each year, as seen from somewhere in the world.

*   *   *

Night sounds echoed through the shell as the two lay together on the floor, different without the tent's cover, yet welcome with the walls' protection. "You know, Boy, if I keep gazing at the stars and trying to figure out the sounds of the night, we'll never get to sleep; I'd better roll over and gaze at my pillow, and forget about the krill of the crickets and the backyard gossip of the other creatures." She mused, The fact is, they're saying, check-it-out; we've a new neighbor on the edge of the meadow. The black anodized aluminum hut with no roof must have looked strange. With all the constant construction noise and activity, they probably wondered when the hell the doll and dog were going to quit making so much racket.

As with Boy's usual nightly habit, he stuck his nose under Leigh's hand several times until she yielded. If he lifted it up to where he knew she would let him under her palm, she would then stroke his soft muzzle and lay her hand on his head; he was at peace—she was not alone; his predictions came true—her hand was his.

They now drifted toward sleep, her thoughts of the excitement of the uncharted future, his with the comfort of Leigh as his mistress and his role as the vigilant sentinel of the hut at the meadow's edge.

Unbeknownst to both, a bruin was foraging for roots in the nearby swamp.

A deep sleep engulfed the shell as nocturnal animals both large and small continued to sing in the night—after all, they do *rule the night.*

Chapter 4

An Ill Omen

The scream of the turbo-fan could be heard over the nine pounding radial cylinders as the bird made its downwind pass at full power. Full flaps, nose up; 'D' ring pulled, package released, chute deployed, and another portion of the hut was on Mother Earth at 50 degrees North Latitude. "DC2 this is DC 1, over," Ford exclaimed as he approached the river basin.

"DC l, this is DC 2, hear you loud and clear; nice shot, dear; we're anxious to start closing her up," Leigh said with appreciation for the system of chute drops working so well. "Hey, how's civilization? Over."

"Good, but could be better with a friend at my side, both day and night—at least you've got Boy. Over."

"Poor baby . . ."

"Okay, I do have the boys; you've got Boy. I'd rather switch. But, you know, I may just get used to this unattached single life with the boys and loose women in town; look out, girl."

She gave him no slack. "I doubt it, and you'd never survive very long without me. None of you men do very well sans women. Anyway, I'm better than any ten you'd find in town."

"Enough of your raid on manhood. What are you, a proselytizing feminine feline female or a wanna-be man? Over."

"You buggar. No, I do not need your plumbing to survive. Stop it! I miss you. And guess what—a white wolf with an orange spot on the chest had a stand-off with Boy yesterday, without any problems, and sure enough, I think a bear went through here last night. Later on we'll see where it went and check scat and tracks. It may be a roving black or even a Grizz. We'll see. Over."

"Damn, it didn't take long for the neighbors of the Tongass to visit. Be careful yourself. This is DC 1. Out."

She knew only too well how dangerous Alaskan flying could be. "This is DC 2, Roger. Out."

*　　*　　*

Leigh exclaimed, "Dang, this unfolding roof is neat. Look, Boy, the guys left a note again." With skepticism, she read, "Pray when you pull the lanyard for deployment of the roof sections when elevated on the 'pod,' and if secular, grab a rabbit's foot, and hold your mouth in a good pucker. Lots of luck, Dave and Milt, 'Da Sages' of FFS.

"Damn, this is quite an engineering operation. Stand back, Boy ... Here goes; I'm pulling." *Swoosh-Flip-Click-Snap-Clunk.* "Damn, the fab boys had it right." The four triangular sections unfolded and fell into place and locked. The moon-shaped roof hung in suspension as if a huge winged serpent looking for a place to roost. It was an awesome sight. She noted, Well if this isn't something; another note dropped out saying: "You did it! See? Anybody, even a woman and a dog, can deploy our design. See? Aren't we good? If you've gotten this far, the rest is a cakewalk. (Signed) 'Da Boys.'"

"Smart asses, every one of those virile fabricators. Ford probably had a hand in these notes, too." They were right; the wing-like section was hanging high and looking for a home, and that was her next task. She had to nestle it into the edge of the shell and lock the center onto the pillars already in place.

"Okay, Boy, let's do it! I'll slowly lower the unit and use this line to align the outer edges the first time. Jesus Jenny, the July sun is right behind the mass of the roof and the dangling wing-like sections look like a serpent ready to descend on us. Here, I'll tie this hoisting line off and engage the mounting points using this other line. Damn, the line slipped. Okay, girl; don't hurry, just do it again.

"Let's see. I'll use a couple of half-hitches after wrapping the line around the trunk twice. That's what I needed to do the first time—dummy. Dad told me to always double-wrap a tie-down before knotting with hitches or a bowline, his and my personal favorite; it never lets you down. Oh, well, it's been a while; I'll get it right soon, probably just when the erection is complete. Isn't that the way with most of life's tasks? You excel at them through trial and error just about when finished with the task. Ha! No sweat, that's life. Most uncharted events never occur exactly as before, but every event, especially while making your own decisions, adds to your databank of knowledge for the next task."

Kerplunk. Down it came. *Clunk. Flop.* One more in place. Leigh quickly moved to get the locking pins to secure this unit before it moved or slid off the guide pins.

Locked in place, the hut looked great from the roofed side, and like a half-eaten pie from the other. She wondered if everyone else stood back to get the big picture. She suspected it was true.

She was damn proud of those sages of aluminum even with their macho notes and elitist style; she could just hug every one of them. Imagine, a 600-square-foot hut assembled in sections with one tripod w/winch, and a determined woman. She'd soon have a Base of Operations for the long-term sojourn of solace and discovery in the wilds of Alaska. She was truly blessed in having health and friends to support her quest for a new life.

*   *   *

Exploring the area west of camp, Leigh and Boy approached the edge of the enigmatic swamp. She exclaimed, "Over here, Boy. See the broken limbs on these dead cedars? There's a ragged path-like tunnel through here—yep—there are bear tracks also. Damn! They're huge. What do you think, Boy? Any scent?"

Tail wagging, nose to the ground and legs churning, Boy added to the air of excitement and tension as he hunkered down to some serious tracking.

"Wait! Slow down, Boy. We're just checking, not chasing. That bruin is long gone (I hope). It must have been here hours ago. It's a wonder you can still sense his presence. Look, a bear has bedded down over here. There's matted grass and bent shrubs under that hemlock. Why the hell did he stay here? You can see our camp from here. I hope it was just a coincidence of being tired or sleepy near our camp. I wonder if he was feeding or checking out our camp on the edge of the meadow. You know, I question if we could survive an attempt by a bear to enter the hut—I think so. We're pretty well closed in, but not really. The walls that are not tied into a roof are still rather flimsy and I suppose they could still be pushed down if a bear cared to do so. Well, that's not our concern. This one is long gone, I think.

"Come back, Boy! We're not going on any extensive hike or explorations until the hut is closed in and we have a base of operations."

Their plan was to be explorative, but passive and non-aggressive in and around the foothills of the coastal range. They knew the animals were all descending from altitude, as fall turned to winter and they sought the shelter of the lower climes. All the animals needed to be near feeding areas in the wind-protected lowland swamps, swales, and river bottoms.

She thought, And that's where we are. But guess what, this is the source of clean water. We're here because we have to be close to water that is clean and drinkable. Nevertheless, Leigh had planned to sanitize all ingested water with antibacterial pills unless it was boiled before use. You can never tell what lurks upstream. For example, a dead and rotting animal (with disease) or a sudden break in a backwater (generally after a storm) or excessive rain and flooding could contaminate the water. Being alone required caution as her guide in all activities, whether eating, drinking, or exploring. But, she did have an excellent first-aid kit, and a firm yoga body.

They wandered down the trail just a little farther to see if there was another opening in this lower area; it was very wet, much like a pre-swamp condition. If they sank too deep, they would have to go back. The hemlock and cedar thickets made for excellent cover. As it grew darker and darker, they proceeded into an almost cathedral like passage, and the overhanging branches and thick canopy above were also cave-like in appearance. "Oops," Leigh exclaimed, "I'm up to my ankles in muck! I can hardly see you. Damn. It's dark. It's wet. It's dangerous. Let's get out of here. I can only see about twenty meters. That's enough; back we go. Boy, you even look like a black bear cub. I know, I know, you want to go on, but this habitat does not favor us and does favor the bears. Remember, Boy, you're only two feet tall and I'm five and one-half feet, so I can't get through this stuff like you. And there will be no funny funk on my knees with this trunk—no way. Yep, let's check out the bruin on terrain of our choice where it's drier, brighter, and we can see at least a hundred meters.

"Son of a bitch!" Leigh fell flat on her ass. She slowly extracted herself from the muck and, thoroughly disgusted with herself, swore again. Boy froze in place as if on point. He knew something was wrong. "We're okay, Boy; it's just me tripping over myself. You know me—Miss Grace, the Klutz."

Half black with muck, she stumbled out of the swamp and into the half-light and then full day light, then decided quickly that she was going for a three-pronged plunge into the Bitterroot to wash clothes, hair, and her filthy body from the foreboding odor of the pre-swamp lair of the bear.

"Woo, this water is cold, but who cares, the alternative is unacceptable: Black-ugly-putrid-stinking-muck. It is all over my body. I stink! Let's get these duds off and get decent. Quick, Boy, fetch my brassiere; I've only got two of those harnesses. Hurry, it's going down stream."

He looked, got the point, and off he went splashing and thrashing the stream until the light blue-laced Victoria's Secret was in his mouth. "Bring it here. Come on, Boy. Damn, good dog. You've even got a tender mouth for my undies as well as quail. Good boy. I won't even tell Ford this story. I don't need any more 'Guess what happened to Leigh' jokes."

She thought, If Ford could only see me now . . . bare-assed again, half black and chasing clothes, trying to keep my footing on these rocks, scrubbing goose-bumped skin, dunking my hair into the drink . . . more like a loon. "A sight for sore eyes," as Mother used to say. She was glad to be alone.

Unfortunately, they *were not alone*.

*   *   *

Lurking in the shadows at the edge of the lowlands was an inquisitive large female grizzly bear. She had backtracked through the swamp in typical fashion of bear-ranging habits, returning to precisely the same spot she had rested in and foraged the previous evening. Her primary intent in returning was to continue foraging for the succulent roots of the Dog-Toothed Violet.

The sound of activity in the stream was not of any particular interest, but it did catch her attention as their scent filtered through the swamp grass. She was just a little confused by the smell(s) she was sensing downwind from the river. The canine scent was typical of the local population of fox, coyote, and wolf, but the human scent was bewildering, if not perplexing. Her curious nature, versus aggression, caused her pause as she fed at the edge of the swamp . . .

The Grizz was now getting a little more confused as the human scent grew stronger, which was rare in the Tongass while foraging. She was not certain of the threat by the two, but didn't like the situation at all. She was nervous. As for the canine scent, there was no doubt it was a threat. She just wondered what was going on. Her nervous beady little yellow eyes now saw a naked, white-skinned human, carrying something, and a canine at her heels. Her head thrust up; she stood on her hind feet and sniffed the downwind breeze. Puzzling to be sure, again she shook her head. What's going on here? Is there a threat? Should she depart? She lowered her massive body and continued feeding, but she huffed, snorted, and paced. She grew more nervous and uncomfortable as she tore into the root beds with increased vengeance!

She reflected, and now remembered *that scent*, as a yearling with her mother and brother. They had been chased by a pack of wolves and that trauma returned with *that scent*. They had escaped, but the anguish of the chase and danger she experienced while her mother fought for their lives had left an indelible fear on her defenses against the horror it represented to her. The anguish of her escape prevailed.

She mused, What is wrong? Why do I feel so threatened? No one is near. There is no hostile action. My territory has not been violated—relax.

*   *   *

Leigh, still stark naked, said, "Okay, Boy, you stay out here until dry. I'm going in to rid my body of these king-size goose bumps. I'll be out with some dry clothes and we'll take a walk to dry your hair and mine. I'll only be a minute." She entered the hut. While lying in the sun's warmth, Boy had almost drifted off to sleep when his sensitive nose detected an intruder. His ears picked up; his head and eyes rotated and turned to the edge of the swamp as if a gun turret on a tank, sharp and purposeful. He sprang to his feet. The wind must have shifted. He sensed a threat. It was a bear.

Regrettably, Leigh was not there to stop him. His protective instincts were about to run amock—his responsibility to protect Leigh about to be miscalculated. The bear was no threat at 100 meters. Nevertheless, without Leigh's counsel, a deep-throated growl emanated through his now bare fangs, which was a universal announcement of his intentions to defend or attack. Unfortunately, he chose the latter. In an instant, and at a dead-run while barking, Boy raced toward the brown mass at the edge of the tree line.

Startled, the bruin now rose again to her hind feet as Boy closed the 100-meter gap. At 50 meters she roared. Her head swung from side to side as if flailing at the attacker with her head . . . a typical warning to all those who dared approach. Her canines flashed in the sun as she chomped her teeth to indicate serious aggressive behavior.

Boy had a narrow-minded survival instinct. His territory had been violated, and he must defend it. He was now ten meters from the howling bruin.

Still on her hind feet, she roared. Few in the forest could match her prowess. She was holding firm and not running.

Fearlessly, Boy leaped ten feet into the air at her swinging, snarling head. Steadfast and inflamed, the bruin held her own and swung at the leaping canine, partially tearing his belly open before Boy's fangs made contact with her throat.

Simultaneously, a shot rang out, and a slug ricocheted though the treetops above the bear's head. She looked to where her paw had dashed the canine to the murky swamp water. The impact luckily off-center, Boy was thrown about ten feet, not unlike a rag doll, and lay in a heap of whining and moaning pain.

The bruin was on him in a second, rolling the limp body over with her mammoth paw and razor-like claws, then sniffing it as if looking for life.

Boy felt his life slipping away.

*   *   *

Leigh fired again. It made non-lethal contact to the bear's rib cage. She reared up and roared at the approaching figure with a gun. Stunned and startled, she swung her head to and fro again to announce her intention to fight while chomping her teeth. Another shot impacted her chest. She whirled and retreated down the swampy path from which she arrived. It was like an *explosion* of splashing water and muck combined with breaking limbs and dead trees in her path. Her pace still had a trace of arrogance. Leigh fired another. The slug tore through the limbs above the bear's departing path.

Immobile, Boy looked up at Leigh as she approached his side. "Don't move—keep your head down—I'm here to help. We'll get you back to the hut shortly. I certainly don't want you taking on the entire forest again on my account.

"We're a team, you know. Next time bark at me for help. Poor baby, you're all torn up and broken, but don't worry, you'll make it; I'll get you back into shape in no time at all. It's pretty clear you've got several broken ribs, massive contusions, and a tear in the hide of your belly.

"Don't move; I'll wrap your chest and make a sling big enough to carry you back to camp." She removed her shirt and wrapped it around his bleeding wound and made a sling of her tunic. "Hold on, Boy, we'll get some painkillers in you soon. Away we go; you're a lucky dog!" Carrying Boy to the hut was quite a workout. She really needed a helper to make a game pole-type litter carry as she had seen in Tarzan films of the '40s.

"Okay, Boy, we made it. I'm going to roll you over real slow and dress these wounds. This hypo will help relieve the pain and ward off infection—just a little prick. All done; now to clean and sew you up. Okay, hold on, one more suture and I'll be done. Good dog." Leigh poured the rest of the 10% iodine solution on the incision and left some of the muck on his upper body in place, total cleaning would come later. Rest and repair was the most important priority now. He was already asleep—no need to transfer him to his blanket. There's no doubt he'd be able to sleep on rocks if necessary.

She mused, I wonder if he knows that a dog at 90 pounds hasn't a chance against a 500- pound grizzly. One thing is sure; he's got a lot of heart and a big serving of fortitude. Apparently, one claw tore a six-inch-long opening in his belly. Just think if she had connected with all five. Not wanting to take any chances Leigh used thirty stitches to close the wound, plus the benefits of a first-class first-aid kit with many painkillers and infection-fighting drugs.

Luckily, the fractured ribs had not penetrated any lung tissue, and there were no compound fractures. He was breathing okay, and the opiates had knocked him for a loop. For certain, this dog would be out of action for many days.

Her clothes were dry now, so she donned her blood-stained tunic and left Boy to rest awhile. The night was, as always, calm and beautiful both to the horizon and the zenith. Venus said "hello" again as she climbed the bright indigo riches of the twilight. Mercury would rise later with less drama or beauty, so she shifted her eyes to the faithful North Star, Polaris, a constant companion and friend to mariners and explorers; you could always plan on its guidance when in need.

Leigh looked to the edge of the meadow and the spot where Boy had attacked the bear. She could not continue to look . . . it was too painful. Boy could have been killed, and she felt partially at fault. She had left him alone. That should never have happened; she'd try not to repeat the situation again. She knew better, but events change standard procedures, and it may happen again. So what could she do about it?

"Well, one thing appears certain, I cannot change or alter Boy's defensive and protective nature. That apparently has been built in over millennia of survival instincts both by interbreeding and nurtured phylogeny of all canines. Since I am the one who introduced him to this habitat, it's my responsibility to avoid a confrontation like today. He cannot change, nor should it be expected. However, I can modify or alter my activities with him to minimize situations that expose him to sure death by an animal with an overwhelming advantage. It is clear, and has just been proven, that Boy will attack any intruder wandering into or near the campsite—for my protection. So I owe it to him to safeguard those areas. That means being armed at all times. This may even mean putting a chain on him for short periods, for his own protection."

As she wandered toward the stream her thoughts drifted to her rich life experiences with the family, work, her loves, her losses, and of course, Ford. She believed, now more than ever, that indeed you need love, by someone—anyone—to sustain life. Without love, life is mechanical and of less worth, at least to her. That is why she found Ford, or did he find her?

Ah ... to love and be loved ... our quest for thousands. Nothing had changed. She mused, After the love of your children, there is no greater love than romantic love. She wandered over to the bench. The Bitterroot sang its melodic song to her as it babbled to the sea. It was a lovely night along the river.

Her meadow by the river was just what she needed to resolve who she was and how to embrace the future. She really shouldn't say *her meadow*; it is our forest, our river, and our stunning hillsides of beauty. Leigh pondered as she realized very few people even knew where she was camped, which was of no concern and fortunate for her. She loved the silent solitude beneath the boughs of great conifers reaching out over the river. She felt the strongest compulsion to claim this place as if she were planting a banner for some sovereign liege.

The sense of discovery does swell greatly when setting foot on an island in the forest, because one never knows what one will stumble upon as the first to be experienced by man. However, she hoped there would be no more repeats of today's confrontation. She also noted there had been few traces of past human activities in this area. There was the altar, with shards of clay pots, and remnants of a fallen sacrifice, or witness to a deity—not sure. She'd explore that beautiful but eerie sacred clearing soon, but no rush; however, she would certainly be here a while. Right now, the bench on the 'Root was her optimum solitude.

As she looked upstream through the dim tunnel of light, the glow was interrupted by occasional brilliant swords of moonlight passing through breaks in the trees.

Shoes off, she waded at the edge of the swirling water. A duck-like mud hen scurried from its feeding, dodging left and right to cover in the reeds. Muskrats dipped and surfaced in silence, Siskins (yellow finch) flitted about, and in the distance a Great Blue Heron slowly rose on its broad wings and sought renewed solitude upriver. Little did the Heron know how alike they both were in their quest to be alone.

There was not, from her vantage point, a human within 100 km—only water, mountains, forest, and sky. She might as well be in the Amazon Basin or the Congo.

It struck her that if they could return, the Native Americans of a thousand years ago who once fished and hunted this area and transited this land would immediately recognize all of the area as home—so little had changed. The only minor change was her little hut amongst the giant firs, pines, lesser oaks, maples, and birches. A change only for a short time, she would not stay long.

Now donning her shoes, she slowly meandered along the path to the hut in a melancholy shuffle to the resting canine friend while thanking the night for this moment of reflection on her life. She bid the evening "good night" as she entered the hut to check on Boy and to sleep. Huddled in a fetal position, Boy seemed to be breathing well. She whispered, "Good night; sleep tight." It had been quite a day for both of them.

She slid into her bag next to the "warrior of the meadow" while still overcome with her guilt for having left him alone outside, but thankful for his survival and blessed that she was able to chase the bruin away and save his life. Shalom, my friend, sleep well.

What a sight, the half-covered roof offering a spectacular view to the stars and sky above. It was early in the evening, so her mind danced in the past while thinking of those she loved and respected: her parents, her relatives, her mentors, her friends, her children, and her lovers. It was so wonderful to have the ability to reflect on the positive and not-so-good experiences. She had another today, to add after the traumatic encounter with the bear and Boy. She just could not sleep. Ford had noticed when she was in a funk or melancholy mood, too, and would say, "What up?" And if she were "elsewhere" mentally, he'd respect her mood and "stand down."

Ford was so much like her dad, so subtle, as she remembered the evasive and sneaky show of affection by her dad to her mother. He would pass behind her at the sink, grab her ass without missing a step, and she'd act as though it was improper and respond with negative body language but smile with radiance that beamed, "Ah, he still loves me and cares by showing it in his not-so-skillful way." Ford was like so many men, a little overbearing, but she knew that immediately. Women knew. She really thought she loved him for his imperfections. Yes, the reverse is true, too; she used to be kind of a prude. Thank goodness she met him . . . she never knew *what* he'd do next.

Her dad had given her many rich lessons. It's just too bad that all kids do not share the indirect exposure to a caring and loving couple by way of subtle, respectful-yet-loving acts through casual observations of their parents.

She drifted back to the loves of her life; well, not so much her loves but unusual episodes that were funny now but sensitive then. Her recollections brought a smile to her face as she drifted to her past:

There was John, who said it would be okay to neck in the sawmill yard after the movie. Well, it was more than okay; it was romantic, plus lots of fun. But . . . when she walked into the front room, at home, and told her dad she enjoyed the movie, her dad said, "You did, huh? Your seat must have been on Murphy's Mill sawdust pile . . . your back is full of sawdust."

Or the time she got a little carried away while on a lover's lane, and the police shined a flashlight into the car and saw her bra in the front seat, John and her in the back. He was quick to respond, "I'm going to ask you to get into the same seat as your bra, when *it's on*, and you, young man, get her home by the time the clock strikes one." The answer was simple: "Yes, sir." In those days the good-old-boys at the station did what was right without a lot of fanfare. They may even have told her dad, and he too let it go, no harm done; it was their little unspoken secret. Dads and daughters have an understanding. They knew the *hard* rules and the *gray* rules. They knew our limits.

How could she ever forget the night I climbed to the top of an abandoned windmill, after being "over-served" some fermented grape, and after rescue by her date, John, and his friends, was told by his parents to sleep it off right then and not go home. John stayed with her all night—in the same bed to be certain she was okay—and she knew nothing could have happened, even if they had wanted some action. She passed out, and he watched her until he too fell asleep. She reclaimed her body in the morning, woke John, and they went about their business . . . without apology, nor did he need to; no harm was done.

Screeeech!

"What is that? An owl? Strange, I wonder why it just dropped into the hut. Hell, wise old bird, how are you doing? Your presence on the outer wall is inspiring and quaint—kind of like a visit or a look-see as to how we're doing. Dang, don't leave, but there you go. Thanks for the visit, y'all come back, ya hear!"

She knew she only had half a roof, but had forgotten. She was recounting her past and drinking deeply of her old fun relationships and experiences. "Thank God, this will be the last week that I'll be looking at half a roof."

She mused, Come on, Leigh, give the past a rest. Quit reliving your conquests; get some rest. Ford's dropping in tomorrow afternoon—dream about a roll in the hay; that will make you sleepy— better yet, as Ford would say . . . a "BNR, Bare Naked Roll-around."

Sleep followed this thought; dreams would overtake her consciousness.

*   *   *

"Good morning, sun," Leigh groaned. "Good morning, Boy." No response.

Considering her day without Boy, since he was still doped up, she reviewed her "to-do list."

Reconnoitering the ridgeline to the east was selected. It looked like a short walk from camp—a piece of cake. With the sun three fingers off the horizon and Boy knocked out, it would be a good day to explore. No sweat, she thought; she'd be back in a few hours.

Her map showed no trail to the ridge, as expected, and she only wanted to see how difficult it would be to get to a higher elevation for a multiple set of circumstances, such as vision, transmitting, and rescue. She knew the ridge to the north would work—it was at least one-hundred feet higher than where the altar stood. That ridge was also closer to Skagway and their antenna systems for radio transmissions.

The map showed it was less than a kilometer upstream to the bend in the river and another kilometer to the ridge. She really didn't give it a second thought, to go beyond the second ridge alone; she'd turn around and come back in short order. In east, out west . . . right? Simple as one, two, three . . . well, not always. Conditions change; compass readings are just part of the formula for a successful return from whence you came.

The forest floor was initially clear except for ferns, so she anticipated no problem seeing a long way through the trees. Beautiful in any season, the forest was highlighted by the red, orange, and yellow of early autumn, plus the ever-present green conifers. Her map indicated much of the land in the interior had been purchased by the state to become part of the four-million-acre forest system.

Pht. Pht. Wop. Pht. Pht. shattered the quiet trail. Startled, she froze as a Willow Ptarmigan exploded up around and through the lower limbs, then leveled off while banking left and right to escape the intruder and clear the area. Then another bird, maybe its mate, exploded from the brush and headed in the same direction, so she assumed the pair was now together again elsewhere. She thought, What a gorgeous area for all kinds of animals, a real cornucopia of wildlife.

Virgin stands like this are virtually unpopulated without roads; there are few people and the terrain too rough for loggers to extract the giants of the forest, be it Douglas Fir, White Pine, Western Hemlock, or other minerals from the earth. As she reached the edge of the ridge and before she knew it, the walking became more laborious. She noticed that the forest floor was now completely tangled with mountain laurel. When she reached the edge of the ridge, the going was getting even more cluttered.

Then suddenly the sky clouded up and the sun slipped away. As a result, she could not see very far—not at all; this could be a problem. She now reached the summit of the eastern ridge, and the fog thickened. She could see no more than 50 meters; it was "socked-in." Concerned, she turned around and started back toward what she hoped was her starting point at the bend in the river. Previously, she had a directional heading with the sun as a guidepost; it was now absent. In addition, the sun no longer even gave a hint of its location. Everything was gray to dark slate. The laurel now not only clogged her path, it obliterated her vision also. She had no idea what direction was "back." She mused, Well, girl, don't be acting so proud; you could soon be walking in circles; get out your compass. It is hardly a weakness to use a magnetic dead-reckoning.

Leigh started talking out loud to herself as a way to minimize fear. "Okay, relax, in east and out west, no sweat. Settle down, girl. I need to return about one kilometer . . . about a 25- minute hike, so keep calm; you'll hit the river one way or another. But, girl, you'll want to be at the right point on the river. Enough planning—get going, girl, aim as well as you can—how about that crooked pine—yep that will do. When you get there, you can sight another closer aiming point—get going."

She moved out smartly with a new feeling of confidence. But deadfalls and laurel continued to clog her path as vision declined. "Oops! Damn, there I go again, ass-over-teakettle and on my butt again. As Dad would say, "Did you trip on your own feet?" "Oh no, this is no simple fall; I think I've sprained my ankle, or at least something in that realm. Son of a bitch, God damn, sonofabitch! What a klutz!"

Soaking wet now, she sat on a fallen two-foot cedar, removed her shoe, and looked. Yep, it had already started turning a beautiful reddish-blue and started to swell. Trying to keep her wits, she thought, Put the shoe on loosely, get a walking stick, and get back to the hut quickly. Now prepared to hobble out PDQ, she noted the laurel was getting thicker and turning into a built-in obstacle course . . . by nature. Off she went and within fifteen minutes found the crooked pine, then rested. Ringing wet, she continued through the fog with one more sighting straight ahead, a tall hemlock, which was due west. She had to keep moving since she knew the ankle was going to get bigger whether she stayed out or got back to the hut. She must keep moving; pain can be suppressed. She had been there, done that, many times in the last 60.

Unknown to her, a pair of yellow eyes followed every move she made.

Leigh trudged on over, around and through the brush, and as last reached the river. "There you are, old man river, and I'm right at the bend; what luck. I'll follow it back to camp, which is just about one kilometer or six-tenths of a mile." The animal's eyes continued to observe every move.

Finally, an hour later, hurting and wet with sweat and fog, she made it back. Sighting the camp, the white wolf quickly retreated into the forest.

Hobbling into the hut, Leigh checked on Boy and noticed he sure looked good. Those big dark brown eyes told her he was better, tail singing, and whomping to say so, too. She told him that "Mother" was banged up, too, and they were both members of the same Klutz Club of the Tongass. "Down, Boy. I'm going to get off these feet, sit on my ass, and stick this damaged hoof in Epson salts, just like grandma did 80 years ago . . . and me 40. It cures a lot of ailments."

To her benefit and sound judgment, she had brought several items to treat injuries like this; salts took care of the appendage, and a triple shot of Crown Royal (w/o water) handled the pain. As she downed her first fix, she thought, Why waste aspirin when the booze handles both pain and pleasure? "Whew! That was good."

Her first sojourn into the forest alone had not gone very well. Yes, she returned but in a lesser capacity than at departure. She'd be less than 100% for several days . . . "Cripe." This was a good warning; anything can and will happen when you're exploring, and it generally does. It's the rule of numbers: The more you do, the more it will do to you.

At that, she was unaware of the *curious* stalk of the white wolf.

Any moralists worth their salt would use this occurrence as a teaching moment, as the made-to-order parable Paul wrote in his letter to the Romans:

> "My behavior baffles me.
> That, which I would do,
> I don't do."

At least she was in good company . . .

She mused, The morning's exploration was a bummer. Sure, she had reconnoitered the ridge to the east, but now she had to figure out, with a bum ankle, how she would:

Meet Ford's airdrop at the stream;

Move the pallet to the hut;

Erect the last sections of the roof; and

Tie it all together.

All with a lame-duck woman, but somehow she'd do it. "Boy, are you awake? I've got to get you up for another shot."

She administered 5cc of penicillin, waited 15 minutes, and rolled him over on his folded legs so he could drink. He certainly did; his tongue was moving faster than a preacher at the end of a failed fund drive. Boy lay back down to savor the refreshing feeling.

It was nap time for both.

The Crown Royal and fatigue gave her a good 90 minutes of off-and-on sleep. She awoke startled and confused—it was 1400 hours. She had to get ready for the 1600-hour drop. She thought about her trek to the drop zone by the stream.

She rose slowly. "Jesus Christ, just look at it, just look at it . . . damn; it looks like the foot of a Clydesdale. Back down you go, girl; better sit a while and figure how you are going to hobble to the drop zone."

Down went another five Tylenol, and up she rose, then out to find a better crutch in the woods. "Miss Grace, I am not." She had to find a better branch with a "Y" shape for her arm at about five feet, and two inches in diameter. She'd be using it for several days, so it had to be a good one. She found one that fit, and guess what? It was not unlike a protective club. "En Guard!" she said, as she acted out the King's Tournament of Jousting as if a Knight of the Round Table. However, her high school track experience was finally paying off, as the Ace wrap was holding up very well under the circumstances.

"It's going to be a real bitch pulling the pallet up, and operating the winch and tripod. But we'll find a way. We will close up the hut today. We will! We will do it together . . . just watch. Our home on the meadow will soon come *alive*."

Chapter 5

The Gentle Man

Ford lived and worked in the small town of Skagway, population 700, at the northern tip of the Alexander Archipelago, about 100 km NW of Juneau.

Not unlike Leigh, Ford was also living an alternate lifestyle so common with the hardy souls who moved north to escape the rat race of the lower 48. Casual and almost primitive, Skagway was much like the little town Cislie, as portrayed in the 1990 TV sitcom, *Northern Exposure*, sans Roslyn Cafe and the "gang." Much like Cislie, a visitor would also see a moose or bruin brethren wandering in and around the docks, it being a seaport and main street at the terminus of the Lynn Canal.

A contrast of primitive and hi-tech, Skagway embraced a lifestyle of the 19th century but operated telecommunications and guidance instrumentation effectively on their boats and aircraft at the state-of-the-art 20th-century level.

This beautiful seaport town maintained its quaint turn-of-the-century atmosphere in the face of modern innovations, primarily due to its history as "gateway" to the Klondike Gold Rush. In the late 1800s, it served as a portage to the north via Altin Lake, Whitehorse (in the Yukon), and finally to the "mighty" Yukon River to Fairbanks.

Historically, Skagway was a haven for milking visitors—through a cutthroat business of swindlers and thieves. Generally, 1880 businessmen made much more money than miners in the fields, since the real money was made in supplying the miners with the wherewithal to stake and work their claim.

One colorful man, Jefferson Randall "Soapy" Smith and his gang of con-men swindlers knew how to enhance the position as a benefactor while "robbing them blind." He gave money to widows, gave credit to down-and-out miners, and later "took" their claim, then robbed them with crooked cards, dice, and shell games. One of the most devious scams was epitomized by the man's artifice through his telegraph office. "Soapy" charged five dollars to send a message anywhere in the world. Eager to send news of their adventures to folks back home, no one bothered to peer behind the shack where the telegraph wire petered out in the brush. Yet within hours of sending a telegraph, a reply was bound to come—collect, of course.

Like any excessively corrupt operation, chaotic business climate, the scam, and personal abuse of townspeople came to an abrupt end when the vigilantes sent Frank Reid to talk with Soapy. The talk was short-lived as both were mortally wounded in a gunfight. Reid was honored with an enormous tomb on "boot hill," and Soapy cast to the wolves in the brush where his telegraph line terminated.

Skagway's lawless days were over, but the 20th-century townspeople mandated a turn-of- the-century National Historic Park that duplicates the street scenes of the 1880's. In a way, the locals are still fleecing visitors of their gold, but they're called tourist- (not gold-) crazy stampeders.

A fifth the size of the lower forty-eight, Alaska entered the Union in '59 with its symbolic seven stars of the big dipper and the North Star (Polaris) on a blue field. As kids, people were taught how to find Polaris by following those two "pointer" stars on the open end of the little dipper opposite the handle. Many were puzzled by the seasonal rotation of the dipper around Polaris, saying, Hey, the water's pouring out of the dipper tonight! Secretary of State Seward, (Seward's Folly) in 1867 was *hardly* a "folly" as the U.S. purchased Alaska from the Russians for $7 million. He must be rolling over in his grave as the Alaskan Pipeline transports over a million dollars a day from Prudhoe Bay in the Arctic to Valdez, 1500 miles south to the Gulf of Alaska. Oil literally makes the wheels go round in Alaska.

The 49th is now and has always been a valuable resource of fisheries, lumber, minerals, recreation, and national security of the U.S., not to mention the hardy souls who want to start anew. All know how valuable the 49th state is to the lower 48 and the world thanks to Seward.

Ford had developed a sense of "escape and rebirth" above 50-degree latitude as he needed a new lease on life to play out his last twenty years on good old Mother Earth. Not a fatalist, he was just realistic about being 60, single again, and ready to start over. Blame the Brownian Movement, but it was true that most of his goals had been accomplished; he had two lovely children, sons-in-law, and grandchildren. Two of everything . . . except for only one severely bruised heart. He was very proud of his girls, Lee and Lynn, who were downstate raising their families and working in their chosen professions, including wife, mother, homemaker and professional breadwinner.

Grandsons Mark and Allen were certainly growing like weeds and, at ages four and six, "the boys" had already pushed the envelope of expectations. As host Garrison Keiller, on The Prairie Home Companion Radio, says, "Here in Lake Wobegon . . . all the children are good looking, and above average." Mark and Allen were certainly that. Maybe the girls are just patronizing when they say, "*You know, Dad, both of the boys look like you.*" When he heard that, it was like the pleasurable sound of Armstrong's foot touching the lunar surface in '69. His chest would tighten with the crush of pride; he felt so high. It was as if his eyes were clouded over while scanning the vistas on Mt. Everest. As such he always made sure he saw the families once a year during the winter holidays.

*   *   *

It was noon and Ford was getting ready for another flight to Leigh's Tongass Camp, but the pallet had not been agreeable to lock and release properly between the pontoons of the C-190. The unit was puzzling but not unusual, being the second half of the roof panels. Many mounting techniques required a few "tunks" with a ten-pound hammer, but this one was as difficult as fulfilling a mother-in-law's goals for her daughter's husband. *Impossible.* A perfect fit was not necessary, but a good fit was, for he wanted no Icarus at the drop zone. So he told the boys to remove the entire unit and take a look at the dimensions. The sages of KSC grumbled but knew Ford was right. Another check in the mounting fixture would clarify any fit-check problems. Working under the aircraft had its shortcomings including the "thin" skinned fuselage near the back swing of the hammer and awkward working conditions.

Resolved to do it right, they pulled the pallet with an estimate that it would take an hour or so to correct the interfaces on the "check" fixture, just as with all NASA pre-flight units. Milt and Dave were as competent as they come, needing no watch dog to ensure the unit was properly mounted, but Ford had to fly it as PIC (pilot in command).

Ford had arrived in Skagway via Juneau, in 1996, as an aging pilot/entrepreneur looking for a Flying Service to work for and purchase, over time, as he honed his skills in the bush. At 60, his days were numbered as a pilot, but he could live to 90. But who wants to? He was looking for a place to shoot his last bullet that involved aircraft, adventure, and ownership. Romance was *not* in his sight picture.

He brought a lot of skills to the table. He was a safe and conscientious pilot. Remember this old and true saying: "THERE ARE NO OLD BOLD PILOTS." He had experienced some close encounters with Mother Nature's variable weather patterns, but none he could not handle by being "humble" and avoiding ego-driven decisions. He had already denied many a hunting party's request to leave camp during inclement weather, no matter how unpopular he had been at the time. They all lived to fly home—a day late.

One thing for sure, he'd had no CFIT incidents, Controlled Flights Into Terrain. Sadly only 2% of these CFIT encounters with Mother Earth lead to walking away. CFIT is digging holes into the terrain or mountainside, which frequently occurs when the pilot thinks he is at altitude, and in reality he is not, with a propeller and motor at terminal velocity. Some call it "auguring in."

With thousands of accidents a year, a separate business had sprung up which

Ford thought about getting involved in: Salvage Reclamation, which involves retrieving flight wreckage in the bush away from the airports. Hired by insurance companies, the salvage operator moves in right after the FAA clears the crash scene. Salvage? Good Parts? Was it worth it? If the craft *has not* been involved in a fire upon impact, it is worth it, since there are many components that survive and are perfectly good—motors (costing $10K new), flight instruments, radios, and myriad assorted avionics. They are expensive and worth retrieving way out in the bush, for insurance reasons or resale, after a little rework.

How do they get the stuff out? Most CFIT or similar events occur within 10 miles of the airport or landing site due to weather, mechanical problems, or lack of fuel. At that distance, a helicopter can drop into the site at reasonable expense, or a snow-mobile can reach it when weather permits. Snow is the only way to get to some locales in Alaska.

Most old time pilots chasing around a local beer tavern wish *flight* had a canary, as in the coal mine, that helped their brothers in deep-earth mining. They didn't. Pilots frequently fly in the face of FAA warnings when they should not! Due to many dumb factors, nevertheless real, they fail to deal with these options objectively. For example:

- A wealthy client needs to get home from a remote hunting camp to close a deal worth millions. "I'll pay you triple your costs to fly." Visibility was 200 feet. *Dead for sure is a deal with a dead dealer—CFIT.*

- The storm front will have moved on before I get to the lodge, so the pilot says, "Let's go; it's only a 40-minute flight." *It didn't move; the gas gauge did—CFIT.*

- The pilot says, "Go ahead, put one more elk carcass on the rack. I can still lift off the lake with a 1000-foot distance." *He did off-lift the lake, but did not clear the trees—CFIT.*

Ford's Flying Service (FFS) started in late '99 under unfortunate circumstances. A Skagway flight service owner had a growing business that became available, through the bank, after the owner "augured-in" during an unexpected storm on the coast near Haines, SW of Skagway.

As with any risk-oriented businessman, Ford had no hesitation to go head-over-heels in debt and purchase the operation in Skagway. Sad over the circumstances, yet glad for the opportunity, he felt compelled to retain all existing personnel, including the owner's widow; there were no children. That fact consoled his feelings about opportunistic entrepreneurship; plus the hangar boys, Milt and Dave, were much like himself, down-staters seeking adventures and a new life. With a month of fix-up and paint-up, the Ford Flying Service (FFS) would be the best on the coast.

Milt and Dave were both pilots and certified FAA mechanics, so FFS could perform certified engine overhauls, frame work and, of course, charter service to the various hunting and fishing camps in the northern lakes. There are few airfields for aircraft, so it's water in the summer and ice or snow (with skis) in winter. FFS had a 2,000-foot runway, but the Lynn Canal was the primary surface. Most aircraft are "tail-draggers" with huge balloon tires (6.00 X 20) for operations on rough fields as well as gravel and hard-packed sand beaches. Pontoon operations are self-evident and very versatile on inland lakes, rivers and, when pressed, the rougher conditions on the ocean. As such, the planes were plagued with inordinate drag and mass, which restricted not only speed but also weight factors. Increased probability of sideslip and stall speed problems are some of the additional negatives of a bush pilot's aircraft. And pontoons have to be drained weekly, or water pumped out or blown out with compressed air. Add to this how difficult it is to get the birds flying in sub-zero (-30) weather, even with electric oil pan heaters.

Communications with a "tower" are almost nonexistent when landing, since they are few and far between and, in fact, Automatic Terminal Information Service (ATIS) is not available in much of the air space. When it is, the requisite English is garbled, vague, quick, and marginally understandable. Ford remembered an Aleut Indian controller helping him one day as he departed from a "towered" field in Yakuatat, on the coast. Over the scream of an unmuffled engine he heard:

> "Cessa190maintainheadingatthe(*Squawk*)outermarkeronefivezerodegreesradialturnleftheading(*Squawk*)twofivezeromaintainthreethousand(*Squawk*)zerooneout!"

Many pilots thought that the controller in the tower must have just had an accidental lobotomy since the pilots sometimes had no clue of what the dude just said.

Everyone is nice to each other in the flying community, since anyone may have to return and need to be welcomed back again. So everyone always thanked the controller to the field in an emergency, but thought maybe pilots should sing to each other, to help understand the words. Music is a universal language!

One, Two, Three o'clock, Four o' clock rock . . .

Okay, so Bill Haley and His Comets may not work.

Ford's "beat-up" but serviceable '73 CJ-5 Jeep, with a 360 hp V-8, called "Blue Boy," ambled down Main Street (a stretch of the word *main*) of Skagway toward FFS. Every toy or mechanical wonder had a contrived name by The Boys at FFS. The C-190 was called "Big Red Bird," and of course the dog simply "Boy," which was pretty weird. Like, come on, Boy, or Boy, come over here. Oh well, it's not a perfect name, but what is perfect? Nothing, except a mother-in-law.

Ford had stopped by his cabin to check the mail and calls on the voice mail and e-mail, never knowing who wanted something and for what. In business, he had to keep checking on customers, and if necessary, tend to their needs, even when it was unwarranted. He almost tried out the satellite cell phone to Leigh since he'd be a little late at the drop zone, but changed his mind; one hour is not an item up here. He looked for a piece of paper, and being impatient, grabbed an envelope to use in organizing his informal flight plan. Grinning, he discovered it was an invitation to receive *Playboy* magazine at reduced prices. Hummnm, maybe FFS should subscribe to *Playboy*. Not a bad idea; there's still more bear in Alaska than bare women, and the Boys just might read it for the latest sexual philosophy. Ha, that's an old line; he knew it was the photos they wanted. Ford remembered the good old days of Vargas Girls in colored pencil that looked every bit as good as new air-brushed nudes, with headlights ablazing and pubic hair. He cared not to see. Times change, some things not for the better. . . . It was 1300 hours.

He went over his checklist:

Depart Skagway 1400 hours, to Tongass Camp.

Winds SW at 10 mph, no weather fronts within 300 miles.

Bearing 2600 west (SW), altitude 3,500 feet.

Flight time, at 80 mph = 2 hours, 160 miles (w/minimum wind), to longitude 138'W: latitude 59'N, the camp, with alternate at Klukwean; tanks at about 1/2 or 80 gallons. When loaded with a short flight you *do not* top-off the tanks that hold 150 gallons. This flight only needed 60 gallons + 20 gallons (1/3 for reserve). Consumption should be about 60 gallons (4 hours @ 15 gallons/hour = 60) plus, reserve of 20 gallons for your future use; this little data point: Gasoline, 6.0 lbs/gal; Oil, 7.5 lbs/gal; Water, 8.3 lbs/gal.

Now he could plan load factors.

Arrive Tongass Camp, 1600 hours.

Loiter time, 15 minutes.

Depart Camp, 1615 hours bearing 80° NE.

Remember, add or subtract 180° to get the back azimuth for a return flight (260°-180°=80°).

Arrive Skagway, 1830 hours with expected headwinds, but without the 1,000-pound pallet jettisoned at the camp, so Big Red should move right along.

Always available when needed, either Milt or Dave would be waiting at FFS to assist in securing the Old Bird upon arrival on Lynn Canal. He would call Base about 20 miles from town. FFS had a 50-foot transceiver antenna that reached out into the bush about 100 miles.

Arriving at "The Bar," another name for FFS, Ford checked the pallet mount that the boys had successfully modified. "Big Red" was ready to go. His looks registered "Well done, Boys." It appeared as though the pallet would now release at the site.

He thanked the Boys and was ready to go! Milt and Dave's body language indicated: "Did you have any doubt?"

Arms akimbo and with a wry face, Ford's grimace said it all. Could you imagine coming back to Skagway with a "hung-up" unreleased pallet? It would be a disaster waiting to happen. It would be a UFIW, Uncontrolled Flight Into the Water of Lynn Canal, not a C.F.I.T.

Milt pushed the Bird away from the dock, and Ford fired up the radial nine.

While taxiing on the water, Ford thought he'd need at least 1,000 feet of water into the wind to clear the big pines to the north. As such, he'd better taxi farther back toward Passion Point. His thoughts had been there recently, as reflected, if not cherished, by the moments with Leigh on the bench.

Ford had met Leigh at FFS a month earlier when she was inquiring about transport options to a remote locale in the Tongass. At first he was a little stand-offish, due to her bold and aggressive personality and speaking style. Very direct and to the point, she minced few words with her inquiry about Ford, FFS, and their capabilities.

1. She needed a yurt type HABITAT (a hut) transported to the Tongass Site. She had plans for a knock-down (KD) air-lifted (with pallets) hut, and cost was not a factor.

2. She also needed counsel on the optimum method of getting to her campsite, approximately 100 km SW of Skagway.

3. FFS had been recommended because of its fabrication shop, personnel with KSC (Apollo) experience and unique metals/fabrication shop, and finally—its flight skills.

Ford was overwhelmed with Leigh's request. In ten minutes she had as much as told him FFS was the one to do the job . . . and when could he start? He felt she was a bit pushy and possibly a "femi-Nazi" (Rush Limbaugh's label), too hot to handle for FFS's good-old-boys style.

Through all this aggressive, unfeminine behavior, there flowed a "trickle" of attractiveness that tapped into Ford's testosterone, but having been bruised earlier by these hormonal urges, he shut it down. *This is a business deal; down, boy; behave—she's got do-re-me ($) and that suits me.* No sense loading the cannon in his loins over this broad.

But, best-laid plans do go astray and after two days of intensive preplanning, Ford found himself on a small bench at the tip of Passion Point—with her at his side. They were not holding hands, but they had embraced each other's life encounters, families, and uncertain but exciting future. The ebb and flow of life experiences brought them together despite themselves. On the fourth night, all plans had been settled. She would fly to and parachute into the Tongass at week's end and start her two-year sojourn to restructure herself, write, explore, and discover the hidden beauty of nature's unspeakable wealth. Was she a little "romantic" or altruistic about nature's open arms? Maybe, but who could challenge her attempt to find her own Chautauqua—in the Tongass.

He imagined they were on the bench again. They had *grown* close . . .

Unsure but driven, he held her tonight. It seemed so natural; she hesitated, but his arms soon felt the invitation as she relaxed in his grip. She did not resist. His cannon was loaded now, but the trigger was on safe/lock.

He paused and enjoyed the moment, but remembered, Go slow. She laid her head on his chest and looked at the stars. They both knew the sky's heavenly bodies.

"Look, the dipper is dumping on us, see?" Leigh said. "Yep, I think it's affecting my hormones, you know. I see nothing wrong with that—we're consenting adults, aren't we?" she cooed.

"Come to think of it," Ford said, "we can't even be arrested for sitting on a bench in a county park at midnight; we're both over 18, for crying-out-loud! Yep, old Sheriff Wright would just love to bust a young couple out here on the bench after midnight. He'd sneak up, shine his six-cell in your face, and say, 'What's going on here?' Then he'd say, 'OOPS, it's you, Ford (gulp). Sorry; good evening, miss!'" Ford exclaimed.

Leigh repositioned herself on his lap. It was as if she were inviting him to take her soft moist red lips to his. She stared at him with wide-open eyes as if focused on his thoughts. Neither said a word; it seemed like minutes but was only seconds. He moved slowly and surely to the moisture of her parted mouth of ruby-red richness. The warmth and gratification added beats to this heart. Strange, there was no wind, but chimes rang out. As they surfaced for air, his hands explored her beauty and he sighed.

She did not resist but said, "Are you sure you want to do that?"

"No, I'm not sure, but I do enjoy you, your lips, and the beauty of your womanhood," murmured Ford.

"I'm glad you do; you know I'm not sure about this, either, but we are aware of what we're doing and of the consequences, right?"

"Yes and no. This started to be a business deal," he said, "but I am absolutely enamored with you and your mind."

"So am I about you, but let's move slowly."

So, slowly, he continued to explore her beauty . . . and she his manhood.

The silence on the Lynn Canal was deafening; animation was absent everywhere. A sound came from the water. They both rose up and strained their eyes to the water's edge, then exclaimed in unison, "What could it be?"

Luckily it was Boy, out for his nightly run on the beach. He had stopped for a moment, sensed someone on the bench, and was headed that way at high speed. Little did he realize it would be Ford and his newfound friend Leigh, whom he was starting to like more and more. Ford gave him a warning. "Hi fella," he said, just a little upset by his activities being interrupted. "Surprised you, didn't we?" He looked at Leigh, truly believing this intrusion was probably preordained. They were getting very intimate. Actually, he did *both* a favor. "Well, Leigh, Boy saved the day," he mused.

"Stop, Ford, don't analyze the night too much. *Just let it be.* Nothing needs to be said. No one was hurt. You are sure one hell of a guy to relax with, or should I say be charged up by? I can now see why they call this place Passion Point!"

Boy sat at her feet; he wasn't going anywhere but right there tonight. He was at home wherever these two were. He was not moving. Ford related, "Guess what, Leigh, my dear friend, I've just decided my interest in you and your safety at the camp has increased twofold. As such, until we decide otherwise, you'll have Boy with you at the Camp as another keener pair of high-fidelity eyes and ears. You need him more than I do while you're at the Camp, and he already loves you." Leigh's expression indicated that this was too much of a sacrifice. "Don't argue; he's your insurance . . . and Boy is going home with you tonight, as much as I wish I were in his place. Let's call it a day and turn in."

"Good night, Boy; night Leigh; sleep tight." Ford sighed as he walked back to his cabin. The night swallowed their experience and anticipated future encounters alone, but not now, maybe later, not now.

She walked home with Boy happily dancing at her side.

Blue Boy then took an infatuated pilot to his lonely bachelor cabin.

*   *   *

The sun was at four fingers and Big Red had already been preflight-checked as Ford slowly turned at Passion Point to head into the wind, then gave her the final preflight checks. Feather prop, run up to full throttle at 4500, OK; Magneto check, both, then left, and then right, OK; Carburetor heat on/off, OK; Fuel rich then lean and reset to nominal, OK; Altimeter (barometric pressure) set at elevation 29.92, OK; Running lights on, collision avoidance on, OK; Pontoon rudders functional, OK; Flaps, tail rudder, elevators, and ailerons, OK, but stiff; Emergency survival kit, on board, OK; Pallet interlock (green) light, OK; Flaps at 10°, prop reset, take-off area clear, OK.

Throttle at full, the Bird burst to life. She shuddered, shook, and the aluminum vibrated as the wake foamed on the surface. The Bird started "pushing water" prior to rising on plane from the water's "grip."

It takes much more horsepower to break the drag from suction of pontoons on the covetous water. Add the pallet's mass between the struts of the pontoons . . . this was no typical water take-off.

Forty knots, pontoons on a level plane, sixty knots, vibration stopped as her resonance frequently silenced the rivet/fastener chatter, eighty knots, pontoons now skimmed the water, Vr (rotation speed), yoke back ever so slightly, and "with a leap" the Bird was airborne. Flaps up, power to 80, AOA 120(VX), altitude 100 feet, cleared the trees, manifold pressure nominal at

16 Hg, check radio frequency, key hand microphone.

"Base Ops, this is DC #1, over."

"DC #1, this is Base Ops, hear you loud and clear, over."

"Base, I've just cleared the outer marker (the tall pine) at 1,000 feet, and turning to 260° W and climbing to 3,500 feet; see you in 4 or 5 hours, out."

"Have a good flight, old timer, and throw that gal a kiss from us, too. And give Boy a wave from us. This is FFS Base, out."

Ford was now cruising at 3,500 feet, 70% power, 3,000 rpms, and headed west at 260° true course (TC), which is the corrected magnetic north (MN). It was tough when correcting the TC way up here, for lines of longitude "bend" or converge at the poles to true north, which is unfortunately not the same point as MN.

Out the port window a flight of geese joined in a "V" formation at about 3000 feet. "Welcome," Ford said, as the Earth's rotation moved the sun to the west over the continent.

At this elevation, Flight Service Station (FSS), from Juneau's facilities (at 121.5 Freq), provided a variety of services to a pilot, which included weather briefings and excellent weather data. FAA also related to specific needs when provided the following information: 1) Type of flight, VFR or IFR (visual or instrument flight rules), 2) Aircraft number and your name, 3) Aircraft type, 4) Departure point, 5) Route of flight, 6) Destination, 7) Estimated time of departure, and 8) Estimated time en route or estimated time of arrival.

Even without a transponder signaling a towered airport, no pilot is ever alone. FSS have awareness of flight plans regardless of whether filed or not. Ford had not, but "The Boys" at Base knew. They had his flight plan written on the *Playboy* envelope. Yes, he was flying alone, but "others" were with him electronically. *Thankfully*, the flight of geese had departed his air space.

The horizon to the west billowed with resplendent cumulus clouds at least to 35,000 feet while unfolding their constantly changing splendor.

Ford had fallen—big time—for Alaska, the Last Frontier. The Aluets called it Alyeska, the "Great Land." And great it was, with 58,600 square miles, though sparsely populated; Alaska still numbers 620,000 habitants. The more remote villages have not been untouched by civilization, but they still bear many marks of the primitive heritage of the native people. Larger cities on the limited "road system" are more modern—those that are not are *very primitive.*

Anchorage, the largest city, where half of the state's population lives, laid to the WNW as Ford cruised WSW to the Tongass National Forest. He reflected on his first meeting with his two mechanic/pilots, jack-of-all-trades brothers Milt and Dave Hughes. Half Aleut and half Russian, they were shuffled around by many relatives on the Kenai Peninsula and finally, to their benefit, were raised in the local churches' non-denominational Juneau Children's Home. With good fortune on their side, and outstanding scholarship, they were sent by the Children's Home Benefactors to Southwestern College in Waxahachie, Texas. That is how they became involved in the nation's space program at the Manned Spacecraft Center (MSC) in Texas, and Kennedy Spacecraft Center (KSC) in Florida.

They had returned to their "roots" after seeing the world with the space program. Ford mused, very fortunate, I am, as they had decided to move back to their roots after a very successful sojourn in the lower forty-eight. Very private, Ford did not press or probe them about their family background or life experiences, unless they volunteered, which they did on occasion. There was a hard and fast rule up here: don't ask about the past. Why? Many were here to forget the past.

Ford learned early in life to limit personal questions or statements. It started when an embarrassing query occurred at his aunt's wedding. It sure fixed him good when he went over to the bride and stated: "My mother wondered how you could wear a *white* wedding dress . . ." The sisters were still not speaking.

At least they did not have to return to their prior families' subsistence standard, where water was still hauled-in, and a honey bucket was found in the bathroom, or fishing with the Yupik and Inupist Eskimos here, or Beluga whaling and walrus or seal hunting on sleds.

Ford played the "looks like" face shapes game with himself at 3,500 feet with the surging mercurial cloud formations. He mused, It's enjoyable searching for cloud formations, but much more enjoyable on the ground with a woman looking up while on our backs with a six-pack before getting in the sack. Okay, okay, a little corny but he mused, "It had been a long time between drinks!"

There is one fine Bull, sure enough with long sharp horns massive snout and "eyes" as if ready to charge and throw a matador over his back. He thought back to his adventures with El Toro, The Bull, in Mexico and Spain in the early '60s.

Ford was where he chose to be, in his mistress of the sky, cruising along without a care—while programmed to descend to his newfound mistress in the Tongass. He alerted ATC of his descent: "Juneau ATC tower, this is Cessna-190, N6401 at 1500 hours SW of Klukuan River; this is 01, over."

"This is Juneau ATC, Roger to standby. C-01, Roger, Out."

Chapter 6

A Visitor

"If a man does not keep pace with his companions, perhaps it is because he hears a different drummer. Let him step to the music which he hears, however measured or far away."

—H.D. Thoreau, 1846

The "bench" on the Bitterroot was not unlike the one on Passion Point in Skagway, sans Ford. Leigh sat and thought of the starlit night with him, while on the 'Root resting her sprained ankle. Ford's arrival was estimated to be about 1700 hours from the east. She remembered that he would probably approach into the wind on his final to maintain maximum lift and control, so might be coming right out of the sun to the west. With the wind blowing to the west, she most likely would not hear his approach. She thought, Better get my hand-held handy; he generally calls about five miles from the drop zone.

"Ford." She mused, What does he really think *of* me?

How do I relate to his attraction *for* me?

How should I react to his attraction *with* me?

How should I react if I want him to be involved with me?

Romance and sex at 63, with me?!

I do not need another man under or over me!

You are *too old* Leigh!

What to do . . . I did not *want* this to happen.

"Damnit, Leigh."

Then again, she mused, A woman is never too old if she can be moved emotionally by a man of her own age. Still reflective, she thought, Damn you, Ford. Isn't there enough on my plate? Not sure, she felt she would like to add Ford to the buffet-of-life experiences.

"Behave, Leigh, you've got a mission in the Tongass. It does not include another man in your life. Damn men. Christ, I don't even have any progesterone in my system, so, 'What's Up, Babe?' You know better."

Just stop it!

"Yeah . . . easier said than done. Wait a minute; I'm no teenager in my first musk attack. What's wrong with a shameless relationship in your 60's?

"I like him . . . but haven't figured out why . . . maybe I just want mindless sex. Huh?"

The roar of a radial engine broke the silence of the Bitterroot's calm. It was the 190. At times, when at full power, the engine appeared to be consuming itself with each piston slamming to the crank with alternate radial explosions of fuel driving a propeller through the resisting air. "DC2, this is DC1, over."

"Yeah, he's on his downwind approach."

"DC1, this is DC2; I hear you loud and clear—yeah, you've made it, Babe! I've missed you! Over."

"Fine, just one more drop after this one and we will have the hut finished. Bet you're anxious to button up the hut with this pallet! Over."

"You bet; it will take a little longer though; I've sprained my ankle, and Boy is recovering quite well from a bear attack, over."

"What?! Is he okay?"

"Don't worry, Ford; we'll be fine."

"I wondered where your four-legged friend was. Are you okay? What happened? Over."

"I fell while exploring. It was my fault, and Boy attacked an intruder in what he felt was his area. I was never in danger, and we must get the roof on. It's just going to take a little more time. Damn, I don't quite know what to say, over."

"Okay, I'm turning and will make the drop and be back in two days. I wish you luck closing in the hut with half a body on the ground—damn. Okay, here she comes." *Klunk! Plop. Whoop. Swing. Splash!*

"Yeah, she's swinging on down in a billow of silk."

"Great. Lots of luck, girl; stroke Boy, and yourself, over."

"Okay, you hunk, will do, but how 'bout your stroke? I'll throw one up, over."

"Okay, I felt it—gotta go; this is DC1, out."

"Okay, see you later, I miss you; I'll think about that stroke tonight; this is DC2, out."

The 190 and Ford disappeared again as the Bird flew over the coastal range to the east. Her eyes looked along the path to the hut; then she cast her eyes to the pallet on the edge of the water, then back to the hut; damn, it's at least 100 meters. *No matter how you look at it, my body is going to suffer.* Within 30 minutes and 25 meters along the path, now soaking wet, her eyelids dripping with sweat, she plunked down to rest. "Damn this ankle."

Actually she wasn't doing too badly. Worse case, she'd have the pallet at the hut in just over two hours—that is, if she continued at this pace and nothing or no one "raised the bar."

Now she knew how the lonely and separated Captain Ahab felt while carrying on with his command aboard ship; at least with her, there was no white whale involved. "One thing is certain; it will be dark at 1930 hours, by the time old "peg-leg" Leigh gets to the hut. And that will be the end of my day. My left arm feels as though it's been stretched and is now longer than the other, my left leg shorter from being jammed by using only one side for the last couple of hours. Frankly, without these tough knobby boots, gloves, and a handmade 'T' handle on the line, I could not have made it at all.

"Rest now, girl; we'll close her up in the 'morrow. The agonal journey is over for now. Tomorrow's another story. Mounting the roof will be difficult while hobbling, but certainly doable."

When she entered the hut, Boy was standing at the doorway. A surprise—she wondered how he could have recovered so fast and gotten up to meet her—and was sure he had to pee. She helped him down the stairs; he didn't resist, and sure enough he peed like a racehorse. He certainly had to go! The clean-up routine in the hut had ended, and he was up and about—carefully.

Still in pain, his eyes resonated the hurt loud and long; he could barely wag his tail without pain.

"Up we go," she said as she carried Boy up the steps and into the hut. She felt the warmth of his body and soon-to-be-experienced closure of this incident.

- Boy would survive.

- Leigh's ankle would soon be 100%.

- The hut would be closed in tomorrow.

- Appliances and furnishings would "drop in" on Sunday.

- A "normal" camp at the meadow's edge was developing.

- What a great feeling, and she wasn't even there yet, but the flash of joy that bordered on rapture dominated her thoughts.

She hugged her sleeping bag as if it were Ford. "We're close now, Babe." Then she felt the returned warmth of her dog's body. Boy was once again at her side, sore ribs and all. "Goodnight . . . don't let the bed bugs bite. Hey, check out those stars, Boy; it's the last night I hope that we'll be able to see them from here." Then she had a good idea, maybe with a little help, a series of star patterns could be painted on the ceiling with the little dipper holding water.

Sleep slowly enveloped their bodies as the mighty denizens of the forest came to life while stars rotated around Polaris in much the same fashion as millions of years ago.

*   *   *

"Oh no! What's that?" Leigh cried out. A long, wet, and aggressive tongue was at her face, all over her face. Boy was not only up on all fours, he was genuinely loving her; he was signaling, "I've got to pee." Some things never change. He was certainly making up for lost time; it was as though he'd been sleeping off a three-day drunk.

"Okay, Boy, let's go. It looks as though you're getting around much better now. Great. Wait! Don't go down the steps alone; save your breath. Oops, too late." He'd gone down the steps and was already in the three-legged stance, even before she could hobble to her "cute" little outhouse. It was a simple log positioned over a hole, and would you believe, a little modesty curtain to shield her little "butt" from what . . . she did not know, maybe the inhabitants of the forest? Yes, it was goofy to hide from the meadow side, but it just wasn't right to display her butt on the throne! Some things do not require a logical explanation. She was in charge here; she'd do whatever.

Like a "good camper," she shoveled over her current latrine deposit, for many reasons including odor, human scent, mammalian scat from animals of the forest—they know, insect control and just good camping practices. Maybe this weekend she'd have the chemical toilet inside and she could close the "pit" for good.

The next thing she did seemed damn pointless and risky, but nevertheless both Leigh and Boy humped all the way from the hut to the river's edge. They were used to doing so every morning when they were healthy, so they continued to do so; it was a routine. After all, that's where the refreshing water and birds were for Boy. He always chased the birds; little did he understand that *would not* be the case today. He'd be lucky to be able to amble down the bank to drink. Boy was by no means healed; he was just feeling better. Of course there was always his inquisitiveness in checking the calling card "prints" of nocturnal visitors to the riverbank. That was always an "event!" And yes, there were many today, both large and small, but both Boy and Leigh just could not repeat their normal routine. It normally consisted of a two-mile run along the river, *in* the river, and *across* the river—then while soaking wet, a dash to the meadow to "flush" every nesting bird in sight. That made the birds' morning pure hell. If she chose not to traverse the meadow, she retreated directly to the hut and said, "Go get 'em, Boy" and off he'd go alone, rousting anything and everything in his path while she attended to camp chores. By the time Boy finished his hell-raising mission in the meadow, scores of animals would be sounding off and pissed off.

Today, he knew the difference as he hobbled up the bank and looked at her. He wanted to "sweep" the meadow, but joined her in the "hump" back to the hut. The ptarmigans and songbirds would not have their peace shattered today. Boy looked at the meadow as he sauntered by; his standing down today was temporary; terror would soon return. He seemed to think, "Don't get used to the calm of today, for I'll be back next week." Both went back to the hut, since Leigh had lots of work to do, and Boy had to rest.

As they trudged back like a couple of drunken sailors, she thought of Ford. Her fascination with Ford still puzzled her—why did she do this to herself? Who knew? Ford sure didn't . . . *Montaigne* said it well:

"If you press me to say why I like him,
I can say no more than it was because
He was he and I was I."

Maybe it was because he was frank and truthful. "What you see is what you get." She could hear from him the truth of his life and experiences; there was nothing to hide. He kept saying, in so many words, *simplify*. Simplify your life; get rid of the excess baggage that's pulling you away from your goals. Not unlike the teaching of the Buddha: eliminate desire and the pain that goes with it, and you will be at peace. Something like that. Well, guess what, that was part of her plan. To rid herself of the "flotsam of life" and live her "Walden" in the little hut in the meadow and keep in touch through the latest in telecommunications equipment. She was alone, by choice.

Solitude was a choice.

*   *   *

The hut would be closed in today! She walked the tripod over the opening and lowered the cable hook to the pallet. Moving slowly due to her bum ankle, she secured the tripod to the pallet and centered it over the open half of the roof. She was getting good at this now, and finally getting the hang of it after two weeks of construction. She now came to the hard part . . . getting enough leverage to lift and then hold onto the "flying-wing" as it deployed over the engagement points. All this on one good leg and foot. It wasn't going to be pretty since the section is always the toughest. There would be swearing . . . so better get started.

She had to move Boy to a safe area first. No telling where the roof section would end up if things went asunder. She asked him to please move his wrapped-up and stitched body over by the distant birch trees while trying to explain why he wouldn't want to be anywhere near the elevated roof section. She helped him move, telling him not to worry, he'd be able to see everything from the birches. Thanking him, she muttered, "Now watch this bitch set this pitch without a hitch." The block and tackle line was now attached to a sturdy oak, the guideline to the neighboring maple. That should do it. Up you go, Protector of Fine Women and Dogs, up to shield us from the elements. Being careful and with TLC, it should just fall in place, no sweat.

"How's the view from the orchestra pit?" she teased Boy. It was too soon to see an outstanding show, just wait and see.

Unimpressed, Boy yawned, laid his head between his outstretched paws, and lifted his eyes up in their sockets as if to say, "Show me, woman; I'm from Missouri."

"You certainly have an attitude problem, Boy." She'd show him. She held up for a moment and checked the lines and bet the other animals were also watching from the meadow. They know when a good show is about to occur. "Stand back—here goes; this Jessie is about to be closed in."

In no hurry for the final insertion of the roof, she first poured a triple of Crown Royal and Tylenol chaser. Her chemical assist was out of the way, so she decided it was time.

Checking again, line around the oak, snub on the maple, up the roof went as planned, and as if *on command* the panels unfolded, locked, and assumed a "bat-wing" position. She then pulled the entire assembly over with the guideline and positioned it for placement. Then slowly down it went, easy does it, slow, slow, "slip" damn, just take it easy. Okay, no harm done, down she comes, one more foot, *Clunk!* Success! "Well done, girl." She had only one thing on her mind—rest the ankle, *now.*

It was down and she was done. Both tie-offs held the roof in place now, and she could rest before going inside to "knock her" into place. After resting a few minutes, the ankle did not stop throbbing, so she decided to continue working.

With her ten-pound hammer and her ankle aching for the next two hours, all Boy could hear was: "Bang! Damn you, bang! You'd better lock in, you bastard, bang! Ha, got you that time. Bang, bang, you SOB, you better get in there. Ha, finally. Now once more, get your cotton-pickin' butt in there . . . don't you dare drop out . . . okay, got ya! One more and I'm done. There you go—get in—now that's more like it! Done!"

For two hours, that was the monologue the meadow's residents and Boy's ears suffered as the roof unit was finally "tied in" successfully. Boy wanted no part of her until she cooled down.

On a ladder with a ten-pound hammer, twenty guide pins, and forty bolts, all fighting for a "good" fit that ended up being "fair" fit after packaging on the pallet, Leigh was using words Boy had never heard before today. Well, maybe in the FFS shop by Milt and Dave; they *really* knew how to swear. However, even the FFS guys had never topped one of Leigh's earlier expletives: "You SOB, if you don't go in, I'll kick your ass into next week—you F____head bolt!" They must have heard her, since all forty bolts were in, screwed tight, and the hut was now solid as a rock.

It was time again for a "fisherman's special." Out came the Crown Royal and Schnapps, and she poured two fingers of each. Before the alcohol could leap into the air, down the hatch it went with the resulting, "Oh, that's good," response. She had now taken care of the inside; now the outside, so she took off her boots. "Just as I thought, the old Clydesdale is red as a beet and swollen again." She expected as much, so out came the pail and Epson Salts in water, to ready herself for a long soaker.

Still outside, she sat and soaked as the trees cast their shadows across the meadow. The rest had also become silent as if the daylight sounds halted and a respectful silence buffered the evening before night sounds began. It was as if in the eye of the hurricane. Two friends remained sitting outside on the porch with their eyes on the sky. Leigh lingered with an unknown reluctance to leave. Boy was resting, and their twinkling friends were starting to appear as they had every night for the last few weeks. She'd miss their celestial beauty rotating around the zenith of their little section of the Tongass. But, realistically, the romance of sleeping under the stars had to yield to the less splendid view of the hut's ceiling and its security.

"Look, Boy, there's a good sign; the Little Dipper is holding liquid tonight. One thing is for sure; I've had enough booze to chase the pain and invite a snooze. Let's hit the sack; I'm ready to drop. Ok, you can slide over here by me, and guess what? This ceiling doesn't look so bad. We can paint stars on it next week. Sounds corny, doesn't it? Maybe not," she whispered.

The last memory of the day was a nose probing under her sleeping bag searching for her hand. She lifted it out of the bag and it fell on the soft muzzle as if a natural and expected occurrence. Leigh faded away to positive dreams of the past.

Her home was now complete, and Leigh felt much like the young Indian boy, Little Tree, from one of her favorite books, *The Education of Little Tree*. She remembered this poem, which described his home in the mountains much like hers on the meadow, "Going Home":

"See the mountains humping and rolling high

Rimming the day birth and busting the sun
And tucking the fog sheets 'round her knees
And strumming the wind with her finger-trees
And scratching her back against the sky.
Watch the cloudbanks roll and stroke her hips
Dripping whispers of sighs from the branch and bush
Hear her womb-hollows stir with the murmur of life,
Feel the warm of her body, the sweet of her breath
And the rhythm of mating that thunders and cries.
Deep in her belly the water veins pulse
And nipple the roots that suckle their life
And streams from her breasts in liquid flow
Giving life to her children she cradles in love
And adding a lilt from her spirit mind
The melody humming of water's song."

—Forest Carter, 1976

*   *   *

The sun broke over the meadow, the dawn of a new day.

He sat at dawn's early light in the ritualistic sitting position, legs crossed, arms extended, hands open with ramrod straight posture as in the Lotus Position. Alone, as directed by his ancestors, the native Healer (Shaman to some) "Walkswithwater" gazed at the horizon to offer thanks to the Creator. It was his custom to greet the day in this way not only for himself, but also for his people. The new dwellers, at the edge, did not know of his presence. It was early morning nautical twilight, five o'clock; only the birds were active. He was well aware of their activities over the last few weeks, but that was not the reason for his presence at the center of the meadow. His visit had a much more important mission.

He sat at the center of the ceremonial meadow where his forefathers had conducted sacred rituals since the early 1800s. He sat as one of the few surviving native healers or medicine men who were becoming an endangered species. Many tribes had abandoned the role and function of Native (Tribal) Healers, and the title had almost become extinct—primarily due to the crazy and rapid advancement of technology, science, medicine, and European religions, be they the popular Christian or Islamic myths. This is precisely why he was at the Sacred Meadows to continue to speak to the sacred mountains from the ceremonial grounds, holy places and former encampments.

He sat on the sacred ground the Creator gave them many years ago. It was here he came to seek visions and guidance, acquire knowledge, conduct sacred

rituals/ceremonies, and gather medical and spiritual needs. Unfortunately as civilization expanded, it encroached upon, desecrated, and destroyed the natural resources that Natural Healers needed to make their people healthy and well.

He sat and thanked the Creator for giving them the power that comes from
their relations in Nature; for they were the spiritual advisors and allies, much like
the Jews and Christians used mythical angels, burning bushes, parting waters, and
evening stars.

Animal hides, claws, furs, teeth, and feathers were their spiritual tools, as
other myths use symbolic candles, a cross, and saints via statues as figures to
worship.

- They used animal tools and their powers for healing, for ritual
  enhancement, ceremony, and humbleness to help keep the spiritual *in balance.*

- They were *keepers* of the land and had the vision to maintain all
  of the Creator's species.

- They did not own the land but were only *temporary caretakers*; they
  were there to preserve the land by protecting it from harm and
  damage so future generations could enjoy its bounty.

He sat knowing a Nature Healer must also be a leader, which is much different today from the ones in the past.

Natural practitioners are mysteriously selected to their calling usually with a
dream followed by a mystical experience of enlightenment, an illness, an accident,
a disease, or even a near-death experience. Their "spiritual" power is derived from
the planets, stars, sun, moon, and animals such as the raven, hawk, eagle, bear,
wolf, deer, salmon, and other physical entities such as wind, lightning, and thunder.

Many things in nature seen and unseen, as with European myths, have been
considered a source of spiritual power.

- *Hawks* are a spiritual source of power, protectors,
  strong fighters, and they travel long distances against
  great odds.

- *Bears* are wise, survive under great adversity, and select
  many herbs to balance and improve their longevity.

- *Wolves* are scouts, or when in a pack they provide strong family structure and survive all the adversities of nature.

The Elements

* Father Sun

* Mother Earth

* Cyclical Moon

* Winds That Blow Away Sickness

* Clouds that purify

* Fog the protector

* Plants for healing

He sat and reflected the earlier years while he was in training and serving with the elder sages as an apprentice healer, and how he used the spiritual powers of nature to help his people.

The powers are symbolically reflected in the tools of the trade the native Healer uses. For example, he might wear a bear hide or wolf hide and use an eagle wing fan while dancing and singing over a patient as others pray to a supernatural unseen god. When he does, he becomes that power; the power speaks through him. So the regalia the native Healer uses is not simply "fetishes" for magic and trickery; they are real physical and spiritual power "tools of the trade" being employed similar to a preacher's vestments, or the same way a modern homeopathic or chiropractic practitioner or psychiatrist use natural chemicals, manipulation, drugs, or counseling.

He thanked the Creator as his morning witness ended. He lowered his head and thanked Mother Earth for her bounty.

As the days of fall deepened, this ritual of Thanksgiving to the Spirits of his Forefathers was performed with vigor, not only by Walkswithwater, but also by his father and grandfather over the previous century. The "Nation" had long been disbanded; nevertheless, second and third generation survivors still honored their memory. That is why he was worshipping on the meadow. It was not obvious to all who traversed the meadow that this was the last winter campsite of the Tlingit

Nation before contraction in the 1700s. A keen eye would see the natural reasons for the location such as land mass elevations providing protection from the NW winds, water provided by the Bitterroot, and an adequate setback from the polar winds to the Pacific Coast to the west.

All human inhabitants north of 50 degrees latitude moved their encampment from the coastal waters inland for at least six months in the fall (October to March). Activities shifted from fishing and boating to hunting and trapping and, quite frankly, survival. It was a hard life 200 years ago. Only the skillful, strong, and communal survived. However, even though they had survived their diurnal seasonal lifestyle with adequate shelter and food, they could not survive the invasion of Europe's pseudo-philosophy of Manifest Destiny . . . "This land and people are ours to be taken. We know what's right for this land and these people."

Political misdeeds relating to land fraud and broken promises, intolerances to attitudes of religious beliefs and fatal disease via co-mingling, including sex, destroyed the tribe. Many tragedies squeezed the life from the Nation's communities along the coast and in the forest of what we now call Alaska. The Native American subsistance lifestyle never had a chance.

From his position in the center of the meadow, he now rose while his eyes moved to the unique features that made this location such a special encampment. Few knew it was the "last stand," or final encampment of the Tlingit's efforts to live on the land through harvesting the natural bounty of animals provided by the Great Spirit.

Years ago, on this meadow, Grandfather shared the story about the 500 Nations that lived in the New World now known as the Americas. He would wave his hands in the air and say, "From the beginning of time, as far north and as far south as the sun shines and wind blows, our people have lived in this land and were one with the land, lived in peace, and we lived according to our ways. We safeguarded the Sacred Fire Beliefs until the very end and finally had to disband our sacred trust at this meadow."

Walkswithwater meditated in the prescribed sitting position—legs crossed, arms aside—to Manitou:

> "Do not fret, my brothers; we tried to carry out trading expeditions and obey the new, white man's law, without any gain of still maintaining our identity.

> "Do not fret, my brothers; we will carry on our traditions individually with the pride we had as a Tribe. You will succeed individually; it is in your blood.

"Do not fret, my brothers; the change is necessary for our children to survive; they could no longer do so with our old ways. They will do well."

Finally:

"My brothers, remember this place and treat it as sacred, for it is the resting place for our historic soul. Great Spirit, bless these people of the Three Fires as they start a new life."

Walkswithwater assembled the contents of his medicine bag that he had laid out in precise order, then stowed its mystical "fetishes" for future use. Amulets of the bear and the raven were then returned to his body for protection. The beautiful foot-long beaver-pelt medicine bag with beaded decor was slung over his shoulder as he backed away from the center of the sacred meadow. Backing away was a respectful gesture learned from Three Bears, his grandfather.

His eyes now traveled over to the ridge on the NW rim of the meadow. The *sacrificial altar* was located on the western promontory. *No one* knew of its location or purpose, nor would they ever know. He would, however, later in life, pass on the mystery of the altar to his surviving children when they were adults. One may even become a Healer, if the spirits were to visit . . . Time would tell.

His eyes now traveled to the black, metallic, eight-sided yurt-like structure that many mobile tribes used, at the edge of the meadow. He knew who the inhabitants were. There were two options in dealing with their presence:

- Visit the altar and leave, or

- Visit the altar and visit the woman in the yurt, then leave.

He chose the first. There was no need to violate the woman's privacy in the Tongass. She had no idea the meadow was a sacred place to his forefathers and him. Furthermore, from what he had heard, she had no intention of altering any part of this hallowed area. It's better for her not to know where she is located, so it didn't affect her perspective of her work in the Tongass.

How did Walkswithwater know so much about the woman and dog?

How did he know about the "yurt" being near the meadow?

The employees in the Department of Natural Resources (DNR) knew him as Jack South and his Tlingit name, Walkswithwater.

Jack had been working with the DNR in the capital, Juneau, for twenty years and was in a key management position both in the Tongass National Forest and

Glacier Bay National Park. His associates knew of his tribal ties and were slightly informed of his yearly pilgrimage to the former home of his forefathers in the Tongass. Today was such a day. They knew he was in the Tongass, but not where. He did not share, nor did he see a need to, the significance of the meadow or its exact location. That was personal and consecrated to surviving tribal members only, and of no concern to his duties as a Conservation Officer (CO) in the DNR.

He did not even mention or let on when he processed Leigh's camping application to the DNR for a two-year permit. It was a startling request, to say the least, due to the location at the edge of the tribe's sacred meadow, specifically for up to three years with an air-dropped, prefabricated hut. At the time, he reflected, somewhat stunned, then closed the file, excused himself from the office, and went home to ponder his next move.

Why there?

There were a thousand other locations near an "opening" in the forest and near a stream that's also protected from winter's NW winds.

Why there?

What could he do? If anything, he would reveal the true meaning of the meadow. Can't do that! What to do?

After some serious soul-searching and discussions with his tribal leaders, he decided. *Say nothing about the meadow's ceremonial ties to the tribe.* He would process the application as though it was typical and not mention the significance of the meadow to the Tlingits.

The fee was enclosed; environmental concerns were addressed and in order. The hut would be removed in three years, and the area of the encampment returned to its original conditions. Everything was in order.

The application was approved.

This was his first visit to the site since her arrival.

Avoiding the hut, he headed to the ridgeline at the NW edge of the meadow. He was at least 100 meters to the east as he neared the edge of the meadow and started up the ridge toward the site of the altar in the clearing.

Chapter 7
A Different Drummer

The altar site still retained its reverence even though inactive for countless years. Nevertheless, the shrine-like atmosphere remained. Walkswithwater examined the site and still stood in awe of the historic aspects of its significance to the tribe.

In doing so, he noticed that it appeared as though animals had recently disturbed the area since last year by digging at the base of the site by the table-like slab. No problem, most of the site had been degraded and eroded over the years of seasonal weather cycles. Walkswithwater prepared for Meditation:

- Facing westward, he lowered himself to the sitting position.

- While concentrating, he started the requisite slow breathing exercises, inhaled deeply, held, exhaled slowly, held, and repeated the cyclic pattern.

- He brought his right leg to the half-lotus position.

- He brought his left leg to the full-lotus position.

- He retrieved the Tobacco, Cedar Bark, Sage sprigs, and Sweet Grass from the Beaver Medicine Bag, placed the ceremonial elements in a dish, and introduced fire by flint to start the smudge of smoke for cleansing.

- Deliberate rhythmical strokes of the Raven Wing brought the cleansing smoke to his face for purification by the Spirits. He felt His presence; he would soon be "with Him."

- Each arm was extended forward and down with open palms.

- His eyes were focused to the west and infinity.

- Deep breathing continued to regulate and prepare the body for accepting the Spirit.

- He started a "chant" to thank the Creator for the gift of the Earth, Sky, and Life itself.

He raised his Salmon Fetish and asked for its blessing and continued gift of life for his people.

He had achieved homeostasis, a neutral point of the mind and body now unified to accept the Great Spirit. He was not only beckoning the natural Spirits, he was also enticing the Spirits of his Native American forefathers. He felt honored to be the shaman assigned to reach out to the Spirits of his forefathers' deity. There were still many unanswered questions:

- Who were the First American Tlingits of the "Three Fires"?

- What were they like?

- Why did they come to Alaska's Tongass?

- Wasn't the "Gateway to America" covered with a sheet of ice? How did they overcome the glaciers or dense forest with deadfalls and hungry carnivores?

It's only speculation, but many were certain that Alaska was the gateway to the New World from Siberia as his forefathers most likely crossed the Bering Strait.

When? Probably 14,000 years ago, but recent discoveries have indicated additional migration from the Atlantic Maritime region, also. In fact, discoveries in the past decade have cast doubt on old concepts, while others have not fully developed to take their place. Most do agree that first Americans arrived by walking across the land-bridge connecting Siberia to Alaska, then traveled south through an inland corridor between continental ice sheets. Yet today scientists and experts disagree on some fundamental parts of that story. Instead of arrival 14,000 years ago, some now place humans in the Americas 20- or even 30,000 or more years ago.

Anthropologists have found two distinct forms/shapes of stone tools and arrowheads based on the origin of that tribal group. Whether it be an Asian Clovis *thick-point* or European *thin-point* tools and/or arrowheads, radiocarbon dating of fossils and plants or skull shape reconstruction, it appears, based on earlier discoveries, that early man came to America in a complex series of waves over many years. Still, radiocarbon dating becomes less reliable after 50,000 years, but is accurate for many physical and cultural anthropologists.

He was certain; he knew where his people were from since most of their stone tools/arrowheads were of the thicker Clovis type. He also realized that those farther south and east in the Americas may have been from Europe. All established theories are shaken to their roots now, and new ideas are stacked all over the place; realistically scientists don't see much resolution soon. This big picture of origin did not affect his or the abstract theories of supernatural religious belief. Those concepts and myths were all over the various realms, for there are a thousand beliefs generally revolving around "hero-worship," death and resurrection, and anecdotal stories and power-hungry charlatans. For example:

- *Judaic-Christian creation story* (after the mythical creation of the universe and earth).

    o   . . . then God molded man from the dust of the ground, breathing into his nostrils the breath of life; this was how man became a living being.

    o   . . . while he slept, He (God) took one of his ribs . . . and shaped it into a woman. (Biblical myth, Old Testament, by Moses, Genesis, Chapter 2, verses 7, 21-22)

- *Cheyenne creation story.*

    o   Now where they came in the south, the land was barren, and food and water was not plentiful. So the Great Power taught the people to hunt and make clothes to cover themselves against the cold, and they had a good life.

- *Pomo creation story.*

    o   Madumda made new people from willow wands, taught them to hunt with bow and arrow, how to make baskets, and how to eat, and then he went home to the north. But these people became bad, so Madumda sent ice down to kill them all.

(There are countless *additional* origin stories.)

Varied beliefs were based on historic mythical fears of deities, cultural ignorance, weak-minded dictators (corrupt popes, who sold an entrance to the mythical "heaven"), and confused spiritual "needs" of the time. He certainly
understood the "leap of faith" necessary to embrace an afterlife or "fertility blessing." He understood, but didn't accept. Walkswithwater was now more secular,
but did respect and honor his forefathers' beliefs, so he continued the Tlingit's

historical and mythical rites. He also recognized the dynamics of change due
to migration and growth of the Alaskan population.

He understood change, for however man was created or evolved, one thing
was clear:

With two billion people on earth when he was born in 1970, six billion now
in 2000 (tripled in 30 years), and projections of 12 billion in 2020 (doubled in 20
years), it would cause a lot of institutions, people, and relationships to change or
they would disappear like the People of the Three Fires.

He stood erect.

He redirected his attention to the location of the former altar, and then to
the western vista and its magnificent view.

He pondered as to how the site may have appeared in his forefathers' days in
the past. Values and worship to the spirits were much like a celebrations; shamans
and priests were led to believe that the gods expected sacrificial offerings to appease their wrath upon the people.

He reflected on the corruption of the sacrifice objective, to give damage control over the potential wrath of the gods. "Bull crap!" With an alphabet of emotions, he felt humiliation and a sense of frustration and shame for his forefathers'
ignorance.

He pictured the terrible introduction of blood sacrifice first from chicken
blood then to calves and large animals, once again to appease the gods and fend
off natural disasters. How absurd.

He held his head in shame as he recalled the story of one deranged shaman
who suggested the crowning spiritual sacrifice would be a human, a young female,
a virgin. This troubled shaman got the tribal leaders all worked up over the logic
for this ultimate sacrifice to appease the gods.

At this very site it happened, unfortunately; this rite to the gods was described
to him by his forefathers as follows:

The Shaman exclaims, "I bring you a virgin . . .

- Her prosperity and fertility are of the ultimate feminine form.

- Her legs carry the receptacle into which the seed must be placed.

- Her swelling womb reflects the growth that occurs in the dark of earth.

- Her breasts are the rains that nurture the fields.

- Her beauty and bright smile are the sun that warms the world.

- Her flowing hair is the cool breeze that keeps the land from parching.

"Brave young Warriors give their life in battle for our people and our god; it is expected for a young virgin to be honored to do so, too."

In principle, the tribe embraced a gentle, thankful religious belief labeled *Animism*: the attribution of conscious life to objects in and phenomena of nature or to inanimate objects. But there was a blind spot in the logic: the shaman convinced the tribe's elders that they could guarantee regeneration through sacrifice. Their mystery of sexual procreation was so profound it was not difficult for the shaman to convince the tribe that the sacrifice of a beautiful virgin would assure a reproductive future for the tribe. After all, in battle, the death of young braves ensured their survival from war parties attacking the village . . . *both were a type of sacrifice.*

The concept of man presenting a virgin to the gods worked hand-in-hand with productivity of the tribe's population and, as such, ennobled this sickening philosophical construct. The homage that the Fire God demanded was so persuasive that all were eager to participate. The ritual continued:

Once a virgin was selected, certain rites commenced:

- Flowers rich in pollen adorned her hair.

- Young animals were brought to her side.

- Maidens danced seductively before her.

- She was fed from the best the fields offered.

- Drumbeats started for her pleasure.

At the appropriate moment, the next celebration, which had been cunningly arranged by the shaman, was triggered by the increased sound and tempo of the drums to a vivid crescendo. While the drums' syncopation influenced the tribal throng, he slowly moved all the celebrants to the promontory on the ridge where the altar was stacked with dry wood and grass. He halted the tumult, and while raising his arms above his head, he cried, "After death, comes life. After mourning, joy." Those present began chanting happily; their words spoke of growth and fertility for the tribe, the animals, and the fields. Others not convinced that what was about to take place was appropriate left the hypnotic horde and returned to their lodges.

"HE DECLARED!"

"Men are born to die gloriously in battle and protect and feed the tribe, and women to fulfill future fertility of the tribe. In this hour of sacrifice it is obligatory for us to remember life. Now in this hour of death, life is born again!"

Light the Fire! Light the Fire! Light the Fire!"

She was an exquisite human being, for no man could look at her provocative form without seeing her as the sublime representation of fertility.

He signaled for the music to cease as his hands began taking away her garments, one by one, allowing them to fall like petals until she stood nude.

She kept her hands folded and her eyes downward. The altar was set aflame.

"Let it be," he said, "Let it be!"

Her lips formed in a silent prayer as she was lowered onto a stretcher, carried to the flaming altar, held aloft as a fruitful offering, and slowly lowered while shrieks of terror and pain echoed through the black vault of the atmosphere; she was sacrificed to the Fire God for the tribe's future fertility.

He raised his arms to bless the event, then turned to the crowd as they began a hushed chant to praise the virgin's sacrifice.

A nighthawk darted through the ether, his hunger for flying insects of more concern than the tumult below. To him the fire merely lured insects for his feeding. Little did the hawk know the reason for the fire . . . as he darted among the searing golden ash and stunned novice members of the tribal clan.

A gibbous moon cast its spell over the walkway from the ridge to the meadow as the remaining tribal members and their shadows filtered silently one by one to their dwellings for what surely would be a solemn, sleepless, and fretful night. Thankfully—*it's over.*

Walkswithwater remembered only too well this sickening story. He had an elemental impulse to cut into the earth of this terrible site. His anger grew. Yes—the knife. Unsheathing his blade, he knelt down and thrust the steel into the earth, lacerating its breast, then again and again and again in an initial violent act that resulted in self-induced pain to his body and mind, so that in doing so he could heal his distaste for this ancient rite.

- Oh yes, *it's over.*

- The site is covered over.

- The "Sacrifice" is over.

- But the terror and torment of this site (tomb), is not.

- *He continued to thrust his knife into the earth* . . . how obscene the ancient rite; he collapsed in pain as the stabbing motions drew blood to his hands, and his shoulders weakened from distressing pain.

He wept and slumped to the ground. And thus was born the contempt that he could not shed for the blunders of his forefathers' ceremonial sacrifices for *no good reason* other than fear of the supernatural mythical gods. Ironically, it had stopped many years earlier, but had been an inane mythical rite many thousands of years ago, too, by early Islamic, Jewish, and later Christian "religious" frauds called "priests" (or swindlers); for example: simony was rampant in the early Roman Catholic Church; you could literally purchase forgiveness of sin to control and demonize the masses with God's twisted edicts.

Overwhelmed by the additive effects of the previous year's visits to this site, he remained in the fallen position reflecting on tribal rites. A sensitive man and sure of his beliefs, he did not hesitate to embrace Mother Earth and savor her closeness. Other faiths had similar acts of faith—they prayed. Christians wore crucifix tokens (on their cars' dashboards) like amulets and pretended to drink and eat their Savior's body through the Eucharist; Islamic tenets thought less of females and oppressed women as second-class humans; Buddhists had their prayer wheels and after-life concepts. All these cultural differences were doing well to serve the culture at *that point in time and location*! Yet it had to be thrust on others as "the only way." What would appear on the scene next? One never knows. He only wished the Christians would have let his forefathers' tribal customs remain. No, he did not like interference. The other religions brought more unusual beliefs than Nature worship or the Animism of his forefathers.

He was fond of this sacred place, not because of the contemptible ancient sacrificial ritual, but for its location in viewing the high mountain valley to the west. Even the grassy meadow below was perfect, punctuated by a bubbling river, surrounded by protective ridgelines, with air so clear it's as if the blue sky comes right down and meets the ridges around him. It's functional. When not on his annual visit to the site, he daydreamed about its beauty. It's a beautiful bastion of solitude that you run across only once in a lifetime. It is now covered with additional pines, firs and hardwoods that spread out and disappear as they migrate closer to the meadow. However, the center remained thick with grass and orientated parallel to the prevailing winds. Yes, a tough, lightweight "bush plane" could land here, but getting out is another story. The visits were reassuring because it provided that "link" to his past and his obscure future. He would bring his eldest child to the site someday, for someone would have to continue the tribe's vigil.

He collapsed in frustration—in sorrow.

*   *   *

"Stop! Stop!" Walkswithwater bounded to his feet to protest an intrusion to his thoughts by way of a wet tongue to his face. His eyes bulged and strained, focused on what appeared to be a wolf or dog!

It was a dog!

Boy had been roaming the meadow and had picked up the Indian's earlier location with the aroma in the meadow. He knew this scent was at least partially human, so he tracked him up the ridgeline to the site of the altar.

"Damn! You scared the hell out of me, dog! I thought you were a wolf or coyote for a few moments." Boy started barking; he tried to calm him down. "Come on, dog, settle down; no one's going to harm you; come on, come over here, come on."

His barking abated and his bobbed tail gave in to acceptance. He sniffed the unusual smell of earth mixed in with the smudge smell that permeated the man's native dress. The outfit was not ostentatious, just native deerskin and nominal decor. The beaver medicine bag had most of the interesting scents that piqued Boy's interest as it also had in the meadow. Boy mused, *This guy does not appear to be a threat, but smells like a log taken out of a fire.* He was more accustomed to the smell of the boys at Ford's Flight Service; they smelled pretty normal, to him—like aviation fuel, greasy food, coffee, and sometimes whiskey. The tobacco, sage, cedar, and sweet grass of the spiritual cleansing smoke were different from the Flight Service, but pleasant. One thing was for sure, it was like a K-Mart "blue-light" special; boy, he knew where the stranger was located, and he looked different in his native dress.

*   *   *

Leigh's sense of smell was not what brought her to the ridge; the barking and voices were enough to know Boy was on to something, hopefully not a bruin—plus his ribs were not fully healed either. So up the ridge she went, lickety-split, .44 in hand. She saw a man and Boy, and abruptly halted at the ridgelines.

"Good morning," Leigh said, "this is indeed a surprise; I hope my dog was not a threat to you and your travel along the ridge."

"No problem," he said. "In fact, the dog and I have finally become friends; he has let me pet and relax with him now."

"Glad you met my dog, Boy. I'm Leigh." She attempted to ease into a conversation that would delve into his purpose in the Tongass and explore via eyes and words before she explained herself. She wondered who this guy was, dressed in deerskin; he did not appear to be a threat; in fact he was attractive, polite, and unarmed, from what she could observe.

"My name is Jack, Jack South," he said while clearly approving of what he saw. He explained the historical tribal reasons for being on the ridge at the former altar site and earlier in the meadow at the former encampment, then apologized for the disturbance. He mentioned that he tried to avoid contact and visit the site without disturbing her camp. However, trauma at the altar and Boy's keen smell prohibited his stealthful arrival, worship, and departure.

"But, ah, ah, I'm not clear, ah, your native clothes and the altar—are they a part of your life today, also?" Leigh stumbled with probative words without being too forward.

"Walkswithwater" is my Tlingit tribal name," he said. He further explained that, by being in the Family of native healers and living in Juneau, he was obligated and in fact chose to honor his forefathers' wishes to give praise to the vestige of his tribe's final encampment, and also to give thanks to the Great Spirit at this site as he had been doing for ten years.

As an employee for the DNR, he explained that he knew of her long-term camping request, where it was, and in fact, approved it, knowing very well it was located near his forefathers' tribal grounds.

Boy wanted no part of this chitchat, so having already accepted Jack, he took off on his morning swing to the river, his ribs slowing him down only a little. He was healing quickly. "Let's go with Boy," she said, and they did indeed walk down to the yurt for an earlier agreed-to cup of coffee.

"You'll have to excuse my primitive abode," she mentioned while brewing the bean. "All the provisions and household equipment are being air-dropped in today at around four o'clock if favorable weather and flight conditions prevail."

Now at the bench by the river, they chatted with coffee and enjoyed Boy's hyperactivity, acting as though he was a River King by chasing ducks, barking at bugs, and chomping at sticks that were meandering down the river to its Pacific outlet 80 miles downstream.

By now, almost all their backgrounds had been shared, and it was amazing how similar their lives had been. Both were married, now divorced, still in contact with children and grandchildren with a similar need to get away to find a new and refreshing life of rebirth and solitude.

Still hobbling, Leigh's ankle was bothersome, so Jack, thinking to himself, decided he would help her, if asked, to bring the first pallet of supplies to the yurt and unload the contents before heading back to civilization.

He had walked in from Klukwan (population 200) to the east as a yearly trek, taking about four days in and three days out to the mouth of the Tatshenshini River to the southwest. The Bear Study Group (on DNA identification) was camped there, and his visit would be part of his job to perform on-site monitoring of the camp, their progress, and personnel. He would then hitch a ride back to Juneau with their weekly boat shuttle, prearranged for them by other personnel in the DNR office.

The DNR assignment was almost perfect as a second career choice, but there was a lingering void that crept up on him periodically when alone at night, or when walking the shore of the Pacific; he reflected—his life was still wanting . . . incomplete.

After hours of very sensitive conversation with Leigh, he looked at her while she wrapped her ankle. "May I help?"

"You sure can! I'm getting tired of doing a half-ass wrap from the ass-side of my foot." He knelt down in front of this beauty on the bench with mixed emotions. He pushed her pant leg up to her knee with his hand as she held it in place with hers. Their hands touched; he rubbed her ankle prior to wrapping. "That felt good . . . do that again," she whispered.

They sat motionless; what was happening? Whatever it was . . . they did not halt their thoughts. Her eyes could not conceal her emotional tension or his; his eyes telegraphed pleasure. How could there be so much joy from a mere ankle-wrap?

It had only been six hours since they had met. Was she that starved for companionship? Husbandry, yes, but there was something *else* in the air.

He thought, Damn, her eyes are omnivorous, and consuming of the rest of her features by dissolving them with the warm aquamarine liquid in her pupils.

He was motionless again.

Color flooded her cheeks.

"Sorry, I hope I have not offended you. I'm a little confused."

"Don't worry; I, too, am starting to feel confused when near you. I'm not much of a talker when it involves feelings," Jack noted.

"Then you should mask your eyes," she cooed.

"What do you think they say?"

"Things that please me," Leigh sighed. "Then tell me, I carry no mirror."

"For certain, something lurks, but we will move slowly—what we know is our secret."

He felt a little exposed for showing emotions that had been previously re-strained. Yet, she was captivatingly different and alluring.

The "wrap" complete, he lowered her pant leg and put on her hiking boot and laced it up. "There. That should hold you for a while."

"Thanks, how much do I owe you?" she said, noticing his hands were still very red and ragged from the altercation at the altar.

"I've been paid . . ."

Her eyes grasped the message. "Say, did you notice, Boy is right over your shoulder, Jack, kind of "on-point"?—*and has been ever since* I asked you to wrap my ankle. He's not sure yet if he likes someone that close to his mistress.

It's okay, I gave him the OK hand signal about 30 minutes ago. It's okay, Boy; come on over . . . it's okay, come on, fellow!" Licks and whines of approval now deferred to leaps and bounds at the stream's animal life. The ducks' quick respite was short-lived; they had no chance of peace with Boy around their home-stead, even with his bruised ribs.

"Jack, since we've gabbed this late, would you mind standing by for another hour to help me pull the last pallet to the hut?"

"Does a bear poop in the woods? Of course! I forgot it was almost four o'clock. Absolutely!" he exclaimed.

He wondered where they would wait. How would they know when Ford was coming? Did she have a radio? He wondered if Ford would be upset with his presence. "Where do we wait, Leigh?"

"Right where you are. Just plunk your butt on the bench with me, and listen; you'll hear Ford's 190 screaming over the treetops from windward. He'll call me on that downwind leg and turn downstream about a mile south and drop the last pallet in the stream, or sandbar, +/- 50', on his final approach. "Seriously, Jack, thanks for staying; it means a lot to me."

With a colorful laugh, she related how unique some of the less-coordinated earlier flights were over her bare-assed-naked body while she was washing and bathing in the stream. "You guessed it. Ford was early and took in the tit and ass show at 200 feet and 90 knots. What chaos—I had to run and get my handheld and hold off the dog. Anyway, it was a hilarious scene—funny now, chaotic then."

Hysterical now, Jack joined in the laughter as Leigh related the blunt talk from Ford in the plane: "He enjoyed it! Matter of fact, if dogs could talk, I'll bet Boy might even have laughed himself . . . he is male, you know! Why don't you go for a swim? I'll hide my eyes; remember, like we did as kids and peeked a little?"

"DC 2, this is DC 1, do you copy? Over."

"It's Ford! Come on, let's go!"

"DC 1, this is DC 2, read you loud and clear. Hi, Babe! Good to hear your voice, how are you? Over."

"Fine, for two reasons—I get to see and hear you, and this is the last flight to the Tongass, Yeah! You'll soon be all snugly and secure for the winter. Over."

"You bet, Babe; I'll forever be thankful. Guess what? I have company; Jack South is passing through and will help me with this last pallet. Over."

"Good, I know Jack. What's he doing in the Tongass? Over."

She thought, It's too complex to explain the meadow's origin and the altar of the Tlingits. So she didn't.

"Oh, he's hiking through from Klukwan to the mouth of the Tatshenshini to link up with the Bear Study Group. Half work, half play, I think. Over."

"Good, say, I'm about to turn for my final approach; I'm getting busy—talk to you in a minute. Over."

"Roger, standing by."

As the loaded and powerful 190 approached the drop zone, Jack wondered how close Leigh and Ford really were, and what Ford thought of his presence with Leigh. Jack was aware of Ford Flight Service in Skagway, so at least they knew of each other. However, guilt was his silent partner in this encampment on the Bitterroot; he could not ignore the feelings he had for Leigh. "Damn, it's only been eight hours, and now I'm staying overnight. Why the conflicted feelings?" he mumbled to himself. It was simple; he respected the rights of another man's woman and her relationship with him. In this case, *Leigh* and *Ford.* There would be no problem. There would be *respect* for Ford's relationship with Leigh.

It was the *way* of the Tlingits.

*   *   *

The roar of a full-power release, while at a high AOA just before a stall, was deafening. It was a good release; down the pallet came with a full chute deployment, *Swoosh, plop, and splash.* Contact, Mother Earth! The 190 roared into the air now free of its impediments, now almost at 30 degrees AOA, the old red bird soared like an eagle into the ether. Ford bellowed, "Good job, old girl, you're a winner; let's go home." He banked to a NE 40-degree azimuth with Skagway in his sights.

"DC 2, this is DC 1. Well, gal, you are on your own now until you call or October arrives, whichever comes first, and the snow permits a snowmobile trek with supplies. Use that propane with care; that's your limiting factor out here; you have enough to last for at least six months. I'm on my way before weather gets in my way; say 'bye to Jack, and remember—love you, miss you."

"Me too, Babe, be safe. I'll call or see you in October; either way, take care, my love, this is DC 2 out."

"This is DC 1, out."

*   *   *

For some reason, he made another pass and dipped his wings. *Unusual*, Leigh mused; he had never done that before. . . .

The Doppler Effect—a change in frequency at which sound waves reach an observer from a source in motion, *with respect to the observer*, like a train going by with its whistle blowing—made the 190 variable roar "sing" into the blue and white mountains to the east as it passed overhead.

Jack and Leigh worked all afternoon retrieving the pallet from the river, unloading the furniture, equipment, and consumables until the horizon stole daylight. All assemblies were retrieved and found undamaged from the drop.

The recycling (bio-mass) toilet was "charged" with anaerobic bacteria; the stove and refrigerator hooked up to the propane tanks; the furnace likewise, and vents attached to the chimney; the table, chairs, and bed were moved three times before finally being placed where they had been at first; all the foodstuffs were stocked on the shelves; and a 4x4 foot solar panel assembly mounted on the southern exposure of the roof, with a small battery attached. It would power a small light, AM/FM radio, and transmitter/receiver. Main lights were gas-operated with a lantern-type chimney design just like in "the good old days." In fact, Jack "screwed up" several silk-bag lanterns while setting up camp . . . some things never change.

They had bumped butts and rubbed shoulders all afternoon while setting up the hut. They ended up being quite a Yin/Yang duo.

"Yea, we are done! We're finished! Yea, and it's only nine!" Leigh exclaimed.

Boy barked since he had not received much attention in the last six hours and welcomed the celebration. *Woof.*

"Let's celebrate this occasion the *right* way—with some good wine," she proposed.

"Okay, where is it?" Jack replied.

"I'll get it." She rummaged through a barrel of sawdust.

"While you're doing that, I'll go set up my mountain tent and get ready for the evening. I'm bushed." He went outside with Boy. She watched him silently. *Quite a pair*, she thought.

For some reason, she froze physically and mentally for a moment. Was it about her day with Jack? She was not certain, but . . .

The tent was erected with Boy at Jack's heels. "Okay, Boy, I'm set up now; how's it look? Come on, let's go down by the river and get a last look and final drink before the animals take over the night."

Upon returning to the tent with Boy, Jack approached the opening and started to secure his rucksack—he felt something at his shoulder. The faint smell of a woman embraced the night.

Startled, he whirled about abruptly.

He stood motionless, as her eyes consumed the night . . . and the opportunity before him. She had an oversize MICHIGAN T-shirt on—it came down to her thighs; her hair was now at her shoulders as if a maiden of the mist. Braless, her nipples welcomed the cool evening air with paired erections.

"Jack, you are *not* sleeping out here tonight. Come in, the wine is waiting . . . for us. Come . . ."

They entered the hut as the pines in the cool clear evening whispered to the star-filled Tongass sky . . .

Chapter 8

Terror In The Tongass

"The best and most beautiful things in the world cannot be seen or heard or touched . . . but are felt in the heart."
—Helen Keller, 1880-1968

She had been cautious with her attraction to Ford, but that was not the plan tonight . . . His feet were reluctantly carrying him to the inner circle of Leigh's domain—it did not seem right.

Why the overt move by Leigh?

Why the caution on his part?

Why the doubts?

There she stood, her oversized T-shirt much like a peignoir of silk, her auburn hair hanging loosely down her back, almost to her shoulders, without cosmetics or jewels, smiling, feminine, and her face-sculptured beauty framing her whole body . . . more desirable sans ornamental trappings.

After her inviting oblique glance to the glasses, he moved toward the table of wine; they both sipped a symbolic toast to the completion of the hut, and preamble to conquest. They stared at each other, speechless, yet their eyes spoke volumes of an understanding for what was about to take place.

In a moment, without further analysis or reason, they were in a passionate embrace—their bodies merging, knees and hips meeting, breasts to chest, union of both mouths moist and sweet, glued—drinking deep. Their arms now had the power of an unquenchable life force, crushing each to the other in a total pulsating time and place and sense—annihilating embrace.

She led him to her berth, looked in his eyes, and without words indicated it was okay. She knew what she was doing; she felt the arousal of his manhood . . ."
Come, dear, we're both ready . . . come to Leigh."

He mused, *She's been schooled.*

He paused at bedside. "But, is it safe?" he whispered.

"Yes, do not worry," she sighed.

He paused at the berthing place again.

"Jack, we own the night; let's not concern ourselves with the 'morrow."

That did it; his hands found her sexual ripeness. He breathed deeply . . . as both tenderly engaged their hormonal urge. A hushed silence overcame the pair—now linked in an interwoven union. It was like penetrating deep into a lush lagoon of robustness with the pounding live thrust of wave after wave beating upward through the warmth. With a surprising urgency, she uttered a long piercing cry.

The coyotes along the ridge halted in their canter through the forest, and momentarily looked to the meadow, then continued their nightly pursuits along the ridge.

His whole body became a heavy column while penetrating ever deeper and deeper into furrows of her soft warm and welcoming body until he reached the explosive supreme moment.

All of his fluid strength, energy, desire, and passion had been poured into the nascent form. The restrained hand of lust had responded, giving off its inner heat and substance and tender form, until at last the amorous urge had coalesced and each became one, an organic unity, each fulfilling the other in the greatest act of love known to humans.

Coyotes, once again howled on the distant ridge.

She whispered, "I needed that . . . you do good work, my dear friend. Please don't leave me now; don't let me go; don't go; hold me. . . . "

He complied; their union remained intact.

They rested.

She slept.

He thought. . . .

*   *   *

Rising early, he carefully eased his way out from under the arms of his unexpected lover. Standing directly at the foot of the bed, he stared at her sculptured voluptuous figure; she still appeared young, fertile, and very desirable as if the cradle of man. Her exquisite head rested its delicately arched neck, eyes closed resigning to sleep, as the darkness with a slight umbra of moonlight moved freely over the contours of the milky female form. The air-hardened nipples and ripe breasts were as if a fount of sustenance. The magnificently robust thigh, and the arm were pulled sharply behind the back to turn the breast and present it proudly outward. It was every man's dream of a bounteous female body in deep sleep after captivating love. They truly had "owned the night!"

Dressed now, packed and ready to move on at 0500 hours, Jack looked down on the resting beauty of the meadow one more time and likewise checked the resting canine. He had learned Boy was in fact Ford's dog, offered for her protection and companionship. She was not alone and certainly, after last night's experience, did not need, nor desire, some types of protection from man's desire . . . she could handle herself. That had been proven.

The day and night with Leigh had been blissful, with a great and fulfilling happiness of passion he had experienced in the past . . . with his now-lost love. Her passion shared some aspects of the spiritual joy of his ceremonial offerings to his forefathers, which made it even more of a gratifying journey in the Tongass. But, it was time to move on. Staying even one day longer would be much too complicated for both lovers of the meadow. There would be no note explaining his departure, or comments of satisfaction; the words would not do justice to his feelings—a bard he was not—the words would not do justice to his feelings; they were too beautiful and complex to write anyway. Maybe they would come at a later date. He would certainly see her again. But, maybe not.

Subdued, yet content, he opened the hut door slowly and urged Boy to continue his nap, saying, "Down, Boy; it's okay." While ensuring the door was locked, he moved aggressively to pack his tent and head down the path to the river, but halted as he felt obligated to turn his encumbered body and direct his eyes to the hut, ridgeline, and meadow with a thankful appreciation to his forefathers for the last forty-eight hours. The hut appeared quiet and content. Satisfied with both experiences, he repositioned his rucksack and continued down the path to the river, but once again paused. Many wonderful moments were shared on this simple wooden whistle-stop in his life.

"Thank you." He nodded to the bench and moved sharply down the familiar path along the Bitterroot to its western flow and ultimately the Pacific and the Bear Study Group.

While walking along the river, he mused about the experiences of the last two days that would probably never happen to him again in this lifetime. As with most dramatic romantic encounters between men and women, their mutual but separate analysis of the impact of these events would be futile. . . .

"Would I have done something different?" Probably not . . . nothing different, he thought.

It was perfection.

So, he trudged on while pondering the sentiment of the night with Leigh, remembering it for future reflection.

*   *   *

Following the river to the ocean required many crossings and departures where the lower flood plain elevation turned the beauty of the swamp to impassable undergrowth and thickets. It was all good concealment for hiding solitary animals, but unacceptable for walking. But he was walking in an open area where he could see ahead; he was not going to be the one to dislodge a sleeping bruin at ten feet; that would be too close/soon to react and he'd be bruin breakfast, lunch, and dinner for certain. Leigh's bear-sighting story was enough to keep him alert since he was now traversing on the same migration route the bears used to move to lower elevations in the fall. That time is now. Anyone who knew anything about bears knew there was only one winner in a bear chase through a swamp quagmire, and it wasn't man!

When the river narrowed through immovable rock formation in the highlands, Jack departed the flow and again traversed the rock-lined, elevated route offering broad views of immeasurable vistas of pristine beauty. The aspens, oaks, and birch started turning from yellow to orange to red, making for a stunning artist's palette of color.

A bright half-moon sat on a high ridge to the east just above the early embers of the sky, framed by a slight breeze; the ridgeline leaves cast multiple faces on the hills in black silhouette. Early Morning Nautical Twilight (EMNT) welcomed him to the forest's mighty might.

It was an "intoxicating" morning, with summer's grandeur fading and falling, heralding one of nature's subtler lessons: less is more. The first thing Native Americans and travelers would notice was that walking in some places along the river would be nearly impossible in the growing season. Underbrush, generally clinging, cloying, checking the rest of the year, was now bare, stripped, and easily passable.

He also noticed the ground along the banks was now exposed, and no wall of vegetation blocked the view. With less rain after June's high-water mark in the watershed, the ponds, marshes, bogs, and wetlands were lower and more revealing of their arcane mysteries of life. Clearly, he knew only too well the necessity for the clear plotting of routes that bypass such hiking hazards. Low-lying nests and burrows, which were covered before now, appeared along the river. Peering in one nest, he noticed seeds, dozens of them, from a nearby berry bush. The seeds were part of the lining; it was built there to serve as a food cache, also. So this was how smaller birds hunker down in a winter blizzard. He could now see, as well as hear, the woodpeckers' *rat-a-tat-tat*, their drilling plainly visible sans foliage; the forest was now one big Swiss Cheese.

Surely, some squirrels would lose their homes with the wider holes; there was no rent control here, or deeded property. If a Great Horned Owl desired occupancy, no other creature in the treetops could stop the avian bully. Observing trees standing along the river's edge, he imagined nesting wood ducks six months hence, their eggs hidden from predators, the chicks protected until their first traditional plummet to the ground.

He continued his crisp walk as the sun was now four fingers high in the eastern dawn, and insects were now seeking a place to hide from the light as their nightly dancing ended. The river was also changing its face at dawn's early light as it moved in no particular hurry to the sea. The slap of a fish resonated as its head turned in the water, slowly rolling . . . and then waiting, in silence. Then another rolled to the surface right in front of Jack. Another leaped for a fly and slapped against the water like a breaching whale. Silence again, as the annual breeding process started on stone beds full of spawn and milt, linked one to another interwoven for future life. Then Jack became aware of the hidden sounds of *toosh, toosh, toosh* by males defending a self-assigned breeding territory. In all cases it would be their last valiant struggle, for death would follow and the life cycle would soon continue as the young smolt moved downstream to continue the life cycle of the Pacific Salmon. Soon the smaller brookies would take over, or take back, their domain without the need of the migration to the ocean to complete their breeding cycle.

Such moments of Nature's beauty defy words, but he had to move on, so he quietly slipped along the banks on his way to a rigorous three-day trip ahead. Luckily he knew the area as well as his mother's face. He had walked the stream for years, in all weather and seasons; every footfall had been tread. He knew the river's hazards both in day and at night, and in all seasons of the year, even when it did not welcome his presence. No matter, he was not deterred. Inclement conditions were a mere challenge to him. He stopped and donned his rain slicker as the typical Tongass drizzle got more intense. It rained almost daily in the Tongass rainforest; and he was used to the constant heavy mist on the shore, to inner shoreline drizzle, full sprinkle inland, and a heavy rain with wind at elevations.

He hoped to expose his children to the beauty of the forest, to know the secret places, the smell of an evening campfire, balsam pitch aroma, the sunset over the coastal range, and the simple solitude of the tall timber. His children had not been with him for some time now, but he was still trying to rendezvous with them to share the more subtle aspects of camping. He would teach them to know when they were near the ocean as gulls appeared in the thermals. Would they know by the change in the smell of salt-watered air near the shore? Did they know lichens grew thicker on the shaded north side of the trunk in North America? Did they have the skills to survive in the forest if they were unexpectedly thrust into this hazardous environment? Would they know how to live off the land? He didn't know; they were now in their teens, with their mother, in Anchorage.

Without a wife to share his knowledge, he was ever so anxious to do so with his children. One small example was knowledge of the helpful trees his ancestors utilized in the area:

- The Balsam Fir—to stuff under bed rolls; its flat fragrant boughs, and adhesive pitch were very beneficial.

- The Spruce—used for oars, bows, arrows, and its roots gathered to tie birch bark canoes.

- The Cedar—the wood resisted decay and was used for boats and keeping insects at bay.

And all of these were fodder for animals in the cold of winter . . . and humans, when desperate.

Somehow Leigh now slipped into his thoughts. She, too, may never have had the exhilarating experience of moving under the shadow of the canopy of pines at noon, or never have seen the half-moon at midnight, or a fish jump and roll at night, or a ray of sunlight break through the protective clouds with its startling rays blasting upon the earth and eyes. It was his nirvana; he loved the variety of events in the tall timber of the Tongass. He felt a little strange now, for after one night of passion he wanted to share these experiences with Leigh, too.

Unsure of the rainy weather ahead, he moved up along the ridgeline to explore the hillside of his first campsite. He'd need at least two overnighters for his three-day outbound trek. In the big timber he always made camp in the daylight, and the sun was now two fingers off the horizon; it was time, plus he wanted one of those beautiful Bitterroot trout as part of his main course tonight.

His pace slowed while approaching an opening in the canopy; the sun also broke through the clouds, creating a spectacular island of light in the shadowy forest.

"Say, this is a stroke of luck; look at all the blueberries!" he exclaimed. They, too, would share his table of delights. About depleted due to the late date, they still had that fresh "sings in your mouth" taste . . . so welcome in the rather passive freeze-dried camp food in his pack. Not to complain, he thought about the limits of the food his forefathers carried: kippered beef, fried fish, and cracked corn—now that's dry! Nevertheless, he'd bet the farm; they, too, folded in berries du jour.

It was no surprise to Jack that the berry patch had been molested and roughed up by a bruin or two—recently! They literally had chomped off the entire terminal branches, and basically trimmed the entire growth pattern by eating their way through the patch. Their presence was very noticeable, and an unwelcome threat to the area in which he was about to camp. "Just my luck, it was probably a mother with her cubs," he lamented. Jack recalled that the mother bear stays with her cubs for the first year (winter), then kicks them out in late summer of the second year. She was obviously fattening up in the berry patch for her winter sleep.

He had gathered enough berries for dinner and turned to leave the inundated patch— A blood-curdling roar exploded in the air!

He froze in place, then slowly rotated his body to face an angry silver-tipped Grizz at least ten feet tall. He instinctively drew and pointed his 9mm at the bruin and fired two shots. The slugs' impact on the furry mass of flesh echoed with a morbid sound of *wap* . . . wap. Luckily, the Grizz spun around and ran into and across the river. It stopped, turned, growled, turned around again, and exploded into the thicket.

"Gone . . . and I hope forgotten—lucky again—I guess," he sighed. "I'd better camp up a little higher on the ridge toward that escarpment of overhanging rock. It will give me a little more protection from the elements, animals, and bear, to my rear. That was one hell of a scare, son-of-a-bitch!" A person could talk to himself/herself out here, as long as he/she didn't carry on a conversation of political or religious nature . . . that caused controversy, or excessive pondering of "what if" on the latest lost love due to male clumsiness in the pursuit female amour. Changes in strategy, yes, but self-pity on failure, no; for no one has yet to understand, much less successfully devise a battle plan that is foolproof as to what works in the conquest of female favors . . . Gentle? Polite? Fatherly? Rough? Subservient? . . . Who knows? Certainly not many. Men just keep throwing the dice until seven-eleven penetrates her psyche. Isn't that why men have embraced a sure-thing mistress such as a bristol boat, fast car, far-reaching airplane, or unquestioning paramour? Jack had all these toys . . . but that was before Leigh upset his comfort zone with them—she was different. What was it about her allure? Maybe there was still time to sort out the differences between his comfort with his toys versus her assertive, yet passionate tenderness. Hurt once by affairs of the heart, he'd be very careful to ensure that it wasn't his loins doing the thinking, for short-term conquest.

The outcrop would provide 180 degrees' frontal vision, rear security, and protection from the wind, too. It would also provide a perfect view to the eastern path of the Bitterroot and the morning sun—should he be so fortunate to live that long?

He took less than fifteen minutes to land a three-pound trout with a rod in one hand and the other close to his 9mm at his side. He was still nervous. Quickly depositing the offal in the stream, he moved briskly to the safer venue of the campsite and its welcoming fire. While the fire was maturing to coals of substance, he made a bed of freshly cut balsam boughs in his tent—smell good too—and started boiling some river water on a base of a small rock in the fire. Tonight the cuisine included: Entree (surf and turf), freeze-dried fillet of beef, fresh fillet of trout, au gratin potatoes, and biscuits; Dessert (rice pudding with fresh blueberries); wine and fresh-perked coffee. Plus, a beautiful view and great smell of the Tongass.

As he sat on a fallen cedar log with the massive outcrop rising upward behind him, the solitary evening meal had all the trappings of a mountain man's perfect sojourn with the natural environment. It was a welcome reflection. An uncluttered life. The optimum solitude of the Tongass.

But this was not entirely true; Jack's life was far from the appearance of the true, alone-by-choice Mountain Man. Unlike Jeremiah Johnson, played by Robert Redford, Jack did not want to be quite that isolated.

His previous life was wonderful, with a beautiful family in Anchorage. He missed their up-close and personal interaction and love. Yes, the kids still loved him, but he left his roots to avoid the pain of seeing his wife with a younger man that stole her and a large part of his life. The move to DNR Headquarters in Juneau had provided a new start, frequent promotions, and a return to his first love of fieldwork versus riding a paper-desk all day. His adjustments were not without pain as many activities were performed alone; he reflected on participating in various activities with his family. He avoided certain family conflicts as a result. As the old cliché goes, out-of-sight, out-of-mind, he thought. But it wasn't working; he was very lonely.

As the fire's sparks lifted, glowed, and extinguished while dancing in the brisk evening air, he started to prepare the campsite for the evening. He approached the river carefully with the flashlight beam and 9mm leading the way. He cleaned the evening dishes and discarded the scraps in the river, then returned to the camp to douse the fire and ensure the campsite was clear of human and food odors. He zipped the tent up with everything inside. Yes, you can get used to granola products, without chocolate, and a lot of water, but it gets a little boring; however, a person must put up with this "cuisine" for a short trek through bear territory.

He certainly could still be a bear's dinner, but noted they were basically herbivores, and omnivorous only when at the river in the fall's seasonal salmon run or when starving and stumbling across an accidental carrion in its path. As noted by all those who are briefed before entering the Tongass alone: stay away from thickets and lowlands with limited vision. When sighted, give 'em at least 100 meters of right-of-way; don't crowd a silvertip, and finally—pack iron, at least to scare 'em away and, if necessary, terminate their attack should one be so unfortunate as to face a charging bruin. *I don't even think I hit the bear very hard; who knows? But I did notice it already had a mangled and deformed paw . . . from a fight? A hunter's shot? A trap? In any case, the Grizz appeared very irritated, and in some pain? Not sure.*

Leigh had related how she saved Boy's life by firing at the bear that had a run-in with the dog in the swamp at the edge of meadow. And the challenge today was certainly thwarted either by the bear's memory of the sound or actual feeling of lead "smacking" fur and flesh. He could have challenged and charged, whether shot or not, but chose not to this time. It was his lucky day indeed.

Jack's tent encampment along the river was melodic indeed, not like a country radio station's "easy listening," but a lot of night sounds—wolves baying socially at each other across the ridges; nighthawks screeching while diving, turning and banking after illusive insects, including the stoic owl hooting from his aerial perch prior to silently gliding to the unsuspecting terminal rodent; and coyotes' wailing cry filling in the background with their similar cry of pain, or was it anger? All this backdrop of instruments combined with the strings of the dancing and weaving upper boughs of the evergreens—in true symphonic harmony. It surely beat country or the hip-hop music played on the late AM dial bemoaning, "My lover done left me and I'm so alone; please, Lord, show me the way—only my horse knows the way." Another smell was thankfully absent—spilled beer and cigarette smoke. "Aahhh for the smell of pine pitch. The only better smell is the scent of a wanting woman, such as Leigh." He relived the previous night with her as he drifted off to sleep, falling off like a rock, hoping his dreams would be of Leigh and not about bears in the area. He had, again, escaped the realities of temporary predation in the food chain and permanent lust for the female of his species. His dreams would certainly be conflicted tonight, for his only bedmate was his cold and hard 9mm at his side—quite a contrast to the soft alluring, sensual fragrance on the neck . . . and in the hair . . . he consumed last night with Leigh.

*   *   *

Less than ten miles east, Leigh was also experiencing a reflective but confusing day about the previous night with Jack. It was a day off for her. She was still outside looking to the stars for wisdom in handling affairs of the heart when it turned a little too chilly to romanticize about the night with Jack, and Boy was getting a little restless, too.

"Okay, Boy, in we go; I can see no solutions in the sky; I'll sleep it off," she mused. She smiled, thinking, What a way to christen the hut. Jack and I did it up very well with food, wine, sex and a deep sleep—not bad if I do say so myself; plus, lust with a native healer—can you believe? Some night, all right. How many times would an older woman have a day with a young, attractive, modern shaman and experience a night with him . . .

Testing his other side, the romantic side of this stoic, yet modest, native savant.

*   *   *

Boy's ears perked up. She has certainly been acting strange today, he thought, and now chatting to herself—women! I'll never be able to figure them out! I wonder if it's related to the Native American that stayed overnight; I wonder. Boy thought, Oh well, she seemed to have a good time, but was certainly melancholy today; hope she snaps out of this funk soon.

He lowered his head, knowing she would continue talking to herself and Jack all night if she wanted. After a time, Boy stealthily moved from his bed to Leigh's; leaning against her body much like her previous bedmate, his muzzle found her hand and her hand found his head and ears . . .

They slept.

*   *   *

About one-hundred miles to the northwest, Ford was daydreaming, too, but of a lesser involvement with Leigh than he had hoped for. He had stayed over at Yakutat on the Pacific Coast after a cargo flight from Juneau. Yakutat was a 280-degree heading from Juneau, the capital of Alaska, which took him right over the Tongass camp on the previous day's flight; he wondered what she was doing while he passed over at 5,000 feet. She could neither hear nor see him at that altitude, but if cloud cover had not prohibited it, he would have buzzed the meadow. Little did he know what was going on that day—and night. In fact, with the winter weather and its Arctic winds, many flights would be at higher elevation to fly over the weather below. Summer's Visual Flight Rules (VFR) would soon change to Instrument Flight Rules (IFR) to navigate the hostile terrain, mountains, and storm fronts that would frequently appear out of nowhere. His wings would be clipped very soon and he would revert to snowmobile travel—which was also risky. Nevertheless, he would get to the meadow—somehow—some way; he needed her more than just a little. Ironically, his flight back to Juneau was the back azimuth of the flight to Yakutat, i.e., 280 minus 180 equals 100 degrees and directly over the camp. "Damn, I hope the weather permits a buzz at the meadow. I wonder where she is now, I wonder . . ."

Sleep engulfed his hopes for the next day.

*   *   *

Ford was performing preliminary preflight checkout tasks while moving along the channel taxiway with his old C-190. Yakutat had only one main route through the marked water-runway. Base operations were quiet today; he even had to push off from the dock himself. Yakutat did not have a control tower or station manager so he was on his own with the ground- based Flight Service Station (FSS) automatic weather data at 122.9 MHz. Under VFR he was not required to, but would when airborne, he would call Juneau ATC and relate his flight plans to Skagway: 100 degrees azimuth at 2,500 feet; DPT 0900 hours; Estimated Time of Arrival (ETA) 1130 hours; alternate landing site, #1 Klukwan, #2 Juneau. FSS weather: 20 degrees Fahrenheit, wind WSW at ten knots, ceiling 6,000 feet, visibility twenty miles. ATC clearance was not required for the majority of his flight path in Class E airspace above 1,200 feet, but a courtesy call to Juneau was always given by bush pilots since all were flying over hazardous terrain and exposed to the sudden arrival of unpredictable storm fronts from the NW, plus the ever-present overcast, rain, and drizzle of the Tongass rainforest. Prior to run-up at the end of the markers, Ford checked one other important on-board item—the Flight Survival Bag. It had a variety of charts, spares, and first-aid kit, and there were a few more items that were a must for Alaskan cross-country pilots: portable GPS, even though one is dash-mounted, four flashlights, flite-lites (green cyalume chemical sticks), Swiss Army knife, duct tape, tie-wraps, fuses, flare gun, binoculars, PFD, and one-man raft, plus a lot of miscellaneous nuts, bolts, and screws.

Engine run-up complete, Ford set the variable pitch prop to its full-power setting, and poured the coals to the Big Red One. The C-190 roared to life as if an explosion of power as the pontoons parted the water and strained to be released from the aqueous vacuum. Pushing water slowly and then with more force, the pontoons rose higher from the water's grip, and finally after 600 feet of water-runway, the captive pontoons escaped the water and the Big Red lurched into the air with only a trailing wake as a memory of the water's previous capture. There seemed to be a little stiffness in the yoke as the beauty trailed a Niagara of water while climbing slowly to the rising sun to the east. "Come on, girl, let's go home; you'll rest better in your own little bed at Skagway," Ford related as the yoke, again, seemed to be a little tight. "You're probably cold from staying outside all night. You'll be home by 1200 hours. Hang in there, Babe."

After arriving at altitude 2,500 and setting the autopilot to 100 degrees AZ, he turned the radio to Juneau ATC: "Juneau ATC, this is C-190, at 2500 feet MSL, 100 degrees AZ, to Skagway at 1030 hours, over." "C-190, this is Juneau ATC, copy your traffic, have a good flight, ATC out."

"Roger, ATC, thanks for the comeback. This is C-190, out."

Ford relaxed a little as the resonant hum of the 190 was music to his ears. You would have to be an old-timer in the left seat with at least four digit hours to understand how a good plane is like a good woman; you take good care of it and it will take care of you. If married, it's your mistress. Big Red was that, certainly, and more.

Ford looked down at the beautiful desolation and rolling terrain of the Tongass. It all looked the same from 2,500, and locating the meadow could only be done with a GPS. In fact, he'd see few reference points until later in the flight when the town of Takutat would appear on the port side and Haines on the starboard at about an hour and a half into the flight. Nothing looked familiar at this height. Nothing, not even rivers or camps carved out of the forest. Nothing.

Fuel burn was approximately fourteen gallons an hour. He planned for enough fuel for his alternates at 60 gallons, so he felt secure of any unexpected headwinds or weather-related problems. The nine-cylinder radial engine was humming as sweet as ever at 7,000 rpm at 80% power, maintaining True Air Speed (TAS) of 90 knots, and Ground Speed (GS) of 80 mph. The flight was going well on autopilot while Ford monitored engine temperature, oil pressure, manifold pressure, and a dead-on AZ of 100 degrees. The old bird, as a rule, flew herself; she had balance, power, and lift to spare. Her normal configuration was altered only by the added drag of the huge pontoons, but they were a necessity in Alaska. Likewise, she flew with large skis in winter. The 190 was his only true love now, and his only source of true adventure—his sixth sense of exploration. A *personification of the inanimate*, true, sans apology . . . no matter, Carl Jung would understand.

His thoughts returned to Leigh as the plane approached the campsite near the meadow. He checked he GPS readings and determined he was about ten miles west of her camp, dead ahead. Since he was flying on VFR authority, he did not notify Juneau ATV that he would be descending soon for a quick buzz of Leigh's camp at 500 feet AGL.

After a 360-degree visual check for other aircraft, and seeing none, he slowly pushed the yoke forward to descend to a lower elevation. The elevators responded, controlling the attitude or pitch of the plane. At 600 feet he eased back the yoke to bring the nose up and level off.

Nothing happened.

Nothing.

He pulled the yoke to the rear again, but there was no response—in fact, the yoke was loose, too loose, without any resistance of cable/pulley travel—nothing at all!

"Damn. What's going on?" Ford cried.

"God damn, son of a bitch, the cable must have snapped, slipped, or fractured."

Cycling the yoke did nothing, so he rotated the wheel on the yoke to actuate the ailerons while also pushing hard on the rudder pedals, and the plane turned.

"Bitch!"

Now in a turn, without any change in elevator movement the plane was 45 degrees nose down at 400 feet. The elevators, apparently, were not going to move. He cut power, and lowered wing flaps to slow the descent and grabbed the mike. He was about to have a "you-see-FIT" *Uncontrolled* Flight Into Terrain, with trees and all—if the controls didn't start responding . . . and they did not.

Ford hurriedly keyed the mike . . . "Mayday, mayday, this is C-one ninety over the 'Root in the Tongass about to auger in . . . going down, controls jammed . . . May Day!"

Silence followed.

Ford's silence yielded to his unconscious flashback of his early life, his family, his life experiences . . . he braced, white-knuckled, for impact.

Silence.

Then a terrible shattering crash of the treetops enjoined the engine's propeller mass as it pushed through the pines like a blunt ballistic missile; the engine sheared off and came to rest suspended by control wires as if hung on a gallows; the wings broke off with a terrible tearing sound as they folded and dropped like matchsticks; the pontoons snapped off like little twigs and fell to the limbs below taking half of the plane's aluminum belly with them. The 190 continued on as if a warrior's spear thrusting through the thicket of trees like a knight in armor—decapitating an intruder.

Big Red slammed to rest in the soft ferns and sphagnum moss of the forest floor, then as if in a slow motion film, she rolled over slowly and gently lay on her side. She was now the shape of an accordion—compressed. The ninety was now a zero.

Total silence followed.

There was little movement except for the dangling struts, wires, and the drip-drip-drip of aviation fuel . . . and the subtle crackling and hissing sound of the motor's cooling-down process.

Ford remained in his seat.

He did not move; nor did his broken watch, now reading 1100 hours.

The Tongass—and Ford's silence—was deafening.

But not for long; he would not be alone very long; there had been witnesses to the fall.

Chapter 9

Resolution

Jack had risen early, fished, and fried two tasty brookies while enjoying his morning cuisine from the Bitterroot; he marveled at his current place in life. He was doing exactly what he wanted vocationally, yet he remained lonely. His thoughts returned to Leigh, as they had throughout the last thirty-six hours. Their brief encounter had been overwhelming, not only in his unconscious mind, but in his conscious thoughts, too.

Having started his day a little late at 1030 hours, he was busy getting his rucksack ready to head west for the second day of his three-day trip to the Pacific. A late start was no problem; he'd make up the time along the river's path by not hunkering down as often and do a little less random exploration. He already missed Boy, and appreciated the logic and common sense in Ford's decision to let Leigh use the dog during her sojourn on the meadow. "Assuredly they're close, or why would he let his best friend, Boy, stay with her for such an extended period of time? I'll bet they're *very* close. Oh well, so were we. She was certainly assertive. But why did she get involved with two men?" He reflected, Maybe there was a reason, maybe there were fewer rules in Alaska, and at sixty . . . who am I to judge?

"Okay, Jack, get your butt in motion and hit the trail; daylight is a-burning."

In his element now, he started whistling an old Indian chant, which served as his companion for many years while hiking through the Tongass.

Within moments he seemed to blend into the timber . . .

He heard the sound first. Then he saw the floatplane.

Something was unusual about its flight path; something was wrong.

Everything was wrong: It was too low, in a forty-five degree nose-down attitude, and descending too fast—it appeared out of control.

Puzzled, he ran forward to a clearing that would provide a better view. The plane continued down, the engine stopped, and the plane shuddered; the plane acted as though the pilot may be having trouble with the controls without any apparent success; the plane was banking and turning as if totally out of control. The sun flashed on the side of the fuselage as it turned back west—wait a minute; it's red.

"Oh no!" he screamed. "That could be Ford's plane!"

The 190 was in serious trouble, and if it was Ford, he would be, too.

"Pull up! Pull up, Ford! Ford, pull up! Get the nose up!

"Son of a bitch!"

Obviously Ford couldn't control the plane, or it would react to his efforts. In a confused panic, Jack knew only too well that the plane was about to break up from excessive velocity for the airframes' maximum stress factors, or for sure snake its way through the canopy and into terra firma.

He ran as fast as he could to the expected impact point. He felt sick, helpless, angry, and sad as he raced through the underbrush.

This could be a deadly crash. Big Bird was falling fast.

He faintly heard the intrusion of the prop and metal into the forest canopy—and the awful absence of sound that followed. The silence was deafening. "Wait, that's good," he cried. He knew that a fire would end it all—and there was no smoke-crackling or ear-splitting demonic noise of an explosion upon impact.

"Thank you, Manitou!" he exclaimed.

Running as fast as his feet would permit against the resisting underbrush, Jack leaped through the forest at breakneck speed.

"Damn—Please, Manitou—let Ford live—please!"

Dejected, he thought gravity sure has an overwhelming advantage in flight; the plane fell like a rock.

*   *   *

Leigh was in a melancholy mood after rising a little late; she dragged herself slowly out the door and left it ajar so Boy could "rock & roll" on the river and any other thing that looked like a challenge. She needed a change in her morning routine, so she wandered alone up the ridgeline to the altar site for the first time since meeting Jack where she discovered him *flailing* the earth in frustration for the acts of his misguided plebeian forefathers. She recalled how upset he was on that day and still how sensitive he appeared to be, especially to her. Boy would find her, not to worry; he'd find her up on the ridge.

"What a view," she sighed. "This panorama has been observed for thousands of years, still basically unchanged. The vista to the west was even more awe-inspiring than when I sat on this very log with Jack." Even with the sun low on the horizon and at her back, the rays enveloped many of the arcane canyons beyond the river, and the mountains were lit with a welcome to the morn. This was too beautiful for words.

Enjoying the bliss of the moment, her eyes wandered to the north.

"Wait. What is that?" Eyes straining, she looked again.

About six miles away and at least two thousand feet elevation was a plane, a floatplane in a rather sharp-angled, nose-down attitude. The plane was descending way too low for a safe pullout speed.

"What the hell is going on? That plane is right in line with the river, but can't possibly land there; something is terribly wrong!"

She screamed as the plane appeared to be ready to auger into the forest canopy miles away. Unable to hear very well at that distance, and barely able to see any detail, she nevertheless knew the plane was in trouble and she was unable to do anything about it.

The sun flashed on the side of the fuselage—it was red.

"Wait a minute, what if it's Ford's plane?

"Son of a bitch!"

Panicked, she ran down the ridge, hollering for Boy as she ran, then fell ass-over-teacup, got up, fell again, and continued running. She met Boy at the hut.

While holding his head and looking into his eyes, she said, "We've got a job on our hands! Someone, maybe Ford, just crashed about six miles down the canyon by the river. Don't worry, Boy, if it is Ford, we'll be there to help."

Confused, Boy whined. He'd heard Ford's name in a manner that was *not good*; plus Leigh looked worried.

"Manitou, please, please, help the pilot!"

She threw together an overnight survival pack with first-aid items, slammed the hut door, and headed west by way of the river, Boy leading the way. Thumping, tromping, leaping, running, and jumping, they started making good time. She thought, Six miles at twenty minutes a mile (best case) means about two hours. It's now 1100 hours; with luck we'll be there just after 1300 hours. Thank goodness there appeared to be no fire.

Away they ran, as agile as any one of The University of Michigan's "stable" of football tailbacks—twisting, weaving, swerving, and doing whatever was necessary to move forward over, under, and through the underbrush.

After three miles of almost sprint-like speed, she hunkered down to rest and reflect. "I've made a few mistakes, Boy; I forgot to pack food, my satellite phone, and rain gear—oh well." Boy cocked his head as if knowing something was wrong; for they had been going someplace in one hell of a hurry and he didn't know why, except he'd heard Ford's name several times. Also, it was very unusual to be this far from camp without a lot more preparation. Leigh had literally thrown together some items as they took off.

She thought of her exciting, mentally rewarding, and romantically active weeks with Ford at Skagway. Yes, it was the boy in Ford who wanted to "christen" the plane, Big Red Bird, properly; after all those years, she thought she was probably not the *first* in simulating sex at 5,000 feet in the back seat. She played along to please him, but never doubted for a moment his purpose for showing her the Bird. It was to have her join the mile-high club.

"Men!"

At the time it seemed a little peculiar but in hindsight it was a riot with legs one way, then another, a yoke lever against her pink ass, and upon completion of the christening . . . he stood on the doc and announced to the sleeping town (she hoped they were sleeping) that, on this night: "The Big Red Bird has been properly honored to ensure a safe flying season . . ." and finished by blessing the Lynn Canal, from the dock, with his pee. "So be it," he finally shouted down the canal, and swaggered back to the plane where she was respectfully hiding from his boasting.

She was not sure of her newly gained fame, but went along, as she noted, so this child-like hunk of a man could get a glow-on. She had no regrets, for adventuresome nights with this kind of a man are not presented very often at her age, and Ford was one of a kind; his type seldom come across a woman's path in Alaska. He was not only brilliant, he was funny, and loved to play hard and work hard at everything he tackled. She happened to be the tackled one . . . that night.

"Drink up, my dear, we've nothing to fear, for Ford is here, hear, hear!"

It was indeed a great night; the Bird was now called "Leigh's Bird" in honor of the "honors" bestowed by her that night.

He immediately climbed into the cockpit of the plane and labeled the start-engine button "Leigh's Button." Men! Of course, he'd said it would remind him of "turning her on" when pressed . . . her button was his, too . . ."

When queried, she said, "Yes, dear, I know I'm supposed to start my engine, too . . . when my magic button is pushed." Aaaggghhh, men!

"Enough rest, Boy, I'm starting to dream of old times; let's get a move on." She and the dog continued their trek toward the wrecked aluminum and fabric bird. Due to increased difficulty, they diverted from the edge of the river's pathway and traversed up to the high ridgeline to the north. "Damn, this is tough going," she exclaimed. From this new height, the opposite mountain where Ford's plane crashed seemed to have moved closer to them. The hollow below, now basked in red, yellow, orange, and mixed evergreen, became a narrow slit revealing the meandering river. It was as if the edge of an axe had sunk into the earth to create the cleavage for the Bitterroot's journey to the west.

Resting while moving slowly over the top of the ridge, the leaves of the self-made trail spewed from the spongy earth as if no one had trod there before—which could be true. As they moved out from under the canopy, the sun hit them like a flash, an explosion of light, and sent showers of sparkling rays into the air.

Leigh boasted, "Good move, Boy, our shortcut up the ridge saved us at least a half-hour."

Suddenly, a raven sounded his presence on the knoll by sending three hard calls through the air, "Caw—caw—caw," letting them know that he was there.

Leigh and Boy moved down the ridge like a wave as the sun cast eerie shadows of their arrival to the river bottom below. As they reached the foothills, the ridgelines were coming to life as the sun burned off residual fog lurking over the river and valley below. Trees stretched their limbs like arms as if released from the bonding cold of the night, and animals murmured as the rays of heat impinged their fur and feathers.

Both silence and a new fear for Ford's safety gripped her thoughts as they moved down the path to the floodplain. Their presence was the only break in the silent low whistle of the throbbing trees and the late morning rustle of foot-thrown leaves.

Silhouetted against the icy blue sky, she strained her eyes in search of a sign of the crash. "Not to worry, I'll find you, Ford; hold on a little longer."

All her energies, both mental and physical, were now totally spent as they moved along the riverbank. An extreme oxbow indicated they would have to cross the 'Root. "Well, Boy, we're going to get wet, so let's not pause too long." She caught her breath and away she went, holding her carry bag on her head. Boy was already on the opposite side while she moved carefully into the water to her waist, sloshing and lunging as she overcame obstacles on the riverbed. "There, made it, got to catch my breath, Boy." She checked her pockets for lost items and found algae and water plants instead. Hoping for a sound from the crash site, she held Boy close to keep his noise to a minimum. Nothing.

"Quit licking, I'm trying to listen." He got the drift and lay down as she strained to hear something—anything.

At this lower elevation, the exact crash location was not obvious. The thick brush prohibited seeing beyond fifty meters. "This is going to be a best-guess direction, Boy; I'm just not sure which way to go, but one thing is for sure, the site is near the river to the west, so let's go."

Just before taking off, a raven sent out three calls through the air as before, "Caw—caw—caw."

Leigh stopped and reflected on the earlier calls. *Could this be the same raven that flew in the direction of the crash site?* She wondered if his presence meant someone was nearby. She wondered if it could be telling them where to start their search. "Come on, Leigh, you're thinking *way* outside the box. No way." But yet, Jack had convinced her that animalistic beliefs were valid, if not *more so* than other religious myths. She did believe that many spiritual powers were in Nature and many animals were part of that mandate to help humankind since their actions were directed by the Creator. In short, natural indigenous aspects of the world had souls—and could relate to humans in a dramatic fashion through any and all of God's creations. As with Thoreau, she felt that the *Divine was within* everybody, and those who believed in this concept *did not* need institutional churches, dogma, or creeds laid down by the ancient writers of Biblical times.

She was now almost certain the raven was a symbol sent by Manitou, and more than that, a beacon to guide them to the crash site. The raven knew that they had seen him. It leaped from its perch and flew silently to the southwest ridge along the southern (windward) side of the river.

"It's Him; I know it's Him; the raven is a messenger. Come on, Boy, let's follow, come on!" and away they went.

She thought, There's a better way to climb up a steep ridge. Her dad had shown her long ago; it's an easier and faster way. You don't run straight up—you run along the side and angle up as you go. You place your feet on the topside of the underbrush, roots, and mounds so you will not slip down as much. The technique worked, and with the adrenaline rush and mystic guidance, the ridge became smaller . . . and conquered in no time flat. "Good dog! We both made it; now let's see if we can see the crash site from this higher vista." Tired as hell, they caught their breath for just a moment before finding the best viewing site to the southwest.

She then noticed something strange. The raven, which had flown ahead in leapfrog fashion, was nowhere to be seen or heard. She thought she had seen him land over toward the west. "Wait." She wondered if there was indeed a call in a slightly different cadence. Not sure, she listened . . . and listened; yes, there was a change in his call. One thing was certain, other than the bird's call, the forest was absolutely silent—mysteriously silent. It was as if something had gone wrong, and the animals sensed the change in the forest's atmosphere—its tenseness.

The silence was deafening, eerie, and just damn troublesome to her.

Then it happened. First in a quiet manner, and then with more volume and frequency. Was it about a quarter mile away to the west? Maybe.

"Larrrupp! Larrrupp! Larrrupp!" Frogs were signaling an intrusion into their area of the riverbank . . . several meters downstream.

"Who-who-who-who Are You-oooooo!" An owl signaled an intrusion into his area downstream also.

Both sounds came from the same area, due west . . . something was over there.

Boy reacted first. His head lurched up, ears perked to their peak; he leaped to all fours. His whine signaled Leigh to this kind of sound that meant an intruder had been scented upwind. Something had disturbed the frogs, owl, and now Boy.

"That's enough for me, Boy; let's get going and check it out. Right now. There is something down by the river, and we have to investigate it, no matter what . . .

"Let's be careful, it could be many things—a grizzly, wolf, another person, Ford, or whatever; we've got to find out."

Without hesitation to the unknown, they barreled down the ridge, determined to find out who or what was causing the disturbance at the riverbank.

*   *   *

Jack arrived at the crash site about fifteen minutes after impact. As he moved into the scene, he was stunned at the spectacle that resembled a typical junkyard scene, sans dog. Flabbergasted, he paused a moment to survey the site.

Looking up, he noticed:

- The pontoons hung at the apex of a one-hundred-foot pine where they had been snapped off in the plunge.

- The motor/prop power plant, severed by another stately Douglas fir at fifty feet, was leaking oil while pointed skyward as if ready to soar again.

- Both wings had been sheared off with dramatic sharpness, leaving the effect of a temporary suspension at thirty feet as if wings of a moth ready to fly away.

- The fuselage and tail structures behind the passenger compartment separated and hung vertically at twenty feet tail-down as if a blunt nose rocket ready to launch.

- The passenger compartment built stronger by plan was also partially collapsed at five-feet, upside down, between two arm/hand-like pine tree limbs . . . not by accident, holding on to the pilot's compartment carefully, as with the insurance company's advertisement: "You're in good hands with Allstate."

- Other equipment and debris had been cast off to the forest floor in total disarray.

The wing tanks were still leaking aviation gas, so this hazard had to be considered. Luckily for Ford, the hot exhaust on the manifold of the motor was higher in the canopy and not near the leaking fuel; nevertheless, fumes always have the potential to ignite when in higher concentrations. In light of these concerns, he moved quickly to the cockpit.

Jack's eyes now focused on the body hanging partially out of the window of the pilot's side of the aircraft. The silence was noticeably present again, in a word—eerie—as he moved carefully toward the limb held compartment. "Ford! Ford!" Jack cried.

"*Caw—Caw—Caw.*"

The sound startled Jack as he approached Ford's suspended body at the same time the raven announced his presence. He had a pretty good idea that the bird was, in fact, a representative of the Creator's Spirit; yes, a messenger, leading others that could help rescue their fellow man.

While avoiding the broken glass, he reached up and checked for a pulse. He found one at the carotids in his neck. "Thank God/Manitou—he is alive!" A cursory exam showed no bleeding beyond cuts and scratches on his face and hands. It must have been a blood-curdling series of events that he just experienced. Similar to having his own Valhalla with the thread holding the Sword of Damocles breaking and descending . . .

Jack was thankful that Ford was breathing, though somewhat irregularly. He wondered if he should leave him knocked out cold or awaken him while trying to extract him from the twisted metal, formerly called the Big Red Bird. It was now a crushed and decapitated shish kebob of parts, each piece pierced by tree limbs, as if ready for cooking. The future use of the Bird's structural remains appeared simple—permanent birdhouses in the Tongass. Jack quickly addressed the most pressing problem; how to extract a 210-pound body out of his mistress, alone, probably seriously injured.

"Ford! Hey, Ford! Ford! Ford!"

Nothing, no response.

Risking movement of damaged limbs, back, and ribs, Jack shook Ford's shoulder a little, and then a little more. Nothing.

Another idea, being only thirty feet from the river, he ran over to its bank and filled his hat with clear cold water. He splashed the aqua tsunami into Ford's face, drenching everything including his neck, chest, clothing, and entire body. It got some of the blood off, but . . . nothing moved, although he appeared a little more presentable now, being clear of leaves and other debris.

There was a first aid kit in the passenger compartment. It should have ammonia smelling salt capsules to bring that Van Winkle around. Come to think . . . a Budweiser might also work for this old fly-boy.

Climbing carefully atop the wreckage, he opened the twisted passenger-side door, propped it open, and crawled in. "Damn, what a mess. It looks like both feet are trapped; lucky I'm here to help, and I'll bet the pain was so intense that he is in shock. It looks like the twisted rudder pedals have forced his feet against the side wall and flight deck metal. Damn, he would probably never have gotten out of this bear trap alive—at least not without help in a reasonable time." He rummaged around the rear seat looking for the first aid kit, moving boxes and overnight bag, and sure enough, there it was, strapped to the sidewall where it belonged. He retrieved a capsule and reached over Ford's body with TLC to preclude any additional damage. Now the trick—how to break the ampoule under his nose without lying on him. He reached as far as possible, crushed the retained spirits of ammonia, and waved it gingerly under Ford's nose.

That did it! Ford not only shook, he wiggled and threw his head back to escape the inhalation of the smelling salts. Startled, he looked up around the cockpit, then down at his trapped feet, and finally at Jack, saying, "Damn, it's about time someone came to pry me out of this crumpled can!" He blinked, shook his head again, and checked his entrapment, undaunted, and looked at Jack again. "That was one hell of a rough landing; I bet it's going to be a real bitch flying this thing out of here."

Jack forced a smile. "You'd better be thankful you survived, fella. Your former mistress is scattered all over the limbs of the Tongass timber."

Ford lamented, "Damn planes; they just don't make 'em the way they used to."

"You know, Ford, we've got a lot of trouble here; you'd better get serious. How are you anyway? How do you feel? Where do you hurt? Can you move?"

"One thing is for certain, my feet are locked in a Cessna Bear Trap and that's a bitch—they hurt so bad I'm about to scream."

Jack looked at Ford's entrapment again, and immediately evaluated what he needed to free Ford's legs and feet. Meanwhile, Ford leaned into the copilot's seat to give Jack room to operate and likewise check on his facial damage. His nose appeared to be broken and his right eye orbital socket fractured. Jack mused, better keep a positive slant in the face of Ford's injuries. But Ford beat him to it. "No dates tonight, Jack, I don't want any woman roughing me up for a while."

Jack retorted, "Yep, you already look as though you've lost the main event at Madison Square Garden, a likeness to Jake LaMotta, except he was better looking."

"Hey, enough of that talk, I'm a bruised and banged up puppy."

"You asked for it with your banter about dating; remember, boy, we've got to get out of here first."

Both had gotten the humor off their chests and discussed the seriousness of Ford's situation, then got down to some critical thinking. Priority number one was to free his legs from the scrap heap below the flight deck, so Jack scrounged around the crash scene to find a lever or pry bar to remove or push away the entrapments. He reflected on how close they had come to mentioning Leigh's name, and how he avoided the seriousness of their crisis. "But, what the hell, I'm working at his release; only, there's no need to mention my nights at her camp. Leigh's name need not come up not at all, she's elsewhere anyway, we may not see her for months," mumbled Jack.

Ford kept yelling down to Jack, asking whether or not he found a pry bar or lever, and Jack was patient, knowing very well how much pain Ford was experiencing. He had given him several Tylenol IIIs and a few 15 mg Valium pills from the kit. Still searching, he thought to himself, how the hell are we going to get him out of here with him all crippled up?

"Hey, Jack, can you bring some more water up here? Not sure why, but my mouth feels as if a herd of camels just rode through. I know we're in grizzly territory, but do I have to live like one?"

"Okay, okay, wait a minute, you think you'd just had a baby or something; you only just crashed into the Tongass at 180 knots—and survived. I'm coming with a jerry-rigged pry bar, and water . . . right now."

"Yeh! You know, forgive please. I would probably have died without you happening along today; my bullshit is only the surface of a deeper thanks to you."

"Christ, don't get soft on me, Ford; I wouldn't know what to think. You know that leg/foot trap you're in may have saved your life, too, by not letting you fly out of the compartment—who knows?"

"Yep, could be, or maybe I'm too damn thick-skinned or ornery to die; we'll soon find out what I'm made of when you pry me out of the scrap-heap, but I'm tough, am I not?"

"Okay, now bite on this wooden stick, this is gonna hurt."

"Wait, doesn't this cheap outfit have a couple shots of Crown Royal to help soothe the pain?"

"You know better, Ford; historically, Indians like me are not allowed to have whiskey, thanks to white men like you."

"Okay, I wasn't flying first-class anyway, but the good news is I can feel one ankle, the bad . . . I don't even know where the other one is; is it still there? I certainly cannot feel it!"

"Yeah, it's there, but your comment affects how we get out of here. For Christ sake, couldn't you have done your see-FIT closer to the coast, or better yet, near Skagway."

Not feeling the ankle was not good news.

Ford, with a little more seriousness, explained his VFR flight plan and May Day call with destination and time of impact—the latter, of course, seen by Jack, also. All the while Ford talked, Jack was trying to find a way to release his foot with minimum damage—that was the most difficult and tense for Jack.

Strange, the forest was silent as if the animals, including the raven, knew the tension in the cockpit. There were sounds, certainly, but they were Ford's moans of pain as Jack moved the impinging pieces away from his torn boot, flesh, and bone. Were the animals aware of the trauma? Were they sensitive to man's pain and tribulations? Jack was always quick to answer: Yes. It is the way for Nature to help all animals of the forest, man included.

"Damn sure going to put morphine in the kit next flight, even though it's not authorized; this pain could be treated."

"Ford, you know FAA will not allow an ER-type, drug-laden Rx in the kit. If they did, everyone would be misusing the drugs."

"Unfortunately, you're right; maybe I'll have to see Doc Jones, the dog's DVM, for help. Speaking of animals, how was my dog, Boy, doing—and Leigh?"

Fortunately, an event prevented an answer, the pry bar had finally freed his ankle.

"It's loose, it let go, I've got it," Ford explained, and immediately passed out from the intense pain.

No sooner had Ford blacked out than he recovered to relive the intense pain.

"What the hell do you mean, I've got it," Jack said quite puzzled.

"Well, dumbkopf, it means I have my leg back from the trap," Ford cried.

"Okay, just sit here a while; don't move; I'll make a splint and a crutch. How bad is it?"

"It couldn't be worse, I believe it's fractured," Ford groaned.

Ford took four more Tylenol III capsules and reviewed the options they would have to consider while trying to survive out here with one good body, and one with a fractured right foot. Jack headed to the scrap pile of Bird parts to make a splint. Remembering the priorities in the FAA guidelines for surviving a crash, it was fortunate that Ford had enough presence of mind to report the crash to the local ATC.

In fact, while Jack was scrounging up a splint, Ford was mentally going over the reporting/survival process in his mind:

- First, call Skagway-ATC . . . every pilot's nightmare, and report the see-FIT. He'd already tried that, and couldn't raise them with the damaged equipment on board, and the hand-held radio was low power, with a short antenna, and limited line-of-site transmitter . . . but he continued keying in a locator signal—of distress.

- Check to ensure the Electronic Locator Transmitter (ELT) was emitting a signal. The unit was pulsing at 121.5 MHz as designed, since it automatically does so upon impact of 500 pounds or more, here it had that for certain, maybe 3,000 pounds.

- Check for filing of flight plan. It was only VFR, but was acknowledged by ATC in Juneau. He noted: The typical response time for rescue of a VFR flight plan was about *fifteen hours* to find the crash site, and *five* hours to access and assist at the site, meaning it could be *twenty-five* to thirty hours in their case. A IFR flight plan was much better due to radar contact; in fact, ATC would find you in *two hours* and assist in less than *three*, especially along the coastline between Anchorage and Juneau. In Alaska, it's not if a plane will need help in a given day: it's just when, and how many. Flying in Alaska is the most hazardous air space in North America. Alaska has it all: frigid temperatures, rain, fog, wind, and mountains shielded by all these climactic variables.

"Now, where are we with our plan? If it's thirty hours to assistance; we've got to get going and try to walk out, hobble in my case, to the coast," said Ford.

Sure, he thought, I sent out a May Day, but how do I know ATC even heard it? Damn, we're between a rock and a hard place, but one thing is certain, no one will spot us down here under this canopy of pines—no one! "Walking out is the best scenario. I hope you agree, Jack. Dave and Milt will be checking at FSS since I'm overdue now, and they will be checking with ATC, the DNR, and field in Yakutat, and yes, the governor . . . knowing them. You want those guys on your side, they would be out looking until I'm found, dead or alive. Okay, once more, what are our survival needs:

- Water is the most important, no sweat, we'd be on the Bitterroot for some time, we would be walking along its route for up to three days.

- Shelter against extreme temperature, wind, and precipitation. We've got lots of blankets in the plane plus many tarps and ponchos and a two-man raft if we need it."

However, Ford had no plans of staying very long in the area; somehow he and Jack would team up to get out. Nevertheless, his life was now certainly marginalized with the injury, the distance to the coast, the elements, the animals, and further injury or infection. Jack was the common denominator for successfully escaping from the grip of the Tongass.

Review of FAA guidelines also directed them to do more analysis:

- Move clear of the aircraft. Do not use it as a shelter. It is not stable enough for overnight protection.

- Administer first aid.

- Communicate with FAA, ATC, base operations, locals . . . anyone. And assume the ELT is working.

- *Do not leave the crash site* for at least twenty-four hours; the search is focused at that location via the ELT, the May Day call and ATC reports. It's critical to the rescuers that you're there.

Jack had hustled back to the cockpit with some braces and cloth ties for a temporary splint. Ford could not be removed without a substantial one. While he worked on his leg, they both agreed to further discuss their options in a methodical way:

- They needed to carefully extract Ford from the 190, which would be very difficult at five-feet in a tangle of limbs.

- He had to get him away from the wreckage before it moved or fell to earth in a strong wind.

- Jack had to determine the extent of Ford's injuries, which affected his next evacuation move.

- He needed to perform first-aid tasks with the limited supplies and a lot of ingenuity.

Finally, they had to determine how long to stay at the site, and the most effective way to march out. They had flight charts, and Jack knew the area very well. The operational question was: "What can Ford do?"

"Augh! Ow! What the hell did you do, Jack?"

"Not much; I just tightened up the splint; apparently it is tight enough, is that my understanding?"

"You're damn right, it is!" Ford yelled with tears in his eyes.

"Okay, we'll tell the coach you're not running the one-hundred-meter dash today, maybe tomorrow. Now grab my hand and then my shoulder, we'll crawl over the seat and you can sit on the edge of the door opening while I go below to catch you. No hugging now, this is rescue, not affection . . . okay sweetie, come on," Jack cooed.

"You know, when I'm better, I'm going to kick your ass into next week!" Ford responded as he moved to the edge of the opening.

"Okay, sweet lips, let's give it a try; less abusive speech would help; come on down!" As Jack spoke he came down with a controlled human crash landing—step one was accomplished. Knocking Jack off his feet with the impact, Jack yelled, "Damn, get off me, Ford; I don't want anyone to see us in this position."

"Okay . . . thanks for the catch, but a Little League shortstop could do better."

Successfully extracted, Ford hobbled with Jack's help to the river under the watchful eye of the raven. Ford collapsed at the water's edge, removed his shoe, and started soaking his ankle in the cold waters of the Bitterroot.

They both knew how serious their predicament was, and the verbal horseplay was their way of releasing the tenseness of their serious plight, especially since the coastal camp could take at least three days to reach with Ford's disability. Normally a one-and-a-half-day trip, Ford's problem created this new timeline. Did Jack have any other options? Yes, but he didn't give it a second thought; he couldn't leave him for the rescue team . . . it could take days for them to find him. He would get both of them out, one way or another, whether rescued . . . or walked out.

As with Aurelius, in 100 C.E., this Roman Emperor also stated in his Meditations, "You just play the cards you're dealt; no one ever said life is fair. Men exist for the sake of one another." Two thousand years has changed little in man's commitment to his fellow man.

Yeah, all this right in the middle of the grizzly migration along the coastal range. It was now 1130 hours, and his May Day call to ATC was at 1100 hours; everyone listening would certainly be aware of Ford's absence by now and someone, somewhere, would be planning a search plan, also.

While Ford soaked his broken ankle, they started discussing their options again on how to escape the vice-like grasp of the Tongass. Jack also wondered to himself if their mutual attraction for Leigh would be revealed as they trudged to freedom.

Probably not.

Hope not.

"Caw—Caw—Caw!"

The apparent guide/messenger called out again as the troubled pair made plans while Ford continued to soak his ankle in Mother Nature's aqueous balm.

The sound of the raven was quite different . . . did it mean something?

Did the raven have a specific reason for its cry? Was it signaling for others? For them? They both looked . . . and wondered.

Chapter 10

Precarious Journey

The raven called again: *"Caw—Caw—Caw."*

Leigh spoke, "I'll bet a hundred bucks that bird is still directing us to the crash site. Let's hustle—Oops!" She went down and up again in a well-executed Parachute Landing Fall (PLF), down, roll, and up . . . "All the way," as Ford would say. He was always flaunting, with pride, his service in the 82nd Airborne Corps. Boy stopped and waited for her to purge the leaves from her trunk and limbs. "No problem, man," she said, although appearing like the mysterious lost tree women of the Tongass.

Rounding the bend at warp speed, Leigh shouted, "Hey!"

They both stopped in their tracks. They were now witness to the goal of their search, but still could not believe their eyes. Stopping to savor the moment, they checked to see if they were dreaming; it was as if frozen in time . . . a theatrical tableau. No one moved.

She wanted to embrace this scene emotionally, but still couldn't believe it. Boy froze, too, with ears perked up while uttering a low growl like a lion: "Grrrr . . ."

Both shocked, Jack and Ford also stared back at Leigh and the dog.

Boy's menacing growl was an audible warning to demonstrate his protection of Leigh, and a warning not to mess with him, no way. Dogs have a built-in bluff factor, and he was using his now.

Little did he know, he had nothing to fear. It was his injured master and a recent friend and lover of Leigh's, both with whom she had been intimate in the last month. There was a no threat short of the timeless undying jealousy found in a triangle of too much love being proliferated among an excessive number of lovers . . . within a very narrow time period.

"Leigh!" yelled Jack.

"Leigh!" yelled Ford.

Shocked and as if in concert, they yelled in unison: "What are you doing here?"

Boy recognized Ford first, and bounded gleefully toward his fallen master. Almost too physical, Ford had to fend off Boy as the licks and hits of Boy's emotional water release at the river's edge created a waterspout. He quickly realized

Ford was injured, and in a lightning change of emotion lay at his side in a passive posture. They knew each other very well. "Good boy!" was all the rugged teary-eyed master could muster as he continued to hug his four-legged canine friend.

Leigh was also in tears. The emotional release was overwhelming as she saw him alive, safe, but obviously hurting. Reaching her objective was a crushing relief. She had been at a dead-run for hours. She needed release . . . so she hugged Jack and quickly moved to Ford and hugged him, water and all. All three ended up wallowing in the river with hugs and kisses spread around. It was hard to let go now since she thought he had been killed.

In his typical style, Ford said, "It's about time I got some attention, but be careful, I'm broke."

"Okay, baby, you've had enough of me for now!" she explained.

It appeared that Jack had saved his life, whether she had reached the plane or not. She was a grateful woman . . .

Then there was the raven, whom she was certain had led her to Ford. Who else could have directed their efforts?

It must have been The Great Spirit, Manitou. Yes, it had to be He. She was certain, she could sense His presence.

A natural organizer, Leigh suggested they all rest, grab a bite to eat, and make plans. She would be working very close to both.

The resulting scene had many elements of a double-edged sword—with a sharp leading edge for the forward thrust, but as in many relationships, considerable damage could be inflicted on the back swing. She was the sword, and she loved both of them.

They had both seen Ford's plane go down, had found Ford alive, and would most likely soon discover that she had been involved with both. No matter, they now had to get Ford's injury treated, and get him out—ASAP—but . . .

They were two or three days from any medical help in the middle of difficult terrain of the Tongass. The raven flew away with a barely audible "*Caw—Caw—Caw.*"

Was the bird's mission complete? Probably not. He'd be back.

It was 1300 hours.

After many animated conversational catch-up sessions while eating some of the snacks found in the demolished bird, they got down to work to develop a survival/rescue plan.

Ford participated aggressively in formulating the rescue plan by analyzing the many questions in the "what if" category. As more options and problems were discussed and factors linked, several ideas were revealed as facts or variables:

Facts:

- Ford would need a lot of help to survive the two-hour hike to the ocean.

- The splint and crutch were definite factors. Could he move over the trail with enough mobility without further traumatizing his ankle/foot?

- With Leigh volunteering to go along with Jack, they had enough support.

- They had adequate tarps, ponchos, and foul-weather gear.

- Jack had found Ford's handgun, so they were well armed.

- The handheld radio *appeared* to be working, but was questionable.

- FAA probably heard the May Day call, so planes would be searching, weather permitting, and others may be walking in from the coast.

Variables:

- The ELT was pinging, but its power/range was very limited in the mountains.

- Without radio contact, they didn't know what the FFS boys were doing.

- They did not know the extent of Ford's injuries.

- They did not know the weather forecasts, such as how good would flying weather be for them and search planes? Alaska is infamous for being socked-in 50% of the time, whether by fog, wind, or excessive winds.

- They were uncertain of the terrain that Jack could find to allow Ford to traverse successfully, hoping he would not need a litter-carry mode.

- Finally, they did not know the grizzly bear movement . . . a problem indeed.

After weighing the facts and variables, the Tongass Three reviewed all the options and added one more: They could *return to Leigh's hut* on the meadow, and while there, hope Ford would return to better health for later travel to the coast.

"Absolutely not!" said Ford.

He explained how the critical needs of his treatment would be better served by hiking out to a place where there were complete medical facilities.

Nothing more was said.

Against FAA recommendations, they also decided not to wait any longer at the crash site. They did so because even if spotted there was no way to rescue them through the tall, dense canopy. They'd walk along the flattest terrain possible next to the river with Jack leading the way. He knew the forest well, and should be able to find a path to accommodate Ford's hobbled condition. He knew where the elevated drier routes were, and best shortcuts through swampy areas to the coast. His knowledge could save them at least six hours.

It was 1500 hours.

Packed, anxious, and eager to get started, away they went—Jack in front, followed by Ford and Boy with Leigh bringing up the rear. Then, typical of Ford, he made a rear-end joke Leigh thought was in bad taste . . . as he indicated, "Those must be buns-of-steel under those Levis and a better fanny to follow than Jack's skinny ass. Leigh gave him a wily look. "Well, it's true!" Ford exclaimed, "You need not give me a sly glare of displeasure."

The crutch/plunk, step, swing bad foot; crutch/plunk, step, swing bad foot, and so on propelled him through some of the most beautiful but also most difficult country to transit in Alaska. However, Ford was hurting and was having difficulty in maintaining any sort of mobility while conquering the trail, and that objective was taking its toll on him. Yet, he kept saying, "Let's keep going; we're burning daylight."

To compensate for his discomfort, he kept pointing out the changing colors of the canopy as the yellow birch and red maples provided a diversion from the obvious. He was experiencing severe pain.

"Let's stop and rest awhile, Ford." Jack threw down his pack. "This natural outcrop of rocks looks like it was made for seating some tired hikers." Jack mentioned that they were all tired, which was untrue, but it would sound good to Ford. Jack glanced at Leigh and winked; she got the message through this unspoken cue . . . the stop was for Ford. He was abusing his ankle, leg, and whole body.

The wink, blink, and nod was unseen by Ford as he lay on the grass totally exhausted. Man's best friend lay with him for comfort. The look in Boy's eyes reflected an almost human sense of caring and friendship as he surely knew the injury was changing Ford's personality.

"How you doing, Ford?" Leigh said as she moved over to see if she could comfort him through a little conversation and attention to his needs. "How 'bout this drink of water?"

"Oh, just what I needed, thanks. You know, I don't know what I'd do without you . . . I love you."

"Yes, I know. Do you need anything other than my love?" said Leigh.

"Yeah, but not here, dear."

"Men! Or should I say pilots, engineers, designers . . . the whole lot; you're all interested in the same thing . . . Come to think of it, you all point at us like a bird dog, as if we were game birds. The lot of you are like Neolithic Man—your romantic actions dictated by your loins!"

"Well, are you not the fair game? Okay, I'll stop, only if you stop being the most beautiful female in the Tongass."

The pained look in his eyes belied his words; they spoke depths of deep pain behind his bravado. He could not hide his deteriorating condition. "I'm kinda hot," he said. "Do you think we ought to take my temperature?"

"Good idea; I'll get the thermometer. Quit talking and open wide, or I'll put it elsewhere, where the sun don't shine, my dear." She retrieved the probe, held it to the light, rotated it to the numerals and said, "Not bad." She lied; it was 103 degrees. "It's close to 100—could be worse."

Jack took over now by saying that it would be best to move on while it was light, and hike about two more hours, until 1700 hours. Jack turned to Ford, "That will give you several hours to soak your foot, grab a bite, and get some well earned rest, okay?"

Agreed, they continued along the river with periodic moves to high ground and game paths to provide easier going for Ford. Nevertheless, Ford showed additional pain and tension by venting his anxiety with crisp swearing as a way to ease his pain. Boy was first to feel his wrath, but seemed to understand Ford's temporary shortage in patience.

At 1600 hours a plane flew over at about 5,000 feet indicating that at that altitude most likely above the weather, it was *not* searching for the crew below.

Jack, who had been calling at half-hour intervals anyway, sent out another transmission on the hand-held: "This is C-190 rescue team, along the Bitterroot, thirty miles east of the coast, walking out with injured pilot Ford Harrison. We need medical help for Ford." He hoped they . . . someone, heard the transmission.

Ford rolled over, having noted the wind shift. "You know, folks, I do believe we're getting an on-shore breeze and the pea-soup weather that goes with it." He continued, "And that could be the reason there are now low-level search planes at 500 feet; they may know the front is coming in tonight. If it does, visibility will be zero/zero for the duration—in other words, fog, which is basically a stratus cloud on the ground."

They hiked up a little higher and would be looking for a campsite within the hour. Poor Boy; he could not quite grasp the severity of Ford's condition, but continued to move from person to person while spending most of the time with Ford. He was not at the comfort level he was used to.

Ford was miserable and bad company now. Being former military and a bush pilot, he was used to pushing the envelope, and now it was time to forebear the acute pain. There was no other option. He was not accustomed to complaining and was not going to start now. He knew his fever was rising. He was burning up, but would not burden Jack and Leigh now. The rest tonight would be the measure of whether he'd improve or degrade. He would soak his foot and rest, and probably improve with a good night's sleep.

Again, crutch/plunk, step, swing bad foot; step, swear; crutch, . . . etc. His temperature continued to rise; he was burning up. "Got to get to camp. Got to keep moving. Get out of my way, Boy." Unbeknownst to Ford, Jack had started to look for an overnight camp—immediately. He felt Ford must rest his foot. Boy cowered and moved away from Ford. Leigh said, "It's okay, Boy; come over here, come on; Ford will be okay. I hope so," she said softly, "I've never heard him talk like that to Boy."

Finding a small sloping meadow at the edge of the river, Jack and Leigh started making camp as Ford soaked his painful, pulsating foot. His humor was on the wane as he immersed his hoof in the soothing rapids. There was a little joke now and then, but very few, as the entire appendage started to lose its sensitivity. This was a bad sign. "Damn, this feels like the Holiday Inn whirlpool, except the water is fifty degrees colder—hot it's not!"

Ford added, "Say, I've got an idea. Let's just rig a canvas fly overhead, right here by the river, and I'll not have to crawl back and forth to the tent. Yep, let's do it. Just tie off the poncho and tarp in a lean-to fashion."

"Good idea," Jack commented.

The river was snowmelt water at approximately 50 degrees Fahrenheit, and it basically neutralized any sensation due to the chill. Ford may or may not have known how bad an indication this was for him. It was hard to know what he knew about his injury or what he was letting on to what he knew. Masking his emotions was an old trick of his. He could "act" when necessary.

Leigh reminded him of the critters, both large and small, that roamed the

Tongass at night. "Are you ready to fight off a sow bear that falls for you?"

"Shoot her in the butt; yep, but no kissy face with a grizz; my girlfriend to-night goes by the name of Colt .45."

"Okay, but don't be howling at the moon all night!"

With the fire started and camp set, Leigh moved over to help Ford while Jack started boiling water for their freeze-dried cuisine entrée. She removed his splint and took his temperature again. It was 104 degrees, not good, and the pulse was at 120, not good either.

"How did I check out, Doc?"

"Not to worry, dear. We'll get you fed and to bed as soon as possible."

It was 1800 hours.

Jack knew she was telling him lies about his health, but had few options to treat his fever, so she was giving him the mental goose of a positive series of comments.

"Okay, big fellow, get that hoof out of the water and take this batch of pills; it will ease the pain and swelling."

Jack helped Leigh while the freeze-dried spice pellets, rock-hard noodles, and granite-like meat chips soaked in the communal pot of hi-tech stew, sans Char-donnay and éclairs for dessert. The leg's appearance wasn't good. Its color was red to blue to yellow and swollen from the trauma of hiking for the last four hours.

"What do you think, Ford?"

"It doesn't look good!" Jack said.

"I agree, it does not look good," Ford said. "I've got to get to a medical facility very soon, but I'll be all right tonight."

None of them liked the looks of the leg's degraded appearance. It appeared to be a thrombosis, or coagulation of the blood in the leg's circulatory system. He really needed blood thinners. His pulse was still at 120; he remained a very sick man.

"I've got an idea, Leigh. Let's assume Ford should not walk anymore to save pressure on the ankle; it is clear that the crutch/splint is not acceptable. As such, we are going to make a little carrier so we can carry him out."

"Damn good idea; we'll make a carrier after chow. I'm starving," noted Leigh.

"Why don't you head up to the fire and I'll look for some long, firm poles to build a carrier. It will only take a minute. Come on, Boy, you can be my apprentice in litter building." Each would be carrying at least one-hundred pounds on their shoulders or arm, whichever way they decided to help the bush pilot. "This pair will work, Boy. We've got twine and rope so let's set these aside and go eat. I'll get Leigh to help later; she wants to assist, also. We'll be right back with some grub, Ford; hang tight. That fly over your head will be needed, but I can get that in the morning and finish up the carrier then."

"You know, Jack, I could make it walking. That litter-carry idea is a lot of work for both of you."

"Enough talk; it's settled, we're going to build it; I'll go get your bowl and we'll all eat the meal du jour in the evening sunset along the beautiful banks of the 'Root together."

"Here we are, folks; everything we need: great friends, a great setting, and great, well kinda great, grub," Leigh exclaimed.

"Damn plan, damn foot, damn bad luck, damn everything . . . except you, Boy," Ford said. Boy had left his side for a moment, but quickly returned when beckoned; the Tylenol must have kicked in. "Thanks much, folks; I may not make it, but one thing is for sure, if you had not come along when you did, I'd probably be wolf or bruin bait by now." The humble man revealed himself with grace.

"Oh, oh—son of a biscuit—we've got company," whispered Leigh.

"Ford, hold on to Boy; be quick about it."

"Okay, I've got him, what's up?"

"Grab his muzzle too, and don't move."

"Damn, what's up?" both Jack and Ford said in unison.

"Fellows, there's a bear glaring at us, downwind, to the west, in the river; he is now sniffing the air, and has caught scent of us now, for sure. Ford, keep holding Boy tight; it may be the bear that attacked Boy last week. He's still checking us out while on his haunches. Don't move; are your guns handy?"

"You're right, it is too late to do anything else, and yes, both of us have our guns at the ready now." Three pistols had been stroked, *ker-chunk*, as a live round entered Leigh's .44, Jack's 9mm, and Ford's .45 firing chambers.

The bear was still standing in the river about forty feet downstream without the appearance of being threatened, but while on his rear feet, the ten-foot mass looked dangerous.

Leigh said, "If this is the same bear Boy encountered, it will remember the attack. If so, we're in trouble if he scents Boy."

Thankfully, the bear snorted, returned to all fours, snorted again, and slowly lumbered away downriver. They relaxed. Then, the bear unpredictably stopped, turned, charged at them for about twenty feet with the characteristic head wobble, back and forth, and roared . . . but, put on the brakes, stopped, snorted, and pounced on the water's surface with its paws, one of which was deformed; he spanked the water again, then spun around, and ran off into a thicket. They breathed a little easier.

"I guess he had to show how lethal he could be, and we better not forget it!" Leigh said.

Both Jack and Ford returned their guns to their holsters, and Ford released pressure on Boy, but did not let go entirely. Boy appeared to know something was amiss . . . but had no idea of the bruin's threat; Ford made sure of that. He was well aware of Boy's last attack; Leigh had told Ford of the incident by the swamp. He would have, no doubt, attacked the bruin again . . . to protect his mistress . . . again.

Jack looked to the sky and thanked The Great Spirit for protecting them from fellow animals of the forest. He was suspicious Manitou had been involved in the bear's decision—in not attacking. All creatures had their place, and as demonstrated today, every animal could share the beauty of His creation.

As if related to his comment, a raven landed above the Tongass Three, plus Boy, and cried, "*Caw—Caw—Caw.*"

Jack noted the presence of the raven whenever there was stress or resolve, as if a messenger of the Spirit. "I'm not absolutely certain . . . but feel it was not a coincidence; it was part of His larger plan to regulate or mediate tension within His Kin(g)dom."

This natural environmental hazard, showcased by the bruin, triggered everybody to be on alert, yet focused on the business of their trip: to get out of the Tongass alive. More specifically, with Ford alive.

"Yes sir," Ford said with a mock French accent, "prime cuts served in the dinner/theatre of the Tongass, tonight by master French Chef Jacquard the Magnificent and my consummate assistant Leigh of Paree. No applause, please, just eat it all so washing the dishes will be easier—thank you in advance for your positive comments."

It was 2000 hours.

Just nine hours ago the Big Bird had knifed its way into the canopy of the forest and dramatically affected all their lives. No matter what happened, their relationship and future would be altered, indelibly altered. Grateful and emotionally stressed, Ford exclaimed, "You're both beautiful people; I love you very much; no matter what happens, I owe you a lot; I owe you my life."

"Egads," Jack groaned, "We're not that good, and besides, we're doing the same thing you would do under similar circumstances. Don't think we're unaware of some of your deeds, fella; I've heard some of the stories of your rescuing both local native tribal members of the Tlingits, plus many down-staters that have been in trouble . . . word gets around. Let's say it's payback time and you're just calling in those chips owed . . . Las Vegas-style." There was a palpable sense of tension in the air, but no one was talking about Ford's declining health and serious condition. It was as if there were a two-ton elephant in camp, and no one was admitting it. At least to his face. Maybe that was the case, they knew—he knew, so they were just going to bear down and get him out to medical facilities without a lot of fanfare.

"Come on, Boy, clean this plate; it will take less work in the 'Root. Good boy, we'll need very little soap, leaves, or sand out here with your skill."

All three sat around with the dog licking dishes, making idle talk about the past three decades, three years, three months, three days, and three hours. Each had a unique story leading up to their union on the 'Root and the wonder of the Tongass Forest at night. Ford needed the catharsis of this special union. He needed the strength-building therapy. He needed the kinship. He needed their conversation and help as his health declined. He was not clear about the future. He needed to embrace and hold on to this night. He needed to talk. They sensed it, and provided for his personal need. He needed to be close to Leigh, to her musk. Only men know what the smell of their lover's scent does to rejuvenate their soul and relieve their lust. He was basically cuckolded by Leigh now, but could do little about it; after all, Jack and Leigh had saved his life. He seemed resolved to his vulnerable position, a strange peace with whatever might come his way, for which Jack and Leigh played a major role.

"You know, my friends—my cuadrilla—if I forget to say it, be aware, you are the troupe I'd go into the bullring with," mused Ford. "The cuadrilla always made up for, or filled in for, the matador's obvious needs or weakness in the ring, dear friends—that's you."

"You know, Ford, you've told us about your work with the Apollo Program at NASA, but you've never talked much about those earlier years while training in Mexico and Spain. Have you heard any of those stories, Leigh?" Jack said.

"No, matter of fact I have not, other than how broke he was and how wealthy matrons kept him fed. Wonder if that's all . . . Ha! What say you, Ford? Come on. How long did you stay? Was it that difficult? Were you ever hurt? Was it as expensive as you indicated?"

"Well, I cannot tell the whole story, but I'll give you a real short series of events and descriptions of what it's all about. I'll have to provide you with a little terminology too, so you can understand the three-year quest for El Toro—The Bull.

"Many do not understand how much luck is involved when you're an Americano competing with the locals. Some of the things I did were embarrassing, but necessary. For example, I had to have a calling card to present to the many operatives, including the organizers, the men in the cuadrilla, the ladies, the matrons, and yes, the bartender. I've got one here. It's kinda worn; take a look:

FORD G. HARRISON – Esquire.

Matador de Novillos

Hernando Colon   *At your service*

30, Sevilla, Espana

"Not bad, huh? Kinda takes me back to relive some of the 'good old days' when I run across it in my wallet. Well, wait a minute, they were not all good.

"I generally lived in a cheap second-floor walkup, whether in Spain or Mexico, since I was stone-broke and frequently lived on cold gazpacho soup. Why? I had no hot plate in the room. Now that's bare minimum living, but remember, I was invited out frequently to adorn the parties of wealthy matrons of the upper class. Nevertheless, it was not easy to do, especially when your character was that of a proud, athletic, and fearless matador in training. Eighty percent of my time was spent positioning myself for a chance to fight. And yes, an aspirant matador was constantly tempted by the daughters of the social elite who wanted to simply put a mark in their diary next to my name, got him tonight. That was not my reason to train; I was dead serious about getting fighting time in the bullring.

"As I mentioned earlier, there are many new terms related to bullfighting; it may be necessary to explain a few to understand the complexities of the business.

"The matador is responsible for *all* expenses in the battle with the bull. The entire compliment of the taurino battle, like you guys, is the Caudrilla, or team to support the matador.

"The Torero includes men engaged in the fight, whether matador, picador, peon, or banderillero—'a' for female. I had to hire all of them, only I was free.

"After the Corrida, the running of the bulls from the pens to the arena, six bulls were allocated to three matadors by random draw for the six flights of the day with the Senior Matador fighting the first and fourth, the Junior Matador fighting second and fifth, and the Aspirant Matador, me, fighting third and sixth. Yep, selection is a big factor; bribes were common to get a big bull with little action in his head and horns that curved in, and were blunt. I could not afford a bribe, so frequently I got two of the most dangerous bulls to fight. Yes, at a few arenas, I did hire a few thugs/peons to sneak into the pens at night or before the fight to bribe the rancher so he'd look the other way while the bulls selected for me had their horns filed down a bit to make them blunt. They also dropped one-hundred-pound bags of grain on their upper backs, from the walkway or loft, to weaken their neck muscles. This was done to level the playing field when I had drawn the worst bull possible. Sorry folks, that's the way it goes.

"It takes about twenty minutes to complete a fight, so I only paid the caudrilla for the two hours they had to be at the arena. It was extra if I failed to kill the bull and they were pummeled with beer, cushions, and debris from the angry spectators in the arena. Worse than that, if you did poorly and did not kill the bull after several thrusts and several swords, they would not work for you again. Not a pretty picture, is it? Well, I guess they throw things like an octopus on the ice at a bad NHL game, but it's a little more dangerous in the arena.

"Equipment is so expensive that I borrowed a padded and decorated matador uniform, skin tight of course, with a catcher's cup, but I did purchase a cape and muleta. The cape is magenta on one side and yellow on the other, and used by the two or three peons to work the bull, and also the matador to show his stuff while tiring the bull alone. This generally takes about ten minutes and serves another purpose: determining the head action of the bull. The muleta is a small red flannel cloth which is used with the sword as a support, hiding the death therein, and in the final phases is, of course, more difficult to use since the matador is closer to the bull.

"Am I boring you guys with all this detail and high-jinks of the bullring?"

"Heavens, no! Continue, please!"

"Okay. The fight is a drama in three acts. Starting with the picador weakening the bull's shoulder muscles on horseback, padded on one side by driving the pic, a twenty-foot pole with a barb on the end, into the shoulders, then the peons test the bull's head action and skill with the cape while the matador observes the action of the bull's head from behind the wall. By the way, a picador or peon is a has-been or injured bullfighter who is in his twilight years of fighting or an aspirant who never made the grade as a matador.

"Next, a younger or the fastest peon, then acts as a banderillero with a pair of decorative banderillas; he charges the bull, and at the last possible moment, thrusts the hooked points of the shafts into the bull's shoulders and spins out of the way. Sometimes he's so close, his colorful outfit is covered with caked blood that is weeping from the damage done by the picador's shoulder-weakening pic thrusts. Get the picture? There's more. A second pair of banderillas is thrust into the bull to ensure his neck and shoulder muscles are weakened.

"After the picador and banderillero have finished weakening the bull, a peon performs a few cape passes while the matador observes the bull's head action. When he's satisfied with the attendant's work, the matador struts into the ring!

"I acknowledge the senior person in the arena, normally a mayor or governor, and casually adjust the cape and prepare to challenge the bull by strutting defiantly toward the irritated and exhausted beast.

"The crowd roars with encouragement for both the bull and matador. I position my body as close as possible to the passing horns while working the bull with the cape with conventional passes . . . getting closer and closer; not only to fatigue the bull, but to please the crowd; I then challenge him with a veronica—it's executed with the cape held behind the body with both hands. I was also expected to show the bull my back, carefully, and also kneel in front of the 2,000-pound animal and dare him to charge . . . if he did, I would roll away with class and grace—of course. By now my legs and arms are tired and covered with caked blood from the close passes. At the right moment, when the bull is worn out, I would retrieve the muleta and sword from an assistant and prepare for the kill."

Leigh interrupted, "Do you have any film of killing a bull, or worse yet, being gored or tossed over a bull's head like I've seen in foreign newsreels?"

"No motion picture film—the State Department will not allow scenes that show killing the bull in U.S. theaters or TV. I do have lots of photos performing all the classic moves in the ring, and yes, some show me being damn near killed. Just think how much damage the bull could do if not weakened in the shoulders and neck . . . and exhausted by the time the matador performs the—coup-de-grace. Yep, that bull damn near killed me a couple of times.

"I could not afford to continue at the young age of twenty-three, always broke and sometimes broken from injuries, always begging for a chance to fight; I bid adieu to the chance of being a Great Senior Matador.

"You may not like this part: finally, the kill.

"With the sword wrapped by the muleta, the fight moved to the epilogue, or final act called the Faena. If everything went right, I would stand in front of the muleta extended, sword at my side, and when he charged with his last bit of energy to kill me, I would raise the sword and point it at his shoulders, right behind his head. In that position I was essentially challenging him to charge the muleta with the sword ready for insertion between his shoulder blades and into his lungs and heart. It was a waiting game, but he would charge. It was just a matter of time.

"Then it happened; I aggressively thrust the sword into the magic spot with as much strength as possible, step aside with a spin, and casually strut away, indifferent to the carnage that followed. If the sword was correctly inserted, the bull would stand in place, cough, vomit blood, wobble, fall to his knees, bawl, and roll over to die by drowning in his own blood. It is so grotesque to many production companies, it is seldom seen in the U.S. This type of kill earned the matador at least two ears and maybe the tail. In that case he would prance around the arena to receive accolades, wine sacks, flowers, hotel keys from the ladies, and acclaim—plus a guarantee of a huge fee for the next appearance. This is all happening as a team of horses drags the bull out of the arena to the local butcher shop.

"Conversely, if the peon had to help kill the bull, by spinning him around, or inserting an additional sword, you might be plummeted with debris and seat cushions and have to run out of the arena, and out of town! The bullfighting crowd does not embrace failure, but as with most sporting events, they forget, and you can appear again in a few weeks or in another distant arena. Most are half drunk when they're throwing things at you, and don't even know your name—just that you are a failed matador.

"Check this out. I knew one matador that stitched his own wounds between fights, doused the cut with sulfa, and returned to the ring—the bull's horns are filthy—to complete the appearance.

"Did you notice the word—appearance? That's what it is, much like a popular singer in the U.S. You are paid to entertain, and also kill the bull with skill; just as Johnny Cash was paid to sing very well, you are expected to kill the bull cleanly. But, after all the abuse the bull had been exposed to, he surely didn't have a chance. Right?

"One thing is for sure, I had a shot at it and will never have to say that I wish I had tried. I did. Well, that's probably more than you wanted to know about bullfighting and my attempt to break into the ranks; but remember, it's much like professional sports in the States. Many try—few succeed."

"Damn, that was a great story, sounds like something I'd have done too, especially the girls, parties, and travel to the arena of Iberia," exclaimed Jack.

"Men," Leigh said. "Some things never change. If you two were in the Garden of Eden, Eve would probably be hounded by both of you . . . eating all the forbidden fruit and probably slaying the serpent before it had a chance to report the mythical original sin!"

In unison, "Women!" the men pronounced.

After Ford's story-telling, the silence in the Tongass turned eerie. The stillness was palpable—not a whisper of the wind in the trees, or nary a rustle at higher elevation. That was unusual since the setting sun generally changed the thermal layers, and movement was expected as coolness acted as a catalyst and warmer air was displaced by cooler wind-driven breezes. Jack knew, the stillness indicated the presence of the spiritual; Manitou's spirit was among them.

The sky was clear and the evening stars were coming out with the moon and its friend Venus accompanying each other across the southern sky. Brighter than ever, poor old Polaris never had a chance to match her brilliance but was sure critical to guide all navigators, always being due North. Partial to Alaska, they all felt the sky was much easier to read north of the 50-degree latitude. It was true, since there was little particulate suspended in the air, and likewise very little light pollution. No one spoke. They reflected on the beauty and solitude of the moment.

Ford was worried about his health, his future . . . Jack was concerned about Ford's survival . . . Leigh was hoping Ford would survive the night . . . Boy's saddened eyes said what they all were thinking: Would all of us make it out together?

Ford felt alone, truly alone in the group of healthy hikers on the 'Root. His loneliness was not totally of their doing. He was isolated through their activity to save him, measuring his chances, and his inherent feeling of sinking away from the embrace of life. It is hard to feel alone with friends, but he was so preoccupied with the possibility of not reaching his personal goals, he collapsed on himself. Although not listening to his subconscious, it told him again and again that he had lost Leigh's true passion for him—to another man. He mused to himself, "I've got to break out of this depression and mental isolation that is separating me from my friends. I've got to stay connected."

Jack chimed in, "Folks, let's call it a day and get these tired bones into a horizontal tuck position." Then he moved about, policing for any food scraps that Boy had missed, and rinsed the dishes in the 'Root. Leigh made the fires safe and started organizing the tent's sleeping arrangement. "All set, Jack, the Ritz is ready for some big-time, tired-body sleeping!"

"Come down here, Leigh, and we'll tie off the fly for Ford's fart sack. I've just put some pine boughs down and with your help we can shoe-horn him in." To Jack's surprise, Ford was at the river's edge.

As Leigh walked to the river, she saw something at the river's edge. "Ford! Is that you? What the hell are you doing standing up over there by the water?"

Ford responded, "Oh, I'm just writing my name in the pool of water; not bad if I do say so myself. Just call me Michelangelo of the Tongass. I could even do the ceiling of the chapel, absent gravity, if asked to do so."

"Jack, get that character into the sack before he hurts himself. No more amateur-hour water painting tonight—men, just cause you have a pointer, you think you've got to use it for everything. Men!"

"Okay, I'll go. Not the rack again, please!" Ford cried.

"Now this kiss will get another in the morning—if you behave and get a good night's sleep. Love ya. Sleep tight; don't let the bedbugs bite." Leigh departed.

"Okay, do you have the clip in the gun and with you in the sack? And if so, don't hesitate to use it. And another thing, do not move around tonight. Stay put and get some rest, and no peeing without help. You know, we may be at a medical facility tomorrow. Good night, and don't expect a kiss from me." Jack tightened up the canvas fly.

"Can I pee . . . if Leigh helps? Just remember, my boy, I'll be asking Leigh in the morning if you've touched her; better not or I'll limp up to the tent and rescue her." Little did he know, he'd been hurt before and now . . . again; so be it, his current struggle was for life—not passion.

From Leigh in the tent area, "Jack! Quit talking; get up here and get to bed. You guys can talk tomorrow."

Jack yelled, "Okay! Come on big boy, take these pills from Dr. Jack, MD—meaning 'Mean Dude'—call me if you have any problems. Seriously, Ford, take care and sleep well. We both need you to recover. Good night, my dear friend."

As Jack moved toward the tent, he stopped, turned to the North Star Polaris, raised his hands and eyes to the sky, paused for a minute, and asked The Great Spirit to care for his friend through the night.

He quietly chanted to Manitou:

> "O, hale, Oh, hale! Awhiz haye,
> Shichi hadahiyago ninya,
> O, hale, Oh hale! Tsago degi nal eyea
> O, hale, O, hale!"
> (Through the air I fly upon a cloud toward the sky, far, far, far. There to find the holy place, and, now the change comes o'er me.)

Tribal Medicine song: *Find the Holy Place.*

The wind wooshed across the campsite and bent the young firs as the force of the wind seemed to race up the ridge. He watched as the tops of the trees moved . . . as if in concert with a rhythm of reverence. Was it the wind, the late hour, or the response to Jack's chant for the injured man by the river? Was the spirit responding to the Tlingit's message? You be the judge.

A raven perched on the tall fir at the river's edge—*Caw*. Strange for a raven to reveal himself so late in the evening. It appeared as if the bird was going to stay for the duration. Had Manitou sent the bird? As many know, Indian totems praise the sun and the raven and believe the raven has the power to change form as the Spirit wishes.

Boy laid his head on Ford's cheek, sensing he should not leave his side, nor sleep this night. He would stay close to protect his friend and just be with him tonight and as long as he needed his care.

It was later that evening that Boy raised his head as Ford's breathing became irregular . . . Boy lowered his head and hoped for the best.

It was not a good sign.

Chapter 11

Travail

"The lonely sunsets flame and die; the giant valleys gulp the night; the monster mountains scrape the sky, where eager stars are diamond-bright."

—Robert Service

Long before light introduced the morning and engulfed the site, a strange sensation of noiselessness enveloped the camp. The greatest of the tall trees and aspirant monarchs of the Tongass appeared motionlessness as eastern rays started to bleed through the openings like swords of light.

Ravens had transformed the wooded campsite with a spectacular display of dominance over the setting. On every available perch around the camp appeared a huge black bird in stoic silence as if part of totem. Yet, there was mysterious silence, no rustling of feathers, no cries, no movement, no sound at all. What did it mean? What had happened to bring the birds? Why here? Why now? Boy made the first sluggish movement.

Boy faintly remembered Jack checking on Ford's condition sometime in the middle of the night.

He repositioned his head on his master's arm that had fallen outside the bag during the night. He expected an immediate response as in the past when they slept together under the stars. There was no reaction. Boy repositioned himself more aggressively near Ford's shoulders. There was no acknowledgement. Boy stood and licked his face, as he had done so often when Ford claimed he had been overserved at the bar . . . but there was still no response.

Boy sat up, slinked around Ford's body, sat down, whined, sat up, whined again, then in frustration walked very slowly, head down, toward the small tent on the rise in the clearing. He stopped and looked back, hoping for movement under the fly . . . there was none; disappointed, he continued walking to the tent.

It was at this moment Boy seemed to notice the change in the din of the forest. The silence was deafening. He stopped dead in his tracks, squatted, and slowly looked up to the canopy of black in the dawn's early light. It was full of birds. He was puzzled, but he rose and continued on; he had an important mission; he continued as if knowing he had to get help for Ford. Something was terribly wrong. His master always responded.

The birds were not affected by Boy's presence. Nary a bird moved as Boy approached the tent. He listened and whined; no one was moving. No one seemed to be there to hear or understand his plea. He looked up again. He felt a sense of panic. He was not used to being alone. He looked back at the motionless fly and stillness of the little alcove by the river and the figure that remained. He looked at the tent entrance again and barked . . . nothing.

Panic took over his body now. *Woof! Wooof! Woooof!* . . . Frustrated, he jumped on the tent in a frantic effort to get some attention.

It was 0600 hours.

Again, not a sound by the birds. Did they know? Finally, Jack heard the commotion outside the tent. "Hey, big fella, what's up out there? I'll be out in a second . . . hold on!"

Jack unzipped the entrance flap and burst through clad only in BVD's, yawning, face in stubble, straggly hair hanging on his shoulders sans the normal exquisitely braided tail, and stocking feet. He exclaimed, "What are you looking for, Boy? How are you? How is it we are honored with a personal wake-up call? How's Ford?"

Boy would not let Jack pet him; he barked again and ran down to the river where Ford lay. Jack mused, "This is not Boy's normal 'I need some attention' act. It is not like him at all. His whole body is shaking like a leaf."

Boy barked while standing near Ford's motionless body. "Ford probably needs some help; don't worry; I'll be right there."

He threw some clothes on, then sensed the aura emanating from the campsite, a blanket of ravens in the trees. Perched without movement, without a sound . . . they were everywhere.

He finally realized what was going on . . . and what must have happened.

"Oh, no! Leigh, get up! Leigh!"

Manitou must have spoken through the ravens' presence. It was His way of speaking to mankind on Earth.

He remembered only too well how many tribal legends and prophecies place the raven at a grave or perilous scene. They frequently honor the passing of one of His followers and escort the subject to the mythical afterlife. A rebirth. A new life. In silence the ravens had spoken to those who knew of the ways of the Spirit. Clearly, there was soon to be a loss of life in camp . . . or there had already been one.

"Leigh! Leigh, get up! Leigh!"

Jack ran down to the river where Boy was looking at Ford as if on point. Boy's emotions were conflicted, and his unconscious behavior had taken over. He was confused; he now had a sickening look of sadness in his eyes. He knew.

Ford's appearance answered any doubts; he was gone, looking at peace, his skin tinted blue. His fingers, lips, and eyelids were the same color. This condition is called The Mask of Death.

Jack's fingers probed for his carotid; there was no pulse. . . . Ford's needs were past and Boy's in the present, so Jack held him to console the loss of his master.

Half-dressed, Leigh arrived at their side. She had not noticed the birds. Taking Boy in her arms, she held him ever so tight, for she too needed the support of a friend. Without a word to Jack, she knelt next to Ford and said, "Love you, dear; rest well; you fought the good fight; you fought hard and proud; your family would have been proud of your tenacity to live; you'll always be in their hearts and ours, too; my love for you is forever." She leaned over to kiss his cold lips. She stayed at his side, still holding Boy as the pines whispered in the wind as if a requiem mass in the timbers for Ford.

Jack stood in the shadows at a respectful distance to Leigh, Boy, and Ford. They needed some time alone.

Silence.

Moments later, he approached the trio slowly and spoke to Ford's body. "Buddy, your name will be recorded as an Alaskan legend—one of the brightest engineers, managers, and pilots; an entertaining man, unselfish, and one of the most talented personalities of the north. Rest well, my friend." Jack bowed his head in respect for his fallen comrade.

Silence.

"You'll be okay, Boy; come along."

"*Caw—Caw—Caw.*"

Now in flight, the ravens soared above the clearing to the thermals at 500 feet, silently circled, and with a muffling sound swooped low over the clearing, circled the treetops, fluttered in place, and rose again, then headed west as if a symbolic gesture of completion; their task had been accomplished.

An eerie silence followed their departure.

Boy, Leigh, and Jack stood next to Ford as if frozen in time. Jack surmised that a blood clot may have let go and passed to his lungs or heart, causing instant death. While standing in reverence, their experiences with Ford flashed across their consciousness from the mind's long-term memory.

Leigh noted, "He had such a good evening with us last night. He talked more about himself than ever before. He must have known. His pain must have been overwhelming. His passive, yet joking manner was another one of his masks to keep his personal problems from others. What will we do, Jack?"

Jack hesitated. "I see us in a difficult and anxious hike for life turning into a somber death march with a lifeless body to the coast. I'll try to call FAA again to report Ford's death, but don't expect to transmit successfully; I think the VHF radio is broken. I'll also start rebuilding the litter poles. You had better continue to give Boy some TLC, and start breaking camp."

"Okay. Come on, Boy, I'm now your permanent mistress. Not as good as Ford, but I'll try. Thanks to his perception of my needs, we're already off to a jump-start with our couple weeks together. Come on, baby, he's gone—we've got to move on. We tried; we all tried. It just was not to be; his injuries were worse than we thought, and the trauma caused by his hike-out was just too much. I believe you know, Boy, he died where he would have chosen—under the stars—in the forest he loved. Come on, Boy! Come on with your new mistress."

Boy would not move from the body. He showed his fangs to Leigh. She backed away from the confused canine.

"Jack, he won't leave him!"

"Okay, let him stay. Go break camp without him and I'll watch Boy while fixing the litter-carry framework down here by the river. Let's not rush him."

"Okay." Leigh broke camp in a robotic manner with her thoughts elsewhere: the trip to FFS in the summer; Ford's macho, "My way or the highway" assertive manner—before he met her kind; listening to stories about families' accomplishments; at the bench by the canal—what a bench it was—as they grew emotionally close; his beat-up knock-about Jeep that everyone recognized and asked, "Why does he drive that bucket of bolts?" She knew. He loved old traditional things that still worked; just look at the C-190 float plane; it was 20 years old—but reliable, except for the recent tragedy; the simple cottage; Skagway bars versus five-star restaurants, where it was hard for him to even pay for a drink; doing favors gave him *carte blanche* power of payment, or don't even try to pay—"it's on us"—and finally the baloney of christening the Big Bird's back seat the night she became his mistress of the Tongass. He was unabashedly full of bull crap at these times, but many let him get away with his skullduggery just to hear where the next story was going, and yes, many times right down the gutter. He always played hard and worked hard. He was also brilliant, in contrast; that's why so many loved him.

In reflecting on her beautiful experiences with Ford, she thought of her dad's favorite poem by Ardis Whitman, which he read often to her when events had not gone her way:

"Hope for the moment. There are times when it is hard to believe in the future, when we are temporarily just not brave enough. When this happens, concentrate on the present. Cultivate *le petit bonheur*, the little happiness, until courage returns. Look forward to the beauty of the next moment, the next hour . . . the likelihood that tonight the stars will shine and to-morrow the sun will shine. Sink roots into the present until the strength grows to think about tomorrow."

She did not move for ten minutes; she still lay supine on the packs at the campsite; she gazed to the clouds in the east, which she imagined were probably parked over her empty hut on the meadow. Designed by Ford and her, she would now call it H², Harrison's hut in his honor.

Jack walked part way up to the campsite. "Are you okay, Leigh?"

"Yes, I guess. So much has happened so fast since our lovely discussion last night—I just need time; I'll be there in a minute."

"Okay, babe."

Not sure of his status emotionally with Leigh, he did not go to her. She needed time, time to be alone, time to reflect, and time to think about the future.

He turned and walked back to the river to continue his task.

Leigh deserved time alone to work out their new relationship—and adjust to her loss of previous relationships.

Jack wondered where he would fit in her plans, or if there were any plans at all. Maybe not. He knew her as an independent, self-starting, smart woman who may have no plans for a long-term relationship with any man. After all, she came to Alaska to avoid individuals and groups, then became involved emotionally and romantically with both Ford and himself; he'd bet that was not planned, and that she had no playbook, but modified her behavior to fit the moment—you can do that after 60. Being beautiful didn't hurt either.

Jack thought about his recent relationship with Leigh and concluded that there seems to be a virginity that, in theory, you only bring *once* to a relationship. They certainly had *taken* that shot. Now that relationship was in the shadow of Ford's death and his memory. Respectfully, he would accept whatever emotional base she chose for the next few days. The first of those, while hiking out, were going to be very difficult physically as well as emotionally. Carrying Ford's lifeless body to the coast would not help her healing process. Then there would be the difficult union with Milt and Dave in Skagway and possibly his family after delivering the body to a mortician.

Jack silently petitioned The Creator, Manitou, to provide her spiritual support during her difficult days ahead. They would know more about Ford's personal requests . . . a will? . . . and details later with Milt and Dave.

"Well, Leigh, are you up to it? With any luck we'll be there tonight at sunset."

"Yep, what options are there? None. Let's go."

It was 0700 hours.

Boy was still distraught, which was expected, but his actions caused Jack some concern: growling and body language of aggression when they wrapped Ford in the poncho, tied it up, and transferred it to the pole. Boy could no longer see him, and that left him very infuriated, angry, and confused.

Jack just kept talking and consoling Boy as well as he could and maybe, just maybe, the dog would figure out Ford's demise, then shift his total affection to Leigh.

*   *   *

At approximately 50 degrees latitude north and one hundred forty degrees west, a hut by a meadow echoed an emergency call from a rescue plane. Leigh always left the receiver ON for emergencies that might arise near the camp. The speaker was broadcasting the following alert:

"C-190 with Ford Harrison, this is C-182 with Milt and Dave of FFS control relay; do you read? Over."

Silence . . .

"C190 with pilot Ford Harrison, this is C-182 Milt and Dave of FFS at 500 AGL, 50 miles inland on the Bitterroot Basin; how do you read? Over."

Silence . . . more silence . . . nothing.

Negative contact to C-190; this is FAA relay, to standby."

No one heard the transmission in the hut; no one heard the transmission along the river; worse yet the plane was 30 miles east of their location. Out of sight and line-of-sight, they would not have heard them anyway.

The Tongass Three, or should it be Two . . . were now unfortunately about 50 miles west of Milt and Dave and out of transmission range, just 20 miles from the DNR camp on the Pacific. It would have been nice for Milt and Dave to know where they were, and their condition, but realistically, in the wet Tongass rainforest, there would probably not be a rescue in the next 10 to 12 hours. They would most likely have successfully walked out of the rain-drenched wilderness by then.

Jack wondered: Which of us knows the direction of his/her life? What will tomorrow bring?

*   *   *

Still distressed, Boy growled again as the pole with padded ends was hoisted to Jack's and Leigh's shoulders and checked for clearance to the ground as they took a few steps. Leigh asked if Ford would start decomposing while being carried out. To which she received a quick "No," just swelling from gaseous buildup. Jack would not tell her, but he'd puncture his skin later, if needed, to relieve pressure and drain fluids.

"Looks okay to me, what do you think."

Leigh responded, "Fine, let's go; daylight is burning. Was that saying from you, Ford, or John Wayne . . . whatever?"

Jack sensed it was going to be a long day without much talk, for good reason; Leigh was still troubled and they were now cast in the position of unsolicited pallbearers, sans mortuary services.

Friends do what is necessary for their fellow man. Jack was not that close to Ford, but still felt much like the novelist McMurtry's character, Woodrow Call, in *Lonesome Dove*, with his commitment to his friend, Augustus McCrae. Call had given his word earlier to return McCrae's body to Texas if he didn't make it back on his own from their Montana cattle drive. Call followed through, as promised, and returned his body under extremely hazardous conditions. However, rather than one thousand miles on a buckboard through Indian Country, Ford's body had to be carried 20 miles to the coast, in big timber, through bear country. Luckily, transport from the DNR camp would be easier. Once there, provisions would be provided to fly Ford to Skagway. In fact, Milt and Dave would take over at that time . . . assuming they got there without difficulty. The only hindrances would be adverse weather, diminished physical health, and aggressive bear attacks; however, they had faith in the grace and vigilance of The Great Spirit, Manitou, along His path on Earth to the Pacific.

"Caw—Caw—Caw."

A lone raven dipped a huge wing at them with a hoarse cry of notice, an announcement most likely that he was here to provide protection and keep watch over their route to the coast.

"Greetings," Jack said to the raven. "You're certainly welcome to join us as we forge west. Let's go, Leigh. Come on, Boy!"

Silent and disposed in thought, the three moved along the 'Root. He reflected on Ford's life and thought of one of his favorite sayings by T. K. Whipple: "Study Out the Land."

> "All America lies at the end of the Wilderness road, and our past is not a dead past, but still lives with us. . . . We live in the civilization our forefathers created, but within us the Wilderness still lingers. What they dreamed, we live, and what they lived, we dreamed."

He mused to himself, "Dream on, Ford; we'll get you there soon."

Leigh's thoughts were internalized also. She wondered what her life would have been with Ford in Skagway while she was at her Walden in the Tongass stimulating her rebirth by writing and other adventures. Ford was to be part of the latter. Now, here she was trudging through the difficult terrain of the Tongass with Ford's lifeless body. Life was indeed complex. Yes, there is guilt, too. Whoever would have thought she'd be carrying a dead lover and walking with the other; life certainly was not fair.

This gentle man, the Tlingit, had been invited, and accepted somewhat carefully—with a little hesitation—an invitation into her adventure. Yes, it was while she still remained emotionally tied to Ford, but the romantic rules of behavior had changed for her after 60 years of trial and error. No, she did not live for the day, for tomorrow we die, as the soldiers of fortune claim; it was just that the rules become more vested in self-interest as one approaches the twilight of life. Yep, he was a gentle man and a good man, and she felt he would participate in some of her experiences over the next two years. Time would tell. Then again, she had sworn off men once or twice before. She certainly did not need a man around all the time! She would be quite happy alone, by choice, in her solitude. She mused to herself, "I sound like I'm over-compensating for the obvious; I do like men, but on my terms, which will never happen. Oh well, we'll see; it's hard to admit that you really do like 'em."

"What did you say, Leigh?"

"Nothing . . . just talking to myself, nothing."

Boy walked at the heels of Jack, rather than in the lead; he had lost the spring in his step and any interest in exploring their path. That was Jack's job now. He stopped frequently to gaze at the mass wrapped up in the green poncho that swung to-and-fro on the ropes tied to the game pole. He sniffed the lifeless body frequently to ensure himself of Ford's presence; it was sad to witness Boy's pain, for at times the swinging action of Ford's body struck Boy, and knocked him off his stride . . . unfortunately there was nothing to do to prevent this terrible scene as they walked in silence . . .

"How's it going, gang? Wanna rest awhile?" Jack said, sensing a need for a break. They had been hiking for four hours along the 'Root and seemed to be making good progress. "Well, it's about ten hours to the coast at twenty minutes a mile, which means arrival at sunset or at about 2000 hours. We've got our work cut out for us. How's the shoulder holding up, Leigh?"

"Not too bad; I shift sides frequently, and took my bra off since the nylon strap was roughing up my shoulders and hide; I replaced it with a handkerchief."

"Good idea; I'll do the same . . . with the handkerchief, not the bra; I need the support it provides ever since I had surgical implants."

"Glad you've got some humor left. Under these conditions I guess we'd better retain a little. Just remember, Romeo, hiking in this mist with these clothes on you'll see little of my natural breasts, sans implants, or the nipples through my clothes; they're too pooped to pop anyway. Wait, I take that back; present me with a warm fire, mulled wine, and soothing music—and my nips might swell a little."

Jack retorted with a chuckle, "At least now I know what that swinging noise is that I've been hearing back there; it's your a rocking and rolling chest!"

"Stop it, Jack. Men!"

Ignoring her complaint, he said, "Come on, Babe; let's rock and roll. It's good for our soul!"

As she groaned again, Jack still pressed the point, "Now, how to get Boy out of his funk. Look, he's a little better already; he knows we're at least talking to each other now. The silence over the last four hours had affected him, too."

Leigh replied carefully because Boy knew when he was being discussed; as with any three-year-old, his head would cock sideways and lean into the words; he was clever and his eyes and ears also revealed his understanding.

"Okay, Jack, let's grab some butt time on this old cedar log and I'll give him some TLC for a bit."

"Good idea. I'll call again, but I'm almost certain the hand-held transceiver is not working. FAA control, this is Jack and Leigh with deceased C-190 pilot Ford Harrison—about fifteen miles from the Bitterroot outlet at the coast—we continue to hike west to the DNR camp, over."

They discussed the possibilities of FAA hearing their call versus the unknown associated with the fact that they could be transmitting but not receiving—a remote chance, but possible. Maybe they knew what was going on below the canopy. Just maybe. So they tried again. No harm trying.

Jack repeated the call to FAA control, again . . . no response.

"Okay, Boy, let's go; come on, get up, let's get going!" He was having trouble getting the message; he had continued to lie on Ford, and preferred not to move . . . but that was not an option. Still reluctant, Jack moved over and carefully coaxed him to alter what would be considered normal behavior as guardian of his master's lifeless body. An admirable trait, but there was no time now for grieving here in the forest. Later, yes. He growled at Jack.

Observing the problem with Boy, Leigh had an idea. "Come on, fella. Milt and Dave are going to meet us soon and have some pizza and beer for you."

That did it. He leaped to all fours and looked at Jack, then Leigh, with anticipation of the old times at FFS. He had been with Leigh for two months, but his true buddies of the belly were at FFS, and he'd been raised on beer, pretzels, and pizza—not recommended by the AKC, but who cares among men in an Alaskan adventure. Not to worry about Boy's diet, Leigh added, his normal diet was supplemented with frozen road kill. Ford would butcher the tenderloins, backstrap, and hind quarters of a deer or elk, bring it home, and make damn good dog food for his friend. Leigh mused, Many a time Boy ate better than Ford. Still, she quickly refused Ford's offer for some of Boy's road kill *du jour*. "Why not?" he'd say. "I eat it."

They moved on with a little more spring in their step as the morbid shadow of the body was less of an issue to Boy.

As they moved on, the overcast sky cooled the forest floor. They tread in game paths seldom used by man. Intermittently, multiple lances of light lay on the trailside virgin sphagnum, untouched by man. The ropes on the pole tugged on the body with a sound not unlike the hawsers on a docked ship. Was there much difference? Both were lifeless—at dock.

An anvil thunder cloud approached from the coast, bringing rain with it, no doubt, as lightning flashed weirdly in the clouds and across the sky and to one another, again and again. The thunder followed, rolling among the sullen hills, and rain whispered among the darkened pines and over pitch-black swamps. Step by step they carried the body along the narrow way, each footfall taken with anticipation of what lay ahead. Lightning hurled its flaming glow against the hillsides again, ripping apart the curtain of the sky with writhing fire-snakes that raced along the naked ridges.

The hammer of the storm beat on their path; rain lashed their faces and pounded their backs. The forest was dismal, with a web of black branches interlaced overhead and a faint path marked by glistering pools of water giving the arbor the look of a cathedral with fonts below. In the distance the rain lay across the ridgelines like sheets of steel. A slight breeze stirred the few leaves remaining and rattled skeleton fingers among the bare trees. Anything and everything could turn against them in a moment's notice, even though progress was good so far . . . vigilance must be their constant companion.

Boy's improved attitude gave back an additional pair of keen eyes and sensitive ears for detection of the unknowns ahead.

Jack felt he'd have to work hard to maintain a positive attitude since the trauma of the last 48 hours had drained his perspective of his life path. It was as though he was waking up from a dream full of nightmares and felt a sense of losing touch. That involved being in touch with himself through mindfulness, meditation, and its applications for people whose lives were dominated by stress, pain, and illness.

As a Native American, he knew of that pain, so he meditated to understand it with Manitou's guidance. Leigh would certainly fit that mold now and in the future; she had suffered, and he could help her through meditation. The key to this life path lies not only with Native American belief, but also with the works of transcendentalists—R. W. Emerson and H. D. Thoreau, plus the explanation of many religious myths by Joseph Campbell. With this knowledge and appreciation for the present moment, he would cultivate an intimate relationship with her through a continual attending to her needs, taking nothing for granted. He would address Leigh's stress as they developed and not ignore her pain.

With this basic logic, his understanding of life was fundamentally about being in touch with his own deepest nature and letting it flow out unimpeded. It sometimes got him in trouble with his colleagues, since it had to do with waking up and seeing things as they were in the hear-and-now—such as Nature's blessings through the spirit of Manitou, teaching to be awakened to his or her own true nature. But he had always stressed not to automatically alter behavior to suit the mass logic of achieving position of wealth by violating known standards of self-control. All great scholars know how easy these options, if not carefully managed, cause pain and suffering.

Jack's meditation helped him on how to help people get out of life's current lack of planning as so often happens by just sitting on the bank, listening to the flow, and not learning from those mistakes, and then just moving on to a better life. He knew very well that one who has position and wealth must have a purpose, and perspective through formal or informal meditation to help in life's constant trials. The divine is internal—within—and not as inculcated by varying institutional religious myths that frequently change for the needs of the ruling elders.

His awareness of his life's path was triggered by Leigh's passionate approach a few days ago. Did it fit? Was it acceptable? Would it result in problems greater than the gain? He reflected . . . guess not. He did get involved one night, but knowing very well a long-term intimate relationship must be closely examined and did not automatically embrace personal needs. Lust is unconscious thought that must be placed in the category of mindlessness—yet okay, in certain circumstances. Was *Leigh* that circumstance? He would soon enough discover the answer—as the loss of Ford modified the formula of heartfulness to provide hers, if any, for a man, and his, if she chooses to reach out to him. Their relationship remained complex, for sure.

He trudged along, engrossed in his private thoughts, so quiet; the next sound he heard startled him.

"Jack, are you okay? You have not spoken for a long time; are you okay?"

"Yeah, just mulling over the last two days; it's as if a bad dream has turned into reality."

"True."

"Though we may resonate on different spiritual frequencies, I was in quiet contemplation with the Spirit while in this solitude among nature's beauty. I was reflecting on my forefathers' teaching and my experiences in life, and especially the last 48 hours, while trying to gain spiritual understanding to clarify truth and how I can turn my vision into reality. I feel our need for each other to complete this task will lead to a warm, loving, and intimate relationship. I now feel deeply for you, and would take pleasure in serving you in practical ways. It is the way of our people and our fellow man. We speak our minds."

A pause . . . silence.

He added, "But let me suggest to you, these are my feelings that incorporate my peoples' openness to emotional truth. Your mind is clouded now by necessary things. So find your peace. Discover what is in your heart, and when it is in bloom for me, call. I will know and come to your side and give you my heart."

"Well, I'm so glad I asked! That was lovely, Jack. I'm impressed with our emotional openness; I'm almost in tears from your tender and direct message. It was not only captivating, it was *lictio divina*, of divine words; and yes, after we move through this period in the darkness of death and into the light of life—and a bloom for you swells in my heart—I will call, and you'll soon find a thousand petals of my caring flower captivating your heart. Thank you, my dear," Leigh sighed.

"Thank you," Jack said.

Silence.

More silence—but there were many internal thoughts about Jack's comments. At this point in time, their decisions for life's path were still on the personal level, uncertain, and did not require speech. Both of their thoughts had been spoken with eloquence.

More silence.

Above the rim of the farthest range, at the terminus of the coastal mountains, a dramatic new weather system enveloped the peaks. Afternoon winds picked up moisture from the Pacific; as if a wall, the pink fog rolled across the range to the east, obscuring the sun and driving it in a heaving and moving pattern through the Tongass. It happened so quickly; it was as if someone had turned half the lights off.

It was 1300 hours.

A weather change along the coast could cause problems for the trio. The fog was now so thick, vision was limited to less then 50 meters. Long-range sightings would not be available for validation of navigation to the coast.

This was not good, Jack said to himself; they sure didn't need any additional variables. The shocking lack of vision and illumination occurred so rapidly that even the birds stopped their hustle, bustle, and fluttering among the lower limbs of the canopy. The jay's call was also muted. The squirrels no longer chattered and leapt across them. The wind that shooshed across the old firs now stood silent as in military formation, ramrod straight, without motion. The fog looked as if alive. The entire forest turned into a tranquil cloud on earth.

The sky was now dark gray with a western sun painting a rainbow of colors like with a paintbrush peeking through the moisture in alternating streaks of red, orange, yellow, green, blue, indigo, and violet as if afire. This spectacular show was always noted by forest denizens and hikers who always stopped and stood in awe of the power of this dramatic natural phenomenon.

However, the splendor of the fog did not help Jack's and Leigh's—the J&L plan—plan to move to the coast in an expeditious manner. They could only see about 20 meters now. They were socked in along with the animals, birds, and airplanes of the area. It was time for most animals to lie low and wait for the front to pass through. But that was not an option in the J&L plan; they must keep moving through the encumbered paths of the Tongass.

"Jack, what are we going to do? Isn't the fog too dense to travel?"

"Yes and no. We're close enough now that the game trails are more defined and easier to find and follow. That's the good part, since I know this area very well. The bad part involves not being able to see any animal we may want to avoid. A skittish moose, prowling cougar, or angry grizzly bear could certainly sneak up on us now. All three animals would feel threatened due to the lack of vision, and we as an unexpected surprise would startle their feeding. Yes, that includes the black bear, too. However, blacks are more predictable and normally take off to avoid man's penetration into their lairs. Another queer factor of a stationary front such as this is the lack of wind. As such, an animal cannot scent us downwind and flee. We could just happen upon them and scare the hell out of them. That could be lethal to us.

"Well, let's go, and let me suggest we both watch Boy's head, ears, and general body language, for he'll hear and smell changes in the trail before we do. Vision, in this case, is better for us, since we're about five feet higher and I know the overall lay of the land."

"Didn't you say some of the DNR's DNA collection/rub-cribs are along the 'Root through here?"

"Yep, this ten-mile stretch is frequented by many bruins as they migrate through and visit the river where the salmon spawn in the late summer. The salmon run is over now, but it was an excellent placement for their rub-crib used to gather hair samples. I do believe they also use molasses to draw them in, so they may linger for a little dessert, too. Now that was a dumb thing to say; we could be their dessert."

They forged ahead on a wider and improved trail, but Leigh was starting to show signs of fatigue and soreness in her shoulder and back, not to mention her legs, which were unaccustomed to hiking for hours. It had been seven hours over rough terrain that had no effect on Jack, but was taking its toll on her body. A nighthawk swooped low—probably confused with the darkness in the fog.

Jack stopped, and they rested. "The fog thickens.."

"True . . . unfortunately," she responded with her heart loudly beating out the sadness from the emptiness within.

"Leigh, do not fret; before us lies a black forest of desolation and terror, but tonight we will tread the shores of the Pacific. I will be your guide and protector." Then in a voice that scarcely seemed his own—and surprised him—he said, "We will be together someday."

In the thickening fog, there was a moment, a moment when neither moved or spoke, but simply stared at one another across the pole; they were mutually astonished by Jack's words. The moment arrested time, and then she spoke quietly. "We will look at the stars together . . . when we escape the clutches of the forest . . . and then see where the stars lead our hearts."

"I will deliver you safely, and the stars will rule in my favor, and I will have you forever."

For a moment they were eye to eye; then he turned and they swept away to the path in the fog.

He mused over his abrupt pronouncement to Leigh. Was he influenced by his favorite writers of historic romantic literature? It did occur to him that many authors gave romantic advice to lovers. As when the prince is wooing the lovely princess, he advised:

> "A man need know but two sentences to survive:
> First tell the woman his need for food.
> Second to tell her he loves her.
> If he must dispense with one or the other, by all means let it be
> the first.
> For surely, if you tell a woman you love her, she will feed you."

Leigh was hesitant to say anything; it had been a tense few moments, but she knew her feet were blistered, her shoulder bruised, and now her neck hurting.

All that concerned Jack was extraction from the Tongass, ASAP—today—at dusk . . . before the blackness of evening. He did ask of her condition at times, but just assumed that she was in good shape; she was not. She had decided earlier not to say a word until reaching the camp at the coast; physical pain she could accommodate; it's the emotional strain that was difficult.

Jack froze in place. Boy growled while slinking forward.

"Hey, what's up?" Leigh asked. "What's up? Did Boy see something?"

"Yes, he's going on point now and not responding to my command. Let's hold up and wait here a moment. Are you okay?"

"Yep."

"Okay, new rules with the fog and Boy's point; unsnap your gun retaining strap on the holster and be ready; you never know."

Leigh sighed, another problem—she had her own .44, and didn't even want to carry Ford's .45, but Jack insisted. He felt with Ford's body slowing them down and their intrusion through the bruin's navigation route, it warranted both being armed—to the teeth.

"What is it, Jack?"

"Not sure; hold tight. Boy is creeping forward now. I'll put my gun at the ready with a round in the chamber. *Kerchunk.* Did you get yours ready to draw?"

"Yep."

Crack-Shuffle-Leap-Bound-Stomp-Stomp-Stomp.

Boy looked back at Jack with a look of relief and pride as a huge bull elk crashed through the fallen logs and underbrush toward the river, then disappeared into the fog-laden borough below.

"Thank goodness," said Leigh. "I've never been frozen in time like that, and sure enough I had my hand on the forty-five all the time."

"Okay, let's continue on," Jack said. "We've got our work cut out for us and you know why; we'll have many encounters like this because Boy can't pick up a scent at distance in this fog, and as I said earlier the animals can't scent us very well, either; we can't see very well and they are blinded, too. Add another factor—we're moving on their trails, and population density thickens near the coastal flood plains of the 'Root."

"Do you have *any* good news?" Leigh asked, shaken. "This is terrible weather."

Jack answered, "No. Hang in there, Babe."

As they moved on, Leigh reflected on the absurdity of her current plight. If they failed to reach the DNR camp, she couldn't fathom the complexity of an over-nighter with Ford's body starting to bloat. She was aware of life's unfairness, but this—all she wanted was her two- to three-year Walden alone by the meadow. Despondent, she continued trudging through the dark, dreary, rain-soaked swale with Jack.

She had enjoyed a wonderful life, and certainly was not a fatalist, but she realistically assessed her current plight and remembered one of Montaigne's writings that applied to her predicament.

> "Whenever your life ends, it is all there. The advantage of living is not measured by length, but by use; some have lived long, and lived little; attend to it while you are in it. It lies in you, in your will, not in the number of years, for you to have lived enough."

She never thought her life would exist on such a slippery slope that she'd feel as though she was not just chum for the grizz of the Tongass, or BB: "bear-bait."

Maybe she was overly concerned about the remaining six-mile trek. The fog seemed to be getting thicker, Boy more responsive to scents and sounds ahead. Jack, now with gun in hand, made for an uneasy state of affairs. What did Jack know that she did not? If asked, she knew what he'd say, "Better be over-prepared so the unexpected can be served."

"*Caw—Caw—Caw*," a fog-hidden raven cried.

"Well, you're still with us, friend; bless you, Manitou." The symbols that influenced Jack, whether a raven, thunder, a wolf, or other natural events, varied in their purpose. Some were sent to arouse, others to warn of violence, some to alter actions leading to . . . submission. These symbols stood alone and did not seek to integrate with a person's religious doctrine or secular group-consciousness. They sought to liberate man from any state-of-being that was too fixed or final. In other words, they concerned man's release from confining patterns of existence—or transcendence of traditional thought.

Jack had become a shaman, a medicine man, whose practices of intuition stamp him as a master of leaving the body to understand the needs of Manitou's domain. In this case, the bird that just spoke was a symbol. It represented the peculiar nature of the Spirit's capability to know of distant events, or facts, of which those involved knew nothing—but were alerted by the bird's presence. The bird's call could be a warning to be careful, or to immediately terminate their actions. Jack's insight and training gave him the knowledge to know whether or not to proceed.

One thing was certain from reading Leigh's body language: under these conditions, her search for adventure was being over-served.

However, being with Jack had a special consoling significance. He was one of the few men for whom the unattainable had been met, and he had a special attraction, ambition, strength, and spiritual faith strong enough to cast aside the doubts of his mysterious past. They had many common traits including faith in themselves, great determination, and love of their fellow man. Plus, if anyone could get through this fog to the coast, it would be Jack. That kept her focused on enduring the fatigue, shoulder and neck pain, and fear as they forged ahead.

It was 1500 hours.

At times the trail opened up into small plains only to contract into a thicket of slender, quick-growing, yellow-leafed poplars of the willow family. Boy's ears were working as if another appendage as he scanned the surroundings, bobbing up and down like a radar dish swings at an airport as if to say, "Something's out there—I hear it but can't see it! I know it's there, but this dampness makes its scent almost neutral. Damn fog!"

Silence embraced the trio as they journeyed through the thicket; all eyes and ears were tuned to anything unusual in shape or sound.

More silence.

Jack broke the tension by shouting, "Leigh! How's that lovely body holding up?"

"As well as can be expected under these conditions. Every tissue in this body is as tight as a drum, and and boobs to lie down and be quiet, so as not to arouse you and your animal instinct."

"Ah, yeah . . . just wondered."

"Well you can wonder no more; keep your mind on that trail ahead, and I'll take care of the rear, and I don't mean yours!"

It worked, he said to himself; he felt he had to get under her skin to break the tension. She could shift her emotional strain to him and get their current plight off her mind for a while. Bawdy talk does that to women; it gets their hair to stand up on their puritanical necks—always has, always will. One thing for sure, it was normal for her to be on a worry route with the extremely dangerous conditions they faced. He felt he must keep doing something to keep her mind off the perilous path she was riding. She would need a distraction or two, for the fog was getting thicker and the willow denser as they moved into a thick swale on the edge of a clearing. They would need to be alert to survive the next five miles to the DNR camp.

Due to the seaside conditions of temperature change along the coastline, the fog was getting thicker as they approached the Pacific.

An eerie silence continued to embrace the clearing ahead.

It was 1600 hours.

As they traversed a small swale, Boy turned his head suddenly, and his eyes changed to brittle, yellow, demonic-like jewels, seemingly full of fear and aggression. He spun and raced toward and around her while uncharacteristically aggressive, knocking her off balance and bounding toward the rear. Leigh fell sideways and crashed into the underbrush. The weight of Ford's body and pole on her shoulder drove her down with his lifeless body, now lying on her legs.

She saw Jack, who had dropped his end of the pole, race by, pistol drawn with the same terror in his eyes that Boy had revealed.

"Stay down!" was all Jack said as he started firing. She leaned up at the waist with the pole still across her body and looked down the trail. To her horror, Boy had just jumped at a huge Brown Bear that must have back-tracked and sneaked up on them from behind in the dense fog; at the instant she looked, Boy was savagely disemboweled with one swipe of the claws on the deformed forepaw of the powerful bear.

"Yip!" was the only sound heard as Boy went down with a dire, lifeless, slumping, fatal wound. His entrails flew out of his body cavity over the bear's shoulder.

"Come back, Boy . . . Come back!" Jack yelled, emptying the entire clip of nine rounds into the charging terror. He was trying to scare him away. She thought she would, in fact, no longer be here if Boy had not turned and attacked. She was last in line and would have been the first to be hit if he had not run by her to attack the bear.

"Christ." Now kneeling, pistol in hand, Leigh had the misfortune to witness the bruin continuing the charge after being hit with many of the nine rounds. He stood, leaped, and grabbed Jack as he pivoted to withdraw, but he was too late; the bruin enveloped his body first with one paw and then the other as Jack struggled and struck the bear's snout with his empty pistol. The bear reacted violently to his blows, bellowed, then slammed Jack to the ground and quickly bit his neck, breaking it with a crunching, snapping sound.

Jack lay immobile.

The bear looked up, roared, and swatted again at his wounds in frustration—then with wanton abandonment bit Jack's head viciously; it was a merciless disregard for life.

Jack's lifeless body made no sound as the bear rolled it over and over again with a paw, then lay motionless as the bear roared and gurgled blood through his muzzle.

His baleful tiny red eyes dimmed as he coughed again, as he pawed the ground, then stood facing Leigh.

Screaming at the bear, she fired again and again at the hairy mass.

Now twisting and clawing his body wounds, the bear staggered and stumbled into a tree at a full gallop, then started to bite at the bark, his wounds, and the lower limbs in a rage. He spun again, coughed blood, and collapsed to his knees, tumbling over and over in the once verdant sphagnum moss . . . now blood red. He struggled to his feet, stood on his hind quarters, roared again, froze in place, looked around as Leigh's final rounds struck the bear's chest . . . and fell backwards to die with the sound of a rasping gurgle of death. It was over.

Silence embraced the clearing, the trail, and Leigh.

The carnage had now taken everything she loved.

She slowly emerged from the ferns, ran to the clearing, and stood next to Ford, then walked over to find Jack and their faithful dog, Boy—and finally the murderous bear. Breathless, she broke down. It all happened too fast.

She started to shake as she glanced at the killing fields along the trail of blood and entrails. "How could all this happen in less than thirty seconds? How could this happen to us? We were so close to the coast. Why me?" she cried. Her two close friends and their dog were taken from her. Boy had charged again to save their lives, and Jack to save her life . . .

"Dear Lord, why? Manitou . . . please help me!"

Hyperventilating now, her breathing accelerated much too fast. Her vision tunneled . . . turned gray, and narrowed to a black hole; she could not overcome the immensity of the tragic events any longer. Her system was about to shut down for her own protection. Nature took its course, and prior to true cardiac arrest—her eyes rolled up . . . and she passed out and collapsed on the bloody trail in the Tongass. Her body lay crumpled as if it were a rag doll.

She was in shock.

An eerie silence embraced the killing fields.

A raven appeared in the clearing . . .

"Caw—Caw—Caw."

Chapter 12

Determination

The sword-like shards of sun penetrated through the base of the clouds. The front had passed through an hour ago, and Leigh's recall of earlier events was uncertain. Slow to awaken and very confused, she felt cold and moist as she sensed the presence of the afternoon's low angle rays on her face. The sun was trying to pierce through the tall timber and cast its pillar-like shadows on the entire scene. She detected an eerie feeling in the forest. She sensed it, felt it, and now she heard it. Almost afraid of the consequences, she opened her swollen red eyes.

"*Caw—Caw—Caw*," cried a raven among the flock.

The birds had returned. She heard the rustle. Hundreds of birds encircled the killing field below. Recalling the afternoon's carnage, she quickly raised her head, lunged to her knees, jumped to her feet—only to be shocked again at the horrific sight along the trail. She looked away . . . then remembered only too well the bruin attack and resulting loss of life. Body aching, mentally bewildered and confused, she stumbled across the blood bath in search of Jack.

He now lay at her feet as if resting in the afternoon sun.

"What am I going to do? Why was I saved?" She mused, "I'll tell you why. Both Boy and Jack ran by me and attacked the charging bear—Boy leaping to his death—Jack firing and charging the bear, in a frontal attack. That's the reason I'm still here. They saved me.

"Somehow, for some reason, I just don't like myself after all this. Ford's death could also be linked to me. It was, in part, my doing, too. Why?

"When he descended with Big Bird and the elevators jammed, it was to buzz me at the meadow. It was to signal Boy and me that he was passing through. It would not have happened otherwise; I just know it. He'd have just routinely flown to Skagway. I know it! I just know it!"

She still mumbled to herself while walking among the carnage . . . still placing blame on herself.

"Now look. Just look at this massacre. Look at what I've done. Look at my negative influence on man . . . on mankind.

"I'm not worthy of this life.

"It may happen again.

"This may happen again.

"I'm sick . . . sick of it all."

Her vomitous upheaval was brief but complete, as she retched again, and again; her headache worsened.

Now at Jack's body, she said, "Jack dear, thank you. You saved my life—I love you." She looked around for Boy.

Silence enveloped the clearing.

Now at Boy's side, it was difficult looking at his disemboweled body; the memories of his love overwhelmed her. She moved away in disgust of the waste, the absolute waste, the cherished value of Boy's shepherding that saved her life.

"Thank you, dear; you'll always be in my heart—I love you, Boy."

The sun drenched her movements as she moved across the clearing in the shards of light. She approached the demonic fur-bearing monster, screaming at the top of her lungs:

"God damn you, son of a bitch! Bastard!

"What the hell did we do to you?

"You bastard!

"You've killed everything I loved."

She fell to her knees in disgust, withdrew her pistol—*Ka Pow, Ka Pow, Ka Pow . . . Ka Pow!* and emptied it into the bear's lifeless body. She rose, walked around the carcass while reloading and kicked him in the face, the rump, and his ribs.

"In thirty seconds you've screwed up my life, you bastard." She leaned over and examined the gigantic mass of fur, claws, muzzle, and teeth caked with blood. Upon closer examination she noticed the mangled front paw. This may be the bear that Jack had had a run-in with while in the blueberries. She also wondered if it could have been the bear that Boy attacked in the swamp by the hut. The wound appeared to be that of a wire foot-snare, causing a deformed, swollen, infected, and torn paw. The bear must have been caught earlier—who knows when, and by whom. The bear must have broken loose and suffered ever since . . . and been filled with hatred.

"That gave you no right to attack us, bastard!" she cried.

The clearing maintained its silence but for the whispering pines. She moved over to the game pole and Ford's body; not knowing why. . . . She had enough pain. Did she talk to him? To see if he was okay? Who knows?

It was 1800 hours.

Staggering back to the center of the butchery, she tried to concentrate on some action, some resolve, some move to attend to the crisis in front of her . . .

She cried at the top of her lungs. "Please. God . . . Manitou . . . The Creator! Whoever, whatever legend or myth is out there—please! Please provide me some peace—please! I see ravens as a representative of your Spirit—so please give me some guidance—please!"

She collapsed again in a veil of tears and emotional pain.

*   *   *

It was now 1815 hours; fifteen minutes had elapsed since the worse experience of her life. A strange and silent movement took place while Leigh's face lay buried in her hands.

It happened.

In a flutter of clatter, ravens descended from their perch in the canopy to the forest floor—just as quickly, an owl mysteriously appeared in their place. The forest turned silent. Suddenly, she felt the birds' presence next to her, then looked around and up toward the perched white owl. Before she could completely comprehend what had taken place in the clearing, the owl spoke:

> "My child, you have been part of and witness to many traumatic events in your life; and this may the worst. But remember, the shadow of death was not of your hand; do not give up; hold your course; do not fret; the pain will depart. Attend to your departed friends. Do find your inner self and be strong. My child, you will overcome this grief because I know you are strong. Continue your quest of discovery in the land you love; solitude will be yours.
>
> "Now go, my dear, be at peace and continue the love in your heart for all. You will survive."

Speechless and motionless, she felt as if every eye was on her from the hundreds of birds on the ground and the Great Spirit's representative—the owl—in the tree. The wind started singing again in the treetops.

Then suddenly, with a swoosh, the birds leaped into the air, circled as before, descended, circled the clearing again, rose to the thermals in the West, and vanished. She looked to the majestic fir to see the owl, but he, too, had disappeared. Silence returned to the clearing.

Was she dreaming? Hallucinating? Or had the Great Spirit sensed her anguish and interceded to calm her soul and remind her the carnage was not, in fact, of her doing.

What was His mandate? Was it the shadow of death reflected today as typical, and the expected exposure she would experience in the Alaskan wilderness lifestyle? Didn't she know about the hazards of planes, weather, and carnivores? Did He imply that trauma is a part of Alaskan life? So maybe His message was to tell her she must forebear this exposure, and to continue her quest of solitude.

Reflecting on all that had just transpired was difficult; she wasn't even sure of what she had experienced. She thought, Many Bible stories, legends, and myths relate similar messages from the Gods or God. And certainly, Manitou's appearance in the form of an owl was just what she needed to forge on and understand what really happened.

Still feeling the guilt of survival, she sadly mused, "There would have been no remote crash, without immediate help, downstate, in the city. There would not have been a need for Boy or Jack to intercede in the city. Conversely, there had been an earlier bear attack, and they were in bear country. Christ, maybe I should just give up and go back to the mess of city living."

She thought . . . and silence permeated the now sun-drenched clearing. "Hell, no. I'm staying, at risk . . . yes. I chose this location, and I'm damn well going to stay! Death of this magnitude was not planned, nor will it likely repeat—so stay I will—and if death visits me I can say that I have stayed the course to live my life as I choose.

"As with mythical Biblical voices from the burning bush, I surmised that when mankind is on the edge of life, and all looks hopeless, as with me, many imagined and wishful dioramas are visualized. I'm just not sure what happened a moment ago, but something somewhere heard me, and through my belief, need, and/or leap of faith, sensed an audience with Manitou—through the owl—was necessary. I needed my head screwed on straight, and he did it.

"Oh, believe me, it was not on that tight yet, but now it was at least attached a little better. I understand now. I no longer desire death with my friends."

Silence embraced the bodies and standing survivor in the setting sun. She heard a sound . . . a repeating percussion-like beat. She looked to the distant western horizon, leaned into the sound, and strained her eyes. In the valley below she heard a rhythmic beat of a drum, a deep-throated base drum, as if spirits echoed across the ridgelines. *Drruum . . . Drruum . . . Drrumm . . .*

It was beautiful . . . spellbinding in tone, rhythm, and cadence. Straining to the West again, she picked up another melodic complementary accompaniment . . . a musical flute rippled its high-pitch song through the ether. It was a hollow, wooden, hand-made, pipe-like resonance as its slow-moving notes permeated the clearing.

She reflected on Jack's comments by the fire one night. "The spirit frequently comes in the form of music as well as an animal form . . . and speaks when the souls of His fellowmen are in a crisis."

This symbol, she presumed, represented help from what Jack called the four directions. She never asked him details about certain spiritual things, for she thought there would be time later to learn more about the spiritual ways of medicine men and shamans. He also said four-leggeds and two-leggeds are visited by the musical spirit to realign their approach to other cultures and creeds for peace and support; he said we must shed our exploiting of each other. It is time for forgiveness and wisdom to replace false fear, mistrust and narrow-mindedness, even for the Washichu.

She remembered his comments very well, and being Washichu (white person), she took his advice to heart.

She remembered Jack's instructions for the ritual in responding to a spiritual visit of music . . . *Let me see; I kneel, face the direction of the music, and sing my response.* She faced the western horizon, knelt, and sang the following:

> "Great Spirit,
> thank you for your visit.
> Behold me,
> for now I am in
> a sacred manner.
> I will walk
> in your wisdom.
> Behold me."

The spiritual music of a melodic flute and rhythmic drum continued, and in time slowly faded as the sun cleared the horizon and chased the Pacific shore.

She remained kneeling in place while contemplating her next move.

It was 2000 hours.

"Can you believe what I'm expected to do? Stay alone, with two departed friends and lovers; my loving dog, Boy; a demonic bear; all overnight—damn it. Plus, the Spirit tells me it's time for forgiveness, eliminating mistrust, and false fear among His animals . . . yet everything I've experienced has been very traumatic, frightful and horrid . . . and laced with death. Oh great one, I'll try to impart your wisdom. I'll try.

"Leigh, get yourself together. Shape up; you've got double, no triple, the responsibility; look at the bodies, so shape up, get a hold of yourself.

"Okay, for Christ's sake—what's first?"

She started planning:

Communications: "The radio doesn't work, so I'll use a fire to signal my location."

Protection: "I'll retrieve Jack's nine millimeter, and I've already gotten Ford's forty-five."

Shelter: "I've got Jack's tent, plus his trail gear."

Light: "Let's see—three flashlights, matches, and flint; plus a signal fire should do the job."

Food: "No problem; I'd better be out of here by tomorrow."

Sleep: "Yep, Jack's bedroll will do, but I don't see me sleeping much."

She mused while gathering wood, "I can't believe the predicament I'm in. Six miles from help, yet isolated overnight in bruin country and unable to move without my male companions—all dead, at 200 pounds or more.

"If I can just get through the night, somehow I'll get out with or without the bodies. I'll solve that problem later on; on to the first priority now: a signal fire, or fires. Yep, I'd better build two. Multiple fires are better for rescue/signaling, and they lighten the clearing a little more for defensive reasons. Scavengers will most likely sense the blood scent downwind and probe the site of the carnage tonight.

"It's wet enough that sparks won't be a problem, so I'll start a pair at about twenty feet apart and put the sleeping gear on the third leg of the triangular footprint in the clearing."

Leigh approached Jack's body.

"Okay, fella, I've got to get this rucksack off; here you go, over now, easy does it." Rigor had taken over his flexibility, adding to her anguish.

"You fool, quit talking to the dead. No, you're no fool; you'd better talk as a means to maintain any sanity out here. Okay, now you're talking back—answering yourself—idiot." She smiled at herself through tear-swollen eyes.

"When isolated and recovering from shock, it is absolutely okay to talk to yourself and trade ideas and opinions," she moaned.

The tent up, she could now inventory Jack's pack, and, as expected, all the items she needed were there: flashlights, food, knives, matches, rope, bedroll, and ammo. What a guy, she thought, a true one in a thousand; a Winchester man will tell you what it means.

"Oh . . . I'd better retrieve the nine millimeter before dark. Here it is."

While cleaning the blood, dirt, and debris off, she reloaded the 9mm clip, slid it into the grip, and laid it on the bedroll outside the tent, then reloaded the .44.

While she dragged smaller and then larger dead limbs to the fire, many a disturbed rodent scurried away, each one sounding to her like a bear. She was still too keyed up, and expected the unexpected to a fault. Yes, it seemed silly, but she had Ford's .45 in hand while retrieving limbs and logs for the fire. With adequate wood in place, she started both fires and dug a perimeter trench around each, with a pointed limb to prevent grass creep beyond the base of the fire. She did not need a forest fire; her plate was already too full.

In due time the fires licked the evening sky at ten feet provided the needed illumination for her next task—consolidating the bodies in the center of the triangle. A nighthawk joined in the sparks, darting, twisting, and dipping for insects. She needed a large fire to ensure that no other animal would be scavenging the campsite, so she kept piling on variously sized logs. The blood scent was not obvious to all carnivores in the area; whether they came in or not is another story. Many animals, including bears, would walk over carrion to get to juicy tubers in a swamp. But a person never knows . . . yes, a sorry state of affairs. Leigh was at this point in time guarding carrion . . . sickening, but true.

Using a thirty-foot nylon rope, she pulled Jack into the center area first and covered his upper body and face with his coat. Trying to be tough did not stop the tears from falling on his face as she covered him. She pulled Ford over with the twenty-foot pole and laid him next to Jack. She couldn't see him in the poncho, so the emotional impact on Leigh had diminished, but he was still present in her heart . . . and always would be. Tasks like these were especially difficult . . . when alone.

The dog was next. He looked grotesque lain open as if a tin can. She severed his hanging viscera, threw them on the fire, and pulled him over to the pile.

She rested while thinking how gross a memory this scene would imprint on her soul. Her next task would be more difficult. The bear lay thirty feet to the west near the tree he had tried to debark during his death throes.

"One way or another, you're going to move where I want you, hairy fat-ass. If I have to slice you up into little pieces, I will; your ass is grass. You will be moved!" At about 400 pounds, the bear was too heavy. Her hands, waist, and shoulders were not strong enough, and traction on the wet grass diminished her ability to pull. Undaunted, she yelled, "You son of a bitch, I'll tear your ass apart. You will be moved."

So very much alone, in the dark of the Alaskan night, she thought, "I must live . . . and stay alive; I must be brave, but more than brave."

She reflected on the writings of one of her favorite historic novelists whose protagonists were frequently isolated, alone, and afraid in a strange land—just as she was, with but a weapon, saying:

> "But what man can claim to be alone when he holds a sword?
> A man with a sword can bring a kingdom down! Many a man
> has a fortune who began with no less, no more. I stand upon the
> outer edge of a continent, and who is to say that continent cannot
> be mine?"

She would rule the night! She knew that they would come—be it bear, mountain lion, wolf, or similar scavengers . . . "They do not know that I am alone, but little do I care; come to me and feel the pain of my weapon; I am not afraid to die, as I will kill you if you try. One against many, no matter . . . come, I'm ready for you."

Under the base of a gnarled and wind-racked oak, with a pounding heart, she grabbed Jack's big 14-inch Bowie Knife and, with two hands, wildly thrust it into the bear's chest and dragged it down to his balls, only to return to the sternum and the thick connective tissue of the rib cage. She impaled him savagely again, totally opening the body cavity. The heat from his mammalian warmth filled the air with water vapor in the cold Alaskan night. With a smirk, she unceremoniously grabbed his maleness, castrated him, and threw his balls into the fire. She was no rookie at field dressing, so she quickly removed the diaphragm, severed the food tube and windpipe, then looked for a rope. Upon tying the two together, she pulled the entire viscera out of his body in one big swoosh, and sploosh. As a final coup de grace, she severed his ass hole to release the mass, and with demonic zeal dragged the mass to the fire to burn as if in Satan's Kingdom.

"Burn, you bastard, burn. Your ashes to hell!

"Okay, you fat ass, let's get your butt over to the fire."

This time it was easier to drag the butchered body, but she still took a few moments to rest between lunges against the rope harness. Her swear words were not wasted, since Leigh's vernacular of words got ample testing and expression to the animals of the night. As she said, "Who's to hear? The squirrels? Other bears? Good, come on in, come on down, there's a forty-five waiting for you, and I don't mean malt liquor.

"Damn . . . done! Now I've got four bodies in sight, the fires are burning very well, I've enough wood for the night, and now to chow down on something that will hold me and keep me awake."

With her hands and arms now covered with blood, she hustled to the river with flashlight and .45, and rinsed the residue of the dead from her skin and clothes. It was as if another peaceful world existed at the river. She rested in the silence of the rippling waters. It was serene . . . a beautiful solitude. Being on its bank kept the positive aspects of the Tongass in her heart.

Hurriedly, she returned to the fires to dry off and reflect on the night ahead and options for the 'morrow. Her return certainly brought her back to reality.

She made a huge queen-like elevated chair from the bedroll and pack that looked good enough for royalty—and her butt, too. She added a few more sweet-smelling cedar boughs. "I might as well be comfortable. I'll have little opportunity to sleep while feeding the fire, watching the triangle for predators, and analyzing plans for tomorrow."

It was 2200 hours.

For the first time in two hours she took a break; drank some water, peed while backed up to the gnarled oak, ate some trail mix, and placed a disposable foil packet of freeze-dried stew mixed with river water near the fire. She then slid it nearer the white-hot embers with a six-foot stick.

"Ah, all the comforts of home—yeah, hardly. Four dead bodies, two human and two animal, and a flashlight in one hand and a .45 in the other. Yep, just waiting for the next crisis. Some night. It's getting colder, too."

Looking up, she noted why the evening was getting so cold. There were no protective clouds to hold Earth's warmth to her outer crust. Her friends were looking down, also . . . Venus was escorting the gibbous moon across the sky as the Earth rotated about its zenith. Always in awe of the billions of stars in the gigantic galaxies, she recalled both Jack and Ford spending hours sorting out the Greek figures in their own distinct pattern—*I never saw Cygnus or Pegasus, but it didn't stop us from trying. It was a cheap date too . . . typical of Ford's frugality.* She did learn how to find the North Star, Polaris, in the Little Dipper and the accompanying Big Dipper and Cassiopeia, the big W. "How'd it go? Follow the edge of the dipper's cup to the North Star or leg of the W to the North Star. I can do that! Matter of fact, I wouldn't put it past Ford to have taken me out star-gazing, just so he could hunker down in a blanket and share some of *his* 98.6 degrees, as he would say. He never really grew up when it came to romance. That's the way I like 'em. With Ford, you never knew what he'd do next. A little boy in a big man makes for a lot of good times, both in and out of bed. Those were the good ol' days. . . ."

"Well, this looks like it's ready to eat. Just like the Ritz, sans Chardonnay, but with one hell of a view—a billion stars, tall timber, Gemini fires—and sadly, four dead bodies." She loved three, hated the fourth.

After throwing away her disposable utensils in the fire, she rebanked the base with larger logs and, with flashlight and .45 in hand, slowly walked around the killing field in the Tongass. "What the hell am I looking for, anyway? If I saw a pair of eyes at this point, I'd probably shoot now and check later. I know I would. Christ, it's as though I'm in a free-fire zone. I'm not even sure I could align the sights in this blackness. I'd probably point, shoot up the woods, and hope for the best.

"Who the hell are you talking to, anyway, girl? Are you going over the edge, or is it typical in this situation? Probably the latter."

She noted the exit and entry of the game trail they were on and decided she'd lay a limb across the trail's pathway so she could determine, at daylight, if any large animal had passed through and slipped by or retreated after seeing the fires. "I do believe it's a good idea to walk this route every couple hours. Why not? I'm certainly not doing anything else, except planning on what to do in the morning to get the hell out of here."

As she approached her throne, she observed it was now occupied by a cute little field mouse with no plans of moving; and having probably never seen a human, her scheme was not to relinquish her newfound berth.

"Scram," she said in a gentle voice. Not choosing any more death along the trail, no matter how small, she pleaded. "Please . . . get!" That did it, and the little visitor scurried into the cedar boughs to escape the wrath of Leigh.

"Okay, girl, you can stay down there. That will give me someone to talk to tonight." Then, as if on stage, the mouse appeared at her feet while feeding on seeds from a cedar cone.

"Ah ha, there you are again. Hello, gal, what's up in your life? You sure don't want to hear about my last couple of days—what's with you? Now isn't she a perfect little animal with clean gray and white fur, humanlike hands, and eyes as black and wet as anthracite coal?

"How's dinner, gal? It sure sounds good." Her chewing was the loudest thing besides the crackling fire and a few wolves crying over the ridgeline. She disappeared and reappeared several times, each time repositioning herself in front of Leigh. There must have been cache nearby, and Leigh wondered why she kept returning as if on stage. A beautiful animal, she was welcome to visit.

"I'll bet clumsy old Leigh has pitched her tent right over your home in the ground—sorry 'bout that, my dear. But it does appear you have a protective access route.

"Strange, she stopped crunching for a moment when I spoke, and held her seed at bay. She then looked directly at me as I talked. Did she understand that I was speaking to her?" Leigh talked to her again, and sure enough, the mouse stopped eating and looked and listened. Leigh did it again, and the mouse listened again.

"Damn, I think many in the Tongass Animal Kingdom and Spiritual World are aware of my plight and are anthropomorphically relating to my needs to forebear the crippling effects of this crisis, and they're talking or listening to me.

"I did see and experience as a first-hand witness to the testimony and actions of the ravens and the owl. Now, this mouse does appear to be very friendly, and maybe it hears what I say. I'm either nuts, or desperate with this witnessing of spiritual power that transcends human logic of reasoning. Is it another leap of faith?

"Whatever, I may have been hallucinating or dreaming with the owl, and the little mouse here was probably just hungry and looking for food. I'm certainly not one to put a spiritual spin on various natural phenomena, but what's going on? It's probably just us girls, with our mutual pheromone attracting her and me together.

"You know, girl, this would not be such a bad experience if I did not have to look at those bodies along with the tall timber, indigo sky, and twinkling stars. It was a beautiful commingling occurrence when the fire's yellow sparks mixed with the white stars millions of miles away and appeared to be in the ether. Yet, from my vantage point below, they danced together for a short time in the evening breeze, only to be extinguished at thirty feet. The only other movement was the flickering fire as its yellow spectrum of radiance and eerie shadows danced on the big timber as if a lattice work of a scary drama at the Metropolitan."

It was 0100 hours.

It was the third day after Ford's plane crash.

It was six hours since the terror of death subsided.

It was six hours to sunrise and critical decisions on the best way to seek help and return to civilization . . .

Many options still had to be analyzed.

"What is it, girl? All your life there has been an expectation to do the right thing and to just be there if extra effort were required. Right? I guess. What would others have done? The same, I'm sure. What other options were there? None! Of course, my dear, the hut on the meadow was supposed to be my thing—my solitude. I was decisive; I was to explore and write. I did, and here I am. No, I did not count on this type of exploration.

"Look, you babble, my dear Leigh. Don't you think it's time to make some plans—or at least options for the morning? Okay, get a grip on it, girl!"

She reviewed her options for survival, as best she knew; they were:

1) Leave camp with the bodies covered, and dash to the coast, get help, and return ASAP. That would take two hours, or four both ways—assuming good trails, good weather, and freedom from animal attacks. The negatives of this decision: Animals scavenging at the bodies.

2) Hold tight, and keep the signal fires burning—hoping for rescue today. Milt and Dave must be looking for us on the ground by now. Negatives: They may not be looking in the right places.

3) Build a travois, rig a harness to my body, and try to drag the two men out, with one starting to swell. That may be too much weight and take too much time . . . seven hours at least. Unfortunately, the odor of death may also attract scavengers. Sadly, this option was *all* negative.

4) Encircle the bodies with fire, and hope that will ward off any animals, and dash to the coast as before. Negatives: The fire would probably not last five to six hours.

5) Hoist the bodies in a tree and dash to the coast as before. Negatives: Without a pulley system, it's doubtful I could hoist that much weight, and even have that much rope. It would be a human cache.

"That's enough thinking for one night—maybe a little more at dawn to see if there are other possibilities. I've had enough of the macabre exercise for one night anyway."

She scanned the perimeter of the timber with the flashlight and decided to walk the route bathed in the fire's light. Many shadows hid the real view, and the fire masked a lot of the mystery in the riprap of young and old fallen warriors of wood.

It was 0300 hours.

The mouse now slept after having had a nice one-way chat and dinner with Leigh, so there was no one else to talk to at this late hour. Leigh moved around the fires, and then to the trees that her firelight enveloped. Like a sentry, sans password, she probed the depths of the area around the triangle. She lingered a little longer at the entrance and exit of the game trail, and reached into the blackness as far as possible with the flashlight's beam. It truly appeared as if one of Steven Hawking's black holes on Earth. The security branches had not been pushed aside—yet. Of course they were of little value for wolverines, wolves, or other smaller animals; they would just jump over or go under the modest barrier.

To ease the tension and add a little humor, she practiced some of Ford's military service challenges used when on sentry duty, now while penetrating the depths of the timber:

"Halt, who goes there—friend or foe? Advance and be recognized . . . and state your business."

She had no plans to challenge anyone tonight, and had decided to shoot anything of any size whose eyes reflected light. She'd ask questions later. The blood scent was well disbursed along the Bitterroot basin by now, and the fire was easily seen by predators that could ravage her night as easily as the afternoon had been witness to unfathomable carnage.

She looked up to Manitou's beautiful sky as her peripheral vision caught a shooting star passing through the galaxy. "Hello, welcome to our sector of the universe. I'm sure desperate . . . talking to shooting stars.

"Ah, this throne is just what I need, but I better be careful or I'll fall asleep. It must be at least thirty-five degrees; I can see my breath when I exhale."

Her eyes had become fixated on the fire while thinking about tomorrow's trauma, and wishing for some good fortune to come her way. She passed time by viewing the beauty of the galaxies in the clear, cold evening sky with the ever-present nighthawk dancing in the embers of the fire. It didn't take long for her to relive moments like this from her childhood . . . with her dad. As she drained her glass of the last bit of Tang, she toasted the Spirit of the Forest, Yol Bolsum! She remembered the Jewish drinking toast her father taught her so well, as they sat around with their drinking friends: Yol Bolsom *May there be a road* . . .

Silence again.

She first saw its breath reflected in the fire's glow. The animal was standing motionless . . . how long had it been there? What was it? The shape and height belied identification. She lurched forward for a better look. Then it stepped forward into the umbra of light. She grabbed for her gun.

"Oh no, not again!"

At a staggering, stumbling gait, a rangy, emaciated wolf walked into camp from the shadows of the western exit of the game trail. Something was terribly wrong. The wolf appeared to be walking sideways, and stopping frequently to snap at his tail and rump. Strange, not appearing to be a threat, it entered into the brighter light near the fire.

She changed her mind quickly . . . he's sickly. "Oh no, I'll bet he's rabid; that's why all the strange behavior/actions. Or he could be poisoned. Whatever, he's in terrible shape."

Taking no chances, she assumed the kneeling position, left foot forward, right knee down, left arm across the left knee as if a bench-rest. She laid the barrel on her arm, checked the sight picture, and held.

The wolf approached the bodies in a stumbling, half-gaited manner and stopped. He scanned the area with a sickly, watery, and desperate pair of yellow eyes; his head's rotation stopped at Leigh's location. He froze and started to growl . . . as his fangs glistened in the foamy broth of impending death.

He stepped toward her. . . .

Safety off, sight picture on his shoulders, she squeezed off the first round . . . *Ka Pow!* . . . again, *Ka Pow!*

At close range of about thirty feet, the .45 threw the wolf sideways several feet as the 120-grain (.25 oz) lead slug smashed his shoulders into splinters. During the rotation of the body, a second round tore into his throat and exploded his backbone as he collapsed in death throes. Silence followed. The crackling fire was the only calming influence for Leigh as the sickening smell of gunpowder lingered in the clearing.

Safety on, and to her feet, with a cautious walk and careful approach, she examined the torn, bloody mass. With its open cavity of warmth, it released visible condensation of fog-like mist that, only moments ago, was of exhaled breath, but now was the kiss of the mist of death. A nudge with a pole ensured the finality of the kill, and with one quick lift, the rabid wolf was cast into the fire. Sure enough, his mouth was full of foam-like saliva, his coat in ruins from indiscriminate biting associated with the final days of life with rabies. After throwing the contaminated pole into the fire, she once again felt the need to rinse her arms and hands in the 'Root as the smell of death permeated her appendages . . . again.

"This killing business is starting to become a regular routine—one that I don't especially care for. At least in this case, I put the animal out of its misery. DVM's have indicated that actions like biting, a staggered gait, and foaming mouth occurred during the last 24 hours of life. I wish rabies on no animal, and especially beautiful wolves, but this was a clear case of doing what was the only right thing; plus his incineration will prevent the spread of disease through his carrion to others."

While reloading the last shells in the clip of the .45, she wished to herself that the gunfire would be retired for the duration. As she had said before, you never know out here with the denizens of the night; this is their domain; the animals own, and in fact rule, the night.

It was 0400 hours.

Her mind wandered again to the pleasant thoughts and her hut on the meadow. Thankfully, she had had many positive experiences in and around the Tongass to support her decision to live here. While pleasantly reliving those exciting times with Ford, and then Jack . . . she once again saw the breath vapors of something by the fire in the evening air.

"Damn it, not again. What the hell is it this time? Be-Jesus . . . what now!" A coyote danced into the area, then a second, a pair most likely. Two adults, no doubt, probably on a blood scent to see if anything was left for them to scavenge. They kept prancing and dancing around the fire as if at a Saturday night square dance. They moved closer and closer to the pile of bodies while constantly sniffing the air and looking over their shoulders. Did they sense Leigh's presence? Not yet, it seemed, but they were wary of something in the air besides the dead bodies.

Being downwind and unnoticed, Leigh witnessed the probing and withdrawal pattern, back and forth, of scavengers to the point where she had seen enough. Their technique seemed to be based on testing the body, a meal, until they were certain that no life would be in their first bite. As if in a sword fight, they parried and thrust their body at the pile of lifeless remains of man and beast. They were getting too close now . . . at any moment they'd be dragging one of the bodies from the pile.

"Enough . . . when blood needs spilling, for cause, I will gladly be the one." Moving slowly into the firing position, again, she cautiously eased her body forward . . . they had not seen her yet.

Gun up, safety off, sight picture good, hold; she decided to go for two with one shot. Might as well, she thought; their tiny bodies would not stop a round at this distance; with muzzle velocity at about 1500 feet per second (fps), one round would do the job.

"Patience, Leigh, patience; let them play and slow down; they'll soon approach the kill together; patience."

They got too close . . . safety off, *Ka Pow* . . . fire again . . . *Ka Pow*.

The slug exploded the first coyote's body on the opposite side of entry; the second coyote got the now partially mushroomed slug in the side knocking its body four feet sideways while blowing a massive hole through the rib cage.

The second shot entered the first coyote in the chest when turning, and the force gutted his entire body cavity quickly.

Both animals lay still as she approached the lifeless carcasses . . . a mangled mass of viscera and blood mixed in with two beautiful tails. She poked to ensure their demise, and felt the need to talk to them.

"You know, on any other night you could have fed on dead animals in the forest without harm coming to you—that is Nature's way; but tonight was different. You picked the wrong carrion, with the wrong woman at their side. Those bodies are my loved ones and I could not let you scavenge. The bear is another story, but that couldn't happen under these conditions . . . you would be only too welcome to attack his carcass. So, I'm sorry, it just was a bad night to be out; please forgive me."

She removed the tails for some reason; it may have been guilt . . . or a collectable reminder for her wall—whatever. She threw the lifeless bodies on the pyre. Again, off to the 'Root, she rinsed her hands of the smell of death, including the offensive odor of burnt gunpowder. The peacefulness of the 'Root remained, now garnished with the beautiful twinkling reflection of moonlight.

Upon return to the clearing, hearing the snap and cackle of the fat and blood as the coyotes charred to a black mass was a welcome sound. It had indeed been a long day. Hoping there would be no further action tonight, she ambled over to her sentry spot in the triangle.

Dawn gave its first warning through early morning nautical twilight as the eastern sky changed from indigo blue to red, to pink, orange, and finally yellow when the sun's rays joined the shadows of night. Those who ruled the night passed the torch to dawn. They were no more to be seen . . . they rested to restore themselves for the next night.

Leigh had returned to her throne. The mouse was up and about, chomping on the latest gourmet seed in her larder, so Leigh started talking to this great listener about her taxing day. The mouse was all ears as the trials and tribulations were related about the rabid wolf and scavenging coyotes. She canted and nodded her head frequently as if to understand. Leigh checked that all three pistols were loaded to ensure enough firepower was available should there be a daylight bruin . . . or other, who knows what, animal attack.

It was 0700 hours.

The sun rose over the ridge as angry red with streaks of scarlet and gold-laced clouds mixed in with the green pines and indigo sky. The tragedy of the night's primeval darkness was thankfully sinking. The last thing Leigh saw was the flickering fire, the mouse's crunching, and the tunnel vision of impending sleep . . .

Only one in the clearing witnessed the orange horizon . . . Leigh was asleep. The mouse soon realized her aloneness, but continued chewing . . . *crunch, crunch,* pause, *crunch,* listen—and then made a hasty retreat and scrambled from her stage in front of Leigh. Something had scared her into her lair.

"Caw—Caw—Caw," cried the leader of an approaching flock of ravens. Several ravens flew to a commanding perch above the bodies.

Leigh remained asleep with a flashlight in one hand and a .45 in the other, a .44 and 9mm on the bedroll next to her, and half-full coffee cup spilled at her foot.

The mouse said good night before racing through the boughs into her subterranean nest. Scores of ravens were perched above camp as if on watch, or as protectors of the scene below.

At 0800 hours, sunlight bathed the entire clearing to expose the carnage of the previous day.

It was ugly.

*   *   *

They approached the clearing carefully from the western game trail, noting the fire was still burning quite well . . . a good sign, and the clearing was encircled with perched ravens.

They spotted Leigh. The rescue crew approached cautiously . . .

"Be careful. If we approach her too suddenly, she may accidentally use one or several of those weapons she has next to her," Dave whispered to the crew.

"Okay, we'll stand aside when you call her name. Ready? Yep, go ahead, we're all over here—go ahead," Milt said in a hushed voice.

Dave shouted, "Leigh . . . Leigh. Good morning, Leigh . . . Leigh! Leigh, it's Dave; Dave from Ford's Flight Service."

Startled, she snapped her head up, opened her eyes, blinked, blinked again, saw Milt, then Dave, and then the crew from the DNR camp.

She cried, "Are they okay? Are they?"

"Yes dear, they're resting well, unharmed, undisturbed, and well protected; you did very well, my dear," Milt exclaimed.

"In fact, it almost appeared as if the ravens were also protecting the camp *and* you," Dave commented.

"How true; you don't know how close that statement is to being the case—you're right on target . . . Oh my God," mumbled Leigh.

Leigh dashed to the center of the triangular camp, at the point where the tent and the two fires crossed. She looked skyward with hands and arms extended upward, then sang and chanted a melodic message to the sky.

> "We thank you, Great Spirit, for this day
> That we are allowed to live upon
> Our Mother Earth.
> For us two-leggeds,
> You give us courage and endurance;
> These strengths are now ours.
> We are blessed
> As we face tomorrow."

She kneeled, bowed her head, and whispered . . . "Thank you, Manitou." The crew looked at each other, paused to take notice, and bowed their heads, even though they did not totally understand. They figured she was giving thanks to her God, her Creator. They had all seen the Natives perform similar acts of thanksgiving.

Overcome with grief, Leigh collapsed in place and cried uncontrollably. Milt went to her side.

"Oh, Milt, it has been a terrible experience. I'm so sorry about Ford. I know how much he loved you, and you guys him; it's such a loss."

"Listen here, my dear, he died as he would have chosen. You can't do much better than that. He knew the Big Red Bird was an old bucket of bolts. It is we, my dear, that owe you thanks for giving him such pleasure since you arrived on the scene and in his life. So, say no more. That's an order. You have been his final reward, his Omega, his last love. You can tell us about your meeting Walkswithwater, DNR Officer Jack South, later on."

"You're a dear man, Milt; thanks from the bottom of my heart. Come over here . . . I need another hug."

"Gladly."

As if by command, in feeling that they had served their purpose, the ravens leaped to the sky, circled in the thermals, and flew to the western sky. The rescue group of Alaskans and Native Americans did not require an explanation for their presence. They knew . . .

"Milt, you stay with Leigh, and I'll check out the camp first, and then we'll get the details from Leigh," said Dave.

"Okay, fellows, douse those fires, use your hat for water if necessary, and Ron, you strike the tent and pack the gear over by Leigh. Andy, you make three travois . . . for Jack, Ford, and the Grizz. We'll bury Boy here at the campsite. Sam, get that shovel and straighten up the area so it looks as though no one has ever been here."

"I want to leave in a half-hour, say at 0900 hours, so let's hustle; I'll be talking with Milt and Leigh if you need me," Dave explained. "Well, Leigh, I see you've already had some java and trail mix . . . not a steak for sure, but that will come later. Are you ready to roll, or would you like to tell us the details of the last couple of days? Take your time, but can you imagine what we, too, have been going through? Certainly nothing like you've experienced. Are there a few bodies of animals in the fire? How did the bear die? How did you all link up? How did Jack happen to be with you? There I go, getting ahead of myself and your story." Dave pulled-up on his questions, and halted his inquiry.

"Well, first, thank you from the bottom of my heart for all of you just being here. My options for getting to the coast were very limited and complicated. I'll tell you the complete story someday, over a cool one.

"As you may know, Ford's plane crashed about thirty miles upstream to the East due to jammed elevators. Then by luck or spiritual guidance—more on that later, too—I saw him go in from eight miles away to the East. I was standing on a ridge up from the hut. Jack was in the area, also, and saw him go in. Leigh went on to fill in the details, sometimes in tears, her love for the lost friends shining in her eyes.

"As an additional bit of assistance," she added, "a raven helped Boy and me reach the crash site. I'm sure of it now; you've already seen them here today. Right? Say, did you hear any transmissions from the handheld?"

"No," said Milt, "All we heard was Ford's Mayday when he went down; and flights were grounded most of the time due to fog and other weather problems."

"Figured as much!" said Leigh.

"We did, however, see your signal fires last night after the weather cleared while we flew along the 'Root. Good thinking, Leigh."

"Ford must have known how bad he was; he talked half the night about old times, including his days as an aspirant bullfighter. And yes, the ravens appeared again upon his death. Jack knew, of course, of the connection with Manitou, and now I'm certain. You saw it, just an hour ago. A coincidence? Not on your life.

Did you guys know the Manitou speaks through His animals and natural elements; it is His way, and mine now, too?

"From what I've observed this week, regarding formal or fundamental Biblical-based institutional religion, I want no part of its archaic teachings. Oh, I might sing their music, view their early art, and socialize, but would have to reject their myths—it's all related to their narrowness in their personal leap of faith. Sadly, however, many are clearly misguided, and don't even know it, in thinking *theirs* is the only belief . . . I've come to appreciate the simple nature beliefs . . . and their clear statement of nature worship. As Dad always said, 'Live and let live, but if you're a proselytizing Trinitarian, you need not call. Anyway, it was a long night for the mouse and me."

"A field mouse?"

"She's my buddy down under the tent and throne; she kept me company, and, between the two of us, we made a lot of decisions and plans together. She'll be sleeping now, only coming out in the evening. She'll be fine . . . this is her little clearing. Yep, along with the ravens and the wise old owl, sent by Manitou, I've had a lot of friends and support out here."

"An owl?" Dave and Milt said in unison.

"Yes, a wise, talking spiritual owl. He sure gave me the confidence to continue my goals in the face of pain and the trials and tribulations in the Tongass, and he helped me face my future adjustments. I've struggled these days to feel and sense death, to celebrate life.

Dave and Milt looked at each other with that Doubting Thomas glare, but they were not there to challenge her positive feelings; she survived. And it appeared Manitou was part of that survival. Both were deists, so they understood clearly her commitment to individual beliefs.

"Okay, let's get moving; daylight's burning. . . . " Milt changed the subject with hopes to hear more later.

The travois plan appeared to work; the three platforms were loaded and ready; the camp struck with evidence of the last 24 hours obliterated, and the whole crew was ready to hike and drag out the results of terror in the Tongass.

It was now 0900 hours.

Leigh approached the two body bags and whispered to each her blessings and thanks for their contribution to her life.

"Jack South, I love you. Ford Harrison, I love you. May your afterlife . . . your new life bring you the riches of memory mixed with imagination's forwarding light . . . May you sense all of us near whose lives you have illuminated with your example of strength and endurance and love of life."

She stopped, turned, and approached the lifeless grizzly and kicked his ass one last time, then spit on his blood-soaked hide. Turning to rejoin the group, she gave each a hug and personal thanks. Finally, she stood over Boy's grave and blessed him.

Silence enveloped the clearing—After several minutes—Leigh spoke:

"I am also saying good bye."

Startled, they all started to say something, but before being able to speak, she declared, "I'm off—to my hut—east on the Bitterroot while you all travel west to the Pacific. Thanks again.

"Bye!"

"Leigh, you should not do that—alone!"

"Why not? That's what I've been doing. But remember, I have Manitou now as my benefactor, my protector. I'm in good hands, don't fret. Stop in some time, boys; you'll always be welcome in my hut; a cool one is waiting for you all! So long!"

She turned and walked the moss-impregnated turf with a new and refreshing spring in her step; she noticed the clouds cupped in the hollow of the ridges of the East, most likely just above her hut. Renewed strength engulfed her soul as the early morning sounds in the forest invigorated her, as well as the sun catching the damp grass poking up through the frost, turning it a gilded gold on the verdant turf.

With exhilaration, she moved on with her life as fall winds turned the golden leaves along her path and bathed her face in sunlight. Her eyes were clear and focused on the future without the blur of earlier tears. She had indeed learned a lesson or two from the experiences of the last month's activities with man and animals in Manitou's Kin(g)dom.

Montaigne wrote so wisely on life; she would live it as such . . . exactly as he had discussed by the firelight with Jack. "Whenever your life ends, it is all there. The advantage of living is not measured by *length*, but by *use*; some men have lived long, and lived little; attend to it while you are in it. It lies in your will, not in the number of years, for you to have lived enough."

"Caw—Caw—Caw." A raven, soaring in the thermals, descended and headed east along the Bitterroot in front of Leigh. "Welcome, Mr. Raven, I'm glad you've decided to rejoin me."

A comforting silence enveloped the basin as she headed East.

Drumm . . . drum . . . drum . . . drum . . . drum . . . .

"Is that a drumming sound? Yes, and now, a flute. too. . . . "

Leigh had an escort—she was not alone . . .

Chapter 13

A New Friend

Hiking through the forest, Leigh reflected on the bloodshed and terror of the previous forty-eight hours that brought death to her two lovers and devoted dog.

The return trip to her hut in the shadow of Alaska's St. Elias mountain range was more enjoyable now than the mad dash a few days ago while she attempted to assist her mortally wounded lovers. Nevertheless, she scanned the tree line for potential peril in the shadows.

Still mourning the loss of her friends and canine companion, she felt the painful absence of their love. Her heart was still broken, but she knew she must recover. Thankfully, the raven that continued to accompany her was comforting. She appreciated the bird's presence in the anticipation of the chill that could come during these days when autumn warred with winter.

It was clear that if she did not realign her life, her mental and physical stability would soon suffer irreversible damage; and she was not about to allow that to happen. Her near-term objectives were much too important.

She had already accepted her station in life and her time-seasoned looks, much like W. Kittredae's 'unique' aging women:

> They wind up looking fifty
> When they are thirty-seven
> And fifty-three when they
> Are seventy.
> It's as though they were
> Down to what counts
> And just stay there . . .

A stunning beauty, she was fortunate to have her dad's high cheekbones, auburn hair, strong jaw, attractive incipient crow's feet, and blue-green eyes that radiated beauty. Her dad also gave her the highest marks, saying, "Those guys will be so busy looking at your eyes and lips, you'll be home before they notice the allure of the rest of your luscious feminine body."

As she ambled along the banks of the 'Root, her relaxed attitude changed. A muffled sound pierced her ears. Her probing eyes strained as she scanned the forest depths ahead and to the side. Frozen in place for minutes, she heard no additional sounds, then carefully moved on. She certainly wouldn't experience the enormity of a grizzly attack again, at least not on her return trip to the hut—she hoped. Leigh had no plans to alter her ideas for exploring the Tongass National Forest. A 15th-century suit-of-mail was not an option. She knew how to survive now, based on her experience of the last few weeks.

With Boy gone, her new companion was a holstered 9mm. It would be 'at the ready,' rather than in her jacket pocket as in the past. She was not cocky or arrogant, just more knowledgeable of animals. She knew the risk-gain ratios, and was prepared to pay the price.

As F.D. Roosevelt eloquently stated to Congress while war loomed over Europe: "We have nothing to fear but fear itself." He borrowed the phrase, in part, from Montaigne (1500s): "The thing I fear most is fear . . ." She was not afraid, but was very observant and careful.

She also had the additional strength of Manitou. His omnipresence through the animals of the forest and natural wonders of the earth and sky give her plenty of comfort. She no longer felt alone. She spoke to Him frequently, and found new solace in His presence and counsel when He revealed Himself.

Her life was not an island; she still had logistical and administrative contact with Ford Flight Service through Milt and Dave Hughs. She loved and needed both of these characters of the north, though at the moment she felt a little closer to Milt.

"I sure miss Boy. His companionship and protective shield provided doubles of eyes, ears, and nose, in his case with scenting ability at least ten times greater than mine," Leigh mused as she slipped into the shadows of the aspen near the river.

Tired, she got some butt-time on a fallen cedar in a beautiful riverside niche that breathed of nature's grandeur and peace.

"I'm so fortunate. Here I sit in an alcove or cradle of life provided by Manitou."

Her relaxed feeling was short-lived. Hearing something strange, she snapped her head around to the opposite bank of the 'Root, then squinted and strained to a movement. It appeared to be a low-slung wolverine growling and hissing while feeding on an animal carcass. Confident of his dominant place in the food chain of the Tongass, it tore at the visceral mass with wanton abandonment, ignoring her presence. A small carnivore, he needed to devour his food quickly, for another, larger competitor could be headed upwind to join in or take the feast du jour without notice.

"I wonder what it's eating. I'll watch with my number nine out of the holster, just in case."

The wolverine's teeth ripped open the soft belly as if custard in a cone. Body hair seemed to slow down the attack to the animal's flanks and belly, but disembowelment was soon complete. He smacked his lips and shook his head to shed the accumulating hair mass blocking his feast. Rolled over now, the carcass revealed the head of a wolf.

"Damn, that's a large wolf. Stiff and dried out, it appears to have been dead awhile."

Then the wolverine stopped abruptly, regurgitated, rolled over again and again in the carcass, and attempted to bury it with a few paw strokes from the small sandy bank. Then he urinated all over the partially hidden carcass and disappeared into the underbrush.

Holstering her #9, she reflected on the feeding frenzy. The wolverine knew she was there—watching . . . and he seemed to feel no threat whatsoever. Somehow he knew she was not worthy competition, and even ignored her in arrogant and daring ways. By barely acknowledging her, he radiated his confidence and fearlessness, and by subtle body language and a low-muffled growl it seemed to indicate, "Try me if you wish." She knew about the animal's reputation for taking on all who cared to challenge. "Thanks, Manitou." Having no interest in viewing up-close the half-buried torn and bloodied wolf carcass, she remained on the north side of the river. She mused, "What else could there possibly be out here . . . nothing." She closed her eyes and practiced deep breathing (Yoga) exercises.

"What's that?" She snapped her head around again, first left and then right while straining to sense the direction of a muffled whining-like cry. Finally, seeing nothing move, she stood up to seek a better view of the bank and surrounding vegetation. She scanned the dead-falls, cattails, and ridgeline. Nothing.

WWWAAAEEEOINE.

"Damn, there it is again. Wait, it's right under the cedar log I'm on. Wait a minute; there's a small burrow under the log, and something's in there."

She leaped up and looked around to check the area, then kneeled down to look into the narrow black hole under the log.

"Nothing," she said. "No, wait. Something is moving, and now whining again. Be careful, girl."

Straining both eyes and ears, she moved closer and deeper into the opening. The whining sounded more intense, louder, and more guttural now, like a growl. Hesitating for a moment, she said, "Sure enough, I've been sitting on top of an animal den all this time. Damn it, girl, shape up and stay alert. You're alone now. Remember? Boy's nose and ears would have sensed this lair in a second. Shape-up! I'll be damned! No girl up here alone should be the Damocles of the twenty-first century.

"Well, one thing is certain: even though the animal sounds like a youngster,

I'm not going to reach into the den, so start thinking, girl. Why not lure it out with food or drive it out by throwing fire or water down the opening of the den?

"Let's see, it's either a fox kit, wolf cub, young wolverine, badger, or member of the weasel family. Maybe I could make a sound like a 'mother with food' and it would come out. Hmmm, nothing ventured, nothing gained. I'll try my vocal animal skills first."

Leigh opened her small backpack in search of a special young-hairy-wild-animal food. She discovered some of Jack's pemmican, a native American trail-food containing beef, fruit, and suet. Taking it out of the wrapper and down to the water's edge, she immersed the brick-like snack in an eddy current to activate the aroma by Chef de la Leigh, of animal edibles fame. At the water's edge, tracks indicated that the den probably belonged to wolves—both large and small.

While waiting for the rock-hard 'lunch' to soak up some liquid, Leigh felt an overwhelming sense of déjà vu. She had done this or experienced something like this before. So startling was the feeling, she froze and recalled the previous time and place when this scene occurred.

It was 1945, and I was about ten when Dad indicated there must be a litter of puppies hidden somewhere on the farm. They would surely die, since he had just found the mother who had been killed earlier in the week.

Dad noted that the deceased mother's teats were swollen, and told me a litter must be somewhere on our 80-acre farm. He suggested the riverbank since feral dogs generally gave birth near a water source. He also warned me of the realities of survival and suggested that nature would likely take a brutal course. A few might survive, but many would die, and the litter may never be found. I understood, but Dad said I could take a brief sweep of the acreage if it would make me feel better. Sure enough, I discovered the den in a fashion similar to today's. The starving, confused, and whining pups were easily heard as they cried for their mother's milk.

The rescue was quick. We kept the pick of the litter and took the remainder to the dog pound for adoption. Everybody won, and my feral puppy became one of my best four-legged friends over the years.

Leigh's task appeared a little more difficult today. The mother must have been the wolverine's dinner, so Leigh was the cub's only chance for survival. In fact, if Leigh had not been sitting on the wolf's den, the wolverine may just have had the cubs for dessert. She felt strange as life's lessons seemed to repeat themselves. Now she had an opportunity to save more lives if she could lure the little ones out of the den.

"Okay, girl, let's give it a try and vocalize a 'come hither' sound of a mother wolf, ready for them to suckle or her to regurgitate dinner for the little cubs.

"Come on, guys and gals; here's dinner," she said.

She wrapped the pemmican on a short stick and slowly lowered it down the entrance, trying to coax the cubs out via smell and motherly vocalization.

"Here goes:

"HUMM GRRRRAAAHHH WOOOOOOFFF;

"HUMM GRRRRAAAHHH WOOOOOOFFF"

Silence.

More Silence.

In response to the odd sounds and silence, a raven cried out: *Caw-Caw-Caw.*

"HUM GRAH WOOF; HUM GRAH WOOF WOOF!"

Silence again.

Now she carefully pulled the stick halfway out of the hole and repeated several vocalization sounds, adding some panting and huffing noises.

"It's working!"

A furry little body with a shiny, wet, jet-black nose and whiney little eyes emerged in a frantic struggle to lick, bite, and grab the elusive pemmican.

"Okay, fella, come on, just a little more. Come on another couple inches. Come on. You'll be okay. That's right, grab the stick, grab on. Good boy. Bite down, bite it. Yeah! He did it!"

The little fella bit down so hard Leigh could pull the entire body out, clearing the entrance by two feet. This aggressive unyielding attack on the bait was to be his dinner and his alone. An admirable trait at any time of life, he continued to chow down on the stick and bait, plus wrestle both to the riverbank as if an adversary of notable strength.

"Good boy. Eat up and enjoy yourself. It looks like you've a lot of pent-up energy. Have at it, boy. Here's some more chow. Eat up."

She threw the cub enough water-soaked pemmican to keep him busy while she searched the den, shining in as far as possible with her flashlight beam. She discovered two lifeless bodies in early stages of bloat and decay, and wondered how the hell the third cub survived such a dreadful environment. Backing out and cleaning the sand off her jacket, she stood and collapsed the den entrance, then pushed additional riverbank sand over the hole. This would ensure that marauding scavengers would not gain access to the tomb.

"Rest in peace, little ones, and be assured I'll do as much as possible to protect your surviving brother."

Leigh knelt, remained silent for a moment, then offered a prayer to Manitou for the Earth, Sky, and her fellow man. Brief and to the point, she also thanked Him for animals of the forest, blessed His fallen comrades, and thanked Him for the surviving cub. She pledged her personal protection and care for the frisky cub still frolicking with his adversarial food stick on the riverbank. She remained in place and asked for her protection, too.

The stoic raven flapped his wings and called: *Caw-Caw-Caw*.

Rising from her solemn lotus position, Leigh walked slowly to the little cub still chewing on the block of pemmican tied to the tree limb.

"What am I going to do with you, boy?" she mused as the cub finally shifted his aggression from the limb to her boot.

"Whoa," she said. "Not my good boots. Stop it. I might as well save my breath; he'll not respond to any command by me. He was probably too young to have experienced the wolf-pack social order, the Alpha wolf's dominance, the Alpha wolf's leadership of a pack, and the rules of subservience. Oh well, live and learn. My right boot is almost ruined now, and like it or not, this little guy is going into a carry-bag of some sort until I get to the hut. Then I'll have time to work with him. One thing is certain: he cannot stay here without a mother. I'll betcha his mother's demise was related to the defense of the den. On the other hand, the mother could have died of other causes. I'll never know, but it looks as though I've just become the cub's new Alpha mother, sans claws and fangs."

She wrestled with the little fella in an attempt to identify her with his need for nourishment, play, and protection. His skeletal feel belied the beautiful fur coat's appearance; he was emaciated.

"Now the tricky part," she groaned. "I've got to get this biting, whining, growling, peeing bundle of uncivilized wild energy into a bag so I can reach the hut in one piece. Plus, do so without my hands, wrists, and yes, face being bloodied and torn. Come here, you little tiger. Come on, get your butt over here and let go of the rock you're trying to split. Come on, boy."

Then without any rhyme or reason . . . except freedom, the little bugger took off along the riverbank as if there were no tomorrow.

"You little fart. After all I've done for you, you're not taking off on your mother now, so get your little, skinny ass back here."

Leigh ran after him for about one minute while tripping over logs and deadfalls that he had conveniently shimmied and scurried under. With the vengeance of a new mom, she ran and jumped and leaped after him until she suddenly stopped.

"What?"

The little guy was now running back toward her with his tail between his legs, crying as though he'd seen a ghost. With no affection for her—yet—he ran right between her legs and headed for his old lair, the now-closed den site. He lay down and started licking his paw.

"Well now," she said, "I guess you've learned a lesson of some sort upstream. I'll continue on a short distance, just out of curiosity, and see what scared the hell out of this courageous runaway."

Certain the cub was not going to move from the old den entrance, Leigh took only ten steps to discover the odious creature of the Bitterroot that scared the wolf cub. It was huge box turtle about the size of a dinner plate. Unshaken by the aggressive cub, as indicated by the skid-marks of a young set of paws at the sandy doorstep, the turtle had likely thrust his snapping jaws, contacted flesh, and scared the wits out of the fearless Lupus of the Tongass.

"I suppose the little fella has just learned one of a thousand lessons ahead of him. I cannot leave him here. It is not something I could live with."

She ran back to the old den site. Licking the open wound, he lay down with a whine, lick, and growl. "He's certainly going to be a tough guy, a survivor, and a presence to deal with," she mused while watching the little fellow. She noticed his eyelids losing the fight with gravity. The afternoon sun played a part, the warm rays bathing his tiny body with the water reflecting like diamonds on the flowing river's sparkling surface as the foamy mass races to the sea. The absolute silence of the moment was special to her. Within moments, he was asleep on the sun-drenched sand bank of this former lair.

"This is beautiful," she said. "As the wolf cub enters my life, it feels like a new moment in my future. I am blessed. Thank you, Manitou."

She decided to linger awhile and enjoy the moment.

All these moments, in appreciation of the grandeur of the forest, tested her Thoreauian thankfulness for late summer's vestments and Manitou's gifts. The land would soon embrace the turning leaves as the yellows presented a beautiful contrast with the deep-green conifers. Nature's paintbrush of colors would be a welcome change in autumn. All animals would welcome the newfound sunlight through the thinning canopy of broadleaf giants in the Tongass.

As the leaves played follow-the-leader in a light wind, the added light and woodland sounds confirmed a change in the season. Leigh felt that sometimes her nirvana was achieved by just perching on a log in a sunny patch to watch and listen as nature performed its ballet of splendid beauty. A sentimental urge moved her to unsheathe her Bowie knife and carve her initials and date on a fallen birch tree to designate an important aspect of her discovery. It identified the locale of her discovery and, hopefully, of a new animal friend and guardian.

"I'll pass by this 'little niche' again someday." Her best guess was that it was only about two kilometers downstream from the hut. She had always marked special places, places that related to important experiences in her life.

She remembered, only too well, carving her first boyfriend's initials in the silver maple in their backyard at home. It was important then for a girl to recall where 'puppy-love' had led to her first kiss.

"Wait a minute," she exclaimed, "I've got to carve the cub's initials, too. Now's as good a time as any to select a name. How 'bout using Native American logic, which attempts to be descriptive of the behavior or notable activity of the subject, person, or animal? In this case, the cub certainly showed many emotions, but he's predominantly aggressive, combative, and curious. We'll forget the encounter with the tortoise; that's in the category of 'live-and-learn' while young.

"I do remember that Jack's Indian name, Walkswithwater, was given to him by his chief, Three Bears, because he loved to 'frolic' in the streams of the camp, day and night. Wait, I've got it! He survived the abandoned den because he's *tough*. Only a *tough* cub would take the chance to escape the den, lured by food and an unknown at the den's entrance.

"Yep, that's it. *Tough*. The name is kind of unusual, but is it not true that his first few months were also unusual?" She finished the carving that read:

LEIGH & TOUGH 1990

She checked the afternoon sun and estimated the time at 3:00. Close. Her watch said 3:30, not bad for an amateur in the wilderness.

"Better get going, gal. Daylight's burning, and you've got to pack up a sleeping cub and get him to the hut before he awakens."

Laying her poncho down, she gently rolled Tough over onto the center, tucked his bony legs under his body, tied her moist handkerchief around his eyes, and picked up each corner of the poncho, tying them to a six-foot carry pole. Looking around the area for the last time, she imprinted its features on her mind and hoisted the tough guy for his flight to the hut, sans wings, over her shoulder.

"You're not so heavy. I can handle this without a doubt. I hope you can—tough guy."

Trudging off along the high-banks, Leigh moved out sharply and followed the 'Root with added vigor.

A raven made its presence known, cawing amid the crisp creaking of stiff upper branches. They purled together on this gusty afternoon, emerging distinctly from the background chorus of waving Aeolian boughs. The trees talked to Leigh in their individual dialects as she passed the cleft that meandered from north to south below the ridgeline to the meadow. Even closer to the hut now, Leigh heard the babbling voices by the beaver dam just downstream from the forest dwelling.

She visualized Tough attacking the fish, shore birds, and ducks as Boy did in the shallows of the river. He would no doubt adapt to a different path, finding new strategies due to his untamed lupine heritage.

The murmur of the raven's 'caw' added to the noise of the forest as if announcing their arrival at the meadow—a signal of warning . . . a summons. It wasn't necessary to announce their approach to camp; the trees themselves sang the story of their location. She knew the song very well.

Leigh spotted the big owl. It did not feel like a sign. It was as if a response by the woodland denizens to her return. Aspiring Thoreauian's would know that owls are the ombudsmen for sylvan glades, but Leigh knew he was much more. 'Minerva' sat watching them serenely from a high branch of a maple tree, slightly startling them with its direct gaze. He looked at her full face without timidity or shyness, since he was Manitou's representative. She felt honored.

She wondered how long he had been observing her and Tough before deciding to present himself. How did he know their location? Simply put: He knew. The owl now knew they knew he knew. And on every future hike in the forest, they would be expecting an owl or raven escort/guide . . . but not always a sighting . . . knowing He would reveal himself only when necessary.

Just around the bend, the hut's outline would soon be noticeable. She hurried her steps, careful not to start the litterbag swinging excessively.

Spotting the hut, she was overcome for a moment, then moved on to the comfort of the meadow.

Suddenly she stopped.

Startled, Leigh noticed a man's shape on the bench by the river. Then upon looking further down the trail to the hut, she noticed a tent pitched by the woodpile.

Her heart skipped a beat.

At the tent she saw a large grizzly bear and her three cubs sniffing around the area. It appeared as if the bears were unaware of humans downwind.

"Oh no! Not again. Please, Manitou. Allow me to live in peace in your Kin(g)dom. Please. I bring no harm."

She removed her 9mm from the holster and advanced slowly toward the revered bench on the 'Root.

"Tough, we're not alone. Again. Hang on."

A raven landed on a tree limb above the bench.

Chapter 14

A Challenge

"Dear God. Why me!"

Leigh moved stealthily to the high banks behind the bench so she could get a better view of the intruder—or guest, uncertain of which—and still keep an eye on the bears. Crawling through the underbrush and deadfalls was taking its toll on her clothes, skin, and Tough, so she carefully lowered the cub to the ground.

She whispered, "I'll be back shortly; rest well. I've got to be sure the intruder is a benefactor, not a scoundrel, and warn him of the bears. We may be able to help each other.

"Damn," she whispered again to herself, "I wonder if all this precautionary activity is necessary. Okay, girl, just a few more meters, and you'll be able to get a good look at the interloper, and a better feel for your safety."

She finally found an opening in the undergrowth permitting a good view to the squatter on the bench. He appeared to be non-threatening in appearance, with military fatigue-type clothing, expensive hiking boots, long jet-black hair, and aviator sunglasses. He did not look menacing or threatening, and appeared clean-shaven and rather attractive.

"Okay, girl, you've got to make a move and decide what you're going to do. Get with it."

The bears continued to tear apart the woodpile in search of rodents. Deciding to trust her judgment, she would slowly approach the bench. She'd call out 'hello' from about thirty feet with her hand near good ole #9. After all, the land was not hers, and she might stop at a stranger's camp, too, during an extended overnighter. More importantly, maybe they'd need to tackle the bear problem together.

"Okay, girl, walk in like you own the place. Set your jaw of confidence and ironhanded will. Ready? Sunlight is aburnin'; you don't have all day. Plus, Tough will awaken soon."

She carefully stood up and moved toward the path by the bench. Cautious, she took just a few steps. Then, as if an old friend, the figure on the beach sensed her presence, leaped up, and turned to face her.

Both froze in place, but in a strange way she felt safe and finally relaxed.

She did not have time to say 'hello,' feeling a little awkward. "Ah . . ." she said.

"Hello! You must be Leigh. I hope my presence in camp has not startled you," he related with utmost courtesy. "I . . . ah."

She cut him off. "Wait . . . Ah . . . We can't talk . . . I mean, we can talk later . . . There's a grizzly sow and her cubs over by the hut; and I don't think they've seen, smelled, or heard us . . . yet!" Leigh said in a whisper.

He looked toward the hut and saw the quad rummaging through the wood-pile. Whispering, he said, "Duck down here below the bench and talk only when necessary, and then in a whisper. I wonder how long they've been here? Say, what direction did you come from? How long have you been on the trail?" he whispered.

"By the way, do you even know who I am?" he murmured.

She squinted, looked at the grizzlies, then at him—he got the message: there was plenty on their plate right now; answers to questions would have to come later.

"Here is what I'm thinking," he said. "If you agree, I think we should scare the bears away by dropping a round near the sow. The memory of a round impacting and splintering wood will imprint on her and the cubs that this is a dangerous place to search for rodent burgers. If she charges, we can drop her with our sidearms."

Leigh responded, "I agree, that old she bear needs a lesson in ownership—that's my wood. She needs to understand this is no drive-through."

The stranger laid a .45 'across the bow' of the sow's nose, as Leigh also took aim as back-up.

Ka Pow! echoed across the meadow.

The bullet exploded in a dry piece of oak, creating a cloud of splinters. The bear twisted in place, grumbled, stood on her hind legs, sniffed the air, grumbled again, saw nothing suspicious, then slapped the splintered piece of wood. Confused and probably concerned about her cubs' safety, she dropped to all fours and ran down the path—directly toward the bench on the river. The obedient cubs followed ass-over-teakettle fashion.

Little did the sow know she was headed directly at the muzzles of two large-caliber handguns pointed directly at her head and shoulders, at the ready, safety off, with both of the people holding them hoping they would not need to fire.

"I know it sounds risky, Leigh, but that sow is not coming after us. She's headed for the swamp across the river to the south. So . . . hold your fire," he whispered.

He was taking a calculated risk for both of them, but Leigh indicated by her actions that she had confidence in his judgment.

Then suddenly, as an apparent act of husbandry, he threw his arm around her and pulled her to the ground as the furry four passed by the bench and quickly splashed into and across the 'Root' in a thundering cascade of water. It was explosive! Just as quickly, he sat up, and rotated to maintain sight of the escaping sow in case she caught wind of their location and halted. Wisely, she continued into the swamp without hesitation.

"Are you okay, Leigh? Sorry to grab you like that."

Her look said thank you as they both cleared their guns' chambers of live rounds, then holstered. They waited a few minutes, and in an odd scene reminiscent of youthful-boy-meets-girl-silence, waited for one of them to summarize the incident. Leigh broke the ice.

"Thanks a hell of a lot—whoever you are," Leigh said with a sigh.

The stranger replied, "I hope you enjoyed the welcoming. I've been here for several days without any excitement; then you show up and all hell breaks loose. But, you're entitled to an explanation. Some of Jack South's last transmissions were heard in Skagway, and between Ford's Flight Service personnel, primarily Milt and Dave, and the DNR in Juneau, we decided that someone should safeguard your camp, whether you returned to Skagway with the rescue party or returned directly to your hut. We did not know what you'd do. I volunteered to parachute in when it was discovered you and Jack were carrying Ford's body to the DNR camp, on the coast. I feel very sorry for you. And as you may know, your loss is also our loss. My name is Andrew South, Jack's younger brother. I'm also known by my Indian name, 'Walkswithwind,' for you are probably aware the Tlingits settled this area years ago, and many remain here and in Canada. I understand you were the last one to be with Jack."

Leigh's mouth dropped open, and her knees started to tremble. She shuddered and clinched her fists to fight the tremors.

A noticeable silence enveloped the scene.

Andrew appeared immobilized.

It was as if the Earth stood still for Leigh.

Andrew spoke. "Leigh, are you . . . ah . . . okay?"

Before Leigh could answer, she collapsed into a heap at his feet.

*   *   *

Quickly, Andrew laid her out in a comfortable, supine position, then raised her legs with a log. He ensured her airways were clear, then dashed to the river to get some cold water.

"Damn, poor girl, she had not had time enough to overcome the trauma of the recent carnage. I hope I've done the right thing in coming here."

He approached Leigh with a damp cloth for her forehead and pondered his next move. Holding her hand, he took her pulse at 100 and continued to make her as comfortable as possible while keeping cold water on her head compress. Not sure what to do next, he decided it may be better for her on the bench, so he gently moved her and provided a pad for her head and feet to keep them elevated.

"Damn, what now? Wait? Or do something—but what?" he wondered.

That decision was made for him; *another* had decided what was next. Andrew snapped his head around and peered down the path toward the hut.

The whine he heard became a cry . . . and then the high-pitched screech of an alarmed young animal.

"Damned if it doesn't sound like a small canine or weasel," Andrew exclaimed. "What the hell! Would you look?" he said to himself. The wolf cub, wrapped in a poncho with a long pole attached, was trudging up the path as if hobbled to impede his progress. He didn't know what to think, but one thing was for sure: the little fella needed some help to escape Leigh's poncho/straightjacket. He looked like a clown, head poking through one hole, two legs another. He did not appear to be happy about his restraint. He had to rest every five or ten feet by sitting down, wailing loud enough to chill one's soul.

Andrew leaped into action. First he filled his cap with water and threw the entire contents on Leigh's face in an attempt to rouse her.

"What's that? Darn! What's up!" she exclaimed as she sat up, hands to face, and coughed out water. Then she leaped to her feet and coughed again. "What the hell? Who . . .?"

"Okay, girl, it's me you're going to be mad at."

"Oh, don't be silly," Leigh whispered. "I figured the lights went out again, as they have been doing more frequently lately. Not to worry—I understand."

Andrew commented, "Thank heavens, I was not sure you'd appreciate the abrupt awaking. Seriously. How are you? Do you understand why I'm here? I do so want to know of my brother's last few days with you. It is no small matter that you were part of that courageous alliance for my brother and Ford."

Leigh responded, "Of course, I'm all right, Andy. Your perception of my last twenty-four hours is right on target—I'm an emotional mess. Yes, please stay and help me through this transition of exhaling death and breathing in the reality of a new life. I'm okay one minute, and the next a basket case of doubt, fear, and yes, *guilt*. Please, stay and help me."

"Well, without a doubt, I'm here to help," he explained. "So what's the story on that angry wrapped-up wolf cub?"

"Oh, poor little motherless fella, come here. Sorry, I'd forgot about you. God love ya, you've found me. Andrew, I do believe he's tracked us to the bench since my scent was all he's had for the last couple hours. I hid him in the underbrush, fully wrapped up, Tom Sawyer-style, while I was checking you out."

"Okay, girl. The plan? What are we going to do with this chewing, growling, whining bundle of sharply pointed teeth? In all due respect, you may have made a bad decision to bring a wolf cub into camp. You've got an incorrigible and stubborn wild animal to train. I suppose you're already aware this fella is never going to be fully tame by our standards."

"Yes, I do. In spite of that, my options were limited. The alternative was unacceptable, to be the main course for a treacherous wolverine."

"But you're forgetting that, absent your presence, in fact, as we speak, many situations exactly as you describe are taking place in the wilds. Carnivorous animals devour each other to live. Need I mention that only the fittest survive?"

"Okay, okay, you're right, but be honest. Would you have left it to perish by starvation as wolf cub 'du jour' for the next carnivore passing through? I just couldn't do it, Andrew."

She donned her gloves and approached Tough as he continued to chew his way out of her torn poncho.

"Looking at him now, and with all he's gone through, don't you think Tough is an appropriate name?"

"Yeah, sounds good to me. Bet you end up calling him 'Tough Guy' at times when he's doing the right thing, and 'Bad Tough' when he misbehaves. Here, I'll help you wrestle that fellow out of the poncho."

"Hey, Andy, I've got an idea that will help settle him down. I'll give him some moistened pemmican, and he'll chew on it versus my already ruined poncho and boot. Here, take this to the river and soak it for a minute."

Andrew returned and gave Tough the moist block, which he immediately attacked as if a warrior on a personal conquest. His sounds shifted from a whine to a protective growl as his little teeth fractured the edges of the block. He licked the crumbs clean as if it were his last meal.

"Finally," Andrew said, "maybe we'll have a few moments of peace. You know, I'd guess he's about three to four months old. If his parents were in a pack, the Alpha male and female would've mated in February, and sixty-three days later she'd have dropped a litter of four to six pups. Tough would have stayed in the den until three months old and then immediately started eating regurgitated food from the entire pack. Ranging, hunting, and socialization with the pack would follow—and that's what Tough will surely miss. You, Leigh, by deciding to save the cub, will now have the opportunity to replace all that and teach the cub to our ways. It will be a daunting assignment, but as you indicated, the other option is unacceptable. You chose life."

"Indeed," she said, "but many have preceded me with successful taming of a wolf, starting early and training in the style of a dominant Alpha parent. And yes, I know it will be difficult. He'll certainly run off at times, so I've heard, but with love, care, feeding, and a need for his presence as my guardian, maybe, just maybe, I can keep him at my side."

They chatted at some length while watching Tough attack more pemmican, then decided to go to the hut. To bring him along, they tied a string to the pemmican and dragged the growling fur ball along the path. It was quite a sight as Tough ran, jumped, rolled, growled, and leaped at his moving 'prey.'

"He sure is animated," Leigh said.

"True, his style appears to be aggressively Alpha-like," Andrew noted.

"Let's see how he handles the stairs. Come on up, boy; come on."

Tough not only bounded up the stairs, but wiggled by Leigh into the hut, ran around the perimeter several times, then peed like there was no tomorrow, and put the brakes on at Boy's old bed of blankets. He then proceeded to pee again, roll and bark in an infantile yap-yip fashion as though he'd found a new home. He whined again, slowed down, and laid his head between his paws, then raised his eyes to his rescuers, blinked, and raised them again as if indicating: who, what, and where? Soon he lost his inquisitive curiosity and gravity pulled his eyelids closed. Within moments, he was asleep in the succor of Boy's bedstead and his own urine—soon to be his crib.

"Look," Leigh whispered to Andrew, "the little guy wore himself out again. He appears to be in dreamland; maybe we can do some preparation for his co-habitation now while the 'wild one' sleeps."

"Sure enough," Andrew agreed, "we'll need to fashion a collar of some sort and also build a pen either in here or outside. What do you think?"

"True, the collar's my job; I'll modify one of Boy's. The pen will take a little more ingenuity. Any ideas?"

"Sure, I've done it before. I'll just take a few sheets of that half-inch plywood outside by the wood pile and cut it into a four-by-four pen, three feet high. Then you can keep it in here or outside, depending on how you manage the little Terror of the Tongass. I'll make it so it's collapsible with hinged joints. Let's get at it; he may not sleep very long. Plus, I've got some cordwood stacking to do after the bear's explosive search for a rodent burger.

"Okay, Andy. Say . . . would you prefer Andrew?"

"No problem, Andy is fine, and much easier than Walkswithwind, for sure. You can even call me South, Windy, or Hey You. I'm flexible."

"Good." Leigh smiled. "Have you noticed the sun is only four fingers from the horizon? We'd better hustle."

"Sounds good to me; let's roll," Andy answered with excitement in his voice.

"I feel better already. Thank you so much for dropping in. I really don't know what I would have done without your caring support and opportunity to share the loss of Jack to both of us."

They moved together to the woodpile. She had been here before with amorous feelings toward his brother. Strangely, some of her feelings were similar now.

Unsure of his response . . . his acceptance, she embraced Andy in a warm expression of her thankfulness. In the time it took for eyes to meet, she felt a bond had formed.

Andy shuddered.

Yet, he did not resist.

Leigh understood the paradox of intimacy: it is easier to become close to others when *not* trying, but rather while ostensibly doing something else.

One of the pleasures that people discover is the gradual and delicately thrilling way in which two people come to know one another as they talk about themselves, their lives, and life.

He felt he must avoid this entanglement . . . for he had no plans to get involved with a woman . . . again.

He carefully disengaged her arms, and she wondered if he wanted to avoid getting more deeply involved.

They returned to the hut hand in hand. Leigh's advances had been subtly rebuffed, but she moved on . . . concealing her desires, her expectations, her bruised amour propre.

*   *   *

Perched in one of the twin pines by the river, a raven called to let everyone on the meadow know that he had borne witness to the day's activities with Leigh and Andy.

Chapter 15

Reality

The animals of the Tongass were growing restless, sleeping less, and eating more as they moved over the earth seeking a setting for winter's sleep. Likewise, birds forming long ribbons and wedges in the sky while migrating toward a far-off summer in the Southern Hemisphere.

Andrew and Leigh walked along the path to the river while enjoying Nature's grandeur unfolding. Geese passed in the azure sky to the west. The scene reminded Leigh of a similar sunset a mere twenty-four hours earlier, ten kilometers west, as she prepared to protect her lifeless friends from predators during Alaska's chilly night.

The last few days of fear, shock, grief, and despair overwhelmed her. Psychic wounds remained in her thoughts. Her eyes rolled up as she took a deep breath . . . and collapsed . . . again.

Andrew attempted to catch her.

"Leigh, are you okay? Hang in there; I'll be here with you. I'll lay you down here on the wood chips and elevate your legs."

Andrew was also a paramedic, through training in the DNR, and knew very well that it was no accident that Leigh's body responded again to the threatening events of the last twenty-four hours. Unfortunately, the past triggered it while she viewed what appeared to be a similar sunset with a similar person. It was just too much.

"Lie here awhile, girl," Andy said as he held her hand in a soothing manner. "Then I'll take you into bed so you can finally get some needed rest. Hold on just a minute; I'll take Tough's pen into the hut and 'encase' your new friend so he'll not have the run of the hut when he awakens."

Andrew moved the collapsible pen through the door and over the sleeping pup. Standing back to view the encased pup, he noticed it had form, fit, and function to hold in the 'wild one' at least for the near-term needs.

Quickly returning to Leigh, he checked her pupils for extremes of constriction or dilation. As expected, they were enlarged, pulse at 120. Eventually, thank goodness, Leigh would put the traumatic experiences of the last few days behind her. At least Andrew hoped she would, but not all are that fortunate. His training suggested that a third or more of people touched directly by events of this magnitude develop post-traumatic stress disorder (PTSD). PTSD was at least as old as war, but didn't become an official medical diagnosis until 1980. Its causes were still murky, and its course unpredictable, but the key symptoms were unmistakable. Immediately or months after, the original trauma, people with PTSD remained hyper-alert and easily startled. They suffered recurring nightmares and inability to recall the experiences without physically reliving them. Any passing reminder—a similar sound, an old friend's smell, a familiar locale, and a 'special' person could trigger intense distress. Andrew clearly reminded Leigh of her experiences with Jack.

"Leigh, I wonder if my presence as Jack's brother or previous events by the woodpile could have played a role . . .?" *What am I doing? She can't hear me. I better get her inside and start planning my next move—correction, our next move, or recommendation for her next move. Okay, girl, you've earned an all-night and all-day sleep. I'll bring my sack in and sleep on the floor between you and Tough. Which reminds me, I'll probably be the first to 'break him in' on the leash and collar—in the moonlight of the Alaskan night: if he gets up—or maybe he'll sleep till dawn. We'll soon see, won't we?*

Andrew laid her on the bed with extraordinary care and tenderly covered her fully clothed body with a blanket. A quick look at Tough was greeted with grateful snores of total immersion in sleep.

"Finally," he said, "I can roll out my sack and get some sleep, too. I'll just slip out and retrieve a few things and secure my tent."

The air was crisp and refreshing as Andy moved to the tent by the winter's (demolished) stockpile of cordwood. It was fortunate that his tent still remained intact after the bear's attack while searching for rodent burgers. Eyes skyward, he caught sight of early evening flocks of birds that skated like black pepper, then disappeared from view as they banked edgewise, only to appear again with a swooping turn. *Are they practicing formation flying while flocking, and maneuvering before they actually set off for the south? Like the Navy's Blue Angels, they swirl like huge plumes of insects over the treetops. They have no choice, really. Food and daylight start growing scarce, temperatures drop, and they must move on.* Man's choice was to remain.

As early evening nautical twilight darkened the sky, his exhaled vapor clearly showed in the moonlight. He scanned the meadow. A strange feeling had overtaken him near the tent. It was as if he was being watched by someone . . . or something. It was so strong now that he stopped and listened.

Zilch.

He heard nothing . . . other than calving ice at the face of the distant Mendaenhall Glacier to the west. The wind must have been blowing in this direction. He strained his senses while scanning a 360.

Nothing.

Who. Whoooooooyyyyyooooouuuu.

He looked south toward the bench on the Bitterroot, started walking down the path, and scanned the treetops as he moved toward the river's edge. There it was. An owl.

Wwwwhhhooo . . .   Wwwwhhhhhooo . . .   Whooo . . .

At about forty feet from the tree he stopped to concentrate on the owl's location above the branch near the river.

"Sure enough, you're still on location for your troubled subject: Leigh. Oh . . . Ah, Wise One, ah . . . Manitou? I do believe I know of your connection/relationship to Leigh. Thank you for helping. Be assured, I will stay to assist Leigh in every way possible until she's able to fend for herself."

Wwwhhhooo.

Then . . . silence.

A raven landed near the Owl.

Caw—Caw—Caw.

More silence.

Immediately the owl seemed to disappear, yet Andy did not see him fly away. Strange. It was as if the raven replaced or displaced the owl. He blinked and looked around to find the retreating bird, but it was nowhere to be found. There was an unusual feeling along the meadow, and eerie sense of a 'happening' or an incident that was upsetting the normal evening's activities on the meadow. The usual complement of nocturnal animals was absent. He looked around the area to determine if he could see any dramatic changes beyond the woodpile's destruction. The bear's digging did expose a thicket of smaller tress that the pile had previously blocked from view.

Turning back toward the river and slowly walking to the end of the pile, he noticed the mess behind the original stack . . . which now looked like a dumped "rick" of wood.

He mused, "Damn, look at this mess, some of the smaller pieces have been thrown or tossed up to thirty feet."

Without hesitation, he started stacking the logs in the proper way, and piled the building materials on a pair of four-by-fours. As he moved into the thicket of tag elders, deadfalls, and ferns to retrieve a few rogue cords, he discovered another bear excavation . . .

"Oh no . . . I'll be a son of a bitch!" he exclaimed. He took a deep breath and blew it out; that done . . . he froze in place. He thought, "Now I can see why there's an eerie overcast on the meadow tonight."

The bears accidentally, while digging for roots and rodents, dug into one of a series of old Indian burial mounds behind the cordwood pile. They had exposed several skeletons. The mounds had previously been masked by deadfalls, 'tag elders,' and a beautiful, huge blanket of bracken ferns.

Leaning over, he discovered the remains of a ornamented adult body with beads, shells, and weapons which would signify a person of rank. Disjointed now, the skeleton appeared as though the head also had an elaborate crown of feathers—if, that is, the head belonged to the exposed body. There were two or three more bodies partially exposed . . . all with portions of the skeleton disjointed or missing. What a mess. Two of the bodies were encased in degraded animal skin capes, with decorative hair braided around their necks and attached to their pouchlike medicine bags. These two seemed to be of lesser rank, but were still ornamented with bone pipe beads, shell-like amulets, trinkets, and silver-like metal. Andy paused . . . in awe but very disturbed by the find, and the unfortunate exposure of the Indian's sacred burial site. But for the appearance of an errant rodent that must have been uncovered in the burial site and ran to the woodpile, the entire burial ground would have been unearthed, and the bears would never have left the site. Unearthing the mounds could have been worse.

"Now, what to do . . . I'm in a sacred place that has been disturbed. Although no fault of mine, I'm violating local taboos by just being here, so the best thing I can do is close up the site quickly and get away as soon as possible.

The Chinde, death ghost, had already made its presence known in the area. The eerie feeling affecting the area around this intrusion of the burial site was hanging in the mist of the clearing.

He got a shovel and quickly reburied the three disjointed skeletons. He tried his best to ensure each was returned to the same site from which it was unceremoniously removed. The bones had been a mere annoyance to the bears as they dug for the rodents, tender roots of the Swamp Lily, and other succulents of the lowlands near the river. Having done the best he could under the circumstances, he started backfilling the holes in the mounds . . . and then it started.

Wooooooeeeeeeaaaaaa . . . AAAAeeeeAoooo.

A 'Wailing Wind' echoed down the valley floor and across the meadow, shattering the silence of the evening. It seemed to be coming from the plateau. The sound was of a high-pitched feminine nature with undulating warbles of highs and lows. Andy strained for a better look toward the edge of the plateau.

"Well I'll be damned. The death ghost, Chinde, may be a reality. The legend of the Tlingit says: If Chinde's song is heard, a taboo has been violated, a custom wronged . . . and if that sacred error is not corrected immediately, sickness will overtake the body of the violator."

Still looking toward the plateau, Andy saw a dim light shining upward into the ether . . . as if coming from the old altar site.

Woooeeeaaa . . . AAeeAoo.

"I'll be. Now I've heard and seen everything that's been talked about around the fireplaces by my ancestors."

The Wailing Wind continued in a hypnotic fashion as Andy stood mesmerized by the scene. He had been told earlier to expect the spirit to express itself in mysterious ways. His shaman brother, Walkswithwater, had told him of those beliefs often.

He felt stiff. He didn't seem to be able to move . . . He felt as if . . . frozen in time and place. The wailing finally subsided.

Moving a little now . . . it was as if the Wailing Wind had been holding him in place . . . or was it the raven, now staring at his every move. He remained at the mounds, but resumed backfilling. Was the owl at the plateau now? Was it his presence there that triggered the Wailing Wind? Did his brother's words still make sense . . . in this situation? Was he doing the right thing by filling in the burial site? Brother Jack had offered his view of man's combined mythical thoughts. He had always told him that the spectacle of spiritual events pass over the face of the earth, again and again, and its power had impressed him, and stirred him to meditate on the causes of these stunning transformations so vast and wonderful—right here in the shadow of Tongass timber. Even a savage would not fail to see, to perceive how intimately life is bound up with nature, and how the same processes which freeze the stream, strip the earth of vegetation, and incite dramatic events affecting the tribe could menace him with extinction, too. In the course of time, the slow advance of knowledge, which had dispelled so many cherished illusions, convinced at least the more thoughtful in mankind that the spirits were not merely the result of their own magical rites, but that some *deeper cause*, some *mightier power*, was at work behind the shifting scenes of nature. As a result the old magical theory was displaced, or rather supplemented, by religious theory. What resulted was a blending of *religious theory* with *magical practice*.

Andy reflected those thoughts, and how they affected the night, that unique spiritual/magical blending or union: the Raven, the Owl, the Wailing Wind, the Light on the plateau . . . indeed, his current experiences had not wholly succeeded in extricating themselves from the trammels of magic.

"I've always wondered, even as a grown man, if I was doing the right thing. That's where I am again. This situation is different, to be sure. For example: Did the owl hear me? Could I have done things differently? Am I getting too involved with Leigh?"

He decided. Absolutely. Yes. He was doing the right thing.

He knew Leigh's PTSD would linger for a month or more after the impact of the week's trauma. She would need loving care and the comfort of another person to build confidence and coping skills.

He mused, I'm not prepared or trained in the behavioral sciences, but she has no one else. I'd better get prepared for some exhausting days with a woman who will need a lot of emotional support. Strange, isn't it? When something like this comes along, my problems seem less important. On the other hand, in losing a brother, I may have gained a friend. I wonder if my decision to wait at her camp was not accidental, but rather divine intervention of Manitou. We'll see. One thing is certain, I'll be here. Better let the folks in Skagway and Juneau know in the morning of my plans.

Thankfully, he could move now without any sense of being held back.

He turned and started walking back to the hut, then stopped, spun, and looked to the solitary oak where the raven was perched.

Gone, nothing on the oak's bare branches.

He pondered, again, the animal's role in nature's construct of birth, life, trauma, and death. For now it appeared he was a part of their witness to Leigh. This tragedy had brought new insight into relationships and service to Him, and realigned to the front burner of life's many priorities.

He scanned the fringes of the forest and riverbank as he slowly moved to the hut. He felt the impact of the day's activities and responsibilities, and acknowledged that the alternative—to leave—was unacceptable. It was a time-honored tradition among men and women of his tribe to aid those in need.

The meadow was silent now as he closed the door and attempted to grab a few winks. He knew sleep was unlikely, and he also knew very well the cub may rise and whine at any moment. Likewise, Leigh's obvious restlessness was most likely attributable to sorting out the nightmare of terror.

The silence along the ridgeline was broken by the call of a red-tailed hawk circling overhead. Its vision, many times greater than ours, would soon sight some prey and dive, its talons tearing into an unexpecting rabbit or rodent on the meadow. Its sharp hooked beak would then tear flesh much like a surgeon's scapel. This unique carnivore, while capturing animals at the lower end of the food chain would perform its survival task with barely a sound of its butchery.

Likewise, the flocks above would be continuing their journey, aided frequently by hitching a ride on a cold front where the winds would speed them along, only to switch as necessary to other trade winds, like subway lines in the sky.

Wedges of geese would be anxious to reach their southern breeding ground, an overnight rest secondary to their mission. Their silhouette against the moon would appear as nature's geometric lacework, or web of life. At five thousand feet, the air would be frigid, but clear for navigation. Just how did they travel so well and so accurately? As with many aspects of life it appeared simple, when its complexity overwhelms the mind.

Most observers assumed they knew the how, when, and where of migration. In truth, they did not. But most likely they had an inborn sense to use the sun as their compass, which they could locate even on cloudy days; fragrances of familiar marshes, crashing waves against coastal rocks, altered winds at the water line of great seas, and maybe the planet's changing barometric pressures—all were navigational cues.

If all else fails, elders can guide the young flock—so, with one thing or another, they survived what seemed like almost impossible journeys.

Andrew reflected on his fate. The birds had no other choice—did he? No.

He would not migrate.

At least not now.

He would not leave her alone in the Tongass until she could cope.

Silence.

Packs of wolves howled, their voices echoing through the valley above the meadow as if communicating to each other with cries of unknown origin.

Andrew's eyes yielded to sleep as he restlessly fought the day's events.

Leigh tossed and turned in her bed, the cub dozing in his pen.

Were the wolves aware of their loss?

Were the wolf packs following the cub's scent?

Were they aware of the location?

Were they pursuing one of their own?

Were they moving closer to the meadow?

Silence.

The sounds of the packs started again . . . but Andrew was falling asleep.

Silence.

Then . . . *Caw—Caw—Caw* . . . the raven returned to his post.

Chapter 16

Alarm

It was two o'clock in the morning.

"Wa . . . What's that?" Andrew mumbled.

Andrew heard Tough growling and thrashing about in his pen. He leaped up to investigate . . . it was nothing. Tough was apparently having a troublesome dream. While Andrew lingered at the pen for a moment he suddenly felt Leigh's warmth, her presence, her alluring feminine fragrance . . . Half-startled, he turnend toward her bed and caught her eyes very close to his—much too close. Almost touching. . .

"I heard you at the pen with Tough. Is he all right? Is there a problem?"

She wore nothing but a large, well-worn blue "Michigan" T-shirt. Her glimmering auburn hair folded over her shoulders and down her back. The triangle marker was covered at the shirt's hem . . . barely covered. Her chest gave the yellow Michigan letters a saw-toothed range look. She leaned over the edge of the pen at breast height, causing a massive protrusion of the paired beauties . . . He refocused on her question.

"No, he's okay. Just look at him; you're responsible for this noble decision to have him join you. You saved his life. I'm proud to be helping."

"Why, thank you, dear," said Leigh as she moved closer.

Before the conversation got too personal, Andrew shifted to a discussion about icons of Native American mythology. He chose to share wolf stories with Leigh, the legends his dad had told around the tribal fires during his youth. "Leigh, you're looking at a living mythology. Some have called the wolf and its progeny man's best friend.

"Tough is one of the approximately a hundred-sixty thousand wolves worldwide, and one of about ten thousand near the caribou herds at sixty-degree latitude in North America, feeding on local moose, the deer herd, and smaller mammals. Most are gray timber wolves like Tough in the sub-arctic, and fewer arctic or tundra white wolves are near the Arctic Circle. He could eat a third of his weight at one kill, then go for two weeks without food when necessary.

"As an adult wolf, at a hundred pounds, he could bring down any large herbivore alone. It would not have to be young, injured, or weakened with age. Naturally, hunting with the pack or in deep-crusted snow would contribute to a higher probability of a successful kill. The kill is not pretty, but necessary for the survival of the fittest to endure this harsh clime and successfully propagate their species. I have observed many savage kills. That is the way of the wild animals in the Tongass. What appeared to be barbaric to outsiders was normal survival to the pack.

"Native Americans of the forest frequently choose a wolf, and sometimes a bear, as icons due to their images of strength, stamina, and survival in the wilds. They revered them as sacred leaders. Tough would indeed be your protector . . . if training was successful. Many chiefs incorporated wolf and bear into their names, displayed paw prints on shields, medicine wheels, mandalas, or tepees to signify the leader of the tribe or local shaman. Travelers soon learned the chief's or shaman's dwelling not only by the marks on their abode, but by the wolf or bear totems nearby."

Andrew reflected on how his brother, Walkswithwater, as a shaman constantly performed rites to strengthen tribal warriors for battle through special ceremonies, providing the basis for spiritual amulets to shore up their bravery for tribal conflicts. The strength, speed, cunning, and soul of the wolf served this role very well.

"This would be the expectation of Tough for you . . ." Andrew stressed. "The extended soul of man is not merely with inanimate objects and plants. Shamans indicate a warrior occasionally believes to be united by a bond of *physical sympathy*. The same bond, supposed by many tribal units, may exist between a man and an animal so that the welfare of one depends on the welfare of the other, and when the animal dies the man may, at times, also die. The analogy between the custom and tales is all the closer because in both the power of removing the soul from the body and transferring it to the animal is often a special privilege of wizards and shamans. As a result our Tlingit shaman may keep or transfer his soul, or one of his souls, incarnate in an animal, which is carefully concealed from all the world.

"Tlingits believe:

> "The soul of a person may pass into another person or into an animal, or rather that such a mysterious relation can arise between the two that the fate of one is wholly dependent on that of the other.

"Tlingits also believe:

> "A shaman has the power to unite his life with that of some

particular wild animal through rites of blood brotherhood; he draws blood from the ear of an animal—for example, a wolf—and from his own arm, then inoculates the animal with his own blood, and himself with blood of the wolf.

"This alliance was thought to bring the shaman a great accession of power, which could turn to his advantage in various ways. Like a Warlock in fairy tales, the Indian shaman and warrior, who has deposited his life outside of himself in some safe place, now deems himself *invulnerable*. Moreover, the animal with which he has exchanged blood has become his familial, a spirit held as companion to serve or guard, and will obey any orders he may choose to give; so he makes use of it to injure his enemies. For that reason the creature with whom he establishes the relation of blood brotherhood is never a tame or domestic animal, but always a ferocious and dangerous wild beast, such as you, Tough."

"Andrew, are you telling me your tribal leaders believe in, and guide their lives on the basis of familial ties with wolves?"

"Yes and no. Some do, some don't, but those warriors who put their lives on the line for the clan truly believe in the mystic powers of the shaman. The chief enters the fray when the shaman gets out of line with reality."

"Okay, just wondered."

"Here's another mythical idea. Listen up; it's complex: *protection of familials.* The power of stealth or concealing themselves is an indispensable condition of the choice of animal familials since the animal is expected to injure his owner's enemy by furtive means; for example, appearing suddenly and unexpectedly when the enemy is weakened or trapped."

"But, Andrew, how could a warrior avoid killing a familial wolf?"

"It is difficult, but from this it follows that the animal kinsfolk may never be shot at or molested. This did not, however, prevent the people of the area, who had wolves for their animal friends, from hunting wolves. For they did not respect the whole species, but *certain individuals* of it, which stand in an intimate relation to certain individual tribal members; and they imagine that they could always *distinguish* these brothers from the common pack of wolves, which are wolves and nothing more.

"The recognition was said to be mutual. When a hunter who had a wolf as a "blood" friend met the human wolf, as it may be called, the noble wolf would let his identity be known; he'd be separate frequently—a rogue—or move differently than the pack.

"When a tribal warrior names himself after an animal, calls it his brother, and refuses to kill it, the animal is said to be his totem. More commonly the totem is appropriated not to a sex, but to a clan, and its heredity is either in the male or female line. The relation of an individual to the clan totem does not differ from his relation to the sex totem; he would not kill it; he speaks of it as his brother, and he calls himself by its name. Now, if the relations are similar, the explanation which holds good for the one ought equally to hold good for the other. The totem, on this theory is simply the receptacle in which a man keeps his life.

"Natives, unshackled by dogma, are free to explain the facts of life by the assumption of as many souls as they think necessary. For if a native seriously believes that his life is bound up with an external object, it is in the last degree unlikely that he would let any stranger into the secret. It is therefore no surprise that the mystery of the wolf's part in his life remains a secret, left to be pieced together from scattered hints and fragments of their legends and tribal beliefs.

"What do you think of your wolf, Leigh? Fearless and assaultive to man, no. Mysterious, yes. On the contrary, most are careful around man, and would avoid him unless trapped, wounded, or rabid. One thing is certain: they're unpredictable. Training yours will be a real challenge."

"What a wonderful story, a *mysterious legend* to be sure. I don't know what to believe. Thank you, dear. I'll probably dream, too, like Tough. I hope mine are pleasant. Good night, dear."

Within minutes, Leigh fell asleep and Andrew had escaped her advance. It was 2:30.

*   *   *

WWWHHOOOoo.

"Leigh? Leigh? Leigh, are you awake?" Andy called from his bedroll.

Silence.

Tough flopped over in his pen, growled, and continued wheezing in his sleep.

"Oops, better be quiet; I sure don't need him up at three in the morning," he whispered.

"I know the wolves are moving closer. Their cries are louder and more frequent. I wonder if they're headed this way."

Andy lay back down in his sack to contemplate the wolves' activity along the ridgelines to the north. Their cries might have been typical of nightly hunts, but that was hard to determine. The route may have accidentally traversed the cleft to the west of the meadow, then headed this way by chance. After all, the route of the fleeing prey determines the path of those in pursuit.

Not being an authority of wolf-pack habits, he could not tell whether the pack was even interested in the four-legged houseguest in the pen. "I wonder if I should get up and wander around camp and the meadow. The wolves could be chasing just about anything, or just searching."

Slump! Kerplunk! Slump!

It was so loud and happened so unexpectedly that Andrew banged his head on the potbelly stove when he bolted-up from his sack. He stood up, fell, recovered, threw on some shoes, and carefully opened the door, then peered out over a scene of dust and particulate masking the entire area to the west behind the woodpile. His first thoughts were . . . a plane crash, a meteor impact . . .

The particulate suspension was more evident beyond the woodpile, over the Indian burial mounds. Closing the door, he quietly moved down the steps with flashlight in hand. The light beam clearly showed the suspended particulate to the west . . . yet it was clear elsewhere. He pondered his next move.

He slowly advanced around the newly stacked cordwood and furtively moved toward the taboo grounds, now laden with settling dust. He stopped short of the mounds and scanned the area.

He froze when the light penetrated into the mound area.

The mounds had disappeared.

All he could see now was a large sinkhole.

Was this a natural tectonic event?

Could it have been an underground stream collapsing on itself?

Or, Manitou's wrath?

He approached the edge of the sinkhole, then scanned the depression with the light. Ferns covering the surface shielded the depression—as if it had been in place for some time. *That's puzzling.*

Strange, eerie, or serene . . .   The new sinkhole's presence appeared as if an old natural setting.

"Well, I'll be damned. Just look at this display of spiritual prowess. I shouldn't be surprised. There was a violation of the sacred grounds, albeit accidental. All those who know the tribal rules would certainly have predicted something like this . . . at least I escaped His wrath."

Andy sat by the cordwood pile until all the air cleared and then filed the event away in his mind as another learning experience. Cold and tired, he returned to his sack to join the sleeping pair.

Silence returned to the meadow.

Andy's sleep was restless as he reflected on the complex events of the day.

* * *

At 3:30, Andy could not sleep, so he slowly put on his boots and jacket and quietly moved toward the door, flashlight in hand, careful not to awaken the sleeping pair.

The evening was clear, cool, and absolutely spellbinding with its beauty.

Hoo-hoo-hoo. Hoo.

Andy looked up in surprise, his heartbeat quickening at this familiar, yet un-expected call. He had heard the great horned owl while camping with his brother as a youth exploring the Tongass.

The owl hooted again. And again.

He wondered if his call has any significance to the evening's earlier events. He also wondered if Leigh had heard the arboreal screeching. Probably not; she hadn't heard the sinkhole forming.

Hoo, hoo, hoo.

It could be a mating call; he certainly wasn't hunting with all that noise.

Andy moved toward the bird's perch, but paused, hesitated, and stopped. It was as if being struck by a club . . . He halted.

The path had been disturbed within the last hour.

He examined fresh tracks in the frost-coated surfaces around the woodpile and leading to the bench, likewise to the porch of the hut.

He recognized the tracks.

Wolves.

The pack had filtered silently across the meadow into the camp, most likely following the scent of Tough's trail or activities earlier in the day. And, who knew, they may have heard the sound of the sinkhole's formation.

Silence.

He felt as if being watched.

Andy swung his eight-cell beam along the edge of the meadow's tree line.

Nothing.

He then pointed the beam along the path toward the bench on the river.

Wolves.

The vaporizing warm breath of the wolves in the night air was highlighted by the beam first. It was as if a cloud hovered over the ground. A dozen pairs of eyes reflected their orange glow through the mist.

The silence was overwhelming.

It was an awesome sight.

Yet, no one moved.

Fifteen seconds . . .

It was a staredown with no end in sight.

Each pair of eyes was focused on the beam of light as if hypnotized, as if frozen in space.

How many seconds . . . minutes? Who knew? Andy slowly moved the beam away from the pack and swung it left, then right, to determine if others languished in the shadows.

After a 180-degree scan . . . nothing.

Fifteen more seconds . . .

The staredown continued; no one moved.

Were they making a statement by their presence, by their stares, by their posturing?

He was alarmed, but the hut was only twenty feet away, the wolves at least two hundred. He did not feel any peril if these offsets remained.

They might be inspecting the new sinkhole, or maybe all of them had been out and around the area earlier in the day.

Andy spoke: "Well, are we going to be friends? Or am I to assume saving or holding your cub prevents us from doing so? Maybe we can compromise our positions. We'll raise Tough, your cub, and if he chooses to leave at maturity—we'll let him go, if he hasn't already. It will be his decision. Okay? What are you doing, Andy? These wolves have no idea . . ."

Suddenly, a dozen pairs of eyes shifted to the hut's door. Then suddenly each grayish mass followed the Alpha male's nervous half step, and quarter-turn upon hearing and seeing Leigh exit the hut with a flashlight; but then held position—as if her appearance presented no threat. They did not speak, but directed both beams to the bench area.

The Alpha male crouched, lowered his head, and curved up slightly with a low snarl. He looked hostile all right, but not offensive in the sense of being prepared to attack. The remaining wolves held their ground in a curious and attentive stare, as if waiting for the leader's next move.

"Andy," Leigh whispered, "I heard you talking earlier and, for the life of me, could not figure out who you were talking to . . . now I see. What are you—we—going to do? How long have you been out here? Are they going to attack? Do they want Tough?"

"Hold on, first things first, questions later. I'm no wolf psychic. But I think they're just about finished with this, 'checking out the hut routine;' and yes, they've scented Tough, but I'm gonna guess he's not a factor; they'll soon continue their nightly search for food."

"But what do we do now? They're not leaving. You can't stay out here all night—and how 'bout the 'morrow?"

"You're right, but let's try another technique. With a gibbous moon we'll have enough light to see; so let's douse the lights, move to the hut, and just leave them alone. I'll bet they'll depart within minutes and continue their hunt."

"Sounds good. Okay, mine's out," Leigh whispered. Andy killed his eight-cell and stared at the gray mass for a moment, now all erect, ears pointed and noses drinking in the air.

"Keep that door open; I'm going to make my move now."

He turned slowly and walked up the path to the hut, grabbed Leigh's hand, the door, and entered the hut.

Leigh breathed a major sigh of relief. With tear-bathed eyes, she latched on to Andrew and held him tightly. He held her softly and carefully. Trembling at first, he held her for what seemed to be minutes, and when she calmed down, he spoke.

"Leigh, you're going to be fine. Let me put you back in bed. Come on. You haven't even had a straight four hours for days."

Andy gently lifted her onto the bed. Then by plan, it appeared, she removed her flannel shirt 'for effect,' and he carefully and purposely pulled the covers over her partially clothed body. The uncovered skin that shared the night air . . . was indeed beautiful; he moved the blankets higher to cover her beautiful breasts and erect nipples. He kissed her on the hand and sat on the edge of the bed as promised.

"Andy, the wolves?" she mumbled.

"They're gone. I checked out the window. Sleep tight, you'll be fine, and so will Tough."

He mused, a 'white lie,' but they'll certainly be gone by now.

"Okay, thanks; I'm better now. You can sleep, too; no need to just sit with me."

"That's okay. I'll stay with you until you're asleep," Andy whispered. "Also, try to sleep in. I'll take care of Tough in the morning."

Andy crawled into his sack, even though her body language and eyes telegraphed *my bed is yours, too.* He tried to sleep.

"Look at me, Andy."

He rolled over and caught her eyes as she sat up in bed—the halo-like aureole exposed again.

"I'll be okay. I assure you," she said. "This emotional cripple you're stuck with will get better pretty damn quick. I will, I know I will—you'll see. I'm not so bad to be with when I'm one-hundred percent, and that will be next week—for sure. Thanks, and good night, my dear man of the forest."

"Good night, Leigh. I, too, am anxious to see you well. Good night, courageous lady of the meadow."

His 'little white lie' started to bother him, so he waited for her breathing to signal sleep, then quietly went out to ensure his comment was fact.

As expected, the wolves were gone. Walking slowly along the path, he saw the wolves' urine marks on the walkway edges and on the bench. The smell of urine permeated the evening air. They let their presence be known.

Considering the face-off earlier in the night, Andy decided it was not as dangerous as Leigh and he had thought. True, wolves surrounding your house was no picnic, but they probably would have scattered with a loud shout of, "Git!" It was just more interesting to stare them down or observe their behavior without a noisy confrontation.

Hoo-hoo-hoo.

The owl returned, and there was no doubt he was working the magic of his voice on Andy. It reminded him of how much he loved Alaska and the mighty Tongass. To be part of a world that included the owl's voice, wails of the loons, and howls of the wolves was a gift indeed. Their voices expressed wildness and mystery of lives with secrets that are rarely revealed. He wondered if others elsewhere were standing outside their houses, pulled away from the familial responsibilities or technological distractions of TVs, CDs, or computers . . . and listening to Nature's sounds.

The owl's call stopped at the exact moment the wolves' howling started over the ridge to the west. The pack was on the run again, at least five miles downwind. He waited a few minutes to be sure, then sat on the porch. Still under the spell of voices of the night, he savored the moment, knowing years from now he'd remember this night.

Andy pondered the moment; so much was happening to him as a result of Leigh's tragic experiences the last couple days. He stretched his cramped muscles, looked up, and let his eyes capture the Alaskan sky.

"Well, Mr. Owl, it's just you and I. I've never seen such brilliance—no moon, no aurora, no city glare, nothing but thousands of brilliant stars sparkled in the deep blackness. How could I ever describe such an overpowering sight? I certainly need a companion to be with, to share with, to love with on nights like this. My time will come. I just do not want a relationship like that yet. Leigh? No, she'll be treated as a sister in peril, nothing more. I've yet to talk to her about Jack. That will come over time, and I'm prepared to stay with her a week or two . . .

"Tonight was different. I feel like lingering and wandering with my eyes among the Milky Way, the Big and Little Dippers, the Gemini Twins, and the Seven Sisters of the Pleiades. I wish I could recognize more constellations, their origins, their legends.

"What was the story of Orion, the giant hunter? Or Taurus the bull? Many suggest, to say the least, that it's odd so many civilizations discerned the shape of a bear in a specific region of the sky. A bear is stretching it—yet that's exactly what native Americans, ancient Greeks, the Germanic tribes of middle Europe, and others saw in this formation . . . a bear! Why such disparate civilizations should all project the same unlikely 'bruin' onto these stars remains a mystery.

"The myths explaining the origins of Ursa Major vary greatly, yet many North American native groups, including our Tlingit tribe, say that the bear is born in heavens and later becomes an envoy connecting the physical and spiritual worlds. It seems the perfect story for a magical night in grizzly country.

"I find it paradoxical, Mr. Owl, that only we here can observe the night sky since city dwellers cannot see past the light pollution blocking their view.

"Good night, great horned Owl. My watch says four o'clock in the morning; better get some shut eye. I've a feeling another four-legged animal will need my attention very soon."

Andrew sneaked quietly into the hut, checked his two roommates, and collapsed with eyes still seeing stars.

Hooo-hoo-hoo, echoed across the ridge line and bounced back across the meadow, then finally sank in the 'Root.

*   *   *

The stars' brightness faded as a pale yellow glow lit the eastern horizon.

Slowly, a sun-driven shadow of a web-like circle stalked across the floor of the hut toward Andrew, cast from the window above Leigh's head—an Indian "Dream Catcher," most likely given to her by Jack.

Dream Catchers are given to those who believe in the Great Spirit. It is frequently hung above beds to sift dreams and visions. The good in dreams is captured in the web of life and carried with them . . . the evil in dreams escapes through the hole in the center and is dissipated by the feathers so they are no longer a part of their life. Some believe the Dream Catcher holds their destinies.

Andrew hoped for a future with many positive life experiences as he drifted into a deep sleep while the web framed his face in dawn's early light. He also hoped Leigh's web captured the best in her future life.

Silence engulfed the dawn as sounds vanished, but only for the moment . . . daylight will bring new voices and challenges to the awakening of the meadow, ridgelines, and mountains.

Chapter 17

The Plan

Late the next morning, either the rustling of Leigh brewing coffee in the kitchen area, or the smell roused Tough from a deep sleep.

First sounds were soft whimpers, peeing, and more murmurs at a high frequency sound as though he had something caught in his throat.

Leigh walked over to where Andy was still sawing logs, unaware of her activities, the smell of coffee, or Tough's subtle noises. She turned toward the kitchen table.

Then it happened—all hell broke loose as Tough started howling.

"Yip-yip-yip-oooooo-ip-ooo!"

Then again.

And again.

His next "shot" was unexpected. He leaped against the 4x4 hinged enclosure with such force that it toppled over and collapsed in a pancake fashion with Tough as a "pig-in-a-basket."

"Yeeeooowww Yip!" Tough scratched and struggled to free himself from the collapsed pen inches from the waking Andy.

Finally free, he tore around the circular floor, eyes scanning the confines of the walls. He appeared to be looking for something, but not sure of what.

Needless to say, Andy was struggling to escape his sack as Tough leaped over his body like a gazelle escaping a lioness. He had to get a collar or leash on the running/howling cub soon, before everything was turned upside down and inside out.

Tough ran into Andy on the next 'rounder,' glanced off, and continued on while peeing, howling, and yapping without pause for anything in his path. He ran like hell on wheels.

Leigh, too, attempted to get a handhold on the racing furry mass. As she leaped for the cub on one pass, her hastily donned shirt popped open, revealing two magnificent bosoms struggling to get out of their confining lacy blue hammocks. This unexpected 'treat' redirected Andy's thoughts momentarily, but the cub came first. He'd sworn off women anyway.

"Damn club," Leigh exclaimed, as she tried to re-button her shirt.

"Get a sack, Leigh" Andy shouted. "Maybe we can bag the bugger and collar the little rascal."

"One more try!" As she lunged at the cunning cub and missed his tail but snagged his hind leg, she slipped to his paw and held on tight enough to throw him ass-over-teakettle. The capture was short-lived; she released the cub after he awarded her a quick nip on the hand.

"You little devil!" She inspected the trickle of blood on her palm. "You'd think he'd be worn out by now. Okay, here's a bag. I'll hold it open while you herd the little bugger my way. Here he comes!"

They both struggled for position as Tough finally slowed down from warp speed to the speed of light.

Then, with Leigh's flick of the wrist on the open bag and Andy's kick in the cub's butt, followed by a *Yipe*, Tough stumbled into the bag head first, not knowing what had happened. Quiet now, in the dark, he must have wondered if he had returned to the womb . . . albeit burlap.

Andy retrieved the sack and held the canine terror in place while searching for a tie. After tying a 'Gordian Knot' and hoping Alexander the Great was not in the area, he finally lay the sack down—and rested.

They looked at each other, at the mess, and back at each other's eyes as if searching for words, locked in an embrace of visual emotion—totally drained. They started to smile, then laughed and finally collapsed in each other's arms. It was a natural embrace of success—not lust. They had won. Their foe was finally captive. Andy felt good in her arms, but they both had work to do, so they abruptly separated with high fives.

"Got 'em, didn't we?" Leigh exclaimed. "Would you just look at this mess! You fix the pen, Andy, and I'll clean up the clutter."

"Okay, Babe, I'll put Tough's pen back together with locking pins on the hinges and bracing so he can't collapse the darn thing. Knowing him, he'll probably still try to push it around as if a pushcart. We'll tie a rope around it, if necessary, not unlike a shark cage."

"Yipe!" The furry animal in the dry and itchy confines of the sack came to life as the couple rebuilt the pen and cleaned up the coffee, both dry and wet, pots and pans, rugs, bedding, and Andy's peed-on fart sack—what a mess.

"Is that a canine tootsie-roll turd in the corner? Yep, sure is," moaned Andy.

"Damn, what else did I miss?" said Leigh. "I'll mop up all these wolf tracks like-coffee-dye later."

"Are you almost done? I'd like to air out this place," Leigh whispered as if she did not want the cub to hear. She almost spelled "open." "Remember when you were about six years old and could spell, your Grandma would spell words not to be heard by little ears? Like: 'Did you know that Grandpa came home d-r-u-n-k last night?' And you played dumb so you could get the drift of a secret;

and later when a treat was coming and Grandma said to Mom: 'Can I buy the kids some i-c-e c-r-e-a-m?'

"Just look at this place," Leigh said as she opened the door. "I'm sure glad the Limoges china was not on the table; this stainless steel ware is practically in-destructible."

"Sure enough, Babe. Let's carry this pen outside and let Tough frolic in it while I watch him and you clean up. Likewise, he can air out and dry out, too. Did you notice your hands smell a pungent odor of wolf pee?"

"Yes, I'm about to take care of that while cleaning the floor."

"Here, let me rinse my hands off in that soapy water. That bundle of woebe-gone wolf's howl is getting right under my skin. Maybe the fresh air and freedom from his sack will quiet the little trembling warrior of the Tongass."

"Okay, boy, here we go." Andy picked up the sack and carefully carried the struggling womb-bound cub outside.

"You're not to blame for all this, you're just out of your element—and all that goes with it—you'll soon be all right; hang on a few minutes more."

Dumping Tough in the pen was as if an act by Houdini; he actually struggled to remain in the bag. Did he feel safer in the sack's darkness, or was it the com-forting "out of sight, out of mind" reprieve?

"There you go, boy," Andy said as the furry ball fell right on his butt, then froze in place with a faraway look of wonder in his eyes. He appeared to ask: Is this my new domain? Andy stepped back quickly, thinking he'd have a little more time away from watching the pen if the cub didn't see him. He wondered, would he try to jump out, or would he hopefully rest?

Luckily it was like calm after the storm as Tough whined a little, howled, and ended with a weak, guttural *wwwooo-o-o-o*. He soon collapsed into a deep sleep.

As Andy went back inside, Leigh said, "What are we going to do with my adopted son? Is this going to work?"

The doubting look on her face was troublesome. Had she embraced a trou-blemaker that would demand all her time? Would he come around? Would basic discipline through operant training work? *Do what I say and you're fed (reward); don't and you'll be hungry (punishment).*

"Andy, here I am in the middle of nowhere with my primary goals to explore, write, and drink deeply of the wine of solitude, and I introduce this wild animal to the scene. I need my head examined; it may not work. You'll be moving on, and I can see me spending ninety percent of my time civilizing that rambunctious cub . . . What do you think I should do?"

While Andy fashioned a collar/leash from and old belt, Leigh poured some wine. "Andy, we need this boost."

Sensing her frustration, Andy carefully mulled over her options before speaking. She could pack him up and release him near an active den—if she could find one. Or she could just let him go by the hut, assuming he'd run away, and not worry at all. Likewise, she could try to give him basic training with the collar and leash. Tough would probably calm down when he figured out the reward and punishment scheme through eating or fasting. On the other hand, who's to say he would even accept man? However, being rescued so young, maybe he had not learned fear or hatred of man from his mother or Alpha in the pack. Maybe his instinctive escape/flight behavior had run its course, and he'd soon settle down. He had a chance with Leigh. When would he realize his fate? It would be hard to tell. Maybe only time would tell. "Okay, gal, here's what I'd do," said Andy. "This collar is designed as a training/choke type so Tough would know you meant business as any trainer would naturally demand with a young animal.

"First, he needs to know you're boss, and the choke collar will tell him so. Second, you must be the only one to water and feed or care for him. I should not assist you. Yes, that includes stroking, petting, playing around, and roughhousing, too. He needs to know that you're the one he can depend on, look to, and trust. Third, it is fair for you to be demanding while making him conform to your life, through signals, verbal commands, and body language back and forth. After all, scientists have claimed their intelligence is at or near a seven-year-old child's, certainly higher than our simian brothers, the chimps. Now that's damn smart. Anne Dillard wrote so clearly in *Pilgrim at Tinker Creek*, 'do as I say and chomp—don't and fast.'

"Carry a strong but yielding stick or rolled-up paper so that in the event he tries to attack you during training you can smack him. Repeat your aggression, even though your heart feels otherwise, whenever it recurs. Believe me, he'll get the drift of who is in charge! His mother would simply bite him hard. I'll make you a twenty-foot training leash you'll need to enforce your commands.

"The most important command is *Come*," he continued. "He must learn to return to you when his instincts urge him to roam, stray, or explore. Why should he come back versus seeking the freedom of the wilds? Answer: food. Dedication and rank will naturally follow, but he has a built-in urge to breed and would rather mate with that beautiful she-wolf out there, too. Her innate hormonal drive to reproduce and the odor of her pheromones begs him to breed at intervals of six months. In reality, he may forever be excluded from this option since he is now an outcast—which was no fault of his. It sounds cruel, but he'll soon be so dependent on you that he'll stay."

Leigh asked, "Will he come to the command if given by another?"

"Absolutely not—not this half-wild wolf. No way."

"I suppose that's gratifying . . . but I'm not sure about that . . . Oh well."

"The next command is *Down*. He'll want to roam. You'll need the long leash for this command, too. *Down* stops him, and he'll lie down, halting in place. It is also effective when he gets too friendly with visitors and jumps on their new clean clothing—if there is such a thing up here. Plus it halts an attack when you are uncertain of the prey or conditions. *Down* also gives him a chance to stay near the adversary without leaving. Including man.

"Okay, Babe, I'll soon get rid of the leash, you watch, and I can be patienct . . . I think," said Leigh.

"Third, *Attack*, *Sic*, *Now*, or *Get 'em*, et cetera is the final command. You select the phrase that's most convenient for you, but you must stick with it. You're in the Alaskan bush and you may want to deter an aggressive animal, be it two- or four-legged. You'll see that Tough's snarl and the command *Attack* will deter most, and when the effect has served its purpose, you command *Down* and he stops. *Come*, and he returns, maybe with reluctance, but he will.

"In the case of a bear, the charge may be enough to scare the bruin away. You'll want him to stop short of contact for his own good when a bear holds his ground.

"In that case, *Come* saves his life. It takes many wolves, about five, to deter a bear. But he won't be thinking clearly; you will. One wolf will surely die if he/she charges alone. I kinda like *Attack* since it is not subtle, but you decide."

They emptied the entire bottle of Chateau Beaujolais Red and were starting the last glass as Andy wound down.

"Dang, Andy, that was an excellent series of do's and don'ts for a wolf cub—or any canine—as I understand your ideas. Thank you so much."

"One more item, Leigh. Remember the flexible stick to aid in training? It is important that, when really necessary, use it, but *never* use your hand to discipline unacceptable behavior. Your hand is used for a reward, a positive, a stroke of friendship. I envy your next few weeks of training the cub. You'll do well, and Tough will conform to both of your needs: his nourishment and sense of belonging, and your needs for a companion and protector. Oh, a warning: never turn him loose with his choke collar. He could easily be hung up by the throat and choke to death. *You* can release pressure on his neck; an errant, broken limb in the forest cannot."

Leigh poured her glass of wine into his, indicating with her eyes and dour look that she had enough training for the day.

"Finally, you'll soon have an unusual roommate with different needs, and a few situations will occur that will be very irritating, but will not require discipline—only patience. Remember, humans are not free, either. It's more like loose on the planet, and our skill in survival determines how long we live, too. As such, we need to consider the big picture and help others also survive.

"So, once trained, he'll be an asset—not a liability. But for now, Tough may whine and cry when thunder cascades up and down and over the valley of the Bitterroots. So sit up with him, or let him sleep with you. You did so with your parents. How many of your friends sleep with their dogs on a regular basis? It's not an unusual occurrence, and you're his only counsel."

*   *   *

Leigh's eyes had been riveted on Andy for the last hour. She was over-whelmed with his knowledge and sensitivity, and his effort to spend all this time with her. He appeared to be gentle, yet firm in the procedures necessary to fulfill her objectives with not only training Tough, but living in the wilds. He appeared to be a quiet giant of a man, much like his brother, with whom she had shared her love.

As if on autopilot, she spontaneously rose, walked to his side, and with the body language used again and again by women over time, she halted and stood at his chair. He rose as if on command of her hidden signal. Their eyes locked. She reached out and held him close to her warm and soft chest . . . he gradually and carefully joined the embrace. Her head remained on his shoulder, his cheek against her beautiful sweet-smelling hair.

They remained in place as the webbed circle of the Dream Catcher cast its shadow across their union.

Silence prevailed, warmth radiated through their minds and bodies.

Andy seemed very uncomfortable as she tightened her embrace, as if he wanted no part of feminine involvement, but she certainly felt good . . .

Much to her chagrin, further contact did not develop. Exhaustion had over-whelmed the trio, and they hit the sack early and separately in pen, sleeping bag, and her *lonely* bed. She fantasized about what could have been as she anticipated the excitement of the 'morrow's togetherness. Much later, at the 'witching hour,' the moon cast its glow through the pines and shaded the hut as if a paintbrush of blues and grays had redefined the interior. Leigh glanced toward the sleeping bag and watched the mystical shadow of the Dream Catcher as it crept across the floor and framed the man's tranquil, resting face. She had experienced this moment before, with his brother . . . Jack.

*   *   *

The sun was still below the horizon at five a.m. when he left the hut on the meadow. It may not show good judgment and not be right to leave unexpectantly, but he'd have trouble finding acceptable words to explain: *It is time to depart.* He did not want to get involved . . . and she did. He did not relish conflict over affairs of the heart.

Silence greeted his movement to the river.

As if he, too, was a meandering river, his mind thoroughly conflicted by Leigh's attention, Andy sauntered along the Bitterroot in his chosen element: The Tongass. Like Thoreau, Andy had a formal education. He agreed with Henry David. Both would rather be around 'chic-a-chicdees' than PhDs and DDs with their pontificating about mythical religious dogma.

He stopped and stood enchanted by the quiet. The darkness felt damp but pleasantly warm. Stars were still out but looking faint. He could see Orion up there with his dog, Sirius. He soaked up the stillness, a rare luxury at today's hectic pace. He was finally alone. Solace was his to embrace.

Nothing moved for a long time except for a small bat on its way home from the night shift. His silhouette flew against an aspen, clothed in its golden leaves, standing like a goddess against the dark pines and their flat shadows against the early morning sky. A white birch, small but elegant, harbored a squirrel's nest that had been hidden all summer but now yielded itself due to thinning leaves of late summer as gravity thieves their arboreal loft. Likewise, as a reminder of reality, an airplane blinked and hummed its way north along its transparent highway between Earth and the stars.

Ever so slowly, beginning at the top edges of the mountain, the sky changed from light gray to the palest of lavenders, to deep lavender itself. Pines changed from black to dark green. Fallen leaves, appearing as unrecognizable bits of torn paper in this early morning nautical twilight, suddenly assumed their bilateral shape.

As if van Gogh's talent is unfolding before his eyes, the flatness of silhouetted pines slowly changed into shadowy three-dimensional forms of the trees we cherish.

The forest came alive.

He saw the leafless stalks of goldenrod with their fancy fuzzy tops, the white silk of milkweed pods, used for 'natural' life-jacket flotation during WWII, glowing in the half-light.

Two doves suddenly and silently flew directly at him ... startled for a moment, the doves quickly performed a vertical, twisting chandelle to clear his frame.

As if a web of diamonds, the spider's trap of silvery dewdrops revealed its entrapment scheme, soon to vanish as the dew evaporated to the rays and breeze of the golden orb.

Earth was rotating toward the sun, yet he could not feel it any more than he could feel the motion of a sailboat in light air on Skagway's Leland Canal. He rode on a gigantic ball decorated with chains of enormous mountains, waterfalls, oceans, and infinitely more.

Another signal of the night shift terminus startled Andy when a white owl silently sailed by a mere three feet from his position. The owl was not surprised; he knew exactly where Andy stood. The Snow Owl just may be dive-bombing to scare him away from its rodent killing field, or maybe just to announce his presence.

Time would tell.

*   *   *

"Dang," Andy exclaimed, while moving from the protective pike position. "That was close."

"Okay, owl . . . I'm not the big field mouse you need. Sorry for the disappointment, and no, I'm not going to hang out on your mousing grounds—I'm moving on."

Andy knew the avian breed very well. With a wingspan of four to five feet, it generally enjoyed the wide-open areas like this meadow. Unafraid of humans, they appear tame because they rarely, if ever, encounter people in the northern latitudes. The DNR registered about 200 birds in Western North America. All who have seen one on a fence or limb say the same thing: there appears to be a complete absence of color. That was the case as Andy observed the bird perched at the meadow's perimeter: shockingly white and mystical. The bird appeared to be in command of the clearing.

Reflecting on his earlier conversations with Leigh, he wondered, "Could this bird be the messenger of the Great Spirit—Gitchee Manitou? His presence certainly seemed to sanctify the area."

He thought, *Could there be a subtle message in this encounter? The owl would certainly give a sign if he was to have contact, a message, a pronouncement, a declaration . . . I'll stand fast awhile.*

Without knowing why, he dropped to his knees and continued to focus on the owl. Then suddenly a flock of ravens, circling on the warning air currents, descended to the forest encircling the meadow.

The birds directed their attention to the owl.

Andy did likewise.

He had a feeling that Leigh's earlier encounter of a similar scene, in a similar meadow, was about to come to pass.

A hush came over the setting.

The owl looked directly at the kneeling person in the meadow . . .

Chapter 18

Discover

The owl spoke.

"Walkswithwind, I come to you from the spirit of life."

Spellbound, Andy sensed the presence of deity in the Owl's voice as the forest became absolutely silent with his words; the wind subsided, leaves hung limp, and the sky appeared immobilized.

'My friend. Long ago when the world was young, our Native American forefathers had a vision. At that time, The Great Spirit spoke about the cycles of life . . . from infancy, childhood, and then to adulthood. During this privileged life on Mother Earth, He counseled and reminded the people of multiple forces, some *good* and some *bad,* that affect man's character. He directed his people to the *good* forces and steered your life in the right direction. There are many forces and different directions that can help or interfere with the harmony of your place in nature, and the wonderful teachings of the Creator.

"A spider spins his web starting from the outside and working toward the center. You'll note that the web is a perfect circle, but there is a hole in the center. Use the principles of the web to reach your goals and make use of your ideas, dreams, and visions. By believing in the Great Spirit, the web will catch you great ideas, and bad ones will go through the hole. Believers have passed this vision to their kinfolk over the years, and they continue to utilize the 'Dream Catcher' as the web of life.

"*My friend* . . . you have been identified through your recent actions as a guardian of men. Additionally, you have been captured in the dreams of a wanting sister . . . and through our forefathers' teachings and expectations I solicit your assistance to help one of our Anglo friends. You have set aside your own needs to share Leigh West's suffering that you, too, have experienced with your brother's demise.

"*My friend,* a white sister is wanting . . . and you, a red brother, can help.

"You have been snared in Leigh West's web-of-life; you have been captured in her dreams . . . you have been called to serve your fellow man.

"I petition you to be a part of her life, now while her needs are the greatest. You must return to her side. I know you will serve the needs of your fellow man. You'll find she urgently needs you: you must return . . . you *must* return to her side.

"Go. The Great Spirit is with you . . . Go!"

The meadow exploded violently with a massive flight of ravens leaping into the early-morning thermals of the Bitterroot.

Andy shielded his eyes from the force of the flapping wings. A change in the airflow created a maelstrom—a dramatic whirl of wind—totally disrupting the peaceful scene. After the dust, feathers, grass, and leaves settled; Andy looked to the Owl's lofty perch.

Vanished.

He was not surprised. Nevertheless, he scanned the entire rim of the meadow.

He thought Manitou's presence was most likely still there, in spirit, but physically absent in the owl form.

This transcendent concept of the owl as Manitou was now his to embrace or reject, for it was difficult to rationally explain. His brother had explained many times that it takes a 'leap of faith' and 'witness' to understand. He certainly had seen the latter.

He reflected on the religious myths of other people of the world and their transcendent beliefs: Hinduism, Judaism, Christianity, Islam, and Buddhism; and they all share supernatural abstract beliefs from old legends that become mythical canon. As with many before him, what just happened to him in the meadow absolutely, unequivocally transcended rational belief.

Andy paused, knelt, and asked Manitou for guidance. "Great Father, our Creator, I seek your help. I have just been witness to your animal presence, the Owl, and your instructions through him. I will do so, but ask you for help. Unlike my brother's position in the Tlingit's tribal order, I do not have shamanic skills. I have not the religious rituals and magic necessary to summon spiritual help. But I have performed rituals of thanksgiving after successful hunts of our animal kinship, and assisted in healing ceremonies for my sick blood brothers, but have never been asked to act alone. Nor do I have a total understanding of tribal myths and ceremony while utilizing sacred objects, chants, dance, or amulets to favor the gods. Please, help me. Teach me the way to aid our threatened sister. Although not a shaman, I understand the need. *We are all part of the Earth*, and *it is part of us.* One thing we know: *Our god is also her god.* I know this since all of your beings are precious to you. Another thing I know: our spirit will be with me, and no man, be he red, black, yellow, or white, can be left in harm's way. We are all brothers under the same covenant to god. I'm humbled by your request, and will do my best . . ."

He scanned the perimeter of the meadow again with its totem-like tree line. The splendor of the monarchs in the temperate rainforest gave him a certain sense of stability; the Sitka spruce, western hemlock, and Alaskan yellow cedar with their sculpted mass gave his belief system strength. As a Native American child he had made homes, just as wood elves would, in their massive roots. As a man on his solitary walks, he always felt a certain friendship with all of Manitou's Kin(g)dom. He felt blessed just to be alive in His presence, especially now with direct contact and a mission at hand. Overcome, he paused again to organize his thoughts, never doubting . . . his sangfroid in place.

A deafening silence overpowered the ether, the meadow, and Walkswithwind as he meditated . . . asking himself, *Am I capable of this task?*

Chapter 19

Resolve

Leigh had no idea what to try next.

All hell had broken loose with Tough's independent attitude toward discipline and simple training tasks. Andy's absence and the cub's attitude turned her into a physical and mental wreck on a canine iceberg. Training was more than taming.

The wolf cub's actions exploded soon after Andy left the meadow. Tough once again started to rile at containment in the four-by-four enclosure. Thankfully, though, the pen held him captive, but seemed to trigger even more aggressive behavior. Tough now jumped, pushed, leaped, rammed, and thrust his body at the pen's walls. His howl and high-pitched bark added to the tympanic rhythmic drumbeat as his body banged against the plywood pen as if a symphonic snare drum. He appeared to be suffering from claustrophobia or madness from the confinement imposed. He had food and water, but the bowl's contents were tipped over and trampled on from his incessant leaps for freedom. It certainly seemed like he did not sleep very often.

* * *

The commotion awakened Leigh around six o'clock with a shock—a double shock. Not only was Tough's howling ringing in her ears; a quick look to the empty floor space, where Andy slept, revealed his absence. She mused, *Another man leaves me in the middle of the night . . . Damn it!*

Leaping from the sack, she grabbed her favorite old worn jeans and pulled them over her bare ass as she ran to the door. When she realized her boobs were dancing in the air, she ran back to her bed and grabbed her well-worn "M" shirt, then dashed to the door, a little more contained. She bounded down the steps, then headed for the center ring of the circus by the woodpile.

"Okay, fellow, calm down—calm down! I'm here. Relax," pleaded Leigh.

The pup quickly froze in place and leaned against the inner wall of the pen. Stymied at her appearance, it was as though he was seeing a ghost. Slowly the frozen body transitioned to trembling and shakes in a manner alarmed Leigh. His eyes appeared to squint in a demonic fashion; then his ears slowly lay back, and fangs emerged from his muzzle, presenting an offensive yet cowering posture.

The deep guttural growl slowly moved from his inner throat through his glistening fangs, sounding like a steam engine leaking water vapor. He lowered his body to the center of the pen and slowly arched his back, tail between his legs as hair around his neck and back bristled erect. He lowered his head with a slight tilt to maintain eye contact with his jailer. The growl repeated in a rhythmic cycle every few seconds as the hominid and canine stared at each other for minutes.

Leigh thought to herself, *I would never have believed it possible, but now I see it, up close and personal. Here is a three-month-old cub who has, at most, only known his mother or other mature wolves for a couple of weeks, and then as a youngster.* Even with that short-lived experience, the mingling with the pack had been very effective. He had developed substantial defensive and offensive traits. This was probably an excellent example of inborn survival traits that had been passed down to aid in his success alone in the wilds. Whether it was bluff or real, without the plywood pen . . . *I would not be this close. It would frighten me . . . I'd be gone. I would not take any chance against this display of aggressiveness.*

Leigh continued eye contact, being careful not to show any fear in her face or in upper body language. She needed time to determine her next move; at least he was not trying to escape—for the moment. Her father used to say, "Just return the fierce look of the bluffing youngster and your eye will tell him you, too, are a tough sonofabitch."

"So, smart ass, I can play your game just as well as you. At least for a while until I get a better idea on how to manage your fear."

She noticed the choke collar Andy made was still around his neck, his leash nearby, but she had no idea if she would be able to get close enough to join the two.

The cub remained in his cowering, arched stance and gazed at her in a hateful manner while emitting a guttural Tibetan chant-like *ooommmm.* She noticed the empty food dish and water bowl, and an idea hit her. She remembered, her dad trained aggressive dogs by lacing their food with a little depressant. Her first aid kit had many similar drugs.

"Bingo! I'll bet that will settle you down enough to get a leash on your body, and I can start some basic training.

Tough's growl was winding down, so Leigh gave him a final look of authority and backed away from the pen to prepare the jazzed-up food dish.

To offer more enticement for the cub, she mixed some venison jerky and honey in with some of Boy's leftover dog food, then added a triple shot of opiate powder used for pain from the kit. She added enough powder for a 40-pound body. Tough weighed 30.

"This should do it. Get going, girl. He's starting to howl again."

She carefully approached the pen with a new sense of confidence. She once again gained eye contact with the cowering pup and spoke gently while he got used to her Alpha look. The growling was just a little different; maybe he smelled the food; maybe he was weakening; maybe he was getting a little more realistic. She raised her voice this time and spoke with more authority, louder, sharper, and directly with one command Andy had mentioned earlier.

"Down! Come on boy... Down."

He looked left, right, and back at Leigh, then to the inner walls, then back to his apparent adversary—soon to be caregiver. He smelled the aromatic nourishment, or sensed a reward forthcoming. He started to lower his body, the custom in the pack when showing subservience. He had done the same for his mother.

"Down!"

The last command worked very well. Completely off his feet and on his belly, he rolled over on his back. She did not quite know what to expect, but the laid-out position would work for her needs. She lowered the food into the pen. He immediately broke the demonic stare and looked across the pen to capture the food dish in his vision, then stared at the dish.

"Good Boy. Oops, remember KISS, Keep It Simple Stupid."

Leigh backed away from the pen and waited with hopes that her dad's idea would soon work, and the wild one of the Tongrass would settle down to a manageable disposition.

Leigh lamented, "Poor cub. He is not unlike a young child that knows his mother's scent, (her fur), skin odor, a halo of light, strength in her closeness, a voice that trembles with feeling. He has known that warmth, which will no longer be his. He does not know the future, but certainly must realize the past is no longer his . . . he will not wake and have a sharing relationship with his own kind, his mother—no impressions of understanding of the simple and complex facts of a cub's life. No marvel could replace the smelling sweetness of Mother's warm neck, soothing sound, and comforting stability. Mothers are always there—but not for Tough.

"He'll not experience the familiar, yet short-lived strength in the crook of her leg as the forest hazards pass by his little world; those feelings are gone forever. It appeared that in rescuing him, I've also become his surrogate mother—which he has no immediate plans of accepting . . ."

Still standing on the woodpile next to the cub's 'doping' pen, she reminisced about the night at this spot when she approached Jack with passion in her heart. Then . . . so much suffering . . . as if eons ago. She longed for those good times and Jack's comforting ways while explaining the universe as seen through the eyes of Native American Beliefs. They made sense.

She also reflected on the past few days with Jack's brother, Andy, as they sat together on the banks of the Bitterroot sharing stories of their past, and his positive understanding of Indian legends and myths.

One simplistic Indian legend was most appropriate as Tough struggled with his new home and Leigh. Andy told her the story as she voiced doubt that Tough would ever come around to becoming a partially domesticated wolf:

A great and wise tribal chief sat around the late evening campfire with youth of the tribe, enjoying a moment of conversation with his young grandson as they lazily poked small branches into the fire and watched the ends smolder and catch fire. They casually watched the smoke as it drifted toward the heavens above, one of those special moments shared between a boy and his grandfather. The chief was telling his grandson of a personal struggle he had always faced in his own life, one his grandson may face, too.

"Within my heart lives two wolves. They are constantly engaged in a fierce battle with one another," said the chief.

His grandson looked at him without understanding.

"One wolf is filled with love, loyalty, and respect for others," the chief said. "This wolf cares for the elderly and is a mentor for the young. This wolf shares his love with all those with whom he comes into contact. This wolf is good."

"What about the second wolf?" his grandson questioned.

The wise old chief studied the smoking end of the small branch he held in his hand. He blew his breath upon the end of the stick and watched the orange glow.

"The second wolf is full of hatred and contempt for others. This wolf is filled with evil thoughts and jealousies. He cares only for himself, despises the elders, and has no patience for the youth. He is a mean wolf, filled with deep anger."

"Which wolf will win?" asked the young boy.

The mighty chief paused for a long moment before saying, "The one I feed!"

Hopefully, she thought, *Tough will soon see the love in my heart, and I'll win his trust.*

She knew that was also Andy's point. He had decided to feed his loving heart and reject the evil thoughts of a mean heart. He basked in the peaceful light of respect and forgiveness of all people.

She loved to hear the stories and Indian legends that pervaded both brothers' cultural beliefs. The stories were especially holistic, and the people reverent, viewing themselves as extensions of animate and inanimate nature.

Leigh felt very close to the wondrous variety of beliefs, sacraments, and views of supernatural world. She learned from Jack that different tribes of related groups had varying types of deities and spirits: Monotheistic, omnipotent universal spirits such as the Universal *Manitou*; Iroquoian, *Orenda*; and Siouan, *Wakenda*, who were the source of all other spirits, e.g., ghost-like spirits, spirits of natural phenomena, such as rain gods, and benevolent or guardian spirits.

She experienced the Manitou deity through the owl, and certainly the ravens as messengers of the spirit.

*   *   *

It was time to see if the cub had passed out.

"How ya doin' in there, boy?" Leigh said while sitting on the woodpile.

No response from the pen.

"Hello! Anybody home?"

Nothing.

"Hello, boy."

Leigh slowly approached the edge of the pen. It had been almost an hour. The drug certainly would have hammered him by now. After all, she gave him almost a double dose.

Peeking over the edge of the pen with both hands on the upper edge, she smirked, feeling as if she looked like 'Killroy' in the famous WWII drawing.

But no one was looking from the other side. Tough's supine body appeared lifeless, face upward, legs stretched out, his entire body torpid. Leigh worried that the drug may have worked too well. However, she detected his chest expanding and contracting; he appeared to be breathing okay as she leaned over carefully.

"Hello!"

No response. Leigh felt that she could finally remove the pen and get a little more control over Tough. She had the metal chain link choke collar in her pocket to supplement the existing leather one on the cub's neck. It would be needed while training. Simply put: Behave, and you breathe; misbehave, and you don't.

Lifting and easing the pen up and over on its side, she carefully rolled it to a spot along the face of the woodpile. Thank goodness Andy made the sides rigid so they wouldn't collapse.

She knelt by the cub's side, and with love and caring movements of a mother's hands, she raised Tough's head and slipped the choke collar over his muzzle, eyes, and ears. Gently lowering his head, she attached the long leash to the choke collar 'O' ring with an audible "snap."

"Oops, I didn't disturb you, did I?" she mused.

The cub was out cold . . . he didn't hear a thing.

Twenty feet long, the rawhide training leash had a large loop and clip on the opposite end making an excellent handhold. She quietly moved to a solid hemlock near the woodpile and secured the leash. This location would be easily observed from a window in the hut, and it provided just enough distance from the porch to allow for easy feeding and attention to his needs. She stared at the drugged cub, saying, "You're restrained enough now so I can start my day in a little more civil way . . . if there is such a thing up here.

"It also looks as though we're on our own now. Andy's absence clearly stated his feelings of not wanting to get further involved with the camp or me. That's not a problem. I've learned that many men only want a platonic relationship. Well, my dear Andrew, we could try friendship, albeit difficult for me. I'm a lover . . . a serious lover; I like being close to men. Maybe he sensed my antennae transmitting stronger than he expected . . . not sure, but I'll plead guilty of being interested in more than—*friendship*. Well, so be it. Why am I telling you all this, Tough? You're out cold. Again, Andy is much more cautious than his brother . . . and he certainly understood; I did have the opportunity to share my relationship, in part, with his brother, Jack. For crying out loud, they're both single. I'm no home wrecker.

"Hold tight, my friend, I'm going to grab some breakfast, get dressed properly, and prepare for your awakening *without* a pen. I can hardly wait since I've no idea what to expect. Here's a dish of water to rinse out your pipes; I'll be right back. Standby, you fur ball," Leigh proclaimed as she ended her chatter with a little more confidence.

Breakfast was a quick, big-city walk-around type, with an unheated bagel and cheese with ebony coffee.

While cleaning the hut's continual mess, she noticed a strange avoidance behavior pattern. She avoided walking over or cleaning the floor where both Jack and Andy had previously rested in their bedrolls. She smiled at her homage to their 'spot' lingering on her floor, and in her heart . . . and smiled again. With a little deprecation in her tone, she mused, "Leigh, Leigh, will you ever be free of your fascination with men? No one's counting, but three in one month rings a bell. Two will not return . . . and the third a work-in-progress.

"Oh what the hell, I'll skip the bra-and-panty routine. I need to wash anyway. I'll be like a lot of teens: 'She has nothing between her body and her denim jeans' . . . but when they itch it's a bitch. Leigh giggled about erotic sensory symbols. She loved and remembered some of her Dad's racy comments about the realities of people's true feelings and life's verity, which were especially true in high school and college, especially when she worked as a waitress. He reminded her of man's libidinous predictability on tipping waitresses: "The size of the tip is directly proportional to the exposure of the tit." Another: "A visible nip' enlarges the tip." He was such a refreshing voice in her past . . . he let it all hang out. And if she'd care to admit it—and she wouldn't—she'd been trying to replace him in her new relationships, knowing it could not be done, but trying to come close.

"I'll need a pitch fork to comb and manage this rat's nest. Damn hair; I should cut if all off. No one would care out here, and if they did, I wouldn't care. I lie . . . the Joan of Arc style is not my bag," she lamented. "Then again, who cares what

I look like? I don't . . . What's that?"

HOWO-O-O-O

Whine

AAAA-RRRR-OOOOOO

"I'll be a rat's ass . . . there he is . . . Dang, it's over. Wolf time again. Better get my rear end in gear. The hell with my hair!"

She sailed out the door, down the stairs, and scanned the woodpile, but saw nothing. However, there was a train wreck of logs scattered along the path to the river, around the pile, and into the wood lot . . . quite a mess compared to its previous neatness.

"Where are you, boy?" Leigh called.

Knowing she was really talking to herself, she might as well have said: "Come to Mom, little fella."

Following the leash, she sneaked around the north end of the partially dismantled woodpile.

"Stop it, girl! You're the Alpha—get with it!"

She altered her body posture, stood with more erect military bearing, and walked around the pile with a definite I'm-the-gal swagger. She also altered her facial expression to an imperative sneer.

She found him tangled, twisted, and frightened. The leash was wound around his head, and a piece of cordwood woven in so bad the combination held his head to the ground. He looked much like a Puritan in the stocks at Jamestown. On the other hand, he also gave the appearance of a tough but worn-out bull in a Tijuana arena. He looked beat-up. He learned quickly how fighting the collar restricts his airway. Foiled, he could only complain by moaning and whining. Totally defeated, his eyes made contact with Leigh. He blinked as if giving a signal. Rescued at last. His mistress.

With her Alpha female presence, she said, "Down."

Again, "Down."

Body and facial language must have worked. At least something did . . . for he immediately, but reluctantly, dropped his head to the ground, lowered his haunches, and rolled over to a submissive position.

"Well, whatever I did, it worked. I'll have to add this to my resume: female wolf trainer—albeit young ones. Let's see, first things first. There is no reason to release him until I rerail this train wreck. I'll stack the woodpile again, clear the rest of the mess, and look for another tie-up site while he's incommunicado."

HOOOWWWEEELLL

"Okay, boy, keep your pants on; I'm just about finished. Where the heck is your water dish? It has to be here somewhere. Ah, here it is.

"Now, not knowing where I'm going to tie you up, here's some water. You'll want to rinse that opiate from your body. Easy now; no one's going to hurt you. Drink up." She also threw a chunk of pemmican next to the dish.

Although restricted, he managed to drink his fill and, much to her surprise, quit growling while munching on the main course du jour. He must have finally realized that she was . . . okay, her manner and voice was certainly soothing, yet imperative.

"It looks as though you'll have to be tied over by that lone balsam pine tree on the meadow's edge, and you're about to have your first walk with the leash; I hope this works. Let's see now, is everything ready? I think so. The only trick will be to get you untangled and secure so I can start working on basic commands."

She moved to unwind the leash. Unforgiving, the resistance of the leash fought her for every foot gained over the next quarter-hour. Finally, the rawhide loosened, Tough felt the slack, and unfortunately, forgetting the principal of the 'choke,' lunged away and quickly withdrew—to breathe. Submission returned to his body. Just a little smarter, he watched Leigh unwind the restraint.

"Finally, I've got it!" she exclaimed as the end of the rawhide freed itself and relaxed along its entire length. Tough was a little more savvy now. He slowly tightened the leash slack as Leigh moved away from the war zone. She tugged a little and said, "Come." Shocked, he came along, more due to the tug, she thought, than her command. At least he was cooperating. She smiled and moved cautiously with the cub.

"Come on, boy. You're doing fine. Come on. You'll clear that mess in a flash." He jumped and leaped over the wood. "Good boy. You're clean now. Keep coming. This isn't so bad, is it?"

He was no 'heeling' AKC show dog, but he was reading and taking most of his clues from Leigh. A lot of his inattention or reluctance was probably due to his eyes constantly sweeping to every new, near and far, item along the path. Everything in his life was a new experience. The leash pull, and dominance was all new. Free of the area near the hut and stack of cord wood, he felt even more liberated, starting to prance on his toes. He ranged ahead, forgetting the leash, and came to an abrupt halt; and Leigh gave him the *down* command.

"Oops. Sorry, boy," she yelled. He looked at her with a cocked angle of his head.

"How's that, boy?" Leigh asked in a sigh of relief. Tough's ears perked up. He lowered to his haunches and stared at his captor with the body language of, *I'm okay, what's next?* She, in turn, stared at the liberated cub in recognition of their new positive relationship.

Leigh repeated the A, D, C routine and, much to her surprise, he caught on very well—C and D were well done . . . A needed work. Attack was a difficult task to train while alone.

She decided it was time for a little rest.

Leigh sat, removed her coat to use as a back support, and leaned against a tree to rest while enjoying the peaceful moment at the edge of the meadow. Idyllic, maybe not, but the peaceful scene had all the aspects of a new resolve, with former tension absent, and a new amicable union of mutual respect. She and the cub seemed to communicate telepathically while staring at each other and at the meadow, the birds, and an occasional animal traversing the area toward the river's nourishment.

"Well, Tough, it appears we can work something out in this relationship. You're a quick learn, that's certain, and over time I'll bet you'll be at my side both day and night. You're not like Boy, but who knows. He was a pointer. It's going to be difficult, Tough, but we'll make it . . . you can take that to the bank. Who's to say that the ten percent wildness that will never vanish from your blood line will not work for both our interests: your defensive skills, and my protective skills," Leigh proclaimed.

Tough moved to a sitting position closer to the tree and Leigh. He surveyed his new landscape. Finally, totally relaxed, Leigh folded her arms on her chest and watched the distant moon rise. It was full and yellow, slipping gently above the tree line on the eastern ridge, triggering eerie shadows of deep purple in the valley. Shadows drifted along in threads through the cleavage and snaked around the mountainsides. The fog moved as if alive, clumps bumping into each other and melting together.

A whippoorwill started singing near them in a magnificent hemlock. They both turned their heads as they heard wolves howling back along the northern ridge. A screech owl announced its presence along the perimeter of the meadow.

"Hello, my fine feathered friends. Meet my buddy Tough."

What bliss, she mused, as her eyelids yielded to gravity and closed. The moon hypnotically coaxed her to sleep.

Moments later, as the wind whooshed across the meadow, Tough carefully but decisively moved to her side in a placid but attentive posture.

Her guardian.

The meadow's daylight sounds yielded to early evening's calm.

A raven circled the meadow, descended to the lone pine, and perched without a sound to share 'watch' with the cub . . .

Chapter 20

Return

Bathed in the shadows of the tall timber of the clearing, Walkswithwind finished meditating, knowing very well the spiritual presence of Manitou, the Owl, remained. Certainly alone, he still felt as though he was in the center of resplendent tableau.

Raising his head slowly, he searched the arboreal rim for the owl's lofty perch near splintered wood hanging like javelins. As expected, He had vanished, leaving only the thoughts of His charge, His petition, and His plea: for Andrew to return to the side of Leigh.

He rose from the lotus position of worship and paused.

The sounds of the night gave him the feeling of not being alone. Wolves appeared to be on a nocturnal hunt somewhere up the ridge, and another band howled in a very distant pursuit along the river. The full moonlight laid many unique shapes across the clearing, including the long eerie-looking distortion of Andy's, not unlike the mythical humpbacked Kokopelli of Chaco Canyon, sans flute. At times they appeared innocuous, but sometimes looked like animals on the prowl, roaming the forest for a conquest. Not familiar with the forest's sounds and shadows, a novice would indeed fear for his life until dawn revealed the truth at sunrise.

Hemingway wrote so clearly in *True At First Light*:

> . . . a thing is true at first light and a lie by noon . . .
> Absolute trauma seen at night, becomes absolutely beautiful and
> Believable at dawn's early light.

The breeze was moving up the slope past his face. Moving on with a determined stride, he used the moon's glow to guide him along the river back to Leigh's camp.

There was no doubt in his mind what Manitou's petition demanded of him. He spoke not only with clarity, but also with urgency.

The moonlight provided a latticework in silhouette of stationary trees. The fog that enveloped the river bottom would soon yield to dawn as night was defeated by the breeze of thermal radiance, robbing moisture along the river with solar power from the golden globe as it moved across the earth.

The forest came alive as ravens started their cawing again, partially muted by distance, and owls swooped to their secretive daytime arboreal perches.

Andy's pace increased as the forest admitted more light from the rising sun. The truth of first light banished the earlier shadows of doubt along his path.

*   *   *

Tough remained at his post by his dozing mistress at the edge of the meadow.

Vigilant through the night, he maintained an upright position, his head in constant motion, eyes scanning the meadow. He somehow sensed his new role as protector of the sleeping mistress . . . his Alpha female.

Although a mere thirty pounds, Tough's body language and posture seemed to be Herculean, with an intensity of concentration. At times he stood erect as if to defend against an unknown adversary, and then passive at other times as though he had the ability to detect the basic concepts of what is good or evil on the meadow. But how? He hadn't lived long enough to see the potential terror of life that dwelled in the depths of the Tongass.

Had he gained some experience with the pack?

His mother?

Leigh?

Andrew?

It was certainly possible the influence of Manitou, who when His help was required embraced any threatened animal of the forest.

In the case of Tough, Manitou may have very well encompassed protecting Leigh as she slept. The Tlingits know very well how Manitou affects supernatural powers of selected tribal shamans. It's tied up with the Indian concept of good and evil. They believe that life is a kind of wind blowing through each person. Some have dark wind, and they tend to be evil. In human form, they're called "skinwalkers," who change their form to the circumstances.

How does one determine if an animal or person is evil?

How would Tough know?

Manitou.

Manitou would ensure that Tough knew what to look for, such as: wanton killing versus killing for nurture; evil acts for no reason; turning into another evil or threatening animal; performing witchcraft; flying; and disappearing in an instant.

Both Andy and his shaman brother, when asked about their beliefs regarding skinwalkers, answered in similar fashion. They believed evil lurked in the world. They also reflected that on many an evening by tribal campfires, they had observed animal-skinned shamans dance to appease the gods, intercede for the sick, or prepare young braves for raiding parties. They did not like to talk about it much, especially in groups that were not Native Americans. They were kind of uneasy about their private beliefs in the public domain. They did not judge others' supernatural beliefs, and being incredibly polite, did not care to offend the white man's unusual beliefs; such as their creation story . . . six days? virgin birth? etc.

*   *   *

Andy continued along the illuminated Bitterroot in the shadows. This brief period postpones the stars and the green-dawn clarity that sponges them up and diminishes the eerie shadows. At greater than 50 degrees latitude the midsummer days are long, midsummer nights a short darkness.

As his former chief, Golden Bear, related so well:

> The sun drags its feet across the top of the world, for no
> sooner than hidden by the mountains in the west, it races
> as if in a game to surprise you in the east before you are
> aware it had gone to the west.

Comfortable with his life and the assignment from Manitou, he felt certain that he was the most qualified to help Leigh. The Tongass mission fit him like a comfortable, nonthreatening partner. He moved silently through the detritus of the inclined ridges leading to the moon-whited mountains, and the vacant moon-faded sky as the sun slowly dominated the horizon. He heard no cry of bird or animal, no rattle of hooves among the stones, no movement except the reflective ghostly flashes along the uneven surface of the river. Silence claimed him as a friend, a friendship in which city folk know nothing—true isolation—solace—nothing but noiselessness.

The metropolis knows nothing of these quietist and loneliest hours. In the city, automatic ice-makers clunk as they drop ice cubes, automatic dishwashers sigh through changes, jets roar as they descend to the local strip, and the nearest freeway vibrates as vehicles pollute the air. Red and white lights pass along highways and glance off windows. There is always a radio that could be heard in the distance on some all-night station, or a television set of artificial moonlight flickering images of the late show or grade B movie.

Curious, he halted and listened for the sound as the night echoed his movements in the windless air. The glitter of the soundless light of the disappearing moon lit his path in the midst of darkness—his own sliver of earth being revealed by the eastern orb emerging. The game trail along the bank was deceptive and without depth; every shadow's blackness stretched his eyes and cautioned his feet. Moving on, feeling his way, he splashed into a hollow hole and felt the cool of the river chill. Not wanting wetness, he headed to a higher ground, tumbling out of the random section of glimmering pockets of water. He could not see the sunken pits unless surface water angled to the rising sun's light reflected a silvery glow.

He approached the blackness of an elevated overhanging cliff, and the sky opened. A broad strip of silver burned through the canopy, exposing his personal slice of the world's miniature hemisphere. He rested in the whitewash of dawn.

Caught by unusual sounds, he paused, listened . . . strained to listen more intently, but then silence. Nothing. He moved higher under a magnificent red-wood, halted, sat, and retrieved a cake of pemmican from his rucksack. Biting off a piece, he quickly soaked it to a chewable texture with a slug of water from his canteen.

The sounds echoed along the ridge again; this time he sensed the origin from an easterly direction. The sounds were child-like. Puzzled, he thought the noise to be much like young animals, as if whimpering cries of stress, aggression, fighting, or play. So faint were the sounds, he stopped chewing to hear better. The irregular cadence of calls continued unabated.

SLAP

Then silence.

Baffled again at the sounds, he removed his side-arm from the holster, racked a round into the chamber, ensured the safety was on, and returned it to the holster without the retainer snapped in place. His eyes strained toward the shadows de-picting strange shapes. Some appeared to move. He stayed at the same spot a long time with his eyes fixed on the changing shadows at the open pathway where a little light seemed to fall from the horizon's sun. A pine tree moved, and snapped with a subtle "crack" and he stood up watching with even more intensity, thinking it might be a bear, but he saw nothing. He sat down again. He felt he could smell the presence of a hot, rich odor of a predator. Hard to explain . . . yes, but real to him.

And then—a shadow.

A sliding image in the pathway.

There it went, on its belly like a snake. A fox, a wolf, a coyote, a wolverine? He raised his weapon and sighted. Then, it disappeared. He waited for the beast to emerge . . . somewhere. Silence.

After several minutes, he knew quite well what had happened. It had seen him, taken a better look, moved back into the darkness, and escaped.

He had witnessed their skills many times . . . creatures of the forest; stealthily able to dart through brush where a man would or could not tread. So much for early-morning animal encounters. He returned his weapon to the holster.

Moving to higher elevation, he discovered the source of one mysterious sound—not a mystery at all.

A beaver pond.

He now saw the reflection of the moon on the beautiful silver water.

It was marked by the tell-take sign of a flat sharp edge on one side of the dam-induced flood plain. In the center of the meadow, it had all the markings of any idyllic setting of peace and tranquility. It also helped to explain the source of the unusual sounds cascading across the ridgeline to the south.

It was a beaver colony having a rollicking good time.

Kits and young adults roughhoused along the shore, in the pond, and tumbling down the sides of the lodge. Some of the kits appeared to be ramming each other like torpedoes, submarines, and PT boats. The younger ones seemed to be picking on their older cousins who, when having enough courage, would bite or otherwise slam the kits into submission, all this while it appeared that the full-grown adults, or parents, were busily foraging for food or dam rebuilding with material found among the trees along the shore.

Golden Bear had explained to Andrew the importance of the beaver. Their presence and compulsion to spend nights building dams played a critical part in the economic and ecological framework of early settlers, both Native and European in the 1800s. Their fur was used by many for hats and coats, and their constant improvement of habitat was very welcome. They created amazing flood plains, but were appreciated only after they neared extinction in the 1900s.

Andy rested and continued eating while enjoying the splendor of Nature's performance on the pond.

Andy reflected back to when his father gave him an abandoned beaver kit who became one of the best friends during summer fun. Called "Blackie," it followed him around like a dog whenever he went exploring the local forest and streams. However, his pet was always getting into trouble when left alone in or near the house. Blackie would gnaw on, or cut off, the legs of tables, chairs, and beds; pile them together, and while doing so, rearrange everything in his path . . . as if building a dam. As the beaver grew older and sexually mature, the call-of-the-wild and drive to mate lured him away from the homestead. Andy's Dad explained why his departure was a logical conclusion of their relationship. He did not pursue his friend of the summer, for he also knew the beaver as a keystone species in the frontier ecosystem. Beaver dams created ecologically rich wetlands and provided homes, protection, and food for dozens of species from migrating ducks to moose, from fish to frogs to Great Blue Herons.

This moment of reflection was part of the reason he loved the out-of-doors, especially untarnished Alaska. Working for the DNR provided an opportunity to live his love. There was still time to maintain the balance of the land, and in this case to allow Nature's engineers opportunity and protection to do their amazing work. There was no higher calling than to be part of a management team whose goal was to maintain, despite man's destructive force, the pristine glory of the Tongass.

He had a difficult time explaining to his friends the reasons Alaska is a spectacular jewel. He needed to explore the bush to just see what is there, where no man had tread . . . before. And since a man lives on this planet only once . . . he might as well get a *feel* for the place—seize its grandeur and let it seize him.

Splash—Slap—Splash . . . echoed across the valley.

Startled from his daydreaming, he looked toward the pond as it exploded with beavers scurrying to cover.

The sound of an adult's tail smacking the water, and its purpose, was clear. The reaction to this alarm was well known to all, both young and old.

A dozen or so wave forms headed for the lodge, with the large adults appearing to herd the younger to the safety it provided. What seemed to be minutes was really seconds, as the surface of the pond flattened.

Silence.

Andy's eyes searched the shore for the cause of the alarm . . . the intruder, the threat to this idyllic scene.

Nothing.

He leaned forward for a better view.

A Ptarmigan appeared to his left and flew behind him into the protective cedars. Its silent flight may be an indication that Andy was no longer alone. He swiveled around and looked directly into the yellowish-green eyes of a snow-white My-in-gau, timber wolf.

They both freeze.

The wolf must have picked up Andy's scent and quietly traversed up the ridge to discover who was intruding in *his* territory.

Andy had never been this close to Lupus. A mature male, the white appeared long-legged and muscular, with penetrating eyes on a slightly canted forward-reaching head. His ears erect and rotating, they were the only moving parts of this beautiful, powerful, and dangerous-looking canine. A small splash of yellow colored his chest and tail; plus linear scars showed on both ears, the crown of his head, and his muzzle. His legs, paws, and tail were unyielding to movement . . . statuesque, as if cast in bronze.

He had emerged from beneath an enormous fallen log, just twenty feet to his left. Still stunned to stillness, Andy felt it was time to thaw, so he twisted to the left to gain a better view. This new position also ensured a better chance of survival in case he had to escape, or stand and defend himself. He hoped the latter would not develop, since he was armed.

Their eyes remained as if the key had been thrown away. The stare-down had emptied their lungs; the Earth could have stopped spinning and both would have tumbled into the depths of their penetrating eyes. He felt as though his head would soon drop from his shoulders. Who would be first to move? He would not, even as his muscles cried out in pain.

Maintaining the position of his head, he scanned the edge of the timber.

No additional wolves seemed to be present. Only a squirrel frolicked up and down a tree—disturbed at his lair's invasion. Andy felt he would get out of this situation . . . but he'd have to play it smart. He did not ask for Manitou's help because to ask for small favors was against his beliefs. *I am in the hands of Him*, he told himself, *but must do this on my own*.

Slowly . . . his gaze returned to the forest to his left.

The wolf had disappeared!

How could it vanish so fast?

He waited.

Motionless, he thought of his next move. The white could be lurking in the shadows, but the pathway was clear, so he breathed in deeply and exhaled slowly.

The two had shared something preternatural for at least ninety seconds. Now he felt he knew the wolf, and the wolf him.

What goes on in a wolf's brain is unknown, but the two were linked—without threatening aggression, without physical conflict? He also felt certain that if they met again there would be no combat, for they had established a nonconfrontational union. Each yielded to the other . . . without engagement. It was as though they thought alike . . . *I'm blessed Manitou. Thank you.*

As he meandered down the ridgeline to the pond, he remembered teachings of Gitchee Manitou, the Creator:

> "There will be many confrontations in life. Be careful not to at-
> tack for the wrong reasons, such as false pride, ego, or envy . . .
> Your brothers, animals of the forest, such as the wolf, will not
> attack unless driven by survival or protection of the pack. The
> wolf lives as he is meant to, yielding to actions for survival when
> necessary, to dominate the weaker prey as part of his need to
> endure. Many could be your blood brothers . . ."

Andy must have presented the posture of a significantly strong adversary, or an attack was not part of the wolf's plan. Both gained in the stare-down. Andy did not have to use his gun, and the wolf lived for another day.

Did the wolf know of man before this encounter?

Had he encountered other men who meant no harm?

Andy may never learn the basis of the positive encounter. But it worked for him and the wolf this time, and would probably do so again.

He rose, adjusted his pack, located his next aiming point to the east, and moved out.

He turned to take a last look at the beaver pond's beauty, and continued his hike to Leigh and her needs.

*   *   *

Andy wonders, was Manitou present during the confrontation with the wolf? Most likely . . . He has a way of being where potential trouble lurks.

He recalled, very clearly, from earlier encounters, that Manitou gives advice and counsel to those in need, but does not demand giving up personal dignity to serve Him. He seldom requires his followers to lose themselves and turn from all that is not Him. In this way, Manitou stands as distinctive from other mythical, supernatural deities. Manitou needs nothing, asks little, and demands only moderate allegiance. It was an individual decision to respond to his petitions—not for Him—but for the group. He intercedes for the benefit of the populace, not himself.

Conversely, many other spiritual groups tie their beliefs to written law of the ancients and their understanding of the world's deities two millennia ago. They're taught that knowledge of *their* God is the *only* route to eternal life. How ridiculous. Have they no knowledge of the pluralistic world? All beliefs are of value if basic *morality* is taught. Buddhism does so *without* a godhead. They teach that through compassionate living . . . enlightenment will follow.

Manitou does not insist that everyone improve his life, but does provide the opportunity to do so. Will is directed to the needs of the people, not Him. Golden Bear, the Tlingit Chief, used the example of viewing the stars:

> "You do not have to sit outside in the dark.
> If, however, you want to look at the stars,
> You will find that darkness is necessary.
> But, the stars neither require nor demand it."

Life has many similar lessons to be learned. Someone may not like to perform certain tasks, but if he doesn't, the rewards of that decision will not be achieved.

Andy rested on the ridgeline above the pond while determining the distance to Leigh's camp. Only a mile away now, he would be there in an hour cross-county, or a little later by following the river.

He would be heading into the rising sun, Pe-to-se-qa, creeping over the forest canopy to the east. He scanned the tranquil pond and comely ridgelines to the west.

Silence.

Stillness.

No animals appeared to be present, but he felt uncertain.

Several minutes later while making good time along the ridgelines, he still felt something could be stalking him. He glanced around several times, only to be disillusioned.

Nothing.

His mind drifted again . . . did the wolf demonstrate human logic? *No way, I must be getting too spiritual . . . well; we're both just visitors to this land—Earth.*

As the moon displayed its last view to Mother Earth, Andy headed in a easterly route. He was unaware that a pair of yellowish-green eyes still followed as he moved toward Pe-to-se-ga's warmth.

Chapter 21

The Pack

Tough's head snapped around, and his eyes focused to the edge of the timberline with renewed intensity. There appeared to be unusual movement along the eastern edge toward the east. It could be the normal activity of diurnal denizens starting their morning activities related to food gathering, or their scouting and sniffing the terrain for changes that may have occurred during the night. He thought it probably was only hyperactive squirrels or chipmunks. While scurrying in the forest debris, many small harmless animals sound like threatening large carnivores, especially to the preconditioned "ears of fear" by smaller ones in the food chain.

Straining to get a better look, Tough lurched forward and came to an abrupt halt as he reached the end of the leather tether. Pivoting around the end of the restraint, he repositioned himself for maximum vision to the shadowed landscape. The hues of gray to brown to muted greens and lavender blended against the cobalt sky and hid any clear definition needed to determine the source of the continuing sounds. "It" or "something" was still there. A rustle repeated its presence . . . a prancing-like sound. Again, he leaned his body against the tether and focused into the depths of the timber.

There was absolute stillness in the air, due to the absence of any breeze, so no downwind scent was there to help him determine the identity of the intruders.

He started whining.

Nerves took over his body . . . he shook uncontrollably.

His head snapped quickly to the opposite direction as the western edge of the meadow erupted in a cascade of rustling sounds. Disbelieving, as if he had sensed the wrong direction of the noise, he looked back to the east. Nothing. He looked back to the west; there was a commotion in that direction, too. The sounds had now totally encircled the meadow.

Then, as if on cue, he heard a loud . . . *Caw—Caw—Caw*.

His eyes locked on a raven landing on a bough directly above.

He looked at Leigh again, as if to say this situation may require her help. He slowly approached her while frequently snapping his head left and right. He had an intrinsic feeling to awaken his mistress . . . for assistance, for help.

Nudging her foot with his nose, Tough quickly withdrew to a safe distance while waiting for her reaction.

Nothing.

He whined.

Again, while looking toward the mist-laden meadow; his need to waken Leigh was not deterred. He still felt the presence of a mysterious threat.

He whined a little louder, then emitted a yelp.

Now, in a more aggressive fashion, he approached Leigh and gave her a right hook to her boot with his paw.

He withdrew . . . quickly, and sat.

She moved; it worked.

*   *   *

Awakening slowly, Leigh found herself facing directly into sun. She stretched, rubbed her damp butt, and tried to figure out the last couple hours. She rose from her natural bed a little faster now, and quickly glanced around the area. Trying to sense what was happening, she jumped up and greeted the day.

"Tough, you're still here. Good boy!" she cried, as her exclamation echoed across the meadow and ridgelines. "Good morning, I must have slept here the entire night with you at my side as 'guardian' . . . and most likely you woke me up, didn't you?"

It appeared that Tough was preoccupied looking toward the edge of the meadow.

"What's wrong, boy? What are you looking at? What's out there?"

As she approached Tough, he immediately rolled over to a subservient position.

"Well, boy, you need not be so submissive to me. As I see it, you were my hero, my protector through the night. I must have been totally bushed last evening . . . whacked or completely zonked out to sleep through the chill and moisture of the Tongass air."

He sensed the affirmation and thanks through Leigh's soothing tones, then rolled up, stood, and wagged his whole body, muzzle low in respect. They both were still uncertain of their relationship, but were doing very well.

Nevertheless, she carefully sat down just beyond the tether's reach and joined him at eye level. As if on command, he stopped wagging and sat down, too. However, eye contact and small talk was short-lived as he rotated his head first to one end of the meadow, then back to the other end . . . followed by an upward glance at the raven. She followed his eyes, too.

"Good morning, avian friend," she said, knowing very well of the bird's ties to Manitou. Or could the bird be protecting the Golden Bough, in a sacred grove, of the past. "Whichever concept/myth . . . welcome. What's up, boy?"

Tough was certainly preoccupied with some sort of activity by the meadow's edge. He lunged to the end of the tether again . . . and whined.

"Dang, he's serious; there must be something out there."

She looked in the direction of Tough's apprehension. Standing up, she moved toward the end of the tether. The wolf cub's back and neck hairs had become stiff and erect—bristling in the angular rays of the sun. Looking through the dissipating early morning mist was a bewildering task; it was not easy to see just what exactly was drawing near in the vapor, and what Tough feared.

An errant deer with her fawns, maybe.

A hiker . . . unlikely.

They both strained their ears to the renewed sounds . . . a rustle, a clatter, a cadence, a rhythm.

Then, as if in starting blocks, one by one, the predators were unmasked as they seemed to explode from the edge of the mist.

Wolves.

A wolf pack.

Prancing as they emerged from the mist, there appeared to be at least a dozen gray-and-blacks.

Head lowered, Tough growled, his back and neck hairs bristling.

"Hold fast, boy. Stay back; they're just checking out you or us! They want to know your situation, your status, and your condition. They're most likely the same pack that visited us earlier—you would not remember—when Andy stayed overnight. At that time they smelled your presence; now they've got both scent and sight. I'll bet they've been scouting our location all night and waited until dawn to approach.

"Get a good look, kindred souls . . . Damn! It just may be decision time for the cub: me or the pack."

The pack slowed and dispersed in a loosely organized skirmish-line to the front of Leigh and Tough. Stopping now, the wolves strained and stretched their heads to sense the mixed scents of woman and cub, but their coats remained unbristled. That was a good sign. Separated by about twenty meters along a frontal line, to her surprise, she did not feel threatened—yet. The "why" of this encounter was easy to explain: Tough.

They seemed curious, with heads bobbing, canted, and extended as if to get a better view of the cub. They revealed the dried mask of blood, probably from the bowels of an earlier evening kill. Some were so relaxed they started cleaning their muzzles with leg and paw strokes and licking off the transferred succulent blood of the kill.

The smaller gray out front appeared to be the Alpha female. She carried herself in a commanding way, and they all looked to her for direction or permission, a signal, or a physical command of what to do or what they were allowed to do.

She sat.

The big black sat.

A few started to move in circles around their own bodies, or to sit or lie, then get up again and repeat. They appeared to be non-aggressive, but nervous.

Five have passed with no one breaking the invisible line between the Alpha gray and the apparent captives.

"Well, Tough, what do you think we should do next? It appears we've been fully checked out. Trouble is, I'm not certain how long I can participate in this standoff. I'm damn tired of watching while the gray decides what to do. Look, half of them are prostrate now, and the others just hanging around like lounge lizards at the local pick-up bar.

"I've had enough. What say you, boy? Tough! I'm going to make a move toward the hut. I've concluded they want me to let you loose—and I'm not.

"I'm not sure it's your choice, but—*it's mine*. I want you more than they need you. I could be wrong, but right or wrong, that's the way it's going to be."

One of Tough's ears turned to Leigh's pronouncement, one to the pack; his eyes shifted to the gray and back to Leigh. Tough remained at the end of the taut tether, rock-hard rigid legs firmly cemented to the ground.

Five more minutes of licking, grooming, and staring passed.

More silence.

The normal sounds of the meadow were absent since the pack's sudden appearance.

"Okay, boy, here's what we're going to do. I'll slowly move toward my woodland bed and retrieve my walking stick leaning against the tree, then slowly untie the tether. We'll move toward the hut, and see what happens next.

"Ready, here I go."

Looking at the tree and then the pack, Leigh moved slowly toward the four-foot walking stick. As soon as she twisted her shoulders, extended her body, and stepped off—the entire pack instantly bounded to their feet, stepped forward, and held their positions.

She froze.

The wolves paused.

Tough whined.

"Dang, it looks like we've tested their behavior—and it's noticeably not passive. I hope their objective is not to have us as dessert."

She did not step back. The walking stick was still about ten feet away, the wolves about sixty feet. However, if the pack chose to attack, to rescue the cub, having the walking stick in hand before the wolves covered the distance would be of minimal value in holding off the "dozen." *Without question, I'd lose if they were*

serious about disembowelment, she mused. Yet, the confrontational standoff, and apparent clos-
ing-in behavior may be a bluffing tactic. It is a rare occasion indeed when wolves attack humans,
unless starving, cornered, or protecting a fresh kill or young. They also have been known to
ravage human bodies already dead and frozen, but they'd rather run and hide from humans.
The literature is clear; any carrion is fair pickings for wolves or other carnivores trying to survive
in the wilds.

"Tough, I'm a gambler. I've made a decision. We're going to end this stand-off—right now. Here's the plan. I'm going to dash to the tree, grab my walking stick, pivot, and if the pack approaches our location, I'm going to yell at the top of my lungs, charge the pack while swinging the stick, and appear violent, and hope they will turn tail and run. What do you think, Tough?"

Tough was also showing the strain as he looked at her with a puzzled slant of his head. Leigh mentally rehearsed her moves to ensure she'd not made any errors in her logic. Chuckling, she reflected that the entire idea was questionable, but assuming the appearance of a stark-raving-mad woman yelling with a sword-like stick as a deterrent—wasn't this entire scene rampant with single-point failure? She reviewed, again, her steps to the tree, about five; steps to the hut, about twenty; a total of ten or eleven seconds to safety.

Untying Tough would be difficult, but was not a part of the initial plan; that would come later . . .

"What else did I forget? If the charge works, boy, I'll have plenty of time to return and untie you, and beat it to the hut. Yep, the door is unlocked. If neces-sary, the forty-five is on the table, w/clip inserted . . . a quick cycle and a round is chambered.

"Okay, boy, I'm ready. How 'bout you? Do you think I'm nuts?—I don't. We could be at a stand-off for hours without resolve, and guess what?—they would eventually win. Why? They're used to this type of stalking in the wild. We are not!"

About to make a move, Leigh noticed movement in the pack.

Startled, she snapped her head and body around to look at the commotion. The entire pack was following the gray as she circled the site. Not any nearer—yet—they didn't seem any more threatening, but with the circular pattern an encounter would surely be more likely. Leigh and Tough were quickly sur-rounded. Certainly not hurried, the wolves loped, walked and stood at times, con-tinuing their irregular path at a staccato pace. One feature of the pack was not a welcome sight: their heads were now lowered, ears laid back as apparently sig-naled by the gray. An even more extraordinary backdrop was the absolute silence.

Then it happened.

With blinding speed, the gray lunged at Leigh. She screamed as the furry mass approached. Tough growled.

The wolf knocked her down, and they rolled over together in the leaves. The gray bit her on the left boot and held on. It started backing up while trying to drag her toward the pack and away from Tough. She felt a searing pain flash through her foot as the wolf began biting higher and higher on the boot to gain a better hold. It started dragging her on her left cheek of her butt.

She kicked at his face with her other boot, and knowing Tough was tethered, yelled, "Tough! Help me! Attack! Attack! Attack!"

The savagery of the assault continued as the pack started to close in on the struggling pair.

Then something amazing happened. Tough answered her call, and *attacked.*

Tough lunged at the gray's neck while Leigh continued kicking. They tumbled together. The gray released the boot and quickly bit the throat of Tough, and just as quickly released, then returned to the pack.

"Damn, that was close. Good boy," she exclaimed.

Fortunately, Tough was at the end of the tether, cowering and growling as the gray rejoined the bloodthirsty horde.

"That's it. Luckily I've got more gaping holes in my boot than *in* my foot. It's only a matter of time and they'll all be taking another shot at me. I've got to make a move—now!"

Caw—Caw—Caw

The captives froze in place.

The wolves halted.

A new warmth bathed the meadow . . . highlighting the rising vapors from the wolves' bodies.

The wolves looked up, then looked toward the meadow and locked eyes on a new intruder standing at the northern edge.

A larger white wolf.

The gray growled.

Caw—Caw—Caw

"Yea! I wonder where the white came from. Dang, what great timing; I'm curious if it is a former pack member, an outcast, or rogue from another pack. In any case its appearance is welcome. It just may save the day."

Startled again, Leigh was literally bumped and brushed aside as several wolves on the far side ran by. The entire pack broke into a dead run toward the white, following the gray across the meadow.

The white then ran up the ridge toward the sacred plateau and the ancient altar—with the pack in pursuit.

Again, the absence of sound was a mystery, absolute silence except for the cries of the raven.

The meadow's silence may have been the result of fear or respect. A wolf pack in pursuit generally silences all those who have been witness to the chase and the kill. Many know, all too well, the carnage that follows as the pack savagely tears at a victim's flesh. When driven by hunger, their rapacious, plundering ways foster a "killing-field" scene while they fight for their share of the remaining morsels of bloody booty.

The horde disappeared over the top of the ridgeline and headed north along a smaller branch of the Bitterroot.

Leigh glanced up as the raven's call announced his departure while flying across the meadow to the north.

"Tough, we certainly have a lot to be thankful for. That encounter was just a little too close for comfort. Let's clear this area and get into the hut before that rainsquall to the north and the *canus lupus* decide to make another 'social' call . . . or should I say 'killing' call!

"Dang, too late; here she comes as the sky bursts in buckets of torrential rain, damn . . ."

She untied the end of the leash holding Tough and led him toward the hut, feeling a closer bond as a result of the mutual defense. Attacking his own kind was a significant statement of commitment to her.

She had a slight limp from her bite wound. He followed her to the hut without need of the tether . . . prancing at her side. She tied him near the porch, sat down, and removed her boot, exposing a single tooth puncture on the top of her foot and several deep gouges on the bottom.

"Stay here for a bit; I've got to clean up and get us some grub . . . and tend to my foot. We've had a full day already."

Tough drank a gallon of water and gulped some pemican she provided, then collapsed in the rain. Partially covered under the lower step, he anxiously waited for chow. Leigh carefully washed and treated her puncture and scrapes with iodine.

Taking care of business on the throne, Leigh tried to understand the logic or mystery of the morning's events; especially the timing. The pack's interest in Tough made sense, but she wondered how the raven seemed to appear at the right time in many crisis situations: Was the raven sent by Manitou, or was it Manitou transformed? How did He always know when His people were in an emergency, or life-threatening situation? The white wolf could not have just happened along to the standoff. Did Manitou transform into the white to save them from the pack? Is all this happenstance? Coincidence, or spiritual influence, to support the Creator's will? C. G. Jung woud call it synchronicity, coincidental events that seem related but unexplained by conventional logic.

"I'm not sure what to believe . . . but I'm certain all that happened this morning was not accidental. All the elements were too interrelated," she mused. "There you go, Leigh, talking to yourself . . . okay, okay, self . . . I'll log all these interesting events in my diary tonight."

After checking the meadow from the windows and finding the area clear, she grabbed a roll and glass of juice, and headed out to feed Tough. Carefully opening the door, she peeked out. Seeing nothing threatening, she fully opened it and exited with caution. Hidden for a moment, Tough was not visible; she followed the tether under the last step and his rain-safe location was revealed.

There he was, sleeping off a tension-filled morning.

*   *   *

Andrew's rain-drenched trek along the northern branch of the Bitterroot slowed his progress for several reasons. Not only a new route for him, it was beautiful . . . and he had not remembered ever traversing this area before, so he explored several aspects of its rain-soaked grandeur. He still sensed that he was being stalked. As such, his normal pace along with the waist-high ferns and underbrush reduced his progress. It did not bother him; there was no exact schedule up here, no rat race in the Alaskan wilds.

More relaxed now, he felt that whatever appeared to be following him, real or imagined, was suppressed in his thoughts. Sensing his distance from Leigh's camp to be less than two kilometers he took one final compass reading at about 170 degrees SSE and visualized the route by picking out a target tree at that azimuth. As he walked along the riverbed he rehearsed his apology/speech to Leigh . . . she may be annoyed at him for his abrupt departure without saying a word.

"What's that?" he exclaimd.

To the left oblique, in a southeasterly direction, the undergrowth exploded as an animal appeared at full speed hell-bent-for-leather directly toward Andy's location. The undergrowth and incline caused it to tumble uncontrollably for several feet, from which it recovered and continued running downhill.

It was a white wolf.

The same one?

After removing the snap retainer on his holster, he froze in place.

Unaware of Andy, the wolf ran to the edge of the stream, pivoted, looked to the rear, turned upstream to a small branching rivulet, turned again to check the ridgeline, and quickly followed the trickling water into a massive undergrowth of ferns and cedar boughs. He lowered his body and slipped under and through the camouflaged source of the rivulet.

The wolf disappeared.

The area returned to its former tranquil scene as the disturbed rivulet bed slowly returned to its crystal-clear beauty.

Silence captured the moment.

"Well, I'll be damned . . . what the hell's going on here? Let's see, I'll . . ."

Crash

The second explosion along the ridgeline was of greater magnitude.

At least a dozen wolves broke over and tumbled down the ridgeline—as if in pursuit of the white. Andy hit the dirt with weapon in hand and hid behind a fallen log. He peered over the edge to observe the pack cascade down the ridge with a medium-sized gray in the lead.

Andy mused, *Lucky for me, I'm downwind of the pack.*

They halted at the stream, in the stream, and at the far edge. With their noses to the ground, immediate pack disorder ensued. They apparently lost scent of the white in the water. The gray wandered downstream; the large black sauntered upstream toward the rivulet. Yelping now, the black expressed confusion and puzzlement. He spun around and around. The gray also started yelping and whining as the downstream scent appeared to vanish, also. Several members of the pack proceeded across the stream in search of a fresh scent, but found nothing. One, nose to the ground, preoccupied with the search, loped within ten feet of Andy. They all looked to the gray and black for guidance as they congregated in midstream.

None of them found a fresh . . . or old scent.

Nothing.

They all started howling in frustration; then more confusion triggered aggressive fighting/biting among the pack.

The gray made a questionable decision to continue the pursuit across the stream in the direction the white appeared to be headed.

Silent now, they all departed in deadly pursuit.

Andy breathed easier.

"Oh, oh, wait a minute, one just got wind of me . . . damn it!"

A small black stopped, pivoted, and searched the airborne scents, then looked directly to the log where Andy was hugging Mother Earth.

The small black whined, yelped, stepped forward, and rotated his head, searching for the location of the faint . . . unusual scent. He could not determine its origin or identification. He whined again, and started to approach the log . . . but stopped. He looked back at the pack's route, pivoted and quickly rejoined their futile pursuit to the north.

"Damn, that was close."

Silence returned to the area, and the rivulet slowly cleared to its previous crystal clear beauty.

Andy held on tightly for a few moments, uncertain of the black's behavior, and his willingness to follow the false trail with the pack. Luckily, he did. The pack's pursuit was an excellent example of group behavior based on minimal knowledge or facts, "do something—rather than think logically," in this case a true red herring.

Andy slowly rose from behind the log, his eyes searching the horizon, then sat on the log and stared at the rivulet's origin behind the fallen cedars.

As if talking directly to the white, he spoke toward the masked entrance of cedars. Silence prevailed as Andy reflected on his confrontation with a white wolf by the beaver pond.

"You're the one . . . aren't you?

Silence.

"We've met before, haven't we? It was by the beaver pond, wasn't it?"

As if a one-man show to an audience, he assumed the wolf heard his words of counsel and revelation.

"In respect of our last encounter, your current hiding place will not be revealed. Although curious, I will not contaminate its location with my scent by approaching the entrance. I owe you that right and will not violate our mutual esteem.

"So farewell, my friend. I will be moving on. I wish you success in your survival, and for whatever reason finds you living alone, may you live a long and satisfactory life; and if you choose to start a family, I hope you breed successfully and have many sons and daughters.

"Good-bye, fellow denizen of the Tongass . . ."

Silence.

Leaving the stream path, Andy traversed up the ridgeline to the plateau and moved near the small grove that contained what remained of the Tlingit's sacrificial altar.

Unhurried now, he stretched, looked for a seat . . . but halted. He noticed the location of the sun in the sky; the hidden cavern, the stream, and the altar were all aligned along a common orientation. The area around the altar was depressed, like a small basin, and water from the recent showers had settled in its cauldron.

He approached the water-soaked area around the massive slabs. Not wanting to wade, he stepped to the edge of the depression and sensed an unusual sound . . . an echo. The sound of water dripping was new to him. He'd been here many times before, and had not noticed the cauldron or water draining to a cavern below.

He looked again at the alignment of the altar to the white's cave, the rivulet, the stream, the sun, and wondered if there was a connection. He leaned over the largest slab, and indeed did discover an opening that had formed in the earth . . . and the echo of the water's impact to the cavern below.

"Damn. Could the chamber or cavern below be part of the spiritual power of the ancient altar . . . Could there be a connection? Could there be a geological karst below? Could there be a stone cap or a door of some sort covering the cavern? Could this be one of the natural burial caves, an Undercroft of the past? Could there be skeletons, idols, weapons for the afterlife secreted in the cave? Could the cavern below be an archeological treasure of the Tlingit's spiritual history, relating to both life as the 'womb-of-the-earth' and death?"

He listened, gazed into the darkness for several minutes, rose, carefully pivoted around the pool of water, backed away, turned, and moved across the plateau toward the hut with a newfound appreciation of the spiritual landscape of his forefathers.

He mused, *I will return soon to examine the ceremonial altar, the cavern, and its relationship to the subterranean opening at the rivulet discovered by the solitary white wolf.*

Sensing he was not alone, he looked at the arboreal rim of the meadow where he saw at least a hundred ravens silently watching his every move.

He stopped, rotated, sighted Leigh's hut through the trees, and pondered the scene.

He looked back at the birds while quickly departing the plateau, and reflected on the changes that had occurred in his life since meeting his brother's friend, Leigh.

"I'm either going to get more involved with this woman . . . or totally disengaged. One way, or the other, something has to change; this ebb and flow of partial emotional attachment is not working."

As he departed the plateau, the ravens burst into the rising earthly thermals and ascended to the azure cloud-filled sky above the Tongass.

Chapter 22

Reunion

The meadow appeared even more beautiful in its sparkling wetness from the intermittent rays of the sun on the morning's rain; it radiated a calm tranquility like a garden with banks of golden and copper flowers flanked by dark green juniper hedges. The State's flower, Forget-Me-Not, proliferated along the meadow's shaded edge as if to highlight the vast untold natural resources and incredible beauty of this "Land of the Midnight Sun." Adding to its splendor was the river's twisting crooks as if a framed scene in a *National Geographic* photo spread.

However, Andy's concern involved the presence of the pack's back-trail clearly leading across the plateau in the same direction as his dead-reckoning route to the meadow. Picking up the pace, he became more intense as the trail continued down the ridgeline toward the hut.

"Damn, the pack's origin appears to be directly from Leigh's homestead."

He now felt that a worst-case scenario included the wolves passing through and holding Leigh and Tough captive inside the hut, or even worse: being attacked outside along the river's edge.

"Dang, all these events may have occurred a mere kilometer from my own rather passive confrontation, with the white."

He increased his pace to a brisk walk, almost a trot, while slipping and falling on the wet ferns, and moved down the ridgeline. As he walked across the sacred meadow of his forefathers, it occurred to him how few actually knew this location as the last campsite of his Tlingit Brothers in the late 1800s. It was indeed a privilege, an honor, and a blessing to know the origin of this beautiful five-acre clearing. He was also very much aware of his deceased brother's annual obligation to give thanks to the Creator at this site. Walkswithwater had the shamanic background and training that made him duty-bound to do so, and now Andy felt a commitment to continue these rites. Even though with much less training and fewer qualifications, somehow he would find a way to pay respect to his forefathers and take his brother's place as a representative for the tribe. He would find a way to praise and give thanks to Manitou.

He stopped in the center of the meadow, looked toward the grassy border and dripping arboreal heights of the timber, and tried to assess the reasons for the absolute silence. He had always felt ownership to "Reading the Treetops," as one of his many wilderness skills; something was strange; something was definitely not right in the entire clearing. Nothing was moving in the normal manner.

Like a flash, the entire sun exposed itself from the mask of rain clouds.

"Hello, Mr. Sun; looks like you're going to stay out this time . . . welcome!"

He looked at the shaded hut, only to find similar stillness and silence. Moving toward the hut, Andy carefully leaned into the shadows with anticipation of some activity. There was none. He walked around one of the sides, held fast at the corner, and peered around at the porch. Nothing.

"Wait. What's that? Are those wolf's legs sticking out from under the lower step? Tough's? What the Sam-Hell is he doing there? Where's Leigh? What's going on? There certainly doesn't appear to have been any problem here. But why the total silence? If that's Tough . . . I hope he's tied up. I'll soon know."

Crouching now, he stealthily rounded the corner, drawn pistol at this side. Irritated and soaking wet from the rain, he grimaced again as the runoff from the earlier rain trickled down his neck.

"Damn weather."

Finally, a sound, a low frequency rumble. He looked down; it was Tough. He appeared out cold with little concern for the rain dripping over the edge of the bottom step, or the lower temperatures of the shaded entrance. Andy paused for a moment. Tough remained asleep. Strange, he normally would have sensed an intruder's presence by now.

"Well, well, just what's going on here? You're tied outside without Leigh's supervision. That seems just a little unusual, to say the least."

The sun was still chasing the rain away as shards of gold filtered through the treetops. The rays had a dramatic impact on the inhabitants of the clearing . . . as they leaped into action. He paused again to contemplate his next move. A large doe and two fawns marched into the clearing as if to claim ownership. Nostrils in the air, they clawed the turf, marking their possession. Their deep brown to tan coats, ebony eyes and noses, and white breastplates glistened in the warmth of the sun. The doe and Andy locked on each other's eyes. She stomped, snorted, and feigned an escape, but remained to graze with her twins. Apparently, he was not a threat to her meadow or family. Andy accepted her decision and carefully moved up the steps to the porch, halted, and scanned the area and the path leading to the river. Nothing. He turned back toward the door and tried the knob. The door was unlocked and partially ajar. He slowly leaned into the shadows of the hut.

"Leigh," he whispered, "may I come in?"

No response.

He heard another low-frequency, slowly aspirated rumble from the interior. His suspicions were confirmed . . . there she was, on the bed, spread-eagle, fully clothed—passed out. Her snore provided a complementary harmony to the cub's rumble under the stairs, melodic, but certainly not the quality of Neil and Barbra's duet, "You Used To Bring Me Flowers. . . ."

"I'll be damned. If this isn't something. They must have had a physically exhausting night—together—someplace. Thankfully, Tough is tied and secure, but she is not with the door ajar, unless it is to give the cub a little security. Who knows?"

He sat on a chair by the kitchen table. Rather than awaken the pair, Andy decided to make a pot of coffee. Surely the potent aroma would soon trigger the lady of the meadow to stir. While the bean relinquished its flavor to the warming water, he reflected on his current role in life and with Leigh . . . and his future life goals. "Leigh does have and interesting lifestyle here on the meadow. The view . . . the scene outside this window has remained pretty much unchanged for centuries. This is one of the few places you can hear a clock ticking.

"It's a sad thing when a generation loses the sound of ticking clock, when people become too rushed to listen to a knitter's clicking needles, too busy to observe sleeping dogs, or wolves, and the slow rhythmic motion of a rocking chair.

"It's unfortunate that many persons crowd out the sounds of a snapping wood fire, the whistle of a steaming kettle, and they no longer observe patterns made by the sun on a wooden floor. Even a well-filled wood box is a comforting sight, which is almost unknown to most of our young men and women.

"All these delightful things make up a way of life that has just about disappeared in these modern times. But Leigh has these things here. No wonder she embraced this lifestyle.

"Measurement of time, the landscape outside the window, and the annual arrival of seasons have not been altered. *I have.* Spring, with its unusual fresh greenery is followed by summer with its same bright flowers growing in the same secluded places. Fall arrived on schedule with its dazzling array of leaves, followed by bleak November heralding the first white flakes of snow. For ten years I have watched the seasons unfold through these eyes, each scene unchanging from year to year; only my face in this mirror has changed. And on the inside I have changed, too; more mellow, I hope, perhaps more tolerant, less patient, more cautious, but still curious. Sadly, I see no change in my life in Skagway, or at work, or at play. Only I change. Thank you, Great Spirit . . . for being durable, eternal. I hope I'll never become insensitive, bitter, shriveled in soul and mind, but that I'll keep growing, learning, and remain flexible—a moist seed in fertile ground. I certainly have an opportunity to sow my oats with Leigh's fecundity. Look at her, she's a beaut, and I've been sent by Manitou to serve her needs. Maybe it's a time to appraise my future, my relationship with women . . . or maybe not. Once cuck-olded, and by God, my first love did so . . . you better have learned to avoid the fire . . . but maybe one failure does not a lifetime make . . . *Maybe it's time for a change*, and just maybe this fall, the most enjoyable time in the woods will bring calm to my life—with Leigh.

"It is difficult to be upset with the world while walking through the Tongass. Animals stop to stare nervously at you, the breeze ruffles your hair, and the streams murmur beside you . . . and everywhere there is peace.

"If I pause to think at all, it should not be of a grudge held by a one-time love, and the humiliation of that long-ago failure.

"Everything seems to be in a truer perspective here with Leigh. My mental vision is clear, understanding of 'other' a bit stronger, and love wider in scope, broad, and inclusive of more people. I can tolerate myself better where trees are tall, where the forest breathes of life, and beauty abounds.

"Yes, it's time for a change . . ."

It didn't take long for the coffee's steam-driven aroma to permeate through the cabin's interior.

Andy rose and walked to the stove as Leigh began to stir. He poured a couple of "blacks" and carried them to the table. She lurched up to a sitting position. They locked eyes and smiled with an expression of a thousand words known only between friends.

"Hi," she responded while combing her hair though her fingers.

"Well, hello, how are you, dear?" Andy responded with a smile. "How 'bout some wake-up juice?"

Damn, she looks good, he mused.

"Just seeing you . . . all my answers are . . . yes," she said. "You've no idea how good it is go see you . . . Oh Andy, I'm going to break up, after the attack of the wolves . . . and now you, my composure is gonna crack—I'm so happy, so relieved."

She jumped up and stood next to the bed, looked toward the doorway, glanced at Andy, and started to move toward the door.

"He's okay, still sawing logs under the step," Andy responded, having read her look.

"Oh, dear me, what will I do next? I'm so relieved . . . I think I've already said that . . . I'm confused."

She froze in place.

Concerned for her stability, her health, she pondered her next move.

Then, without concern for the consequences, she loosened up and moved toward Andy. A little shocked, Andy returned the embrace as Leigh wrapped her arms and body around his. Just a little unsure of his role, he gave her the complete warmth of his body. She sobbed and murmured in low mumbling tones about the wolf attacks and her fearfulness—her stress levels.

Andy felt as if her embrace lasted a lifetime as he listened to Leigh's conflicted feelings of joy bolstered and aroused by the presence of his comforting arms. His thoughts also shifted to emotions that he had blocked for many years, thinking maybe this was the time to shed the bitterness of past love lost and light the fires of sensitivity again. Some opportunities present themselves only once in life, and this . . . might have been his last chance. It was not the first time Leigh had shown a willingness to inhabit the same heartfelt thoughts; she'd tried many times before . . .

"Leigh, we have some personal business to discuss. Let's move to the clearing for a moment. I'll feel better, with what I have to say, at the meadow's edge. Trust me—come," Andy pleaded.

He dried her tears of happiness and anticipation, took her hand, and slowly eased out the door and down the steps over the sleeping cub. They moved hand and arm toward the center of the meadow.

"Leigh, I'm not real good at emotional pleadings, but if you'll be just a little patient, I need your reaction to the feelings I have for you. I'm clumsy with words, but do know a tribal love poem that expresses my feelings.

"Recitation of the poem must be at a spiritual site as in this clearing of our forefathers, for that's when the soul is awakening and more receptive to the heart-felt pleadings of a suitor.

"Here are my thoughts, my dear, from the words spoken by our tribal deity, Manitou.

"Here is my plea."

He positioned Leigh so she also faced the sun, then stood behind her with arms encircling her nervous body. Andy spoke:

> "I bring you an opportunity for a Life with me.
> Somebody at sunrise will express his love to you.
> Somebody at sunset will demonstrate his love for you.
> When the thunder rumbles, Manitou has spoken to you.
> When the wind whistles, the Spirits have blessed you.
> When the sky rains, Mother Nature has blessed you.
> When the raven calls, he will guide you.
> When the sun shines, the world has accepted you.
> When you look at the moon, it will be your Lover's face for you.
> Let your Soul come to mine so I can love you.
> I offer you a new life of Friendship, Admiration, and Love."

Nervously, he turned Leigh around, lowered his head to hers, found her eyes, sought her tender lips, and touched them with his . . . expressing passion of a determined lover.

Time passed . . . They gazed into each other's eyes with thoughts swimming in the depth of his poetic words, thoughts of hope and pleasure for the future.

"Leigh, you're even more beautiful in the shadows cast by the timber of your meadow . . ."

He held her tighter, and wrapped his body around hers.

Looking up at him, touching his face with her hands, she pressed her body to his to show her love for him . . . that moment . . . she thought to herself, if God lives, God gives us moments like this.

"My dear, we have a tribal tradition that suggests a pause, a reflection, a refrain prior to making important decisions, whether in love or battle. The ceremonial rite involves a spiritual communal fire; in this case, for us. I'll start preparing the fire pit now for our conclave later this evening so we can enjoy the dancing embers and flames licking the sky. I'm urging you to continue for now the sleep I interrupted. You also have a lot to think about . . . Your canine friend, I assume, will remain asleep, so don't worry about him. I'll be around."

For his own reasons, maybe tenderness, maybe closeness, he picked her up and carried her to the hut as she caressed his damp neck and shoulder. Carefully avoiding Tough, he slid inside and gently lowered her onto the bed.

Not letting go of his neck, she whispered, "Why don't you lie with me."

"Later," he said reluctantly.

"Wait a minute . . . at least a kiss, dear," Leigh murmured.

"No, I'm afraid of what might happen. Things are moving fast enough as it is. Do you realize how much emotional territory we've discussed today?"

"Chicken," she whispered.

"Cluck cluck," he responded. "Sleep tight, I'll wake you up in the afternoon, unless I need your help with Tough or an unexpected visitor. Sweet dreams—and think about how you'll respond to the Spirit of the Fire tonight."

Andy left her side, determined to control his feelings . . . for now. Without a doubt, he was ready for love.

*   *   *

Andy moved silently over the sleeping cub to the woodpile, paused, then gathered materials for the campfire.

He whispered to the cub, "I heard the good story about your steadfast resolve last night. Protector, yes, a noble act of love. You have started to rule the wilderness with majesty and fearlessness. Your brothers have long been revered as symbols of mysterious power. According to our Tlingit legends and lore, you are among the most courageous, protective, and cunning creatures of the Tongass."

Andy remained by the wolf, turned toward north, and cast tobacco north, east, south and west, raised his arms to the sky, and gave thanks to the tribal Godhead.

> "Creator—Manitou—our Protector,
> Hear my thanks and my plea.
> Bless this young cub for his courage;
> Provide for his future and give him strength,
> We praise your role in our lives, and
> Let the spirit of the wolf watch over us, too."

As Andy continued his efforts building the ceremonial fire pit, he could not help but notice the beauty of autumn's encroachment, the colorful panorama of leaves, of scarlet maples, bright yellow birches and poplars, all contrasting with the dark green spruce and pine, and lighter green tamarack. They seemed to be bursting into the sun's rays as lingering raindrops sparkled and reflected rainbow hues.

The air was crisp and invigorating as he walked down the path from the hut to the Bitterroot. He decided to build an additional fire pit by the river's edge. Its newness would be identified as their pit, the pit of the newly found lovers. . . .

First placing several large rocks in a circular pattern over freshly tilled soil, he rolled two massive logs into place, which finished the physical aspects of the pit. Ceremonial Rites would be introduced with spiritual blessings later in the day. He collected, stacked, and lit a cedar fire. Relaxing on the bench now, he faced west to the cluster of cattails on the edge of the bank. Muskrats ate the starchy underground stems while the masses of tiny seeds in sausage-shaped heads attracted small warblers and finch. He enjoyed the conspicuous plants with their towering brown "tails" and waving sword-like leaves.

"Hey, I've got an idea," Andy mumbled to the tails. "My mother displayed you beauties every fall in an old discarded galvanized coffee pot that she found in the trash. I'm going to do the same for Leigh."

He quietly strolled up the path and started rummaging around the back of the woodpile.

"Bingo, this number ten empty bean can will do the job. I'll just form it to a somewhat exotic shape, and no one will know the difference. As mom would say, 'It's the thought that counts.'"

Back at the river, he cut about a dozen of the towering tails and leaves, enough to stuff the can plus a few more for a future project. Sitting on the bench he went to work on creating his signature piece.

"Now that looks pretty," he pronounced.

He leaned back on the bench to admire his creation . . .

Tough's whine gave away their stealthful approach.

Jerking his head around, Andy blurted, "Dang you, woman, don't sneak up on me like that!"

"Why, dear, we're not sneaking; we are just *seeking* out my newly found Alpha male. There now . . . how do you like that? Or we can just call you 'The Man.'"

"Okay, Court Jester, maybe I'm down here signing for an FTD air shipment fresh from a florist in Juneau," he replied.

"What have you got there?"

"Nothing," he teased. "Nothing until I get the proper greeting and recognition from you . . . and that wolf."

"Well, you're about to get a big suck-face kiss and hug from me. It looks like Tough already senses who you are, meaning: an 'okay' smell. He's no dummy; I'll bet he knows you, and by his body language, I'm certain he's already accepted you and is looking elsewhere for intruders, two- or four-legged. I'll tie him up here by the bench and you two can talk over old times. You watch, I'm positive he has accepted you; after all, you have been okayed by his Alpha female. How's that for a mouthful? Now where's that Tongass/floral treat? Oops, I forgot, a big wet-one first."

She laid one on Andy and, after surfacing for air, he laid one on her. Already getting carried away with their newly found passion, they fell over into the wet leaves and their legs intertwined . . . then they rolled over again . . . and he lingered a little longer than planned. Their legs interlocked.

"Andy, Andrew South, are you about to dry-hump me in these wet leaves? If you are, fine, but guess what? The bed in the hut is still unmade, warm, and dry!"

He got the message, and giggled.

They both came up for air, rolled on their backs, looked at each other, looked at the cloudy sky, and started laughing at her logical and willing words as well as his own impetuousness.

"Are you sure about this?" he asked. "We're not rushing this are we?"

"Dear, I have never felt so certain of my feelings, for anyone, as I now feel about you. Let's roll," she said, getting up and grappling for his hand.

"Come on, big fella, times awastin'."

Andy bounded up and grabbed her body. She jumped him from the rear, so he carried her piggy-back up the path. "Hold on, boy," she yelled to Tough. "We'll be right back. I've got to ride this bronco to submission."

They skipped the candlelight, wine, and small talk . . . they were too busy undressing each other.

Silence dominated the meadow.

Later on, Tough's head snapped around toward the hut as he heard a robust noise of pleasure from his mistress. He judged the sounds as good . . . so he continued his sentry duties as protector of the compound for both now, with one who appeared to be lingering for some time with his lady.

*   *   *

The sun hung at four-fingers from the horizon.

Drinking in the cattails at the river's edge, Tough quickly raised his head and turned toward the sound coming from the north. He scurried up the bank to investigate the intruders coming down the path. His growl changed to a low whine as he saw Leigh and Andy. He sat and waited for the pair to arrive at the bench.

The combined smell of the pair was not bad, but it *did not* improve hers. His ears pricked up, and he stood to all four, as a smell of a snack filtered to his senses. Pemmican. He rose to his hind feet as they approached. With both front legs on Leigh's waist he snatched the treat, then lowered himself and gave a thankful whine as he tore into the firm cake-like bar.

"You've certainly earned a treat, Mr. Wolf. Thanks for watching the outpost again while Andy and I did some riding," Leigh said.

"Tough has certainly earned his keep over the last couple days. He's a true guardian. He also accepted me as your companion. That's something, just on face value; we both need each other—we all will need each other," Andy responded with a serious look on his face.

He moved toward the fire pit.

"Come on, Leigh, let's christen the new pit. Remember, it's our pit, ours to share over the seasons in the Tongass. This is kinda nice isn't it? Blankets for two, by the fire, should provide a good venue to discuss our present and future plans. I certainly need to let you know what kind of a guy you're about to be involved with."

"Okay, big boy . . . 'show me'; I'm from Missouri."

They snuggled against the log, and under the blankets. Tough also settled into a prone, observant position while tied to the bench. The sun hung at one finger as shadows lengthened across the clearing. The fire's sparks, rising to the ether, were now visible in the fading light. Only upon close observation could their blending be filtered from the emerging stars.

"Leigh, I realize I am a maverick, for I can claim nothing more than being a man in search of the meaning of life—the human search for Spiritual Meaning—my raison d'etre, my reason for justification of my belief system."

Inspired by these thoughts, Leigh reflected on her feelings. "Love is also an interdependent life force, a broad spectrum of significance, from its divine grandeur to its basis as a goal in our search for compassion."

"I agree, dear. I've only recently personally resolved that you can't give away what you don't have . . . you must have love in your heart—to love others. Indifference can have no quarter in a loving heart. May I give you some of my newly discovered sources of strength, for survival, in relationships with others you love?"

He did not wait for an answer; her eyes telegraphed her positive feelings.

"Oh, there's probably more, but here are a few that come to mind, my top guiding principles in my new outlook to life.

"For example, in our case:

> "We should give up our *Personal History*; pack it up and throw it away, and start anew.
>
> "Again, with our newly found closeness: Don't try to solve problems with the *Same Mind* that created them; let's rewrite our approach to problems with a new reality.
>
> "And, although I'm no scholar: Let's avoid thoughts that weaken each other; let's optimize our *Combined Wisdom*; careful thoughts before actions.
>
> "And finally: Love each other for *What We Are*—not what we want another to be; learn *to love* that imperfect person, like the imperfect selves we are.

"There is something distinctively altruistic about the friendship of the Spirit. It operates outside the bounds of duty, function, or office. Of all our relationships, it is the most free, invoking neither the interdependence of the Creator, nor the mutuality of the lover, Eros, but offering a quality of presence and sustenance that allows and empowers the divine 'Evolutionary Dance.' It evokes sentiments of the friend who remains a friend for life . . . that is my hope, that is my wish for us," Andy said with heartfelt emotion in his voice. "Our tribal fathers said it well: 'The needs of the planet are the needs of the person, and the rights of the person are the rights of the planet.'"

"Dear, I want you to join the Dance of Life: Our Dance," Andy continued. "In evolutionary terms, all dances are sacred. For thousands of years before the development of formal religion, our ancestors—our tribe—did not draw the distinction between sacred and secular. In its origin, dance was fundamentally *spiritual*, and I plan to demonstrate to you tonight, its innate function to facilitate contact with the sacred and the divine. I perform tonight for our newfound love, and the love of the spirit that safeguards the tribal altar on the plateau. I dance for you, my dear, and hopefully appeasement of the Creator; for tomorrow we explore the underground chamber below the altar . . . we will need His *forgiveness* and blessings as we explore my tribal history.

He started dancing slowly around the fire . . . increasing his body motions as his step quickened.

"Come, my dear. Join me in the Dance To Our Sacredness."

Their bodies moved in a staccato rhythm, casting a silhouette against the fire's backdrop, undulating, turning, and twisting to the rhythm of the flames.

Andy chanted, and Leigh repeated the words of praise in his native tongue:

> Gi-tchie Man-i-to . . . gi-tchie man-i-to'
> Ah-ki Ah-ki . . . ah-ki ah-ki'
> Gee-sis Gee-sis . . . gee-sis gee-sis'
> Nee-ba-gee-sis Nee . . . nee-ba-gee-sis nee'

They repeated their pleas to the spirits as they chanted through the night; then, overcome by the heat of the fire and dancing, they stripped to their naked beauty and plunged into the Bitterroot. After cooling off, they continued to dance in the glimmering wetness of their nakedness. Again, and again, they twisted and chanted while circling.

Exhausted, they collapsed to the blankets and passionately moved in the rhythm of climactic love, both yielding to each other's needs, giving wholeheartedly of self without reservation.

Andy whispered in her ear, "Just let everything loose . . . let it all go . . . yes, inflame your soul—shake, let your body be erotic . . . let go, connect with yourself—love that body, give yourself permission to be sensual."

"Thank you, my dear . . . oh my dear . . . oh, Andrew."

"I hope you felt a connection with me and our ancestors during the dance."

"Andrew, I not only feel connected . . . the rapture in my loins seeks your linkage 'til the end of time."

Relaxed now, Andy summarized the purpose of the dance ritual.

"My dear, you should be aware that not only did our ancient ancestors dance to the sacred, a practice often dismissed by other myths as pagan worship; they also danced in order to articulate and celebrate what scholars call *The Wonder Of Existence.* External action and inner experience are given symbolic, ritual expression, activating a process of anthropocentric wholeness and integration. Dance becomes the primary medium to explore and express the human search for meaning. Our modern version of the sacred circle dance illustrates something of the effusive, unrestrained richness of these ancient forms, particularly the group dimension, the circular aspect, and the sense of interconnectedness. Nonetheles, I remind you of my sacred pledge:

> "I still leave you free to be
> yourself . . .
> I will not attach
> myself . . .
> Your inner peace is important to me."

"Thank you, dear; that's beautiful. Come to me . . . it's my turn to show you some Ann Arbor-based loving . . ."

Sleep quickly overtook their tired bodies as they made tentative plans for exploration of the sacred cavern on the 'morrow.

Again, Tough, alert to the surroundings, remained vigilant as the entwined lovers slumbered by the fire.

Preoccupied with the safety of his mistress by the fire with Andy, he was unaware of the raven perched silently in the tall pine by the river.

Chapter 23

The Ancients

As the late summer moon slipped over the horizon, the morning sun's rays played across the eight-legged threesome at the hidden entrance to the cave.

"Yes, that's a good idea, Leigh. Tie him to that tree near the stream, which is still close enough to reach the cave's entrance. That will give him a chance to be a sentinel, and also allow him to look in as we explore the cave," Andy declared.

"Okay, boy, here's a pemmican biscuit. Good boy; see you later," Leigh said. She then looked at her newfound love, while waiting for him to clear the entrance to the cave.

She reflected to herself on the previous evening's bliss. "You're some girl, Leigh . . . Once again you are caught up in an affair of the heart. Are you sure you know what you're doing? Oh well, go for it, girl; best not analyze your actions too much. It's not as though I've been in this exact situation before . . . I'll see how the next few days unfold. We're certainly going to be busier together crawling into this tribal burial cavern. It's going to be a test beyond the romantic campfire. We'll see. We'll see how well our camaraderie is sustained while searching for his spiritual past—underground."

"How's that look Leigh?" said Andy. "Do you think there's enough room to get through? Frankly, that's all we'll have anyway. The walls appear to be made of a sedimentary layered material. There seems to be a blockage about ten feet into the cave. No sweat; I can clear a way. The water is still flowing underneath the debris. Look, here is where the white wolf I told you about has been bedding down. All things being equal, just maybe we can leave this little escape venue for him to use again. Time will tell. Did you notice Tough checking out the white's scent?"

"Yeah, his nose is still fired up. He's sniffing just about everything in the area, and around the little rivulet's entrance to the cave. I guess that's normal. Didn't you say that this is also where the pack came through yesterday?"

"Yep," he said. "Most of the scent should be rained away, but he seems to be picking up the residue of their activity anyway. Good nose, boy."

"How are we going to handle a confrontation if the white wolf or the pack appear while we're in the cave? Tough should be okay for a short time, but . . . what if we're delayed inside or the white, or worse yet, the pack attack Tough while tied up. What then?" she lamented.

"You know, I can think of no other way to handle this unique situation. We'll just assume that any commotion or howling can be addressed prior to any dangerous threat to Tough's well being."

"Well, okay," Leigh said reluctantly.

"I'll have this blockage cleared in a minute and we'll be ready to go. How 'bout it, dear; are you ready to crawl on your tummy, in the rivulet's subterranean flow for about fifty meters to the cavern below the altar?"

"I'm not sure if I'm ready, but ready or not, I'm going . . . matter of fact, I wouldn't miss it. We may be the first to explore and examine the death rites of your people from, say, about five hundred years ago."

"That could be right. Some of the older tribal scholars living in Juneau may be able to help with Carbon fourteen dating. Still, this site may have been established a thousand or more years ago. Archeologists have explored Central American temples and other majestic ruins at least that old. Anthropologists have probed the ancient Maya's sacred landscape and have come to realize that this group's belief system invested immense supernatural power in caves and the mountains that surround them. Banks of researchers are piecing together this subterranean, spiritual perspective. In their view, this supernatural terrain permeated spiritual life on all five continents and still inspires faith in many native groups today.

"Caves occupy the focal point of many archeological projects," he continued. "In initial research they discovered that some of the largest North American outposts of the Classic period, which lasted from BCE two-hundred to Current Era nine-hundred, were strategically oriented on and around the natural and human-made caves as entryways for the sacred. It was as if the living earth led to an underworld of gods, mythical creatures, and ancestors, and caves served as spiritual land works. It appears that in these dim chambers, rulers conducted ceremonies vital to maintaining their power.

" I'll bet this cave is a *karst*. It is probably the result of an underground stream slowly eroding the softer limestone deposit from the harder surrounding bedrock. Look ahead; the stream of water still flows at a lesser volume. These cave-like underground caverns are found in abundance in the Tongass and the entire coastal archipelago in a seemingly random pattern. It appears wherever an active flow of subterranean water flows through an isolated limestone deposit it erodes away over time resulting in caves, caverns, and more dangerous sinkholes."

He continued as they both wrapped their knees and elbows. By Current Era fourteen-hundred, tribal leaders were burying their dead in rock shelters and caves like this. Among the contemporaries in North America, a tradition of cave burials included encasing symbols of sacred sacrifices and deceased chieftains in cave-like tombs, so we'd better be ready for more than just artifacts: like body jars and spiritual symbols on the dead bodies. We may see a body or two, or more. . . ."

"Are you finished? You're starting to scare the hell out of me. Let's just get going. I've had enough of your 'what if' stories. I'm ready; let's go!"

She double checked the rawhide tie on Tough, then waded up the rivulet to Andy. Tough stood square, ramrod straight as his mistress moved to the entrance of the subterranean breach. His head tilted in a typical 'not sure what's going on' prejudice.

"Okay, Leigh, the blockage is clear now. I'll go first with the big light. Do you have yours?"

"Yep, this old three-cell is one of my best friends up here. You know the saying I'm obligated to recite since I'm following you, don't you?"

"No, what do you mean?"

"Here it is . . . 'If you're in a line, like a dog-sled team, be sure you're lead. If you're not, all you'll see is ass ends the entire trip . . .'"

"Ha! So that's the best you can do, huh? Dear, all I can say is, Enjoy the view since I've got the best looking tush in Alaska."

"Okay, it's acceptable, but let's not get carried away. From what I saw at the fire last night . . . it could use some work!" giggled Leigh.

"That reminds me of the exercise instructor's comment to the women in his class. 'Remember to get your butts in shape, because it's the last impression you leave when you exit a room,' and you, my dear, by the fire, left a very good impression . . . from all angles," Andy cooed.

"Ha! Before your delusions get off-scale, let's go."

As they crawled into the opening, they noticed the internal structure consisted of a long narrow passageway leading to a dimly lit opening at the end of the tunnel. The rivulet of water was constant and cold as though fed by and underground spring ahead.

The subterranean pair could not see the ravens' approach as they perched above the statuesque canine. By the time Tough noticed their arrival in the treetops, at least a dozen birds had landed. . . .

*   *   *

Leigh mulled over her plight. "I hope I'm doing the right thing. It seems whenever I'm with adventurous men . . . their lives and mine seem to be perched on a slippery slope. Andy's request for appeasement from Manitou is still unknown. We're at risk going into this cavern. Oh well. The loss of Ford and Andy's brother was enough trauma for the whole year . . . for a lifetime. . . . "

The tunnel's dank environment was not only eerie, but its narrowness made movement difficult and claustrophobic, bordering on the cusp of danger. Leigh was a little uncertain of her decision to join in Andy's exploration of the cave. Andy must have sensed a little tension in her voice; he broke the silence with a comment.

"Hey, babe. Aren't you glad we wrapped our knees with rags? Mine are still feeling the stress of last night and the discomfort of cold water over these ragged rocks."

"For sure, and I had no idea we'd be plowing through a bone field, too."

They continued their careful crawl through the rivulet of water and hanging stalactites entangling and what appeared to be a plethora of small animal bones. The symbolic 'generative womb of the earth' appeared to have been violated by many animals, but seemingly unmolested for centuries by large animals—or man.

A series of six-foot square dugout chambers appeared on both sides. Each held a little altar laden with clay lamps of various sizes . . . probably for light or incense. They appeared to be of a spiritual nature. Below them, pools of water reflected an eerie but beautiful symbol of respectful calm and honor.

"Leigh, look at this one," he said, lowering his voice to a whisper. "This chamber has a very small child-like skeleton, adorned with beads and chain, on an altar. I'll bet this one honors the early life of a special child and presents the soul of that body to the spirits for safekeeping, or rebirth. Many of our early ancestors were confused about the causes of life and death, and at times, in awe by the suddenness of death—and the mystery of birth. Some of these altars are expressions of those mysterious beliefs. Each one is a little different, a little eerie, but beautiful and serene. They're especially scary only when illuminated and shadowed by our light beams. I never cease to be amazed at the stamina shown by these earlier inhabitants as they performed all this creative work with primitive tools, simple lamps, and torches.

"The cubical-like chambers," he continued, still whispering, "called 'Chultuns' in Central America, have always been of interest to anthropologists. They generally agree that tribes in both North and South America had similar spiritual concepts. Carbon fourteen dating indicates many of the subterranean cave artifacts are from the Current Era 1000 to 1600. Who knows, we may have stumbled into the first one in North America.

"Leigh, can you see those big clay pots? I'll bet there's everything from a skeletal body, to grain or water in there . . . for the afterlife. What do you think?"

"Not sure. Say, do you realize that you've been speaking in a whisper for the last few minutes? It's a though you do not want to disturb or awaken the sentinels protecting the ceremonial altars."

"No, I hadn't noticed. But now that you mention it, I do feel rather humble and respectful as we probe the sacred ground of my Tlingit ancestors. Dang, do you feel it? Call it what you wish. I feel it, whether it's the Source, Spirit, or One

Power, its nomenclature is not important; it's in the tunnel."

They sloshed through the rivulet, flashlights pointed ahead while jammed into their trousers. Andy halted and listened.

"Do you hear that, Leigh? It sounds like cascading water, like a waterfall . . . do you hear it?"

"Yes, and I also see the light at the end of the tunnel is getting brighter now. We must be only a few meters from the large cave under the altar on the plateau. I hope so. I'm getting cold, sore, and crunched up—I can't wait to stand up and stretch."

"Did you notice that as we get closer to the cave's inner chamber, the honored dead are older and of higher rank? The first chamber held a child, and as we progressed there were a few adults, and now the warrior's chamber. I'm thinking the center cave/dome ahead will contain a chief or two, tribal shamans, or sacrificial virgins. Virgins were sacrificed to ensure the tribe's future fertility . . . to guarantee many births. Don't worry, Leigh; you're no longer a qualified candidate . . ."

"Okay, smart ass. I used to be until men like you *entered* my life."

"Touché'."

*   *   *

Both stood in the domed cavern and immediately collapsed to a sitting position against the walls, not from fatigue, but rather awe. The scene was shocking beyond their wildest imagination, yet beautiful in an ominous way, and still very eerie. A single ray of sunlight exposed the additional chultans in the dome's perimeter; and at least six sarcophagi in a special section toward the rear. In the center, directly underneath the opening in the ceiling, in a stack at least ten feet high, hundreds of skeletal remains from sacrificed bodies had apparently been dropped from above.

Odor-free now, it must have been rather 'rank' when an active site. The decayed flesh now absent, only stable cellulose fibers in the clothing, beads, oxidized green copper, and necklaces remained on the skeletons.

Their flashlights' narrow beams reflected off beadwork, amulets, tombs, and petroglyths on the walls as they explored the cave, their own bodies in situ. They were reluctant to move in the cluttered gravesite. The stack of bones, being the focal point of the room, was an absolute jolt as to what they thought they would find in the cave. The pile spread to almost twenty feet in diameter. The late morning sun's rays were close to an optimum angle as the shards of light impacted the bones and eerily illuminated the cavern below. Their disruption sent dust particles airborne and added to the ghostlike highlights of the sun's path from the ceiling to the skeletal mass below.

The light now adequate, they both turned off their flashlights. They still remained in place, as if unable to move.

"Look at that strange-looking assemblage on the rear wall," Leigh said. "There must be about twenty bodies all lying in a flexed position facing the dome's entrance. Notice they have been placed in that orientation, the remaining merely dropped from above. It's clear that 'rank' has its privileges here, too. Hard telling who's in the wall slots, but certainly of important rank or position. As for the sarcophagi, they've got to be at the top leadership level . . . like chiefs? Queens? Did you notice that several vaults have feminine face carvings? And look at the fresco-type wall paintings. They're stunning and quite beautiful, plus very typical of the icon worship in the hunting culture."

Items placed at the end of the in-wall dugouts included variously shaped pottery, obsidian blades, and practical types of hardware for the afterlife. At the rear of the dome, water flowed out of a natural earthen aquifer, looking very much like a manmade waterfall. At about ten feet up the wall, the cascading flow acted as a cleansing presence for the chamber. In fact, it also carried some debris out with the flow of the rivulet.

It looked like most of the sacrificial bodies were nude at the moment of death. Many of the skeletons were severely burned . . . a fiery sacrifice?

There was some obvious equality in the cavern. Upon dying, "bigwigs" of natural causes and "sacrifices" both gained direct access to join their ancestors.

Near each of the bodies was a dense concentration of shells from freshwater clams eaten by the ancient Tlingit Tribe. Large numbers of these shells had also turned up at the ceremonial altar. Traditionally, Andy noted, the shells were associated with sacred concepts of water, fertility, birth, and death. Modern Tlingit groups continued to revere the clams. He recalled that local morticians still place clamshells in their caskets and graves.

Andy had another idea about rank and placement. He also figured the topmost chambers in the cave probably entombed high-ranking individuals, as the lower-ranking were nearer the floor. This arrangement reflects an attempt to protect their graves from pillaging by invading groups, both in the tunnel and the inner chamber.

He mused, *Well, that includes us, but I do not pillage—pictures only.*

Moving around now, they both carefully explored the wall art together. Many of the images appeared to be portraits of the resident shaman, scribe, chief, or warrior. One appeared to wear a cloth head wrap into which paintbrushes are tucked and quill pens are tied with knotted cords. A painter or artist, no doubt. Another wore a wolf face mask. Another, with a wild hairdo, a ceremonial raven mask typical of a shaman.

"Look here, Leigh: Kokopelli, with his pack and dancing feet, performing the Sower Dance of fertility for both plants and humans. Look, here are the representative animals of the time: buffalo, bear, deer, and smaller animals."

"Yet, and over here the fresh and salt-water fish and mammals. Here's a salmon and some other fish of their spiritual clam. This one is difficult to figure out, but I think it's a seal . . . yeah, a seal with a sturgeon, I think."

"Over here is a larger panoramic of a pilgrimage of some sort . . . a ritual affirming their legitimacy, and supporting their social position, I guess," said Leigh. "Many are women in exotic dress. Queens? The Kin(g)dom's leadership? Look at that. She's holding a cadaceus with staff, wings, and snakes . . . a healer, no doubt."

They slowly traversed the entire perimeter of the dome's moldy wet floor. A black snake slithered away as Leigh moved around the sarcophagus in the center. The ceiling had fallen in many places, and the interior was in ruins. She stopped at the far wall, which had a little niche cut into the stone. At first she thought these were little altars, but they were too small, and she saw bits of wax; evidently, they had been made to hold a candle. She noticed several of these candle niches in the walls. The inner structure of this niche was beautifully carved, with a symmetrical design of birds' wings going up each side. And the carving had not been damaged, perhaps because the heat of the candles had somewhat suppressed the growth of mold. Andy rejoined her from the other direction as they met at the entrance. They stopped, looked at each other, and sighed.

"What do you think?" Andy asked.

"I just don't know what . . . I'm thinking; this is so complex."

Andy paused, and said, "Here's the way I see it. We savor our experience. Avarice plays no role. We disturb nothing . . . in this sacred place. We tell no one of our discovery, no one, not even my fellow Tlingit brothers. We take the visual images of this subterranean landscape to the grave. We take no samples of their art or body parts for Carbon-fourteen dating. We do take a brief series of photos, for personal use only, to document our discovery. What do you think, Leigh?"

"I agree; it is just too sacred, and rare, to exploit. Even the photos do not have to reveal location. Yep, this has been a good day, and this is a good decision."

"Okay, my friend, here's the plan," said Andy in an anxious voice. "Since you're safe in here, you stay, and I'll go get your 35mm Nikon at camp. That's forty minutes on the long side. What do you think? The photos should only take about five minutes, so we can do it all in less than an hour and be back at the hut by . . . let's see, noon. What say you, woman?"

"Let's roll!" Leigh exclaimed.

Andy gave her a quick kiss, ducked into the tunnel, and headed out.

Leigh gave him her best . . ."Be careful, dear—love you."

*   *   *

Andy reflected on his tasks while crawling through the tunnel . . .

"What an experience. The tour of the cave has certainly shown just how serious my ancestors were about their beliefs. They were a little confused in scientific logic, as are most believers, but these are stable people, that is certain. They seem to have drawn inspiration from the earth in this subterranean setting as well as sunlight, moonlight, and starlight. The domed ceiling even displayed the phases of the moon, the north star, and its relationship to the other planets. It seems the mystics, sages, and leaders, both men and women of this culture, sought enlightenment or spirituality through the constant human search for the meaning of life. Mother Earth and Father Sun were featured dominantly in how tribal artists tended to describe their deity, as compared to some modern-day worshippers who spend a lifetime seeking enlightenment. In the evolutionary story, they seem to yield by not competing with natural forces—meaning that if in competition with the Planet Earth, the planet always wins. Mother Earth has an amazing resilience, a very profound intelligence, and can be quite ruthless in maintaining her integrity. They must have discovered, that we are just another species, neither the owners nor the stewards of this planet. Only visitors.

"All the artworks in the cave celebrate that fact, and give thanks for our existence. The true narrative of the cave art is about life on Earth, and the respect for Earth. Yet modern man seems to ruthlessly set out to torture nature until she reveals her last secrets to us. They had best remember that a biblical creator—creation—was a mere construct of the human mind, documented centuries ago by fearful scribes and storytellers to assuage the wrath of god(s) and control people. Many characterize god as a male and anthropomorphize that created symbol; the cave art suggests the reverse. The Tlingits indicate Mother Earth equal to Father Sky and present as a fiercely protective female, for whom passion and justice are paramount; a woman who rages with anger, with her own body, for her offspring, if they are deprived of the basic essentials of love, care, and justice. She is the heroine in several of the panoramic scenes.

"The art suggests a need for modern man to find a new vision, since the current one is very inadequate. I think we need a radical shift in emphasis—a quantum jump—in the human search to find the meaning of life. The Father, Son, and Holy Spirit myth is certainly not working, as religious wars cloud our past and future. Maybe the metaphors suggested in the cave art are more practical and inclusive as: Mother Earth; Father Sky. Mother Earth and other female icons lead the elders' spelling of Kin(g)dom to deemphasize the kin(g) and emphasize *kin*, which is gender neutral.

"That's enough talking to myself, but the impact of the visit to my ancestor's sacred cavern was one of the high points of my spiritual life . . . just think if I could have talked to them . . . versus viewing their thoughts through art and sacred objects. My next concern is whether or not Manitou is going to be upset with our probing into these hallowed grounds . . . there could be repercussions. . . . At least, for me, Leigh would be forgiven as an outsider brought in by me. I knew the rules, and violated them. Curiosity is not justification to disturb the sacred grounds of the dead.

"Woe is me if Manitou shows his displeasure. . . ."

*   *   *

Passage to the opening went very well. Being prepared for the pressure of wet and slimy rocks, Andy made it to the entrance in less than five minutes. The 'plug,' about ten feet from the end of the tunnel, was the most difficult to pass.

Upon reaching daylight, he was shocked—again.

Hundreds of ravens circled above the entrance . . . the stream . . . and the entire plateau above the valley. More were perched on every available limb around the entrance. So dense was their presence, the noonday rays of the sun were partially obliterated. The eerie glow was not unlike the feeling of a partial eclipse.

Tough's watched as the flock continued to gather around the entrance. He did not see Andy emerge from the sacred earthen tomb on his knees.

"Damn. Manitou. Is this your reaction? I'm in trouble. He knows of my penetration into the burial grounds. I should have known. Damn it."

Tough heard Andy and started jumping on all fours, whining a welcome of rescue, or at least, companionship in a threatening setting.

"Okay, boy, hang in there. I'm going to 'de-mud' my eyes in the stream and get over there to you. One thing is for sure, we're going to be getting out of here as quick as possible, finish our little project in the cave, and skedaddle."

Andy moved to Tough slowly and led him away while watching the sky. The birds were just circling or staring at them as they slowly walked toward the meadow. Picking up the pace, Andy and the pup trotted along the stream to the hut. The turnaround at the meadow and the return to the cavern were even quicker. His thoughts were a jumble of concern for Leigh, the aggravation of Manitou, the intentions of the birds, and the safety of all three who were involved with violation of the burial grounds. Manitou could be very decisive and brutal when known rules were broken, especially by his tribal members.

"Okay, boy, let's slow down now and walk up to the entrance very slowly. I'm just not certain what's on the mind of those sometimes nasty black sentinels. I'm going to tie you right here, near the entrance. That way you've a partial shelter with the cave."

It looked like more birds were in the area, but with his preoccupation to get moving, estimating their number was not an option. After double-checking the watertight bag holding the camera, he ducked into the entrance and started crawling toward the cavern and Leigh.

"Hey, Leigh, I'm back. This old cave aficionado is on his way to your rescue. Are you okay?"

"I can barely hear you, but yes, let's just say I survived . . . and I'm not liking it one bit being alone in this burial chamber. How'd it go out there; any problems? How's Tough? What's the weather like? I ask because there is less light coming through the opening in the ceiling. Dark rain clouds must be blocking the sun. What's up?"

Andy mused, "Dang it, what was that? Thunder? Or is that the beginnings of an earthquake? One thing is for sure, the earth is shaking . . . a slight earthquake . . . there it is again . . . that is not thunder! That's all I need—a tectonic shift while underground. We'd better hurry up and get out of here."

Finally at the domed opening, Andy greeted Leigh. "Well, gal, I made it, and it appears to be none too soon. There's a whole lot of trouble headed our way."

"Yes, I feel it, too . . . the shaking . . . not only once, but twice. Could it be a mini-earthquake as Mount Elias rocks and rolls—it has happened before."

"Not sure, babe, but let's get these few photos, and get out of here as soon as possible. How 'bout an indexed panorama from here and a couple from the other side . . . okay?"

Andy did not wait for an answer. He took the first panoramic series and moved to the opposite side, then took four more, including one with Leigh near the dome's tunnel. In a hurry, he misjudged his footing on the moldy rock floor and slipped. Falling, he grabbed the closest item for support, which was unfortunately a femur in the skeleton pile . . . and the entire edge of the skeletal mass cascaded down on him.

"Andy! Are you okay?" Leigh shouted with fear in her voice.

"No, I'm not. But I'm digging my way out of this mass of bones with somebody's leg bone. There, I think I've made a passageway large enough to get over to the entrance. Hang on; I'll be there in a second. What a mess."

The earth shook again, several skeletons shifted, and earthen debris started falling on the apprehensive explorers. Both looked at each other . . . speechless, and must have thought the same thing . . . let's get out of here as soon as possible.

Andy spoke first. "Manitou's at the root of all this activity. We've offended him, and it's my fault. He could be so upset that he's punishing me—us. If that's the case, we've got to get the hell out of here as soon as possible. Especially you, Leigh. This was my idea. You should not be blamed. You go first."

They both tucked and ducked into the tunnel and crawled quickly. At the opening, Leigh grabbed the excited cub, and both ran, shocked at the blackened scene of thousands of ravens. They were everywhere. A few, just a few, left their perches as the earth shook again.

"Wait just a minute, Leigh. I've got to go back and secure the entrance by replacing the plug in the tunnel. It will only take a moment; all the large rocks are there."

"No, Andy, it's too dangerous! Don't!"

Apparently he didn't hear her, for he was already in the tunnel replacing the plug.

Another rumble shook the entire valley and river bottom.

Then again, and again, the reverberation shook the side of the plateau above the entrance . . . and in an instant it collapsed, burying the entire area.

"Oh no! Andy . . . Andy . . . are you there? Andy!" Leigh exclaimed.

There was no response. Dust and debris filled the air.

"Andy! Andy, are you there?" Leigh cried, knowing too well the answer.

She collapsed, holding on to Tough and the hopes of a miracle.

In a maelstrom of rushing air, the ravens rose and circled the site before departing into the sun's rays.

Deathly silence embraced the prone woman in shock, and the confused wolf.

Chapter 24

Commitment

Moments later the dust and debris settled.

The wolf and his mistress remained at the cavern's entrance.

Unwilling to give up, Leigh called, "Andy, can you hear me . . . Andy!"

Tough whined as they approached the earthen slide that obliterated the cave's entrance. He knew something had gone wrong; Leigh's panic was evident.

"Andy . . . can you hear me? Andy?"

Silence.

Then, as if by a remote command, a smaller flock of ravens returned to their perch.

"Isn't this strange," Leigh whispered to Tough.

It's as if the birds have been told to return to the site in a new role as guardians for the pair, now that the threat of the intrusion into the cavern had been resolved . . . tragically. Upon landing, they called once, then remained absolutely silent. Manitou has been known to work in mysterious ways.

"What are we to do, Tough? I feel so helpless. Whether a natural tectonic event or punishment to us from Manitou, the results are the same . . . Andy is gone. For violating the sacred grounds? Is that possible? Would He do that to one of His tribal members? To me? Who knows . . . but one thing is for sure, it is going to take a lot of luck to save him . . . and even retrieve his body if we fail to find him alive."

She made an aggressive but futile attempt, for about a half-hour, to penetrate the earthen mass with her bare hands and a stick. Tough, with a basic instinct to help, joined in the panic to dig. His progress was twice that of Leigh's, but was going nowhere except down, and they needed to go forward, too. Typical of digging in fresh soil, for every bit of progress, the earth kept caving back into the hole. The broken and twisted roots and limbs also thwarted their efforts.

She mused while digging, Why . . . *Why was I spared? It could have been a simple matter of timing, happenstance, or coincidence. But, one or two results appear certain: Andy either escaped to the dome area, or is now entombed as a permanent spiritual guard, an unwilling reminder to others at the 'plug,' which is now completely sealed from the outside world. He could he have been sacrificed as a warning: Do Not Enter Sacred Burial Grounds.*

"Come on, Tough, this isn't going to work. The earthen slide must be at least ten or twenty feet thick at the entrance. Plus the small rivulet of water is no longer flowing, so it's hard to tell what direction to dig. Unfortunately, that means the cavern may be in the process of filling with water now, too.

"Oh look, the camera! Andy must have dropped it. It's covered with mud but appears to be okay. Anyway, Nikons are known to be survivors. In light of the crisis, no one else will ever see these photos . . . no one; they will be our secret—Andy would agree. Thank goodness. At least we now have personal photos of our 'find,' for it may just have been rendered inaccessible. Andy, please be a survivor, too. I need you . . . please be alive.

"Come, Tough, let's get rid of that leash, it's been a pain in the arse, especially now while we're searching for Andy. I don't think we can do anything more down here; let's go up to the plateau and examine the quake's impact on the altar."

Tough's freedom would have allowed him to take off, but he stopped and realized his place was with his mistress. His freedom was a positive statement of confidence from Leigh. He stretched his legs by running around like any youngster would, then followed Leigh up the ridgeline to the plateau.

The afternoon sun crept to the west as they climbed through a new uncluttered route to the brim. Downed trees and recently uplifted soft earth made the going rough for the pair; the slipped earth had leveled a swath about two-hundred feet wide. The "slide" was very selective—as if preordained to the specific area above the cave's entrance, versus a massive slip in surface layers along an existing fault line.

"Look, boy, it appears that the area by the altar has escaped damage from the quake. Let's move carefully to the edge and take a peek into the cave below while there's still enough light."

Slowly and carefully she crawled toward the fracture in the altar's base, with Tough close behind, to look into the opening and view the damage within. She stretched on her stomach to the edge, and peered down.

The cavern has already filled halfway up the bone pile. The natural spring was still flowing into the chamber, and with the outlet plugged it is just a matter of time before the chamber would be full. The tunnel was already submerged.

"Andy, Andy, are you there? Andy?"

Her voice echoed to the walls of the half-filled chamber.

"Andy, please . . . answer me. Andy, please. Dear Lord, make him safe. Andy!"

Silence.

The underground aquifer was also silent now.

"Andy!"

Silence.

Tough whined, looking at her as though he could feel her panic, her fear, as the reality of Andy's demise became apparent. She knew that not even a professional spelunker could survive that chamber.

Leigh cried,

> "His body and soul may already be with his ancestors.
> "His unintended sacrifice complete.
> "His errant deed, by going in the sacred chamber, has sealed his fate.
> "His actions have upset Manitou.
> "His body, in all likelihood, is now pinned at the plug in the tunnel or his body immersed in the cave's aquifer.
> "His soul, most certainly, is now with Manitou . . ."

Leigh looked at Tough through tear-soaked eyes, wondering if he understood the gravity of the situation surrounding Andy's entombment.

"Tough, we've got a real serious problem here. It's dark down there, and this flashlight appears to be worthless. It just reflects on the debris-filled water. All I can see are floating bones and ceremonial debris . . . churning around. I also can't hear anything other than the swirling water, and I'm tired, dirty, and soaking wet. I'll stretch just a little more and get my head closer."

Then it happened.

Crunch—Slip—Karruummpp!

The entire altar, surrounding earth, and small trees collapsed and formed a sinkhole with Leigh at the center of the confluence.

Leigh screamed, crawling and struggling to the upper edge of the sliding earthen mass . . . but could not overcome the force. She slid to the bottom. Worse yet, a tree trunk held her fast to the conical-shaped hole.

"Leigh, you're an idiot!" she screamed, "What the hell are you thinking? What the hell are you doing? Random acts like this just are not wise while alone in the Tongass. Tough! Tough! Are you there?"

Silence . . . a cautious peek by Tough at the edge . . . followed by quick withdrawal.

"Tough!"

"Tough! Come, boy, it's okay! Come! Damn, girl, this is serious."

She spit out a few leaves twigs and sand, then cleaned her eyes partially with her wet and dirty hands. Reaching into the loose sand, she tried to pull herself up and out of the vise-like grip of the granite hooks and wood claws. Nothing. She could not move. Sand and roots slid into the newly formed sinkhole. She collapsed on the slope and mulled over some ideas for extraction . . . anything that had a chance . . . before the entire hole filled in.

Depressed and tired, she almost passed out in frustration.

"Wait. I'll break off one of these dead limbs and use it to gain leverage in the sand or against another tree."

She twisted, stretched, and lunged toward an old dead pine at her side. The idea worked. In a quick twist and pull, an old two-by-four-inch branch snapped off in her tired hands. Quickly, as if a trapped groundhog, she plunged the limb into the loose dirt. Again, and again, she drove her lance-like probe into the surface, but failed to achieve her goal. Digging caused more slides . . . and the sand buried her up to the waist.

Her efforts totally drained her energy . . . and state of mind. It looked hopeless. She wondered, *How can this be happening to me . . . again?*

She rested against the damp debris-strewn sand. Then, whether from the day's activities or Andy's apparent loss, she closed her eyes to the tumult . . . and slept.

The stress was just too much to handle.

Silence dominated the plateau.

No bird's sang, no beasts stirred as shadows fell across the new void in the plateau's surface. Even the quaking aspen expressed no sound as daylight raced to the western sky.

*   *   *

Tough knew where his mistress lay, but he still wandered the area searching for the presence of something . . . someone. He sought the comfort of the familiar. He looked for consolation . . . freedom from anxiety. He needed security. Seeing Leigh half-buried in the sinkhole provided all the opposite emotions. Running down to the former entrance of the cave did not help. Whining, he scanned the valley for answers to the dilemma . . . but found none. However, his eyes caught sight of the hut. Still confused, yet pleased to see a familiar item, he spun in place and raced towards the meadow. At break-neck speed he cleared the stream and dashed through the fallen timber with renewed confidence of finding something . . . someone.

He stopped near the familiar woodpile, the old sinkhole, and scanned the area. Nothing. Much to his disappointment silence enveloped the entire meadow, hut, and stream. Even the trees stood in stoic silence.

Tough thought, Andy must certainly be here. I was just here with him. Just a moment ago. Wait . . . we left together and returned to the cave. Yes, and he and Leigh came out. And yes, he went back into the cave. Dang. He couldn't be here. That's right . . . he never came back out. Leigh was checking on him at the altar site. And the collapse . . . Leigh is in trouble. What's wrong with you . . . wolf, get back to her . . . quickly.

Tough looked at the hut one more time, then spun around to head for the plateau . . . and Leigh.

*   *   *

The white wolf stopped at the stream after noting the complete destruction of the hillside by the former cave entrance. He glanced around the valley in all directions, seeking an answer to the devastation of the hillside. Nothing remained of the bluff. Stranger yet was the absolute isolation of the event. No other trees or earthen slides had slipped into the stream area. All the surrounding ridgelines and topography were intact—totally undisturbed. For some unknown reason, only the area above the entrance was affected.

He cautiously moved toward the earthen slide with his nose searching for an explanation, or a clue to the devastation ahead. Halted now at the fading scent of a canine and human, he looked up and scanned the ridge. The tracks took him to the plateau and its center where he halted again. The stone edifice and grove of trees were also gone—disappeared. Puzzled, he moved on as tracks were leading him to the area where the trees once stood.

He sensed another fresher set of canine tracks departing the area. Not deterred, he continued following the older set of . . . man.

The white halted again as he reached the edge of the sinkhole. He saw the immobile human form below. Confused, he whined . . . scanned the area around the plateau, and glanced back at the figure below. There seemed to be no apparent threat now, but a lingering concern for the unknowns that triggered the two events.

The white whined at the sleeping figure to announce his presence and gain a response. Nothing. No part of the body moved. Silence ruled the earthen depression. Either fatigue or frustration must have provided her escape to—a deep sleep.

The white felt compelled to stay near the trapped human. He circled the edge of the hole clockwise at a trot, paused, then doubled back in a counterclockwise walking pattern and repeated the process several times. Still confused, he stopped and lowered his body. Although the plateau remained as a beautiful and serene area, the lower sun angle turned the clearing into an eerie site of irregular long and perplexing shadows in stark contrast to the grassy surface below. He could not keep his eyes off the immobile figure . . . even though feeling helpless, the white stayed as a sentinel over the victim.

Caw—Caw—Caw

As the sun raced to the western horizon, a couple of ravens announced their presence and perched on a pine at the meadow's perimeter. Then an unexpected breeze blew dried surface-sand in the face of the white.

He heard another troubling sound in the same direction near the base of the pines, more like a shuffling in the leaves at first. He ignored the noise. But, the sound continued, then changed to a trotting and prancing cadence radiating to the white's sensitive ears. He leaped to his feet, spun around to face the sound, and lowered his head as neck and back hairs bristled in his supple fur. He growled at the bobbing heads and pairs of eyes staring back at him from across the clearing.

Part of the pack was back.

The wolves remained at the perimeter of the meadow in a stare-down as if not being sure of their next move.

The white also held fast.

He only saw five—thankfully, not the entire pack. Undaunted, he held his ground. The wolves lowered their heads and advanced at a walk, then trot . . . followed by a loping gait toward the white.

The white howled.

Unnoticed until departing from their perch, a large flock of ravens, who had silently congregated in the trees, flew upward, circled and swooped downward toward the wolves as they departed the perimeter.

The ravens made a low pass over the advancing wolves . . . as if a warning.

Surprised, the wolves appeared disoriented . . . but continued the attack.

The ravens turned in a chandelle and brutallly assaulted the wolves as they jumped and snapped with their sharp fangs at the avian terror. Wave after wave of tearing talons and hacking beaks tore at the wolves' muzzles, noses, eyes, ears, underbellies, and genitals.

Several wolves loped into the timber to escape the onslaught of the black-feathered-terror. Those who remained were not so fortunate. They were mortally wounded, to die on the fringe of the plateau . . . bleeding to death in the cover of the brush. It was not a pretty sight; the killing fields were bloody and strewn with hair and feathers of battle. The Alpha male and female that remained waged a good fight, but they did not have a chance. They were not prepared for the bird's vengeance, or brutal pursuit. Likewise, they probably had no idea the birds were protecting the human in the sinkhole, not just the white, nor who directed the ravens to ensure there was no harm done to one of His people.

The white, too, had never witnessed such carnage as the ravens demonstrated. He returned to the edge of the sinkhole, an observer who entered the fray, but seemed to know his role near the trapped human. His protective feeling had been developed . . . and then, he thought no more of it. He knew . . . it was—Manitou.

Sensing that the dying and departed wolves were no longer a threat, the birds circled the plateau, rose to the late afternoon thermals, and departed to the west with the setting sun.

The white resumed his vigil at the edge, and periodically emitted a loud whine to test the buried human's consciousness . . . her ability to respond, to react, to hear . . . anything.

All efforts fell on deaf ears. He lowered his body at the edge, and stared at the lifeless body below. After some time, he grew fatigued and lowered his head into his paws, fighting sleep as the sun settled closer to the horizon.

A cold wind blew in from the north as evening shadows moved into the plateau.

*   *   *

Moving along the Bitterroot, Joe Bloom, known as "the Brit" at work, was anxious to reach the infamous meadow before total darkness. Thankfully, the full moon would provide a little help in finding his way to Leigh's hut.

"What a delightful sight to watch my yellow pee blend in with the clarity of the stream as it races to the Pacific. It will be bloody well mixed in by a fortnight or so, and the tourists will hardly notice the taste of the recycled pint I had last night. Ah, that felt good. Okay, feet, just a little farther for this tired bloke. The little map here, that I got from Andy's desk, indicates the camp is bloody well right around the bend—it bloody well better be . . . then again, that dimwit Andy could never do a mapping as well as 'the Brit.' He normally leaves me to get on with it, anyway. Not sure why he sketched this buggar up. He's always been a bit dim at board work, but he's good in the field, so that's where he belongs. His kismet. Beejezus, for Christ's sake, what the hell happened to the bloke this time? It's not like him to buggar up a simple three-day survey in the Tongass. He knows this area like the back of his hand, all the Tlingits do, and this is their old stomping ground. Whatever. Maybe Leigh's involved. Rumor has it that he could be 'knob-bing' with her as his brother did . . . oh what the hell, it's no matter to me . . . it's certainly apropos for older consenting adults. I'll tell you right now, you old bloke, no wench would be interested in you after this hike, and you smell a bit grittier than porcupine doo doo.

"He better be around here or I'll have his arse in a sling.

"Anyway, I've snorted my last fag, and will soon get ornery without these stupid smokes. It wasn't my idea to chase him into his bloody woodlot. It's not fair for a pencil-pushing desk jockey to be asked to chase his boss, much less find him, in the bloody woods.

"I told Andy my lot would have been better served to have been the stage manager of the 'Sex Pistols' and make piles of money. Why I left England to work in Canada, and now for the bloody Yanks in the DNR, is beside me . . . bloody bears, bad maps, noisy tourists, and the like. Bullocks! Stop complaining, you old bloke—let's get on with it; you could be cleaning the loo in the zoo," Joe grumbled to himself.

A gruff iconoclast from the United Kingdom, he was not as bad as he sounded. His words emanated from the lexicon of the pubs around the shipping and foundry town of Widnes, near E. Liverpool, on the west coast of England. The DNR in Juneau felt they got the best of the deal when the Canucks let him go . . . "for being too outspoken for the propriety of the local manager of the Royal Canadian Mounted Police." He relished these words, and had them framed and hung on his office wall—as a badge of honor. Andy, the DNR's wildlife unit manager, snatched him up quickly after having several positive working assignments with him to curb poaching along the Canada/U.S. border. At "age" now, close to retirement, his sixty years, of which forty involved wrestling violent humans and animals, provided a lot of value both in the field and primarily at the office. Andy and Joe made a good team since Andy loved field work and Joe, having his fill of the woods, liked his comfortable desk and nearby loo, throne, water closet, or porcelain queen, whatever. He was no sot, but did like his daily "tin" of beer from the local pub. Andy's first encounter with Joe's "King's English" came when Joe told him to move his desk one day by saying: "Put it in the other bloody road." To which Andy said, "Speak English . . . please," to which Joe replied, "I am."

On more than one occasion Joe had embarrassed him in public by offering his unsolicited advice. In a recent public meeting, Joe said in his eloquent style, "Let the other young pups do it; let the other bloody buggars get their feet wet; I've had 'nough; it's your time in the barrel; it's time to be shot of you puppies." He also thought Andy needed him as ballast . . . or he'd float away and get lost in the bloody timber. Needless to say, Joe was not only outspoken, he wasn't about to change his Widnes dock worker's language for anyone. He also still felt it was okay to pinch the butt of the waitress who brought him his pint or bitters or wherever he was drinking; but it didn't work in the U.S. Andy had to bail him out of the local jails, frequently, after the waitress pressed charges. To all this, Joe would say, "You Yanks should get on with it, and start appreciating the arses of all the lassies."

In many ways, Joe was still living in the Twentieth Century.

"It looks like the Bitterroot will bend just beyond the beaver pond, and that is our spot. Mr. Raven, I've noticed you've been following me for the last hour or so. Welcome; it's nice to have someone to talk to rather than this ol' bloody buggar. Not sure what your purpose is, mate, but let's get on with it. I don't think you know it, but I've been informed of your ties to the spiritual deity of the Tlingits. Andy told me to befriend your presence since you've ties to Manitou. I'm bloody well not religious, but do feel a spiritual identity to Native American belief systems. So welcome, you old bloke; welcome aboard this mission to find what the hell Andy's been up to. I need your help—I could use some of your friends—anyone can join us . . . got any more friends? Bloody well, wait a minute; from what I've heard, you could be Manitou. I've heard you can transform yourself to any one of your human or animal followers. So, if this is true, let's pull off some of your magic, some of your tricks to find my friend Andy. Welcome, mate, or should I say Manitou . . . whatever."

Unaffected by the raven's shadowing, he followed the map to the bend in the river, and sure enough the hut appeared on the meadow about two clicks upstream.

With a little more snap in his step, he crossed the river and arrived at the bench by the fire pit. Walking up the path to the hut, he sensed the absence of anyone in camp. A brief inspection of the hut and then the meadow's edge revealed no current signs of animal or human activity unfortunately . . . at least not for the last twenty-four hours; but, the fire pit had been used the previous day . . . some of the charcoal remains were still warm. He also examined the freshly dug hole behind the woodpile rather like a sinkhole.

"Well, everybody on staff says that Andy was headed here to assist his brother's friend Leigh . . . so where the hell are you guys? And where's the wolf cub Andy told me about?"

"I hope the bloody hell I didn't come out here on a bum steer for those blokes in Juneau. They're a bunch of worrywarts anyway. I'll kick their arse if you're okay, and just chasing the lassie through the woods until you convince her to run bare while chasing her to your bear-skin rug. I know about all those Indian tricks. I sure don't like risking my own fat arse . . . if you're playing toesies with Rosie in the posies.

"Well now, here's the tie-down for the wolf cub. Where the hell is he? He certainly can't be trained to run loose this soon. I suppose he's hiding around some log or bush to pounce on me—bloody well, he better not; I'm armed and will get shut of him quickly."

He wandered around the grounds a little more, and plunked down to rest. Impatient, tired, and puzzled, he reviewed the memo received at DNR Headquarters.

EMERGENCY—EMERGENCY: All DNR units, August 09: Priority Message. DNR Specialist, Andrew South, traveling from Haines to the docks at Yakatut, is now three (3) days overdue to meet his team members. He left Haines on the 4th to assess the effectiveness of the bear study, marking stations—and was to meet his team at the Pacific docks on the 6th. His last report was from the camp of Leigh West, in sector VII, on the 5th.

Assignments:

1. DNR aircraft to search the area during daylight hours immediately.

2. DNR specialist Joe Bloom to perform a ground search immediately over the probable route along the Bitter-root.

   a. Plan for a one-week search.

   b. Coordinate results with a daily sked to HQ's in Juneau, on Freq. 121.5.

Be careful, this is movement time for bears feeding on blueberries, salmon, and roots in the marshy areas near streams as they prepare for hibernation.

END OF MESSAGE

Rested, he walked down the path to the stream and bench by the fire pit. By rearranging the residue in the pit again, he noticed that it was really less than 12 hours old; none of it was distributed by nosy animals, weather, or blowing leaves. The water-soaked blankets and footprints also indicated that two people, a lad and lassie, shared the blankets by the fire. Their barefoot tracks to the stream and back, to a circular pattern around the pit indicated a dance or ceremony of some sort.

Well, I'll be dipped in dung and rolled in flour; the old boy had quite a night of it with the dancing, drinking, and dunking . . . and who knows what else! Good show, Andy. I hope you communicated with the spirits and got her in the spirit of things, too."

Caw—Caw—Caw, trumpeted from the magnificent pines.

"You're still at my side, are you? Well, you old buggar, have a pop at it—enjoy yourself singing. I rather enjoy your kick-ass sound," he mumbled to the raven.

In reality, his voice took on the sound of irritation triggered by the sense of vacancy in the area around the camp. He continued to wander and started toward the meadow by a different route.

His field-of-view to the meadow and ridgeline provided a different perspective. That's when he noticed movement on the ridge to the north. He strained to focus on the tree-lined bluff.

"Bloody well, would you believe it's a pair of wolves, standing in ramrod fashion, in a small opening in the foliage? Would you believe they're staring back at me from the ridge? A large white and a smaller gray are clearly checking me out. By their stance, it seems to indicate they're challenging me."

His binoculars provided the same visual feedback—they were definitely exposing themselves for a purpose. They were standing on the ridge—they wanted to be seen.

Then, as if by silent signal, they both spun in place and disappeared into the tall timber on the edge of the plateau.

"Absent anything being here, and figuring the small gray is Tough, let's have a pop at the two—come on you, bloke, you're doing nothing here, and the temperature is dropping as that fat red sun moves to the horizon rapidly."

At the famous British "quick step," he moved across the meadow toward the ridgeline. The raven quickly launched into the air and flew ahead of Joe to an arboreal perch about the plateau.

Caw—Caw—Caw.

*   *   *

While running across the meadow, Tough mused, I'm glad I finally figured out this crisis of people and events.

Arriving at the bluff under full speed, he quickly pulled up when sighting a change in the plateau's population.

The white was back.

Scarier still was his location.

He was standing at the edge of the sinkhole, staring at Leigh in her trap.

Scanning the area revealed a solitary raven. Comforted and strengthened by the raven's presence, Tough slowly moved forward and out of the protective foliage, exposing himself to the white.

Ever so carefully the white turned and positioned his body toward the cub, stepped off in his direction . . . and stopped.

Likewise, the cub moved toward the white, and reflected on his earlier training. "Let's not make the first move." In light of Leigh's dangerous plight, hold fast and wait until the situation unfolds.

It appeared as if they both felt a sense of relaxed cooperative spirit—as if a spiritual dimension has been introduced to their presence. The excitement among the two became palpable as they wagged their tails and approached each other, licking each other's muzzles and gathering together like soldiers ready for battle.

Somehow, maybe for obvious reasons, the two wolves united at the sinkhole to assist Tough's partially entombed mistress. Hampered by canine limitations for the complex task ahead, they would still try to retrieve Leigh.

Perplexed, they relaxed.

Early Evening Nautical Twilight encased the meadow as the sun slipped over the horizon, the orb gone but its rays remain for up to thirty minutes of twilight. Its light created a lattice work of shadows much like a flood of a primeval past, turning everything brittle, and seeming to forbid sound. Shadows quavered and flowed as the wolves by the hole stood and stretched in the shadows. These wolves were not on the prowl; their haunting and surreal presence was for the rescue of Tough's mistress. They were ready to go to work.

As a result of genetic imprinting, or the white's previous experience, possibly with man, they moved easily as a team at the sinkhole. The whining started in hopes of awakening the sleeping/frustrated woman. They kept whining and growling, again and again—without response. Nothing.

Then, without a pause, they simultaneously raised their heads to the ether and howled, then yapped, and howled again. Their cry from the deep past echoed across the Tongass in a chorus of melodious piercing pitch of splendor. The music penetrated the valley below, and finally—Leigh.

It worked. She moaned first. Then she mumbled a bunch of expletives, and then she exclaimed, "What the hell's going on? What am I doing here? Oh Christ . . . now I remember . . . how the hell long have I been down here? What have you gotten yourself into now, Leigh? Dufus! Dummie! Son of a bitch, what to do now.

"Hi, Tough, who's your friend?

"Whoever . . . thanks for the wake up. Christ, it's almost dark—in fact, it will be pitch-black out here in just a minute or two. I wonder how long I've been in here? About two hours? I think . . . dumb broad, you better get your ass in gear and air out this cold, wet, and tired butt . . . the sooner the better."

Lucky for Leigh, while she rested, the lower and heavier slabs and tree trunks slowly settled into the chamber below. As a result, the vise-like grip on her boots and legs was relieved . . . she could now feel a sense of being free of the trap below.

However, she still felt numb and sore in both legs. It wasn't going to be easy to move, much less push against the sand and debris to escape the entrapment of the sinkhole. She was still buried to the waist in wet sand.

Confused by her diatribe, the wolves responded to what they thought was a call for help, and slipped down the side of the sinkhole. Being at least twelve feet down, the resulting slippage of soft sandy soil not only buried Leigh to well above the waist now, but she also had two struggling canines on her small front porch doorstep—staring at her with just as much shock—eyeball to eyeball . . . a little too close for comfort.

"Thanks, but no thanks, fellows; this is entirely too much togetherness for me; and I haven't even met you, big white. But, you're here, so what's next? What the hell are we going to do? Got any ideas? I hadn't planned to be buried alive with two wolves, at least not yet.

"Guess what, in light of your tumble, there is some good news. When you guys fell over me, I felt a slight movement below, as if my feet are no longer completely entrapped. Ah, I'm right. I can move them a little now. Great! Now, what to do so I don't further bury myself crawling out. Damn, life is indeed unfair at times. Dufus, you know that, remember what's happened . . . over the last month of hellish events. How many times has Dad said life is unfair . . . just deal with it, and move on."

"Okay, I have an idea. Since you fellas are here, let's give my idea a try. I can just reach my belt; ah yes, there it is; now I certainly may be able to crawl out with my feet free; but you guys may be able to assist in pulling me out the first couple of feet. If I can get my knees free I'll have a good chance of crawling out with my hands and elbows digging, too.

"Here's the plan. I'd like both of you to grab on to the end of this belt. Here, like this, I hold on to this end, and you guys chomp on to the other, and pull. Go on—grab it—bite it—grab it," she pleaded.

Both of the wolves canted their heads while staring at Leigh. They were having trouble understanding her, to say the least. They started whining to show their displeasure in not comprehending. Yet they knew the purpose for their presence was to extract her—the how was unknown.

"Okay, I've got an idea. Watch this, boys. See? Come on, look! I'm putting this end of my belt in my mouth . . . see? Now you do the same . . . and pull!" she cries.

They didn't move, did not respond . . . nothing.

Leigh collapsed in a frustrated slump.

The plateau remained silent, too, as the pair looked at each other then back at Leigh in the early evening shadows. The sun was long gone, and darkness was creeping across the Tongass.

Tough was the first to sense the stalemate and Leigh's frustration. He mused, *I've got it. We've played games like she is suggesting, many times, by tugging on my leash; she wants us to pull her while she claws and pushes with her legs and feet—I've got it!*

Leigh repeated the entire idea again to the attentive yet puzzled student wolves, but . . . this time they seemed to get it. At least Tough did, and the white joined in. Tough grabbed the belt, and within moments, the white, also.

"Yea! Good boys! Now, back up or whatever you need to do to gain traction; we're going to do this, boys. I'm going to make it with your help. I'm about to start wiggling and waddling like a mole; and if necessary hump my butt like a 'go-go-girl' and pry myself out of here—with you guys.

"Okay, back up . . . here goes. Go ahead—pull!"

It started working. The two wolves pulled while growling and twisting the belt as an adversary . . . but the truth is that their normal aggressive nature did not disallow the growls, even when pulling for Leigh. They were not upset; they were giving it their all . . . with gusto . . . growling was part of their character at work, play, or fighting. It was their wild side . . . check this inbred trait with any domestic canine; they, too, growl when tugging on anything. It's natural.

Leigh twisted, turned, and humped while digging into the sand with her one hand and free elbow. The other hand held fast to the belt.

Her knees finally became free. She lurched out of the hole and lay on her back while the sand slid into the vacated tomb-like cavity.

"Okay, boys . . . Okay! We've made it! You can stop! Okay!"

They finally stopped and the trio of wet, sandy, and tired victors slowly and carefully rested on the slope. In due time they climbed to the top edge of the hole and rested again in the fading light of the plateau's moonlight.

Dead tired, but very thankful, they bathed in the dim light of freedom as the sinkhole slowly filled in.

Leigh reflected on her latest experience. "Would you believe? Look at the white. He's very relaxed in the presence of humans. I'll bet the ranch he's been with 'man' before. He's probably an outcast, a pariah to the pack, since he's most likely been partially domesticated. Look at him; he's at ease with both Tough and me. What an honor; we've become a team, and I've gained acceptance. Thank you, white. Thank you, Manitou. Okay, Tough, thank you, too. I know none of this rescue would have been possible without the 'link' between the invisible and the reality of the visible world. The nexus is Manitou.

"I wonder, could you both, in fact, be Manitou's reincarnation of the Indian Brothers who were named after their characteristics of walking with Water and Wind. The brothers I loved, and who loved me in return. Just maybe. Time will tell.

"In the face of the additional trauma of losing Andy; I've gained a new friend in the white. Your presence may help overcome Andy's loss. Looks like the three of us are together as a team now as I, again, reestablish my life in the Tongass. Manitou, please help to overcome the loss of my friend, mentor, and lover. Please!"

Savoring the moment, she sat in the moonlight with both of her new canine friends, their tired bodies now lying against her tired wet and sandy legs. Then she discovered, much to her surprise, that the white was a female. *Oh well . . . now we can have a small pack*, she chuckled to herself.

The Tongass was silent and beautiful as she turned her head to the evening's starlit sky. A raven landed in a Stika Pine and looked down on the trio. Peaceful silence infected the moonlit clearing.

"Leigh, ol' gal, you are blessed. Thanks for your help, Manitou; as I strive for peace while exploring Alaska, your continued help will be most appreciated. You know, I'm due for some good luck pretty damn soon.

Don't you think?"

*   *   *

The serenity of the night was disturbed as a sound from the bluff echoed across the plateau's calm, and the beam of a flashlight distorted the moonlight's beauty.

"Hey, who's there? Bloody well . . . is that you Leigh? Have I finally found you blokes?" Joe Bloom shouted. "Hey! Is my old kick-ass buddy, Andy, there?"

The wolves leaped up and turned toward the intruder. Their hair bristled as they growled at the bouncing beam of light headed in their direction.

"Who the hell is that?" Leigh sighed.

"I certainly don't need exposure to any more adventurous men . . . especially a Brit."

*   *   *

Notions of "God" and "Divinity" should be used sparingly in life decisions, since these are human constructs that may limit rather than enhance our understanding of life's ultimate source and meaning.

—Diarmuid O'Murchu

Chapter 25

Nature's Way

Three friends, and lovers, all dead over a short two week-time span.

Many enlightened and cultured people live their entire lives without knowing tragic events that transform their souls. Not so with Leigh. In spite of that, people are constantly exposed to trauma, wholly unprepared while embarking upon the second breath of their life. Leigh is that person. She is in her sixties, the last half of hers for certain, and has just survived partial burial in a collapsing cave, under a sacred Indian shrine and resulting sinkhole; and would not be safely resting on its edge if the two wolves that befriended her had not rescued her from the coffin-like cavity.

Both her newfound canine friends: the newly arrived "White," and her companion "Tough," had just dragged her from the sinkhole.

The wolves had also shielded her from a pack of marauding wolves that were ready to attack her and the two wolves as they defended her at the collapsed shrine. Then, she thought, not by happenstance, Manitou, the Native American deity, must have sent a flock of ravens to join in the fight, and in doing so, not only deterred the pack, the birds killed several wolves in the pack as they retreated through their violent wall of relentless aerial bombardment of sharp slashing beaks and razor-like talons.

Nothing in Leigh's former life experiences had prepared her for these events and continued losses: first, there was Ford, the bush-pilot she had known for three months before his fatal plane crash; then, Walkswithwater (Jack), the Indian shaman she met only last month, now torn apart by an enraged grizzly bear; and finally, the shaman's brother, Walkswithwind (Andy), she just met, entombed, trapped in the collapsed cave below. Certainly Andy has perished by now, having been imprisoned by rock and water since late afternoon.

All this, along with the wolf pack attack in the evening, has left her in a state of shock. She felt exposed with a false assumption that truths and ideals learned earlier had not been taught very well in helping her adjust to recent encounters. Was the male portion of her animus missing?

It appeared so; few masculine characteristics appeared to be within her psyche, as C. Jung had suggested, for a balanced persona in the female. Yes, apparently not enough.

Shuddering uncontrollably now, alone with her lifesaving wolves . . . she felt as if panic was about to invade her body again. Wasn't this more than enough proof that she was not prepared for this most recent terror? Maybe she couldn't live in a hostile environment, like Alaska, where there are no guarantees of solace according to the plans of life's morning—for what was grand in the morning may be modest in the evening; and what in the morning was true, will, at evening, become a lie. In the secret chambers of her soul, these fundamental truths had been revealed, and must be analyzed again.

Three lovers . . . gone.

Forsaken by her plight, she cried, a*ll of them gone, gone in two weeks. . . .*

Leigh should have known that in aging, her life was not growing and expanding; conversely, she felt her inner process belied this contraction of life.

*   *   *

The splendor of the crisp and clear starlit night provided a reassuring setting for the threesome as they talked to each other in words, looks and body language, that were comforting as they cuddled in thankfulness of survival, and warmth of their bodies to shield the night's cooling air.

Suddenly shattered, the evening took on an unknown and threatening aura . . . again.

The beam of a flashlight being tossed across their eyes triggered an immediate standing growl by the wolves, followed by Leigh's exclamation, "Who's that?"

A pause . . . followed by silence, and the light targets them again.

"Bloody well, I've finally found you guys! 'Tis me, Joseph-of-Liverpool, be I."

Leigh faintly knew of Joe, a jocund character, from conversations with Andy as he shared some of his more interesting work assignments and personnel in the DNR. Those warmhearted fireside chats were "dear" to her heart; in fact, she had just been reminiscing past experiences with Andy while gathering her thoughts with her four-legged rescuers.

She quickly held fast to both wolves. Tough dropped to the ground upon hearing her command "down," and the white reluctantly followed his lead. However, their pent-up emotion did not abate their growling, nervousness, and involuntary trembles. The wolves, now both defensive, and offensive in posture, were behaving in a normal way after the terror of the afternoon and evening events. The unknowns of the flashlight's beam shielded the voice and body of the mysterious intruder visible only in the penumbra, or partial shadow, in the starry night. Long overdue, while helping Leigh, Joe was searching for Andy.

"Down boys. He's okay. Down!" Leigh exclaims as she fights the wolves' anxiousness to charge the unknown sound. Tough knew many commands including "get 'em," or "sic," turning his head to her constantly, acting as if he was torn between Leigh's cautious command, down! versus his tendency to challenge . . . but seemed resolved that Leigh knew best. He held his ground with the white.

"Please, get that light out of my eyes and let the full moon do its job . . . neither the wolves, nor I, can see you with that damn light enveloping us. I know how terrible I must look, but I'm no gorgon. Come on over here; you'll not turn to stone. It's true, my hair may look like a nest of snakes; but wouldn't you if buried for a couple hours and having just been rescued?"

"Okay, my lady, the flashlight is off . . . and you're jolly well right; I can see a damn sight better now, my lady, with the bloody moonlight," bellered Joe.

Half of the problem for the wolves was solved for the moment . . . the intense light was now absent, but still left the approaching unknown human form that spoke in a "strange" speech pattern. It was not at all like Leigh's soft voice, or the Indian's (Andy's) mellow voice, or the local Tlingit tribe's fluid tonal speech pattern, an accent to which the white was accustomed. Both wolves stared at the approaching figure, then rotated their heads around, in unison, to Leigh—to wait for her next move.

"Is me friend Andy with you, lassie? Is Andy there? Is me mate okay?"

As Joe walked slowly toward the trio, Leigh quickly reflected on how to break the bad news of Andy's loss; he's certainly lost . . . even if he escaped from the collapsing tunnel into the burial chamber—which was flooded—and now filled with earth as the sinkhole collapsed. She mused, What should I say? Dad had a rule: when in doubt—tell the truth as best you know it—and people will understand, they can handle conflict, don't think for them.

"Hold back a moment, Joe. I'll put this leash on the wolves and you can come on in, free of harm, I think. Hold on until they're secure."

"Okay, lassie, I need not another warning my dearie—this bloke ain't no dope—I'm frozen in place. Take your time. I'm staying here, out of the bloody road, like a piece of ice. Bloody well, lassie, make sure your knot is square; no granny will hold those fangs."

Joe mused, there is something wrong here. I don't see Andy. Something is definitely wrong . . . he's not there, and I smell trouble. She wouldn't be out here alone, by choice; I know there's a problem with Andy.

"Okay, Joe, come on in. I'm holding on to the salt and pepper attack team; come on, they'll calm down soon."

"If you say so, dearie, but I still feel as though they see me as dinner."

"Oh well, how do they know? Are they not acting as expected? We were resting peacefully and quietly while reflecting on our recent terror and watching stars dance across the sky—catching our breath—and being thankful for our survival . . . both from the wolf attack, and the sink hole resulting from the cave-in of the cavern below. Sadly, we're also mourning the certain loss of Andy who was trapped in the cave-in. Sorry, Joe. We've been sitting here for hours listening and hoping for a reversal of the inexplicable laws of nature. Unfortunately, gravity cannot be rescinded."

Joe froze in place at some distance, and tried to process the trauma hanging on each word. In typical avoidance reaction to the wound of her words, he too tried to reverse the natural occurrence of the cavern's collapse.

"No, not Andy. We can rescue him. We can do it. Let's try. How long has he been buried? How long has it been since you've heard his voice? Where can I start digging? Come on, lass . . . let's try," Joe stammered with allegro and volume.

"Joe, I know how you feel, but it all happened hours ago. Come on over here—let's talk—the wolves have calmed down now . . . come on."

Leigh fills him in on Andrew's activities with her over the last few weeks and the trauma resulting from exploration of the Tlingit's cave below.

He is devastated.

Joe moves over to the debris around the sinkhole, nods at both animals with guarded acceptance, and sits next to Leigh.

"Joe, please forgive me if what I say offends you. It is truly not my intention, but we must be frank about this . . . Andrew is gone," Leigh sighs as Joe moves toward the wolves to mask his emotional shock. Alone with him now, the wolves are cautious but accepting since Leigh had done so. However, in their classic head-down, back-arched, tail-between-their-legs body language, Joe worked on his collapsed emotional condition hoping it could be displaced, in part, to them. After all, he was not afraid of what the Alaskan Wilds offered . . . having a reputation of killing many attacking animals of the north with his bare hands and a knife. The wolves sensed his confidence and quickly allowed the rough-talking visitor to be part of the group. However, they constantly turned their eyes to Leigh for tacit approval. Still tethered, the wolves lay down as Joe rejoined Leigh and both their eyes returned to the sinkhole's base . . . looking for movement, life? A miracle? Neither expected one nor believed in religious myths that embrace miracles.

Joe glanced at Leigh, and with a startled reaction noted a certain vacuity in her eyes as they now seemed focused at a distant thought, answer, the why, the question . . . Why me, Lord, why me, Manitou, why me? He held his tongue. Wisely, Joe yielded to her need for silence . . . her shock, her need to reflect on the terror of the day. She looked as if questioning. Her glaze, her fixation, her moist eyes, slumped posture . . . her need to process these events in a sane manner, and try to understand why her friends . . . and lovers, had to be taken—again.

Was she drifting off to a condition that would send her body into shock? Joe wisely let the wolves go to her side, and they immediately lay on her feet and thigh . . . to which she responded with both hands.

"Whew . . . I think she'll be okay," Joe murmured to himself.

Joe decided to let the wolves and Leigh communicate by touch, hoping that they could all return to the yurt soon and further investigate the area in the morning. If what she said were true, there would be no need to crawl around the collapsed sinkhole and cavern entrance tonight. Morning would do.

The wolves kept one eye on Joe while cuddling with Leigh as he got in a restful position. It was a strange scene; the white's muzzle still bloody, blackened now, from the run-in with the pack as Leigh had mentioned, yet, look at them now. Tranquil, loving and committed to Leigh . . . and an eye on him. He would try to move her to the yurt before the dampness and cooling of midnight set in.

Joe noticed the blood on his clothes and hands from handling the white and reflected on the lore learned while growing up that taught us to be wary of the animal lurking within. We've all heard of tribal dogs, as gentle as lambs, that would disappear for a few days into the fields and return with bloody snouts and meat on their breath.

The Lakota, Chippewa, Iroquois, Inuit and the local Tlingits, and many other North American peoples tell stories of humans changing form to become seals or salmon, ravens or coyotes, buffalo or wolves. Wayward, tricky, charged with power, these shape-shifters bring wisdom and spiritual medicine to the human tribe from our nonhuman neighbors. We can only guess what our Paleolithic ancestors meant by painting deer or bison or bear on the roofs of the caves, similar to those here, but we cannot mistake the feeling of awe that suffuses those portraits. Although we are clever, these old pictures and tales heard from shamans remind us, we also have much to learn from our fellow creatures, for we are only one tribe in the great circle of life.

Poets assure us, "If the door of perception were cleaned, everything would appear to a man as it is, infinite." Sitting on this clump of soil in midst of the forest with two wolves purled with their mistress, studying the sky for answers, tracking the seasons, listening to the spiritual wind, watching other animals, talking with those for whom you care: these are indeed the riches all around us. They require no electricity, no petrol, no props aside from the Creator.

The Milky Way was looking down on them and every other denizen of the sky, more clearly at this latitude thanks to the absence of light pollution and industrial particulate suspended in the air. There stood old faithful Polaris and Jupiter, wrapped in its bands of clouds like a ball of heathery yarn and Mars chasing the moon across the sky.

Nearly as bright as late afternoon, the Moon illuminated the opening in the forest floor in a brilliance seldom seen below the latitudes of the Tongass.

"No problem," he said, and settled down, for Leigh had chosen wisely to rest . . . and hopefully recover from the shock of the day's trauma.

Glacial air poured down the valleys from the snowfields higher up. The branches of spruce and fir, spreading outward from the clearing, framed the white cascade in green lace. The day was catching up with Joe, too; he could feel weariness gathering in his bones . . . and drew his knees up and wrapped his arms around them for warmth. Still he trembled, not knowing whether it was from the cold or the trauma he felt for Leigh's pain.

After an unknown time of thoughts and dreams, Joe heard something and looked up with a startled expression in the direction of Leigh.

Leigh exclaimed, "Thanks for being here, Joe!"

"My Dearie, this is where I belong."

"Well, fellas, you seemed to have found a good place to lie. Your old mistress is good to have, I see, on a cool evening," Leigh exclaimed as she appeared to be coming out of her funk but still holding on to the wolves as a blanket.

"My Lassie, by God you are wit' us, welcome to the cool Alaskan night. 'Tis a fact that I was 'bout to carry your beautiful bones to the yurt before the dew froze on your pretty eyelashes. Then again, I'm, ahhh . . . not so sure the wolves would let me do so without a lot of convincing that it was the 'right' thing to do. Okay, Dearie, are we ready to call it a day?"

"Oh, yes, I guess so; then again, let's look at the impact the events of the day will have on maintaining my goals here in Alaska. I have embraced a lifestyle that surely invites instability, but the habits of my heart may not fit into this adventuresome life. My generosity and mercy is deep with an abiding concern for others, a delight in nature and human company and all forms of beauty, a passion for justice, a sense of restraint and a sense of humor, a relish for skillful writing, a readiness for cooperation and, finally . . . love of my fellow man . . . as you might say, 'tis causing a wee bit of a problem, I love to love.

"I don't pretend to always live up to those values—I aspire to do so—but will those values have to be altered to live alone, with the wolves, up here?"

"Dearie, do not fret, do not be concerned 'bout these thoughts tonight; we'll give her a shot in the morn. But believe this, my dear, from what I've seen and heard . . . you've had a major serving of bad luck, my lady, and will have to change very little as this old bloke sees it."

Joe noticed as Leigh moved the wolves aside, stood up and stretched . . . statuesque was the only polite word that came to mind for describing her shape. He felt way off, mark, but she did remind him of a travel bureau poster he saw last week, in Skagway, advertising Jamaica's fun in the sun. It showed a woman who looked much like Leigh, in a black bikini, the top undone, a hand cupping a triangle of fabric to each breast, leaning forward with similar eyes, grin, and tawny auburn curls tumbling down over her shoulders. Joe murmured to himself, behave mate—she's no date. Bloody well you'd better behave yourself. Stop it, you're bloody well confused with the confluence of emotions . . . that be it, stop it.

As he rose and moved toward Leigh, he heard a sound as if his movement triggered its response. It was a low, steady whinnying from a hemlock above the ridge. He paused.

"What now," he said to Leigh. "Do you hear that?"

"Yes, what do you think it is? A plane? A ship's horn ?"

"I hope so; we don't need a bone chilling sangfroid—from some atavistic past—tonight in addition to what's come down today. We've already been over-served! They both paused and listened again as the whinnying continued.

"I've got it."

"Bloody well, you know what, mate, after listening more closely, I know . . . it's the single note gargling of a *screech owl*. I would often wake in the wee hours of the night to savor this watery song. Our feathered friend's territory has been invaded, no . . . violated, and the bloke is telling us to move on or suffer the consequences . . . his single-note gargling. We'll not ruffle his style, gone we'll be soon; he needs a little excitement anyway, the Tongass can be pretty quiet at times."

Undisturbed by their presence, the owl went about its wooing.

"I imagine other midnight calls could be more scary. Like wolves, foraging bears, and god knows what. You know, there is a little joy in our screech owl's watery sound."

Then it started . . . a great horned owl called out, another answered across the fog-shrouded valley, and the screech owl chimed in, and the horned owl again . . . what followed was a symphony of the night. All four listened to the exchanges from mist above and across the foggy valley . . . two at point, with heads rotating up, down, and across the now opaque clearing, then down the masked valley.

The evening's moisture, having moved in suddenly, now hung in suspension as if a curtain to mask the nightly process of denizens' activities as part of the food chain—add four more, as Leigh, Joe, Tough, and The White sliced the wall of fog while hiking single file from the clearing to the hut. The queue had true rank order as if in military procession with Leigh in the lead, followed by Tough, then The White, and Joe bringing up the rear.

*   *   *

Joe murmured to himself. You know, while in strange territory like this you will come to what you swear must be the last log-fall before the clearing, and home, but there's another, and another. There will be smells in your nostrils which go beyond description, mixtures of cedar and ferns, and a deep musty odor that sustains you, at times will mistake for the breath of a beautiful woman. This fog tonight is the type you can dip your hands into, squeeze together, and come out with nothing. How strange, you think, not to see your hand at the end of your arm. You conjure up images of yourself going in, parting the fog just enough to slop through, finding that spot on a log near a stream where you are sure she is sitting. She is cupping her breasts in her hands as though once there you could replace the emptiness in your own hands with the directions you are positive must be printed on her chest . . . then you realize it is only a memory of your imagination run wild as suggested by the stimulating vacation poster seen earlier in the week.

It is easy to call mist an apparition. You can bloody well become lost easily in these conditions. All your senses will be distorted. You will think you have walked too far, missed a critical landmark. Your voice will leave your body and make a path through the fog. Birds of prey will appear overhead as fast-moving, dark shadows. You will become so cold you will want to feel the pain of a talon in your neck. If you can still breathe, you'll take in as much air as possible and let the mist become part of you.

I wouldn't put it past Manitou to bring on this blasted fog as a subtle signal of Andy's demise. Leigh need not know, but Andy's last moments would have been *tragic*. His lips would move continuously for air . . . but get water. A voice coming from the deep in his belly pleads for air, but gets water. Assuredly, he could not even move his arms as the water encased his body. More water moves to further entomb. The deep cracks of his skin would fill with the ointment of pure wet coldness, and later troubled in a dream of the fire under his skin, he would wake to the taste of the earth's water, the memory of the cold, as his lips drank it in, the taste of iron turning to blood.

He would hear his voice as he had known it before: rich and flowing, the sound of water mixing with the howl of the wind, his body cupping into itself, then driven upward, a spike of pure direction churning into white light, his body free and clean . . . from earth's yielding grip.

Manitou awaits his spirit in the mystic afterlife of nature's way, knowing very well that returning to earth as one of His subjects is likely.

Didn't Leigh feel strongly that the embodiment of Tough was, in fact, *Jack's* return . . . and The White, *Andy's*, "personification"—both to embolden Leigh and provide additional support and courage to sustain her mission to live in the Tongass.

Bloody well, she implied as much, moments ago . . . and the inference to me is clear. The wolves are, in fact, her former friends and lovers. Faith in the Creator, Manitou, makes anything possible, if you believe. Dearie, we hope you're right 'cause if what you say is true, you've got two top-flight soul mates on her side.

*   *   *

"Are you there, Joe? I can't see you through this fog. Are you there?"

"Bloody well, my lassie, me arse is bringing up the rear. How much longer do we have to slice our way through this fog? Me throat cries out for a brew!"

"Don't worry, you old bloke . . . 'tis only minutes to a little grog for you. Hold on just a little longer, and I'll draw one for your crying body."

Chapter 26

The Search

Having difficulty sleeping, Leigh thought of her favorite Spencer Reece poem,

Midnight

"All these years later and the hill is still bald,
whispering softly as the revolutions of the sea,
echoing with the mouths of the vanquished . . .
If you look closely in the left hand corner,
I can just be distinguished from the blue blue brilliance of
all the land,
a tiny figure, no bigger than a grass blade, a shadow hugged
by shadows,
heading home after a long walk nowhere,
encircled by a halo of rocks, trees, crops, rivers, clouds—
by every blessed thing conspiring together to save my life."

She thought, heading home after a long walk nowhere . . . that's me, alone again.

"However, if I'm correct in the Creator's plan for his Kin(g)dom, Gitchee Manitou has already replaced Jack with Tough; and Andy with The White; and I'm certain that He will replace Ford with a similar animal; possibly another wolf . . . Who knows?

She looked over at Joe's supine form now roaring like the Canadian Pacific Limited streaking through the Alaskan night. She didn't care; companionship out-weighed sonorous noise, when she was ready to sleep nothing would stop her. As if sleeping with one eye open, Tough jerked up his head with Leigh's movement. Not by accident both he and The White were strategically located between Leigh's bed and the guest's bedroll on the floor, used last by Andy, and previously Jack . . . poor Ford never had a chance for an overnight alliance in the hut; else-where, and everywhere, in Skagway, yes, but sadly not here.

She tingled again . . . three men, all gone, all gone in three months.

"Damn! . . . Good fortune, please stop by, please embrace this gal!"

As so many times in the past, with different men, the reflection of the window-mounted Dream Catcher started to cast its shadow from the now-clearing moonlit night; inching ever so slowly across the floor and onto Joe's British features with high cheekbones, graying red hair, freckles and aging spots, and four-day reddish roan stubble. His torso expanded and contracted in a syncopated seventy strokes a minute; the wolves added whizzing in offset rhythm of about forty strokes a minute; and finally the wind-up alarm clock at a predictable sixty tick/tocks a minute. Too tired for sleep, she lies there listening. No wind, no creak of limbs, no grumble of engines, only a distant sound of ice calving from the face of glaciers to the northwest.

Even though she knew better, she kept imagining that if she could only clear the decks of all her previous trauma, then she could renew her life by merely simplifying her life. Sounded easy, but trying to catch up once and for all is like digging a hole in sand: no matter how fast you shovel, new sand keeps pouring in. Unable to make headway, missing her previous life, missing her men friends . . . she began to slide down the slope toward gloom.

Her longing to write inhabited her body, this longing was also a liveliness, an aliveness.

"I must write my words. Words have their own flow, just let it happen, Leigh, don't let all these extraneous events get in the way of the . . . words."

Between the shivers of her depressed thoughts, she tried to practice the meditation exercises she'd learned from the Buddhist monk named Thich Nhat Hanh:

"Breathing in,
I calm my body.
Breathing out, I smile.
Dwelling in the present moment,
I know this is a wonderful moment."

As she murmured the motivating lines of her mantra: You Can Do It—Do It, she realized that this was a wonderful moment, in spite of the shudders, the sleeplessness, the worry . . . the unknown future. She reflected . . . is it ever really known? No.

She fell into a deep sleep as the rhythm of the man, the wolves, and the clock kept time to the movement of the Dream Catcher's silhouette across the floor.

*   *   *

Dawn finds Leigh on the meadow with the racing wolves chasing anything and everything that smells and moves by leg or wing. The operative word for the meadow was—Chaos—by the wolves' violence over the formerly tranquil scene.

The cries, the noise and the terror of winged flight indicated major disquietude. The wolves, being totally consumed by their vigorous pursuits, allowed her to set off by herself on a little hike to the river; they would not miss her, and easily find her later at the time of their choosing. The trail from the meadow to the river was a little more primitive as dragonflies dashed and butterflies lolled over the seed-heads of late summer grasses, over milkweed and ragweed and creamy goldenrod above the purple/blue/green teaberry blankets; she picked a few leaves and chewed the distinctive taste as found in Teaberry Gum of the '50s . . . Do they still make it? She noted that the heart of the meadow was high and dry, as she now adjusted her footfalls to the boggy borders of the river. She lay a while on Mother Earth, her hat shading eyes against the rising sun, with smells and sounds and sights pouring through her soul's inlets.

"Dad, Ford, Jack, Andy . . . I so wish you were here to share this spot . . . oh well."

At this supine level the forest was abuzz. She plucked a spear of grass and chewed the stem's juicy terminus, a sensation she'd loved since her dad intro-duced her to succulent Timothy stalks, the best, while walking the uncut hay fields, alone in July, this was by far the best treat in her youth; the Timothy and alone with Dad.

The meadow was still a dueled agitation of stalking and flight, so after a short spell she dusted off the forest floor, the moss, and picked another grass for the road, and continued on. Beyond the soggy fringe of the meadow she entered a brief wood, mostly hemlocks and pines and birches. The trees had been left in peace long enough to grow thick at the waist and gnarly at the roots. The soil underfoot was spongy from the depth of decay. She shuffled knee-deep through cinnamon ferns and skirted mossy hummocks, filling her lungs with moist and spore-laden air. She soon heard water, a purring hustle that made her heart relax, and a few more steps carried her to the river. It was rocky, a narrow trough of boulders that shredded the current into dozens of riffles and chutes.

"Damn, it was an area like this that Andy and I performed the Tlingit Love Ceremony, (Gi-zah-gin), only days ago; now it seems as if a lifetime ago, yes, just up the river a few meters, the difference being moonlight and firelight . . . what a wonderful memory, our last night—together."

Leaving her moccasins on the bank, and rolling up her jeans, she waded out to a flat stone in the middle of the rapids. There she sat, enveloped in the mist and rushing water sound. Sunlight broke through the canopy of trees, filling the ripples with scoops of silver and pressing warm against her back. Soon she felt the water flowing through her; time slowed, circled, came to a halt.

There she sat, thinking, body laid bare, reflecting on Joe's ritualistic actions last night . . . and his reasons for body mutilation. Tradition? British historical custom? From the Norsemen raiders of 1100 C.E., ancient religious myth? or was it a personal reverence for his fellowman? His explanation escaped her logic . . . but, it was the first thing she noticed on his wrist upon awakening.

*   *   *

He told her the story . . . Joe explained:

"Many years ago, in The United Kingdom, my grandfather, after my father died, pulled me aside as we left the cemetery. My son, he said, it is time to introduce you to a secret, something your father, and my father in years past, and I, have done—in private—after the death of our fellow blood-sport hunters. The 'spirits' have been good to us in sharing the bounty of the earth. We have all hunted together and have shared in this conquest of survival through hunting much like our forefathers. It was something about respect, about giving yourself over."

He then unbuttoned his shirt cuff, and pulled up his sleeve and showed Leigh the inner part of his arm . . . she gasped. His inner arm had a series of approximately one inch narrow scars, all laced in rank and file. One was freshly cut with a new pencil-like scab, and a slight ooze. He opened his pocket knife, and showed her the motion used; not a quick slice over his wrist but a slow, delicate draw over the skin. Each one small, distinct, his left forearm covered with inch-long memories.

"But why?" Leigh pleaded.

"My dear, the bleeding never lasted long, just long enough to let a little blood fall into the river. I mix it slowly with my hand, then wave it along to honor my fallen friends in the hunting grounds of life. Nothing was said, the spirit knew, I only watched the way the blood swirled into the clear water, then dissolved, disappeared, became river. Eight fellow hunters. Eight cuts. The last was for Andrew a.k.a Walkswithwind. Do you understand?"

She looked at her own forearm, thought of the rivers she knew, the men who had passed into the other world, the spiritual world of life after death . . . she felt transformed by Joe's story, his commitment to his fellow man, to his blood-sport friends. She thought of her life, now, again . . . somehow transposed, transported into one of the streams with apparitions of spiritual friends lining the path of the river. She knew what she had to do. She would go to the river, too, kneel down, roll up her sleeve, and make a cut, and begin the process of giving herself over, too.

"Thank you, Joe. What a lovely story, what a lovely way to honor your fallen friends; thank you for sharing."

"Dearie, 'tis no bother; we share with those who care. Did you not know that both Andy and his brother Jack share the ritual? If you had known them longer, they surely would have shared. Good night, my love, we've a big day tomorrow ... sleep tight ... for I don't mind tellin' ya the mark next to Andy—'tis Jack's ... sleep tight."

"Oh! I hadn't thought ..." Another tear formed as she rolled over in bed.

*   *   *

"Here I am, six hours later, with a perfect opportunity to perform the ritual. There's no time like the present, the wolves are busy, Joe's still asleep, I'm in the center of the stream, and I've got a knife."

She completed the ceremony while talking to Andy—she made the cut to honor their lives ... and his death. She gave herself over to the spirit of Andy's life.

She performed the ceremony again, this time talking to Jack—she made the cut to honor their lives ... and his death while trying to save her life. She gave herself over to the spirit of Jack's life.

She performed the ceremony again while talking to Ford—she made the cut to honor their lives ... and his death. She gave herself over to the spirit of Ford's life.

She watched in silence as the blood dissipated and the river flowed clear.

Only as the blood vanished in the silver ripples, and the sun's heat grew more intense did she realize the time was ticking. The wolves would be looking for her soon, so she headed back through the shadowy woods, over the brightening meadow, feeling buoyant but full of newfound energy as though she had already feasted on life in its fullest.

"Tough, Tough, where are you?"

"Over here, dearie, the wolves and I are having a rollicking good time down here by the river; come to us, my lassie, come on, I'm laying in a bloody neat pile of logs for a fire. Come on; I've also a little grog waiting for your beautiful lips, over there on the bench. 'Tis time you washed out that that rusty water from your throat; come on, let's get on with it."

"How thoughtful, Joe. OK, I'm on my way."

The wolves were on her in a minute; they danced around her as she walked to the fire pit, and Joe, too, while he sang some sort of drinking song of the pubs: "Roll ye leg over, oh, roll ye leg over, your olde man's ah coming over to see thee tonight ..."

"Joe!" exclaimed Leigh, "isn't that lyric a little racy, and risqué to the ears of these naive denizens of the meadow?"

"'Tis right you are, my fair lady, but 'tis me favorite, and the only one I can sing in tune. Wait. I could sing me mother's favorite: "The Old Rugged Cross" ... 'On a hill far away, stood the old rugged cross, an ...'"

"No, ah . . . that's okay, let's just chat awhile."

After a little hug, and withdrawal, maintaining a hold of each other's hands, they separated, and looked into each other's eyes and shared an unspoken moment of thanks for Andy. Nary a word was spoken, nor needed; their eyes said it all . . . Andrew was no more; Andrew's gone, gone, their eyes said to each other. Thanks for the part you've played in his life: Joe, as a colleague, and friend, for years in the DNR; Leigh, as a short-term helpmate, appearing at her hut when she needed someone, and yes, her beloved for a short week. Joe's grasp gave her the strength she needed to sustain her emotions.

Before he released her, he did notice three freshly administered one-inch cuts on her left wrist . . . he noted without mentioning it to her that she had performed the blood-rite in the stream in the early morn to honor her friends. He looked at her—she knew—he knew, nothing need be said; she was now a member.

"My dearie, we'll seek our closure together. Let's go to the plateau in the morning's light. Come on, lassie; bottoms on that last bit of grog, away we go."

As they headed up the ridge to the plateau, Joe told her he'd fixed earlier a big brunch—English Style, and it was waiting for them. Then, he explained, after a little rest, they'd have a quiet fire in the evening, for he would be leaving at dawn's early light. He related that he'd taken the liberty to use her transceiver, called Skagway-DNR, reported the unusual circumstances of Andrew's death to his supervisor, and decided that they'd leave well enough alone for now, subject to the daylight inspection. Joe suggested that Andy was where he would have chosen to be, with the spiritual world of his forefathers . . . an afterlife of spiritual wonder, an afterlife of the faithful. His interment would not be violated; the family would understand. A simple memorial service would be held, sans body. Joe would handle the details and inform family and friends.

The examination at the plateau was uneventful, as expected. The rivulet at the base of the earthen slide had forced its way out the cave's collapsed entrance and rejoined the stream flowing into the Bitterroot. The hydrologic pressure in the cave must have forced the underground spring to find its previous course through the plugged tunnel; likewise the sinkhole would probably soon fill with water and find its way to the cavern below. The altar's huge stone slabs were gone, totally buried in the hole. A few trees encircled the spot with no particular significance to a passerby. Then again, a shrewd observer just might notice the sinkhole . . . and the rivulet just over the edge of the plateau . . . may be connected . . . and the circle of hemlocks . . . they were put there no doubt, by man . . . maybe or maybe not . . . depends on who's looking.

The wolf bodies killed the previous night were also gone; all that remained were scattered bones and hair; they most likely had already been scavenged by a gaggle of nocturnal carnivorous animals, including their own kind.

"My dear, could we kneel a moment, right here at the edge of the encircled hemlocks . . . I've a few words to pass on to me mate, Andy. Come on, hold my hand."

They both kneeled in silence; the wolves joined them in mutual respect of the tone of the moment.

Joe spoke:

> "Andy, life is not always fair to us, neither standing by truth nor anchoring one's faith in a transcendent power guarantees that justice will vanquish injustice here and now, nor that righteousness will roll down like an everflowing stream, but it does give one strength to carry on. And if we receive strength from you to carry on the work you believed in, with people we love, in a place we cherish, what else do we need? We thank you for your life . . . we love you. May Manitou embrace your soul.
> Gi Zah Gin."

One solitary raven watched their activities in stoic silence; the bird merely noted its presence with a series of calls upon their arriving, and another series of calls as they left.

*   *   *

As they sat by the fire, Joe thought it important to let Leigh know how thankful he was for the fellowship she had shared with Andrew . . . "I loved the bugger, would have given my life for him, and he for me . . . I sense you would have done the same, Leigh. He was complex you know; as a Tlingit he had his own ways—not always in harmony with the white man."

Joe leaned back, sipped on his "pint," and looked Leigh in the eye as if to ask a question, then turned away and stroked the wolves.

"What is it, Joe? What's on your mind?"

"My dear, I'm leaving in the morn' and I'm not sure you're aware of the history and present day concerns of Andy's and Jack's tribe and the people of the Tongass. Would you care to have me share with you what I've learned? For what's worth?"

"For sure, I'll be here a while, at least two to three years . . . I'd better be informed, and you've been living among the natives for thirty years in the U.S and Canada . . . please do. You're a hell of a lot better source than a book, or dissertation by some Ph.D. Please do!"

"Well then, get comfy, gal. I'll freshen up my pint and tell you what I know. First, it is important you know that I am obviously a non-native spokesman and do not speak for the native people of Southeast Alaska. However, I can try to describe an important force at work within the Tongass. The Tlingit, Haida, and, more recently, Tsimshian Indians have a relationship with the forest and the sea that has formed over the millennia. That relationship continues today and tis at the heart of many of the local concerns that both Andy and I addressed daily.

"At the center of the Native customary and traditional way of life are land and the concept of subsistence. Tis important to understand that subsistence is a white man's word, and it does not capture the traditional way of life. My god, you'd think the word subsistence suggests poverty, or bare survival, while the experience for Alaskan Natives is a rich, vital, and fulfilling way of life.

"Bloody well, it is critical to a discussion of subsistence that I have you understand the 'subsistence life' as it is played out on the lands and waters of Southeast Alaska. The traditional subsistence life forms a deep web of connections between the people, the land, the sea, the wildlife, and the spirit. If we don't kill fish or game . . . we don't eat. On the spiritual level, it uses the surrounding world as a source of materials and sustenance. Hunting, fishing, and gathering provide the people with a protein- and vitamin-rich source of food. Customary and traditional foods are essential to the physical health of Alaskan Natives, and changes away from the traditional diet are believed to contribute to the incidence of diabetes, heart disease, obesity, and cancer.

"In Alaska, and Canada, where I served earlier, relying on subsistence foods for a substantial part of one's diet is a matter not only of choice, but also of necessity. A number of factors, including great distance from other food sources and compromised position in the cash economy, combine to make native communities physically and economically dependent on traditional subsistence resources. Bloody well, like me, I'm sure not slim . . . and would be on a native's diet, you can bet a couple pints on that.

"However, Leigh, it is not appropriate to reduce the traditional subsistence life solely to the act of obtaining food. In addition to providing sustenance, subsistence gathering activities build a network of social relationships within the community. There is a division of labor among harvesting, preparing, and distributing wild foods. At times, me thinks the women drew the short straw . . . they do *most* of the work. The spirit of sharing is central to a successful harvest. Natives often share portions of their harvest with extended family and with Elders, widows, people without boats, and others who cannot obtain their own supply. Subsistence harvests provide the classroom for passing on traditional values to young people. By God . . . I feel we're losing the classroom. This education follows the cycle of seasons and the special foods that come only for a brief period during the year. Young harvesters learn slowly, through seasons of experience, the lore and skills preserved through the generations.

"A life of traditional subsistence is governed by a commonly accepted set of principles. These laws and customs strictly define the rights, obligations, and privileges of tribal members. Traditional law is passed from generation to generation through repetition of legend, observance of ceremonies, and social corrections by community Elders. Subsistence living is not only a distinct way of life, it is also a life-enriching process. Conservation and perpetuation of subsistence resources is part of the traditional way of life, and is mandated in traditional law and custom. Traditionally, waste was not permitted; all remains not used for food, dress, tools, or other purposes had to be burned or returned to the water. On remote assignments, in Canada, by God, I wore fur clothing all winter. The animal spirits then could report to their kind of the respectful treatment by the people, and thus the animal populations were plentiful each season. In addition, Leigh, all things, including animals, fish, trees, glaciers, and the sea itself, possessed a powerful spirit and must be treated with great respect. Isn't our blood-rite an example? True? My Dearie. Do you understand?"

"Absolutely, Joe, the native's lifestyle sounds so logical and independent."

"These Pantheistic thoughts are related eloquently by an old friend of mine, from Juneau, Austin Hammond, Sr., Tlingit storyteller; you'll note his frustration with the white man. It goes something like this:

The Spirit Came to All Things

"All the animals, what's flying, in the water,
All the fish got the spirit.
Everything He threw in got the spirit.
The tree beginning to grow too.
Every year it comes out if you look at it.
They are all alive.
He gave us the spirit.
From the Raven what He threw in.
That's why we talk about it.
To respect everything . . . the tree,
the rock, the ground, everything.
Everything's got the spirit, but
They don't believe us.
They don't want us to talk about the Spirit."

"As you've noted, the literal Tlingit-to-English translation leaves a little to be desired for exact sentence syntax. Nevertheless, Leigh, can you see a doctrine that equates the Spirit with the forces and laws of the universe (pantheism), combined with animistic projections to nature with attribution of conscious life to objects in and phenomena of nature or to inanimate objects; and how this can lead to a life encapsulated by the Spirit . . . anything, and everything . . . everywhere.

"Unfortunately, Leigh, to many non-natives like us, subsistence hunting and fishing refers solely to the effort of providing necessary food. Even a cursory description of the traditional subsistence way of life is much more than putting food on the table; the ability of natives to engage in the subsistence life is a measure of their self-determination.

"Aye, I've said enough to last you a lifetime. But finally, without full access to fish and wildlife, without the ritual and community that revolve around subsistence activities, the way in which natives live would be defined by standards outside their own cultural values. That, my dear, is what I will do when I go back to work with the DNR . . . assisting the natives in their quest for as much of their culture as possible. All of this is very satisfying in helping the natives while trying to urge the white man to step aside and let them be."

"Thank you, Joe. I never quite knew what all you guys in the DNR did for us and the natives. It sounds like a big job: pantheism, animism, and Christian myths, all entangled in the lives of the people. Yep, it must be a full-time job."

Leigh felt the pleasure of these moments by the fire, but could not scour from her vision the darkness that troubled her soul. She had witnessed too much suffering and waste of life in the last month. Not to mention the irony of her departure from the lower 48 to escape what humans are doing to one another and to the planet. Look what's happening to me—here. Sure, hope is our constant companion, but anyone who pays attention to the state of the world knows that we are in trouble—no matter where we live.

"Joe, for my part, I believe that all but the poorest of us could choose to lead materially simpler lives, and thereby do less harm and reap more joy. What endures? What lifts our hearts? What do we possess in abundance? Our truly abundant resources are obvious, and easily measured; the intangibles are difficult to describe and impossible to appraise, and among them are love, beauty, skill, compassion, fidelity, and wildness; we must nurture these powers."

"'Tis true, my dear, as memory grips the past . . . hope grips the future. I will be thinking of you as I hike out tomorrow, and while I contribute to this life with more vigor having known you. I imagine the host of ancestors, human and non-human, whose lives and labors have made this moment possible for those remaining two of us who breathe."

"Yes, my dear friend, let us draw a breath, savor it, and bless those not so fortunate to be with us."

As Leigh, Joe, and the wolves walked toward the hut, a raven leaped from its perch and soared toward the sky.

Chapter 27

Expectations

As Joe trudged westward along the Bitterroot River, with the sun at his back, he thought of the previous evening by the fire; Leigh's ongoing drama, her personal crisis was still on his mind. He could do very little to ease the burden she has experienced over the last couple months, and an equally clouded future.

However, he could, and did relate to her the essential state of conflicts in man as seen by the philosopher Rousseau's unique conception of self-love *amour de soi*. She needed one big serving of self-love. There certainly is a lot of room for more, since she had not one drop of selfishness *amour propre* in her body; he had tried to distinguish the two radically different states for her . . . to help her understand herself, she must embrace *amour de soi* to its fullest, as Rousseau explains:

> "Self-love, which concerns itself only with ourselves, is content to satisfy our own needs; but selfishness, which is always comparing self with others, is never satisfied and never can be . . . the tender and gentle passions spring from self-love, while the hateful and angry passions spring from selfishness."

Leigh knew of the French, deistic philosopher and author from the '60s, her "golden years" at The University of Michigan. He, too, had studied Jean Jacques Rousseau's writings while in London, and felt especially blessed to run into a woman in Alaska who was as well read as Leigh. No wonder Ford, Jack, and Andrew were captivated in her presence . . . which he understood went well beyond her intellect. She was still a foxy lady.

Having been around a long time he never assumed that there was anything certain in life, but Joe did feel that if he reached out to Rousseau's writings as a way to help her, JJR's logic may have bearing for more pleasant fruit in the future. How? By attempting to understand why so many bloody orgies nature had visited upon her. He thought, Bloody well, I too have taken my licks, and have found the world to be intelligible but not necessarily rational, for JJR has also taught us that . . . "the voice of the soul, as the passions are the voice of the body . . . conscience never deceives us; she is the true guide of man, it is to the soul what instinct is to the body; he who obeys his conscience is following nature and need not fear that he will go astray." That is where my dear Leigh should be: between the states of nature which rational man lies. She will do fine, discussions by the fire helped, she'll soon love herself again. She will posit a state of happiness contingent upon a pure autonomy, unaffected by external causation . . . she has to in enabling the simple joy of freedom, untouched by the influences of external untoward forces. She must control her own destiny.

"Bloody well, just as I thought, that's a rain cloud acoming this bloody-road; better get my slicker on, I'm already half wet from tromping along this spongy sphagnum-swamplike surface.

"At approximately three miles an hour following the river out, it should take about twelve hours to reach the DNR's Deer Monitoring Camp on the shores of the Pacific. Bloody well, it will be a long day of trudging through these lowlands along the river . . . just where the bear dig for their succulent tubers, and blueberries . . . dag nab it. What a wretched place to be alone. But, we've done me duty to Leigh, and have honored me friend Andrew . . . the man I loved, and still do. Such a tragedy, but as I told Leigh and the boss, he is where he would have chosen . . . I'm certain; and if any of his family would like to visit his entombment, I will gladly be their guide.

"Come on now, you bloody bloke, you came in this way without problems, you'll get out . . . you've done your job well, if I don't say so myself. Come on self, get your butt in gear, the sooner you get to the coast, the sooner you're be swilling a beer."

*   *   *

At 5,000 feet, and 50 miles due north just above the snow line, two Tlingit hunters were stalking a mule deer through the shadows dappling the black spruce forest, keeping downwind of the animal's trail while striding on flat, tapered snowshoes. The bent birch frames laced with strips of deer hide permitted them to ride the thin crust that firmed the powdery snow—a crust that was too weak to support the heavy deer with pointed hooves, as it forged for scant winter fodder through drifts that occasionally reached as high as its shoulders. Food was sometimes scarce in the boreal forest of northern Alaska. The hunters had traveled hungry for two nights, as they were on an urgent dual mission of great importance to the tribal clan and were hunting en route to the headwaters of the Bitterroot River. However, hunting was secondary; their primary mission was to investigate an incident his local shaman reported to him and the tribal leadership. The shaman had a vision of severe damage and loss of a Tlingit warrior's life at a cave-in near a sacred burial site along the Bitterroot where Tlingit ancestors had been enshrined. The vision was unclear so Chi Mukwa (Big Bear) and his son Chinoodin (Big Wind) were asked by the elders and the shaman to visit the site. The shaman Gete Wabiska (Old White) had also indicated that The Windigo had carried the message to him. The Windigo had apparently appeared in the form of a monster, one of many different forms, but in this case Chi Mukwa was told that he appeared with a heart of ice, bulging eyes, a lipless mouth gleaming with long, jagged teeth. Moving sometimes as a monstrous entity, sometimes as a whirlwind, this phantom of retribution and hunger haunted the shaman's lair as well as all of the Tongass in the winter.

Hunger, yes, as the Tlingit people moved inland from the summer fishing camps on the Pacific Coast, they hunted deer, beaver, and bear—so did Windigo hunt Tlingit men, women, and children. In fact, whenever a hunter failed to return to camp or a child disappeared, it was assumed that Windigo had devoured another victim. In this case, the giant was also aware that something had disturbed a sacred burial chamber.

Windigo was much more than a disturbing presence in the Indians' spirit world—it presented terrible hunger and the cruel choices that hunger forced on people who were desperate for survival, the manifestation of something dark and unspeakable in human need. There were times in the forest when starvation hovered close at hand as dried salmon fillets were exhausted and human flesh was looked upon as the alternative to a lingering death. Succumbing to this temptation, however, carried a terrible consequence: The cannibal developed a bloodlust; he or she "turned Windigo," as the Indians said, and had to be driven away from the band or killed.

The middle-aged, iconoclastic father and his teenage son were typical representatives of the clan who chose to live in the forest like their forefathers in the 19th century, refusing the marginal life of "half-acceptance" and welfare controlled by the white man in the towns and cities in and around Juneau. Less secure and at times near starvation, they chose the forest, and would survive in the Tongass as the modern day brothers of the tribe sought welfare and dependence from the white man versus tribal pride and independence.

The specter of starvation began to evaporate when Chi Mukwa came upon the broken snow marking the passage of a foraging deer.

"Look, Chinoodin, here is where the deer has been feeding on willow twigs, and the animal had stood for some time. Note the angle at which the urine has hit the snow; its shape tells whether the deer is a cow or a bull . . . the circular pool versus an ellipse shape indicates this one is a bull. Good. See the torn branches and partially chewed bark of the willow and over here, the aspen; it is eating well; with luck, it will soon lay down and ruminate; then we can sneak up when its vision is at a lower level."

"True, these fresh pellets also indicate it might be ready to lay down."

"Yes, son, the odor may also mask our scent."

"Yep . . . Dad, it looks like it will double back on its trail and lay down soon, as deer habitually do. Then, predictably, it will turn with its nose pointed into the wind so it can scent any following two- or four-legged predators . . . and we can sneak up from downwind while it is facing upwind."

"Yes, my son, the deer would behave exactly as you have so often observed; they are creatures of habit, and will behave exactly as my guardian spirit revealed to me last night while having an out-of-body experience."

The guardian spirit, himself a deer, had visited Chi Mukwa, in the form of a human body in a dream on many occasions when still a boy. It had told him the ways of the large-antlered animals so that he might hunt them when he got older. In addition, a deer had appeared in his dreams a few nights earlier, a sure signal that the hunt would be successful.

Following the teachings of his spirit, father and son stalked into the wind until they could scent the deer where it lay ahead of them in the snow. They each gripped their birch bows, Chinoodin's horizontally behind a fallen log, Chi Mukwa's vertically behind a large tree; both with fingers holding birch arrows fletched with duck feathers, both arrows notched on the taut bowstring of twisted caribou gut. Chi Mukwa saw the great animal first, then signaled his son with the chirping sound of a wren, followed by arm and hand signals. The great animal, its antlers splendid, was bathed in a wreathed haze of warm steam. The hunters now moved in unison to ensure a lethal killing zone for their arrows, now so close that the deer could hear them. They drew back on their bow strings and froze in place. The enormous creature lumbered to its feet and stood for a moment in its snow bed; then it turned in a majestic manner to face the threat. In that gesture, in that turning toward the fatal arrows, the animal gave itself to the triumphant stalkers.

This self-offering by the animal was the dominant spiritual explanation for the hunter's ability to find and kill animals. They were jittery and shy of human company and could conceal themselves against their forest background; they possessed manifest intelligence and, often, greater size and strength. How could it be killed without its cooperation?

In the tradition of former Tlingit hunters, Chinoodin removed the animal's heart, held it skyward to draw the attention of The Great Spirit Manitou . . . and offered a prayerful chant of thanksgiving:

> "Anewaynee, anewaynee kooo,
> anewaynee, anewaynee que,
> me kay toe, me kay toe,
> An ah wanna choo."

Chinoodin lowered the heart, placed it in a birch-bark container, then re-moved the liver and cut a portion for his dad and himself; they sank their teeth into the bloody warm tissue . . . and together, again thanked Manitou for his gift of life:

"An ah wanna choo!"

A Raven dropped from the thermals and perched above the jubilant hunters as if a sign . . . a messenger, a symbol that Manitou had heard their thankful chant. Or maybe, just maybe, the bird was here to perform the task it had been assigned from the beginning of time . . . clean up—after the kill. Maybe both. Ravens have been called "mystic birds of death" for centuries, following not only hunters, but wolves, and any other successful carnivore.

This was the second kill of the day; they had gratefully downed an elk earlier and had a similar ceremony, then left the meat and hide in a cache over the ridge to the north.

Clearly, there was no greater gift than that of the animal to the hunters. For their part, the hunters would skin, gut, and dismember the deer with ceremonial care—being careful not to leave its blood on the snow, which risked bringing other carnivores to the site—after obliterating the traces of slaughter, they would cache it in a spot where even the wolverines could not find it. Initially, Chi Mukwa would take only the heart and some other token parts, so that when he returned to camp, his wife, Wabun Ahnung (Morning Star), would see that he had found large game. Subsequently, the entire clan of twenty men, women, and children would move to the kill site, and Chi Mukwa would retrieve his cache and honor one of his fellows, perhaps an older warrior who had been less fortunate in the hunt, by giving him the meat and organs to distribute among the band as well as to share with the needs of nearby clans also living a subsistence lifestyle. Chi Mukwa would also see that the younger hunters like Chinoodin learned to treat the remains with respect. Such reciprocations between man and animal are ele-ments in an ageless tapestry of behavior and belief that links Native Americans across the continent.

The hunt was the men's domain, like the fashioning of tools and weapons and the building of sleds, like the important readings of prophecy from fractures in a charred shoulder bone. However, women, led by Wabun Ahnung, did every-thing else, including adding finishing touches to some of the manufactured items, such as lacing the snowshoe frames made by the men. Yes, hunters like Chi Mukwa and Chinoodin sought large game, but women snared rabbits and birds that often kept the clan alive between major kills. When the men returned to camp or they moved the camp to the kills, the women turned the animal into pemmican, dried meat, and other food; women also tanned hides, and manufactured and repaired clothing, moccasins, and mittens. Women picked berries in summer and did most of the fishing, along with the arduous work of cutting and drying fish for winter, which was never very far away.

To an outside observer, the women's lives may have seemed worse than they really were. But, Wabun Ahnung reminded her husband, they were "independent" of the white men and their narrow-minded stifling religion, plus their heavy-handed rules. Furthermore, women hauling water in the winter, collecting firewood, and providing a clean home for the clan is part and parcel of the pleasures of being principal or key aspect of a successful clan; not to mention creative cooking, and fixing a variety of tasty meals.

Chi Mukwa was well aware of certain cruel aspects of the Tongass to the clan and appreciated his wife and the clan's women with multiple skills; it's an inhospitable domain to strangers who choose to linger. Winters are deep, dark, and long, with temperatures plunging far below freezing for months at a time. Summers are short and warm, but in some ways even less tolerable. Voracious mosquitoes hatch by the millions as soon as the snows begin to melt, to be replaced by clouds of black flies. There is the illusion of fecundity that will never abate; although the boreal forest teems with wildlife, its resources are widely distributed, always uncertain, always on the move. For prey and predator alike, the land delivers good times and bad, feast and famine, life and death, on a schedule no one can fully know.

All of these thoughts were on the minds of the clan tonight as they celebrated around the fire, well fed, and at peace with themselves.

Chi Mukwa noted his son's preoccupation with thoughts elsewhere, and sensed a need to address the ideas that must be swirling in his typical young and exploratory mind.

"Son, need we talk? Do we need to discuss your inner thoughts tonight? I am very proud of your actions during today's hunt. Is something bothering you?"

"Yes, and no. I understand the clan's goals for independence, and the benefits of this sometimes cruel environment . . . but I wonder how long it will last. As you know, many of my friends have been forced from—or have given up on—the independent ways of our clan in the Tongass; many have succumbed to the heavy-handed dependent rules of the white man in the city. How long do you think we can survive as the whites continue to violate our lands, our hunting and fishing privileges/rights . . . all guaranteed by the Home Rule Treaties?

"For example, you've informed me that tomorrow we investigate the destruction of our forefathers' burial grounds and sacred altar . . . and that a lady called "Red hairs" has encroached our land with a DNR permit in an area near our forefathers' ceremonial grounds, a sacred area that has been safe and secure all these years; now the white man's presence has altered the formerly undamaged sacred grounds. How long can we maintain this lifestyle . . . this separation from the white man?"

"Son, the history of this region is anything but gentle. Indians have suffered attempted genocide, dispossession on a mass scale, the white man's persistent blindness to injustice, and our dismaying indifference to the possibilities for radical change that now stare us in the face. However, we are inclined to be gentle and self-effacing. Furthermore, many of our elders, in the past, regarded displays of anger, noisy confrontation, or polemical hyperbole as infantile and self-defeating. They preferred to speak quiet truths. On the other hand, politicians' entire way of life is dulled by clamorousness, and they have no difficulty in smiling down with benign indifference on the nice and peaceful natives. Of course, we could also create guerilla mayhem in utterly vulnerable isolated white outposts if we chose to do so. But our tribe response to attack has in recent times been cautious and muted: wherever possible, we keep out of the way.

"My son, sadly, the undeclared objective of this conflict has always been to deprive the indigenous inhabitants of their resources: territory, water, wildlife, fish, language, religion, even our children."

I admit to being very proud of my Tlingit heritage. Our traditions and stories and art forms are cultural aspects I respect and admire in the ancient teachings, though I recognize they can never be mine in this modern Anglo world, nor should many of them be retained in the presence of many life-saving modern scientific discoveries . . . some advanced, but many retrograde to man . . . without knowledge of the negatives of their new technical developments. I'm no Anglophobe . . . I just have no interest in converting to their distorted view of nature, the nexus which spawns from their bible which, to me, is more self-serving to man and written by man . . . with little inspiration by "divinity."

There are plenty of people from my own Western tradition who would tell me I've got it backward, that the land and places belong to people rather than the other way around. The government, after all, claims most land in this region as the Tongass *National* Forest. Understanding that, I think of the story told by Mary Kancewidk in her essay "Of Two Minds" that opens the anthology *From the Island's Edge:* The story about the testimony of the late Tlingit leader Austin Hammond at a public hearing in 1984 about Native land claims in Alaska:

> "The Tlingit elder travels to the meeting to present his people's deed, as recorded on a ceremonial blanket of his Sockeye Salmon Clan. The blanket has been passed from generation to generation in an unbroken line, this history of the land and its people woven into mountain goat wool, from a time before the

Puritans' first Thanksgiving. His granddaughter holds the blanket for him, translating his Tlingit words. Her grandfather tells how the Tlingit land was formed, how Raven made the waters, how the trees and plants came to be, how the people realized their kinship with the sockeye salmon, how the rules governing the use of land and waters came of the need to protect that kinship. Her grandfather shows how the Tlingit people and their land and its resources continued as one for thousands of years, continues to this day. Her father says, *'You say this is your land. Where are your stories?'"*

"Hammond's question is echoed many times a week in my mind, too: the connection between place and culture, and my concern for our species. The paradox that turns inside the concept of belonging, the possibility of taking possession or being possessed . . . these cultural attitudes shape the place we live. Our sensibilities determine what kind of inhabitants we are, and how long the natural community survives. Here I sit, blessed, before the horizon-wide landscape of mountains and glaciers and forests and waters—powerful, indifferent, complex, staggering, sublime. Its vast wildness breathed a fundamental question: What is the appropriate relationship between human beings and the land? The notion had never struck me so starkly or been so compelling. For the first time, my imagination stumbled over the possibility that the boundaries of my life might be defined and supported by the earth itself as much as by other people, and I found myself dreaming of being steadied by those tangible realities embodied in the land."

"I see what you mean, Dad, the poison of "progress" has continued even in the twenty-first century; the war goes on: more land is being stolen today, children are being pressed into alien schools, and a white man's world is offered as a panacea for all ills. Surely, Indian politics have re-emerged from their more forceful posture in the late 1900s. Hasn't "Redpower" caused a little flurry of excitement; aren't there ever-increasing native-rights organizations?"

"True, my son, but meanwhile the economies of the world are losing a vital element of their independence, too: an inordinate belief in ever more growth, newer and better opportunities for all, has weakened old treaties. Let me explain. In our particular case: wood products. Instead of too much, as in the 1900s, there is now too little lumber available to the industrial nations; both Anglo and Asian building needs has accelerated forest stripping. Developers rush to our lands with a new justice to serve their corporate needs, and we are not ready to yield to *their* needs to our established territories, rights to our culture, and *control* of resources left to us through treaties based on eminent domain.

"So, there is part of your answer, my son; our clan stays on the land to preserve the pure form of tribal life in the forest sanctuaries, where our idea of tradition is the formaldehyde in which to preserve what we like about our chosen life.

"My son, we are surrounded by changes that we are yet to see. And we are accustomed to its insidious forms—the stifling of our own cultures and other societies, cruelty to our people, indifference to the elderly, and the killing of our environment. One hope for us all is that the Indian voice, your voice, will continue to be heard."

Silence hung its cloak over the tribe as they reflected on Chi Mukwa's words explaining their reasons for maintaining their tribal sanctuary in the Tongass. In the center of the group sat Gete Wabiska, who slowly turned his head to look at the assembled clan. His face was wide and deeply lined by many moons of experience; even in the darkness the lines were remarkable—great bands of parallel creases that ran from temple to jawbone. It was a sculpted face, but always reflected a watchful, attentive, and welcoming expression. He rolled into a half-kneeling position; then with a decisive precision spoke:

> "Perhaps young people do not understand,
> perhaps some people of all ages do not want to understand.
> The time has come for the Tlingit Nation, for all Indians, to insist on the land, the right to its use, and the right to protect it.
> The land.
> Using the land in the proper way, is inseparable from the people who live here.
> We have no plans to be the penultimate clan of the Tongass."

It was clear, finally and unequivocally, from the way that everyone around that dark campfire listened, from the respectful stillness, from their occasional grunted agreements, that Gete Wabiska spoke with the wisdom of a sage, an experienced elder, a leader . . . not as an old man. He finished what he had to say, and once again, as in the past, passed the torch of leadership, with a warmhearted look to his apparent successor, Chi Mukwa, who rose, and without a sound acknowledged his father, and signaled an end to the evening's events.

As the clan slowly departed the council fire, Chinoodin spoke to his father. "As part of our task to know what's happening in our forest, are we now ready to move on to the headwaters of the Bitterroot and examine the damage to the sacred burial site of our forefathers?"

"I leave in the morning, my son; be at my side at dawn to receive instructions for you will be in charge of the clan in my absence. I will tell Gete Wabiska of my plans and ask if he has had any additional visions before I start out. The young wolf, Sitka, will be my companion. Good night, my son."

*   *   *

Earlier debates reflected the intensity and nature of American Indian society. This debate turned on a central and deceptively simple issue: did or did not the Indian occupants have a way of life that deserved to be respected? In another and later idiom, this becomes a question about whether or not the Indians have a proper social and economic system that European colonists must legally and morally respect. Many who had a wealth of first-hand experience of Indian tribal life argued that they did have a system, and that it should be respected. Others who had never been to the New World argued from first principles and on the basis of universal laws of reason and religion, said that they did not have any such system or rights, and therefore could only benefit from their Christian myth and control—even if it amounted to enslavement. Obviously, Puritanism, with its "planting" agrarian base, would be entirely at odds with the "hunter's" way of life.

In the course of this debate's long history, advocates on behalf of Indians and other "savages" included several figures of immense standing, among them J. R. Rousseau and Carl Marx. These great men were impressed by their social systems. The enthusiasm for the Noble Savage during the Enlightenment had a great deal to do with a vision of simple freedom and a life far removed from degeneracies and hypocrisy of the Europeans. It had very little to do with a resolve that any particular Noble Savages be left their land and economic system.

Again, hear the Sage J. R. Rousseau, who in 1750 wrote:

> "The American Savages who go naked and live entirely on the products of the chase have always been impossible to subdue. What yoke, indeed, can be imposed on men who stand in need of nothing?"

While resting on his tentless bedroll on layers of sweet smelling Hemlock boughs, Chinoodin gazed at the star-studded sky. In the wonder of it all, he contemplated his future role in the Tlingit's tribal world in the Tongass, versus countless additional opportunities available in the modern world ... elsewhere. The decision would be difficult, but it would have to made soon ... would it be with his heart for his needs, for his tribal needs, for his obligation to his father's needs ... or the best for *his* future needs.

"Manitou, my spiritual leader, I'll soon need your counsel."

Perched above the young warrior a placid raven observed the scene below as if it understood the burden of the young man's thoughts.

Chapter 28

Night Music

Leigh heard a sound, listened carefully, raised her head toward the source, and closed her eyes to shut out extraneous noises. Was it The Spirits of the forest speaking, speaking a thousand little sounds among the musical pine boughs . . . dancing in the evening breeze, or, The Voices of the Wind? What was it? The timbre? Its distinctive tone appeared to be carrying a musical message across the boughs on the distant ridge line. She wondered what familiar melody was impacting her senses, her mind, her soul. She was in her private place, her secret place, seeking solace and reflection of the week's events. She sought aloneness—not a wood Satyr with his flute or harp. The sound abated; she paused, took a deep breath, savored her time alone with Tough, then inhaled deeply again the night's beauty . . . grateful for this moment of reflection . . . of thankfulness, her victory over death's grasp.

Alone, yes, somewhat unusual, and discomforting, due to The White having wandered off earlier in the day, and had not been seen all afternoon. No problem, both of the wolves have taken to exploring over the last few weeks; so far, they both returned without incident.

"There it is again . . . my god, it sounds familiar, like Bach's 'Jesu, Joy of Man's Desiring.' How could this be? What games are being played in my mind? Leigh, settle down. It must be mind over matter? Dang! It is one of my favorite songs."

She mused, "Grandma played that song at Christmas while dressed to the nines in her finest . . . normally her choice was a classic guitar by the then-young Spaniard, Carlos Segovia. Now the hands of the Spaniard somehow were recreating Bach in the pine-bough cathedral of this dark secret place . . . but why? Why?"

She felt her heart unfolding to the richness of her youth, and held Tough closer. "Fella, you're my squeeze tonight," she murmured.

Indeed, it was the most beautiful music she had ever heard. What was happening in the forest . . . on this particular night?

She opened her eyes and softly sang the chorus:

"Jesu, joy of man's desiring,

Holy wisdom, love most bright;
Drawn by Thee, our souls aspiring
Soar to uncreated light . . ."

She faced toward the sound of the music, then got up with Tough at her side and moved to the source of the mystery.

"Come, Tough. Come on . . . let's follow the music. Come. Come on, what's wrong? All right, tag along behind me later if you choose, but don't let the music bother you, dear. It's probably just an abstraction of my confused, lonely mind, or the gods truly whispering in the wind to announce an event of significance or, maybe, nothing; but one thing is certain: I'm following the origin of Bach's finest."

She moved out of her secluded, secret place. While following the music, she slid down a moderate slope, slowly approached an aspen thicket, listened, then went down on her knees, looked into the dense thicket, found a small entry hole, lay on her stomach to penetrate the protecting brush, and crawled into a small opening, a small lair, a temporary den.

She gasped, and froze in place.

The music hushed . . . then suddenly fell mute.

She stared at an awesome site—the reason for the music.

Hot tears stung her eyelids; her vision held the arrival of the creator's rendering of the future . . . a mother wolf, The White—suckling a coal black cub. The doctrine of the forest, of Manitou, had manifested itself tonight as it had occurred over the eons of time past . . . to time present.

Leigh spoke softly, "Good girl, you've a beautiful surprise for us. Good girl. I'm as proud as can be . . . bet you're even prouder. Are you okay? Need anything? Oh, Leigh, shape up; she knows what to do. She doesn't need a human midwife."

She lingered quietly, lovingly, and reverently remained with the mother and son. The music did not continue . . . it had served its purpose. It had announced the cub's arrival . . . through the mysterious voices in the Wind. Why Bach? She may never know, but it's certain someone did. Bach's "Jesu . . ." music was to announce the birth of "Emmanuel." The allegory to the cub was obvious. Contrasting with limited or restricted Christian myth, their canon of the ancient disciples, Manitou embraced all creatures in nature as equals, forgoing Egypto-Semitic biblical canon that man was dominant and nature subservient. It worked for her, someone—Manitou—knew her thoughts. Scary, but true.

After Leigh pet both mother and the jet-black moist cub with its shiny cold black nose, temporarily blind, the reluctant cub continued his search for an even faster-flowing teat. With all appearing well, and mother in total control, Leigh slowly backed out of the thicket, while The White finished eating her afterbirth and the little jet-black cub kept pushing mom with his nose to stimulate her mammary glands. Slowly exiting, she backed into the now-inquisitive Tough. There he was, waiting patiently by the entrance, his now-obvious front-row nosy presence not unexpected, not a surprise; his casual air belied his excited body language.

"Hi, fella. You knew, didn't you? That's why you were reluctant to come with me ... you knew, too. I was the only one outside the 'loop,' you stinker. Guess what? I've got a name for that little fella; yes, I know, he's already peed on me from the bottom ... not the rear. What do you think of 'Jet?' He's jet black with a little white star on his chest and four white stockings ... if you agree, it's done. Just think, we'll soon have a gray, white, and black pack running over the ridge lines in the Tongass as if they owned the forest. I can see it now; it's beautiful ... but, slow down, girl; Jet is not even a day old.

Caw-Caw-Caw ... caw ... caw ... caw.

A raven's repetitive, ringing, resonant cry echoed across the ridge lines and down to the campsite below. The bird's posture appeared as if he was staying with the new mother and cub.

"Just as I thought, we have not been alone. The raven's presence is always near when a significant drama unfolds in His Kin(g)dom. Good evening, Mr. Raven; welcome to our recent birthing, 'it's the greatest show on earth,' as if you didn't already know. Nice to see a sentinel at their side."

She felt like a mother, too, sharing the pride of The White. After all, Leigh was her mistress, her trainer, her keeper ... while remaining with her and Tough in camp. True, half-tame, and half-wild, The White gave signals of commitment to Leigh that she was clearly her companion. Yes, she would share the wonder of the Creator's blessing: the birth. They would celebrate very soon and give thanks to Manitou together.

For all Leigh knew, Tough may have been the "Papa." No, wolf gestation is about 63 days. No, not likely, she'd only been in camp about a week. She was well along in her pregnancy when helping to rescue Leigh at the cave-in on the plateau. Yep, she may have joined Leigh and Tough most likely in anticipation of the birth. Having only one cub, probably the first, it may have been due to her rejection by the pack for whatever reason, poor nutrition, and being on the run for months. Nevertheless, The White appeared to be doing well. Leigh not only acted like a new mom, she felt blessed—more like a grandmother ... with no late-night feeding.

As her German grandma so frequently said at these happy birthing times,

> "Was Gott tut, das ist wohligetan,"
> (What God has done is rightly done.)

"Come, Tough, let's return to camp; we'll lay back for a while to see what she plans to do with the cub. I'll bet you she brings the cub down to the hut soon. We'll see. Let's go, she'll be just fine. She now knows that we know. I'll build a shelter, a natural lean-to near the hut. She'll find it; I know she will. In fact, I'll bet she'll be wandering around the hut tonight, checking things out. Isn't it joyful, boy? The joy of birth provides an added texture you can feel; feels damn good, doesn't it, boy?"

Leigh and Tough continued their delightful walk toward the hut, following their new-found bliss. While walking along the Bitterroot, she recalled that both Jack and Andrew had mentioned a Tlingit ceremonial birthing rite: a chant, she thought, performed to honor a new arrival and thankful praise to Manitou for the gift of life.

Arrangements for honoring the cub could be accomplished, but in her tongue, not the natives' structure. It would happen tonight. She had been involved in enough ceremonial chants of thanksgiving with Andrew to know the basic Tlingit rhythm to attract Manitou's witness . . . however, afterward, her message of gratitude would be in the King's English with a slight Midwestern drawl. One way or another, her message would be offered. Heard. But, she felt it would be satisfying for her to express her thoughts to the Creator.

Dang, how to prepare, how to go about the process of thanks. Then she remembered a fireside chat by Andrew less than a week ago, by the Bitterroot at midnight, as he praised the Creator for their union . . . how well she remembered.

It came to her like a tsunami . . . Andrew's words were clear; he stated that Native American Indians were clearly pluralistic, had no one religion any more than they had one way of life or one language. But, certain religious beliefs were widespread. Most important was the belief in the mysterious force in nature. They considered this unseen spirit power superior to human beings and capable of influencing their lives, similar to the varied Judeo-Christian myths. People depended on these spiritual myths for success in the search for food, the wonder of birth, and in healing the sick, as well as victory in battle.

Leigh recalled how Andrew revealed with blinding clarity that he knew whereof he sings when contacting and honoring the Creator through ceremony. She learned that the power might be centered in an animal, a sacred place, inanimate things, making all of nature powerful, and likewise dangerous. Various tribes had a name for the particular spirit in their tradition: Iroquois = Orenda; Sioux = Wakonda; and *many* revere Manitou, but the god belief was always accompanied by a belief in many other spirits, too. Behavior patterns varied with separate tribes; some groups greatly feared the ghosts of the dead, with a prohibition against pronouncing the decedent's name during mourning. Leigh paused, thinking thank goodness I'm not that structured. But, she did know that few gave much thought to life after death, or the fantasy of "heaven." She did believe in a personal spiritual helper called a guardian spirit. As with many younger tribal youths, they went through an initiation ceremony until they saw a vision of their guardian spirit through a "vision quest," . . . abusing themselves, if necessary, to bring a vision. She felt her quest was, in fact, her move to Alaska—and her quest had been fulfilled—with far too many traumatic events. She was now ready for a rest—no more quests. Ceremonies honoring the cub's birth, fine, but no more trauma . . . please.

At times, over the last two months, she felt that her "quest," her "experience," had sucked much of her emotional "blood" . . . leaving very little energy to survive . . . but survive, she will.

The fire had now burned down to a glowing hint of blue, followed by a dash of red on a bed of yellow glimmering base. Both she and the fire were ready to honor the birth.

> "Ana wana ho we, ana wana ho se,
> Gitchee wana ho we, ana wana na te . . . Great Spirit, hear my plea . . .
> It is our understanding, you, the creator, made everything.
> You made everything,
> And, since You made everything, then you must respect everything.
> That's simple.
> As I look upon you, I know that the Creator made me,
> I know that little Jet is an equal.
> He's in every way equal to us.
> I respect him because he is a manifestation of Creation.
> The law says that he must respect us as well.
> In this basic respect is peace.
> That's what's called community.
> I am talking about respect for our people's ways.
> Our land, our language, and our culture.
> We respect community.

> *Silence*

> Great one, I've noticed everything our people do is in a circle, and that is because the Power of the World always works in circles, and everything tries to be round . . . Everything, the Power of the World does is in a circle. Jet chooses to join the circle of

life.

Even the seasons form a great circle in their changing, and always come back again to where they were.

The life of a man and a wolf is a circle from their beginnings and so it is in everything where Power Moves.

We praise you for giving us little Jet, and will bless this event and welcome him to our circle of life. . . ."

Caw—Caw—Caw . . . *Caw—Caw—Caw*, cried a raven across the northern ridge line.

Silence slowly but surely embraced the meadow.

The moon peered over the horizon.

The flickering fire reflected on the celebrants' faces as it slowly extinguished into the night.

The last sounds of the night were the popping cork from a liter of a commemorative 1996 dry white Chardonnay, and Leigh exclaiming, "A toast to your health, Jet; may happiness and joy be yours through life. Welcome!"

Chapter 29

Discovery

Taking a few steps, then hesitating for long minutes to watch and listen, Sikta and I move at a pace only slightly faster than no pace at all. My senses become increasingly engaged, warming up like a runner's muscles. Beside the trail I notice that most of the dainty twigs on a huckleberry bush are pruned to nubs, evidence of deer browsing during last winter's heavy snows. Faint chitters reveal a mob of white-winged crossbills among the boughs high over head, prying seeds from spruce cones and unleashing a shower of flaky brown scales.

Today's excursion started at first light when I stashed enough gear and food for several days, and eased away from camp with Sitka. Leaving my son to help clan winterizing activities will be good for him. I set course to the plateau near the collapsed burial vault, and felt a bit lonely going off without Chinoodin, but he needs the experience in a leadership role by replacing me in camp while I'm gone. I will miss traveling with him, but Sitka has an impeccably sharp eye for animals, whether hunting or being hunted; she loves "still hunting" in a truly meditative, patient style, especially well disciplined for a young wolf handled by man.

As I gaze at the tall timber and the infinity beyond their zenith, I recognize how minute and vulnerable I am—alone—on this remote planet. But I willingly accept the risks, and regardless of consequences, I'd rather be here than anywhere else on Earth . . . Manitou watches over me.

Many times I've yearned to own some part of this land, although it's public and rightly belongs to everyone; this morning I realized the equation is in fact reversed, that the land owns *me*. To this, I freely yield myself.

A buck appeared from the shadows. A mere second after release, the thud of impact echoed through the darkness and over the land's edge. His vertical jump is followed by a circular race through the thicket as he dashes to and fro to escape the impact to his burning lungs. However, it will not happen, there will be no escape, no relief; the arrow is tearing his lung tissue with each stride, hop, jump, and twist. It is shredding his lungs apart as he tries to escape the hunter's razor sharp clovis point on the shaft. Blood is now flowing into his trachea as he wretches for air . . . but is slowly drowning in his own blood as the lungs are being destroyed.

At one-hundred meters, there is a burst and a shock and a jarred half vision of the deer's fall, as if he were completely released, like a marionette whose strands have all been cut at once.

I stand, breathing heavily, and move in a deliberate yet cautious manner toward the empty place between the pines with Sitka bounding alongside. She reaches the spot before me, circles, and snuffles the soft edges of the buck. He lies on a mat of crowberry and bog laurel—soft and quiet and midnight-still—as if the forest had instantly grown calm. At first I hear only silence. Then I hear my heart pounding and the ringing in my ears, and finally Sitka panting at my side, the swashing of wind in the high boughs, the distant howl of wolves.

I kneel beside the deer and touch his warm, sightless eye to affirm the certainty of death. Then I run my hand along his flank, whispering words of thanks that seem inadequate and frail against what I've been given here—a life that will enter and sustain my own. Beaded raindrops roll down over the dry, brittle fur.

Sitka prances back and forth excitedly, looking in all directions for another deer, as if animals fascinate her only when they're running or might do so. I hold her by my side, rub her fur, and nuzzle her wet face. The deer is a prime, heavy, thick-coated buck, bearing modest but lovely antlers, their axe-handle beams stained dark maroon at the base, fading to polished gray on each side of the six elegantly tapered points. I will leave them here, although it's not hard to understand why someone might hang them on a living-room wall. After dragging the buck to a nearby tree, I fasten a rope around both forelegs, loop it over a branch, then hoist the animal off the ground. With my knife, I sever the neck and spinal cord, then make a shallow incision, slightly longer than my arm, down the middle of the deer's belly, being careful not to puncture its stomach, which would foul the inside with spilled contents. Next I reach up into the hot, moist cavity to pull out the stomach, intestines, and fatty mesenteries, leaving the heart, liver, and kidneys in place. Sitka nudges close, trying to lick the blood that drips down, but I shoo her away out of respect for the animal. Later on, when we butcher the deer, Sitka will have her share of scraps.

I take some fat from inside the body, plus a few slivers of meat, and leave them with the viscera for the other animals. It's important, Gete Wabiska (Old White) our shaman, would say, that wild creatures feed on remnants left in the woods by hunters, but other than small tidbits, nothing should be abandoned except parts we can't use ourselves. The eagles and ravens will come at first light tomorrow and within an hour they'll clean up everything but the skull bones and intestinal contents.

I tie the front and rear legs together so I can carry the deer as if it were a pack, putting my arms through the fastened legs and hoisting it up so the animal's belly lies against my back.

With darkness upon us, I start the final trudge to the plateau, Sitka dancing alongside, perhaps anticipating tonight's dinner. No doubt I'll cut a few pieces of fresh venison to fry atop a fire on a stick—the most delicious and elemental feast I can imagine, making the deer a part of me.

In the last stretch of river before sighting the plateau, I put my load in the river and rest before climbing. Sitka slumps against me, finally getting tired. But she perks up a few minutes later when a large doe moves out from the trees and steps to the water's edge, nervously switching her tail. She reaches down and drinks . . . as if I'm one of them.

Moments later, upon arriving at the top of the plateau in total darkness, our plans change. I give Sitka some choice cuts of raw venison, throw the tent up quickly, hoist the deer to a branch of a large tree, and bed down with Sitka at my side.

Awake in my sleeping blanket, I stare into the black fissure of night, listening to raindrops flail against the tent, gusts hissing in the treetops, and wolves howling across the valley floor.

I assure myself that tomorrow's exploration of the collapsed vault and meeting with the pretty red-haired Anglo lady will be uneventful and routine . . . I hope.

Sleep comes quickly to the pair as the denizens of the forest lie low in the rain-soaked night.

*   *   *

Silence.

Eyes blink.

Tired muscles and strained back remind him of the previous day's activities. His eyes open at first light.

The wolf remains in place, still weary of the chase.

The first thing he hears is the absolute silence. The normal morning's presence is not. Something has changed. The absence of sound is deafening.

He muses . . . plateaus, like this one, elevated above the forest, are always busy, always have some sound, always in motion at dawn: a rustle of leaves dancing in the slightest breeze, the echo of a raven's cry at distance, a scurrying mouse returning from his nocturnal hunt . . . searching for the entrance to his lair. Something. Subtle, yes, but something.

Big Bear (Chi Mukwa) bolts upward to a sitting position, noting the chill in the air, then rolls back the deer-hide pelt of his bedroll, grabs his sheathed knife as a matter of habit, and crawls around totally zonked young wolf Sitka. He opens the tent's woven cedar-fiber door flap slowly, and carefully stretches his head out to survey the Earth's newly found silence.

Early Morning Nautical Twilight (EMNT), with the sun just under the horizon, is ready to burst the mask of night, already creating a glow in the sky of pink-to-yellow as the planet rotates and orbits around the Earth's star, the Sun, our source of heat and light.

Shadows from the Earth's Moon, now settling over the horizon, are being replaced by the longer shadows to the west . . . impacting across the plateau's sparkling surface. The earth is now covered with the first virginal snow of the year . . . untouched by man.

"Beautiful. Thank you, Manitou. You've taken my breath away again; there seems to be no limit in your ability to enhance the wonder of the Earth we share."

Big Bear decides to lie back awhile and not rush into the first day of winter's snow. There'd be time to perform the reconnaissance when the sun was higher in the sky, soon to be warmed by early-morning rays. Another hour or two of rest would help repair the strained muscles of the previous day's activities.

He could also use this time for meditation—meditation necessary for awakening genuine compassion in his heart, which would allow him to see more than just obstacles in today's tasks at the collapsed burial site. His first step is to develop compassion for his own wounds and shortcomings so he can take on the suffering of others; he believed that unconditional compassion for ourselves leads naturally to unconditional compassion for others. He had been taught that if he is willing to fit fully in his own skin, and never give up, then he will be able to comprehend the skin of those oppressed, and not give up on their misfortune, which would ultimately lead to mutual kinship with all beings. Most important, if the Woman-With-Red-Hair was involved with violation of the burial site, it would be essential to put these practices into play for mediating inevitable frustrations and difficulties during his inspection. The proper method of unconditional compassionate giving, allowing a lot of space to relax, to be open, was his goal.

Old White (Gete Wabiska), the clan's shaman, had spent many an hour by the camp fire teaching these principles. This had been especially important in his past dealings with the white men, who frequently found themselves in conflict with Native American openness . . . and had no idea of living an open life . . . too often, they lived in the darkness of deceit, leading to misunderstandings.

This time for meditation will serve him well.

"Relax . . . Woman-with-Red-Hair may be like a drifting cloud that only temporarily obscures the sun. Relax. It may take only one blink of the eye to resolve this incident. Remember . . . there's richness in all of the Creator's beings . . . Woman-with-Red-Hair, too."

He relaxed while looking up at the frost-covered cedar-fiber tent interior, reminding him of a similar setting with his girlfriend, Wilma, now his wife, Morning Star (Wabun Ahnung). His mind wandered back to several years ago when they were walking his trap line up north near White Horse and the weather turned bad. "It was dark and we didn't want to take the risk of the long trip back to camp. We were cold and tired and didn't know what we were doing, and God knows where we were. Then we found a hollow where the wind had blown around a stump and we took off our snowshoes and burrowed into the open pocket under the snow. Then we crawled in; it was quiet and completely dark. Wilma lit a candle, and oh my . . . we lay back in awe. It was as if Manitou had guided or provided us to this cathedral encrusted with diamonds. The air was still and the wind was very faint out above the snow. I curled into her arms . . . and melted as if one being. We made love for the first time, out-of-doors, in a snow cave. We made love, again. As we made love, our breath formed a thick crust on the snow. Then we slept the most beautiful, peaceful sleep. When Wilma woke up she never thought of San Francisco as her home again, and she gave her heart to me and Alaska. Undaunted by my concerns, at midnight she insisted on her eyes searching the silent pristine Alaskan expanse. Her first words, 'look, a morning star.'"

She has since been with him for many nights as Morning Star (Wabun Ahnung). That night, and all the following nights have been no less than that first night in nature's natural wonders. He loved Morning Star very much, and wished for the warmth of her body tonight. She never mentioned San Francisco again, marrying Big Bear in a beautiful and very spiritual Native American ceremony, for she loved both Big Bear, Alaska, and the Tlingit Clan's primitive lifestyle.

Their son, Big Wind (Chinoodin), was born the following autumn. At eighteen, he is now heir-apparent to the Clan, having developed into a fine, self-sufficient young man.

He remembered several revealing conversations during their courtship. She was not uncertain of her decision, but did not understand that much about Native Americans or Tlingits. However, her candor was refreshing, saying, "Big Bear, I know enough to know . . . that I know very little. I know enough to know that a person can't make assumptions."

He chuckled at some of Star's comments about Alaska, especially since at some point it becomes subject to one's interpretation on some questions . . . or would it be the answers? One of the most time-consuming questions asked in this part of the country involves where the "real Alaska" is. Most of the people living north of Skagway consider southeastern Alaska to be a suburb of San Francisco, inhabited by drug-addled phonies and the bureaucrats, with a few loggers and fishermen holding on against all odds. The phonies and the bureaucrats have an image of the modern white (Watuchie) resident of the north as a 300-pound Texas building contractor with a 20-pound gold-nugget watchband and an antebellum attitude toward the darker races. Anchorage falls in the middle of this mess.

For example, Anchorage grew up too fast to keep pace with its ability to dress itself properly. Today its buildings mostly resemble monumental subarctic toasters, all reflective surfaces to "steal" the beauty of the surrounding landscape.

Big Bear and Morning Star embraced the beauty of the Tongass and the primitive lifestyle of the Tlingit Clan. Anchorage and the capital, Juneau, were places to visit—not to live in.

"As long as Sitka still appears to be in dreamland, I'll lay back awhile and await her first stirring from what appears to be the sound of a deer chase or a bear being treed. Plus, butchering and hoisting the deer cache tore a few muscles."

A raven's flight over the small hovel on the plateau is masked by winter's first blanket of snow, but raven, the trickster, knows who is in the covered tent, and their purpose . . . Gitchee Manitou knows the intentions of all the denizens of the forest.

*   *   *

The meadow, hut, and river sounds appear to be lessened, altered, quieter.

The sleeping pair in the hut have yet to sense the silence.

The silence is broken; someone, something is stirring.

The first sound is a whimper. Or is it a whine? Or is it a subtle growl? Leigh rolls over to get a better look at Tough. As if by command, they both lock eyes at the same time. And as if in a Yoga class, they rotate their heads simultaneously to the continuing sound at the door, staring at the noise and rotating their eyes back to each other, as if to say . . . "What's that?" The sound is now augmented by a cadence like scratching, one stroke-two strokes-one stroke-two strokes . . . Again, as if in a Yoga move/position, they creep to the door; Tough, in a slow aggressive/offensive crouch; Leigh slowly, too, while throwing on a three-quarter terrycloth cover-up. Both stop at the door and listen as if silent witnesses to an ongoing mystery. Puzzled, they look a each other again. . . .

Tough's nose is first to reveal the identity of the guest. He looks at Leigh and their eyes lock on each other again. He knows. His neck hairs relax from stiffness, and his tail comes up wagging. His mouth opens, tongue out . . . all the indications of open friendliness.

"What is it, boy? Do you know who's come to call?"

Knowing the answer, too, she repeats the question. "I've an idea. Don't you?"

Anxious, Tough leaps up on the door and rests both paws on the door latch.

"Okay, okay, boy, we'll let 'em in . . . you and I both know it's The White and the cub, Jet, who with The White's decision has come to join us at the hut. Wanna bet? She knows she'll be welcome, and for sure the cub will be in better hands with 'Grandma' Leigh. Come on, Tough, hang back a little so I can open the door. Thank you, sir."

"What! Well I'll be darned!"

The giants of the forest and the mountains are staring down on her like Gods.

They are both shocked by the changed landscape of the Tongass. In a hurry to get to the door, she did not notice that winter's first snowfall had blanketed the trees and the mountains. This is beautiful. She now notices the absolute quiet. Wind is absent. Sound is absent. Movement is absent. It's so quiet, no wonder they heard the little one and mom "knocking" on their door.

Sure enough, both the mother and young cub sat on the doorstep in the snow, with a pair of tracks leading from their birthing den. Here they sit, picturesque as a greeting card awaiting their friends in the hut to answer the door. Jet is a little more restless, more hesitant for sure, since he's just along for the ride. His interests are simple, mom's teats and warm body . . . wherever the nipples reside. Being uprooted from the primitive lair in the bush, Jet acts as though he just wants to get away from this cold/white/wet stuff underfoot.

"Well, Tough, it looks as though we have company, a little before we had planned. It's okay by me, how 'bout you?"

As wolves usually greet, The White and Tough lick each other's snout, then sniff butts with equal vigor, both erect, since the alpha leader is not established yet.

Unencumbered by this protocol, Jet ran into the hut between Tough's legs, jumped on the familiar smell of Tough's ragged bed, and lay down.

"Tough, it looks like we're going to have company, and it could be permanent if Jet has his way. Look at him; he's already moving the rags around your 'bed' to fit his little body . . . and, look at that, there goes the White, too. Nursing now, The White looks up at Leigh with a look of resolve that, indeed, they are taking over this portion of the hut . . . at Tough's and her expense.

"Look at her, boy, she knows it has been a sudden takeover, and she is humbled. Can you see it?"

While the "squatters" continued their necessary chores, with Tough now lying on the floor, Leigh bounded around the hut doing her morning chores. Dressing for the new landscape, she threw on an old pair of boots, then rounded up her beat-up Michigan sweatshirt, Mackinaw, and Pluto hat with floppy ear protectors. She thought of the wolves charging into the virgin snow while exploring heretofore unseen animal tracks, private entrances to ground squirrels, and precariously perched song birds. They too would be displaced.

She had seen it time and time again . . . the birds would gather their last bit of reserve, leap in the air to escape the charging duo, fly to the evergreens by the river, find an old thick cedar tree, wiggle into the middle of the thick branches, lock feet onto a limb, puff up feathers until looking like a ball, then lower down until its scraggly legs were covered. A very welcome feeling of warmth would spread all over. It was all worth it . . . to escape the charging wolves. Nodin's (the wind) gentle rocking of the limbs brought on a deep peace. The bird then put its head under one wing and falls asleep most likely with plans to remain until the morning's sun warmed the little body through the cedar's branches.

The new vistas in depths previously unseen is exciting to anticipate, for Nature's blanket of snow has a dramatic cleansing affect; colder, but bolder revelations in Nature's macroenvironment, smothering the micro.

"Here, Tough, chomp on a couple of yesterday's breakfast biscuits. I'm anxious to get out and explore. Here's one for you White, and the last one for me. Okay, okay . . . kinda thrown at you like at the greasy-spoon, it is; I'll make up for it tomorrow. At least they're palatable; I've had some that needed a coffee soak. Anyway, these will be good for your teeth. No coffee today, either; got to get going before the denizens beat us to the virgin flakes."

The White gives Leigh the 'look' of: Me, too? Can I go? I need a break. Jet had just finished his morning meal and was laid-out like a little black round ball, legs extended at right angles from four points. He appeared to have little interest in going anywhere except dreamland. The White stood in place on the bed, awaiting an invitation to explore with Leigh and Tough.

"How's this look, boy? Yo 'Mamma' is ready to explore with cool boots, Paul Bunyan-like winter jacket, and Pluto hat . . . are you ready? Hey, White, with your cub, Jet, long gone; why don't you come along, too?"

White's tail reacted; she made a quick check with her nose of the snoring black ball with little legs, looked at Tough, then Leigh, and they all moved to the door.

The opening door pushed aside the top crust of snow.

Gone!

Neither touched the landing or the stairs as they leaped to the newly fallen snow; both fell ass-over-teakettle, recovered, and raced away in the glittering snow shining like a million diamonds. As she swept the area clear of snow, she noticed that not a single track appeared near the hut, stacked fire wood, or the path to the ridge; the snow's silence seemed to affect the denizens equally . . . sleep in. The only signs of activity were pine-cone husks—cast-off, dropped by the ever-present, always-gnawing, pesky squirrel as he sought the cone's tender germ at the base. It was a mess.

"Hey, you up there, don't be so messy at the dinner table; shuck your cones elsewhere. My porch is a mess," she exclaimed with humor.

"Tough, Tough! Come on in, let's go down to the river. Tough!"

She moved toward the meadow for a better view of the ridgeline in its awesome splendor, and noticed what appeared to be Tough's and The White's tracks.

They had already been to the river, probably for a drink; she was uncertain, but they were now headed out to the meadow, most likely to raise havoc with the ptarmigans, rabbits, and innocent song birds—all minding their own business, waiting for the warmth of the morning's sun, only to be shocked by the presence of stampeding horde, the wolves on the run over the earth's newly fallen blanket of snow. The snow revealed the birds' former hiding spots, so they took action and flew away rather than complain too much, most likely planning to return later that morning.

"Tough!"

The wolves' departure did not bother her too much, for she was enjoying the visual clarity of the day, plus the majestic snow-covered mountains in the distance; seldom noticed in the other seasons as they normally blend into a pallet of yellow-green-red-to-brown kaleidoscope as spring and summer yields to autumn, and the multicolored paint brush captures the landscape.

While following the wolves' tracks, she thought of the dramatic changes winter's storms and snowfall would bring to the Tongass and her activities, now restricted by the snowfall and colder temperatures. Thankfully, grizzlies hibernate.

"So this is what to expect for the next six months. From what I've heard, this four inches is just a 'dusting' of snow compared to the four to six feet mid-winter will bring. That's okay. I'll need more indoor quiet time by then, time to restore this old body, time to reflect, time to contemplate the future; I've certainly been on the fast-track so far this year—too fast a track—it's time to slow down. It's time to write about some of those exciting and not so pleasant encounters with Alaskan two- and four-legged animals."

After meandering all over the meadow, undoubtedly disrupting every peaceful resident, the wolves' tracks appear to halt at the edge of the meadow next to the ridge line leading to the plateau. It seems as though there is a lot of turning, backtracking, prancing, and false starts in several directions, and finally both pairs of tracks seem to explode up the ridge line to the plateau.

In deeper snow on the lee side of the ridge, she followed the tracks in the two-foot bulwark of flakes. She struggled and slipped with limbs and small brush helping her up the slippery slope. Halfway up the ridge she heard a yipping sound . . . silence, and then a growling sound . . . more silence, and then a louder more aggressive bark combined with an eerie howling. Then, the troubling silence.

"I wonder what they've found? Certainly sounds interesting."

Then, Leigh thought she'd better be careful; hazards appear suddenly.

"Hold on!" she yelled. "I'll be there in a minute—hold on!"

The next sound she heard was a shock, and quite unexpected.

"Down girl, back . . . settle down Sitka, come back!" someone said.

Leigh froze in place.

She sensed that someone was on the plateau; it sounded like the voice of a "man." He was calling for something. Puzzled, she listened intently.

More silence.

"Dag nab it! Here we go again. I'd better move on and see what's going on."

*   *   *

Chi Mukwa (Big Bear) had his hands full. Sitka had burst out after the two wolves had found the tent and approached it sniffing and whining, knowing very well what was inside. Big Bear was caught off guard, and Sitka was gone before the sounds of the pair outside the tent awakened him. By the time he got his boots on and fully opened the torn flap completely, the three wolves were running and tumbling while exploring each other. It appeared that aggression was minimal, and the three were doing what all wolves do upon meeting each other. They licked each others' muzzles, sniffed all orifices, growled, chased, and played "pile-on" as if on the goal line. Of course, the alpha leader was not established, so they were quite gentile . . . for now. The gray, Tough; the black, Sitka; and the white, The White, all appeared snow white and full of grass from the plateau's surface. Nevertheless, it did look like a hazard, one you'd avoid by choice . . . after all, these were three fully grown, semi-wild wolves.

"Sitka, come. Come, Sitka! What the heck, there's two of them tussling with her, but apparently not fighting. I wonder if the white and the gray are wild or semi-domesticated—they appear not to be wild. I bet they belong to The-Woman-with-Red-Hair living near the meadow below. I see the vapor/smoke rising from her hut to the south. I might as well hustle and get dressed, break camp, and check in with her first before I start examining things under this blanket of snow. It looks like the elevated cache is secure; I can get it down just before we leave. I'm certain The-Woman-with-Red-Hair will be able to tell me many clues about the horrific damage and the facts leading up to the sacred site's destruction."

He continued folding his sparse supplies into the tent, then folding it into a bundle small enough to fit the rucksack. Now with it secure and tightly packed, he looked for the wolves. "Sitka, come!"

*   *   *

Leigh approached the crest of the plateau while still struggling with her footing—as in two ahead and one back—all the way up the forty-foot-high ridge. As she broke over the crest and onto the plateau . . . she saw him.

It struck her like a bolt of lightning. Except for the blanket of new-fallen snow, it was déjà vu from months past.

She had come across Walkswithwater in a similar manner in the springtime as he visited the Tlingit sacred ceremonial burial site. His visit was part of his responsibility as tribal shaman for the tribe and its forefathers. Unfortunately, a menacing grizzly ended their passionate relationship much too early in his life. His memory still lingered in her heart.

Likewise, she had met his brother Walkswithwind in camp as he sought her with a deeply felt obligation of comforting her sorrow, their mutual loss, and also discover the circumstances of his brother's death. Unfortunately, he too died under extraordinary circumstances in the collapse of the sacred cavern below. Again, she held compassion for him in her heart, too. Maybe the visitor was also checking on both their deaths.

Then, there was the colorful and talkative British subject, Joe Bloom from the DNR by way of Canada, who was a friend of both. After a delightful visit, he departed with the results of his mournful investigation of Walkwithwind's overdue trip. Sadly, he would have to explain his death to the family. At least he survived and is certainly safely back in Skagway or Juneau by now. She wasn't sure, of course, but she had not heard otherwise.

"Well, I'll be darned, this visitor appears to be an Indian, too. I wonder what his interests are. I'll bet he, too, is investigating the collapse/destruction of the Tlingit's sacred burial site . . . right under his feet. Of course, if he's a Tlingit, he knows very well where he stands, and probably wonders by now where the altar is, and what is the cause of the depression where it used to be. I'll bet you a pint of lager I'll soon find out."

She rises above the crest of the ridge, moves onto the plateau, and cautiously approaches the man in native dress.

He senses her presence, stops packing, and turns to face the person coming over the ridge line in a strange hat with flapping ear protectors.

The wolves, rolling over each other in the snow, sense her presence, also. Recovering from their play, they stop and face the person approaching the Indian.

She scans the area, noticing the wolves at bay, the cache in the tree above, and the Indian staring at her.

She speaks first.

"Hello," she exclaims in an appealing tone, "Can I help you?"

As soon as she speaks, they all pause and look above as a silent flock of ravens descend from the thermals to perch on the trees encircling the plateau.

Chapter 30

Veneration

Bête noire was not a forgone conclusion; he was not predisposed to dislike her, but from the stories he'd heard about the The-Woman-with-Red-Hair filtering back to the Clan, both she and Walkswithwind, our brother, were exploring the sacred cavern together. Unfortunately, for some unknown reason, only she escaped unharmed. He would ask some very pertinent questions, but that could wait for the appropriate time. He'd meet her on a genial basis for now, and later on get down to specific questions. Although unlikely, he certainly wanted to know if they disturbed—or took—any of the ancient artifacts. And he certainly wanted to know the status/condition of those items they saw, for no one had been in the cavern for about two-hundred years. He did wonder how much they did see. Her observations and impressions were of value to the entire Clan.

He also wondered what reasons they believed were behind the sudden collapse. Rumors prevailed that it was Manitou's resentment of their actions that triggered the earthquake in a very selective portion of His domain: the plateau. Not knowing where his probative questions would lead, Big Bear would play it by ear, and see how she responded. Many of his doubts about her veracity would be resolved through a wholesome chat.

More important, had Walkswithwind's (Andrew South's) family been informed of his demise; and was his death the reason Joe Bloom from the DNR stopped by last week? Not much happened in the Tongass of which the Clan was unaware.

He could only hope for the best, and from what appeared in front of him she was emerging as no beauty . . . unless the winter garments and unusual 'flapping-eared hat' were concealing it. Nevertheless, not being Native American, she had a lot of Morning Star's attractive facial features.

"Hello. Nice meeting you. I'm Chi Mukwa (Big Bear) and have been anxious to meet you. Did you bring all these ravens with you?"

Leigh immediately relaxed at hearing the pleasant tone of his voice. Her anticipation in meeting him had caused a little tenseness due to her obvious guilt. Guilty. Absolute guilt of exploring the vault with Andrew. True, it was Andy's call to violate his forefathers' resting place, his decision to slip in, take pictures for the Clan, then slip out without disturbing anything. How could he have known a higher power would sense the violation of these sacred grounds, while in progress . . . how could he have known. He just wanted a photo record of the cavern's contents for Clan's records. *How could he have known*; yet, he should have been aware: no reason justified violating the sacred tomb. It sounded so innocent at the time. He thought the elders would understand. They would not disturb or "take" anything. He'd show the photos to the Clan members only.

It was purely accidental in finding the entrance. The White wolf had led them to the cavern's entrance at the head of the stream where the wolf hid, and also rested when evading the hostile pack. It was an accidental happening, just waiting for a major calamity. He should, and she should have known. In reflection, they had had a warning when the whole ridge started to rumble and shake. More guilt. She also knew Andrew made certain she got out before a total collapse. She knew it. He made her leave.

His last task, sealing the tunnel with the blocking boulder, caused the delay; there was just not enough time for both of them to get out. He was trapped in the last twenty feet of tunnel, so close . . . yet so far. She would always remember his last words:

"Leigh, get out of here, quickly, go, get . . . now!"

Those words now haunted her subconscious, traumatized her dreams, and flustered her conscious thoughts. Her guilt would not let go.

Poor Andrew would never know that she too had almost lost her life, at the altar above the cavern when it collapsed, taking her with it. Fortunately, since she was only half-buried, the wolves played a critical part in her rescue.

At least she could show Big Bear the location of the collapsed entrance, and the site of the sink-hole where the altar imploded, collapsed on her, and sunk into the cavern below. Details would be offered later concerning Andy's and her . . . relationship.

For now, she speculated that Big Bear would want to know the present condition of the sealed-off burial site. At least, that's what she anticipated to be the reason for his visit. She'd show him as much as possible under the conditions now hampered by the unexpected and beautiful blanket of snow.

"Welcome," she said. "It's nice to have a visitor. Did you bring all this wonderful snow? I do not know how you feel, but I welcome the change, and it looks like our wolves do, too. They're still romping, running, and racing. Surprisingly, they are getting along just fine. How can I help you? My first thoughts were a hot cup of coffee, what do you say?"

A second transformation occurred; Big Bear also lost his earlier tenseness that had followed him for days. A tense confrontation with Leigh may not be necessary. He hoped not.

"You're so kind. I sure will. Let's round up these raucous wolves and grind some beans. I can help you. Yes?"

With the cache of deer meat remaining in place, and rucksack on his back, wolves assembled and settled, they all descended from the plateau heading for the hut with the wolves leading the way.

The ravens remained stoically unmoved and silent while watching the procession from their aerial perch. They appeared to be immobile, going nowhere until the two human members of His Kin(g)dom revealed their plans. Not a feather rustled. An eerie silence permeated the entire area around the plateau, ridge line, and meadow below. A deafening silence prevailed. The forest became motionless as the sun revealed itself on the glittering facets of each six-pointed flake. The only movement was the shadows of the pines slowly "marching" across the new-fallen snow.

It was apparent that Manitou's demeanor was present.

*   *   *

Coffee, biscuits, marmalade, and relaxed conversation by a crackling fire was much more than Big Bear and Sitka expected. They all sat around the fire pit enjoying an early noon brunch with the four- and two-legged "meadow clan" of four wolves: the female piebald, White; the male gray, Tough; the female black, Sitka; and the male black cub, Jet; plus two humans: the aspirant writer, explorer, Leigh West; and the Tlingit Clan elder investigating the violated burial vault, Chi Mukwa. Brunching by the fire was Leigh's idea so they all could enjoy the beauty of Nature's paintbrush. It took a little more work to lay the fire, get it crackling, and brush the snow off the encircled log-type seating. Add the cabal of four wolves who were better served by the out-of-doors fireside brunch. They were worn out from romping on the plateau, meadow, and dunking/swimming in the Bitterroot to cool off and clean up. Soaking wet, all three were both sitting and standing by the fire drying out while chomping down some of Tough's dog food. By the look in their eyes and belly-to-the-ground posture, their body language stated clearly . . . they'd be whacked out within the next few minutes. Even Jet, now bloated again with his mother's milk, was tired from sucking mom's teats and running around with the gang-of-three, further disadvantaged by carrying a barrel of milk, too.

From his perch above, the lone raven would probably agree the idyllic scene below was a welcome site.

The animated humans chatting like a '50s rock-and-roll jukebox with syncopated volume bursts were much like Bill Haley's "Rock Around the Clock" from 1955. Simply put, they were getting along quite well.

At the time she thought appropriate, the full story would be told, the story he wanted to hear about the unfortunate exploration of the sacred burial vault.

There is never a perfect time or opening to tell a tale like this . . . its trauma, terror, and death, so she just jumped into the tale without his prompting.

Leigh explained how The White had led them to the sacred burial cavern's entrance below the plateau, how Andy discovered the nexus between the altar on the plateau and the cavern below, and how innocent it seemed at the time to just take a few photos of the artifacts for the clan by first removing the blocking boulder, crawling through the forty-foot tunnel to the cavern, taking photos, touching nothing, and withdrawing out of the tunnel quickly. Her pain was evident as she described the quaking that began as soon as they took several panoramic shots of the sarcophagi, artifacts, and skeletal remains. The rest of the story had been told; she made it, and Andy didn't. The earth collapsed around him while he was re-setting the boulder that blocked the tunnel's entrance.

"Thank you, Leigh. I understand. You need not go on; this must be painful to relate to someone . . . all over again. I understand. Your suspicion of Manitou's participation in triggering the earthquake is probably correct. Whether or not it was intended to trap Andy is another story . . . we'll never know, but I doubt it. It could be as simple as uncontrolled timing of the collapse, or not knowing that Andy would linger back so long to replace the boulder. Again, we'll never know. In my opinion, taking Andy's life was not a part of the Manitou's plan. True, He sensed the violation, the penetration of the sacred tomb by both of you, and He did plan to collapse the tunnel to prohibit entry by any future explorers . . . that has happened. What do you think?"

"I agree. I can't imagine Manitou burying one or both of us, but we had erred. He knew, and I knew we were taking a risk to get a few photos for the curious elders of the clan in Skagway. I could, and maybe should . . . be in there with him."

"No. I disagree, and do not think you should be talking like that. No. He is our brother; he, and he alone, knows the Tlingit's Traditions and Sacred Laws, not you. Sorry to say so, but he knew better. Enough said."

"Oh, I guess you're right, but it doesn't help me much knowing very well that except for a ten-second lead in exiting the tunnel—ten seconds saved my life."

"True, but remember, my dear, as you must be well aware by now, life is not fair. We live and die based on variables in life to which we have no control.

"It could have been a natural slip in the Earth's crust; however, you and I both know that was not the case. I lean to Manitou's management of His domain when His intervention is needed—not always wanted—as in this case, Andy's death; nevertheless Tlingit Traditions had been compromised.

"Wica yaka pelo!" Big Bear relates to Leigh. (You have spoken truly.)

"Thank you," she murmurs. "You're the only Tlingit I've told the story to, and it helps to share my emotional burden. As I've mentioned, Joe Bloom, Andy's

DNR colleague, was here and helped a lot. He's informing Andy's family of the tragedy. A nice old fella', his presence earlier this week was a Godsend for me."

"Good, I'd like to meet him. I've heard a lot about his colorful style and language of British origin; he sounds like my kind of guy."

"As I started to say, Tough and I attempted to dig into the collapsed entrance, but failed; it was just too large a mass of dirt and crushed trees. Frustrated, we ran up the ridge line to the plateau since we knew the altar had a trap door to the cavern below. We had heard water dropping into it after a hard rain. Tough and I started digging around the trap door under the altar with desperate plans of lowering myself to the cavern. I thought Andy might have been able to climb out if he made it back to the vault from the collapsed tunnel. Then, all hell broke loose. Tough jumped out of the way as the entire altar area collapsed also . . . pulling me with the dirt, boulders, and small trees. After the stone structure slipped into the cavern below, it kinda blocked the flow downward, but in doing so pinched and trapped me up to my waist. So there I was, half buried, arms free but legs held fast.

"And there he was.

"Tough peered helplessly over the lip of the sinkhole wondering, just like me, what the hell our next move would be. It didn't look good . . . to either of us.

"It gets worse. But, to make a long story short . . . I remained trapped for hours with Tough holding fast at the edge of the hole as the sun, based on the elongations of shadows, appeared to sink to about two hands.

"Then, suddenly, Tough left the edge of the sinkhole and returned with another wolf, a white adult. I thought for a moment and remembered Andy saying that the wolf he found hiding in a den at the tunnel's entrance was an adult white with an orange patch on the chest. He lay down with Tough with body language and facial expression making me think there was a certain amount of domesticity in its character. He definitely was not wild. Luckily, while we contemplated what to do to get me out, the sinkhole slipped down another couple feet and in doing so freed my legs, but, still trapped by dirt and debris. Shortly thereafter, along with the whining wolves and forced innovation . . . I removed my belt, threw the loose end to the wolves, and within one hour of trial and error the 'tow rope belt' worked as they pulled—belt in mouth—and I struggled, crawled, and clawed out of the hole . . . leaving my shoes, pants, and pride in the hole. To fight off the cold, I covered my bare legs with dirt as 'both' wolves shared the victory over death. I was kissed and pawed as if on a date with a horny wolverine 'fratter' in A-squared. This celebration felt good.

"Earlier, for reasons I'll never understand, while 'stuck' with The White, another shock. Slinking towards us on the opposite side of the plateau appeared what seemed to be a marauding pack of six or eight wolves. As they slowly approached and started their circling mode—another surprise.

"From where, I'll never know, a flock of at least one-hundred ravens descended from the ether directly at the wolves with such vengeance . . . again, and again, and again, and when they had deterred the pack and chased them back into the forest, two lay dead, their throats and heads torn by talon and beak. The carnage was lethal and quick; within ten minutes it was all over and The White rested with me.

"It was midnight when we started for the hut and Joe arrived. Can you believe all this happening to me in one day? Well, there's more, but let's save some of these stories for another day, okay?"

"That's quite a story; it's a wonder you've made it this long, my dear; as we've noted and said many times before—life is not fair. On many a fireside chat, Gete Wabiska, our clan's shaman, has warned us of life's realities. He spoke as follows:

> "One of the mysteries of life is why so many people are tested in ways that most of our brothers will never know even in our worst nightmares; whether it be living alone without friends, losing a close friend, outliving your family. Many of our white brothers have adopted several of our basic beliefs, but do not be deterred, do not let the white man's presence alter ours; nature is divine, maintain the course of Gitchee Manitou's teachings, deliver us from the white man's evil. Stay the course, show your brothers the way—and when we fail—give yourself another chance at life, never give up."

"How true." Leigh sighs.

"More coffee, my dear?"

"Yes. Thanks for your ear. I feel better now. How 'bout you? Do you understand my plight?" Leigh sighs again.

"Sure do; thanks for sharing. I've a few tasks to perform as part of the Tlingit's Burial Tradition; let me share with you a few of my plans."

"Shoot."

"Okay. Show me the area of the collapsed tunnel entrance on the side of the ridge, and the sink hole on the plateau. Then I'll be able to offer closure for Andy. While the wolves are still resting, maybe we can return to the area and complete these tasks. This evening we can finish our fireside chat and I can leave in the morning after a good night's sleep. Your offer to stay in the hut tonight is accepted; that will give us a chance to chat a little more."

"It's settled then. Bring your rucksack to the hut while I straighten up the area, and by then the wolves will be raring to go. Say, why don't you bring Jet in; he's still zonked out. We'll leave him in the hut while showing you the destruction around the cavern's collapsed entrance."

They enter the hut together; he beds the cub down on Tough's "former" throne; Leigh grabs the camera as they prepare to depart for the plateau. While looking into the fridge for dinner ideas, he senses her eyes with a not-so-positive feedback of the contents, so he thinks of an alternate idea for dinner.

"Leigh, I've an idea for chow tonight. Why don't I bring the quartered venison in the cache down here this afternoon and butcher it into steaks, chops, and roasts so we can eat 'high on the hog' tonight. In fact, I'll fix the backstrap and tenderloins for ourselves. What say you? It will also lighten my load for the trek back home tomorrow."

"Sounds great; good idea. I'm looking forward to a venison banquet."

*   *   *

After surveying the collapsed entrance area to the former tunnel, they both noticed the small stream was flowing again. Apparently the hydraulic pressure from inside the partially collapsed cavern was sufficient to push the water out through its former routing. Trickling through the freshly fallen snow, it presented a measure of beauty even though its origin was tragic. It most likely flowed over or around Andy's lifeless, crushed body.

"There is nothing more to see here, Leigh; let's take a look at the sinkhole where the altar collapsed. Okay?"

"Sure enough. Follow me; this way will steer us clear of all those fallen timbers. Look, the wolves are already leading the way. Tough is having a ball showing-off his lay-of-the-land smarts. Let's go. I'll follow the wolves, you follow me, and I'll be the final snow plow."

"Leigh, have you noticed above? It appears as though not a single raven has left its perch. They give the area a strange, kinda eerie feeling, don't they?"

"Sure do, but I'm used to them by now. Whether Manitou's messengers, sentinels, combatants—or Manitou personified—it's clear whatever happens here today will be monitored, and if anything is disturbed again, those doing so will be dealt with—harshly. Say, have you seen Hitchcock's *The Birds*, filmed at Bodega Bay, California, in 1962?"

"No. I rarely see movies."

"Well, I was thinking if we were to paint the ravens white and gray, like seagulls, we'd have the same scene—stalking/perching birds driven by a mystical/spiritual force."

"Oh ... I ... ah ... I never see movies."

"Thought so; no sweat."

Upon reaching the plateau and viewing the sinkhole while Leigh finished taking pictures, Big Bear seemed to approach fulfillment of his goals. He paused, looked at Leigh, and asked her in a respectful way to not follow him as he moved to the center of the plateau. Then without a command the three wolves moved toward Leigh and, in an extraordinarily silent motion, lay down and froze in place. At the same time, Big Bear retrieved his medicine bag from around his neck and lowered his body to a lotus-like position, legs crossed, back straight, hands forward, and palms up. He spoke.

> "I am Chi Mukwa, Tlingit Elder of the Raven Clan. Worry not my fine feathered friends; I am here with absolute respect for our Forefathers' breached vault. I am here for closure through prayer and forgiveness for our brother's transgressions. We are also here to honor our fallen Tlingit brother, Walkswithwind."

He rose, opened his medicine bag, retrieved a pinch of tobacco, held it up as an offering, cast it to the east, and said the following prayer in a pleasant sonorous tone to Gitchee Manitou.

> "Hear my prayer as we ask for your forgiveness and your blessing as we walk in the trail of sorrow for Walkswithwind and ask your guidance as we face a new day and new challenges guided by your principles."

He faced to the south, cast tobacco, and repeated the prayer.
He faced to the west, cast tobacco, and repeated the prayer.
He faced to the north, cast tobacco, and repeated the prayer.
Facing the sun, he raised his arms, extended his palms, and repeated the prayer to all His Kin(g)dom. Now lowering his head, arms to the side, Chi Mukwa stood in silence.

Nothing moved on the plateau except the slowly creeping shadows of the pine boughs casting their finger-like silhouettes across the newly fallen snow. The ravens held fast. Leigh stared at the praying Indian with pride, and felt blessed to be a small part of his mission for closure. The wolves remained in place as though chiseled statues of stone.

It was a tableau without motion; the plateau appeared to be a still frame . . . frozen, in the motion picture of life—in the forest's life.

One minute later, or was it five? . . . *the plateau explodes in a maelstrom of leaping birds, flapping wings, and cries of arousal as the black mass eclipsed the sun when they rose to the thermals and flew west.* The message, the symbolism was clear; they all had re-spect for Gitchee Manitou's Kin(g)dom; it had been served. Chi Mukwa knew what was expected of him, and he delivered appropriately in the tradition of the Tlingits' homage to the great spirit.

A silent beauty returned to the once terror-filled plateau.

*   *   *

After retrieving the aerial cache of quartered venison, they all moved down to the meadow, Leigh and Chi Mukwa hand in hand as she expressed to him her pride of being a small part of the ceremony, and the skillfulness of his presenta-tion of the solemn rites to the Great Spirit, Gitchee Manitou. Upon reaching the bench by the river, they all helped with butchering, the wolves in their normal demeanor growling, snapping, and jousting as they fought for the raw trimmings and scraps thrown to them by Chi Mukwa and Leigh. He took over while sepa-rating the muscle groups in the shoulder and rump from its captive, elastic-like sinewy silver. It looked easy, but Leigh knew better as he extracted beautiful masses of undamaged muscle groups that would soon be tied together with a few bacon strips to enhance the flavor, the "main event" in a venison-based banquet.

Leigh scurried around setting up the irons over the fire pit to cook the meat and veggies, cooled the wine in the snow, and threw together a "Tongass Casse-role" of vegetables de jour, and finally some milk and honey biscuit to drive the venison home. A feast for royalty? Maybe, maybe not, but a feast indeed for the Tongass Two, plus four four-legged fur balls . . .

With the weather cooperating at a balmy thirty degrees Fahrenheit, no wind, and a clear sky as the Earth moved away from the illuminating orb to the west.

Very soon, the quad, the pack, the cabal—or was it the "gang"—of multicol-ored wolves stretched out on the edge of the fire pit, stuffed to the gills with their favorite raw, blood-red, venison . . . churning nirvana.

The vigilant raven had not moved from its perch. A Sentinel? A companion? Manitou's presence? All of the above; some questions in life were never specifi-cally answered . . . but you knew. They looked at each other as if knowing each others' thoughts, but said nothing. They knew of her needs as a lone woman in the forest, and had made a decision to be with her—at all times—whether in good times, or bad.

As the plates emptied of the bounty of Mother Earth and their fulfillment gratified, Chi Mukwa felt obligated to share some of his background and his tribal traditions.

"Look at that pile of multicolored cabal of predatory flesh eaters and teat sucker as they sleep off their fictional kill. This may be a good time to give you a little background on our tribe . . . since I'm still planning to leave at daybreak."

"Oh, please do. I've witnessed so much of your tradition, like today's ceremony. Your people have so much richness beyond the value of gold measured in ounces . . . yours is measured in deeds, values, and beautiful traditions. Tell me about your origins, and when the Tlingit people arrived on our northwest shore."

"I'd be delighted."

In an unusual move, the raven descended from its perch in the pines and landed on the bench next to the six animals nestled around the fire pit. In its place, landing in absolute silence, was a snow white owl.

Chi Mukwa placed his blanket around Leigh's shoulders.

"Looks like we've company."

"Yes, I know, and the owl knows that I know who it is."

"As I was about to say, we Tlingits . . ."

Chapter 31

Tribal People

"Their eyes are not our eyes yet we can see ourselves in them."
from *Seeing the Animals*, J. Pruchac.

"My dear Leigh, I've seldom had an opportunity such as this to chat with someone of your stature from the outside world about our people, the Tlingits.

"My brothers, The Tlingit, are the northernmost of the Northwest Coast peoples, which also include others, primarily the islander Haidas and southern Tsimshians, who live much like us traditionally by fishing and hunting marine animals, and building large plank houses, totem poles, and ocean-going dugout canoes. We are all skillful traders who utilize our excess wealth on luxuries, giving splendid feasts called potlatches, which serve to honor the dead and to maintain or elevate the rank of worthy elders in the tribe. The Tlingits comprise four groups or tribes: Southern, Northern, Gulf Coast, and my group, Inland Tlingit. Our history has been one of movement and mixing people. My grandfather, Chi Nodin (Big Wind), told us that our people have occupied southeastern Alaska for many centuries, even millennia, and our language developed about five-thousand years ago. Additional changes occurred in our base about two-hundred years ago when the Haida moved north from Queen Charlotte Islands into the Tongass, along with the southern Tsimshians, who started mixing with our tribe through intermarriage.

"Tlingit oral traditions also tell of our forefathers moving in small family groups, venturing in boats or rafts down the rivers under the glaciers that once arched over the waters, suggesting that early migration might have come from the Asian continent as well as the interior as Nordic Explorers entered our eastern shore, which once again led to mixing with our resident coastal population of Tlingits.

"Natives see themselves as participants in a great natural order of life, related in some fundamental manner to every other living species. Each species has a particular knowledge of the universe and specific skills for living in it. Human beings had a little bit of knowledge and some basic skills, but we could not compare with any other animals as far as speed, strength, cunning, and intelligence. Therefore it was incumbent on us to respect every other form of life, to learn from them as best we could the proper behavior in this world and the specific technical skills necessary to survive and prosper.

"Man was the youngest member of the web of life and, therefore, has to have some humility in the face of the talents and experience of other species.

"We made a point of observing the other creatures and in modeling their own behavior after them. Many of the social systems of the tribes are patterned after their observations of animals, and in those tribes that organized themselves in clans, every effort was made to follow the behavior of the clan totem animal. Some of tribes even developed a psychology of birds and animals, describing human personality traits as being similar to those of wolves, elk, bears and so forth. In your case, Leigh, have you noticed these descriptions of animal habits are amazingly accurate in terms of predicting individual behavior and frequently surprising even the most casual observer? Is the owl's presence a part of this idea? I think so. You know who the owl represents . . . and why. Didn't Manitou send the ravens? Who do you think sent The White? You've told me of the trauma with Ford, the bush pilot; Walkswithwater, the shaman; Walkswithwind, his brother . . . Gitchee Manitou knows, He feels, He cares for you and your safety; He is your guardian spirit."

"You're probably right; I don't have enough time to tell you of the trauma I've experienced . . . likewise, the support I've received from your people, the Tlingits, and others in this Tongass experience. So much has happened, I wonder at times if staying through the winter is a wise move. I wonder."

"Please, if only for my sake, stay. You are much wiser now, you've a cabal of wolves for protection, and many in the outside world know of your presence . . . forebear, my friend, for I too will be there if you're in need.

"You know very well the relationship is so close between humans and other forms of life that it is believed that selected humans, such as shamans, could take the shape of birds and animals for some time in their life, as needed, and after their death. So it is not uncommon, following the death of a tribal member, to see a hawk, raven, or owl circling the camp. Look above, need I say more . . . and you've mentioned seeing him before, under similar circumstances. True?"

"Yes, you're on target, all right; even more self-evident, I've conversed with the raven and owl on several traumatic occasions. You're absolutely right. I've found many two- and four-legged friends in the past event-filled nine months."

"See, I told you . . . interestingly, we Indians see a grand distinction between two-legged and four-legged creatures. Among the two-leggeds are humans, birds, and bears. Bears are included, because when feeding, they often stand on two legs. Since the two-leggeds are responsible for helping to put the natural world back into balance when it becomes disordered, birds, bears, and humans share a responsibility to participate in healing ceremonies, and indeed the cumulative knowledge of these three groups is primarily one of healing. We must carefully accord these creatures the respect that they deserve and the right to live without unnecessary harm. Leigh, you have already shown that sensitivity when you rescued Tough from the wolverine and took The White into your life rather than leave him in the forest as a rogue wolf from his pack. These efforts do not go unnoticed."

"Thank you, my dear friend; your words are of comfort. But, I've always wondered, in this pluralistic society, how do Native American beliefs fit in with the white man's narrowly defined Biblical myth?"

"It wasn't always easy, especially in the early days when the so-called Christians withheld food and blankets unless we acknowledged their myth as the only belief. To this day, the three major faiths are arguing, and actually killing each other, over who has the 'right' canon of belief and salvation.

"Sickening isn't it? It's obscene.

"Traditional peoples in many parts of the world, and the Tlingits, do not make a separation between the world of the sacred and the world we call 'everyday.' There is, in Christianity, Judaism, or Islam, a general belief in the existence of a God who is the ultimate Creator. This God, however, is not seen primarily in human form. Most often God is referred to as a Great Mystery or a Great Spirit, one whose essence is not exclusively male or female, human or animal, but in and of all things.

"The word for the Great Spirit in the Tlingit's belief is Gitchee Manitou, and His presence is everywhere. Everything around us is alive and contains a part of the spiritual presence of the Creator. Our Spirit cares equally for all parts of Creation: humans, animals, plants, and stones.

"We perceive the natural state of the world as a state of balance. The Tlingits are part of that great circle. You, Leigh, are also a part of the great circle, and we *are not* more important than the plants or the animals or the rocks. Animals and plants are beings equal to humans. In some cases, they are described as ancestors, and stories of animals becoming people and people becoming animals are common.

"Didn't you think The White might be the manifestation of Andrew?

"Animals, whether they are connected to people or not, have their own families and traditions. And, along with human beings, they are part of a world that is meant to be in balance.

"This is what I want you to remember: to respect the animals, to greet and thank them, and to keep them in our minds and hearts. Is it so hard to give them greetings and thanks ... I don't think so. What do you think?"

"The beauty of your words are remarkable, I agree; you make a lot of sense," Leigh responded.

"As my grandfather noted many years ago:

"In the path of life, avoid the center, walk the edge of the field, you'll see more; keep your feet and mouth quiet, your mind still and your eyes open."

"Hey Gal! I've been doing a lot of talking about our people; am I boring you? But remember, you asked."

"Are you kidding? I'm loving it; I feel as if I'm in school again, and I wish I'd taken notes. Thank you so much, my dear friend. And just look at the venue out here by the fire in the crystal-white Tongass. Compare this to the bare lecture halls at Michigan's Angell Hall. Geez. You'd have to be there to understand; the building is one-hundred years old, looks it, and the professors match. Okay, I stretch the point. Can you imagine just how many loose ends you have tied together with the summary just given me of your people . . . the Tlingits? It was wonderful! Have you also noticed the wolves have either been lulled to sleep by your euphonious voice, or they are totally zonked from the day's activities and evening feast? Whichever. None of them have moved a muscle, twitched a nose, or jerked a leg. Yep . . . as in 'dog tired.'"

"Your simile is more correct than you may think. Dogs and wolves are part of the rich palette of predators and scavengers that co-evolved with herding ungulates about a million years ago. Canis lupus became the top predator in Eurasia being able to keep up to the horde of migratory herds; the wolves became the first pastoralists, feeding off the herd for survival. At the same time, we the agile tree climber transformed into a swift cursorial ape and adopted a migratory lifestyle necessary for our survival. As omnivorous gatherers and scavengers, we too moved to the steppe of Eurasia and became skilled hunters. Sometime during the last millennium, our ancestors teamed up with the pastoralist wolves . . . right here in front of us. Much like you've experienced yourself, Leigh, you've linked up too, for protection. Adaptive evolution followed, and some humans adopted the wolves' élan as followers and 'herders' of sorts of hoofed animals for the same reason: sustenance—or as we would say: grub. Wolves and humans like my forefathers had found their match, their symbiotic triad of hoof, paw, and foot.

"The first contact between wolves and Indians was truly mutual, and the subsequent changes in both wolves and our people are understood best by the term—'co-evolution.'

"We have evolved to the experiences you've enjoyed with both Tough and The White, not to mention our new member, the cub, Jet. We have the classic symbolic relationship right here between the wolves' needs—a new dependency on us for nourishment, and for us the protection they provide by giving advanced warning, their strength, and tracking skills. Didn't you say The White brought the cub to your doorstep very soon after birth . . . is that not an example of her trust in you versus raising the cub in the wild? She helped save your life, true? Now you can help her raise the cub. True?

"Of course, many are now social parasites and scavenge around our camps and provide little in return, but this troika of yours, plus Sitka, is a good example of mutual benefits for all. Of course, less controllable wolves would remain wild, expire earlier, and inevitably be killed while the tame prevail. I should emphasize Manitou has allowed room for both wolves: the tamer and the wilder.

"As for the reincarnation or humans taking on an animal likeness such as in a wolf, that's for the shamans and other holy men to address. I pass. But, I'll admit to feeling a mystical or eerie sense, a wonderment, a perplexing kind of déjà vu with some animals, a personification as if I experienced this event/condition before. What do you think, dear?"

"True, I do share your feelings, but as for The White, I'm not sure. You see, in her case I thought it more than accidental that she arrived on the scene at the precise time that Andy died and, along with Tough, helped to save me from certain death in the sink hole.

"On the other hand, when I stumbled upon Tough accidentally . . . well maybe, maybe not; he was the lone survivor of a wolverine attack at their den, his later demise a certainty. Was that happenstance . . . or a planned encounter by Manitou? Psychologist Carl Jung calls these encounters a synchronicity, not happenstance, but a planned encounter based on the needs of the cub and my needs being depressed from the loss of dear friends, and being alone, and venturing to the den area, hearing his cries, and the resulting rescue, and over time has surely been a benefit to me. Since that 'synchronic event,' he has saved my life many times. You ask if I believe in the personification of human traits in wolves. I'm not sure. Their attachment to some animals, and the idea of an animal projecting certain human traits, is not a new idea. The answer's still sought . . . will we ever know? Not sure. One thing is certain: wolves and dogs have a special ability to pick up human cues. They get the picture of our intent immediately, much faster than the chimpanzees, who are much slower to recognize and act on visual cues even though our DNA links are almost identical. Yes, the wolf and dog are always the first choice for companionship; there is none better on Earth . . . except for the opposite sex."

"What do you think, dear?" he asked.

"It's hard to know, at times, what to believe . . . When you 'fold-in' the beauty of the 'natural' in Native American belief, as contrasted with beauty of the Psalms . . . sometimes the 'blend' works very well, for as we both know belief systems vary only because of location and culture of that people's Hero, and the creator of these varied myths is more alike than dissimilar. True?"

"Indeed, you're on target. Those faiths that do not adapt to the life's present, and remain in the past, will soon live only in cloistered venues, off the beaten track of life, while unenlightened clerics mollycoddle mystical principles and scriptures of false doctrine that only work in monastic environs on the outskirts of life."

"Well, I've certainly become very comfortable with Nature's way, the Tlingit way, and I thank you again for bringing me on board to the principles of life that have been serving me so well. Speaking of serving, look at the mess around the spread-eagle canines by the fire. They have deer bones strewn all over the place. What should I do with them?"

"They'll be useful later; just gather them up, throw them in a bag, and toss 'em to the wolves every now and them to condition their teeth. Here, I'll help you."

Big Bear moved around the fire pit collecting bones of all shapes and sizes as if on a mission, quickly and with purpose. He tied the bag and wedged it into the crook of a tree above the wood pile. He felt this would keep many of the critters from gnawing them for the rich calcium. Looking at the overnourished wolves and their vulnerability when stuffed, slow moving, and sleeping . . . it reminded him of one last reason for Indians keeping wolves in their camp. He certainly wasn't going to mention it to her, unless she asked, but they were frequently used as an emergency food supply. She probably wouldn't understand how anyone could be so desperate, so hungry, so starved that the wolf that helped them hunt, guarded the camp, and literally provided warmth in bed on frigid winter evenings one night could be 'dinner' the next. He decided to be silent on this topic, unless she asked, and then remind her that Asians still eat their canine friends . . . even when not starving. He felt it would not be in her interest to go to an oriental marketplace where caged dogs, cats, and rats are sold to 'liven-up' the local rice dish. He had already scraped the deer hide, so rather than show her how to stretch the hide tonight, he decided to teach her a neat trick for collecting gold dust. He had learned the trick many years ago from a Russian trapper who also did a little panning for gold. He 'skinned' for gold, too.

"Leigh. Darned if I didn't overlook preparation of the deer hide. Come on over here to the stream with me. I've got the deer hide all scraped, but we need to cure it and try another 'trick.'

"This is the idea. We stake the hide, kinda suspended, in the faster flow on the edge with the hair side up. Okay, now that I've your attention . . . here's the trick: Gold dust suspended in the water passes over the fine hairs and are trapped, adhering easily since gold is very heavy. You may ask if this is for real; well, my dear friend, it is. However, we'll only know if there is gold dust in the stream if in five or six days the hide is laden with it. Believe me, you'll know; the brightness will be overwhelming."

"Okay, if I'm to believe you, how do we harvest our mother lode?"

"Easily, my dear, with the same comb and brush you use on your beautiful auburn locks. Just remove the hide, angle it into a bucket, and wash and comb. The heavy dust will sink as the dirt washes away. Pretty cool, huh?"

"More than cool. I've already ordered a new pair of boots with the proceeds."

"Not so fast, gal . . . we first need a mother lode upstream that releases its bounty to us. Okay, it's a long shot, but how do we know unless we 'lock and load and shoot!'"

They placed the hide in the perfect spot, staked it, and tied a safety lanyard to the hide and then to a local tree.

They returned to the fire and started chatting about his trip back to the clan and the detour planned through his forefathers' camp that was abandoned about 100 years ago. She was a little surprised and unaware of this aspect of his return. For some reason it had never come up in their previous chats whether at the hut, the fire, while eating, or when exploring together on the plateau. A little disheartened, she reflected unnecessarily that she should have been told, or it should have come up during the day's activities. Of course, her concerns were not valid; he had no obligation whatsoever to live up to her expectations of what she was to know . . . and what was just not important to know, or just none of her business. After all, she had just met him twelve hours ago. But she fumed internally over the side trip—this detour—this "interesting" deviation.

Then, in her quiet rectitude of how to express her preoccupation with his 'side trip,' she reverted to what had always worked for her in the past, to say what she was thinking—she wanted to go with him to explore the abandoned campsite. It would indeed be an extraordinary request. Add the fact that she'd have to return alone . . . again. He would probably not only say no, but give her a piece of his mind in being so brazen in her assumption that it was even possible. But she decided to take the heat—been there, done that before—so she decided to "jump into the fire," if necessary, with her request. Nothing ventured nothing gained, she thought; if he gets pissed-off, so be it. She'd pissed-off many others in the past to achieve opportunities on her behalf.

"Hey . . . my dear Tlingit teacher, could we continue my schooling, and take me with you to the old campsite? As you've said, I could never find it myself."

"Of course, no problem."

She slumped in shock, but covered her elation with a casual look.

"Can you be ready to leave in the morning?"

"Yep, I'll leave The White here with Jet; Tough and I will be ready with bells on. Thank you so much. Come on, let's pack some venison jerky from the fire;

I'm sure it's ready; then we can lift the sack . . . wait, how far is it to the old camp?"

Chi Mukwa, in a cautious reply, not wanting to reveal too much about its exact location, replied in an indirect way. "It's about four hours north; don't worry, you'll have time to explore the area in and around the camp, and return by late afternoon."

"Great, let's get some rest; we've a big day ahead of us tomorrow. Come on guys, up and at 'em."

All six, two two-leggeds and four four-leggeds headed for the hut. All six were well fed and relaxed after a full day of rewarding activities. None of the legs could know of the excitement and the trauma that awaited them on the 'morrow.

The lone raven stayed by the radiating heat of the glowing orange coals in the fire pit, probably waiting for the tasks expected tomorrow; the assignment would be the same as before . . . protecting the mistress of the meadow from the vagaries of the Tongass.

As the crew in the hut prepared for their trip north, rippling sounds emanating from the Bitterroot was one of the few sounds broadcasting across the meadow. The sound of gold dust impacting the hide's hair was especially silent as the stream carried its wealth to the hide's sluice.

The full moon's glare enhanced by the freshly fallen snow reflected silhouettes of the six as they paused to sense the direction of the wolves' howling. The cries to each other across the ridge either announced a kill or rejoining of the pack.

"Beautiful, isn't it?" he asked. "Night sounds across the Tongass are music to my ears. How 'bout you, Leigh? It's a melody made no place else; it is a sound unique to the wilds of the north. Isn't it? Look at the wolves. They know the language. I wonder if the pack's call-of-the-wild ever entices them to return to the wilds?"

"I'm sure it has passed their mind," she said. "I too have wondered if Tough has ever thought of taking off to see what's out there. I'm philosophical about it; if he's meant to be with the pack . . . so be it. It's not for me to alter his wishes. However, as you've explained earlier, there is more dependency nowadays as noted in your comments on co-evolution of the species."

Chi Mukwa rounded up the wolves, who had broken to vanquish the denizens of the once-peaceful meadow, Jet lagging behind as usual. He sensed that the wolves all saw a nestling mouse, a settled rabbit, or a nesting bird as an animal to be disrupted. It was as if their motto was: "Let no animal be at rest while we are hotfooting it across the meadow." Wearily, they dragged their tired bodies back to the hut, ate some snow, took a leak, made the obligatory sniff, and tumbled into the hut.

*   *   *

"Would you look at this hut? There's a bundle of fur on most of the floor space. I wonder if I can get to the fridge so we can finish that bottle of wine."

"No sweat, I'll get it. I can reach the door from here. Ah, a Mateus Rosé, just what the doctor ordered. May I pour?"

"You bet. Come on over here, if you can sidestep the canine throw rugs."

"Well, if this isn't a top-notch way to end a day. Cheers to you, Lady of the Meadow, or as I've referred to you before I met you: The-Woman-with-Red-Hair. Cool, hey? Not bad for a guy that had never seen you and, as a matter of fact, had only heard about you from locals.

"Let's talk a little about tomorrow. The hike will be the easy part of the day. The harder part will be for you to lie back and let me complete one of my primary objectives, determining who has been scavenging artifacts from our forefathers' home. You see, it is the second part of my mission.

"The violation and subsequent collapse of the sacred burial vault was the first, to which you were complicit. Thank you for helping me solve that riddle. I will make sure you are not put in harm's way at the site; I see no reason for any tension. The site is abandoned, but one of the hunters noticed a change, an altering of the original layout. I'll investigate his comments.

"Let me give you an example of what you'll see at the abandoned campsite. You may already know by now, the Tlingits are renowned as woodworkers; their communal houses made of cedar logs were often large enough to hold several families. A matriarchal society, we had two main divisions, Ravens and Wolves, with smaller clan groups inside each division. We believed along with our neighbors that these divisions were related to each other, exclusive of tribe. This meant, for example, the Tlingits of the Eagle division regarded themselves as relatives of Haidas of the Eagle division and could go visit those Haida Eagles and be welcomed as relatives—even though their languages were different and they were strangers. This may be where our problem in missing artifacts is rooted. The Tlingits are known for our skills in carving totem poles, boxes, and masks, as well as the famous Chilkat blankets made of cedar bark and mountain goat hair. Our Haida carvers, still aspirants, are suspect; we'll see.

"Before your expectations rise too high, let me remind you the communal log or plank houses have long since collapsed, which is one reason for the site being hard to locate. But, many of the totem poles remain in various states of deterioration, nevertheless enduring with their former beauty. Many have younger trees shooting up alongside their former grandeur and masking their location.

"Therein lies our problem. It has been reported to our clan that several totems are missing. I have been sent to determine the extent of our loss, if any, and who may have violated our property, and our response if items have been stolen. Doesn't sound like a pleasant trip, does it? Still want to go?"

"Yes, of course, but only if I wouldn't be a burden to you."

"Good, we'll still plan on it. Remember, we're not sure the Haidas are at fault. I've been told the Haida feel a sense of ownership in the campsite too, based on the clan identity logic I described earlier. That could, and I caution you not to jump to conclusions, be the source of the problem, a 'taking' of what some people think is theirs; if that's what we find, I hope the conflict in ownership can be resolved peacefully.

"Remember, the red and yellow *cedar* trees of the woodlands are rapidly disappearing, which concerns native cultures in the area. So, with few trees left to carve totems, the business of theft of old totems and *recarving* has been observed. It's quite a trick; they use the same pattern and just carve the characters deeper through the old wood into the new wood. Our short-term objective is to determine if our forefathers' site has been compromised and address that problem. The long-term goal is to put an end to wanton destruction and harvesting of cedar indiscriminately. I for one want my children and their children's children to enjoy the cedar and the totem that it yields under skilled hands of our people.

"You will get your tour, my dear, and it will be a good one, since I'm one of the last to see the campsite before the collapse of the lodge house, and before the Tongass moved into its footprint."

"Sounds good to me; let's hit the sack."

Chi Mukwa lay where others have rested, all of them sent to help the Lady of the Meadow . . . some falling in love. Chi Mukwa was different, or was he?

As with men in the past, the Dream Catcher in the window cast its shadow from the full moon, over the face of the resting Tlingit hunter, elder . . . and good Samaritan.

The raven ruffled its feathers and bedded down for the night, also. Tomorrow would be another exciting clay. Most days with Leigh West were risqué.

Chapter 32

Anxiety

Chi Mukwa turned from his dreams to conscious thoughts and morning musings of the day's activities as the sun slowly broke over the eastern ridge lines.

Repeating the custom for early morning prayers, he quietly rose from his bedroll by the wolves and tiptoed around the furry piles, moving furtively to the fire pit by the river, the door left ajar to aid the wolves needing to pee . . . forthwith.

The crisp morning air was as if a stimulating mental goose . . . a shot to his psyche. He loved the morning's unique shadows and rustling underbrush as the denizens of the Tongass awoke and started their day scampering on top of, underneath, and digging through the snow.

As certain as the sun's rise in the east, the raven appeared from its circling flight, descended slowly while looking for its favorite perch; flaring like a B-1 the majestic bird landed in one of the twin pines by the fire pit. Its cry of arrival echoed across the meadow and ridge lines.

"Good Morning, my fine feathered friend; welcome to the Red Hair's Meadow. I'm sure, by now, you know her well . . . better than I, is certain. We've got quite a bit of activity scheduled for today; you'll be busy. Hope you can keep up."

The raven looked down on him as if the meeting were expected, and more or less expected a briefing of some sort.

Chi Mukwa stood in silence. It was time to meditate.

Facing west, breathing in a deep rhythmical cadence, he maintained a solemn silence, lowered to a modified lotus posture, and prepared to repeat the prayer of his father and his father's father. He prepared to recite the prayer of thanksgiving repeated by his people over the years to Gitchee Manitou.

He carefully dispensed tobacco, cedar, sweet grass, and sage to the four points of the compass with ceremonial eagle feathers, chanting:

> "Atewiopeyata, nawajin yelo, wamayanka yo! Ite, otateya, nawauin yelo.
> (Creator, to the West I am waiting. Behold me! The wind is blowing in my face. I am waiting.)

"Gitchee Manitou, The Creator, Great Spirit, Life Giver, creator of Earth, our island home, you carried across the vast expanse of interstellar space on the back of Great Turtle. All the earth is Turtle Island. This inland home teems with living things. The waters teem with fish, the woods with four-leggeds and crawling beings, and the skies are full of birds, and finally Anishinabeg, the two-legged arrive.

> May the nourishment of the earth be ours.
> May the clarity of light be ours.
> May the fluency of the mighty river be ours.
> May the protection of all the ancestors be ours.
> And so, may a slow wind work these words of love around you,
> An invisible cloak to mind your life."

Silence. Silence returned to the area as Chi Mukwa meditated while thinking over the plans for the trip back to the clan by way of his forefathers' home with Leigh. He reviewed the plethora of items to check on to make the trip as safe as possible for Leigh and the wolves. First things first, he had better put a collar on both, in case they needed to be held back . . . for any number of reasons.

They'd take some of the pemmican and deer jerky, the water jug, and rain slickers in case of a downpour. He had not mentioned his tentative plans to also invite Leigh to the camp of his clan. He would like very much to introduce her to his family and other members so that, if necessary, she would have a support group to help in case of future traumatic incidents. Based on her past experiences, she'd probably be served a smorgasbord of potential episodes of danger or joy. In either case, how she reacts to a dangerous encounter, with tension or even glee, may be improved if she knows the clan is there to share. He pondered the decision to take her to the clan site, feeling the decision could be delayed until he sees how the side trip to the forefathers' camp developed.

"What's that?"

*   *   *

Leigh had slipped out of the hut and, amazingly, passed the snoring wolves without them noticing her; she then crept behind the meditating elder, ready to surprise him with some sort of ambush. But, she wisely changed her mind; this was no time to upset a meditating elder who, at his base, was still an armed warrior and hunter of his tribe . . . to be taken very seriously.

At a safe distance, near the path, Leigh spoke in a melodic manner. "Hello, how are you, my dear? Are we ready to go?"

"Good morning. I guess. I've been meditating and making some plans for today's hike. There are a few items we need to discuss. Okay? How 'bout grinding a bean, getting the wolves up and out, and kicking around a few ideas on which I need your input, your opinion."

"Okay, you've got a date at the kitchen table, such as it is; you can chase the wolves across the meadow until the coffee is ready. Okay?"

After the obligatory chase, pee, and tumbling in the snow, the wolves came in with Jet bringing up the rear. Poor guy, easily bottoming out in the snow. By the time he got halfway into the meadow, the horde were on the way back and literally ran over the ball of black fur. Their board meeting on the kitchen table led to a few basic decisions; one, to leave The White and Jet outside in a more protective shelter along with enough food and water for a day or two. He mentioned the need for collars, and would quickly make a couple and put them on Tough and Sitka before departing. He also discussed plans to take a leash for each wolf, to use only if necessary, noting that one never knows which critter might be out there . . . and object to their presence in their domain. He hated to leash them, but it may be necessary to save everyone's lives. He also recommended taking her sidearm for their trip, and especially for the trip back alone. She replied, unequivocally, that it would be at her side, as it always is when venturing away from the hut.

"Well, my friend, that's settled; do you think we have one more moment to chat about an idea I had this morning by the fire pit? I was going to wait until we were underway, but it may make better sense to ask you now."

"Shoot, what is it, dear?"

"I had not mentioned the location of our clan's camp, as related to our forefathers', and its location relative to your hut on the meadow. It's almost a perfect equilateral triangle. Why do I mention this geometry? It all relates to my request. I would like you to visit our camp, meet our people, my family, and learn a little about the Tlingits."

Silence ruled the moment of deep thought.

Chi Mukwa continued, "You see, if you accept my offer, you'll have to stay overnight in our camp and return the next day . . . alone, over new territory. It is a little more complex. What do you think? Can you fit in an overnighter?"

"Well, let's do what I'm certain both of us have done before . . . Let's look at the downside, for I definitely want to go, most definitely!"

"A couple things. We'd have to leave The White here, alone with her cub, overnight. Secondly, the return trip alone in new terrain is an added risk to your safety in getting lost or stumbling upon an angry critter. Thirdly, an overnight in our camp should be the easiest part; we've a bedroll for honored guests like you. When one of us brings a stranger to camp, it is an honor. And the mere fact that you are invited means all clan members will welcome you as their sister in the Spirit of Manitou's Kin(g)dom.

"What say you?"

"The White will be okay for several reasons. I feed her, house her, and more importantly she won't run away because she feeds the cub, and he is here . . . and, I can find my way home. Give me my compass and a bottle of Schnapps, and that last leg of the triangle will disappear in no time flat. Clearly, in spite of all these variables, I'd love to meet your people. So, what do you think?"

"You're the boss, Leigh, and if in agreement—let's do it! I'm looking forward to our trip."

*   *   *

The four headed north with the Sun at two fingers, leaving The White nursing the cub. She would probably stay and, at worse case, possibly hide the cub and track them if something bothered her and she felt it absolutely necessary to leave. One never knows how the emotions of the pack or fraternity versus motherhood plays out in the canines. Time would tell, but for now the foursome cleared the plateau to the north and entered into unchartered territory, at least for Leigh.

The tag elders, with a little snow on their leafless limbs, had the appearance of stick men in assembly, waiting for their arrival. Under cover of the big timber, the ground was partially free of snow, revealing mat with fallen leaves turned almond brown in the first stages of decay . . . in stark contrast to the piebald snow. The leaves were slick and limber underfoot, beginning their seasonal compost. They pushed their way through thinning limbs into an opening covered by a canopy of older trees. Here, the floor of the forest was a thick mattress of moss dotted with groundcover plants with heart-shaped leaves, and the walking was open through the thin cover of snow. The snow also revealed a few scattered, bare blueberry bushes. This fringe area was maybe twenty yards wide before the slope rose up steeply. On the slope the moss sloughed away slightly and rocks showed through. The spruce and hemlock were fat at the stump and did not seem to taper until high out of sight into the upper stories of limbs. It was quiet except for the wolves, who had a whispered murmur along with constant rotation of their heads right, left, around, and repeating all previous motions. The wolves were very well behaved as they clung to the heels of their mistress and master, but they appeared very nervous.

Chi Mukwa stopped, leaning forward to sense the direction of the sound. He heard the low-lying wheeze of the stream ahead of them, and the light breathing of the exposed roots of streamside trees straight ahead and a little to the left.

A little nervous over their silent journey through the soft forest floor, she asked, "Big Bear, did you know we would come upon this stream ahead?"

"Yep, it's a branch of the Bitterroot, called the Little Root. It meanders throughout the forest and makes it easy to find our fathers' camp. It runs right by it, and served as their source for drinking and cleaning. We'll be following it to the northwest for about two hours and with any luck be there by noon."

They followed a narrow path made by use, soft footing worn down through the moss. Here, where the skin of the forest floor was broken, they could look down to see the mass of roots and organic soil that lay like musculature under the covering of moss. The roots twisted and intertwined in one continuous fabric the entire length and width of the floor. It would be difficult to single out one distinct plant from the whole growing mass.

A gaggle of crows cried as they hopped from the streamside bushes to rocks in the middle of the stream.

"Look, Big Bear, the first sign of life. Matter of fact, where do you think our raven is hiding?   You know the bird is following us somewhere."

"How true. I'll bet it lurks in the canopy of silence—by plan."

Both wolves wanted to chase after the crows, but were held back by a quiet voice command of their handlers. They were given the operant reward of . . . good wolves, good girl, good boy.

The flood plain narrowed as they followed the stream to the west. The slopes were more rocky on either side, with outcroppings of twisted cedars and spruce. They came across one ancient spruce tree that must have been eight feet across at the butt. They stood next to it and looked up its length. All they could see was thick limbs coming off the trunk several hundred feet above. The trunk itself was twisted and gnarled with uneven bark. About ten feet up from the ground there were large gouges or wounds that showed black down into the sapwood, weepy with pitch. Large amber and white cakes of pitch ran toward the bottom of the tree, and claw marks raked down the bark. At the foot of the tree he found the matted and strewn carcass of an eagle with long hollow bones, thigh and shoulder; also, amazingly intricate curved architecture of the wing and the gray-green of feathers and mold. There was no skull, no talons. The claw marks were fresh, the eagle kill aged, but some animal had freshly disturbed the kill.

"Ugh, that's a mess. Wonder who killed it. Yuck. Look, upstream, there's an eagle. Back guys. Stay. Isn't he beautiful?"

An immature eagle walked clumsily along the mud and flattened eel grass. He waddled, muscular and hunched, like a self-conscious young athlete. The crows were pestering him by taking short, swirling dives at his back and veering away. The eagle plodded on toward an elevated elephant-colored rock.

They walked along the edge of the meandering stream below the grass line on the fresh mud. Leigh stepped into firm green bear scat wedged between a group of small rocks near the water's edge.

"Hold it. I've got to rinse off this boot or I'll stink up the forest. Damn, I've smelled some pretty bad old biology projects in the fridge, but this beats them all . . . pooooeee. There, that should do it. Tough, Sitka, get away from that crap! Damn fresh, wasn't it?"

Chi Mukwa did not answer . . . his body language and facial expression said it all; his concern, the threat was obvious.

Undaunted, they continued upstream.

The salmon run in the stream was over, but there were rotted corpses of pink salmon strewn all over the bank, ugly, with hooked jaws and deformed backs. None had eyes in their sockets. Some swayed in the shallows of the clear water, rotted white, with skeins of sloughed flesh twirling into the current, their mouths agape and grotesquely jutting to the surface. The air was thick with the smell of dead fish in the soft mud.

He saw bear tracks in the mud, clear and finely etched. Claws perhaps four inches long, coming from the toughened palm of the pad, headed in the direction they were going. There was nothing unusual ahead of them either on the bank or in the tall grass that ran down into the swampy flat of the stream. They looked again, and listened. Nothing.

"What do you think, Leigh?"

"Well, let's walk a little farther upstream. But first, let's put the leashes on. Do you agree?"

They came to a narrowing point of the stream where the water fell through a short rocky falls into a tidal pool. To their left was a dogleg cul-de-sac of grasslands, and straight ahead was the steep slope of a ridge line of tall timber.

They stopped as the wolves grew agitated, and were considering which way to go when they heard a low grunt from a deep pair of lungs.

*   *   *

When I was young we lived in an old tar-paper shack in Haines that had been a hunting cabin in territorial days. When my father came home from work it was almost of ceremonial significance. I would have the fire burning in the stone fireplace and my mother would have his favorite drink ready. He would share his day with us, and after a while my mother would excuse herself and start to prepare dinner. Dad would then politely inquire about my day at the Indian school. I would give him some evasive but polite reply. He would then move the subject to a hunting trip he planned to make, promising to take me on it. He talked about the duties of a man in the hunting camp and how a bear-hunting trip was no place for immaturity. When I was worthy I could go. He also talked about the bears on Admiralty Island and claimed they could touch the beams of our living room standing on their hind legs. Those beams seemed unbelievably high at twelve feet. I thought the likelihood of my ever being old enough to go on such a hunting trip was slim. I watched him, tasted the smell of burning alder in the fireplace, and saw the bear standing behind him clawing the beams of our house. The presence of a bear that large was forever etched into my childhood imagination, and I had spent much of my adulthood trying to ignore it.

*   *   *

When the bear stood up in the tall grass beside the stream at the bend of the stream, the dream world of Chi Mukwa's childhood house rose out of his body like a cold sweat. The bear stood on her hind legs, exposing three-quarters of her torso. At first she did not move, and it was as if she were more a monument to a bear than an example of one. Then she swayed briefly like the top of a tree being felled. Her fur was matted down by the water she had been wallowing in, and her coat was slick against her torso. She had the well-defined musculature of a middle-weight champion and the height of Brobdingnagian. As she stood there, water ran down her body and etched the pathways of the blood vessels and the knotted bundles of muscle, down the bulk of her shoulders and front legs, down her stomach past the visible row of teats that he could see just above the grass. She stood with apparent grace and power like Mount Rushmore.

Her head swayed; her tiny black marble eyes searched for us. Her coffin-shaped snout twitched and scanned, twitched and scanned. Her ears were erect. He heard the heavy bellows of her breathing and tasted the scent of rotted fish and blueberry shit. He imagined her great warm bowels and the row of blunt teeth that would grind our bones to a slurry. It was like staring into the sun and having to avert their eyes and look down at the mud; they did not run; they did not say anything . . . they listened and waited.

Sitka was the first to break loose and charge, while Leigh restrained Tough. She bounded across the mud flats and stream, then disappeared in the tall grass for a moment. The bear looked down at the same time Sitka rose to the bear's throat. Immediately, the sow's huge arms encircled the wolf while shaking her head from Sitka's fangs in her throat. Chi Mukwa called for her return . . . with no response.

No sooner had the bear's arms encircled Sitka . . . the horrible sound of an extinguished life howled across the grasslands. The bear had summarily squeezed the life, the air, the capacity to breathe out of the wolf's lungs. At her last breath, she released her blood-soaked fangs from the sow's neck and fell into the grass. Unseen, they heard her last howl and the wind pipe's guttural rattle of death.

The sow clashed her teeth again and again, pounced the ground with her forepaws, roared to the ether, and took a defiant last swat at the wolf's lifeless body. She also swatted at the bleeding neck wound . . . Sitka had left her mark.

Tough broke from Leigh as she leaped for the trailing leash . . . losing it as she and the wolf collapsed into the stream. Tough recovered, and attacked.

The sow dashed to the stream's edge and halted as the gray wolf leaped at her groin. She roared and rotated around and around like a cyclone with the new wolf appendage swirling around with her. Snapping and growling now, she continued chasing the wolf still locked on her crotch.

Leigh and Chi Mukwa could only watch as Tough fought for his life . . . he must have known he could not dispatch the bear alone, and if she did not run, her decision to stay and fight would seal his fate. He must have known. Was he protecting the two-leggeds? He must have known he would die; it was just a matter of how, and how soon. She hadn't run away from his attack.

The sow stopped rotating and caught the canine appendage with one paw, held tight, and chomped down viciously on Tough's back. The sound of crunching back bones resonated across the stream to the two witnessing the attack. The next sound was not unexpected. Holding fast, she shook and smashed the howling body into the streamside rocks, and threw the lifeless body over her head into the churning water.

Again, she stomped her paws on the water, clicked her teeth, and rose to her hind feet and roared, then stared directly at the pair.

Chi Mukwa and Leigh remained frozen in place while witnessing the terror, but under the present condition of an enraged bear staring at them, he cued Leigh to slowly, on command, lower themselves into the water and float or swim downstream . . . very slowly.

Tortoise-like, they slowly lowered their bodies into the deeper water and, upon full immersion . . . it happened.

The bear was down and running. Toward them. The snuffling grunts of breath broke through her teeth. Toward them. Running hard and outstretched like a thoroughbred; warm breath, slobber, the stench of rotten meat and tideflat; small, impassive eyes and the black rubbery rind inside her lips. Her teeth. The bulk of her body coming over them like a breaking wave.

While they were submerged, the confused sow literally ran over them, paused on the opposite bank, looked around, huffed, spanked the water, and ran up into dense cover of the alder trees and into the forest. She never looked back.

Surfacing, the submerged pair heard the small trees snapping as she clawed up the steep rock slope, not slowing down or stumbling once. The clattering of rocks and the grunting up the hillside became more and more faint. Was she still chasing her antagonists? They'll never know.

Chi Mukwa shook as the icy hot needles of fear started stabbing up through his body while he lay still on the bank, shaking and muttering.

Silence.

Remorse and sadness captured their souls as they reflected on the last twenty minutes of trauma ... disheartened further as they witnessed Tough's body floated downstream.

Leigh was first to recover enough to speak.

"My dear Chi Mukwa, I'm so sorry for this terror, for your loss of Sitka, my loss of Tough . . . but thanks to your last move, by submerging in the stream, you saved our lives. Are you hurt? She seemed to run right over you."

"She sure did, my pants and shirt are ripped from claws, front or rear. I'll need immediate treatment to head off infection. Bears have filthy habits and eat rotten food as a matter of course. I'll rinse these wounds in the stream and wrap them for our hike to camp. I can get proper treatment there. How 'bout you? Are you okay?"

"Yep, mine are just contusions from falling on rocks and rolling over dead falls. Let me see your wounds. What can I do to help?"

He directed her to the moss beds in the mud flats, and meticulously made a mixture of moss/mud paste, then had her smear it over the claw marks on his back and lower right leg. She wrapped the scrapes as best she could with his and her handkerchiefs, then tied the poultice in place with some string. He sure looked like he had just wrestled a bear and the bear won. Luckily, they concluded, the bear probably threw up so much splash and spray while running in the water, she most likely could not see them, their eyesight being what it is. Or, maybe she'd had enough killing for one day. Whatever, they were lucky ... or was someone looking after their wellbeing?

"Let's get out of here. First I'll bury Sitka under some rocks and pray for her. I'll meet you by the falls in a few minutes."

As he sadly prepared Sitka's gravesite, he noticed how bad his pants were ripped and his thigh bruised and cut slightly where she had pushed off while leaping across the stream. The hard corner of his knife had also dug into his hip. His clothes had the stink of rotten fat where she had touched him. His skin seemed hot but his body was freezing and could not stop shaking. He flexed his fingers and felt them move easily in their sockets. He put his hands over his eyes and ran them down over his face and felt the soft elasticity of his lips. He ran his hands down his neck and chest to feel his pulse beating up along the entire surface of his torso. His ears rang with blood pumping through the vessels; the air seemed sparkling and the newly falling rain glittered like dust.

He supposed that the sow was some distance away by now. He tried to think if her teats showed she had young cubs with her, but he could not make his mind focus. He kept seeing eyes, teeth, and black gums. He tasted reflux and his head ached, yet he felt like he could have sprinted up the mountain after her, his venge-ance was so heavy, but it was a manifestation created by fear—he soon realized he'd have to return from this dream state. He was pulling, pulling on his breath to slow down as he moved to the falls to meet Leigh.

A raven cried in the tree tops over the waterfall where Leigh was waiting.

At the falls, Leigh looked up. "Well, there you are, my feathered friend. I'm certain you're fully aware of what has happened here . . . and, in fact, probably had a hand in our survival. I wonder? Your actions are hard to measure, and are frequently beyond the pale . . . I never know if some of our resolves are happen-stance, or Manitou's Plan . . . you know, don't you? Here I go, talking to birds again; who would have thought a year ago in Ann Arbor that I'd be doing such a thing."

Still saddened over Sitka's death, Chi Mukwa waded across the stream toward the falls.

"There you are. If you aren't a sight for sore eyes. Hey, with the wolves gone, I'll be your partner . . . bet you're ready to move out of this godforsaken place; come on, let's get the hell out of here! Come on, dear friend, show me the way to your camp," Leigh exclaimed.

Chapter 33

The Past

"When to the sessions of sweet silent thought I summon up remembrance of things past . . ."

Marcel Proust

The last leg of the hike was a quiet one, with both reflecting on the terror by the falls whose costs were still being measured, quietly sifting out a way to deal with its reality, the reality of death and life in the wilds of the pristine Tongass . . . resplendent Alaska.

They made better time without the wolves, but missed them terribly, especially considering that the reasons for their demise were primarily based on protecting them. Adding to their grief was the clarity that even though the odds were against them, both without hesitation leaped to their certain death. When helping her over some dead-falls, he held on to her longer than necessary. His actions did not go unnoticed. When they first arrived at the abandoned settlement, the voices heard ahead were quite a shock.

They held their ground by the gurgling stream, then slowly moved into the tag elders for cover while creeping closer to the voices in the center, or was it on the far border of the settlement. Stealth was made easier in the newly fallen snow, but their contrasting dark outer garments were obvious.

"Well, I'll be damned, Leigh, look at that; the settlement has a few guests. And fancy that, they are well supplied with crosscut saws, a large sled, and would you believe—a horse."

"Just look at that; they've even pitched a tent over there," said Leigh.

"Yep, and it looks pretty clear to me what's going on here. They're taking cedar planks from the old lodge house, the newer totems that are not totally decayed by aging, or rotted by moisture, and worse yet it appears that when they cannot dig them out—they're silently cutting them down right through the face of the lower totem animal when necessary. We have to stop this denigration of our sacred totems immediately.

"And you know damn well why the crosscut saw is used, and the horse . . . a chain saw and snow machine would be too noisy for their illicit activities. Plus a snow machine would be too heavy and most likely sink in some of the bogs they'd have to traverse to keep out of the path of law-abiding people in the Tongass.

"Here's the worst part of this already disgusting scene: both of these rascals are Haidas. I've seen them both at the Dead Dog Bar and Cafe in Skagway. The tall one with long black hair hanging loose and tied around his head with a leather band is called Yellow Knife; he's an alcoholic and drifter, moving from one shady deal to another. His Haida brothers do not think much of him either. As we know, there's a few bad apples in every bushel. The shorter one with the big nose and pony tail is called Red Dog; he too has a rap sheet long enough to paper a jail cell. When they're sober, they earn a living poaching game for themselves or for 'downstaters' who hire them to fill their big game license . . . no questions asked. They know the forest very well, having lived with the tribe for years until they were asked to leave. Their presence here is a good example of their cunning; few know the location of the old settlement . . . but they do, and we've got to do something about this intrusion with minimal trauma to either party."

"But, what to do?" she asked. "If they know you, there could be trouble, and quite frankly we've already had a full serving today. I sure don't want anything to happen to you. Can you see if they are armed?"

"Hell no; they're smart enough not to get caught packing iron when committing another felony. That would add another five to their jail time. No, that's not going to be a problem, but we've got to handle this carefully before it gets dangerously out of hand."

"What are you going to do?" Leigh whispered.

A raven glided to a tall cedar, perched, and cried as if announcing its presence for the activities below.

"If you agree, I'm going to walk into the settlement, and tell them to do the following: unload the totems and planks from the sled, return the totems to the ground where they were found, strike their tent, and depart ASAP—never to return . . . and I'll keep this incident quiet, 'between us girls,' and if they ever return, I will tell the elders and warriors of both the Tlingit and Haida Tribes. We take care of these matters without involving the law, and they know it. They also know the law would be easier on their hide . . . they know very well our justice would be more severe.

"Did you notice I said, 'if you agree,' Leigh? Here's why. If I have any trouble, and I don't expect any—they know who I am—as I said, if I see them as confrontational I just might say my armed partner has one of you in the sights of a gun, do you care to argue?"

"Hey, sounds good. I like this, just like a play with one act, and live ammunition . . . let's do it!"

"Not so fast, my dear. Did you understand with my direct approach, these 'nuts' could bolt or dig a gun out of hiding and put me in their sights? Do you understand? You may have to shoot in the air, at their feet, whatever, or 'drop' one or both . . . do you understand?"

"Big Bear, I do understand. And no, I hope I will not have to shoot, but after this morning's experience at the falls, I'm damn mad at bears—and these jack-asses, too. Yes, my dander is boiling over, and thieves—worse, thieves of historical artifacts for resale, artifacts of your clan's history—piss me off. It's time. Let's burn 'em."

"Okay, okay, I believe you; you're ready. I just hope, after hearing and sens-ing your feelings, that they don't cause any trouble. I see what 'they' mean now by red-headed vengeance. However, I think if you send one across their bow, I know one of them, if you throw a slug close to him, he will have to clean out his pants tonight. Why? Because they're both yellow-bellied sapsucking varmints. Okay, let's do it."

"Wait, I hear voices. Maybe they've seen us. No, they're talking to each other in a loud, argumentative tone, in contradiction/interruption style."

*   *   *

"Where's the bottle?"

"How the hell should I know; you had it last. Isn't it over by the sled? You've had enough anyway, Red Dog. Get your butt over by this totem and help me. We've got to get out of here very soon; it's getting late. We can drink after loading is complete."

"Okay, okay, but remember you're not the boss. I've got as much risk in this as you . . . and I'm damn well going to get the same money from selling these artifacts."

Yellow Knife mumbled yes to himself, but it appeared that he was the only one sober today. Too bad he had to put up with such a scumbag, but in this line of work—theft—one could not be too fussy.

Yellow Knife spoke with authority. "Now, let's get those last two short to-tems, the ones we had to cut, over by the sled and roll them up with those ramp logs. Be careful, some of these totems are rotted so bad they're about to fall apart. It's a shame to have to move them. I know one thing for certain: if the Tlingits, or our brothers, discover what we're doing . . . we're in for plenty bad medicine. Needless to say, if the Great Spirit is involved we may wish we had never sold our heritage for a mere two-thousand dollars per totem. But, being desperate, marginal menlike us, we'll take a chance. Come on, let's get humping."

Red Dog responded, "Bitch, bitch, bitch . . . you're always bitching or griping about one thing or another. I'm getting tired of your bossy attitude—punk."

Yellow Knife knew part of the problem was his partner's continual sucking on the whiskey bottle. But he was damn tired of doing most of the cutting, load-ing, and burying cut totem stumps or filling in totems' evacuated holes so the casual observer could not tell several totems had been removed. Dumb, for sure, but smart enough to leave about half the totem poles in place and a lot of the cedar planks from the collapsed lodge. The bickering continued as they finished loading.

"For Christ's sake, is this all the tie-down rope you brought?" yelled Red Dog, with a little more slur in his speech. "How the hell do you expect me to secure this load with these two coils?"

"Do the best you can, blockhead. Use some of the smaller rope from the tent tie downs, cut 'em if necessary, and be sure to lay the tent over the entire load to hide its identity. You never know who's out and about in the forest, or on the two-track back to our cabin. I'll get the horse and hook-up; we've got to get the hell out of here. It's about a four-hour trek to our cabin. Come on, you bastard, hustle!"

"You know, I've had just about enough of your mouth today. I'm doing most of the work, and getting an excessive amount of crap from you. I ought to give you a piece of this fist to straighten you out."

Yellow Knife tried to ignore his drunken partner, but if he kept up the banter a confrontation surely would occur, and it would not be pretty. Both barroom fighters, they followed no rules. While Red Dog struggled, half drunk, with the tie-downs and tent covering on the sled, Yellow Knife stopped suddenly, and looked around the area, scanning the settlement and the approaches from the east and the west, then cautiously moved toward the horse. He stopped again, as though sensing a presence, an intruder. He looked up and immediately spotted the raven and felt a little relieved, but he *still* had a feeling that they were not alone.

"Hello my black feathered friend. What brings you to our camp?"

He knew very well why the raven was here. Ravens serve the two-leggeds in both good and bad times . . . as a blessing, and as a warning. It was pretty obvious what this visit entailed. It was not goodwill. Now it was even more pressing to get the hell out of here. If the Great Spirit knew what was going-down . . . we'd both be in big trouble. It may already be too late. He thought it may be his nerves; they always flared when doing something illegal. He asked himself how the hell the raven knew they were here, what could have cued the bird to their presence at the settlement. The bird's arrival was no accident. He wondered if someone brought the raven here, or it followed them in last night. He wondered.

"Come on, old gal; let's get hitched up and on the way so you can be eating oats in your own stall by sunset. Looks like you've already had a little snack; the cedar branches must have tasted good. Hope you enjoyed them, old gal. Come on, let's go."

As Yellow Knife approached the sled with "old gal" under harness, whiffle-tree in one hand, reins in the other, he saw Red Dog spread-eagle in the snow, passed out, not half-drunk, but totally smashed.

Yellow Knife moved the horse around, backed her up to the tongue, and hooked up the sled alone. He patted her neck and fed his last apple to his friend, certainly more reliable than the drunk lying in the snow.

"You, you son of a bitch. You better get your butt up and get ready to get out of here. I don't like the feeling I'm getting. It's as though we're being watched. Then there's the raven . . . it's not right; let's get going you bum," he yelled, at the same time planting his foot on Red Dog's butt. "Get up you half-baked Indian, get up you soused no good Indian."

After this encounter, all hell broke loose. Red Dog jumped up, staggered, and started flailing at Yellow Knife, falling and stumbling across the snow and sled. The horse lurched against the harness as he fell into her, then under her, causing a little dangerous prancing by old gal. Seeing that he'd sooner or later hurt himself, Yellow Knife dragged him out from under the horse and conked him on the head with a shovel. Then before he dropped, he threw him on the load of poles and planks to sleep it off and out of the way so they could leave.

Just as he took a last look at the ravaged settlement, a figure stealthily stepped into the clearing; Yellow Knife froze.

*   *   *

Leigh whispered, "Big Bear, you'd better step into that fight and stop them before they hurt each other. Look, the tall one just hit the drunken short one with a shovel. What's going on?"

"You're right; I've seen enough, too. I want them in good health to unload that sled and replace everything as they found it, then get 'em the hell out of here before I blow my top. You're right. Cover me as we have discussed. Remember, stay out of sight, but keep the thieves and me covered at all times. When I've got things under control . . . I call you in, okay?"

"Yep, let's do it. You'd better hurry; the tall one just threw his 'conked-out' partner on the sled; he's about to take off."

*   *   *

"Well, if it isn't the Tlingit elder, Chi Mukwa. What are you doing here?"

"I may ask the same. At least I am not stealing Indian artifacts for personal profit. I'm not violating my tribal rules. I'm not a thief. You have few choices, as I see it."

"Maybe I do not care to choose any of your choices," he echoed.

"The way I see it, Yellow Knife, you've just run out of choices. You know why? Your only choice is to unload that sled, replace all the totems exactly as you found them, return the planks, and get out of here while you've still got a chance. I'm the only one who knows about your skullduggery, your thievery, your violation of Native American habitat . . . should I go on? I am going to give you one hour to roust that good-for-nothing partner of yours to complete all these tasks, and if I'm still in a good mood, I'll be the only one to know. We don't need any more tribal conflicts than what we have in honest dealings over fishing and hunting rights. Now step to it; we're burning daylight while I'm talking to you . . . scum. By the way, I'm keeping your horse, and sled, too. Why? I know what you use that rig for . . . pulling in illegal deer for downstaters. My clan can use her for hauling wood and transportation. I'll prepare a bill of sale right here in the clearing to ensure it's all nice and legal. Do you have anything to say that's worth me listening to?"

He did not speak, but went over to the sled, threw snow on Red Dog's face, slapped him around, and dragged him over to where Big Bear was standing.

"Heads up, you Dog; we've got company. We've got to make a quick decision on our forefathers' property."

"It is not the property of the Haidas—and you know better. This is a Tlingit settlement," Big Bear interjected in clear language.

"Well, we're not so sure, and anyway what makes you think we're going to roll over for you? There's two of us. We may just tell you to go to hell," Yellow Knife said, holding a shovel in a threatening position.

"Well, first, I could take you both with one arm tied behind my back and, second, my partner has a gun leveled on one of you as I speak. Want to discuss this any further? As I said, daylight's burning, and you will complete this task today, within the next hour, and get the hell out of my sight while you've still got your clothes on your back; waste any more time, and I'll send you home stark naked."

"He's bluffing! There's no one covering him! He's full of crap!" Red Dog screamed. "He's full of crap. I'm getting tired of his better-than-thou attitude. Let's take care of this problem—right now!" Red Dog jumped toward Chi Mukwa.

At that moment a shot rang out, and the shovel held by Yellow Knife was blown out of his hands as he collapsed. Red Dog also hit the snow, face first.

As the report echoed across the lowlands and down the valley, Yellow Knife looked up at Chi Mukwa narrowing his eyes and stared—then looked around at his miserable partner who was yelling, "Heap bad luck! Heap bad luck! No shoot at him! No shoot! We give you what you want! No shoot Indian!"

"Shut up, you fool, shut up!" Yellow Knife yelled. "Get over here. They shot at me, not you, you fool. Get up and get over here."

"Okay, don't shoot," Yellow Knife pleaded as they both unloaded the sled.

"If you've learned anything today, I hope it's that 'you don't pee in your friend's pool' . . . think about that."

It didn't take long for the two thieves to agree to all the terms presented to them, including unloading and replacing the totems, straightening up the area, and hightailing it to the east . . . all within one hour, so Chi Mukwa let them keep their clothes and boots. Yellow Knife also signed over the sled and horse to the clan for the "going price" of one dollar . . . and services rendered. In other words, he would keep quiet on their attempt to steal Native Indian artifacts.

Leigh never had to show, by plan, so no sense exposing her to these bums. They never even knew who took the "value clarification" shot . . . slamming the shovel out of Yellow Knife's hands. All they knew is whoever shot had a good aim. The next one might have been a blood shot.

"Hello there, what's your name? 'Old gal' is what I've heard. If that's it, may I say welcome to the Tlingit, Raven clan of the Tongass; our tribe will take good care of you."

"Hey, can I come in now? Hey, you, is it clear?" Leigh yelled from the tag elders.

"Yeah, come on, meet my new girlfriend. She's got beautiful brown eyes, long eyelashes, long black hair, and a beautiful white star on her forehead. All that on a beautiful sculpted body . . . like a Greek goddess. Yeah, come on in, sharpshooter. Meet 'old gal,' the clan's new horse."

Raven watched over the settlement where the elegant plank houses and clan totems once stood, totems that magnificently celebrated the fabled bird. The bringer of light to the world gazed over what was formerly the grand structures of solid cedar for which all the totems exalted the raven's high position in Tlingit life. Missing was the former gathering with the chief, Raven in the Moonlight's house for a potlatch, a traditional feast and gift-giving ceremony. Missing were the canoes and horses for safekeeping under the raven's eye. The singers were no longer heard, the dancers, all masked in animal faces, absent. Chanting around the fire and pounding of drums . . . missing. Indeed, the present scene was rather bleak as compared to its past.

The raven's sorrow was heard in its melodic cries across the cedars. Yes, the dancing had stopped forever, but at least some like Chi Mukwa were risking their life to maintain the memories of times past to times present.

"Welcome, my friend. I've missed your presence, but sure needed your back-up. You shot at exactly the right time, and in blowing the shovel out of Yellow Knife's hands, he lost all the little fight that was left in the miserable old bastard. We make quite a team, my dear. But, let's not make a habit of this, right?"

"Right! I was concerned for your safety while those drunken bastards were replacing the totems. I actually got tired holding the pistol in the shooting position. Look, the handle has left its impression in my palm. More than that, I'm still shaking."

She offered her hand to show him. He held it and wrapped his arms around her. It was a very close embrace. He was speechless, she with a small tear in her eye; it had been a rough hour of tension that, thankfully, turned out in their favor. The embrace seemed a little different; more was involved than comforting over the fear. There was a chemistry of the union, a mixture of a quality rarely found. The union remained hard and fast. She spoke. "Big Bear, I can't explain my emotional collapse. I guess it's related to not being used to holding a gun so long, and seeing you in danger. I'm so glad it's over. I'm so glad you're safe." Reluctantly, she withdrew from his passionate embrace and walked through the settlement. "Look at this wanton destruction. Those two should have their balls fried for breakfast!"

"Now, now, Leigh, calm down. Let's relax for a while. Come over here; I'll give you a ten-cent tour of my forefathers' settlement." After a brief walk-around, they approached the collapsed plank house. "This would have been the center of the large central assembly area. Here, sit on this log with me and I'll give you an eyeball look at the settlement. Maybe I can do it in a story-line type of tour. Wanna' try?"

"Sure. Can you do it while sitting next to me? I need a little more tender-loving care . . . I'm still rattled from all this excitement."

"Yep, here goes. Throw this rain slicker around you and lean back for the show. I hope it measures up to your expectations. This is the story of Raven by the Moonlight's Potlatch . . . held right here where you sit, only two-hundred years ago. I've heard the story a dozen times by Three Bears, and several chiefs:

"On a typical evening, several horses and dozens of large cedar canoes were drawn up on the stream's bank under the Raven's eye. They had arrived from villages up and down the coast, bearing men and women of high rank along with their relatives and slaves. All were gathered at Raven in the Moonlight's house for a potlatch, a traditional feast and gift-giving ceremony. That's where we're sitting. Inside the great house, the guests looked on as masked figures danced around a fire to the pounding of box drums and the chanting of singers. Raven in the Moonlight and the invited chiefs sat in the place of honor—a platform at the rear of the house, erected in front of a decorated wooden screen. Carved and painted on the screen was a scene from the sacred history of the house, one in which Raven assumed the guise of a mischievous infant in the house of a spirit chief and stole from him the light that became the sun, the moon, and the stars. A small round opening in the center of the screen led into a cubicle where the treasures of the house were normally kept. On this night, however, the cubicle lay empty. All its treasures—masks, ceremonial bowls, ornamental blankets, wooden helmets, engraved sheets of copper, and other prized items handed down by the host's ancestors—had been placed on the platform in front of the screen for the guests to admire.

"Abruptly, the chanting stopped, and a close kinsman of Raven in the Moonlight, chosen by him to serve as speaker, rose to address the guests. He presented the invited chiefs with a regional delicacy, heaping ladles of oil from the salmon mixed with snow carried down from nearby mountaintops. As the chiefs consumed the rich mixture, several of Raven in the Moonlight's warriors rushed into the house, making menacing, but only theatrical, gestures. Soon the warriors ceased their hostile movements and scattered raven feathers over the heads of the guests as a sign of peace. While his people sang songs that praised the greatness of his house, Raven in the Moonlight directed the distribution of the presents—Chilkat blankets, bundles of food, and for the highest-ranking guests, such finely wrought articles as cedar boxes and canoes.

"As the gift-giving neared its conclusion, Raven in the Moonlight's uncle stood up to address the gathering. 'Raven in the Moonlight has asked me to speak to you about his ancestors and the sacred history of his house,' he explained. 'We all know that raven was a powerful spirit who came from the sky as a shining youth. Here on Earth he learned to eat food and became ravenously hungry. He would do anything to get food, and sometimes he did things that have helped us to this day.

"He taught us to respect other creatures.

"He gave us fish and game.

"He taught us to respect the land.

"He taught us to honor Heaven above.

"But more than these, he brought us out of darkness. He got light for us."

*   *   *

"What do you think? Quite a story, kinda complex, isn't it, Leigh? But the message is clear. The raven's light is symbolized by the distribution of gifts from the Chief through the potlatch, for those with much are to share with others not so fortunate, and believe me from what I've heard the potlatch and celebration went on for days, as it should be. They were only held once or twice in a chief's lifetime."

The beauty of the settlement, even with the forest taking over the footprint of its grandeur, gave pause to the odd pair joined by accident in the forest of his forefathers. She had much to learn, he much to learn about her. The magnificence of the locale urged him to speak to the red-headed stranger as he had not made a practice in doing . . . until now. She was special.

"You know, Leigh, in the still of the night, when others are captive of their dreams, this spot comes to me. Her gentle tree-lined stream, colorful vistas, and many faces dance across my mind, awakening the sounds and sights of a time long past. The Tongass is my first love, and like any true love, our journey together was not always an easy one. I owe to her much of what I consider to be good in myself and to my Tlingit people.

"Many in the Northwest had roots planted here long before the white man knew about these shores. As Indians, we had a way of life that suited us; at its center were the land upon which we walked with the Creator, Gitchee Manitou. After the white man came, much of that changed. When he first came to our land, we accepted his arrival and taught him what we knew so he could survive. We did a pretty good job, because as the years went on, his numbers grew.

"Over time, we lost most of our land and found ourselves struggling to fit into what had become his world. Our days of abundance and freedom were gone. The dark times, foretold in our prophecies, were upon us. These were times into which I was born, the early years in the twentieth century.

"As a young boy, I thought being Indian meant struggling to survive. Now I am an older man and have learned to see beyond those struggles to a deeper meaning.

"The camp you are about to visit is more than a group of subsistence Indians living on a no-name street in the Tongass. The camp is our home away from the problems of urban life and, like our ancestors, we belong to one another. Our working, playing, and struggling together gets us through the hard times. It is my prayer that our story will teach you that the worth of a people can be measured not by what they have accumulated, but only by how they treat one another."

"That was beautiful. I have just relived the Tlingit tradition through your story of words and facial expressions."

"Facial expressions?"

"Yes, your words drew me to your facial expressions. They were beautiful and resplendent as you proudly told your people's story. By the way, may I call you Bear?"

"Thank you for the comment, and yes you can call me anything you want."

"Bear, isn't it time for us to move out and plan the route to camp with our new 'purchase,' or should I say our gift, our four-legged friend."

"You're right, but we are in luck. The route to our camp will be easy for 'old gal' to traverse. In fact, my good friend Leigh, load your butt on the sled. I'm going to be your carriage/sled chauffeur, without top hat and tails, but everything else that they've got in New York's Central Park. "Up gal, let's go, daylight is a burning."

Chapter 34

Bridge To The Past

"The great law of culture is to let one become what they were created to be."

D. Rexford, Barrow, Alaska

Hemlock and cedar provide a beautiful contrast for the lighter aspen and birch plus an occasional Great Redwood intertwined as their shadows lie across the fresh snow as if to double the forest's density. The late afternoon sun with its growing shadows offers a wondrous setting for the couple as they forge ahead to Chi Mukwa's home, the Raven Clan Camp of the Tlingit Tribe.

The route from the former settlement to his camp is a little more arduous than they planned. The horse is not the problem; old gal's surefootedness prevails. It is the runners on the sled that are unable to "track" along the foot path and behind the horse. The sled keeps sliding off the path and from behind the horse, taking Leigh with it at times into snow drifts, windfalls, and bogs. Nevertheless, Leigh and "Bear," Chi Mukwa's new nickname, trudge on, chiefly following the branch of the Bitterroot River called the Root, or Little Root. Bear leads the way for old gal, and Leigh rides, the sled reins in hand.

Bear indicates they are about halfway to camp, and should be at the outer markers at about four fingers of horizon to the sun. After falling off for the third time, Leigh comes up with an idea to improve the movement of the sled through the irregular path along the stream.

She remembers, while working with her dad picking stones from farmers' freshly plowed fields, they frequently used a "stone boat" type of sled much like this one. It too did not run or track true unless it had weight on it. The snow is like the freshly tilled soil, and throwing stones on the "boat" solved the tracking problem there, so it would here, too.

"Bear, I've an idea. Let's throw some large deadfalls on this sled. That will give it some weight for tracking and give old gal a constant pull versus the present 'wig-way, slacky-tacky, marshmallow, lightweight sled,' she's pulling now. I only weigh about one-hundred fifty pounds soaking wet, and that's not much. What do you think? You'll need some firewood anyway. Okay?"

Bear nods with a "sounds good" look.

"Whoa, gal," as Leigh unhitches the sled.

"Not a bad idea. Let's rest before we load and all go down by the stream to get a drink. Come on, grab that whiffletree and we'll walk her down. Do I have to call you Mule Skinner, Wrangler, or Coachwoman now? Here, let me hold your arm so you don't fall in; it's slippery on these rocks. Say, we could throw some rocks on the sled, too. Yeah, good idea. You gals had enough to drink? Hey this ain't bad, traveling alone in the wilds with two beautiful gals, a two-legged and a four-legged. So, let's hitch her up, 'Skinner Leigh' . . . or is it 'Leigh the Mule Skinner?'"

"Are you just about done calling me names, my friend? . . . You know, Chi Mukwa is no cakewalk to pronounce."

"Say, if I had not known better, at a distance you must have looked like a beautiful red-headed nymph drinking from nature's natural, nourishing natatorium—or better yet, a red-headed doe. Red Doe, Red Deer, and, with wolves in camp, The White, Jet, you could be called: 'Red Deer Runs with Wolves.' That's more like it . . . Or 'Runs with Wolves.' I see a naming ceremony coming up, my dear. Yes, if you agree, we'll do so while you're at camp. Yes, madam, that's it: 'Runs with Wolves.'

"That's better than what others have been calling you, such as: Woman-with-Red-Hair. It could have been worse. Some of the tribal members call me a lot of names that are less flattering, when we disagree. I've heard 'Bad Bear' many times behind my back, never to my face.

"Before we load the sled with deadfalls, would you join me in a prayer for our departed four-leggeds, the wolves? We'll ask Gitchee Manitou to accept them into an afterlife, their new life, and thank Him for the wolves' short time with us. Okay?"

She nods yes, thinking of his tenderness contrasted to his outer appearance as a Tlingit warrior and elder. His commitment to the Spirit shows. She is anxious to participate in thanking the Spirit for the wolves' life, and to bless their passing. As they sit on the sled together, he holds her hands in a ceremonial fashion, looks at her . . . focusing directly, singularly concentrating on her eyes as both assume a modified lotus position, facing each other.

The omnipresent raven now reveals itself, making its presence known by extending its wings, flapping them wildly, and crying loudly in announcing his location in the valley.

"Good afternoon, my black friend; welcome to our trek along the Root. I knew you were around here . . . somewhere," says Leigh. Silence follows, with minimal rustling of leaves and gurgling of the Root.

Bear begins:

"Great Spirit, we are thankful for your creation of Earth and its inhabitants. Today we mourn the passing of two of our and your four-legged friends, Sitka and Tough, courageous wolves who blessed us with their presence. Bless them in their afterlife."

Leigh speaks:

"Creator, Lord of the Universe, bless us and the animals that you have given us to sustain our life. We especially thank you for our departed friends, Tough and Sitka, magnificent wolves in our care and now in yours. We thank you."

They remain silent upon completion of their thanks to the Creator while Bear chants quietly a mournful melody, and Leigh hums her favorite song from the protestant hymnal, "Open my Eyes" . . . "Open my eyes and I will see spirits of love come true to me; open my eyes and I will see spirits divine." It was her father's favorite, and hers, too.

The sled is loaded with good old dried out dead wood and about a dozen large rocks for multiple uses around camp. Leigh has made herself a little driver's seat and appears ready to "strap 'em on and move 'em out."

Then, to her surprise, old gal, for some unknown reason, starts fidgeting and prancing, ears erect and rotating like a radar antenna, head and neck stretching back . . . looking back down the stream and acting nervous.

"What do you think is bothering her, Bear?"

"Not sure, but the wind is blowing this way from downstream; maybe she's picked up the scent of an animal to which she's uncertain . . . or knows, and has had a run in with in the past. It's hard to tell. Quite frankly, there must be many scents of various animals that are predatory. I'm not sure what this one could be."

He thinks the worst. Horses react rather violently to the scent of bear for good reasons; they're just like an elk to a hungry grizzly.

"Wait, Bear, listen. Can you hear that? It's a whimper or groan. Kinda guttural isn't it?

"Yeah. I hear it now. That's what's bothering the horse, I'll bet. It's coming from the path behind us. It's silent now. Strange. No, wait. There it is again. You hold, gal, and I'll go see what it is. Wait here; I'll be right back."

"Be careful, hard telling what's back there. Whoa, gal, it'll be okay. Whoa. Settle down." Leigh dismounts the sled and moves to Gal's head.

Silence follows, with a slight whisper in the wind. The *Spirit of the Wind*, comes down from the northern climes, across the stream, rattling the drying oak leaves as they cling to their last breath of life. No matter, they will soon fall, some sooner than later . . . as with man.

An eerie silence prevails; Leigh has not heard from Bear for a while. She starts to worry a little, and wonders if it would show too much tentativeness to call out for him. After all, she wants to demonstrate her toughness.

Silence. More silence. The sound is deafening.

She starts to tie gal to a tree and find him . . . and it happens all at once.

"Leigh! Come quickly!" Bear shouts.

"Whoa, gal, settle down. I'll be right back."

"What is it, Bear?"

Leigh quickly ties the horse to a branch and takes off down the path. Her nerves at their peak intensity, she wonders what Bear has found. As she rounds a small bend, she sees him. Bear is kneeling over a mass of fur along the path.

"What is it, Bear? What have you found? What is it?"

Bear looks at her without speaking; his facial expression is complex. It's an amalgamation of joy and sorrow . . . such as she has rarely seen in any man. The face is what one might see on relatives at a funeral, glad to see you, sad for the reason. Bear is at a loss for words to express his joy and sorrow. She discovers why.

"Bear! It's Tough! He's alive! Is he? Oh Bear, he's survived the attack, the stream, and has tracked us for several miles . . . Oh Bear."

Leigh collapses to her knees next to Bear and tenderly holds the head of the gray wolf. Indeed it is Tough, breathing with difficulty, and appearing barely alive as he struggles for air . . . but shows a little glint in his eyes that he has found his mistress. He now has a chance of surviving. Hardly a pretty sight, his fur is caked with dirt and dried black blood, ice, and snow from the stream's mudflats.

"Leigh, the good news is if he has made it this far, he'll probably make it with the care we can provide. However, the bad news is, this trip to find us may have pushed the limits of recovery. But, one thing is certain, our skills and the Great Spirit will do everything possible to save this tough wolf. His ribs are fractured, breathing is difficult, but—by God—he survived, and we'll ensure he lives. Yes, he was half dead, but his quest to find you, and now having seen you I can almost guarantee his effort to live, to have a life, will be realized. With loving care, nourishment, and a little help from Manitou, my money is on the wolf; as you've said many times, he's tough. You're a fortunate woman, Runs with wolves."

"Oh Bear. Oh dear. What can I say? Let me hold him?" She carefully raised his head slightly, and he whined. "Well, that's enough, boy. Here, I'll lay you down. Can we clean him up? I suggest that we do not until we've wrapped his chest and rib cage, and get him to a warm place to eat and rest. Then we can make him look clean and pretty. It won't hurt to leave him with this disheveled look for a while. Let's move him to the sled and get him to camp and a warm bed."

"Before we move him, let's wrap up his chest so there's no more damage or fractures to his ribs, now or during the ride on the sled," says Bear.

Leigh doffs her coat, removes her outer shirt, and tears it into strip-like bandages. In doing so her inner body is clearly revealed under the old bleached Michigan T-shirt. Since she rarely, as today, wear a bra to cup her beautiful breasts, they too sense the chill in the air as her nipples clearly speak of their presence behind the M and N, in MICHIGAN.

None of this sideshow of tearing cloth, spreading arms while tearing, and the resultant bouncing boobs are lost on Bear. He pays attention. In fact, he moves toward her to help. He feels just a little guilty, being married, but . . . just a little.

"Here, I'll help you tear some of those strips. You grab this end and I the other; we'll get these last couple tears together. There, finished, can I help you on with your coat? You must be chilled. It's lucky for Tough that you wore two shirts."

"You bet, thanks. Damn, it's chilly. The old sun is getting lower in the sky. We'd better get a move on. You know, being alone with you out here, it's lucky for both of us that I wore two shirts . . ."

They both work on Tough, she wrapping his chest while he holds him up. They make a small litter-carry of limbs and tie-downs and roll him carefully over on it, then lay it on the sled. While Bear leads old gal, Leigh sits next to Tough and they move the last couple miles to the Raven Camp of the Tlingits.

Her thoughts are of Bear's body language, his closeness, his caring.

His thoughts are of Leigh, her beauty, and her last comment . . . "It's lucky for both of us that I wore two shirts . . ." He wonders if she had only worn one shirt, if she would have taken it off and torn it up, regardless of the consequences.

*   *   *

The last five miles went well. Suddenly a couple of domesticated wolves ran out to meet them at what Bear called the half-mile marker. After jumping and licking his hands, growling at the horse, who casually threw a hoof in their direction, the two wolves approached Leigh and Tough with utmost caution. They circled the sled a couple of times, ears back, then seemed to get less defensive and followed the sled to camp without incident.

The clan came forward and after a quick greeting to all. Bear pulled the elders aside and gave the small group, including his wife, a brief overview about the last three days as he surveyed the collapsed and violated burial vault; Leigh's reasons for visiting the camp; the terrible grizzly bear attack costing Sitka's life, Tough's injuries; the incident at the abandoned settlement with Yellow Knife and Red Dog stealing artifacts, chasing them off, yet buying their horse, and finally the marvel—the omen—of Tough's surviving the grizzly attack and finding them on the trail just a few miles back. Finally, how anxious he was to return to normal life in camp.

His wife, Morning Star, greeted him with a smile, but lowered her eyes in an unusual manner. Bear could not judge her strange body language. Was it Leigh's presence? Or something else? There were a few more questions, some answered, some deferred for Leigh to answer later.

Big Wind, Bear's teenaged son, was elated with the opportunities that the horse would provide. He went directly to her, patting her neck while talking to her. He asked her name, and took her to a shelter for food and water. He had found a new friend.

Morning Star went directly to the sled to help bring the injured wolf to the fire pit and warmth. With Leigh's help, they both carried him gently to an elevated area near the fire just outside the plank house. Bear approached the women and asked how Tough was doing.

"Leigh, would you please come with me to the plank house? It's a custom to introduce you to the senior elder, the shaman, Old White, soon after arrival in camp."

They left with Morning Star caring for Tough; she nodded as if understanding Bear's next task, but again lowered her eyes without contact with Bear as she attended to Tough. Her attitude toward Leigh was certainly cautious, but by no means appearing to be jealousy. While attending Tough together, she did mention knowing of her location south of the clan's settlement. Like a well-trained nurse, she wrapped his chest after cleaning him up, and noted that the shirt torn for the initial wrapping of his chest was not Bears. She did not ask if it was Leigh's . . . the answer was pretty obvious . . . she wondered if Leigh had anything on under her coat.

As they approached the plank house, Leigh's eyes gathered in the magnificent totem pole out front. She walked through the ceremonial entrance to the house, more than 90 feet wide and nearly twice as long, built of tightly joined 2-foot-wide cedar planks. The totem that fronted the house was a towering cedar pole with crests symbolizing the lineage of its inhabitants. Bear explained how this particular structure reflects a culture that is rich in the material and spiritual resources of life. As Bear and Leigh walked into the center of the house, he explained the four smaller corner totems symbolizing their legendary brothers in the Earth: the Bear, the Wolf, the Eagle, and the Whale, representing sea creatures like the salmon and halibut. The lower floor in the center contained the fireplace, with a smoke hole above. Although Leigh could not attend the ceremonial services, he showed her where a sky pole was inserted into the ground by the fire, and how the shamans made contact with their ancestral spirits through the smoke hole. He climbed the pole to dramatize his access to the sky powers.

"Sounds kinda strange, or should I say different, doesn't it?" he spoke to the red-haired woman in a partial trance.

"Not at all. I'm just trying to picture in my own mind the beauty of the ceremony . . . trying to place myself in it. Oh, Bear, you misjudge me; I think it must be—beautiful."

"We are now proceeding to the revered and decorative rain wall that separates the chief from his people. As you can see, it represents the raven, with claw-like feet and human arms outstretched from the opening that serves as the entrance to the house leader's chamber. The large decorated chest contains clan regalia, emblems of rank, dancing headdresses, masks, and other images. The chief also uses it as a seat during ceremonies.

"The chief is behind that large circular hole at the base of raven's claws in the center of the rain wall; he's waiting for us. Are you ready?"

"Ready and anxious, my dear. Thanks for the grand tour; this house is amazing for more reasons than one . . it's loaded with as much mystery as culture."

"As it should be, my dear, it represents the center of the universe for our kinship group, the Raven Clan, that inhabits it. Did you notice the house faces east, and the back door the forest where the remains of the dead are interred in individual little wooden death houses? I'll show them to you later. Ready? Let's crawl through the entry hole.

"Gete Wabiska (Old White), I present Leigh West, per our custom, for she is an overnight visitor. Her purpose for living in the Tongass, ten miles south near the sacred burial vault, is to explore the Alaskan wilds and write of her experiences. She chose to make part of that experience a knowledge of Tlingit life, and to expand on the relationship for our mutual benefit, friendship, and aid if it ever comes to pass," explained Chi Mukwa.

"I'm pleased and honored to meet you, sir. It is indeed a once-in-a-lifetime opportunity to be with you and your Raven Clan. May I present this small gift in thanksgiving for being with your people," said Leigh.

He took the Bowie hunting knife with the grace of a chief, showed it to Chi Mukwa, and set it aside with a nod of thanks.

"The honor is ours, my dear. Thank you for the practical gift; I so often receive unusable trinkets from guests who mean well. I have heard of your presence, and have been calling you, The Red Haired One, or something like that. We meant no disrespect; we call 'em as we see 'em, as you down-staters would say. My son indicates the elders will soon take care of that with a naming ceremony, maybe tonight. Their name seems to be: Runs with Wolves. From what I've heard about you, it's accurately descriptive. Yes? If there's anything else I can do for you, let me know through my son. And, let me thank you again for your interest in our clan, and the Tlingits. I will see you again soon, in fact tonight, at the tribal camp fire. There is much serious business to talk about tonight."

"There is one request. Since Chi Mukwa is married, would you give permission for him to give me a tour of the entire settlement. I would not like to be in conflict with his wife. Only you, I understand, can give him permission to do so. I so want to record a visual memory of every inch of this beautiful settlement."

"Chi Mukwa, is this possible?"

"Yes, father; I will tell my wife of your decision."

"Thank you," Leigh directs to Gete Wabiska.

"I will see you this evening. Please sit at my right hand as an honored guest." He nods and indicates their meeting is over.

*   *   *

Leigh and Bear walked around back of the plank house to view the "death houses" built over each burial spot, unique indeed. The next stop was by the huge wood pile where an older man called Running Deer was working on their favorite dugout canoe of cedar, although redwood was also used.

"Running Deer, would you mind giving Leigh a walk through of how you create such a beautiful vessel?"

"Certainly. We split it along its center with wooden wedges. The round sides are charred and stripped with an adz. Both the inside and outside are scraped, chiseled, and rubbed smooth to two-inch thickness; the dug-out portion is widened by putting hot water inside, adding hot rocks and burning hot fires near the outside to heat the wood so inside braces can be wedged into the cockpit to further widen it. Sometimes we cover the dug-out cavity to hold the heat in, widening more of course in the center than the bow and stern. After the desired shape is formed, we let her dry out, sand the sides with stone and sharkskin and decorate in with totemic designs of choice. The medicine man would come along next to capture a soul and give it to the vessel. What do you think?"

"I'd love to order one; do you think I could afford it?"

"No question. Place your order with Chi Mukwa."

"Thank you. Maybe next time, though; carry on. We're moving on."

"We can't see everything before dark, so let's take a look at the fish traps in the Root."

A youngster ran up to the pair as they walked down toward the stream.

"Hello Wind Spirit, how are you today? What's on your mind?"

"Can I go with you and Red Hair?"

"Sure," said Leigh, with a concerned look from Bear.

"Is it okay, Bear?"

"It's up to you, dear," he said in a less-than-positive tone.

It was as though his voice indicated that he secretly wanted to be . . . *alone* with Leigh. She picked up on the tone and stored it away, for now. She felt as though they must be careful under the circumstances . . . they'd already been alone for more than two days.

"Here we are. Take a look at the heart-shaped weir with vertical sticks pointed upstream. It blocks three-quarters of the stream. The fish are directed into the center of the heart guided by the roundness of the top section of the heart . . . once in, they linger, eat a little, and do not panic, and every day they are dipped out since the exit opening is indeed hard to find without any guides, like on the entry."

"Neat, can we see if there are any in the trap?"

"Sure, but it's used primarily for the salmon run in late August when they are spawning and swim with reckless abandonment. Yeah, look, there's a few in there."

"Come on, Wind Spirit," Leigh challenged. "Let's go down to the stream; we'll find a few. Come on, I'll race you to the bottom!"

Bear did enjoy watching the two frolic on the edge of the stream, looking into the weir's heart-shaped trap. She certainly didn't look or act like someone who'd seen sixty years or more. He felt that she was a winner, to be sure.

"Yep, you're right . . . 'notten; they've all bailed out for the season, I guess. Do you see any, Windy . . . are there any down by you?"

"No, my name not Windy, me . . . Wind Spirit!"

"Oh, I know, I just shorten a lot of the Indian names for my convenience . . . sorry 'bout that. I'll do better."

"Come on, you chatterboxes. Let's get going. Daylight's a burning. Come on. That boy's so close to falling in the drink . . . he's within sniffing distance."

"Red Hair," said Wind Spirit, "Chi Mukwa sure talk funny at times. Me have problems understanding him."

"I understand. He verbally shoots from the hip a lot."

They all gathered at the top of the stream, and Leigh made them all join hands as the three returned to the camp with the sun at one finger off the horizon. It's getting late; the nightly ceremonial meeting by the fire will begin very soon. And rumors indicate the chief has an important announcement.

*　　*　　*

Indeed, it was a somber night; you could tell by the body language of the chief and his demeanor when he talked. He was polite all right. It was just that everyone noticed the solemn style that was not typical of Gete Wabiska. They were all seated, the chanting complete, when he asked Chi Mukwa to start the *naming ceremony* for the Woman-with-Red-Hair, Leigh West, who sat at his right in her new and very valuable gift from the tribal women, a hand-woven Chilkat blanket. He asked her to stand and, in an unusual display of affection for the chief, held her and kissed each cheek as was the custom with some Europeans. Taking her hand, he led her to the center of the grouping around the fire and gave it to his son. Gete Wabiska's reserved emotional presence was noticeable, or was it a more caring style demonstrated tonight.

Chi Mukwa called forward the witnesses who had met Leigh. Much to her surprise, Wind Spirit had been granted special permission to be part of the ceremony as a witness. He was elated at the honor bestowed on him by Chi Mukwa. The drums started beating a melodic rhythm with variable soft and loud volume.

He cast tobacco to the four corners, chanted to the Great Spirit, Gitchee Manitou, and presented the clan's candidate for naming. He gave her qualifications, the basis of her name, her non-Indian background, her own medicine bag with instructions on what its contents should be, and finally, her name: *Runs with Wolves*.

After joining hands in a circle, each witness spoke for her non-Indian membership in the tribe and offered her a gift of welcoming. She hugged Wind Spirit after giving her a hand-carved salmon amulet. Runs with Wolves spoke last with an elegant pleading to share their heritage with her due to its rich tradition. Not in the ceremonial plan was her kiss of each witness.

> "Thank you, my brothers and sisters of the Raven Clan, Tlingit Nation. I am humbled in your presence. I hope to learn your traditions, understand your spiritual beliefs, your subsistence skills and the proud walk of the clan. Hear me, Manitou. Bless these people of the Earth and bless their welcoming to me."

Again, Leigh altered the standard ceremony by embracing the witnesses, Chi Mukwa, and his father, Gete Wabiska . . . a highly unusual and unexpected act. She did not return to the Chief's side. Instead, she sat with her witnesses to the naming ceremony . . . which included Chi Mukwa and Wind Spirit.

*　　*　　*

Gete Wabiska rose. The gathering grew silent as he cast tobacco to the four points of the compass, raised his arms to the sky, and prayed to Manitou. "My fellow clan members, although we still number just over thirty men and women, we have unity that many in any society would envy. The council has reviewed our subsistence lifestyle that we have maintained for the last fifty years and unfortunately decided against its continuance. Due to the needs of our children, their education and long-term enrichment, security issues, health concerns—survival-type living in this primitive, yet enriching life must come to an end. The separation from the white man has come to a bitter conclusion, and for that I am sorry, but nothing in life is permanent.

"As you know, our forefathers founded the Alaska Native Brotherhood in 1912, and we received a cash settlement in 1971; that's in the bank and invested locally to rebuild our lives in modern-day industry and give up our subsistence ways.

"The council has decided to use that money, form a corporation, and utilize the natural wonders of our land without despoiling them as the white man might do. We have been approached by our brothers the Haida and Tsimshian to form the TriAlaska Corporation. I have accepted the offer to be a part of this progressive brotherhood which will concentrate on forestry and fishing interests. Why? Because we are the best that this Earth can offer. And, we will respect the land more than outside interests.

"I urge you to keep practicing your traditional crafts, such as making totems, canoes, Chilkat blankets, and baskets . . . all of which are highly prized the world over.

"Thank you, my fellow Raven Clan brothers and sisters. I bid you peace and comfort tonight as you plan for the future as this clan moves from the forest but retains its roots of ownership and management. And, most important of all, we will retain our unity . . . but, out of the forest, in a new lifestyle. Good night."

The rustle in the treetops and the subtle cries signaled the arrival of a flock of ravens. He, the Spirit, was here, too.

"My God, a lot has happened in my three days' absence. Now I know why so many people were kinda tentative . . . the evasive eyes of Morning Star are understood; she knew, and knows that I will not leave the forest . . . she knows."

"What will you do, dear . . . what will *we* do, my dear?" Leigh asked with a sigh.

*   *   *

A white owl circled the assemblage, screeched, and landed in the tall cedar.

Chapter 35

Resolve

"Do not go where the path may lead, go instead where there is no path and leave a trail."

Ralph Waldo Emerson

The Raven Clan members paired-off in couplets or as family units when departing the tribal fire, all thinking of the impact on each of them with Old White's message. The Raven Clan would be leaving the settlement in the forest, leaving the subsistence way of life, leaving their independence of the white man—now to depend on the white man for their livelihood. Be it forestry or fisheries, they would lose the 'clan' identity and by default would have to integrate into the white man's restricted way of life. Although many knew their independent days of living in the settlement were short-lived, the tribal council's decision announced tonight was unexpected. No matter whether expected or not—it was a shock.

Indeed, Chi Mukwa had his work cut out for him, and very little time to do it or to fine-tune the options in and around what was best for Leigh, Morning Star, and their teenage son. He needed time to think, to think through the best decision for all parties. In the past, he always yielded to the family's desires first. That may not be the case, this time. He had announced that he would not leave the Tongass, and it may affect all three of the people he cared for: Leigh, Morning Star, and his boy, Chinodin. He had to move fast.

"Leigh, you'll be staying with Gete Wabiska tonight as his guest of honor. I'll take you there in a minute. Hold tight. I'll find the family and arrange to meet them after I take you to the Chief's lodge. While waiting, look at the moon and see if there are any answers up there for me. I think you know what I mean."

"Will do. Don't be long: I may get moonstruck . . . and that'd be a problem."

Bear ran off, and Leigh watched as the tribe passed her by, mumbling and discussing the effect of the chief's decision on their lives.

Many knew the reality of entering the industrial competition against the white man's fisheries or lumbering would be a two-sided coin, positive and negative.

In fisheries they'd have to start working as laborers on the boats; in the canneries, at the same place . . . the bottom. This would be necessary before being licensed, a trawler purchased, fighting for dock space with the whites, and finally training a

Native Indian crew . . . and then starting to battle the mighty Pacific.

They had money to start right away, but the "establishment" would probably resist another boat, especially Indian, entering the "fleet's" fishing grounds. However, the Indians had one advantage, their skill in catching various species in the Pacific was known around the world, and luckily the DNR prescribed the area to fish and the limited seasonal times that fish could be netted—or trapped in the case of King Crab. Add the dangers of winter storms and the Indians rose to the top of the competition, also.

Likewise, lumbering options were based on allocations of the "type" of cutting, clear or select, and many existing firms competed for their permits from the capitals, be it Juneau or Washington D.C. However, Indians did have one leg up since the Indians had treaty rights to lumbering activities on Native Lands in the Tongass Forest and the islands of the archipelago. And the U.S. Forest Service recently opened 9.4 million acres of coastal rainforest to lumbering of the total 16.8 million full growth timber available, and Native Americans had the first opportunity for logging. Lumbering could start immediately upon purchase of minimal cutting and handling equipment, plus extraction vehicles, including boats for logging on remote islands.

Nevertheless, these options gave the council an opportunity to leave the subsistence life in the forest, and to gain the positive aspects of the white man's society . . . unfortunately, along with the negatives.

Several negatives bothered Gete Wabiska more than the obvious loss of control he had in the close-knit settlement; his discipline would be replaced by the local sheriff and judiciary. Tribal members will now be exposed to alcohol, gambling, prostitution among the few, plus theft . . . none of these present in the settlement. Yes, they had adultery, assault, and grand theft in the settlement, but infrequently and acted on quickly by the council. These worries had come and gone . . . the irrevocable decision was made; they would survive the move.

Chi Mukwa directed Leigh to the far end of the lodge by the rain wall, asked for Old White's assistant, Yellow Bird, to tell the chief that Leigh was present. He asked her to wait, and departed through the access hole to contact the chief.

While Leigh waited by the rain wall, holding hands, she gave Bear a sensitive good-luck look and a wink as he departed to meet his wife.

Chi Mukwa returned to his family as planned, who waited for him by the fish weir on the Root. He had one of the most important pleadings in his life ahead of him.

Yellow Bird returned with a bedroll and luxurious furs for her bedstead. After laying out the area and leaving a water vessel and small towel, he asked her to return with him to the chief. She followed him into the beautiful chamber lit with multiple candles, with a small iron pot in the middle over glowing coals, and a kettle of tea suspended by an "A" frame. A round window allowed a small beam of light to impact the chamber's suspended particulate and paint its presence on the wooden floor. As her eyes adapted to the darkness, she sensed others in the room.

"Welcome, Runs with Wolves. We are honored by your acceptance of our invitation. Let me introduce the council I have invited to meet you."

She noticed at least four or five men sitting around the fire, all wrapped in blankets and dressed in their best regalia. Old White in the position of honor motioned for her to a place at his right, the only vacancy in the circle.

"Yellow Bird, would you bring Runs with Wolves a Chilkit blanket for her shoulders. Thank you. My dear, the council sits to my left, Double Runner, followed by Middle Calf, Bear Child, Many-White-Horses, Mad Wolf, and Gives-to-the-Sun.

In front of Old White lay the sacred Beaver Bundle. It contained the skins of beaver and other wild animals which were believed to contribute power to the chief. It was opened during ceremonies, given in behalf of various celebrants to cure the sick or on other important occasions. Around the chamber, beaded clothing, with long leather fringes and beautiful designs hung from the lodge poles. A Chilkat blanket hung from the ceiling.

Old White was a noble specimen of Indian Chief. His long gray hair fell loosely over his shoulders, and his face had a kindly and benign expression. He was large in stature and of majestic presence, with broad forehead and high cheek bones, keen eyes, and firm mouth. From the waist up his body was bare. He had broad shoulders, and his chest and his arms were muscular and well formed like those of a young man. He wore leggings of deerskin, moccasins decorated with colored porcupine quills, and necklaces of deer bone and bear claws. A medicine whistle, with which he led his beaver ceremony, hung by a thong from his neck.

All sat in silence, apparently waiting for someone to speak.

"Council members, I am pleased to meet you. I've had such a delightful day touring your settlement, talking to the women and men who all seem to be crafting something for the good of the tribe. I witnessed totems being carved, canoes being made, fish being caught in the weir, and Chilkat blankets being crafted from, what still is amazing to me . . . cedar bark and sheep's hair. They are a prized possession indeed, with their yellow, blue, green, and black design symbols of the raven, your clan's spirit animal. I've been told that legend says if you listen, the blanket actually talks. What a wonderful day. I'll be forever thankful for being with you, and visiting with the people you all represent. I'll confess, I've fallen in love with one of your members."

Startled, they all turned their heads to Old White with a puzzled look written on their faces . . . Then . . . they all looked at Runs with Wolves.

She spoke. "I've fallen in love with Wind Spirit, the orphaned twelve-year-old boy. He escorted me around today, along with Chi Mukwa, and even with the stress that must be apparent in his life, he is exciting, talkative, jocular, and comforting to my needs. I'd like a few more like him, although I've already raised three."

Silence followed as they all looked at the chief.

"My dear woman, my dear complicated woman of the meadow, my dear beauty of the Tongass, my dear survivor. I have brought you here tonight with these noble witnesses to ask you to serve as the legacy of our tribe as we depart the Tongass and you remain. I ask you to become part of our Nation . . . a member of the Tlingit Nation. I ask you to represent us as the sole survivor of the clan, who remains in our stead, as we leave. How do we do this? How do we hope to implement such a plan? Simply put, by being *my* kin . . . my progeny.

"I've asked you to be my daughter . . . I've asked you to be my adoptive daughter. Are you prepared for this responsibility?"

Silence permeated the chamber. There was a strange stillness. The air was sultry, with wind, birds, and insects silent.

"I am."

"I've asked for a lot of you tonight, my dear . . . but, important decisions and important events do not come easy. I have thought through my request with the help of our Great Spirit, Gitchee Manitou, who knows you well. He has witnessed your character first-hand and is proud to claim you as a sister among us. The council concurs. The entire Raven Clan would be proud to have you represent us in the Tongass as the last resident. I know this is a sudden and arduous request. But, my heart begs you to embrace my offer. I would be proud to call you . . . *daughter;* I hope you, too, will call me . . . *father.* I await your answer."

Silence followed as Leigh's eyes lowered, her head bowed, and her hands covered her eyes in embarrassment as they welled up with tears . . . of joy.

She wished for Chi Mukwa's arms, she wished for advice to confirm her affirmation to Old White, she wished for counsel, she felt so alone, reflecting on her dad's advice decades ago. He had said, "When in doubt, and unsure of yourself, judge with your heart." That had always been her way . . . and it would be hers tonight.

More silence radiated from the shadows of the firelight as the stoic yet noble men opened their hearts, through their eyes, to Leigh. They waited. Tension mounted.

She raised her head, dried her tears, then turned to the chief and spoke.

"Dear Father, Gete Wabiska, I am proud to be your daughter. I'm proud to be called a Tlingit woman. I am anxious to be formally confirmed."

With the answer breaking the tension in the chamber, both of the principals rose to embrace, and each of the council passed by in gratitude to her affirmation.

They returned to their seats and sat in silence, waiting for the ceremony of adoption to begin.

Old White nodded, and Yellow Bird brought forth a forked stick. He lifted a live coal out of the fire and placed it in front of the chief, who burned sweet grass on it. As the fragrant perfume-like incense filled the lodge, they all began to sing a low chant in a minor key.

Then the chief purified himself by placing his hands over the rising smoke, and rubbed it all over his body, then breathed it in, purifying himself without and within.

He turned to the small window with the burning sweet grass in front of him. He raised his hands and chanted:

> "See! Our Father, the Sun, shines into the lodge.
> His power is very strong.
> At night, our Mother, the Moon, shines into the lodge.
> Her power is very strong.
> I pray Morning Star to shine into the lodge and bring a long life."

The chief took a willow branch, which was painted red, and placed it on each shoulder, and prayed for a long life. Runs with Wolves was asked to do the same while he prayed to the Sun that she might live to be old, too. The branch was passed to the council, who also prayed for a long life. The Chief loosened the thongs on the bundle, opening it slowly while singing a monotonous song. A red pipe was revealed among many beautiful animal hides. Again he chanted, moving the pipe in time with his song:

> "Pity us! O Sun! O Moon! O Stars!
> Mother Earth! Pity us! Pity us!
> Give us food and drink.
> Bless our children; may their trails lie straight."

The chief retrieved the pipe and passed it around to receive the prayers of each member. Some prayed aloud, others silently. Finally the pipe came back to the chief. He arose, danced around the fire, and blew on his medicine whistle to the four points of the compass. He lit the pipe, sat down, and invited all to smoke. While the pipe passed to each member, Chief sang:

> "Hear! Above-Spirits and Underground-Spirits, birds and ani-
> mals, our secret helpers. This woman with red hair, let her live.
> Care for her and let no harm come to her from evil men or wild
> animals. May all her relatives live long and have plenty. Let our
> young people grow, and our men, women, and children have a full
> life and be happy."

At the end of the prayer all the council united in a long-drawn "Ah-h-h-h-h," meaning Amen.

The Chief brought forth a small pouch of red clay, the sacred paint. There was a long silence while he prepares his hands and said: "Now is the time for my new daughter to come forward."

He motioned to her; she went before him and knelt while he painted her forehead, chin, and both cheeks, describing a circle and representing the sun's daily course through the heavens. He took a beaver skin from his sacred bundle and passed it down both sides of her head, shoulders, and arms; then ended with an upward sweep, by which he imparted his blessing and prayed:

> "Before you, my Father, Great Sun Chief,
> I now adopt this white woman as my daughter.
> Let the red paint be like the sunlight,
> To protect and bring her health and strength.
> May all my people be kind and help her,
> That she may be happy, as long as she remains among her
> Indian brothers and sisters.
> My Father, the Sun, keep her from harm,
> When she goes again to her home toward the rising sun.
> Give her the light by day,
> That her path may be free from danger.
> If she should go into the wrong trail,
> Lead her safely back,
> That her path may be firm and downhill to old age."

After the prayer, Chief and Yellow Bird retrieved rattles of rawhide from the bundle and distributed them to all, including Runs with Wolves. He said, "You are now my daughter and should take part in the ceremony." Then while kneeling with the Council, she joined in the chants and in beating time with the rattles on her hand and on her leg. One song was about a beaver at work, another about a war eagle soaring down on its prey. The men were surprised by her dancing around the fire and at each council member's area.

Gete Wabiska brought the ceremony to a close with this prayer:

> "Father, the Sun. Continue to give us light,
> That the leaves and grass may grow.
> May our cattle increase, and our children live to be old.
> Mother, the Moon. Give us sleep,

May our hearts feel good toward our white sister,
We are all your children."

"May I remind you all," said Gete Wabiska, "Indians may pray in the direction of the sun, but not to the sun; we pray to the Spirit of the Creator that dwells *beyond* the sun. The Spirit of the Creator fills and exists in all spaces in creation—it's in outer space or inner space within all living or non-living things."

After the feast of soup made of berries and tongue, Chief made a sign that the ceremony was over; and all rose, embraced Runs with Wolves, and filed out of the lodge.

*   *   *

Runs with Wolves was standing by the rain wall next to her bedstead when Gete Wabiska approached, lingered, and chatted in a manner quite unexpected for the late hour. They'd already had a full evening of ceremony and celebrating. She pressed her point first. "Dad. How do you like that sound? Dad! Do you have something on your mind? Feel free to ask. The council has left; we're alone."

"You are indeed very perceptive, my dear; I do have a few items to discuss. But first, hasn't it been a wonderful night? I'm so grateful for your positive decision, my dear daughter. I'm blessed. There are a few points.

"We'll be moving several artifacts to a Native American museum in Skagway over the next few weeks. Within the year we will open a Tlingit Raven Clan show-room there, along with an actual working craft shop staffed with our talented people. They will demonstrate and actually manufacture totems, boxes, blankets, and various other popular items for tourists. Now, to my point. Morning Star, being older and having similar responsibilities here, will manage the shop for the clan. She will move to the tribal apartments with her son; he will work in the craft shop and go to school, also. She and her husband, Chi Mukwa, have discussed with me their separation, since he has decided *not* to leave the forest. This decision has put a strain on their marriage; the isolation will not help this tension. A rumor indicates he has taken a job with the DNR through a British/Canadian person called Joe Bloom, who was looking for a replacement for the DNR chap who died in the sacred burial vault. I believe his name was Andy North. Now, again, to the point. My dear, what have I said? You look flushed. Why are your eyes awash with tears?"

"I'll be okay. Go on," Runs with Wolves sighed.

"Now, to my point. Have you noticed any signs by Chi Mukwa toward you that would indicate his interest is more than graciousness to a guest in our settlement. It appears to this old trained eye that his heart, his emotions are involved in his thoughts about and to you . . . would you care to respond?"

Her eyes dropped; her body stiffened.

Silence.

She finally relaxed, looked up, looked at his still probative eyes; he was no rookie in "affairs of the heart." Gracefully, she answered honestly, since *he knew*. "Emotional relationships between two people are hard to measure. Conscious acts, the visible, are at best difficult to evaluate, and without question the most difficult to quantify are the subconscious thoughts toward another being."

Silence.

"As to your question. My heart is open to the tenderness and the strength he has shown to his people, animals, the environment . . . and, yes, to me."

Silence.

"With all due respect, your question can only be answered in its totality . . . by him. You will have to ask him."

Gete Wabiska grasped her hands. His eyes spoke volumes as he replied. "My dear daughter, you have spoken clearly and with gracefulness. I will chat with him, as you suggest. May I suggest you, too, clarify the feelings you have for each other? Let your hearts speak to each other. He is indeed a fortunate man, but he'll need to address his obligations here, and he will do so. My sources indicate he may be doing so as we speak. I see the family is not in the lodge. Sleep tight, good night."

"Dear father, thank you for your comments, your wisdom, your suggestions. They will be discussed in the morning. If not by he, me. Good night."

He received a kiss on the lips, the first in years.

*   *   *

Chi Mukwa's family gathered in the moonlight by the river.

"This is indeed a difficult time for all of us. I had no idea the council's decision was this close. I yield to their wisdom on what is best for the Raven Clan to which we owe our past livelihood lifestyle and now an altered future.

"I must be honest to myself and likewise to my extraordinary wife and son, whom I'm very proud to serve, love, and respect. However, it may not come as a surprise to you that I am totally opposed to this move, have passed my view to council, without ears, and now must suffer the consequences. Why? I saw it in your eyes when I returned from my three-day assignment for the council. From earlier discussions we all knew that if the clan moved both of you would shift to town and I would, unfortunately—not. For that resolve, my heart bleeds in sorrow. However, we have discussed the consequences; now is the time to implement them to our mutual need.

"Chinoodin, you are our prime concern, and school in Skagway will serve yours and our interests in training for the future. The move is good for you. You can always come back to hunt and explore the Tongass, your first love.

"My dear Morning Star, we have discussed your options and final decision to manage the Tlingit Museum for the chief in Skagway. I support this effort, for our son can live with you and assist you when and wherever it's needed. The clan's condo/apartment complex sounds beautiful and downright exciting.

"As for me, I've tentatively agreed to work for the DNR as specialist in their conservation group, monitoring lumbering, fisheries, and hunting regulations in the Tongass and the archipelagos north of Juneau. Joe Bloom, DNR Supervisor, is meeting me this week to discuss the job vacated by a Andrew South, who perished in the burial vault a week ago.

"Neither you, nor I, have left the clan; we've only separated from their location in Skagway. I'll always be a Tlingit. I will not see you for a while, but will stop by frequently at the museum and school.

"May the speed of the Creator whisk you both to happiness and good fortune."

They walked back to the lodge holding hands, knowing the future was at best unknown and certainly difficult . . . but they all knew life was not fair; you did the best with what comes your way. The emotional consequences to the heart, the mind, the soul will take time to adjust to life's realities of separation.

They settled down with the restless clan, all knowing it was the last night in the plank house, the settlement, the Tongass, the Tlingit world.

From his bed Bear remembered the nights under the stars searching for his favorites coming slowly out above the dark battlements of the mountains. Tonight he heard overhead nighthawks feeding, pitching about and diving with a rushing sound of their wings. Thoughts returned of ducks on the lake or the solitary beaver swimming in the twilight. After dark the night wind began to blow, sighing through the branches of the pine trees. He heard the calving of the glaciers like distant thunder as the windblown sound traveled from the Malapina fields in the Saint Elias Range.

*   *   *

There is no sweeter chorus than songs in the early morning by wrens and chickadees at dawn. They also heard thrushes and purple finches in the willows and western yellow-throats and evening grosbeaks in groves of quaking aspen. They all felt dawn in their bones; those who lived out-of-doors knew.

It was Chi Mukwa's idea to go skinny dipping in the Root at dawn. It would be the last time for the family to swim together in the Root's swimming hole. Donning their blankets, dad, mom, and son silently slipped out and slid by the uncaring wolves. The horse looked on in an uninterested fashion, and they ran the last leg to the stream. Doffing their blankets at shore, they all jumped in, naked as jaybirds—as was the family tradition. Their noise rousted the white-crowned sparrows with a sweet uplifting melody. A raven cried to let them know of its presence.

A sunrise swim is luxuriously cool . . . some say cold. They dove deep and gazed through the depths of the clear green water while bubbles floated around their bodies; they came into the sunlight and floated on their backs as the bubbles ran across their skin while gazing into the sky, turning from black to a deep midnight blue . . . soon to be purple.

For a moment they all lay still as their bodies seemed to leave them; then they cut to the sandy shoreline where the sand felt warm on their feet and the cool air tingled their bodies from head to toe.

"Whew! Let's go, Dad!" Chinoodin said while shivering in his blanket.

"Go ahead, son. We'll catch up."

"Okay, Dad, see you at the fire. I'll build it up," he said all wrapped up, jogging back to camp, refreshed but chilled.

"My dear, I've an idea. The white-crowned sparrow's mating call has caught my attention as I, too, feel a need to call my mate. Let's lay the blankets out, lie out, roll up for warmth, and celebrate the dawn."

Morning Star blushed, paused, then smiled . . . she knew all his tricks by now, her maneuvering lover, her husband, her love.

"Come to me, Big Bear; you'll catch a cold just looking at me. Your lover is waiting to warm your body . . . all your body parts."

"Well, I'll tell you dear, the landscape looks pretty good from here. Look out, here I come, goose bumps and all . . . ready to go."

They rolled up and over, and over again, as they had done many times in the past under the morning sun. His leg found her soft moist spot in her loins as their lips expressed their desires and their bodily need for satisfaction.

"Hold it right there, dear; you're at the right spot, my man. Your woman is about to take care of your needs. Ah, there you are. Give that to me; I'll help you. This blanket is so confining." She reached down to his manliness and placed it where it would gratify her needs.

"Thank you, dear. Now that we're warmed up, let's unroll this blanket—now that we've 'captured' each other."

"All right, bet you can't do so without decoupling."

"Ha, watch me, my dear."

They rolled out of the confining blanket to the warmth of the morning sun . . . without detachment.

"Ha, I win."

"Ha yourself, I win, too," she responded with a sheepish grin.

Now in their favorite position, a symbolic phenomenon unfolded as Venus, their star, the great western star, was sinking over her head and the snow-covered mountains.

"Come down here, Venus; you're too far away . . . that's more like it. Now, you hold me, dear."

"Oh Bear, I love you, and I already miss you, and you're still part of me . . please come back."

"I will, my dear. Your love is part of my soul . . . and always will be."

They relaxed in silence until the chirping crickets, and the rushing river, eddying and swirling in the deep pools caught their attention. They arose, embraced, and wrapped themselves in the blankets and returned to the lodge.

He stopped in a thicket halfway there and spoke, "I love you now, as I did your eighteenth year. Your love is equal if not enriched from your years of fulfillment."

Again, he wondered if he'd made the right decision.

A raven cried on the totem as they entered the lodge where residents were just rising to make ready for the move.

*   *   *

Runs with Wolves slept next to Tough, who appeared to be better but still moving very carefully with his cracked ribs.

"Good morning, my friendly four-legged with sore ribs. Ready to travel a little, and get back to the meadow? Come on, let's both pee, pack a snack for the trail, and I'll build a sled to pull you along. Okay, okay, I'll move slower."

After securing Tough, she returned to the rain wall to say good bye to the chief. She knocked and requested entry. Yellow Bird answered and let her in. The chief rose, embraced Runs with Wolves, and wished her good health and safe passage; she wished him success in Skagway as the clan established themselves in town. She tried to kiss him good bye, but the chief raised his hand. He needed to say more before their final kiss.

"My dear, we must talk again."

"Yes, but . . . what is it?"

"My dear, your life is about to become more complex or more exciting—whichever way you determine it to be. Chi Mukwa came to me very late last night. He has resolved his differences with his family in an awkward fashion. Since they still love each other but cannot live together under the circumstances, he has, in effect, let her go, go to a better life, a life she deserves. Likewise, his son. He has indeed an awkward path to walk the next few months until his path is clear. He is certainly an example of R. W. Emerson's words, 'Do not go where the path may lead, go instead where there is no path and leave a trail.'

"My dear, read the content of Emerson's words with care. You may find in them a message from Chi Mukwa to you. I could be wrong, but do spend some time searching for Chi Mukwa's subconscious thoughts expressed through his actions. He is a risk taker; you are that risk. As we said last night, lead with your heart if you are uncertain.

"He is planning to guide you back to the hut on the meadow, if you agree;

whether or not he stays will be up to you. He did not ask me to inform you one way or the other, but asked permission to stay with you . . . if you agreed. I gave him my thoughts; those will stay with he and I. However, as my daughter, I am obligated to inform you of his interests. That, my dear, I've done. You, and you alone, can make the decision that's best for you.

"At that, good morning—not good bye. I will visit you at the meadow when I can. A dad has to keep tabs on his daughter, right?"

She kissed him and hugged him and ran out the lodge to find Chi Mukwa standing by old gal hitched to the sled, Tough bound and tied to the sled . . . all raring to get going.

"Come on, gal, daylight's a-burning. Come on, Runs with Wolves, we're headed south. Wanna come?"

She ran to him, embraced him and asked, "Who said you could come, anyway?"

"Well now, you'll need a guide . . . and that's me, like it or not . . . Cool face paint gal!"

She noticed all his personal possessions and bedroll on the sled, along with many of the gifts received from the Tlingits. She thought he had a strange way of asking if he could stay with her . . . just assume, she thought, until she said otherwise . . . ugh, men, will they ever change?

They turned to the lodge area, waved good bye, and thanked them for their hospitality, then Runs with Wolves suddenly stopped and ran to the crowd, picked up Wind Spirit, embraced him, and told him he can visit any time he chooses. The invitation was acknowledged by his uncle. She ran back to Bear, and they departed into the forest as the sun rose to its zenith.

As they moved through the blinding, shadowless, white forest floor, suddenly everyone halted.

A voice, a young voice, somewhat tentative, echoed across the valley, a boy's frail but heartfelt chant:

"I love you, Runs with Wolves,
I love you, Runs with Wolves,
I love you . . ."

Her eyes filled with tears. He held her tight. She looked at him and said, "If you and I work out, my dear, maybe we can assist in his needs."

He nodded silently as they turned and continued along the path.

*   *   *

About an hour into the trail, she mentioned to Bear, "I see you've brought your personal belongings as well as your bedroll. Planning on staying awhile?"

"Yes, if I'm permitted; you'll need someone to cut wood, haul water, pour drinks, and keep you warm."

"You're certainly not bashful, my Tlingit brother."

Silence.

He looked at her ... their eyes did not meet. She appeared to be in deep thought.

"It sounds good to me, yet ... it appears you've made a deal before any rules have been discussed. I suspect I'm supposed to just play it by ear. Is that it?" Leigh groused.

"Yep."

"I had better confess. I know we both talked to Gete Wabiska. He shared part of your conversation with him, and some of your options," she grumbled.

"Yep, I knew he'd talk to you. He says some things better than I, especially in expressing affairs of the heart. I might as well tell you ... he clearly thinks we're already sleeping together," Bear chuckled.

"I don't suppose you told him—*we're not*. Is that what we are ... an affair—of our hearts?"

"Yep, you could say so."

"So, is it my understanding, Bear, we live together, see how it goes, and if it goes okay we continue in some fashion? Is that the deal?"

"Yep."

"Men, sometimes wolves talk more than you clunkheads."

"Yep."

She gave him a peck on the cheek. He grabbed her bottom ... without objection.

She mused, This is certainly going to be an interesting experiment, but I think I'm going to enjoy it. He's pretending with this "Yep" stuff. The truth is, he can talk the base off a totem pole if he chooses. Men!

*   *   *

A raven leaps from a cedar and follows the couple, the horse, and the sled with the injured wolf, Tough, as they push through the snow to the meadow ...

A white owl joins the raven, hoots across the valley as a message to the denizens of His Kin(g)dom ... They're on the way. Be aware, and protect them, for they are members of our dominion ...

The last of the Tlingits to live in the Tongass.

The Fresh Ink Group

Publishing
Memberships
Share & Read Free Stories, Essays, Articles
Free-Story Newsletter
Writing Contests

Books
E-books
Amazon Bookstore

Authors
Editors
Artists
Professionals
Publishing Services
Publisher Resources

Members' Websites
Members' Blogs
Social Media

www.FreshInkGroup.com

Email: info@FreshInkGroup.com

Twitter: @FreshInkGroup

Google+: Fresh Ink Group

Facebook.com/FreshInkGroup

LinkedIn: Fresh Ink Group

About.me/FreshInkGroup

INTREPID LADY:

A Woman's Alaskan Quest for Native American Spirituality

By Mark Allen North

In the second novel of *The Lady Trilogy*, auburn-haired Leigh West continues her adventures in Alaska's majestic and mysterious Tongass National Forest in search of self-discovery and harmony with nature. In her journal, she chronicles becoming the Spiritual wife of Chi Mukwa (Big Bear) and guardian of two Tlingit teens. It is through Native American spirituality that she sparks new passion within herself, a new appreciation for others, and a life filled with love.

www.FreshInkGroup.com
ISBN: 978-1-936442-13-3

VALIANT LADY:

A Woman's Alaskan Quest for Native American Spirituality

By Mark Allen North

In the third novel of *The Lady Trilogy,* auburn-haired Leigh West continues her adventures in Alaska's majestic and mysterious Tongass National Forest in search of self-discovery and harmony with nature. In her journal, she chronicles all she learns from native Tlingit tribesmen. She marries one and adopts two, fights a devastating fire, and promotes environmental concerns all in those transforming seasons of the region's glorious landscape. It is through Native American spirituality that she sparks new passion within herself, a new appreciation for the physical world, and a life filled with love.

www.FreshInkGroup.com
ISBN: 978-1-936442-14-0

PAPALA SKIES

By Stephen Geez

Chicago native Rochelle DuFortier likes to imagine the future, her world a series of picture postcards so vivid they sometimes seem real. When a foolish mistake at thirteen causes her mother's death, she's sent to a secluded Hawaiian valley, an outsider "haole-girl" among pidgin-speaking boys who hurl flaming papala spears under the full moon to summon her mother's spirit. After boarding school and a prestigious university back east, the ambitious young woman is torn between chasing new career opportunities, discovering her mother's heritage in a remote French village, and meeting obligations pulling her back to Hawaii.

On this island steeped in ancient mythology and modern superstition, Rochelle tests the possibility of sharing pieces of her life with those whose beliefs she barely understands and never intends to embrace. She dives the depths of a pristine coral lagoon, conceals bodies in a subterranean lava tube, and challenges the eruptions of a living volcano, even as she deciphers the truth about her mother's death and struggles to satisfy new debts born of old betrayals.

Papala Skies is the story of a young woman who makes all the right choices, only to find herself living an unexpected life. It is about the need to belong, and seeking one's own version of truth amid such differing cultures' responses to wrenching loss and abiding grief. It is about yearning for a sense of place, yet having to confront new ways to honor the love of family and friends.

Will Rochelle lose what matters most, or might she learn what the smart octopus already knows?

www.FreshInkGroup.com

ISBN: 978-1-936442-07-2

JAZZ BABY

By Beem Weeks

While all Mississippi bakes in the scorching summer of 1925, sudden orphanhood casts its icy shadow across Emily Ann Teegarten, a very pretty young teen.

Taken in by an aunt bent on ridding herself of this unexpected burden, "Baby" Teegarten plots her escape using the only means at her disposal: a voice that makes church ladies cry and angels take notice. "I'm gonna sing jazz up to New York City," she brags to anybody who'll listen. 'Cept that Big Apple—well, it's an awful long way from that dry patch of earth she used to call home.

So when the smoky stages of New Orleans speakeasies give a whistle, offering all kinda shortcuts, Emily soon learns it's the whorehouses and drug joints promising to tickle more than just a young girl's fancy that can dim a spotlight . . . and knowing the wrong people can snuff it out.

Jazz Baby just wants to sing—not fight to stay alive.

www.FreshInkGroup.com
ISBN: 978-1-936442-10-2

BEEN THERE, NOTED THAT:

Essays In Tribute To Life

Observations, Inspiration, Remembrance, & Noteworthies To Share

By Stephen Geez

The simple lives of everyday people in a mundane world prove extraordinary in this collection of 54 personal-experience essays by novelist Stephen Geez. The eclectic mix of memoir, commentary, humor, and appreciation covers a wide range of topics, each beautifully illustrated by artists and photographers from the Fresh Ink Group. Geez catches what many of us miss, then considers how we might all share the most poignant of lessons. *Been There, Noted That* aims to reveal who we are, examine where we've been, and discover what we dare strive to become.

www.FreshInkGroup.com
ISBN: 978-1-936442-05-8

www.ingramcontent.com/pod-product-compliance
Lightning Source LLC
Chambersburg PA
CBHW030543260626
47157CB00006B/2171